THE GOSPEL
ACCORDING TO THE
APOSTLES

W PUBLISHING GROUP™

www.wpublishinggroup.com

A Division of Thomas Nelson, Inc.
www.ThomasNelson.com

THE GOSPEL ACCORDING TO THE APOSTLES

The Role of Works in the Life of Faith

John MacArthur

THE GOSPEL ACCORDING TO THE APOSTLES

ISBN 0-8499-4212-8

Printed in the United States of America

To Lance Quinn

a Timothy to me in every sense—who fulfills my
goal by going beyond his teacher.

The grace of God has appeared, bringing salvation to all men, instructing us to deny ungodliness and worldly desires and to live sensibly, righteously and godly in the present age, looking for the blessed hope and the appearing of the glory of our great God and Savior, Christ Jesus.

Titus 2:11–13

The Lord knows how much I owe (and every reader owes) to Phil Johnson for this book. He is my dear friend and the perfect complement to me in every aspect related to writing. He carefully, skillfully pulls my voice out of the air and transforms it into ink. I could not do it without him.

Contents

Introduction

This is not a typical sequel. It is more of a *prequel*, a start-from-the-beginning approach to the subject it deals with. It fleshes out the framework of doctrine that was only hinted at in its predecessor, *The Gospel According to Jesus*. That book was an analysis of Jesus' evangelistic ministry. It contrasted our Lord's preaching, teaching, and private ministry with the methods of twentieth-century evangelicalism. This book deals with the apostles' doctrine of salvation, showing that the gospel according to Jesus is also the gospel according to the apostles. Thus the entire New Testament message stands in stark contrast to the hollow "gospel" many are proclaiming today.

Perhaps you are thinking, *No, thanks. I'll leave the doctrinal studies to professional theologians. Give me a good devotional book instead.*

But please read on. This is not a technical study or an academic treatise. It is not a textbook for theologians. It is a message that has burned in my heart through all the years of my ministry. Far from being a dry dissertation, it is a passionate look at the most essential of all Christian truths. If salvation is important to you (what could possibly be *more* important?) you cannot afford to ignore the issues this book addresses. If you are inclined to think that a "doctrinal" book is the antithesis of a "devotional" book, I hope to change your mind.

I believe Christians today are starved for doctrinal content. Five years ago, when I was writing *The Gospel According to Jesus,* this issue came to the forefront of my thinking. Several publishers warned me that the book was "too doctrinal" to sell. The whole point of the book was to answer a doctrinal controversy that had festered beneath the surface of evangelicalism for years. I could not write the book without plunging into doctrine. When I finally completed the book, I had to admit it seemed rather like a textbook. It employed theological terminology you might encounter in a Bible college or seminary classroom, but is unfamiliar to many laymen. It was set in small type, heavily footnoted, and began with a critical appraisal of some dispensationalists' soteriology—not the kind of reading the average lay person wants for daily devotions.

In the end the book was published as an academic study, edited and marketed by the publisher's textbook division.

Naturally I hoped the book would gain a broader audience, but I admit I was astonished when it became one of the most widely read Christian books of the 1980s. It was the first "doctrinal" book to become a bestseller in years. It was obvious that *The Gospel According to Jesus* struck a chord—or hit a nerve, depending on which side of the debate you stand.

Almost immediately after the book was published, I began to get letters from lay readers asking for more on the subject. They wanted practical advice: *How should we explain the gospel to children? What tracts are available that present the way of salvation fully and biblically?* They wanted help understanding their own spiritual experiences: *I came to Christ as a child and didn't surrender to Him as Lord until several years later. Does that invalidate my salvation?* They wanted spiritual counsel: *I've been struggling with sin and lack of assurance for years. Can you help me understand genuine faith and how I can have it?* They wanted clarification: *What about Lot and the Corinthians who lived in disobedience? They were still redeemed people, weren't they?* They wanted simplified explanations: *I don't easily understand theological terminology like "dispensationalism" and "soteriology." Can you explain the lordship controversy to me in plain English?*

This book is for those people. It's a simpler treatment, which is appropriate, because the gospel itself is simple. Moreover, I contend that the biblical issues at the heart of the lordship controversy are all very simple as well. It doesn't take an accomplished theologian to discern the sense of difficult passages like 1 John 2:3–4: "By this we know that we have come to know Him, if we keep His commandments. The one who says, 'I have come to know Him,' and does not keep His commandments, is a liar, and the truth is not in him."

I am once again using footnotes, mostly to document the quotations a book like this requires. I have again included a section on dispensationalism, because I wanted to explain in more detail what it is and what bearing it has on the lordship controversy. Nevertheless, this is a book for every Christian. It is not meant to be an advanced study. Each key term is defined the first time I use it, and I have included a glossary. My goal has been to explain the issues so that even a newcomer to the faith can understand what I'm talking about.

Unfortunately, the lordship controversy has become needlessly muddled by complex arguments couched in theological jargon. All of this tends to intimidate people who sincerely want to understand the issues. Many lay Christians—and some Christian leaders—have concluded that the issues are too deep to fathom. Others have allowed themselves to be misled by oversimplified arguments or distracted by emotionally charged rhetoric, rather than thinking through the issues carefully for themselves. I hope this book will help provide an antidote to the confusion and garbled logic that have commandeered the lordship debate over the past half decade.

My purpose is not to answer critics. I have a file drawer full of reviews of *The Gospel According to Jesus*. Most have been positive, and I appreciate the encouragement and affirmation. But I have also read very carefully all the negative reviews (and there have been many). I have studied them with an open heart, asked my staff and the faculty of The Master's Seminary to evaluate every criticism, and returned to Scripture to study prayerfully the biblical issues. The process has helped sharpen my thinking, and for that I am grateful. Some readers have noticed that later editions of the book have included some wording changes that clarify or refine what I was saying.

Overall, however, I must confess that I have been deeply disappointed with the *quality* of the critics' response. The overwhelming majority of criticisms have nothing whatever to do with biblical matters. Some reviewers have complained that the lordship issue is too divisive, the message too hard, or my position too dogmatic. Others have argued semantics or taken exception to my terminology. Some have feigned indignation, claiming *The Gospel According to Jesus* is an unfair personal attack on them, their friends, or this or that organization. A few vocal critics have declared the book unbalanced, accused me of paving the road back to Rome, said I am abandoning dispensationalism, labeled me a hyper-Calvinist, faulted me for being too Arminian, or (most grievously) denounced me as a teacher of works-salvation.

To all who have asked me to reply to those charges, I have simply said read the book for yourself and judge whether they are fair complaints. I believe they are all answered by *The Gospel According to Jesus*.

The problem with all such criticisms is that none of them deals with the *biblical* particulars. As I said in that first book, I'm not really troubled if what I teach messes up someone's dispensational chart. I'm not ultimately concerned with whether something is compatible with a particular system of theology. Nor is my agenda to promote some novel theological scheme. My only aim is to discern and teach what the Scriptures say. I make no apology for that. If we're going to discuss doctrinal matters, let's allow the Bible to settle the question.

Many critics were willing to condemn "lordship salvation" for calling sinners to full surrender, but not one bothered to explain why Jesus Himself said to the unsaved multitudes, "If anyone wishes to come after Me, let him deny himself, and take up his cross, and follow Me" (Mark 8:34). Several called me a legalist for teaching that a transformed life is the inevitable consequence of genuine faith. But no one offered any other possible explanation of 2 Corinthians 5:17: "If any man is in Christ, he is a new creature; the old things passed away; behold, new things have come." Many were eager to argue theological fine points, hypothetical cases, logical ramifications, rational premises, semantic differences, and so on. Almost no one has been willing to grapple with the pertinent biblical texts.

Modern evangelicalism seems poorly equipped to handle controversies like the lordship issue. We have been conditioned to hear only brief, insipid "sound bites." In considering issues of this magnitude, we need to listen, reason, and ponder matters carefully, then come to resolution and agreement. Many seem to think the lordship controversy ought to be settled through a public showdown similar to the televised presidential debates. I have been repeatedly challenged to match wits with leading no-lordship advocates in a public forum. I have consistently declined, and I want to explain why.

My experience with such debates has convinced me that they are not particularly edifying. Listeners come away thinking they fully understand the issues, but the typical debate format allows time only to scratch the surface. The real issues are not going to be settled in one-and two-hour sessions. In practice, the real issues rarely are dealt with. Instead, public debates tend to major on the minors. Debates, in the end, merely offer the most clever participants a forum in which to score points. Worst of all, debates contribute to the perception of personal hostility.

A speech contest cannot resolve the differences in this controversy. Moreover, such an approach has no biblical warrant. I know of no occasion in Scripture when debate was used to come to a proper understanding and consensus on a doctrinal question.

In *The Gospel According to Jesus,* I expressed a desire that the book would be a catalyst for discussion and ultimate resolution of the issues. Since the book's release I have met privately with a number of key Christian leaders from the other side—and my door remains open. I don't view any of these men as enemies, nor do I regard our disagreement as a personal feud. In the scope of all that we believe, we agree far more than we disagree. But there's no denying that these matters pertaining to the gospel are fundamental and therefore our disagreement on them is a serious matter. Surely everyone involved will agree that we cannot simply act as if nothing of importance is at stake.

Ultimately, the best forum in which to air this kind of doctrinal dispute is through careful, biblically reasoned dialogue, preferably in written form. It is easier in writing to measure one's words carefully, to be comprehensive, and to avoid the kind of divisiveness we all are rightly concerned about. We need to clarify the issues, not escalate the emotional pitch of our disagreement.

My desire is to present the case biblically, clearly, graciously, fairly, and in terms that every Christian can understand. My approach will be to examine some of the key passages from the epistles and Acts that reveal how the apostles proclaimed the gospel and how they unfolded the truths of salvation to the early church. There is so much clear revelation on this theme that you may feel you are being given the same thing over and over—and you are—because it is so crucial to the Holy Spirit's purpose in communicating the matter of salvation that these truths are woven into the fabric of many epistles.

I think you'll agree that the gospel according to the apostles is the same gospel Jesus preached. I believe you'll also be convinced that their gospel differs dramatically from the diluted message popular with so many today. And I pray you'll find this book an encouragement as you seek to put your own faith to work.

1

Prologue

In the gospel, I find satisfaction to my mind that I find nowhere else. . . . There is no problem of my life but that the gospel deals with it and answers it. I find intellectual rest and an answer to all my questions.

And, thank God, my heart and my desires are also satisfied. I find complete satisfaction in Christ. There is no desire, there is nothing that my heart can crave for but He can more than satisfy. All the restlessness of desire is quelled by Him as He breathes His peace into my troubles and problems and restlessness. . . .

So I am given rest in spite of my circumstances. The gospel enables me to say with the Apostle Paul, "I am persuaded"—which means, I am certain—"that neither death nor life nor angels, nor principalities, nor powers, nor things present nor things to come, Nor height, nor depth, nor any other creature shall be able to separate us from the love of God, which is in Christ Jesus our Lord" (Rom. 8:38–39). That is perfect rest which is independent of circumstances; that is to be calm in the midst of storm.

D. Martyn Lloyd-Jones[1]

*W*hile I was writing this book my whole life suddenly changed.

One afternoon while waiting for my son to join me at the golf course, I received a telephone call informing me that my wife, Patricia,

[1]D. Martyn Lloyd-Jones, *The Heart of the Gospel* (Wheaton, Ill.: Crossway, 1991), 165–66.

and our youngest daughter, Melinda, had been involved in a very serious automobile accident. Patricia had been gravely injured and was being airlifted to a hospital about an hour away from where I was. No other details were available. Inadvertently leaving my golf clubs on the practice tee, I immediately got in my car and headed for the hospital.

That hour-long drive to the hospital will be forever etched in my memory. A thousand thoughts flooded my mind. I realized, of course, that I might never see Patricia alive again. I thought of the gaping hole that would exist in my life without her. I reflected on the essential part she has had in my life and ministry over the years. I wondered how I could ever manage without her. I remembered when we first met, how we grew to love each other, and hundreds of other little things about our life together. I would give anything to keep her, but I realized now that choice was not mine to make.

A supernatural peace flooded my soul. My grief, sorrow, uncertainty, and fears were all enveloped in that restful peace. I knew that Patricia and I were both in our Lord's hands, and under the circumstances that was the only place I could imagine any sense of safety. I did not know His design. I could not see His purposes. I could not understand what had happened or why. But I could rest in the knowledge that His plan for us was ultimately for our good and for His glory.

When I arrived at the emergency room, I learned that Melinda had been badly bruised and cut but was not seriously injured. She was severely shaken but not in any danger.

A doctor came out to explain Patricia's injuries to me. Her neck was broken. Two vertebrae were severely crushed. The damage had occurred above the crucial nerves in the spinal cord that control breathing. In most cases like hers, the victim dies immediately. But our Lord had providentially spared her.

She had also sustained a severe blow to the head. The impact of the roof crushing down on her head as the car flipped was powerful enough to have killed her. They were giving her massive doses of a new drug designed to stop swelling in the brain. The surgeon was concerned that the head injury could yet prove fatal. He had used more than forty sutures to close the wound in her scalp. Her jaw and several bones in her face were broken. She would not be out of danger for several days.

Emergency room personnel were about to move Patricia to surgery, where doctors would attach a steel halo to her head by means of four bolts drilled directly into the skull. The device would suspend her head and stabilize her neck while the vertebrae healed. She would wear the halo for several months and after that undergo a grueling program of physical rehabilitation.

In the next few days doctors discovered additional injuries. The right collarbone was broken. Worse, Patricia's right arm was paralyzed. She could move her fingers and grip things, but her arm hung limply and she had no sensation in it. Her left hand was broken and needed a cast. That meant Patricia could not use either hand.

This all has brought a wonderful opportunity for me to serve my wife. All our lives together she has cared for my needs, served the family, and ministered to us in a myriad of ways. Now it is my turn, and I have relished the opportunity. My love for her and my appreciation of all that she does has grown by magnitudes.

As of this writing, Patricia is still in the halo. It is a remarkable contraption, a huge steel yoke that suspends her head by resting the weight of it on four steel rods rising from a plastic upper-body vest. It holds her head and neck immobile in traction.

I am glad to report that she is out of danger now. If God graciously permits, by the time this book is published she will be out of the halo. She has regained some use of her right arm, and doctors tell us she could be on the way to a full recovery.

This whole experience has been the most difficult trauma of our lives together. Yet through it all both Patricia and I have learned again—in a very practical way—that faith works. Our faith in Christ—the same faith with which we first trusted Him as Lord—has remained strong and enabled us to trust Him through this trial.

We have understood as never before the sweetness of our Lord's invitation in Matthew 11:28–30: "Come to Me, all who are weary and heavy-laden, and I will give you rest. Take My yoke upon you, and learn from Me, for I am gentle and humble in heart; and you shall find rest for your souls. For My yoke is easy, and My load is light." We have found again and again that though the yoke does not always *seem* easy and the burden does not always *feel* light, living under the precious reality of Christ's lordship offers the only truly restful life, no matter what.

That is, after all, the heart of the gospel according to Jesus. The apostles knew this truth both from the Lord's teaching and from their own experience. It was the heart of their message to an unsaved world. They preached that faith *works;* it cannot fail or remain passive, but immediately goes to work in the life of the believer. It works *for* us and *in* us and *through* us. Faith is sustained and it sustains us in the midst of life's trials. It motivates us in the face of life's difficulties. It carries us through life's tragedies. Because faith works, it enables us to enjoy a supernatural spiritual rest.

Our experience throughout Patricia's ordeal has given me a new vigor for this book. I am constantly reminded that my confidence in the lordship of Jesus Christ is the foundation and the support of my life. The immense provision of His saving grace enables us to endure.

The lordship of Christ is not some dry and musty abstract doctrinal subject. The gospel is not an academic matter. Faith is not a theoretical pursuit. The grace of God is not a conjectural reality. How we understand the truths of the gospel will ultimately determine how we live our lives. All these issues are dynamic, intensely practical, and supremely relevant in our day-to-day lives. Please bear that in mind as you study these pages.

2

A Primer on the "Lordship Salvation" Controversy

> Beloved, while I was making every effort to write you about our common salvation, I felt the necessity to write to you appealing that you contend earnestly for the faith which was once for all delivered to the saints.
>
> Jude 3

*W*hy do you want to do another book on 'lordship salvation'?" a friend recently asked. "Hasn't that issue been beaten to death?"

I admit that a part of me echoes that sentiment. Originally I had no intention of writing a sequel to *The Gospel According to Jesus*. That book was in preparation for several years, and when I finally completed it I was eager to move on to something different. Although I felt there was much more that *could* be said, I was satisfied that the book adequately covered the subject. I was not trying to place myself at the nucleus of an ongoing debate. Most of all, I did not want the "lordship salvation" controversy to become the single focus of my ministry.

That was five years ago. Today I sense something of what Jude must have felt when he penned the verse quoted above. An urgent prompting in the deepest part of my soul constrains me to say more.

Is This Really a Crucial Issue?

A major reason for my concern has to do with some popular misconceptions that cloud the whole controversy. "Lordship salvation" has

21

become the most talked about and least understood theological topic in evangelical Christendom. Nearly everyone seems to know *about* the debate; few truly understand the issues. It is easy to find strong opinions on both sides. But ferreting out people with genuine understanding is another matter. Many suppose the whole thing is a superficial conflict and the church would be better off if everyone forgot about it. One very well known Christian leader told me he had purposely avoided reading any books on the matter; he didn't want to be forced to take sides. Another told me the issue is unnecessarily divisive.

Yet this is not theological trivia. How we proclaim the gospel has eternal ramifications for non-Christians and defines who we are as Christians. Nor is the lordship question a theoretical or hypothetical problem. It raises several fundamental questions that have repercussions at the most practical level of Christian living.

How should we proclaim the gospel? Do we present Jesus to unbelievers as Lord, or as Savior only? What are the essential truths of the gospel message? What does it mean to be *saved*? How can a person know his or her faith is real? Can we have absolute assurance of salvation? What kind of transformation is accomplished in the new birth? How do we explain sin in the Christian's life? How far in sinning can a Christian go? What relationship is there between faith and obedience? Every area of Christian living is affected by one or more of those questions.

Of course, that's not to say the lordship discussion is purely pragmatic. A number of crucial doctrines have surfaced in the debate: dispensationalism, election, the *ordo salutis* ("order of salvation"), the relationship of sanctification and justification, eternal security, perseverance of the saints, and so on.

Don't be put off. You may not immediately recognize some of those terms or be able to define them all, but if you're a Christian, every one of them is important to you. You ought to have a basic understanding of what they mean and how they relate to Scripture and the gospel message. Doctrine is not the exclusive domain of seminary professors. All true Christians must be concerned with understanding sound doctrine. Doctrine properly understood can never be a merely academic pursuit. It is the discipline of discerning and digesting what God is saying to us in His Word so we can live lives that glorify Him. Doctrine forms the belief system that controls and compels behavior. What could be more practical—or more important?

Let's keep that perspective in mind as we approach this controversial topic. Do we disagree on doctrinal matters? Let's look together at what *God's Word* says. Theological systems, polemics, elegant rhetoric, or bombast and bravado may persuade some people, but not those who seek to know the mind of God. God's truth is revealed in His Word, and it is there we must ultimately go to settle this or any other doctrinal issue.

What Is "Lordship Salvation" All About?

The gospel call to faith presupposes that sinners must repent of their sin and yield to Christ's authority. That, in a sentence, is what "lordship salvation" teaches.

I don't like the term *lordship salvation*. I reject the connotation intended by those who coined the phrase. It insinuates that a submissive heart is extraneous or supplementary to saving faith. Although I have reluctantly used the term to describe my views, it is a concession to popular usage. Surrender to Jesus' lordship is not an addendum to the biblical terms of salvation; the summons to submission is at the heart of the gospel invitation throughout Scripture.

Those who criticize lordship salvation like to level the charge that we teach a system of works-based righteousness. Nothing could be further from the truth. Although I labored to make this as plain as possible in *The Gospel According to Jesus,* some critics continue to hurl that allegation. Others have imagined that I am advocating a new or modified doctrine of salvation that challenges the Reformers' teaching or radically redefines faith in Christ. Of course, my purpose is just the opposite.

Therefore, let me attempt to state the crucial points of my position as plainly as possible. These articles of faith are fundamental to all evangelical teaching:

- Christ's death on the cross paid the full penalty for our sins and purchased eternal salvation. His atoning sacrifice enables God to justify sinners freely without compromising the perfection of divine righteousness (Rom. 3:24–26). His resurrection from the dead declares His victory over sin and death (1 Cor. 15:54–57).
- Salvation is by grace through faith in the Lord Jesus Christ alone—plus and minus nothing (Eph. 2:8–9).
- Sinners cannot earn salvation or favor with God (Rom. 8:8).

- God requires of those who are saved no preparatory works or prerequisite self-improvement (Rom. 10:13; 1 Tim. 1:15).
- Eternal life is a gift of God (Rom. 6:23).
- Believers are saved and fully justified before their faith ever produces a single righteous work (Eph. 2:10).
- Christians can and do sin (1 John 1:8, 10). Even the strongest Christians wage a constant and intense struggle against sin in the flesh (Rom. 7:15–24). Genuine believers sometimes commit heinous sins, as David did in 2 Samuel 11.

Alongside those truths, I believe Scripture teaches these:

- The gospel calls sinners to faith joined in oneness with repentance (Acts 2:38; 17:30; 20:21; 2 Pet. 3:9). Repentance is turning from sin (Acts 3:19; Luke 24:47). It is not a work but a divinely bestowed grace (Acts 11:18; 2 Tim. 2:25). Repentance is a change of heart, but genuine repentance will effect a change of behavior as well (Luke 3:8; Acts 26:18–20).
- Salvation is all God's work. Those who believe are saved utterly apart from any effort on their own (Titus 3:5). Even faith is a gift of God, not a work of man (Eph. 2:1–5, 8). Real faith therefore cannot be defective or short-lived but endures forever (Phil. 1:6, cf. Heb. 11).
- The object of faith is Christ Himself, not only a creed or a promise (John 3:16). Faith therefore involves personal commitment to Christ (2 Cor. 5:15). In other words, all true believers follow Jesus (John 10:27–28).
- Real faith inevitably produces a changed life (2 Cor. 5:17). Salvation includes a transformation of the inner person (Gal. 2:20). The nature of the Christian is different, new (Rom. 6:6). The unbroken pattern of sin and enmity with God will not continue when a person is born again (1 John 3:9–10).
- The "gift of God," eternal life (Rom. 6:23), includes all that pertains to life and godliness (2 Pet. 1:3; Rom. 8:32), not just a ticket to heaven.

- Jesus is Lord of all, and the faith He demands involves unconditional surrender (Rom. 6:17–18; 10:9–10). He does not bestow eternal life on those whose hearts remain set against Him (James 4:6).

- Those who truly believe will love Christ (1 Pet. 1:8–9; Rom. 8:28–30; 1 Cor. 16:22). They will therefore long to obey Him (John 14:15, 23).

- Behavior is an important test of faith. Obedience is evidence that one's faith is real (1 John 2:3). On the other hand, the person who remains utterly unwilling to obey Christ does not evidence true faith (1 John 2:4).

- Genuine believers may stumble and fall, but they *will* persevere in the faith (1 Cor. 1:8). Those who later turn completely away from the Lord show that they were never truly born again (1 John 2:19).

That is my position on "lordship salvation." Anyone who supposes I have some deeper agenda has misunderstood what I am saying.

Radical or Orthodox?

Most Christians will recognize that the points I've listed are not new or radical ideas. The preponderance of Bible-believing Christians over the centuries have held these to be basic tenets of orthodoxy. They are standard precepts of doctrine affirmed, for example, by all the great Reformed and Calvinist creeds. Though our Wesleyan brethren might disagree on a few of the particulars, most of them would quickly affirm that the lordship of Christ is at the heart of the gospel message.[1] No major orthodox movement in the history of Christianity has ever taught that sinners can spurn the lordship of Christ yet lay claim to Him as Savior.

The truth is, the no-lordship gospel is a fairly recent development. Although most advocates of the no-lordship view write and speak as if their teaching represented historic mainstream evangelical Christianity, it does not. Except for a circle of North American pastors, authors, and conference speakers, practically no church leader in the world defends no-lordship doctrine as orthodox. Until recently in

---

[1]Wesleyans believe, for example, that genuine believers can fall away from the faith, but they generally teach that those who do fall away lose their salvation. Their system makes no room for "Christians" who live in continuous rebellion against Christ.

Eastern Europe and the Soviet Union, for example, being a Christian could literally cost a person everything. There the notion of faith without commitment is unthinkable. In England and the rest of Europe, Christian leaders I have met condemn no-lordship teaching as an American aberration. The same is true in other parts of the world I'm familiar with.

This is not to say that no-lordship teaching poses no threat outside the United States. Over the past three or four decades gospel tracts, how-to books on witnessing, radio and television broadcasts, and other media have carried the no-lordship message to the uttermost parts of the earth. The so-called simple-faith gospel—no repentance, no surrender, no commitment, no changed life—has had a horrific influence on the vocabulary of evangelism. Because no-lordship terminology ("accept Jesus as Savior" now, "make Him Lord" later) has become familiar and comfortable, many Christians' thinking about the gospel is fuzzy. When so many of the purveyors of no-lordship salvation brashly level charges of heresy against those who oppose their teaching, is it any wonder sincere Christians are genuinely confused? Which system represents true orthodoxy?

What Does the No-lordship Gospel Teach?

I have listed sixteen beliefs of lordship salvation. The first seven are tenets every major no-lordship advocate would also affirm:

- Christ's death purchased eternal salvation.
- The saved are justified through faith in Christ alone.
- Sinners cannot earn divine favor.
- God requires no preparatory works or pre-salvation reformation.
- Eternal life is a gift.
- Believers are saved before their faith produces any righteous works.
- Christians sin, sometimes horribly.

On that much we all agree. Those who espouse the no-lordship position, however, differ dramatically from lordship salvation on the remaining nine points. Instead they teach:

- Repentance is a change of mind about Christ (*SGS* 96, 99).[2] In the context of the gospel invitation, *repentance* is just a synonym for *faith* (*SGS* 97–99). No turning from sin is required for salvation (*SGS* 99).

- The whole of salvation, including faith, is a gift of God (*SGS* 96). But faith might not last. A true Christian can completely cease believing (*SGS* 141).

- Saving faith is simply being convinced or giving credence to the truth of the gospel (*SGS* 156). It is confidence that Christ can remove guilt and give eternal life, not a personal commitment to *Him* (*SGS* 119).

- *Some* spiritual fruit is inevitable in every Christian's experience. The fruit, however, might not be visible to others (*SGS* 45). Christians can even lapse into a state of permanent spiritual barrenness (*SGS* 53–54).

- Only the *judicial* aspects of salvation—such as justification, adoption, imputed righteousness, and positional sanctification—are guaranteed for believers in this life (*SGS* 150–52). *Practical* sanctification and growth in grace require a postconversion act of dedication.[3]

- Submission to Christ's supreme authority as Lord is not germane to the saving transaction (*SGS* 71–76). Neither dedication nor *willingness* to be dedicated to Christ are issues in salvation (*SGS* 74). The news that Christ died for our sins and rose from the dead is the *complete* gospel. Nothing else must be believed for salvation (*SGS* 40–41).

- Christians may fall into a state of lifelong carnality. A whole category of "carnal Christians"—born-again people who continuously live like the unsaved—exists in the church (*SGS* 31, 59–66).

- Disobedience and prolonged sin are no reason to doubt the reality of one's faith (*SGS* 48).

---

[2]Throughout this book, I will use the abbreviation *SGS* in reference to Charles Ryrie, *So Great Salvation* (Wheaton, Ill.: Victor, 1989).

[3]Charles C. Ryrie, *Balancing the Christian Life* (Chicago: Moody, 1969), 186.

- A believer may utterly forsake Christ and come to the point of not believing. God has guaranteed that He will not disown those who thus abandon the faith (*SGS* 141). Those who have once believed are secure forever, even if they turn away (*SGS* 143).

Some of the more radical advocates of no-lordship doctrine do not stop there. They further stipulate:

- Repentance is not essential to the gospel message. In no sense is repentance related to saving faith (*AF* 144–46).[4]
- Faith is a human act, not a gift from God (*AF* 219). It occurs in a decisive moment but does not necessarily continue (*AF* xiv, 107). True faith can be subverted, be overthrown, collapse, or even turn to unbelief (*AF* 111).
- To "believe" unto salvation is to believe the *facts* of the gospel (*AF* 37–39). "Trusting Jesus" means believing the "saving facts" about Him (*AF* 39), and to believe those facts is to appropriate the gift of eternal life (*AF* 40). Those who add any suggestion of commitment have departed from the New Testament idea of salvation (*AF* 27).
- Spiritual fruit is not guaranteed in the Christian life (*AF* 73–75, 119). Some Christians spend their lives in a barren wasteland of defeat, confusion, and every kind of evil (*AF* 119–25).
- Heaven is guaranteed to believers (*AF* 112) but Christian victory is not (*AF* 118–19). One could even say "the saved" still need salvation (*AF* 195–99). Christ offers a whole range of postconversion deliverance experiences to supply what Christians lack (*AF* 196). But these other "salvations" all require the addition of human works, such as obedience, submission, and confession of Jesus as Lord (*AF* 74, 119, 124–25, 196). Thus God is dependent to some degree on human effort in achieving deliverance from sin in this life (*AF* 220).

---

[4] *AF* refers to Zane Hodges, *Absolutely Free!* (Grand Rapids, Mich.: Zondervan, 1989).

- Submission is not in any sense a condition for eternal life (*AF* 172). "Calling on the Lord" means *appealing* to Him, not *submitting* to Him (*AF* 193–95).

- Nothing guarantees that a true Christian will love God (*AF* 130–31). Salvation does not necessarily even place the sinner in a right relationship of harmonious fellowship with God (*AF* 145–60).

- If people are sure they believe, their faith *must* be genuine (*AF* 31). *All* who claim Christ by faith as Savior—even those involved in serious or prolonged sin—should be assured that they belong to God come what may (*AF* 32, 93–95). It is dangerous and destructive to question the salvation of professing Christians (*AF* 18–19, 91–99). The New Testament writers *never* questioned the reality of their readers' faith (*AF* 98).

- It is possible to experience a moment of faith that guarantees heaven for eternity (*AF* 107), then to turn away permanently and live a life that is utterly barren of any spiritual fruit (*AF* 118–19). Genuine believers might even cease to name the name of Christ or confess Christianity (*AF* 111).

Appendix 1 (pages 213–17) is a chart in which the major differences and similarities of the various views are shown side by side.

What Is Really at the Heart of the Lordship Debate?

It should be obvious that these are real doctrinal differences; the lordship controversy is not a semantic disagreement. The participants in this debate hold widely differing perspectives.

Nevertheless, the issues have often been obscured by semantic distractions, distorted interpretations of lordship teaching, mangled logic, and emotion-laden rhetoric. Often it is easier to misconstrue a point than answer it, and sadly that is the tack many have taken. All it has done is confuse the real issues.

Please allow me to address some of the most troublesome fallacies that have hampered understanding and resolution of the lordship question.

The lordship controversy is *not* a dispute about whether salvation is by faith only or by faith plus works. No true Christian would ever suggest that works need to be added to faith in order to secure salvation. No one who properly interprets Scripture would ever propose that human effort or fleshly works can be *meritorious*—worthy of honor or reward from God.[5]

The lordship controversy *is* a disagreement over the nature of true faith. Those who want to eliminate Christ's lordship from the gospel see faith as simple trust in a set of truths about Christ. Faith, as they describe it, is merely a personal appropriation of the promise of eternal life. Scripture describes faith as more than that—it is a wholehearted trust in Christ personally (e.g., Gal. 2:16; Phil. 3:9). Not merely faith *about* Him; faith *in* Him. Note the difference: If I say I believe some promise you have made, I am saying far less than if I say I trust *you*. Believing in a person necessarily involves some degree of commitment. Trusting Christ means placing oneself in His custody for both life and death. It means we rely on His counsel, trust in His goodness, and entrust ourselves for time and eternity to His guardianship. Real faith, saving faith, is all of me (mind, emotions, and will) embracing all of Him (Savior, Advocate, Provider, Sustainer, Counselor, and Lord God).

Those who have such faith will love Christ (Rom. 8:28; 1 Cor. 16:22; 1 John 4:19). They will therefore want to do His bidding. How could someone who truly believes in Christ continue to defy His authority and pursue what He hates? In this sense, then, the crucial issue for lordship salvation is not merely authority and submission, but the affections of the heart. Jesus as Lord is far more than just an authority figure; He's also our highest treasure and most precious companion. We obey Him out of sheer delight.

So the gospel demands surrender, not only for authority's sake, but also because surrender is the believer's highest joy. Such surrender is not an extraneous adjunct to faith; it is the very essence of believing.

Lordship salvation does *not* teach true Christians are perfect or sinless. Wholehearted commitment to Christ does not mean that we never disobey or that we live perfect lives. The vestiges of our sinful flesh make it inevitable that we will often do what we do not want to do (Rom. 7:15). But commitment to Christ *does* mean that obedience rather than disobedience will be our distinguishing trait. God will deal with the sin in our lives and we will respond to His loving chastisement

---

[5]Though, curiously, no-lordship doctrine is often married to a view that sees postsalvation works as meritorious. Zane Hodges, for one, holds this view. He teaches that eternal life may be obtained freely by faith, but the abundant life of John 10:10 is a reward that may be acquired only by works (*AF* 230).

by becoming more holy (Heb. 12:5–11). I labored to make this clear in *The Gospel According to Jesus*. For example, I wrote, "Those with true faith will fail—and in some cases, frequently—but a genuine believer will, as a pattern of life, confess his sin and come to the Father for forgiveness (1 John 1:9)" (p. 192).

Nevertheless, a few critics have tried to portray lordship salvation as a thinly disguised form of perfectionism. One dear brother—a Christian radio personality—wrote me to suggest that qualifying comments in the book like the one I just quoted are actually inconsistent with my overall position. He assumed that these were "disclaimers" added by an editor trying to "tone down" my book. He evidently surmised that my real intent was to teach sinless perfection as the test of true salvation. He had missed the point entirely.

Of course Christians sin. They disobey. They fail. We *all* fall far short of perfection in this life (Phil. 3:12–5). "We all stumble in many ways" (James 3:2). Even the most mature and godly Christians "see in a mirror dimly" (1 Cor. 13:12). Our minds need constant renewing (Rom. 12:2). But that doesn't invalidate the truth that salvation in some real sense makes us practically righteous. The same epistle that describes the Christian's hatred of and battle with sin (Rom. 7:8–24) first says that believers are free from sin and slaves of righteousness (6:18). The same apostle who wrote, "If we say that we have no sin, we are deceiving ourselves" (1 John 1:8) later wrote, "No one who abides in Him sins" (3:6). In one place he says, "If we say that we have not sinned, we make Him a liar, and His word is not in us" (1:10), and in another, "No one who is born of God practices sin, because His seed abides in Him" (3:9).

There's a true paradox—not an inconsistency—in those truths. All Christians sin (1 John 1:8), but all Christians also obey: "By this we know that we have come to know Him, if we keep His commandments" (1 John 2:3). Sin and carnality are still present with all believers (Rom. 7:21), but they cannot be the hallmark of one's character (Rom. 6:22).

Scripture clearly and repeatedly confirms the lordship viewpoint on this matter: "Beloved, do not imitate what is evil, but what is good. The one who does good is of God; the one who does evil has not seen God" (3 John 11). That speaks of *direction*, not *perfection*. But it clearly makes behavior a test of faith's reality.

The sinner's role in salvation is *not* the main issue in the lordship controversy. The heart of the debate deals with how much *God* does in redeeming the elect.

What happens at regeneration? Is the believing sinner really born again (John 3:3, 7; 1 Peter 1:3, 23)? Is our old self really dead, "crucified . . . that we should no longer be slaves to sin" (Rom. 6:6)? Are believers really "partakers of the divine nature" (2 Pet. 1:4)? Is it true that "if any man is in Christ, he is a new creature; the old things passed away; behold, new things have come" (2 Cor. 5:17)? Can we really say, "Having been freed from sin, [we are] slaves of righteousness" (Rom. 6:18)?

Lordship salvation says yes.

This, after all, is the whole point of redemption: "Whom He foreknew, He also predestined to become conformed to the image of His Son" (Rom. 8:29). Does that conforming work of God—sanctification—begin in this lifetime? Again, lordship salvation says yes.

Scripture agrees. "We all, with unveiled face beholding as in a mirror the glory of the Lord, are being transformed into the same image from glory to glory" (2 Cor. 3:18). Though "it has not appeared as yet what we shall be," it is nevertheless certain that "when He appears, we shall be like Him. . . . And everyone who has this hope fixed on Him purifies himself, just as He is pure" (1 John 3:2–3).

There's more: "Whom He predestined, these He also called; and whom He called, these He also justified; and whom He justified, these He also glorified" (Rom. 8:30). Notice God's part in salvation begins with election and ends in glory. In between, every aspect of the redemptive process is God's work, not the sinner's. God will neither terminate the process nor omit any aspect of it.

Titus 3:5 is clear: Salvation—all of it—is "not on the basis of deeds which we have done." It is God's work, done "according to His mercy." It is not merely a declaratory transaction, legally securing a place in heaven but leaving the sinner captive to his sin. It involves a transformation of the disposition, the very nature, through "the washing of regeneration and renewing by the Holy Spirit" as well.

The question is *not* whether we're saved by grace, but *how* grace operates in salvation. No-lordship advocates love to portray themselves as champions of grace. But they characterize grace in an anemic way that misses the whole point. God's grace is a spiritual dynamic that works in the lives of the redeemed, "instructing us to deny ungodliness and worldly desires and to live sensibly, righteously and godly in the present age" (Titus 2:12). True grace is more than just a giant freebie, opening the door to heaven in the sweet by and by, but leaving us to wallow in sin in the bitter here and now. Grace is God presently at work in our lives. By grace "we are His workmanship, created in Christ

Jesus for good works, which God prepared beforehand, that we should walk in them" (Eph. 2:10). By grace He "gave Himself for us, that He might redeem us from every lawless deed and purify for Himself a people for His own possession, zealous for good deeds" (Titus 2:14).

That ongoing work of grace in the Christian's life is as much a certainty as justification, glorification, or any other aspect of God's redeeming work. "I am confident of this very thing, that He who began a good work in you will perfect it until the day of Christ Jesus" (Phil. 1:6). Salvation is wholly God's work, and He finishes what He starts. His grace *is* sufficient. And potent. It cannot be defective in any regard. "Grace" that does not affect one's behavior is not the grace of God.

Repentance is *not* incidental to the gospel. What is the gospel, after all, but a call to repentance (Acts 2:38; 3:19; 17:30)? In other words, it demands that sinners make a change—stop going one way and turn around to go the other (1 Thess. 1:9). Paul's evangelistic invitations always demanded repentance: "God is now declaring to men that all everywhere should repent" (Acts 17:30). Here's how Paul described His own ministry and message: "I did not prove disobedient to the heavenly vision, but kept declaring both to those of Damascus first, and also at Jerusalem and then throughout all the region of Judea, and even to the Gentiles, *that they should repent and turn to God, performing deeds appropriate to repentance*" (Acts 26:19–20, emphasis added). Repentance is what leads to life (Acts 11:18) and to the knowledge of the truth (2 Tim. 2:25). Thus salvation is impossible apart from repentance.

Advocates of the no-lordship position frequently suggest that preaching repentance adds something to the biblical doctrine of salvation by grace through faith alone.

But faith presupposes repentance. How can those who are mortal enemies of God (Rom. 5:10) sincerely believe in His Son *without* repenting? How can anyone truly comprehend the truth of salvation from sin and its consequences, unless that person also genuinely understands and hates what sin is? The whole sense of faith is that we trust Christ to liberate us from the power and penalty of sin. Therefore sinners cannot come to sincere faith apart from a complete change of heart, a turn-around of the mind and affections and will. That is repentance. It is not a supplement to the gospel invitation; it is precisely what the gospel demands. Our Lord Himself described His primary mission as that of calling sinners to repentance (Matt. 9:13).

We often speak of the salvation experience as "conversion." That is biblical terminology (Matt. 18:3; John 12:40; Acts 15:3). *Conversion* and *repentance* are closely related terms. Conversion occurs when a sinner turns to God in repentant faith. It is a complete turnaround, an absolute change of moral and volitional direction. Such a radical reversal is the response the gospel calls for, whether the plea to sinners is phrased as "believe," "repent," or "be converted." Each entails the others.

If someone is walking away from you and you say, "Come here," it is not necessary to say "*turn around* and come." The U-turn is implied in the direction "come." In like manner, when our Lord says, "Come to Me" (Matt. 11:28), the about-face of repentance is understood. Nowhere does Scripture issue an evangelistic appeal that does not at least imply the necessity of repentance. Our Lord offers nothing to impenitent sinners (Matt. 9:13; Mark 2:17; Luke 5:32).

Again, repentance is not a human work. Jesus said, "No one can come to Me, unless the Father who sent Me draws him" (John 6:44). It is God who grants repentance (Acts 11:18; 2 Tim. 2:5). Repentance is *not* pre-salvation self-improvement. It is *not* a question of atoning for sin or making restitution *before* turning to Christ in faith. It is an inward turning from sin to Christ. Though it is not itself a "work" the sinner performs, genuine repentance will certainly produce good works as its inevitable fruit (Matt. 3:8).

The lordship salvation controversy is *not* churchwide. Because of the publicity given to the lordship debate over the past five years, one might get the impression that the entire worldwide evangelical movement is split over these issues. But as I noted earlier, modern no-lordship theology is primarily a North American phenomenon. Certainly it has been exported to some parts of the world by missionaries and others trained in American schools, but I know of no prominent Christian leaders from outside North America who have undertaken to defend the no-lordship view on doctrinal grounds.

To be even more specific, the modern lordship controversy is primarily a dispute among dispensationalists. Appendix 2 explains dispensationalism and why it is at the heart of the lordship debate. Without getting into a technical discussion about theology at this point, let me simply note that one arm of the dispensationalist movement has developed and defended no-lordship doctrine. Their influence on the evangelical culture has been widespread. As the lordship controversy has been debated on radio talk shows and in other popular formats, it has begun to seem like a monumental conflict threatening to divide Protestant Christianity in a major way. The truth is, only one branch of dispensationalism has risen to defend the no-lordship view.

Who are the defenders of no-lordship dispensationalism? Nearly all of them stand in a tradition that has its roots in the teaching of Lewis Sperry Chafer. I will show in Appendix 2 that Dr. Chafer is the father of modern no-lordship teaching. Every prominent figure on the no-lordship side descends from Dr. Chafer's spiritual lineage. Though Dr. Chafer did not invent or originate any of the key elements of no-lordship teaching, he codified the system of dispensationalism on which all contemporary no-lordship doctrine is founded. That system is the common link between those who attempt to defend no-lordship doctrine on theological grounds.

The New Testament epistles do *not* present a different gospel than Jesus Himself preached. One of the hallmarks of Dr. Chafer's brand of dispensationalism was the way he segmented the New Testament, and particularly the teachings of Christ. As we'll note in Appendix 2, Chafer believed many of our Lord's sermons and evangelistic invitations were intended for people in another dispensation. He contrasted Jesus' "kingdom teachings" and His "grace teachings." Only the "grace teachings," according to Chafer, can be legitimately applied to this present age.

Many dispensationalists have abandoned that kind of thinking, but some still do not believe the gospel according to Jesus is even relevant to the discussion of lordship salvation. "Of course Jesus taught a lordship message," one old-line dispensationalist brother wrote me. "He was preaching to people under law. Under grace we must be careful to preach a grace message. We must preach the gospel according to the apostles."

So for the remainder of this book we will focus on the apostles' preaching and teaching. We will take an especially close look at the apostle Paul's teaching. We will examine what the apostles taught about the key doctrinal issues in the lordship debate: faith, grace, repentance, justification, sanctification, sin, works, assurance, perseverance, and the gospel message. A clear fact will emerge: The gospel according to Jesus *is* the same as the gospel according to the apostles. The faith it calls for is not dormant, but dynamic; it is a repentant, submissive, trusting, enduring faith that works.

3

Without Faith, It Is Impossible to Please Him

Faith is the acceptance of a gift at the hands of Christ.
. . . It is a very wonderful thing; it involves a change of the whole nature of man; it involves a new hatred of sin and a new hunger and thirst after righteousness. Such a wonderful change is not the work of man; faith itself is given us by the Spirit of God. Christians never make themselves Christians; but they are made Christians by God.

. . . It is quite inconceivable that a man should be given this faith in Christ, that he should accept this gift which Christ offers, and still go on contentedly in sin. For the very thing which Christ offers us is salvation from sin—not only salvation from the guilt of sin, but also salvation from the power of sin. The very first thing that the Christian does, therefore, is to keep the law of God: he keeps it no longer as a way of earning his salvation—for salvation has been given him freely by God—but he keeps it joyously as a central part of salvation itself. The faith of which Paul speaks is, as Paul himself says, a faith that works through love; and love is the fulfilling of the whole law. . . . The faith that Paul means when he speaks of justification by faith alone is a faith that works.

J. Gresham Machen[1]

*A*t the heart of the no-lordship error is a disastrous misunderstanding about the nature of faith. No-lordship teaching depicts faith as

[1]J. Gresham Machen, *What Is Faith?* (New York: Macmillan, 1925), 203–4.

inherently inert—even antithetical to works, obedience, and surrender to the will of God. The disciples of no-lordship doctrine have much to say *about* faith. After all, "simple faith" is the foundation of their whole system. Unfortunately, most rely on sketchy definitions of *faith* ("being convinced or giving credence to something or someone," *SGS* 156) and *believe* ("to hold something as true," *SGS* 155). Many are loath to define the words at all. One has written,

> In every other sphere of life, except religion, we do not puzzle ourselves with introspective questions about the "nature" of our faith. . . . Let it be clearly stated here that English words like to "believe" or "faith" function as fully adequate equivalents to their Greek counterparts. There is not some hidden residue of meaning in the Greek words that is not conveyed by their normal English renderings. . . .
>
> It follows that a Greek reader who met the words "he who believes in Me has everlasting life," would understand the word "believe" exactly as we do. The reader *most certainly* would not understand this word to imply submission, surrender, repentance, or anything else of this sort. For those readers, as for us, "to believe" meant "to believe."
>
> Surely it is one of the conceits of modern theology to suppose that we can define away simple terms like "belief" and "unbelief" and replace their meanings with complicated elaborations. The confusion produced by this sort of process has a pervasive influence in the church today (*AF* 27–29).

Those statements summarize the thesis of a chapter titled "Faith Means Just That—Faith!"

All right. Let's suppose that *faith* and *believe* are satisfactory equivalents of the Greek words *pistis* ("faith, faithfulness") and *pisteuō* ("to believe, entrust"). What do English dictionaries say about *faith*?

The *Oxford American Dictionary* says faith is "1. reliance or trust in a person or thing. 2. belief in religious doctrine. 3. a system of religious belief, *the Christian faith*. 4. loyalty, sincerity."

Wait a minute. "Loyalty, sincerity"? Would no-lordship teaching grant that those are elements of true faith? Aren't such concepts specifically excluded from the no-lordship definition of faith?

We turn to the authoritative *Oxford English Dictionary* (OED), which lists more than a full page of meanings for *faith*. It defines faith as "confidence, reliance, trust"; "belief proceeding from reliance on testimony or authority"; "the duty of fulfilling one's trust; allegiance owed to a superior, fealty; the obligation of a promise or engagement"; and "the quality of fulfilling one's trust; faithfulness, fidelity, loyalty." The OED even includes a theological definition:

> That kind of faith (distinctively called *saving* or *justifying* faith) by which, in the teaching of the N. T. a sinner is justified in the sight of God. This is variously defined by theologians (see quots.), but there is general agreement in regarding it as a conviction practically operative on the character and will, and thus opposed to the mere intellectual assent to religious truth (sometimes called *speculative faith*).

Would no-lordship doctrine be in agreement with those definitions? Certainly not. The patrons of no-lordship salvation redefine *faith* precisely to strip the word of any idea of loyalty, faithfulness, allegiance, submission, duty, fidelity, obligation, and "things of this sort."

So the no-lordship partisan finds no support in an appeal to the standard English meaning of the word *faith*. What about *believe*?

According to the OED, *believe* is a verb meaning "to have confidence or faith *in* (a person); and consequently to rely upon, trust to." The dictionary notes that *believe* is derived from root words that mean "to hold estimable, valuable, pleasing, or satisfactory, to be satisfied with."

To be satisfied with Christ. Coming straight from the English dictionary, that frankly is a better definition of *believing* than those who plead for no-lordship salvation have yet proposed. It explicitly sets believing apart from mere abstract acquiescence to academic facts. It describes a faith that *cannot* be placed in opposition to commitment, surrender, repentance, delighting in the Lord, and "things of this sort."

Ultimately, however, it is not the dictionary, but Scripture, to which we must turn for a definition of faith. One chapter in the New Testament, Hebrews 11, is given to us for the express purpose of defining and describing *faith*. The writer to the Hebrews tells us precisely *what faith is* and *what faith does*. Here we find that the faith represented by no-lordship teaching bears little resemblance to the faith Scripture speaks about.

What Faith Is

Hebrews 11 begins, "Now faith is the assurance of things hoped for, the conviction of things not seen. For by it the men of old gained approval. By faith we understand that the worlds were prepared by the word of God, so that what is seen was not made out of things which are visible" (vv. 1–3).

The entire chapter deals with the supremacy and superiority of faith. It confronts the Pharisaism of first-century Judaism, which taught that righteousness, forgiveness from sins, and ultimate salvation could be achieved only through a rigorous system of meritorious works. Jewish tradition had so twisted God's law that most Jews saw it as the way to earn favor with God. Even after being shown the basic truths of Christ, some of the Hebrews were unwilling to abandon their religion based on works-righteousness.

Works-based salvation is and always has been despised by God (cf. Rom. 8:3; Gal. 2:16; Phil. 3:9; 1 Tim. 1:9). God has never redeemed man by works, but always by faith (cf. Gen. 15:6). "The righteous will live by his faith" (Hab. 2:4), is not a truth about the New Covenant alone. As Hebrews 11 makes clear, from Adam on, the instrument of God's salvation has been faith, not works. Works are a byproduct of faith, never a means of salvation.

Habakkuk 2:4 is quoted three times in the New Testament: Romans 1:17, Galatians 3:11, and Hebrews 10:38. Romans explains what is meant by "the righteous." Galatians is something of a commentary on the words "will live." Hebrews 11 plumbs the depths of the phrase "by faith."

Habakkuk 2:4 forms a bridge from Hebrews 10 and its great theme of justification by faith. The saints named in chapter 11 are examples of people who were justified by faith and who lived by faith. Faith is both the way to life and the way to live. Faith is the *only* way; without it no one can please God (v. 6).

What is faith? "Faith is the assurance of things hoped for, the conviction of things not seen" (11:1). That verse is a couplet of Hebrew-style poetry. It defines *faith* in two parallel and almost identical phrases. It is not meant to be a full theological definition. Nevertheless, all the crucial elements that summarize the biblical doctrine of faith are suggested by this verse and the examples of faith that follow.

Faith is the assurance of things hoped for. Faith transports God's promises into the present tense. In other words, real faith implicitly takes God at His word. Faith is a supernatural confidence in—and therefore reliance on—the One who has made the promises. It is not an uncertain hope for something that may come to pass in a vague, indefinite hereafter. It is a trust that brings absolute here-and-now certainty to "things hoped for."

The word translated "assurance" (Gk., *hupostasis*) appears two other times in Hebrews. In 1:3 it is rendered "nature" in the phrase "exact representation of His nature," speaking of Christ's likeness to the Father. In 3:14 the word is "assurance," as in 11:1. It refers to essence, substance, real content—reality as opposed to mere appearance. *Hupostasis* is made up of *stasis* "to stand" and *hupo* "under." It refers to a foundation, the ground on which something is built. A Greek dictionary notes that *hupostasis* was used in ancient Greek literature as a legal term referring to "documents bearing on the ownership of a person's property, deposited in archives, and forming the evidence of ownership." That is the sense conveyed in Hebrews 11:1. The Greek dictionary offers this translation: "Faith is the title-deed of things hoped for."[2]

In a similar vein, the King James Version's rendering of Hebrews 11:1 is a good one: "Faith is the substance of things hoped for, the evidence of things not seen." Faith, far from being ambiguous or unsure, is concrete conviction. It is the present confidence of a future reality, "the *assurance* of things hoped for."

The assurance this verse describes is not personal assurance of salvation but rather absolute certainty with regard to the gospel message. It is saying that faith is a God-wrought conviction about the truth of the Bible's promises and the trustworthiness of Christ. The verse is not saying that faith automatically guarantees full assurance of one's personal salvation.

One question that has been raised by the lordship debate is whether the essence of saving faith is personal assurance. Radical no-lordship doctrine teaches that faith is assurance and assurance is faith. "A person who has *never been sure* of eternal life has *never believed* the saving message of God" (*AF* 51). Also, "It is utterly impossible for us to give credence to the gospel message without knowing that we are saved" (*AF* 50). On the other hand, if you are sure you are saved, you must be: "People know whether they believe something or not, and that is the real issue where God is concerned" (*AF* 31). That teaching makes no place at all for the possibility of *false* assurance.

In chapter 10 we will deal with this matter more thoroughly. As we shall see, there is much more to full assurance of one's salvation than simply believing the objective promises of Scripture. There is much more to faith than a feeling of assurance. Hebrews 11:1 simply means

[2]James Hope Moulton and George Milligan, *The Vocabulary of the Greek Testament* (Grand Rapids, Mich.: Eerdmans, 1930), 660.

that faith is a supernatural certainty about the truth of the gospel and the reliability of Christ.[3]

This sure faith must be God's work in us. Although the truth of the gospel is confirmed by many evidences, human nature is predisposed to reject the truth about Christ. So apart from the work of the Spirit in us, we can never believe in the sense this verse describes.

Hebrews 11:1 faith is not like the everyday faith that we speak of. We drink water out of a faucet, believing it is safe. We drive our automobiles in freeway traffic, trusting that the brakes will work. We submit to the surgeon's knife and the dentist's drill by faith. When we drop film off at the drugstore, we trust that the prints will be ready at the promised time (cf. *SGS* 118). We believe in the basic integrity of our governmental leaders (*AF* 27–28). The capacity for that kind of faith is intrinsic to human nature. But it is not the faith Hebrews 11:1 describes.

To begin with, natural faith rests on an object that is not necessarily reliable. The water *might* actually be tainted. The brakes *could* fail. Surgeons *do* make mistakes. The drugstore *may not* deliver your prints on time. The president *probably will* default on some of his campaign promises. But when we believe unto eternal life, we trust something more real and Someone more trustworthy than anything or anyone we could ever comprehend with the natural senses. Our senses may lie; God cannot (Titus 1:2). People fail; God does not (Num. 23:19). Circumstances change; God never does (Mal. 3:6). So the faith described in Hebrews 11 is focused on an infinitely more dependable *object* than any of the day-to-day varieties of faith.

Also, the *nature* of faith is different in the spiritual realm. Natural faith relies on the physical senses. We tend to believe only what we or others can see, hear, taste, and feel. When we trust the water, our brakes, the surgeon, the drugstore, or the president, we do so because our senses and human experience tell us these things are generally worthy of our confidence. Hebrews 11:1 faith, on the other hand, is a *supernatural* conviction—a solid, unshakable assurance that is contrary to human nature. It includes a capacity to lay hold of spiritual reality imperceptible to the natural man: "A natural man does not accept the things of the Spirit of God; for they are foolishness to him, and he cannot understand them, because they are spiritually appraised" (1 Cor. 2:14). Hebrews

---

[3]Hebrews 11:1 certainly affirms that *an element* of assurance is at the heart of faith itself. As we shall see in chapter 10, saving faith in Christ is the foundation of all assurance. One's sense of personal security grows deeper and stronger with spiritual maturity, but the seed of that assurance is present even at the beginning of saving faith.

11:27 characterizes Moses' faith the same way ("he endured, as seeing Him who is unseen").

The clear implication of all this is that faith is a gift of God. If faith were a mere human decision, it would be no assurance at all. It might be a bad decision. If believing were merely a function of the human mind, faith would be no grounds for confidence. The mind can easily be deceived, mistaken, deluded, or misinformed. Real faith, however, is a divinely implanted assurance that rises above the natural functioning of the human mind. After all, the natural man *cannot* see Him who is unseen (v. 27).

But seeing the unseen is the nature of faith.

Faith is . . . the conviction of things not seen. This parallel phrase carries the same truth even further. *Conviction* implies a deeper manifestation of the inward assurance. People of faith are prepared to live out their belief. Their lives reflect a commitment to what their minds and hearts are assured is true. They are so sure of promises and blessings yet future that they behave as if those promises were already realized (Heb. 11:7–13; cf. Rom. 4:17–21).

"Conviction of things not seen" echoes the apostle Peter's description of saving faith (1 Pet. 1:8–9): Although we have not yet seen Christ, we love Him. Though we do not see Him now, we believe in Him—we are committed to Him—with inexpressible and glorious joy, obtaining faith's outcome, the salvation of our souls. Such faith is unassailable. No matter what tests it, no matter the cost, this faith endures. In fact, all the examples in Hebrews 11 show people whose faith was severely tested. In every case, their faith remained strong. To those examples we could add Job, whose faith Satan tried to destroy with the severest kinds of personal tragedy, and Peter, whom Satan sifted like wheat—but his faith didn't fail (Luke 22:32). To this end, Jesus prayed for Peter. He prays just as successfully for *all* the saved (Rom. 8:34; Heb. 7:25; 1 John 2:2). No matter what attacks this faith, it cannot be destroyed.

How can such faith fail to be life-changing? It can't. This faith is a firm and supernatural conviction that governs the true believer's behavior, as the examples in Hebrews 11 also demonstrate. People of faith obey, worship, endure, sacrifice, and work *by faith*. Our works are not fleshly efforts, but the inevitable byproduct of a rock-solid conviction that the "things not seen" are nevertheless real. We obey because we are committed to the object of our faith.

Commitment is the disputed element of faith around which the lordship controversy swirls. No-lordship theology denies that believing in Christ involves any element of personal commitment to Him. It is impossible to harmonize the no-lordship view of faith with Hebrews 11. The whole point of this chapter is to highlight examples of people who were *committed* to what they *believed*. More precisely, they were *committed* to the God they *believed* in—even to death.

Systematic theology usually recognizes three elements of faith: knowledge (*notitia*), assent (*assensus*), and trust (*fiducia*). Augustus H. Strong and Louis Berkhof both refer to *notitia* as the "intellectual element" of faith. *Assensus* is the "emotional element." *Fiducia* is the "voluntary [volitional] element."[4] Real faith therefore involves the whole person—mind, emotions, and will. The mind embraces *knowledge*, a recognition and understanding of the truth that Christ saves. The heart gives *assent*, or the settled confidence and affirmation that Christ's salvation is applicable to one's own soul. The will responds with *trust*, the personal commitment to and appropriation of Christ as the only hope for eternal salvation.

This "trust," or *fiducia*, faith's volitional component, is the crowning element of believing. It involves surrender to the object of faith. It is a personal appropriation of Christ as *both* Lord and Savior. Standard theology universally affirms this. Strong defined *fiducia* as "trust in Christ as Lord and Savior; or, in other words—to distinguish its two aspects: (*a*) Surrender of the soul, as guilty and defiled, to Christ's governance. . . . (*b*) Reception and appropriation of Christ, as the source of pardon and spiritual life."[5] Berkhof echoes Strong at

---

[4]Augustus H. Strong, *Systematic Theology* (Philadelphia: Judson, 1907), 837–38; Louis Berkhof, *Systematic Theology* (Grand Rapids, Mich.: Eerdmans, 1939), 503–5.

In *Absolutely Free!* Zane Hodges claimed I had "seriously distort[ed]" Berkhof's definition (*AF* 207). "*Assensus* is *not* an 'emotional element,'" Hodges protested. But those are, after all, Berkhof's own words. Note that Strong, for one, held an identical view. Even Ryrie agrees (*SGS* 120). By "emotional element," Strong and Berkhof meant that *assensus* goes beyond considering the object of faith in a detached and disinterested way. Berkhof wrote, "When one embraces Christ by faith, he has a deep conviction of the truth and reality of the object of faith, feels that it meets an important need in his life, and is conscious of an absorbing interest in it. . . . It is exactly the distinguishing characteristic of the knowledge of saving faith" (Berkhof, 504–5).

John Calvin defined *assensus* as "more a matter of the heart than the head, of the affection than the intellect." He equated assent with "pious affection"; see John Calvin, *Institutes of the Christian Religion*, trans. Henry Beveridge, 3:2:8 (reprint, Grand Rapids, Mich.: Eerdmans, 1966), 1:476.

[5]Strong, *Systematic Theology*, 338–39.

this point almost word for word.[6] B. B. Warfield, noting that *trust* comprises some element of commitment to its object, wrote, "We cannot be said to believe that which we distrust too much to commit ourselves to it."[7]

Saving faith, then, is the whole of my being embracing all of Christ. Faith cannot be divorced from commitment.

Radical no-lordship theology dismisses all of the above as unnecessary "psychoanalysis" of what should be a simple concept. "No one needs to be a psychologist to understand what faith is," Zane Hodges has written. "Still less do we need to resort to 'pop psychology' to explain it. It is an unproductive waste of time to employ the popular categories—intellect, emotion, or will—as a way of analyzing the mechanics of faith. Such discussions lie far outside the boundaries of biblical thought" (*AF* 30–31).

But all three elements of faith are clearly implied in our text: *knowledge:* "By faith we *understand*" (v. 3); *assent:* "faith is the *assurance* of things hoped for" (v. 1); and *trust:* "faith is . . . the *conviction* of things not seen" (v. 1). The men and women profiled in this great Hall of Faith were all fully committed—mind, heart, and soul—to the object of their faith. How could anyone familiar with this chapter ever devise a notion of faith that lacks personal commitment?

Faith is believing that God is. Hebrews 11:6, a landmark verse, gives still more insight into the nature of faith: "Without faith it is impossible to please Him, for he who comes to God must believe that He is, and that He is a rewarder of those who seek Him."

Absolutely nothing we do can please God apart from this kind of faith. Without faith, pleasing God is *impossible*. Religion, racial heritage, meritorious works—everything the Hebrews regarded as pleasing to God—is utterly futile apart from faith.

The beginning of faith is simply believing that God *is*. This certainly means far more than believing in an unnamed and unknown supreme being. The Hebrews knew God's name as I AM (Exod. 3:14). The phrase "he who comes to God must believe that He is" is a call for faith in the one God who had revealed Himself in Scripture. This verse does not ratify belief in some abstract deity—the "ground of being," the "man upstairs," Allah, the "Unknown god" of the Greek philosophers

---

[6]Berkhof, *Systematic Theology,* 505.

[7]Benjamin B. Warfield, *Biblical and Theological Studies* (Philadelphia: Presbyterian & Reformed, 1968), 402–3.

(Acts 17:23), or any of the other manmade gods. It is speaking of faith in the one God of the Bible, whose highest revelation of Himself is in the Person of His Son, the Lord Jesus Christ.

Clearly, true faith has objective substance. There *is* an intellectual content to our faith. Believing is not a mindless leap in the dark or some ethereal kind of trust apart from knowledge. There is a factual, historical, intellectual basis for our faith. Faith that is not grounded in this objective truth is no faith at all. On that, I think everyone on both sides of the lordship question is in full agreement.

But no-lordship teaching is inclined at this point to two serious errors. First, it strips faith of *everything but* the objective, academic aspect, making the exercise of faith a simple head game. Second, it tends to pare down the objective content of faith to the barest minimum, making the ground of faith so meager that one need scarcely know anything about who God is or what Christ has done. It is a minimalist approach to believing that has no warrant in Scripture.

How far will no-lordship apologists go in divesting the gospel of its essential content? A recent article in the leading no-lordship fraternity's monthly newsletter suggested that "a person can place his or her trust in Jesus Christ and Him alone without understanding precisely *how* He takes away sins." Therefore, the article stated, "it is possible to believe savingly in Christ without understanding the reality of His resurrection."[8] The man who wrote the piece maintains that neither Christ's death nor His resurrection are essential to the evangelistic message. It is enough, he says, "to present only the core truth of the gospel: namely, that whoever believes in Jesus Christ has eternal life."[9] Evidently he believes people can be saved who have never even heard that Christ died for their sins.

But the apostle Paul said, "If you confess with your mouth Jesus as Lord, and believe in your heart that God raised Him from the dead, you shall be saved" (Rom. 10:9). The resurrection was central to Paul's gospel: "I make known to you, brethren, the gospel which I preached . . . that Christ died for our sins . . . and that He was buried, and that He was raised on the third day according to the Scriptures" (1 Cor. 15:1–4). There are many false christs (Matt. 24:24). The only One who grants eternal life rose from the dead to make salvation possible. Those who worship a lesser christ cannot be saved: "If

---

[8]Bob Wilkin, "Tough Questions About Saving Faith," *The Grace Evangelical Society News* (June 1990): 1.

[9]Ibid., 4.

Christ has not been raised, then our preaching is vain, your faith also is vain" (1 Cor. 15:14).

The crucifixion and resurrection are the most vital facts of the gospel (1 Cor. 15:1–4). When Hebrews 11:6 calls for "believ[ing] that He is," it is requiring that we believe in the God of Scripture, the One who gave His Son to die and rise again. Granted, Old Testament saints did not have full revelation about Christ's death and resurrection. They were saved through their faith based on what God *had* revealed. But since that first resurrection Sunday, no one has been saved except through believing in Christ's atonement for sins and His subsequent resurrection.

So the phrase "believe that He is" speaks of faith in the God of Scripture, based on an understanding of crucial truth about Him. This is *notitia*, knowledge—the objective side of faith. But as we are seeing, there is more to saving faith.

Faith is seeking God. It is not enough just to believe that the God of the Bible exists. It is not enough to know about His promises or even intellectually believe the truth of the gospel. In order to please Him it is also necessary to "believe . . . that He is a rewarder of those who seek Him." That phrase brings together assent (*assensus*) and trust (*fiducia*) to make the picture of faith complete. *Assent* goes beyond a dispassionate observation of who God is. The assenting heart affirms the goodness of His character as "a rewarder." *Trust* applies this knowledge personally and practically by turning to God in sincere faith as a seeker of *Him*.

It is not enough merely to postulate a supreme being. It is not enough even to accept the *right* God. Real faith is not just knowing *about* God: it is *seeking* God. In fact, "seeking God" is often used as a synonym for faith in Scripture. Isaiah 55:6 is a call to faith: "Seek the Lord while He may be found; Call upon Him while He is near." God Himself told Israel, "You will seek Me and find Me, when you search for Me with all your heart" (Jer. 29:13). "For thus says the Lord to the house of Israel, 'Seek Me that you may live'" (Amos 5:4). "But seek first His kingdom and His righteousness; and all these things shall be added to you" (Matt. 6:33).

Perhaps someone will object that Hebrews 11:6 simply says we must *believe* that God rewards seekers; it doesn't say we must *be* seekers of God. But why does God reward those who seek Him? Because of their works? No, "all our righteous deeds are like a filthy garment" (Isa. 64:6). God rewards only those with faith—without faith it is impossible to please Him. This verse thus identifies seeking God as the epitome of true faith.

Seeking Him leads to finding Him fully revealed in the Lord Jesus Christ (Matt. 7:7; Luke 11:9).

The attitude described here is the antithesis of works-righteousness. Instead of trying to earn favor with God, faith pursues God Himself. Instead of bartering for God's approbation, faith follows after *Him* as the soul's greatest pleasure. Far from making faith a human work, this definition emphasizes that faith is the abandonment of seeking to please God through works—and the adherence to God, who manifests what pleases Him by His works through His people.

Faith, then, is seeking and finding God in Christ, desiring Him, and ultimately being fulfilled with Him. Another way of saying it is that faith is wholly leaning on Christ—for redemption, for righteousness, for counsel, for fellowship, for sustenance, for direction, for succor, for His lordship, and for all in life that can truly satisfy.

Notice that we have come full circle to the definition of faith suggested by the English dictionary: Faith is being satisfied with Christ. Jesus Himself said so: "I am the bread of life; he who comes to Me shall not hunger, and he who believes in Me shall never thirst" (John 6:35). There is no way a genuine believer can ultimately fail to be satisfied with Christ. After all, God Himself has declared His beloved Son fully satisfying (Matt. 3:17; 17:5). How could sincere faith deem Him something less?

How do you suppose this kind of faith behaves? The rest of Hebrews 11 gives an unequivocal answer to that question.

What Faith Does

Faith obeys. That, in two words, is the key lesson of Hebrews 11. Here we see people of faith worshiping God (v. 4); walking with God (v. 5); working for God (v. 7); obeying God (vv. 8–10); overcoming barrenness (v. 11); and overpowering death (v. 12).

Faith enabled these people to persevere to death (vv. 13–16); trust God with their dearest possessions (vv. 17–19); believe God for the future (vv. 20–23); turn away from earthly treasure for heavenly reward (vv. 24–26); see Him who is unseen (v. 27); receive miracles from the hand of God (28–30); have courage in the face of great danger (31–33); conquer kingdoms, perform acts of righteousness, obtain promises, shut the mouths of lions, quench the power of fire, escape the edge of the sword, from weakness be made strong, become mighty in war, and put foreign armies to flight (vv. 33–34). This faith has overcome death, endured torture, outlasted chains and imprisonment, withstood temptation, undergone martyrdom, and survived all manner of hardship (vv. 35–38). **And faith endures.** If anything is true about Hebrews 11 faith, it is that it cannot be killed. It perseveres. It endures no matter what—holding to God with love and assurance no matter what kind of assaults the world or the forces of evil might bring against it. No-lordship theology posits an altogether different kind of faith. No-lordship faith is a fragile, sometimes temporary, often nonworking faith. No-lordship faith is simply being convinced of something or giving credence to historical facts (*SGS* 30). No-lordship faith is confidence, trust, holding something as true—but without any commitment to the object of faith (*SGS* 118–19). No-lordship faith is the inward conviction that what God says to us in the gospel is true—that and that alone (*AF* 31). No-lordship faith is "a single, one-time appropriation of God's gift." It won't necessarily continue believing (*AF* 63). In fact, no-lordship faith might even turn into hostile unbelief (*SGS* 141).

Is faith merely the illumination of human reason, or does it transform the whole being? Some advocates of the no-lordship view resent the accusation that they see faith as merely a mental activity. But they consistently fail to define believing as anything *more* than a cognitive function. Many use the word *trust*, but when they define it, they actually describe *assent*.

Charles Ryrie, for example, cites approvingly Berkhof's section on *notitia, assensus,* and *fiducia*. He even quotes Berkhof's definition of *fiducia,* trust: "a personal trust in Christ as Savior *and Lord, including a surrender of the soul as guilty and defiled to Christ,* and a reception and appropriation of Christ as the source of pardon and a spiritual life" (*SGS* 120, emphasis added). In the same paragraph, however, Ryrie makes the curious assertion that "Berkhof does not inject or speak to the issue of the mastery of Christ over one's life." As Ryrie continues his own explanation of "trust," it becomes clear that he actually wants to abridge Berkhof to this: *Fiducia* is "a personal trust in Christ as Savior . . . and . . . as the source of pardon and [eternal] life." In fact, when Ryrie further explains what he means by "personal trust in Christ," he continually falls back on language that speaks only of believing facts: "To believe in Christ for salvation means to have confidence that He can remove the guilt of sin and give eternal life" (*SGS* 119). That is *assent*, not *trust*. Assent is the acceptance of truth *about* Christ; trust is a turning *to* Him in full self-surrender (cf. Deut. 30:10; 2 Kings 23:25; 1 Thess. 1:9). That was Berkhof's point.

Here is the typical no-lordship appeal to sinners: "trust in the gospel" (*SGS* 30), "believe in the good news" (*SGS* 39), "believe that Christ died for our sins" (*SGS* 40), "Believe that He is God and your Messiah who died and who rose from the dead" (*SGS* 96), "believe that Christ can forgive" (*SGS* 118), "believe that his death paid for all your sin" (*SGS* 119), "trust in the truth" (*SGS* 121), "believe that Someone . . . can take away sin" (*SGS* 123).

No-lordship doctrine inevitably makes the gospel *message* the object of faith, rather than the Lord Jesus Himself. Contrast the no-lordship appeals with biblical language: "Believe in the Lord Jesus, and you shall be saved" (Acts 16:31). Sinners are called to believe in *Him,* not only the facts about Him (Acts 20:21; 24:24; 26:18; Rom. 3:22, 26; Gal. 2:16, 20; 3:22, 26; Phil. 3:9). Faith certainly *includes* knowledge of and assent to the truth about Christ and His saving work. But saving faith must go beyond knowledge and assent. It is personal trust in the Savior. The call of the gospel is to trust *Him* (cf. John 5:39–40).[10] That necessarily involves some degree of love, allegiance, and surrender to His authority.

Does this mix faith and works, as some are fond of saying? Not at all. Let there be no confusion on this point. Faith is an *internal* reality with *external* consequences. When we say that faith encompasses obedience, we are speaking of the God-given *attitude* of obedience, not trying to make *works* a part of the definition of faith. God makes the believing heart an obedient heart; that is, a heart eager to obey. Faith itself is complete before one work of obedience ever issues forth.

But make no mistake—real faith will always produce righteous works. Faith is the root; works are the fruit. Because God Himself is the vinedresser, fruit is guaranteed. That's why whenever Scripture gives examples of faith—as here in Hebrews 11—faith inevitably is seen as obedient, working, and active.

No-lordship theology reasons that to be truly free from works-righteousness, faith must be free from all obedience, including an *attitude* of obedience. In no-lordship thought, it is unacceptable to require that faith include even a *willingness* to obey.[11] But willingness

---

[10]Ryrie occasionally speaks of Christ as the object of faith, but inevitably defines what he means in a way that nullifies the whole point. For example, when he says, "the object of faith or trust is the Lord Jesus Christ," he immediately counters with: "The issue about which we trust Him is His ability to forgive our sin and take us to heaven" (*SGS* 121).

[11]Charles C. Ryrie, *Balancing the Christian Life* (Chicago: Moody, 1969), 169–70.

to obey is precisely what sets genuine faith apart from hypocrisy. Warfield wrote, "It may be very fairly contended that 'preparedness to act' supplies a very good test of the genuineness of 'faith,' 'belief.' A so-called 'faith,' 'belief' on which we are not prepared to act is near to no real 'faith,' 'belief' at all. What we are convinced of, we should certainly confide in; and what we are unwilling to confide in we seem not quite sure of—we do not appear thoroughly to believe, to have faith in."[12]

Faith and unbelief are states of the heart. But they necessarily impact behavior.[13] Jesus said, "The good man out of the good treasure of his heart brings forth what is good; and the evil man out of the evil treasure brings forth what is evil; for his mouth speaks from that which fills his heart" (Luke 6:45). The state of one's heart will inevitably be revealed by its fruit. That is a key lesson to be drawn from Hebrews 11 and its chronicle of faithfulness.

---

[12]Warfield, *Biblical and Theological Studies,* 379.

[13]That faith necessarily has practical moral results is seen in the cause-and-effect statements of John 8:36–47 (emphasis added):

> "If therefore the Son shall make you free, *you shall be free indeed.* I know that you are Abraham's offspring; yet *you seek to kill Me, because My word has no place in you.* I speak the things which I have seen with My Father; *therefore you also do the things which you heard from your father.*"
>
> They answered and said to Him, "Abraham is our father."
>
> Jesus said to them, *"If you are Abraham's children, do the deeds of Abraham.* But as it is, you are seeking to kill Me, a man who has told you the truth, which I heard from God; this Abraham did not do. *You are doing the deeds of your father.*"
>
> They said to Him, "We were not born of fornication; we have one Father, even God."
>
> Jesus said to them, *"If God were your Father, you would love Me;* for I proceeded forth and have come from God, for I have not even come on My own initiative, but He sent Me. Why *do you not understand* what I am saying? *It is because you cannot hear My word.* You are of your father the devil, and *you want to do the desires of your father.* He was a murderer from the beginning, and does not stand in the truth, because there is no truth in him. Whenever he speaks a lie, he speaks from his own nature; for he is a liar, and the father of lies. But *because I speak the truth, you do not believe Me.* Which one of you convicts Me of sin? If I speak truth, why do you not believe Me? *He who is of God hears the words of God; for this reason you do not hear them, because you are not of God.*"

A key to that passage is verse 42: "If God were your Father, you would love Me." Their *saying* that God was their Father did not make it so. Their behavior and affections reflected the spiritual reality.

A crucial point must be made here. The works described in Hebrews 11 are *faith works*. These are not fleshly efforts to earn God's favor. The works described here are in no sense meritorious. They are the pure expression of believing hearts. *By faith* Abel offered a better sacrifice (v. 4). *By faith* Enoch walked with God (v. 5). *By faith* Noah built an ark (v. 7). *By faith* Abraham obeyed (v. 8). *By faith* he lived in a foreign land (v. 9). *By faith* he offered up Isaac (v. 17). *By faith* Isaac, Jacob, and Joseph persevered to the end of their lives (vv. 20–22). *By faith* Moses' parents hid him (v. 23). *By faith* Moses spurned Egypt in favor of the reproach of Christ (vv. 24–26). *By faith* he left Egypt without fear (v. 27). *By faith* he kept the Passover (v. 28). *By faith* all Israel passed through the Red Sea (v. 29). *By faith* they conquered Jericho (v. 30). *By faith* Rahab welcomed the spies in peace (v. 31).

> What more shall I say? For time will fail me if I tell of Gideon, Barak, Samson, Jephthah, of David and Samuel and the prophets, who *by faith* conquered kingdoms, performed acts of righteousness, obtained promises, shut the mouths of lions, quenched the power of fire, escaped the edge of the sword, from weakness were made strong, became mighty in war, put foreign armies to flight. Women received back their dead by resurrection; and others were tortured, not accepting their release, in order that they might obtain a better resurrection; and others experienced mockings and scourgings, yes, also chains and imprisonment. They were stoned, they were sawn in two, they were tempted, they were put to death with the sword; they went about in sheepskins, in goatskins, being destitute, afflicted, ill-treated . . . wandering in deserts and mountains and caves and holes in the ground.
>
> Hebrews 11:32–38, emphasis added

Works-righteousness? No. "All these . . . gained approval through their *faith*" (v. 39). Hebrews 12:1 identifies these people as a "great . . . cloud of witnesses surrounding us." Witnesses in what sense? They give testimony to the validity, joy, peace, satisfaction, power, and continuity of saving faith. The writer, then, calls on all to run the faith-race (vv. 1–2).

In spite of this monumental testimony to faith works, no-lordship apologists often claim that viewing works as the inevitable expression of faith is tantamount to setting up a system of works-righteousness. Zane Hodges argues this way:

> Lordship salvation cannot escape the charge that it mixes faith and works. The way it does so is succinctly stated by MacArthur: "Obedience is the inevitable manifestation of saving faith."
>
> But this is the same as saying, "Without obedience there is no justification and no heaven." Viewed from *that* standpoint, "obedience" is actually a *condition* for justification and for heaven. . . . If heaven really cannot be attained apart from obedience to God—and this is what lordship salvation teaches—then, logically, that obedience is a *condition* for getting there (*AF* 213–14).

But the folly of that line of reasoning is immediately evident. To say that works are a necessary *result* of faith is *not* the same as making works a *condition* for justification. Hodges himself surely believes all Christians will ultimately be glorified (Rom. 8:30). Would he accept the charge that he is making glorification a *condition* for justification? Presumably, both the lordship and no-lordship views agree that all believers will ultimately be conformed to the image of Christ (Rom. 8:29). We differ only on the timing. Lordship salvation maintains that the process of becoming like Christ begins at the moment of conversion and continues for all of life. The no-lordship view allows for the possibility that practical sanctification may stall short of its goal, or not even begin until this life on earth ends.

Meritorious works have nothing to do with faith. But *faith works* have everything to do with it. As we shall see in chapter 9, faith that does not produce works is dead faith, inefficacious faith. Faith that remains idle is no better than the faith the demons display (James 2:19).

Here we must close this chapter with a clear and careful distinction. Faith works are a *consequence* of faith, not a *component* of faith. As we observed earlier, faith is an entirely inward response and therefore is complete before it produces its first work. At the moment of salvation, faith *does* nothing but receive the provision of Christ. The believer himself contributes nothing meritorious to the saving process. As J. Gresham Machen stated in the quotation with which I began this chapter, "Faith is the acceptance of a gift at the hands of Christ." Better yet, faith lays hold of Christ Himself. In no sense is this an issue of works or merit.

But true faith never remains passive. From the moment of regeneration, faith goes to work. It doesn't work for divine favor. It doesn't work against God's grace, but in accord with grace. As we "work out

[our] salvation with fear and trembling" (Phil. 2:12), we discover that "it is God who is at work in [us], both to will and to work for His good pleasure" (v. 13). True faith keeps our eyes fixed on Jesus, the author and perfecter of all genuine faith (Heb. 12:2).

4

Cheap Grace?

Cheap grace means grace sold on the market like cheap-jacks' wares. . . .

Cheap grace is not the kind of forgiveness that frees us from the toils of sin. Cheap grace is the grace we bestow on ourselves.

Cheap grace is the preaching of forgiveness without requiring repentance, baptism without church discipline, Communion without confession, absolution without personal confession. Cheap grace is grace without discipleship, grace without the cross, grace without Jesus Christ, living and incarnate.

Dietrich Bonhoeffer[1]

*C*heap grace. The term itself is offensive.

"Why do you use that expression?" a friend asked. "It just seems to denigrate the grace of God. After all, grace isn't *cheap*—it's absolutely free! Isn't perfect freeness the very essence of grace?"

But "cheap grace" doesn't speak of God's grace. It is a self-imparted grace, a pseudograce. This grace is "cheap" in *value*, not cost. It is a bargain-basement, damaged-goods, washed-out, moth-eaten, second-hand grace. It is a manmade grace reminiscent of the indulgences Rome was peddling in Martin Luther's day. Cheap? The cost is actually far more than the buyer could possibly realize, though the "grace" is utterly worthless.

---

[1]Dietrich Bonhoeffer, *The Cost of Discipleship* (New York: Collier, 1959), 45–47.

The term "cheap grace" was coined by a German Lutheran pastor and Nazi resister named Dietrich Bonhoeffer. Bonhoeffer was hanged in 1945 by SS guards, but not before his writings had left their mark. Bonhoeffer's theological perspective was neo-orthodox, and evangelicalism rightly rejects much of· his teaching. But Bonhoeffer spoke powerfully against the secularization of the church. He correctly analyzed the dangers of the church's frivolous attitude toward grace. After we discard the neo-orthodox teachings, we do well to pay heed to Bonhoeffer's diatribe against cheap grace:

> Cheap grace means grace as a doctrine, a principle, a system. It means forgiveness of sins proclaimed as a general truth, the love of God taught as the Christian "conception" of God. An intellectual assent to that idea is held to be of itself sufficient to secure the remission of sins. The Church which holds the correct doctrine of grace has, it is supposed, *ipso facto* a part in that grace. In such a Church the world finds a cheap covering for its sins; no contrition is required, still less any real desire to be delivered from sin. Cheap grace therefore amounts to a denial of the Incarnation of the Word of God.
>
> Cheap grace means the justification of sin without the justification of the sinner. Grace alone does everything, they say, and so everything can remain as it was before. "All for sin could not atone." The world goes on in the same old way, and we are still sinners "even in the best life" as Luther said. Well, then, let the Christian live like the rest of the world, let him model himself on the world's standards in every sphere of life, and not presumptuously aspire to live a different life under grace from his old life under sin.[2]

Cheap grace has not lost its worldly appeal since Bonhoeffer wrote those words. If anything, the tendency to cheapen grace has eaten its way into the heart of evangelical Christianity. The no-lordship movement has led the way in legitimizing and institutionalizing cheap grace in American fundamentalism. No-lordship teaching tragically misconstrues and misapplies the biblical doctrine of grace. While verbally extolling the wonders of grace, it exchanges the real item for a facsimile. This bait-and-switch tactic has confounded many sincere Christians.

No-lordship theology utterly ignores the biblical truth that grace "instruct[s] us to deny ungodliness and worldly desires and to live

---

[2]Ibid., 45–46.

sensibly, righteously and godly in the present age" (Titus 2:12). Instead, it portrays grace as a supernatural "Get Out of Jail FREE" ticket—a no-strings-attached, open-ended package of amnesty, beneficence, indulgence, forbearance, charity, leniency, immunity, approval, tolerance, and self-awarded privilege divorced from any moral demands.

Supergrace is fast becoming the most popular bandwagon in the evangelical parade. Those who make allegiance to Christ's lordship optional are leading the way. They have even begun calling their teaching "grace theology" and refer to their movement as "The Grace Movement."

Yet the "grace" they speak of alters believers' *standing* without affecting their *state*. It is a grace that calls sinners to Christ but does not bid them surrender to Him. In fact, no-lordship theologians claim grace is *diluted* if the believing sinner must surrender to Christ. The more one actually surrenders, the more grace is supposedly watered down (*SGS* 18). This is clearly not the grace of Titus 2:11–12.

No wonder Christians are confused. With so much contradictory and obviously unbiblical teaching continuing to gain popularity, we might wonder about the future of biblical Christianity.

What Is Grace?

Grace is a terribly misunderstood word. Defining it succinctly is notoriously difficult. Some of the most detailed theology textbooks do not offer any concise definition of the term. Someone has proposed an acronym: GRACE is *G*od's *R*iches *A*t *C*hrist's *E*xpense. That's not a bad way to characterize grace, but it is not a sufficient theological definition. One of the best-known definitions of grace is only three words: God's unmerited favor. A. W. Tozer expanded on that: "Grace is the good pleasure of God that inclines him to bestow benefits on the undeserving."[3] Berkhof is more to the point: grace is "the unmerited operation of God in the heart of man, effected through the agency of the Holy Spirit."[4]

At the heart of the term *grace* is the idea of divine favor. The Hebrew word for grace is *chēn*, used, for example, in Genesis 6:8: "Noah found favor in the eyes of the Lord." Closely related is the verb *chānan*, meaning "to show favor." In the New Testament, "grace" is a rendering of the

---

[3]A. W. Tozer, *The Knowledge of the Holy* (New York: Harper & Row, 1961), 100.

[4]Louis Berkhof, *Systematic Theology* (Grand Rapids, Mich.: Eerdmans, 1939), 427.

Greek *charis,* meaning "gracefulness," "graciousness," "favor," or "gratitude." Intrinsic to its meaning are the ideas of favor, goodness, and goodwill.

Grace is all that and more. Grace is not merely unmerited favor; it is favor bestowed on sinners who deserve wrath. Showing kindness to a stranger is "unmerited favor"; doing good to one's enemies is more the spirit of grace (Luke 6:27–36).

Grace is not a dormant or abstract quality, but a dynamic, active, working principle: "The grace of God has appeared, bringing salvation . . . and instructing us" (Titus 2:11–12). It is not some kind of ethereal blessing that lies idle until we appropriate it. Grace is God's sovereign initiative to sinners (Eph. 1:5-6). Grace is not a one-time event in the Christian experience. We stand in grace (Rom. 5:2). The entire Christian life is driven and empowered by grace: "It is good for the heart to be strengthened by grace, not by foods" (Heb. 13:9). Peter said we should "grow in the grace and knowledge of our Lord and Savior Jesus Christ" (2 Pet. 3:18).

Thus we could properly define grace as *the free and benevolent influence of a holy God operating sovereignly in the lives of undeserving sinners.*

Graciousness is an attribute of God. It is His nature to bestow grace. "He is gracious and compassionate and righteous" (Ps. 112:4). "He is gracious and compassionate, slow to anger, abounding in lovingkindness, and relenting of evil" (Joel 2:13). He is "the God of all grace" (1 Pet. 5:10); His Son is "full of grace and truth" (John 1:14); His Spirit is "the Spirit of grace" (Heb. 10:29). Berkhof observed, "While we sometimes speak of grace as an inherent quality, it is in reality the active communication of divine blessings by the inworking of the Holy Spirit, out of the fulness of Him who is 'full of grace and truth.'"[5]

Charis is found in the Greek text 155 times, 100 times in the Pauline epistles alone. Interestingly, the term itself is never used in reference to divine grace in any of the recorded words of Jesus. But grace permeated all His ministry and teaching ("The blind receive sight and the lame walk, the lepers are cleansed and the deaf hear, and the dead are raised up, and the poor have the gospel preached to them" [Matt. 11:5]; "Come to Me, all who are weary and heavy-laden, and I will give you rest" [Matt. 11:28]).

---

[5]Ibid.

Grace is a gift.[6] God "gives a greater grace. . . . [He] gives grace to the humble" (James 4:6). "Of His fulness we have all received, and grace upon grace" (John 1:16). Christians are said to be "stewards of the manifold grace of God" (1 Pet. 4:10). But that does not mean that God's grace is placed at our disposal. We do not possess God's grace or control its operation. We are subject to grace, never vice versa.

Paul frequently contrasted grace with law (Rom. 4:16; 5:20; 6:14–15; Gal. 2:21; 5:4). He was careful to state, however, that grace does not nullify the moral demands of God's law. Rather, it fulfills the righteousness of the law (Rom. 6:14–15). In a sense, grace is to law what miracles are to nature. It rises above and accomplishes what law cannot (cf. Rom. 8:3). Yet it does not annul the righteous demands of the law; it confirms and validates them (Rom. 3:31). Grace has its own law, a higher, liberating law: "The law of the Spirit of life in Christ Jesus has set you free from the law of sin and of death" (Rom. 8:2; cf. James 1:25). Note that this new law emancipates us from *sin* as well as *death.* Paul was explicit about this: "What shall we say then? Are we to continue in sin that grace might increase? May it never be! How shall we who died to sin still live in it?" (Rom. 6:1–2). Grace reigns through *righteousness* (Rom. 5:21).

There are two extremes to be avoided in the matter of grace. We must take care not to nullify grace through legalism (Gal. 2:21) or corrupt it through licentiousness (Jude 4).

Two Kinds of Grace

Theologians speak of *common grace* and *special grace*. Common grace is bestowed to mankind in general. It is the grace that restrains the full expression of sin and mitigates sin's destructive effects in human society. Common grace imposes moral constraints on people's behavior, maintains a semblance of order in human affairs, enforces a sense of right and wrong through conscience and civil government, enables men

---

[6]This is contrary to Zane Hodges' staggering claim, "It is inherently contradictory to speak here of 'grace' as the 'gift of God.' The *giving of a gift is an act* of 'grace,' but 'grace,' when viewed as a principle or basis of divine action, is never said to be a 'gift,' or part of a gift" (*AF* 219). Scripture is filled with statements that contradict that assertion: "The Lord gives grace and glory; no good thing does He withhold from those who walk uprightly" (Ps. 84:11); "He gives grace to the afflicted" (Prov. 3:34); "He gives a greater grace" (James 4:6); "God is opposed to the proud, but gives grace to the humble" (1 Pet. 5:5; cf. also Rom. 15:15; 1 Cor. 1:4; 3:10; Eph. 4:7).

and women to appreciate beauty and goodness, and imparts blessings of all kinds to all peoples. God "causes His sun to rise on the evil and the good, and sends rain on the righteous and the unrighteous" (Matt. 5:45). That is common grace.

Common grace is not redemptive. It does not pardon sin or purify sinners. It does not renew the heart, stimulate faith, or enable salvation. It can convict of sin and enlighten the soul to the truth of God. But common grace alone does not lead to eternal salvation, because the hearts of sinners are so firmly set against God (Rom. 3:10–18).

Special grace, better called *saving grace,* is the irresistible work of God that frees men and women from the penalty and power of sin, renewing the inner person and sanctifying the sinner through the operation of the Holy Spirit. Normally when the New Testament uses the term *grace,* the reference is to saving grace. Throughout this book when I speak of grace, I mean *saving* grace unless I specify otherwise.

Saving grace "reign[s] through righteousness to eternal life" (Rom. 5:21). Grace saves, sanctifies, and brings the soul to glory (Rom. 8:29–30). Every stage of the process of salvation is governed by sovereign grace. In fact, the term *grace* in the New Testament is often used as a synonym for the whole of the saving process, particularly in the Pauline epistles (cf. 1 Cor. 1:4; 2 Cor. 6:1; Gal. 2:21). Paul saw redemption as so utterly a work of God's grace that he often used the word *grace* as a blanket term to refer to the totality of salvation. Grace oversees all of salvation, beginning to end. It never stalls before concluding its work, nor does it ever botch the job.

What we're really saying is that grace is *efficacious.* In other words, grace is certain to produce the intended results. God's grace is *always* efficacious. That truth is rooted in Scripture. It was a major theme of Augustine's teaching. The doctrine of efficacious grace is the bedrock of Reformed *soteriology* (teaching about salvation).[7] Charles Hodge defined efficacious grace as "the almighty power of God."

No-lordship theology is fundamentally a denial of efficacious grace. The "grace" described in no-lordship teaching is *not* certain to accomplish its purposes—and most often, it seems, it does not. Under

---

[7]This explains why Reformed theologians universally agree on lordship salvation. Many of them consider the no-lordship arguments somewhat silly, because they correctly understand that faith, repentance, surrender, and holiness are all part of God's gracious saving work.

no-lordship grace, key parts of the process—including repentance, commitment, surrender, and even holiness—are optional aspects of the Christian experience, left up to the believer himself (cf. *SGS* 18). The believer's faith might even grind to a screeching halt. Yet no-lordship grace tells us we are not supposed to conclude that "he or she was never a believer in the first place" (*SGS* 142). Well, then, what *are* we to conclude? That saving grace is not efficacious? It is the only reasonable conclusion we *can* draw from no-lordship theology: "God's miracle of salvation in our lives, accomplished by grace through faith without works, makes ample *provision* for the lifetime of good works for which he has designed us. *But it does not guarantee this*" (*AF* 73–74, emphasis added).

One could legitimately characterize the whole lordship controversy as a dispute over efficacious grace. All points in the discussion ultimately come back to this: Does God's saving grace inevitably obtain its desired effects? If all sides could come to consensus on that one question, the debate would be settled.

Sovereign Grace

It is clear from all this that the sovereignty of God in salvation is at the heart of the lordship debate. The irony is that the so-called Grace Movement denies the whole point of grace: that it is *God* who effects the complete saving work in sinners. Redemption is *all* His work. God is wholly sovereign in the exercise of His grace; He is not subject to the human will. "For He says to Moses, 'I will have mercy on whom I have mercy, and I will have compassion on whom I have compassion.' So then it does not depend on the man who wills or the man who runs, but on God who has mercy" (Rom. 9:15–16).

Don't misunderstand; we are not idle in the process. Nor does saving grace force people to believe against their will. That is not what *irresistible grace* means. Grace is not coercion. But by transforming the heart, grace makes the believer wholly willing to trust and obey.

Scripture makes clear that every aspect of grace is God's sovereign work. He foreknows and foreordains the elect (Rom. 8:29), calls the sinner to Himself (Rom. 8:30), draws the soul to Christ (John 6:44), accomplishes the new birth (John 1:13; James 1:18), grants repentance (Acts 11:18) and faith (Rom. 12:3; Acts 18:27), justifies the believer (Rom. 3:24; 8:30), makes the redeemed holy (Eph. 2:10), and finally glorifies them (Rom. 8:30).[8] In no stage of the process is grace thwarted by human failure, dependent on human merit, or subjugated to human effort. *"What then shall we say to these things? If God is for us, who is against us?* He who did not spare His own Son, but delivered Him up for us all, how will He not also with Him *freely give us all things?"* (Rom. 8:30–32, emphasis added). *That's* grace.

Many people struggle with the concept of sovereign grace, but if God is not sovereign in the exercise of His grace, then it is not grace at all. If God's purposes were dependent on some self-generated response of faith or on human merit, then God Himself would not be sovereign, and salvation would not be wholly His work. If that were the case, the redeemed would have something to boast about, and grace wouldn't be grace (Rom. 3:27; Eph. 2:9).

Furthermore, because of human depravity, there is nothing in a fallen, reprobate sinner that desires God or is capable of responding in faith. Paul wrote, "There is none who understands, there is none who seeks for God; all have turned aside, together they have become useless; there is none who does good, there is not even one. Their throat is an open grave, with their tongues they keep deceiving, the poison of asps is under their lips" (Rom. 3:11–13). Note the metaphors involving death. That is the state of everyone in sin. As we shall see shortly, Scripture teaches that sinful humanity is dead in trespasses and sins (Eph. 2:1), "separate[d] from Christ, excluded from the commonwealth of

---

[8]I am not explicitly suggesting an *ordo salutis,* or order of salvation, in these comments. Much has been written on the *ordo salutis,* but it is beyond the scope of my purposes in this book to deal with the question. One of the better treatments of the issue is found in Anthony A. Hoekema, *Saved by Grace* (Grand Rapids, Mich.: Eerdmans, 1989), 14–27.

Hoekema shows that salvation is not so much a series of successive steps as a simultaneous application of several aspects of saving grace. The *ordo salutis* must be primarily a logical, not a chronological, arrangement, for in the same moment that we are regenerated we are converted, we repent, we believe, we are justified, we are sanctified, and we embark on a life of faith and obedience that will persevere unto glorification.

In the broad sense, *regeneration,* or the new birth, is a term sometimes used as a synonym for salvation (Titus 3:5; cf. John 3:3, 5, 7; 1 Pet. 1:23). In its specific, theological sense, regeneration is the work of the Holy Spirit that imparts new life to the sinner. The word is never in the New Testament used of some narrow prefaith act by God which can be separated out as an autonomous event or a stand-alone commodity. From the viewpoint of reason, regeneration *logically* must initiate faith and repentance. But the saving transaction is all a single, instantaneous event.

The crucial point to be made in respect to this is that it rules out making sanctification, consecration, Spirit baptism, or any other aspect of conversion a second-level experience. No phase of conversion is postponed or offered as a second work of grace.

Israel, and strangers to the covenants of promise, having no hope and without God in the world" (v. 12). There is no escape from such a desperate predicament, except for the sovereign intervention of God's saving grace.

By Grace Are You Saved

The classic text on salvation by grace is Ephesians 2:8–9: "For by grace you have been saved through faith; and that not of yourselves, it is the gift of God; not as a result of works, that no one should boast." Let's look at those verses in their context and try to understand better how Scripture describes the salvation that is by grace through faith in the Lord Jesus Christ.

In Ephesians 1, Paul's central point was God's sovereignty in graciously saving the elect. He wrote that God chose us (v. 4), predestined us (v. 5), guaranteed our adoption (v. 5), bestowed on us His grace (v. 6), redeemed us (v. 7), forgave us (v. 7), lavished riches of grace on us (v. 8), made known to us His will (v. 9), obtained an inheritance for us (v. 11), guaranteed that we would glorify Him (vv. 11–12), saved us (v. 13), and sealed us with the Spirit (vv. 13–14). In short, He "has blessed us with every spiritual blessing in the heavenly places in Christ" (v. 3). All of this was the work of His sovereign grace, performed not because of any good in us, but simply "according to the kind intention of His will" (v. 5, cf. v. 9) and "according to His purpose who works all things after the counsel of His will" (v. 11).

Here in the first ten verses of Ephesians 2, Paul chronicles the process of salvation from eternity past:

> And you were dead in your trespasses and sins, in which you formerly walked according to the course of this world, according to the prince of the power of the air, of the spirit that is now working in the sons of disobedience. Among them we too all formerly lived in the lusts of our flesh, indulging the desires of the flesh and of the mind, and were by nature children of wrath, even as the rest. But God, being rich in mercy, because of His great love with which He loved us, even when we were dead in our transgressions, made us alive together with Christ (by grace you have been saved), and raised us up with Him, and seated us with Him in the heavenly places, in Christ Jesus, in order that in the ages to come He might show the surpassing riches of His grace in kindness toward us in Christ Jesus. For by grace you have been saved through faith; and that not of yourselves, it is the gift of God; not as a result of works,

that no one should boast. For we are His workmanship, created in Christ Jesus for good works, which God prepared beforehand, that we should walk in them.

Paul's focus in those verses is solely on *God's* work in saving us, because there is no *human* work to be considered as a part of the saving process (vv. 8–9). These verses describe our past, present, and future as Christians: what we were (vv. 1–3), what we are (vv. 4–6, 8–9), and what we will be (vv. 7, 10). The passage reads like a tract on lordship salvation. The apostle Paul names six features of salvation: It is from sin (vv. 1–3), by love (v. 4), into life (v. 5), for God's glory (vv. 6–7), through faith (vv. 8–9), and unto good works (v. 10).

Salvation is from sin. Paul writes, "You were dead in your trespasses and sins, in which you formerly walked according to the course of this world, according to the prince of the power of the air, of the spirit that is now working in the sons of disobedience. Among them we too all formerly lived in the lusts of our flesh, indulging the desires of the flesh and of the mind, and were by nature children of wrath, even as the rest" (2:1–3). There is perhaps no more succinct statement in Scripture on the total depravity and lost condition of sinful mankind.

Because we were born in sin we were born to death, "for the wages of sin is death" (Rom. 6:23). People do not become spiritually dead because they sin; they are sinners "by nature" (v. 3) and therefore born without spiritual life. Because we were dead to God, we were dead to truth, righteousness, peace, happiness, and every other good thing, no more able to respond to God than a cadaver.

One afternoon early in my ministry at Grace Church I heard a frantic pounding on my office door. I opened the door and there was a little boy, breathless and crying. In a panicked voice he asked, "Are you the Reverend?" When I told him I was, he said, "Hurry! Please come with me." It was obvious something was terribly wrong, so I ran with him to his house, about half a block away and across the street from our church.

Inside, the boy's mother was weeping uncontrollably. She said, "My baby is dead! My baby is dead!" She quickly took me to a back room. On the bed was the limp body of a tiny infant. He had evidently died in his sleep. The body was blue and already cold to the touch. The mother had been trying desperately to revive him, but nothing could be done. The child was gone. There was absolutely no sign of life. The mother tenderly held the tiny body, kissed it, gently touched its face, spoke to it, and wept over it. But the child made no response. A crew of paramedics arrived and tried to get the child breathing again, but it was too late. Nothing had any effect. There was no response because there was no life. Even the powerful love of a heartbroken mother could not evoke a response.

Spiritual death is exactly like that. Unregenerate sinners have no life by which they can respond to spiritual stimuli. No amount of love, beseeching, or spiritual truth can summon a response. People apart from God are the ungrateful dead, spiritual zombies, death-walkers, unable even to understand the gravity of their situation. They are lifeless. They may go through the motions of life, but they do not possess it. They are dead even while they live (cf. 1 Tim. 5:6).

Before salvation every Christian was in precisely the same predicament. None of us responded to God or to His truth. We were "dead in [our] trespasses and sins" (Eph. 2:1). "We were dead in our transgressions" (v. 5). "Trespasses and sins" and "transgressions" here do not speak of specific acts. They describe the sphere of existence of the person apart from God, the realm in which sinners live. It is the eternal night of the living dead. All its inhabitants are totally depraved.

Total depravity does not mean that every person's lifestyle is equally corrupt and wicked, or that sinners are always as bad as they can be. It means that mankind is corrupt in every regard. The unredeemed are depraved in their minds, their hearts, their wills, their emotions, and their physical beings. They are utterly incapable of anything but sin. Even if they perform humanitarian, philanthropic, or religious deeds, they do them for their own glory, not God's (cf. 1 Cor. 10:31). Sinners may not always sin as grotesquely as possible, but they cannot do anything to please God or earn His favor. Sin has tainted every aspect of their being. That is what it means to be spiritually dead.

A hundred cadavers in the morgue might be in a hundred different phases of decomposition, but they are all equally dead. Depravity, like death, is manifested in many different forms. But just as death itself has no differing degrees of intensity, so depravity is always absolute. Not all people are manifestly as evil as they could be, but all are equally dead in sins.

How do people get around in this state of spiritual death? They walk "according to the course of this world, according to the prince of the power of the air, of the spirit that is now working in the sons of disobedience" (Eph. 2:2). Satan is "the prince of the power of the air." He governs the realm of sin and death ("this world") in which the unredeemed function. It is a realm that features many different and apparently competing religions, moral systems, and standards of behavior, but ultimately they are all under the control and in the grip of the devil. "The whole world lies in the power of the evil one" (1 John 5:19).

Thus the unredeemed—whether they realize it or not—have a common lord, "the prince of the power of the air." Satan is the *archōn,* the prince. He is "the ruler of this world" and will reign until the Lord casts him out (John 12:31). All those in this realm of sin and death live under his dominion, share his nature, are conspirators in his rebellion against God, and so respond naturally to his authority. They are on the same spiritual wavelength. Jesus even calls the devil the father of those under his lordship (John 8:44).

Note that the unsaved are "by nature children of wrath" (Eph. 2:3). People are not "all God's children," as some are fond of saying. Those who have not received salvation through Jesus Christ are God's enemies (Rom. 5:10; 8:7; James 4:4), not only "sons of disobedience" but consequently "children of wrath"—objects of God's eternal condemnation.

Paul's purpose in Ephesians 2:1–3 is not to show how unsaved people live—though the teaching is valuable for that purpose—but to remind believers how they *previously* lived. All of us *"formerly* lived in the lusts of our flesh, indulging the desires of the flesh and of the mind, and were by nature children of wrath, even as the rest" (v. 3, emphasis added). The realm of sin and death is a past-tense experience for the believer. We *were* hopelessly subject to the world, the flesh, and the devil (vv. 2–3). We *formerly* walked as sons of disobedience (v. 2). We *were* dead in sins and trespasses (v. 1). Now all that is in the past.

Although we were once like the rest of mankind, by God's grace we are no longer like that. Because of His saving work in us, we are presently and eternally redeemed. We have been delivered from spiritual death, sin, alienation from God, disobedience, demon control, lust, and divine judgment (vv. 1–3). That is what saving grace accomplishes.

Salvation is by love. "But God, being rich in mercy, because of His great love with which He loved us . . . made us alive together with Christ" (vv. 4–5). God's mercy is "rich," measureless, overflowing, abundant, unlimited. Some who struggle with the concept of sovereign grace believe God is unfair to elect some and not save everyone. That is exactly opposite from right thinking. The truth is, *everyone* deserves hell. God in His grace elects to save some. *No one* would be saved apart from God's sovereign grace. The thing that keeps sinners from being reconciled to God is not a deficiency of mercy or grace on God's side of the equation. It is *sin,* and sin is a human problem. Rebellion and rejection are in the nature of every sinner.

The two words "but God" affirm that the initiative to save is all God's. Because He is rich in mercy toward us, and because of His great love for us, He intervened and provided a way by grace for us to return to Him.

God is intrinsically kind, merciful, and loving. Love is so integral to who He is that the apostle John wrote, "God is love" (1 John 4:8, 16). In His love He reaches out to sinful, corrupt, impoverished, condemned, spiritually dead human beings and blesses them with every spiritual blessing in the heavenly places in Christ (Eph. 1:3).

Not only does God love enough to forgive, but also enough to give His Son to die for the very ones who had offended Him: "God so loved the world, that He gave His only begotten Son, that whoever believes in Him should not perish, but have eternal life" (John 3:16). "Greater love has no one than this, that one lay down his life for his friends" (John 15:13). God's love for those who do not deserve it makes salvation possible and fills salvation with every mercy. It is the epitome of sovereign grace.

Salvation is unto life. "Even when we were dead in our transgressions, [God] made us alive together with Christ" (Eph. 2:5). The saving transaction begins the moment God gives spiritual life to a dead person. It is God who makes the first move. Jesus said, "No one can come to Me, unless the Father who sent Me draws him" (John 6:44). Of course! The unsaved are *dead,* incapable of any spiritual activity. Until God quickens us, we have no capacity to respond to Him in faith.

When sinners are saved, they are no longer alienated from the life of God. They become spiritually alive through a miraculous, God-wrought union with Christ. They become sensitive to God for the first time. Paul calls it "newness of life" (Rom. 6:4). Now they understand spiritual truth and desire spiritual things (1 Cor. 2:10–16). Now they have become partakers of the divine nature (2 Pet. 1:4). They can pursue godliness—"the things above"—rather than "the things that are on earth" (Col. 3:2).

This new life is "in Christ Jesus" (Eph. 2:6). He *is* our life (Col. 3:4). "We . . . live with Him" (Rom. 6:8), in the likeness of His resurrection (6:5). Our new life is actually His life lived in us (Gal. 2:20). It is utterly different from our former life and the supreme manifestation of God's sovereign grace.

Salvation is for God's glory. "[God] raised us up with Him, and seated us with Him in the heavenly places, in Christ Jesus, in order that in the ages to come He might show the surpassing riches of His grace in kindness toward us in Christ Jesus" (Eph. 2:6–7). Salvation has a particular purpose: that we might enjoy and display His glory, showing forth the riches of His grace (cf. Rom. 9:23).

Our new citizenship is in heaven (Phil. 3:20). God raises us up with Christ and seats us with Him in the heavenly places. We no longer belong to this present world or its sphere of sinfulness and rebellion. We are rescued from spiritual death and the consequences of our sin. That is pure grace.

Note that the apostle describes this heavenly life as if it were already fully accomplished. Even though we are not yet in full possession of all that God has for us in Christ, we live in His domain, just as we formerly lived in the realm of sin and death. "Heavenly places" clearly implies the full sense of God's dominion. This expression cannot be read in a way that makes His lordship optional. To dwell in the heavenly domain is to enjoy full fellowship with the Godhead. It is because we dwell in this realm that we enjoy God's protection, His day-to-day provision, all the blessings of His favor. But no one dwells there who still walks according to the course of this world, according to the prince of the power of the air, and under the control of the spirit that now works in the sons of disobedience. We are no longer "children of wrath" but "children of God" (John 1:12; 1 John 3:1) and citizens of heaven (Eph. 2:19).

Just as in the old realm of sin and death we were subject to the prince of the power of the air (v. 2), so in this new realm we follow a new Lord. Just as we were "by nature children of wrath" (v. 3) and "sons of disobedience" (v. 2), so now we are by nature "alive together with Christ" (v. 5) and "in Him" (v. 6).

God's ultimate purpose in our salvation is to exalt His sovereign grace "in order that in the ages to come He might show the surpassing riches of His grace in kindness toward us in Christ Jesus" (v. 7). So our loving Father glorifies Himself even as He blesses us. His grace is the centerpiece of His glory. From the first moment of salvation throughout "the ages to come," we never stop benefiting from His grace and goodness to us. At no point does grace stop and human effort take over.[9]

Salvation is through faith. "For by grace you have been saved through faith; and that not of yourselves, it is the gift of God; not as a

---

[9]A major flaw in no-lordship theology is its tendency to make grace operative in justification only and make works the ground of sanctification. Zane Hodges teaches that "God's gift of life" and the "potential" for sanctification are "absolutely free" gifts of grace. "But from there on" growth, fruitfulness, and practical sanctification require arduous human effort (*AF* 74).

result of works, that no one should boast" (2:8–9). Faith is our *response,* not the *cause* of salvation. Even faith is "not of ourselves"; it is included in "the gift of God."

Some no-lordship advocates object to this interpretation.[10] They point out that "faith" (*pistis*) is feminine, while "that" (*touto*) is neuter. Grammatically, the pronoun "that" has no clear antecedent. It refers not to the noun, *faith,* but more likely to the (understood) act of believing. It could possibly refer to the whole of salvation.

Either way, the meaning is inescapable: Faith is God's gracious gift. Jesus explicitly affirmed this truth: "No one can come to Me, unless it has been granted him from the Father" (John 6:65). Faith is also spoken of as a divine gift in Acts 3:16 ("The faith which comes through Him has given him this perfect health in the presence of you all"), Philippians 1:29 ("To you it has been granted for Christ's sake, not only to believe in Him, but also to suffer for His sake"), and 2 Peter 1:1 ("Simon Peter, a bond-servant and apostle of Jesus Christ, to those who have received a faith of the same kind as ours").[11]

"Not by works" is not contrasting faith versus repentance, faith versus commitment, or faith versus surrender. In fact, the issue here is not as simple as faith versus circumcision or faith versus baptism. The contrast is between *divine grace* and *human merit.*

Human effort cannot bring salvation. We are saved by grace alone through faith alone in Christ alone. When we relinquish all hope except faith in Christ and His finished work on our behalf, we are acting by the faith that God in His grace supplies. Believing is therefore the first act of an awakened spiritual corpse; it is the new man drawing his first breath. Because faith is unfailing, the spiritual man keeps on breathing.

Obviously, if salvation is entirely by God's grace, it cannot be as a result of works. Human effort has nothing to do with gaining or sustaining it (cf. Rom. 3:20; Gal. 2:16). No one should boast, as if we had any part in bringing it about (cf. Rom. 3:27; 4:5; 1 Cor. 1:31).

But we cannot stop here, for there is one more crucial point in Paul's line of reasoning. It is the principal thesis to which he has been building.

---

[10]Charles Ryrie may be an exception to the rule on this point. In one place, he acknowledges that "the whole of salvation, including faith, is the gift of God" (*SGS* 96). Unfortunately, he mentions this crucial reality only as "an interesting sidelight" and does not deal with the implications of it in his system.

[11]Contrast Hodges' declaration: "The Bible never affirms that saving faith per se is a gift" (*AF* 219).

Salvation is unto good works. "We are His workmanship, created in Christ Jesus for good works, which God prepared beforehand, that we should walk in them" (2:10). That is a verse no-lordship theology cannot adequately explain. Many no-lordship books have simply ignored it. Verses 8 and 9 may seem to fit easily into the no-lordship system. But without verse 10 we do not have the full picture of what Paul is saying about our salvation.

It cannot be overemphasized that works play no role in *gaining* salvation. But good works have everything to do with *living out* salvation. No good works can *earn* salvation, but many good works *result* from genuine salvation. Good works are not necessary to *become* a disciple, but good works are the necessary *marks* of all true disciples. God has, after all, ordained that we should walk in them.

Note that before we can do any good work for the Lord, He does His good work in us. By God's grace we become "*His* workmanship, created in Christ Jesus for good works." The same grace that made us alive with Christ and raised us up with Him enables us to do the good works unto which He has saved us.

Note also that it is God who "prepared" these good works. We get no credit for them. Even *our* good works are works of *His* grace. In the previous chapter we called them "faith works." It would also be appropriate to call them "grace works." They are the corroborating evidence of true salvation. These works, like every other aspect of divine salvation, are the product of God's sovereign grace.

Good deeds and righteous attitudes are intrinsic to who we are as Christians. They proceed from the very nature of one who lives in the realm of the heavenlies. Just as the unsaved are sinners by nature, the redeemed are righteous by nature. Paul told the Corinthians that God's abundant grace provided an overflowing sufficiency that equipped them "for every good deed" (2 Cor. 9:8). He told Titus that Christ "gave Himself for us, that He might redeem us from every lawless deed and purify for Himself a people for His own possession, *zealous for good deeds*" (Titus 2:14, emphasis added).

Remember that Paul's primary message here is *not* evangelistic. He is writing to believers, many of whom had come to Christ years earlier. His point is not to tell them how *to be* saved, but to remind them of how they *were* saved, so that they could see how grace is meant to operate in the lives of the redeemed. The phrase "we are His workmanship" is the key to this whole passage.

The Greek word for "workmanship" is *pōiema*, from which we get *poem*. Our lives are like a divinely written sonnet, a literary masterpiece.

From eternity past, God designed us to be conformed to the image of His Son (Rom. 8:29). All of us are still imperfect, unfinished works of art being carefully crafted by the divine Master. He is not finished with us yet, and His work will not cease until He has made us into the perfect likeness of His Son (1 John 3:2). The energy He uses to accomplish His work is grace. Sometimes the process is slow and arduous; sometimes it is immediately triumphant. Either way, "I am confident of this very thing, that He who began a good work in you will perfect it until the day of Christ Jesus" (Phil. 1:6).

Cheap grace? No way. Nothing about true grace is cheap. It cost God His Son. Its value is inestimable. Its effects are eternal. But it *is* free—"freely bestowed on us in the Beloved" (Eph. 1:6)—and "it abounds to many" (Rom. 5:15), elevating us into that heavenly realm where God has ordained that we should walk.

5

The Necessity of
Preaching Repentance

Our ears have grown accustomed to hearing men told
to "accept Jesus as your personal Saviour," a form of words
which is not found in Scripture. It has become an empty
phrase. These may be precious words to the Christian—"personal Saviour." But they are wholly inadequate to instruct a
sinner in the way to eternal life. They wholly ignore an essential element of the Gospel, namely repentance. And that necessary ingredient of Gospel preaching is swiftly fading from
evangelical pulpits, though the New Testament is filled with
it. . . .

Paul confronted the intellectuals of Mars' Hill by preaching, "God now commandeth all men everywhere to repent"
(Acts 17:30). This was no optional note on the apostolic
trumpet. It was the melody, the theme of their instructions to
sinners. Merely to talk about "accepting a personal Saviour"
eliminates this crucial imperative.

Walter Chantry[1]

Over the past five years or so, I have had opportunities to minister in
many of the nations that we used to call "Iron Curtain" countries. There
I have encountered a surprisingly vigorous evangelical church—solidly
biblical, doctrinally orthodox, and *alive*. Western Christians generally do

[1]Walter Chantry, *Today's Gospel: Authentic or Synthetic?* (Edinburgh: Banner of Truth,
1970), 48–49.

not comprehend or appreciate the vitality of Eastern European churches without visiting them firsthand. The churches are full—often uncomfortably packed—with crowds standing outside looking through windows. The people are earnest in their commitment to Christ in a way that is rare among Western Christians. Their services are worshipful, subdued, yet intensely passionate. Spontaneous weeping is as common as laughter. Prayer for the lost and personal evangelism are on the hearts and minds of these people more than social activities and sports. The focus of their message to the world is a clear call to repentance.

Eastern European Christianity typically refers to new Christians as "repenters." When someone comes to Christ, fellow believers say the new Christian has "repented." Usually new believers are given the opportunity to stand before the church and verbalize their repentance. In nearly every church service I have attended in the former Soviet Union, at least one new convert has made a public confession of repentance.

It is entirely biblical for the church to make repentance the chief feature of its message to the unsaved world. After all, the gospel calls people to come to the One who can deliver them from *sin*. People who don't feel guilt and want to be delivered from the power and penalty of sin wouldn't even want a deliverer.

Did you realize that our Lord's Great Commission demands that we preach repentance? Luke alone of all the Gospels records the *content* of the message Jesus commanded His disciples to preach: "that repentance for forgiveness of sins should be proclaimed in His name to all the nations" (Luke 24:47). As we shall shortly see, repentance was the substance of the church's message to a hostile world throughout the Book of Acts.

The Bible is clear: Repentance is at the heart of the gospel call. Unless we are preaching repentance we are not preaching the gospel our Lord has charged us to preach. If we fail to call people to turn from their sins, we are not communicating the same gospel the apostles proclaimed.

The Western church has subtly changed the thrust of the gospel. Instead of exhorting sinners to repent, evangelicalism in our society asks the unsaved to "accept Christ." That makes sinners sovereign and puts Christ at their disposal. In effect it puts Christ on trial and hands the judge's robes and gavel to the inquirer—precisely opposite of what should be. Ironically, people who *ought* to be concerned about whether Christ will accept them are being told by Christians that it is the sinner's prerogative to "accept Christ." This modified gospel depicts conversion as "a decision for Christ" rather than a life-transforming change of heart involving genuine faith, repentance, surrender, and rebirth unto newness of life.

A. W. Tozer wrote,

> The formula "Accept Christ" has become a panacea of universal application, and I believe it has been fatal to many. . . .
> The trouble is that the whole "Accept Christ" attitude is likely to be wrong. It shows Christ [appealing] to us rather than us to Him. It makes Him stand hat-in-hand awaiting our verdict on Him, instead of our kneeling with troubled hearts awaiting His verdict on us. It may even permit us to accept Christ by an impulse of mind or emotions, painlessly, at no loss to our ego and no inconvenience to our usual way of life.
> For this ineffectual manner of dealing with a vital matter we might imagine some parallels; as if, for instance, Israel in Egypt had "accepted" the blood of the Passover but continued to live in bondage, or the prodigal son had "accepted" his father's forgiveness and stayed on among the swine in the far country. Is it not plain that if accepting Christ is to mean anything there must be moral action that accords with it?[2]

The "moral action" Tozer was referring to is repentance.

Repentance in the Lordship Debate

Repentance is no more a meritorious work than its counterpart, faith. It is an *inward* response. Genuine repentance pleads with the Lord to forgive and deliver from the burden of sin and the fear of judgment and hell. It is the attitude of the publican who, fearful of even looking toward heaven, smote his breast and cried, "God, be merciful to me, the sinner!" (Luke 18:13). Repentance is not merely behavior reform. But because true repentance involves a change of heart and purpose, it inevitably *results* in a change of behavior.

Like faith, repentance has intellectual, emotional, and volitional ramifications. Berkhof describes the *intellectual* element of repentance as "a change of view, a recognition of sin as involving personal guilt, defilement, and helplessness." The *emotional* element is "a change of feeling, manifesting itself in sorrow for sin committed against a holy God." The *volitional* element is "a change of purpose, an inward turning away from sin, and a disposition to seek pardon and cleansing."[3]

---

[2]A. W. Tozer, *That Incredible Christian* (Harrisburg, Pa.: Christian Publications, 1964), 18.

[3]Louis Berkhof, *Systematic Theology* (Grand Rapids, Mich.: Eerdmans, 1939), 486.

Each of those three elements is deficient apart from the others. Repentance is a response of the total person; therefore some speak of it as total surrender.

Obviously, that view of repentance is incompatible with no-lordship theology. What do no-lordship teachers say about repentance? They do not fully agree among themselves.

Some radical no-lordship protagonists simply deny that repentance has any place in the gospel appeal: "Though genuine repentance *may* precede salvation . . . , it *need not* do so. And because it is not essential to the saving transaction as such, it is in no sense a condition for that transaction" (*AF* 146). This view hinges on making the "saving transaction" nothing more than forensic *justification* (God's gracious declaration that all the demands of the law are fulfilled on behalf of the believing sinner through the righteousness of Jesus Christ). This single-faceted "saving transaction" does not even bring the sinner into a right relationship with God. Thus the radical no-lordship view offers this peculiar formula: "If the issue is simply, 'What must I do to be saved?' the answer is to believe on the Lord Jesus Christ (Ac 16:31). If the issue is the broader one, 'How can I get on harmonious terms with God?' the answer is 'repentance toward God and faith toward our Lord Jesus Christ' (Ac 20:21)" (*AF* 146).

The insinuations underlying those statements are staggering. How or why would anyone who is unrepentant raise the question, "What must I do to be saved?" What would such a person be seeking salvation *from*? In what sense is salvation a separate issue from "get[ting] on harmonious terms with God"? Is it possible to obtain eternal salvation with no sense of the gravity of one's own sin and alienation from God? That is the implication of radical no-lordship teaching.

But the predominate no-lordship view on repentance is simply to redefine repentance as a change of mind—not a turning from sin or a change of purpose. This view states, "In both the Old and New Testaments *repentance* means 'to change one's mind'" (*SGS* 92). "Is repentance a condition for receiving eternal life? Yes, if it is repentance or changing one's mind about Jesus Christ. No if it means to be sorry for sin or even resolve to turn from sin" (*SGS* 99). Repentance by that definition is simply a synonym for the no-lordship definition of faith. It is simply an intellectual exercise.[4]

---

[4]Though Ryrie, to his credit, *does* acknowledge that repentance "effects some change in the individual" (*SGS* 157), he takes such great pains to describe repentance as *only* an intellectual activity that he seems to contradict himself.

Note that the no-lordship definition of repentance *explicitly* denies the emotional and volitional elements in Berkhof's description of repentance. No-lordship repentance is *not* "be[ing] sorry for sin or even resolv[ing] to turn from sin." It means simply "changing one's mind about his former conception of God and disbelief in God and Christ" (*SGS* 98). Again, one could experience that kind of "repentance" without any understanding of the gravity of sin or the severity of God's judgment against sinners. It is a remorseless, hollow, pseudorepentance.

Repentance in the Bible

Does the no-lordship definition of repentance square with Scripture? It clearly does not. It is true that sorrow from sin is not repentance. Judas felt remorse, but he didn't repent (Matt. 27:3). Repentance is not just a resolve to do better; everyone who has ever made New Year's resolutions knows how easily human determination can be broken. Repentance certainly is not *penance,* an activity performed to try to atone for one's own sins.

But neither is repentance a solely intellectual issue. Surely even Judas changed his mind; what he didn't do was turn from his sin and throw himself on the Lord for mercy. Repentance is not just a change of *mind;* it is a change of *heart.* It is a spiritual turning, a total about-face. Repentance in the context of the new birth means turning from sin to the Savior. It is an inward response, not external activity, but its fruit will be evident in the true believer's behavior (Luke 3:8).

It has often been said that repentance and faith are two sides of the same coin. That coin is called *conversion.* Repentance turns from sin to Christ, and faith embraces Him as the only hope of salvation and righteousness. That is what conversion means in simple terms.

Faith and repentance are distinct concepts, but they cannot occur independently of each other. Genuine repentance is *always* the flip side of faith; and true faith accompanies repentance. "The two cannot be separated."[5]

Isaiah 55:1–13, the classic Old Testament call to conversion, shows both sides of the coin. Faith is called for in several ways: "Come to the waters . . . buy wine and milk without money and without cost" (v. 1). "Eat what is good, and delight yourself in abundance" (v. 2). "Listen, that you may live" (v. 3). "Seek the Lord while He may be found; call upon Him while He is near" (v. 6).

---

[5]Berkhof, *Systematic Theology,* 487.

But the passage also enjoins repentance: "Let the wicked forsake his way, and the unrighteous man his thoughts; And let him return to the Lord" (v. 7).

As that verse demonstrates, the issue in repentance is moral, not merely intellectual. What repentance calls for is not only a "change of mind" but a turning away from the love of sin. A leading New Testament dictionary emphasizes that the New Testament concept of repentance is *not* predominately intellectual. "Rather the decision by the whole man to turn around is stressed. It is clear that we are concerned neither with a purely outward turning nor with a merely intellectual change of ideas."[6] Another principal theological dictionary defines repentance as:

> radical conversion, a transformation of nature, a definitive turning from evil, a resolute turning to God in total obedience (Mk. 1:15; Mt. 4:17; 18:3). . . . This conversion is once-for-all. There can be no going back, only advance in responsible movement along the way now taken. It affects the whole man, first and basically the centre of personal life, then logically his conduct at all times and in all situations, his thoughts, words and acts (Mt. 12:33 ff. par.; 23:26; Mk. 7:15 par.). The whole proclamation of Jesus . . . is a proclamation of unconditional turning to God, of unconditional turning from all that is against God, not merely that which is downright evil, but that which in a given case makes total turning to God impossible. . . . It is addressed to all without distinction and presented with unmitigated severity in order to indicate the only way of salvation there is. *It calls for total surrender, total commitment to the will of God.* . . . It embraces the whole walk of the new man who is claimed by the divine lordship. It carries with it the founding of a new personal relation of man to God. . . . It awakens joyous obedience for a life according to God's will.[7]

Repentance in the Gospels

One argument against repentance that is invariably found in no-lordship books goes like this: The Gospel of John, perhaps the one book in Scripture whose purpose is most explicitly evangelistic (John 20:31),

---

[6] *The New International Dictionary of New Testament Theology,* ed. Colin Brown (Grand Rapids, Mich.: Zondervan, 1967), s.v. "conversion" (1:358).

[7] *Theological Dictionary of the New Testament,* ed. Gerhard Kittel (Grand Rapids, Mich.: Eerdmans, 1967), s.v. "metanoia" (4:1002–3, emphasis added).

never once mentions repentance. If repentance were so crucial to the gospel message, don't you suppose John would have included a call to repent?

Lewis Sperry Chafer wrote, "The Gospel by John, which is written to present Christ as the object of faith unto eternal life, does not once employ the word *repentance*."[8] Chafer suggested that the Fourth Gospel would be "incomplete and misleading if repentance must be accorded a place separate from, and independent of, believing. No thoughtful person would attempt to defend [repentance as a condition of salvation] against such odds, and those who have thus undertaken doubtless have done so without weighing the evidence or considering the untenable position which they assume."[9]

More recently, Charles Ryrie has written,

> It is striking to remember that the Gospel of John, the Gospel of belief, never uses the word *repent* even once. And yet John surely had many opportunities to use it in the events of our Lord's life which he recorded. It would have been most appropriate to use *repent* or *repentance* in the account of the Lord's conversation with Nicodemus. But *believe* is the word used (John 3:12, 15). So if Nicodemus needed to repent, *believe* must be a synonym; else how could the Lord have failed to use the word *repent* when talking with him? To the Samaritan harlot, Christ did not say repent. He told her to ask (John 4:10), and when her testimony and the Lord's spread to other Samaritans, John recorded not that they repented but that they believed (verses 39, 41–42). And there are about fifty more occurrences of "believe" or "faith" in the Gospel of John, but not one use of "repent." The climax is John 20:31: "These have been written that you may believe . . . and that believing you may have life in His name" (*SGS* 97–98).

But no one camps on this point more fiercely than Zane Hodges:

> One of the most striking facts about the doctrine of repentance in the Bible is that this doctrine is totally absent from John's gospel. There is not even so much as one reference to it in John's twenty-one chapters! Yet one lordship writer states: "No evangelism that omits the message of repentance can properly be called the gospel,

[8]Lewis Sperry Chafer, *Systematic Theology*, 8 vols. (Dallas: Seminary Press, 1948), 3:376.

[9]Ibid., 3:376–77.

for sinners cannot come to Jesus Christ apart from a radical change of heart, mind, and will."[10]

This is an astounding statement. Since John's Gospel *does* omit the message of repentance, are we to conclude that its gospel is not the biblical gospel after all?

The very idea carries its own refutation. The fourth evangelist explicitly claims to be doing evangelism (John 20:30–31). It is not the theology of the gospel of John that is deficient; it is the theology found in lordship salvation. Indeed, the desperate efforts of lordship teachers to read repentance into the fourth gospel show plainly that they have identified their own fundamental weakness. Clearly, the message of John's gospel is complete and adequate without any reference to repentance whatsoever (*AF* 146–47).

Hodges suggests that the apostle John was purposely *avoiding* the subject of repentance (*AF* 149). He finds in the Gospel of John

> not a word—not a syllable—about repentance. And if ever there was a perfect place for the evangelist to inject this theme into his gospel, this is the place.
>
> But his silence is deafening! . . .
>
> The silence of chapter one persists to the very end of the book. The fourth gospel says nothing at all about repentance, much less does it connect repentance in any way with eternal life.
>
> This fact is the death knell for lordship theology. Only a resolute blindness can resist the obvious conclusion: *John did not regard repentance as a condition for eternal life.* If he did, he would have said so. After all, that's what his book is all about: obtaining eternal life (*AF* 148).

What are we to think of this suggestion? Is the apostle John's "silence" on repentance really a death knell for the lordship position?

Hardly. H. A. Ironside responded to this issue more than fifty years ago. He wrote:

> The arrangement of the four Gospels is in perfect harmony. In the Synoptics [Matthew, Mark, and Luke] the call is to repent. In John the emphasis is laid upon believing. Some have thought that there is inconsistency or contradiction here. But we need to remember that John wrote years after the older Evangelists, and with

---

[10]Hodges at this point is quoting from my book, *The Gospel According to Jesus* (Grand Rapids, Mich.: Zondervan, 1988), 167.

the definite object in view of showing that Jesus is the Christ, the Son of God, and that, believing, we might have life through His Name. He does not simply travel over ground already well trodden. Rather, he adds to and thus supplements the earlier records, inciting to confidence in the testimony God as given concerning His Son. He does not ignore the ministry of repentance because he stresses the importance of faith. On the contrary, he shows to repentant souls the simplicity of salvation, of receiving eternal life, through a trusting in Him who, as the true light, casts light on every man, thus making manifest humanity's fallen condition and the need of an entire change of attitude toward self and toward God.[11]

Zane Hodges' assertion that "the fourth gospel says nothing at all about repentance" (*AF* 148) is demonstrably false. It is true that John does not use the word *repentance,* but as we observed in the previous chapter, our Lord did not use the word *grace.* One suspects no-lordship theologians would recoil from any suggestion that the doctrine of grace was missing from Jesus' teaching.

Repentance is woven into the very fabric of the Gospel of John, though the word itself is never employed. In the account of Nicodemus, for example, repentance was clearly suggested in Jesus' command to be "born again" (John 3:3, 5, 7). Repentance was the point of the Old Testament illustration our Lord gave Nicodemus (vv. 14–15). In John 4, the woman at the well *did* repent, as we see from her actions in verses 28–29.

Isn't repentance included by implication in the following Johannine descriptions of saving faith?

> *John 3:19–21:* And this is the judgment, that the light is come into the world, and men loved the darkness rather than the light; for their deeds were evil. For everyone who does evil hates the light, and does not come to the light, lest his deeds should be exposed. But he who practices the truth comes to the light, that his deeds may be manifested as having been wrought in God.
>
> *John 10:26–28:* But you do not believe, because you are not of My sheep. My sheep hear My voice, and I know them, and *they follow Me;* and I give eternal life to them (emphasis added).
>
> *John 12:24–26:* Truly, truly, I say to you, unless a grain of wheat falls into the earth and dies, it remains by itself alone; but if it dies, it bears much fruit. He who loves his life loses it; and he who

---

[11]H. A. Ironside, *Except Ye Repent* (Grand Rapids, Mich.: Zondervan, 1937), 37–38.

hates his life in this world shall keep it to life eternal. If anyone serves
Me, let him follow Me; and where I am, there shall My servant also
be; if anyone serves Me, the Father will honor him.

To say that John called for a faith that excluded repentance is to
grossly misconstrue the apostle's concept of what it means to be a believer. Although John never uses *repent* as a verb, the verbs he *does* employ are even stronger. He teaches that all true believers love the light
(3:19), come to the light (3:20–21), obey the Son (3:36), practice the
truth (3:21), worship in spirit and truth (4:23-24), honor God (5:22–
24), do good deeds (5:29), eat Jesus' flesh and drink His blood (6:48–
66), love God (8:42, cf. 1 John 2:15), follow Jesus (10:26–28), and
keep Jesus' commandments (14:15). Those ideas hardly concur with
no-lordship salvation! All of them presuppose repentance, commitment,
and a desire to obey.

As those terms suggest, the apostle was careful to describe conversion as a complete turnabout. To John, becoming a believer meant resurrection from death to life, a coming out of darkness and into light,
abandoning lies for the truth, exchanging hatred for love, and forsaking
the world for God. What are those but images of radical conversion?

Loving God is the expression John uses most frequently to describe
the believer's demeanor. How can sinners begin to love God apart from
genuine repentance? What does *love* imply, anyway?

Finally, remember that it is the Gospel of John that outlines the
Holy Spirit's ministry of conviction toward the unbelieving world (John
16:8–11). Of what does the Holy Spirit convict unbelievers? Of "sin,
righteousness, and judgment" (John 16:8). Wouldn't it seem that the
Holy Spirit's ministry of convicting people of sin and its consequences
has the specific purpose of laying the groundwork for repentance?

Repentance underlies all John's writings. It is *understood*, not necessarily explicit. His readers were so familiar with the apostolic message
that he didn't need to dwell on the issue of repentance. John was emphasizing different facets of the gospel message than those highlighted
by Matthew, Mark, and Luke. But he most assuredly was not writing to
contradict them! His aim certainly was not to devise a no-lordship doctrine of salvation.

In fact, John's purpose was exactly the opposite. He was showing
that Jesus is *God* (e.g., 1:1–18; 5:18; 12:37–41). John's readers clearly
understood the implication of *that:* If Jesus is God and we must receive
Him as God (John 1:12), our first duty in coming to Him is to repent
(cf. Luke 5:8).

Repentance in Apostolic Preaching

Even the most cursory study of the preaching in Acts shows that the gospel according to the apostles was a clarion call to repentance. At Pentecost, Peter concluded his sermon—a clear lordship message—with this: "Therefore let all the house of Israel know for certain that God has made Him both Lord and Christ—this Jesus whom you crucified" (Acts 2:36). The message penetrated his listeners' hearts, and they asked Peter what response was expected of them. Peter said plainly, "Repent, and let each of you be baptized in the name of Jesus Christ for the forgiveness of your sins" (v. 38).

Note that he made no mention of faith. That was implied in the call to repentance. Peter was not making baptism a condition of their salvation; he simply outlined the first step of obedience that should follow their repentance (cf. 10:43–48). Peter's audience, familiar with the ministry of John the Baptist—understood baptism as an external corroboration of sincere repentance (cf. Matt. 3:5–8). Peter was not asking them to perform a meritorious act, and the whole of biblical teaching makes that clear.

But the message he gave them that day was a straightforward command to repent. As the context of Acts 2 shows, the people who heard Peter understood that he was demanding unconditional surrender to the Lord Jesus Christ.

In Acts 3 we encounter a similar scene. Peter and John had been used of the Lord to heal a lame man at the Temple gate (vv. 1–9). When a crowd gathered, Peter began to preach to them, rehearsing how the Jewish nation had killed their own Messiah. His conclusion was precisely the same as it had been at Pentecost: "*Repent therefore and return,* that your sins may be wiped away, in order that times of refreshing may come from the presence of the Lord; and that He may send Jesus, the Christ appointed for you, whom heaven must receive until the period of restoration of all things about which God spoke by the mouth of His holy prophets from ancient time" (vv. 19–21, emphasis added). The King James Version says, "Repent . . . and be converted, that your sins may be blotted out." Again, Peter's meaning was unmistakable. He was calling for a radical, 180-degree turning from sin. That is repentance.

In Acts 4, the day after Peter and John had been instrumental in the healing the lame man, they were brought before the Sanhedrin, the ruling body of Israel. Boldly, Peter said, "Let it be known to all of you, and to all the people of Israel, that by the name of Jesus Christ the Nazarene, whom you crucified, whom God raised from the dead—by this name this man stands here before you in good health. He is the stone which was rejected by you, the builders, but which became the very corner stone. And there is salvation in no one else; for there is no other name under heaven that has been given among men, by which we must be saved" (Acts 4:10–12). While there is no mention of the word *repentance* there, it was Peter's obvious message to these rulers. They had rejected and killed their rightful Messiah. Now they needed to do an about-face: turn from the heinous sin they had committed, and turn to the One whom they had sinned against. He alone could grant them salvation.

When Peter was called of God to proclaim the gospel to Cornelius and his household, the message had a different emphasis: "that through His name everyone who believes in Him receives forgiveness of sins" (Acts 10:43).

But did Peter overlook the issue of repentance in his ministry to Cornelius? Not at all. It is evident that Cornelius *was* repentant. When Peter later recounted the incident to the church at Jerusalem, the church leaders responded, "Well then, God has granted to the Gentiles also *the repentance that leads to life.*" (Acts 11:18, emphasis added). Obviously the entire Jerusalem church understood repentance as tantamount to a saving response.

No-lordship advocates usually gravitate to Acts 16:30–31 to find support for their view that repentance is not essential in the call to saving faith. There the apostle Paul answered the Philippian jailer's famous question, "Sirs, what must I do to be saved?" What did Paul tell him? Simply, "Believe in the Lord Jesus, and you shall be saved, you and your household." Evidently Paul did not call the jailer to repentance.

But wait. Is that a fair conclusion to draw from this passage? No, it is not. The jailer knew very well the cost of being a Christian (vv. 23–24). He was also obviously prepared to repent. He was about to take his own life when Paul stopped him (vv. 25–27). He had clearly come to the end of himself. Moreover, Paul gave him a more extensive gospel presentation than is recorded for us in Acts 16:31. Verse 32 says "they spoke the word of the Lord to him together with all who were in his house." Ultimately the jailer *did* repent. He proved his repentance by his deeds (vv. 33–34). This passage cannot be used to prove that Paul preached the gospel without calling sinners to repentance.

Repentance was always at the heart of Paul's evangelistic preaching. He confronted the pagan philosophers of Athens and proclaimed, "Having overlooked the times of ignorance, God is now declaring to men that all everywhere should repent" (Acts 17:30). In his farewell message to the elders of Ephesus, Paul reminded them, "I did not shrink from declaring to you anything that was profitable, and teaching you publicly and from house to house, solemnly testifying to both Jews and Greeks of *repentance toward God and faith in our Lord Jesus Christ*" (Acts 20:20–21, emphasis added). Later, when he was hauled before King Agrippa, Paul defended his ministry with these words: "I did not prove disobedient to the heavenly vision, but kept declaring . . . even to the Gentiles, that they should repent and turn to God, performing deeds appropriate to repentance" (Acts 26:19–20).

Clearly, from the beginning of the Book of Acts to the end, repentance was the central appeal of the apostolic message. The repentance they preached was not merely a change of mind about who Jesus was. It was a turning from sin (3:26; 8:22) and a turning toward the Lord Jesus Christ (20:21). It was the kind of repentance that results in behavioral change (26:20). The apostolic message was nothing like the no-lordship gospel that has gained popularity in our day.

I am deeply concerned as I watch what is happening in the church today. Biblical Christianity has lost its voice. The church is preaching a gospel designed to soothe rather than confront sinful individuals. Churches have turned to amusement and show business to try to win the world. Those methods may seem to draw crowds for a season. But they're not *God's* methods, and therefore they are destined to fail. In the meantime, the church is being infiltrated and corrupted by professing believers who have never repented, never turned from sin, and therefore, never really embraced Christ as Lord *or* Savior.

We must return to the message God has called us to preach. We need to confront sin and call sinners to repentance—to a radical break from the love of sin and a seeking of the Lord's mercy. We must hold up Christ as Savior *and* Lord, the one who frees His people from the penalty *and* power of sin. That is, after all, the gospel He has called us to proclaim.

6

Just by Faith

The difference between Rome and the Reformation can be seen in these simple formulas:

Roman view
faith + works = justification

Protestant view
faith = justification + works

Neither view eliminates works. The Protestant view eliminates human merit. It recognizes that though works are the evidence or fruit of true faith they add or contribute nothing to the meritorious basis of our redemption.

The current debate over "Lordship/salvation" must be careful to protect two borders. On the one hand it is important to stress that true faith yields true fruit; on the other hand it is vital to stress that the only merit that saves us is the merit of Christ received by faith alone.

R. C. Sproul[1]

*I*n the 1500s a fastidious monk, who by his own testimony "hated God," was studying Paul's epistle to the Romans. He couldn't get past the first half of Romans 1:17: "[In the gospel] is the righteousness of God revealed from faith to faith" (KJV). He wrote:

---

[1]R. C. Sproul, "Works or Faith?" *Tabletalk* (May 1991): 6.

> I greatly longed to understand Paul's Epistle to the Romans and nothing stood in the way but that one expression, "the [righteousness] of God," because I took it to mean that justice whereby God is just and deals justly in punishing the unjust. My situation was that, although an impeccable monk, I stood before God as a sinner troubled in conscience, and I had no confidence that my merit would assuage him. Therefore I did not love a just and angry God, but rather hated and murmured against him. Yet I clung to the dear Paul and had a great yearning to know what he meant.[2]

One simple biblical truth changed that monk's life—and ignited the Protestant Reformation. It was the realization that God's righteousness could become the sinner's righteousness—and that could happen through the means of faith alone. Martin Luther found the truth in the same verse he had stumbled over, Romans 1:17: "Therein is the righteousness of God revealed from faith to faith: as it is written, *the just shall live by faith*" (KJV, emphasis added). Luther had always seen "the righteousness of God" as an attribute of the sovereign Lord by which He judged sinners—not an attribute sinners could ever possess. He described the breakthrough that put an end to the dark ages:

> I saw the connection between the justice of God and the statement that "the just shall live by his faith." Then I grasped that the justice of God is that righteousness by which through grace and sheer mercy God justifies us through faith. Thereupon I felt myself to be reborn and to have gone through open doors into paradise. The whole of Scripture took on a new meaning, and whereas before the "justice of God" had filled me with hate, now it became to me inexpressibly sweet in greater love. This passage of Paul became to me a gate to heaven.[3]

Justification by faith was the great truth that dawned on Luther and dramatically altered the church. It is also the doctrine that brings equilibrium to the lordship position. Critics usually claim that lordship salvation is salvation by works. Justification by faith is the answer to that charge.

Because Christians are justified by faith alone, their standing before God is not in any way related to personal merit. Good works and practical holiness do not provide the grounds for acceptance with God. God

---

[2]Cited in Roland Bainton, *Here I Stand* (New York: Abingdon, 1950), 65.
[3]Ibid.

receives as righteous those who believe, not because of any good thing He sees in them—not even because of His own sanctifying work in their lives—but solely on the basis of *Christ's* righteousness, which is reckoned to their account. "To the one who does not work, but believes in Him who justifies the ungodly, his faith is reckoned as righteousness" (Rom. 4:5). That is justification.

Declared Righteous: What Actually Changes?

In its theological sense, justification is a forensic, or purely legal, term. It describes what God *declares* about the believer, not what He *does to change* the believer. In fact, justification effects no actual change whatsoever in the sinner's nature or character. Justification is a divine judicial edict. It changes our status only, but it carries ramifications that guarantee other changes will follow. Forensic decrees like this are fairly common in everyday life.

When I was married, for example, Patricia and I stood before the minister (my father) and recited our vows. Near the end of the ceremony, my father declared, "By the authority vested in me by the state of California, I now pronounce you man and wife." Instantly we were legally husband and wife. Whereas seconds before we had been an engaged couple, now we were married. Nothing inside us actually changed when those words were spoken. But our status changed before God, the law, and our family and friends. The implications of that simple declaration have been lifelong and life-changing (for which I am grateful). But when my father spoke those words, it was a legal declaration only.

Similarly, when a jury foreman reads the verdict, the defendant is no longer "the accused." Legally and officially he instantly becomes either guilty or innocent—depending on the verdict. Nothing in his actual nature changes, but if he is found not guilty he will walk out of court a free man in the eyes of the law, fully justified.

In biblical terms, justification is a divine verdict of "not guilty—fully righteous." It is the reversal of God's attitude toward the sinner. Whereas He formerly condemned, He now vindicates. Although the sinner once lived under God's wrath, as a believer he or she is now under God's blessing. Justification is more than simple pardon; pardon alone would still leave the sinner without merit before God. So when God justifies He imputes divine righteousness to the sinner (Rom. 4:22–25). Christ's own infinite merit thus becomes the ground on which the believer stands before God (Rom. 5:19; 1 Cor. 1:30; Phil.

3:9). So justification elevates the believer to a realm of full acceptance and divine privilege in Jesus Christ.

Therefore because of justification believers not only are perfectly free from any charge of guilt (Rom. 8:33) but also have the full merit of Christ reckoned to their personal account (Rom. 5:17). At justification we are adopted as sons and daughters (Rom. 8:15); we become fellow heirs with Christ (v. 17); we are united with Christ so that we become one with Him (1 Cor. 6:17); and we are henceforth "in Christ" (Gal. 3:27) and He in us (Col. 1:27). Those are all forensic realities that flow out of justification.

How Justification and Sanctification Differ

Justification is distinct from sanctification because in justification God does not *make* the sinner righteous; He *declares* that person righteous (Rom. 3:28; Gal. 2:16). Justification *imputes* Christ's righteousness to the sinner's account (Rom. 4:11b); sanctification *imparts* righteousness to the sinner personally and practically (Rom. 6:1–7; 8:11–14). Justification takes place outside sinners and changes their standing (Rom. 5:1–2); sanctification is internal and changes the believer's state (Rom. 6:19). Justification is an event, sanctification a process. The two must be distinguished but can never be separated. God does not justify whom He does not sanctify, and He does not sanctify whom He does not justify. Both are essential elements of salvation.

Why differentiate between them at all? If justification and sanctification are so closely related that you can't have one without the other, why bother to define them differently?

That question is crucial to the lordship debate. It was also the central issue between Rome and the Reformers in the sixteenth century.

Justification in Roman Catholic Doctrine

Roman Catholicism blends its doctrines of sanctification and justification. Catholic theology views justification as an infusion of grace that *makes* the sinner righteous. In Catholic theology, then, the ground of justification is something made good within the sinner—not the imputed righteousness of Christ.

The Council of Trent, Rome's response to the Reformation, pronounced anathema on anyone who says "that the [sinner] is justified by faith alone—if this means that nothing else is required by

way of cooperation in the acquisition of the grace of justification."[4]
The Catholic council ruled that "Justification . . . is not remission
of sins merely, but also the sanctification and renewal of the inward
man, through the voluntary reception of the grace, and of the gifts,
whereby man of unjust becomes just."[5] So Catholic theology confuses the concepts of justification and sanctification and substitutes
the righteousness of the believer for the righteousness of Christ.

This difference between Rome and the Reformers is no example of
theological hair-splitting. The corruption of the doctrine of justification
results in several other grievous theological errors. If sanctification is
included in justification, then justification is a process, not an event.
That makes justification progressive, not complete. One's standing before God is then based on subjective experience, not secured by an objective declaration. Justification can therefore be experienced and then
lost. Assurance of salvation in this life becomes practically impossible
because security can't be guaranteed. The ground of justification ultimately is the sinner's own continuing present virtue, not Christ's perfect
righteousness and His atoning work.

Those issues were fiercely debated in the Reformation, and the
lines were clearly drawn. Reformed theology to this day upholds the
biblical doctrine of justification by faith against the Roman view of justification by works/merit.

Justification in Reformation Teaching

Advocates of no-lordship theology often suggest that lordship salvation has more in common with Roman Catholicism than with Reformation teaching. One outspoken advocate of the radical no-lordship
view has repeatedly voiced alarm that lordship salvation is "not paving
the road back to Wittenberg but, rather, paving the road back to
Rome."[6]

The suggestion ignores both church history and the real issues in
the contemporary lordship debate. No advocate of lordship theology I

---

[4]Henry Bettenson, ed., *Documents of the Christian Church* (New York: Oxford, 1963),
263.

[5]Philip Schaff, ed., *The Creeds of Christendom*, 3 vols. (reprint, Grand Rapids, Mich.:
Baker, 1983), 3:94.

[6]Earl Radmacher, "First Response to 'Faith According to the Apostle James' by John
F. MacArthur, Jr.," *Journal of the Evangelical Theological Society* 33/1 (March 1990):
40.

know of denies the doctrine of justification by faith. Rather, lordship theology represents a refusal to disengage justification and sanctification. On that we are in full accord with every significant Reformer.

Reformation teaching was clear on this issue. Calvin, for example, wrote,

> Christ . . . justifies no man without also sanctifying him. These blessings are conjoined by a perpetual and inseparable tie. Those whom he enlightens by his wisdom he redeems; whom he redeems he justifies; whom he justifies he sanctifies. But as the question relates only to justification and sanctification, to them let us confine ourselves. Though we distinguish between them they are both inseparably comprehended in Christ. Would ye then obtain justification in Christ? You must previously possess Christ. But you cannot possess him without being made a partaker of his sanctification: for Christ cannot be divided. Since the Lord, therefore, does not grant us the enjoyment of these blessings without bestowing himself, he bestows both at once, but never one without the other. Thus it appears how true it is that we are justified not without, and yet not by works, since in the participation of Christ, by which we are justified, is contained not less sanctification than justification.[7]

Elsewhere, discussing James 2:21–22 ("Was not Abraham our father justified by works, when he offered up Isaac his son on the altar? You see that faith was working with his works, and as a result of the works, faith was perfected"), Calvin added,

> It appears certain that he is speaking of the manifestation, not of the imputation of righteousness, as if he had said, Those who are justified by true faith prove their justification by obedience and good works, not by a bare and imaginary semblance of faith. In one word, he is not discussing the mode of justification, but requiring that the justification of believers shall be operative. And as Paul contends that men are justified without the aid of works, so James will not allow any to be regarded as justified who are destitute of good works. Due attention to the scope will thus disentangle every doubt; for the error of our opponents lies chiefly in this, that they think James is defining the mode of justification, whereas his only object is to destroy the depraved security of those who vainly pretended faith as an excuse for their contempt of good works. Therefore, let

---

[7]John Calvin, *Institutes of the Christian Religion,* trans. Henry Beveridge, 3:16:1 (reprint, Grand Rapids, Mich.: Eerdmans, 1966), 2:99.

them twist the words of James as they may, they will never extract
out of them more than the two propositions: That an empty phan-
tom of faith does not justify, and that the believer, not contented
with such an imagination, manifests his justification by good works.[8]

Martin Luther championed justification by faith as passionately as
any Reformer. Did he believe sanctification was optional? Not at all.
When some of Luther's associates began to teach *antinomianism* (the
idea that behavior is unrelated to faith, or that Christians are not bound
by any moral law), he opposed them. He called their teaching "the
crassest error," designed to "grind me under foot and throw the gospel
into confusion." Such teaching, according to Luther, "kick[s] the bottom out of the barrel" of God's saving work.[9]

Someone reported to Luther that one of these men, Jacob
Schenck, "had preached carnal license and had taught: 'Do what you
please. Only believe and you will be saved.'"[10]

Luther replied, "This is a wicked disjunction. Turn the matter
about: 'Dear fellow, believe in God, and then afterward, when you
are reborn, are a new man, etc., do whatever comes to hand.' The
fools don't know what faith is. They suppose it's just a lifeless
idea. . . . It's impossible to be reborn of God and yet [continu-
ously] sin, for these two things contradict each other.[11]

Although many more examples could be given, I'll just mention
one other. The Formula of Concord, the definitive Lutheran statement
of faith, written in 1576, dealt extensively with the relationship between
justification and the believer's obedience. This document reveals that
the questions at the heart of the contemporary lordship controversy
were also on the minds of the Reformers. The Formula of Concord, like
every other significant Protestant creed, refused to divorce justification
from sanctification, though it underscored the distinction between the
two.

According to this creed, "the renewing of man . . . is rightly
distinguished from the justification of faith." The Formula stated

---

[8]Ibid., 2:115.

[9]Martin Luther, *Table Talk*, in *Luther's Works*, ed. Helmut T. Lehman, trans. Theodore
G. Tappert, 55 vols. (Philadelphia: Fortress, 1967), 54:248.

[10]Ibid., 54:289–90.

[11]Ibid., 54:290.

explicitly that "antecedent contrition [repentance] and subsequent new obedience do not appertain to the article of justification before God."[12]

But it immediately added, "Yet we are not to imagine any such justifying faith as can exist and abide with a purpose of evil. . . . But after that man is justified by faith, then that true and living faith works by love [Gal. 5:6], and *good works always follow justifying faith, and are most certainly found together with it.*"[13]

The Formula of Concord repudiated the teaching that *justify* means "[to] become in very deed righteous before God." But it also condemned the notion "that faith is such a confidence in the obedience of Christ as can abide and have a being even in that man who is void of true repentance, and in whom it is not followed by charity [love], but who contrary to conscience perseveres in sins."[14]

The well-known Reformation epigram is "Faith alone justifies, but not the faith that is alone." F. W. Robertson adds, "Lightning alone strikes, but not the lightning which is without thunder."[15] On these matters the principal Reformers all agreed. Only the antinomians taught that true faith might fail to produce good works.

Justification in the Lordship Debate

Contemporary no-lordship doctrine is nothing but latter-day antinomianism. Although most no-lordship advocates object to that term,[16] it is a fair characterization of their doctrine.

Zane Hodges misses the point when he calls *antinomianism* "Reformed theology's favorite 'cuss word.'"[17] He writes,

---

[12]Schaff, *The Creeds of Christendom,* 3:117–18.

[13]Ibid., 3:118 (emphasis added).

[14]Ibid., 3:119.

[15]Cited in Augustus H. Strong, *Systematic Theology* (Philadelphia: Judson, 1907), 875.

[16]J. Kevin Butcher, "A Critique of *The Gospel According to Jesus," Journal of the Grace Evangelical Society* (Spring 1989): 28. Butcher believes that by describing Chafer, Ryrie, and Hodges as antinomian, I am implying "that these men (as well as the view they represent) are only concerned with populating heaven, showing a disdain for holiness and a consistent Christian walk." But that is not what the term *antinomian* means, as the discussion on these pages shows.

[17]Zane Hodges, "Calvinism Ex Cathedra," *Journal of the Grace Evangelical Society* (Autumn 1991): 68.

We could define "Antinomianism" in the way the American Heritage Dictionary (2nd College Edition, 1985) does as "holding that faith alone is necessary for salvation." If that were what was meant by the term, I would be quite comfortable with it. Unfortunately, because "Antinomianism" implies to many minds a disregard for moral issues, I must reject this designation. I urge my Reformed counterparts to drop this term because of its pejorative, and often unfair, connotations and overtones. But I will not hold my breath waiting for them to do so![18]

It is important to understand the term *antinomianism* in its theological sense. I do not use the word to be derogatory. To say someone is antinomian is not necessarily to say that person spurns holiness or condones ungodliness. Most antinomians vigorously appeal for Christians to walk in a manner worthy of their calling; but at the same time they minimize the relationship between obedience and faith. Antinomians typically believe Christians *should* yield to the lordship of Christ; they just do not believe surrender is a binding requirement in the gospel call to faith. Antinomians do not necessarily despise the law of God; they simply believe it is irrelevant to saving faith. They suggest that obedience to the righteous principles of the law might not become a pattern in the Christian's life (cf. Rom. 8:4; 10:4). In short, antinomianism is the belief that allows for justification without sanctification.

Antinomianism makes obedience elective. While most antinomians strongly *counsel* Christians to obey (and even urge them to obey), they do not believe obedience is a necessary consequence of true faith. Zane Hodges, for example, includes a chapter on obedience entitled "The Choice Is Yours" (*AF* 117–26). The leading theologian of the no-lordship movement has written, "The unsaved person has only one course of action—to serve sin and self, or to leave God out of his life—while the believer has an option. He may serve God, and as long as he is in a human body he may also choose to leave God out and live according to the old nature."[19] Clearly, no-lordship theology *does* make obedience optional. And that is what makes no-lordship theology antinomian.

---

[18]Ibid., 69.

[19]Charles C. Ryrie, *Balancing the Christian Life* (Chicago: Moody, 1969), 35. The context of this quotation is a section arguing that believers have two natures. Ryrie suggests that carnality can be a continued state of existence for the Christian (ibid., 170–73). When he speaks of those who "choose to leave God out and live according to the old nature" he is clearly speaking of something more than temporary failure.

This kind of antinomianism tends to see justification by faith as the whole of God's saving work. Antinomians minimize sanctification or even render it noncompulsory. Antinomian discussions of salvation typically omit any consideration of practical holiness. They emphasize justification by faith and Christian freedom to such an extreme that they become unbalanced, fearful of talking about personal righteousness, obedience, the Law of God, or anything but the purely forensic aspects of salvation.

No-lordship theology is classic antinomianism. There is no way around that fact. Because it is important to understand the no-lordship view in the context of Reformation teaching, we cannot avoid the term *antinomianism*, even though proponents of no-lordship teaching find it offensive. Their view is, after all, firmly in the tradition of historic antinomianism.[20]

One other point must be made about the no-lordship tendency to downplay sanctification. Most no-lordship advocates acknowledge the necessity for *some* degree of sanctification. Dr. Ryrie concedes that "every Christian will bear spiritual fruit. Somewhere, sometime, somehow. Otherwise the person is not a believer. Every born-again individual will be fruitful. Not to be fruitful is to be faithless, without faith, and therefore without salvation" (*SGS* 45).

Even Zane Hodges has lately affirmed that "some measure or degree of sanctification *will* indeed result from justification [and] that final sanctification *is* an inevitable result of justification."[21]

But those disclaimers must be understood in context. Ryrie, for example, is quick to add that some believers' "fruit" may be so meager

---

[20]There are many parallels between modern no-lordship theology and the other forms of antinomianism that have emerged from time to time in church history. These include, for example, the teachings of Johann Agricola, whom Luther condemned, and the Sandemanian cult that flourished in Scotland in the 1700s.

[21]Hodges, "Calvinism Ex Cathedra," 67. In a footnote Hodges implies that he expressed this same view in *Absolutely Free!* (213–15). But in *Absolutely Free!* Hodges never made such an assertion. Turning to the section of *Absolutely Free!* Hodges cites, we find that, ironically, he begins by condemning me for writing, "Obedience is the inevitable manifestation of saving faith" (*AF* 213). He concludes incongruously by stating, "We must add that there is no need to quarrel with the Reformers' view that where there is justifying faith, works will undoubtedly exist too" (*AF* 215). But that is precisely the view Hodges *is* arguing against! Hodges concludes that it is only "a reasonable assumption," that works will follow faith. And such works might be invisible to a human observer: "God alone may be able to detect the fruits of regeneration in some of His children" (215).

and so fleeting as to be invisible to everyone around them (*SGS* 45). Elsewhere Ryrie seems to suggest that *practical* sanctification is by no means guaranteed. He quotes Romans 8:29–30 ("Whom He foreknew, He also predestined to become conformed to the image of His Son, that He might be the first-born among many brethren; and whom He predestined, these He also called; and whom He called, these He also justified; and whom He justified, these He also glorified"). "But what of sanctification?" Ryrie asks.

> Nowhere does it appear in Paul's list in Romans 8:29–30. Only predestination, calling, justification, and glorification. Could it be that Paul didn't want to base our guarantee of ultimate glorification on our personal sanctification? Assuredly it does not rest on that, for the many sons who will be glorified will have exhibited varying degrees of personal holiness during their lifetimes. Yet all, from the carnal to the most mature, will be glorified (*SGS* 150).

Ryrie outlines three facets of sanctification—*positional sanctification,* "an actual position that does not depend on the state of one's growth and maturity"; *progressive sanctification,* or practical holiness; and *ultimate sanctification,* perfect holiness that will be realized in heaven (*SGS* 151). It is clear that Ryrie views the first and third aspects of sanctification as guaranteed. But he evidently believes *practical* sanctification can be forfeited or bypassed, for he makes room for "believers" who fall into utter carnality and permanent unbelief (*SGS* 141).

Hodges holds a similar view. If anything, his tendency to depreciate the practical aspect of sanctification is more pronounced than Ryrie's. Hodges' most extensive book on the lordship debate, *Absolutely Free!* omits any discussion of sanctification as a doctrine.[22] What Hodges does make clear from the beginning to the end of his book is that no measure of practical holiness is guaranteed in the life of a child of God.

Although no-lordship doctrine may give lip service to the necessity of sanctification, it seems certain that most no-lordship proponents do not really believe *practical* sanctification goes hand-in-hand with justification.

---

[22]In my reading of *Absolutely Free!* I could not find a single occurrence of the words *sanctify* or *sanctification,* except in one quotation from my book. Nor is sanctification dealt with in either of Hodges' other major works on the lordship issue, *The Gospel under Siege* (Dallas: Redención Viva, 1981) and *Grace in Eclipse* (Dallas: Redención Viva, 1985). Hodges evidently views practical holiness and growth in grace as purely the *believer's* work (*AF* 117–26). We shall deal with the issue of sanctification at length in chapter 7.

That is, in fact, the fundamental point no-lordship advocates want to make. They have dismembered the biblical doctrine of salvation by severing justification from sanctification.[23] They are left with a crippled antinomianism that cannot guarantee any measure of holiness in the Christian experience. Therefore they have utterly missed the point of the biblical doctrine of justification by faith as it is closely related to sanctification.

Justification in the New Testament

Justification is the heart and soul of New Testament soteriology. Realizing that is the case, a friend asked me why my book *The Gospel According to Jesus* had virtually no discussion of justification. The reason is that Jesus Himself had very little to say explicitly about justification by faith. That doctrine was first expounded in its fullness by the apostle Paul. In his epistle to the Romans, it is a major theme.

The first half of Romans divides naturally into three parts. Paul begins by showing that all men and women have sinned against God's perfect righteousness. This is his theme throughout the opening chapters of the book: "There is none righteous, not even one" (3:10). Beginning in 3:21 through the end of chapter 5, he explains in detail the doctrine of justification by faith. "Therefore having been justified by faith, we have peace with God through our Lord Jesus Christ" (5:1). In chapters 6 through 8 he expounds the doctrine of sanctification. "That the requirement of the Law might be fulfilled in us, who do not walk according to the flesh, but according to the Spirit" (8:4).

So Paul talks about sin, saving faith, and sanctification. Or, as a friend of mine has said, Romans 1:1–3:20 speaks of *God's righteousness defied* by a sinful world. Romans 3:21–5:21 shows *God's righteousness supplied* for believing sinners. Chapters 6 through 8 focus on *God's righteousness applied* in the lives of the saints.

Justification by faith is the means through which God's righteousness is *supplied* on behalf of believing sinners. I wish there were space in this book for a full exposition of these crucial chapters (Romans 3–5), which make up the core of biblical truth about justification. But that

---

[23]R. T. Kendall, whom Hodges frequently cites for support, is explicit about this: "It is true that sanctification was not a prerequisite for glorification, or Paul would have placed it in line with 'calling' and 'justification' (Romans 8:30)." R. T. Kendall, *Once Saved, Always Saved* (Chicago: Moody, 1983), 134. Note the similarity between Kendall's statement and the paragraph quoted above from Ryrie (*SGS* 150).

would require multiple chapters, so instead we will focus only on one section, Paul's main illustration of justification by faith—Abraham—found in Romans 4.

Here Paul writes,

> What then shall we say that Abraham, our forefather according to the flesh, has found? For if Abraham was justified by works, he has something to boast about; but not before God. For what does the Scripture say? "And Abraham believed God, and it was reckoned to him as righteousness." Now to the one who works, his wage is not reckoned as a favor, but as what is due. But to the one who does not work, but believes in Him who justifies the ungodly, his faith is reckoned as righteousness.
>
> Romans 4:1–5

Several crucial truths rise from this text.

True salvation cannot be earned by works. There are, after all, only two kinds of religion in all the world. Every false religion ever devised by mankind or by Satan is a *religion of human merit*. Pagan religion, humanism, animism, and even false Christianity all fall into this category. They focus on what people must *do* to attain righteousness or please the deity.

Biblical Christianity alone is the *religion of divine accomplishment*. Other religions say, "Do this." Christianity says, "It is done" (cf. John 19:30). Other religions require that the devout person supply some kind of merit to atone for sin, appease deity, or otherwise attain the goal of acceptability. Scripture says Christ's merit is supplied on behalf of the believing sinner.

The Pharisees in Paul's day had turned Judaism into a religion of human achievements. Paul's own life before salvation was one long and futile effort to please God through personal merit. He had been steeped in the Pharisaic tradition, "a Pharisee, a son of Pharisees" (Acts 23:6), "a Hebrew of Hebrews; as to the Law, a Pharisee; as to zeal, a persecutor of the church; as to the righteousness which is in the Law, found blameless" (Phil 3:5–6). Paul understood the religious culture of his day as well as anyone. He knew that the Pharisees revered Abraham as the father of their religion (John 8:39). So he singled him out to prove that justification before God is by faith in what God has accomplished.

By showing Abraham as the ultimate example of justification by faith, Paul was setting Christian doctrine against centuries of rabbinic tradition. By appealing to the Old Testament Scriptures, Paul was showing that Judaism had moved away from the most basic truths affirmed by all believing Jews since Abraham himself. He was seeking to anchor the church so that it would not follow the drift of Israel. Abraham's faith was the foundation of the Jewish nation and the basis for God's covenant with His chosen people. For the Pharisees' tradition to be at odds with Abraham was unthinkable. But, as Paul was about to prove, Abraham did not practice the Pharisees' religion of merit.

Boasting is excluded. If people could earn justification by works, they would indeed have something to boast about. The doctrine of justification by faith is therefore a humbling truth. We do not merit salvation. We cannot be good enough to please God. There is no room in God's redemptive plan for human pride. Even Abraham, the father of the faith, had no reason to glory in himself: "If Abraham was justified by works, he has something to boast about; but not before God. For what does the Scripture say? 'And Abraham believed God, and it was reckoned to him as righteousness'" (Rom. 4:2–3).

Paul was quoting Genesis 15:6: "[Abraham] believed in the Lord; and He reckoned it to him as righteousness." That single Old Testament verse is one of the clearest statements in all of Scripture about justification. The word *reckoned* shows the forensic nature of justification. In Romans 4, *reckoned* is translated from the Greek word *logizomai,* a term used for accounting and legal purposes. It speaks of something put down to an account.

This reckoning was a one-sided transaction. God designated righteousness to Abraham's spiritual account. Abraham *did* nothing to earn it. Even his faith was not meritorious. Faith is never said to be the *ground* for justification, only the channel through which justifying grace is received. Abraham believed God, and so God imputed righteousness to his account.

Again, the forensic nature of justification is clearly evident: "Now to the one who works, his wage is not reckoned as a favor, but as what is due. To the one who does not work, but believes in Him who justifies the ungodly, his faith is reckoned as righteousness" (vv. 4–5). Those who attempt to earn justification by *doing* something will find a huge debt on their ledger. Those who receive God's gift by grace through faith have an infinitely sufficient asset applied to their account.

Faith, then, means the end of any attempt to earn God's favor through personal merit. God saves only those who do not trust in themselves—those who trust "Him who justifies the ungodly." Therefore, until a person confesses that he is ungodly, that person cannot be saved, because he still trusts in his own goodness. That is what Jesus meant when He said, "I have not come to call the righteous but sinners to repentance" (Luke 5:32). Those who are righteous in their own eyes have no part in God's redemptive work of grace. Consequently, those who are saved know they have nothing to boast about.

Justification brings the blessing of forgiveness. In verses 6 through 8 Paul quotes David as support for the idea of righteousness by imputation: "David also speaks of the blessing upon the man to whom God reckons righteousness apart from works: 'Blessed are those whose lawless deeds have been forgiven, and whose sins have been covered. Blessed is the man whose sin the Lord will not take into account.'" Paul is quoting from Psalm 32:1–2. The blessedness David refers to is salvation.

Notice that David speaks of both a positive and a negative accounting: righteousness is reckoned to the believer; sin is not taken into account. Justification has both positive and negative elements: the reckoning of righteousness to the individual, and the forgiveness of sins. This forgiveness would not be possible if our sin had not been paid for by the sacrifice of Christ's own blood. His death paid the price so "PAID" can be written on the believer's spiritual invoice (cf. Col. 2:14).

As our sin was imputed to Christ (1 Pet. 2:24), so His righteousness is imputed to the believer. No other payment or reimbursement is required.

Abraham was not justified by circumcision. Paul anticipated the question that Jews would be asking themselves at this point in his argument: *If Abraham was justified by his faith alone, why did God demand circumcision of Abraham and all his descendants?*

Most Jews in New Testament times were thoroughly convinced that circumcision was the unique mark that set them apart as God's chosen people. They also believed it was the means by which they became acceptable to God. In fact, circumcision was considered such a mark of God's favor that many rabbis taught that no Jew could be sent to hell unless God first reversed his circumcision.

Genesis 17:10–14 records God's instructions that circumcision was to be a mark of God's covenant with Abraham and his descendants. On the basis of that passage the rabbis taught that circumcision itself was the means of getting right with God. But as Paul carefully points out, Abraham was not made righteous by his circumcision. When God commanded him to be circumcised he had *already* been declared righteous:

Is this blessing then upon the circumcised, or upon the uncircumcised also? For we say, "Faith was reckoned to Abraham as righteousness." How then was it reckoned? While he was circumcised, or uncircumcised? Not while circumcised, but while uncircumcised; and he received the sign of circumcision, a seal of the righteousness of the faith which he had while uncircumcised, that he might be the father of all who believe without being circumcised, that righteousness might be reckoned to them, and the father of circumcision to those who not only are of the circumcision, but who also follow in the steps of the faith of our father Abraham which he had while uncircumcised.

Romans 4:9–12

The chronology of Genesis proves that Abraham was declared righteous long before he observed God's command to be circumcised. At Abraham's circumcision he was ninety-nine years old and Ishmael was thirteen (Gen. 17:24–25). But when Abraham was justified (15:6), Ishmael had not even been conceived (16:2–4). At Ishmael's birth Abraham was eighty-six (16:16). So Abraham was justified at least *fourteen years* before his circumcision. When Abraham was declared righteous he was actually no different from an uncircumcised Gentile.

Circumcision and other external rituals—including baptism, penance, holy orders, marriage, celibacy, extreme unction, fasting, prayer, or whatever—are no means to justification. Abraham was in God's covenant and under His grace long before he was circumcised, whereas Ishmael, although circumcised, was never in the covenant. Circumcision, a sign of man's need for spiritual cleansing, was only a mark of the covenant relationship between God and His people.

Paul had already stated in Romans 2:28–29: "For he is not a Jew who is one outwardly; neither is circumcision that which is outward in the flesh. But he is a Jew who is one inwardly; and circumcision is that which is of the heart, by the Spirit, not by the letter; and his praise is not from men, but from God." Only justification by faith makes someone a son of Abraham (4:12).

Abraham was not justified by the law. "For the promise to Abraham or to his descendants that he would be heir of the world was not through the Law, but through the righteousness of faith. For if those who are of the Law are heirs, faith is made void and the promise is nullified; for the Law brings about wrath, but where there is no law, neither is there violation" (4:13–15).

Again the chronology of Scripture proves Paul's point beyond dispute. Obviously, the law was not revealed to Moses until more than half a millennium *after* Abraham lived. Abraham clearly did not become righteous by means of the law.

Justification has never been through ritual *or* law. God's law "is holy, and the commandment is holy and righteous and good" (Rom. 7:12; cf. Gal. 3:21). But the law has never been a means of salvation. "For as many as are of the works of the Law," that is, seek to justify themselves on the basis of keeping the law, "are under a curse; for it is written, 'Cursed is everyone who does not abide by all things written in the book of the law, to perform them'" (Gal. 3:10). The law demands perfection. But the only way to obtain perfect righteousness is by imputation—that is, being justified by faith.

The purpose of the law was to reveal God's perfect standards of righteousness. At the same time, it sets a standard that is impossible for sinful humans to live up to. That should show us our need for a Savior and drive us to God in faith. Thus the law is a "tutor to lead us to Christ, that we may be justified by faith" (Gal. 3:24).

God has never recognized any righteousness but the righteousness of faith. The law cannot save because the law only brings wrath. The more someone seeks justification through the law, the more that person proves his or her sinfulness, and the more judgment and wrath is debited to that person's account (cf. Rom. 4:4).

Then comes the climax.

Abraham was justified by God's grace. "For this reason it is by faith, that it might be in accordance with grace, in order that the promise may be certain to all the descendants, not only to those who are of the Law, but also to those who are of the faith of Abraham, who is the father of us all, (as it is written, 'A father of many nations have I made you') in the sight of Him whom he believed, even God, who gives life to the dead and calls into being that which does not exist" (4:16–17).

The gist of this entire passage is stated in verse 16: "*it is by faith, that it might be in accordance with grace.*" The dynamic of justification is God's grace. Abraham's faith was not in itself righteousness. Faith is only *reckoned* for righteousness. Justification is wholly a work of God's grace.

Again, we see here the purely forensic nature of justification: God "calls into being that which does not exist." The King James Version says that He "calleth those things which be not as though they were." That is a fascinating statement about God.

If you or I were to declare "things that [are] not as though they were," we would be lying. God can do it because He is God, and His decrees carry the full weight of divine sovereignty. God spoke, and the worlds were created. "What is seen was not made out of things which are visible" (Heb. 11:3). He spoke things that were not, and behold! They were. He can call people, places, and events into existence solely by His divinely sovereign decrees. He can declare believing sinners righteous even though they are not. That is justification.

But justification never occurs alone in God's plan. It is always accompanied by sanctification. God does not declare sinners righteous legally without making them righteous practically. Justification is not just a legal fiction. When God declares someone righteous, He will inevitably bring it to pass. "Whom He justified, these He also glorified" (Rom. 8:30). When justification occurs, the process of sanctification begins. Grace always encompasses both.

As we shall see in chapter 7, Paul clearly taught both truths. He did not end with a discussion of justification and forget the matter of sanctification. The salvation he described in his epistle to the Roman church was not a single-faceted, merely forensic reckoning. But the forensic element—justification—was without doubt the footing on which Paul based the whole of Christian experience.

7

Free from Sin, Slaves of Righteousness

> You cannot receive Christ as your justification only, and then, later, decide to refuse or to accept Him as your sanctification. He is one and indivisible, and if you receive Him at all, at once He is made unto you "wisdom and righteousness and sanctification and redemption." You cannot receive Him as your Saviour only, and later decide to accept or refuse Him as your Lord; for the Saviour is the Lord who by His death has [bought] us and therefore owns us. Sanctification is nowhere taught or offered in the New Testament as some additional experience possible to the believer. It is represented rather as something which is already within the believer, something which he must realise more and more and in which he must grow increasingly.
>
> D. Martyn Lloyd-Jones[1]

A dear friend of mine once ministered in a church where he encountered a retired layman who thought of himself as a Bible teacher. The fellow would seize every opportunity to teach or testify publicly, and his message was always the same. He would talk about how "positional truth" had given him new enthusiasm for the Christian faith.

The "positional truth" he spoke of included the perfect righteousness of Christ that is imputed to believers at justification. The man also

---

[1]Cited in Iain H. Murray, *D. Martyn Lloyd-Jones: The First Forty Years* (Edinburgh: Banner of Truth, 1982), 375.

loved to point out that all Christians are seated with Christ in heavenly places (Eph. 2:6) and hidden with Christ in God (Col. 3:3). He was eager to remind his fellow Christians that we all stand before God as "a chosen race, a royal priesthood, a holy nation, a people for God's own possession" (1 Pet. 2:9). Those "positional" realities *are* true of all genuine Christians, regardless of our level of spiritual maturity. Our unassailable standing in Christ is one of the most precious truths of Christian doctrine.

But this particular man, obsessed with "positional truth," lived a deplorable life. He was a drunkard. He was addicted to cigarettes. He was ill tempered and arrogant. He was unloving to his wife. He had created division and strife in several churches over the years. He was completely undisciplined in almost every way. My friend once visited the man's home, and signs of his ungodly lifestyle were all over the house.

To this man, "positional truth" evidently meant truth that has no practical ramifications. He had wrongly concluded that since our *position* in Christ isn't altered by our *practice*, Christians really needn't be bothered about their sins. He evidently believed he could be assured of the promises of the Christian life even though none of the practical fruits of faith were evident in his walk. In short, he loved the idea of justification but seemed to give scant attention to sanctification. My friend rightly encouraged him to examine whether he was truly in Christ (2 Cor. 13:5).

Nowhere in Scripture do we find positional righteousness set against righteous behavior, as if the two realities were innately disconnected. In fact, the apostle Paul's teaching was diametrically opposed to the notion that "positional truth" means we are free to sin. After two and a half chapters of teaching about "positional" matters, Paul wrote, "What shall we say then? Are we to continue in sin that grace might increase? May it never be!" (Rom. 6:1–2). In stark contrast to the man who concluded that sin must be OK since our practice doesn't alter our position, Paul taught that our position *does* make a difference in our practice: "How shall we who died to sin still live in it?" (v. 2).

What is no-lordship theology but the teaching that those who have died to sin can indeed live in it? In that regard, no-lordship teaching rests on the same foundation as the doctrine of the "positional truth" zealot I have just described. It separates justification from sanctification.

Second-Blessing Spirituality?

No-lordship theology demands a two-level approach to the Christian experience. Because of the presupposition that faith has nothing to do with surrender, no-lordship teaching about obedience and spiritual maturity must begin with a postconversion experience of personal consecration to God. This is analogous to "deeper life" theology, which in turn echoes the Wesleyan idea of a "second blessing," or second work of grace.

Charles Ryrie is candid about the no-lordship approach to spirituality:

> Before any lasting progress can be made on the road of spiritual living, the believer must be a dedicated person. Although this is not a requirement for salvation, it is the basic foundation for sanctification. As we have pointed out, *dedication is a complete, crisis commitment of self for all of the years of one's life.* Such dedication may be triggered by some problem or decision that has to be faced, but it concerns a person, the child of God, not an activity or ambition or plan for the future. A dedicated person will have dedicated plans and ambitions; but dedicated plans do not necessarily require or guarantee dedication of the planner.
>
> *Dedication is a break with one's own control over his life and a giving of that control to the Lord.* It does not solve all the problems immediately and automatically, but *it does provide the basis for solution, growth and progress in the Christian life.*[2]

Dr. Ryrie includes a diagram that illustrates how he views typical progress in the Christian life. It is a line that rises and falls to show the peaks and valleys of the Christian life, always with an upward trend. What is significant about the diagram is that the line is flat—indicating no growth whatsoever—between the point of conversion and the "crisis" of dedication. Only *after* dedication does practical sanctification begin.

According to no-lordship theology, it seems, conversion alone does not "provide the basis for . . . growth and progress in the Christian life" or "the basic foundation for sanctification." A second-level experience is necessary before practical sanctification can even begin. Thus no-lordship theology divides Christians into two groups—the haves and the have-nots. The terminology is slightly different, but this theology is nothing but a repackaging of second-blessing sanctification. It sends Christians on a futile quest for an experience to supply what they already possess—if they are truly believers.

---

[2]Charles C. Ryrie, *Balancing the Christian Life* (Chicago: Moody, 1969), 186–87 (emphasis added).

More than a century ago J. C. Ryle correctly analyzed the chief fallacy of every two-step approach to spirituality:

> Sudden, instantaneous leaps from conversion to consecration I fail to see in the Bible. I doubt, indeed, whether we have any warrant for saying that a man can possibly be converted without being consecrated to God! More consecrated he doubtless can be, and will be as his grace increases; but if he was not consecrated to God in the very day that he was converted and born again, I do not know what conversion means. . . .
>
> I have sometimes thought, while reading the strong language used by many about "consecration" that those who use it must have had previously a singularly low and inadequate view of "conversion," if indeed they knew anything about conversion at all. In short, I have almost suspected that when they were "consecrated," they were in reality converted for the first time!
>
> . . . By all means let us teach that there is more holiness to be attained and more of heaven to be enjoyed upon earth than most believers now experience. But I decline to tell any converted man that he needs a second conversion.[3]

All no-lordship teaching hinges on a two-stage theory of the Christian life. Stage one, conversion, is receiving Christ as Savior. Stage two, consecration, is surrendering to Him as Lord. In between is usually a period of time during which the "carnal Christian" lives like a pagan before he or she makes the "decision" to become a "disciple."[4] One needs only to listen to testimonies to see how pervasive this teaching has become in American evangelicalism: "I received Christ as my Savior at age seven, and didn't make Him Lord until I was in my thirties."

I am convinced that such testimonies reflect people's misinterpretation of their own experiences. There are many degrees of sanctification; hence many levels of commitment to Christ. But no one who truly has trusted Christ for salvation is *un*committed in principle to Christ's lordship, and no one who perpetually lives in conscious and purposeful rebellion against Him can truly claim to trust Him.

As I have pointed out, God justifies no one whom He does not sanctify. No second work of grace is necessary for those who have been

---

[3]J. C. Ryle, *Holiness* (reprint, Durham, England: Evangelical Press, reprint), xxv.

[4]Hence Zane Hodges writes, "The rich young ruler was not ready for a life [of reliance on Jesus' lordship], but the born-again disciples of the Son of God were" (*AF* 189).

born again. The apostle Peter could not have stated it more clearly: "His divine power has granted to us *everything pertaining to life and godliness,* through the true knowledge of Him who called us by His own glory and excellence" (2 Pet. 1:3, emphasis added). Sanctification is not a second-level experience entered into sometime after conversion. Paul addressed the Corinthians as "*those who have been sanctified* in Christ Jesus, saints by calling, *with all who in every place call upon the name of our Lord Jesus Christ,* their Lord and ours" (1 Cor. 1:2, emphasis added). He reminded them, "By [God's] doing you are in Christ Jesus, who became to us wisdom from God, and righteousness and sanctification, and redemption" (v. 30). He told the Thessalonians, "God has chosen you from the beginning for salvation through sanctification by the Spirit and faith in the truth" (2 Thess. 2:13).

If the *positional* aspects of God's truth are applicable to a life, His *practical* sanctifying work will also be operative in that same life.

What Is Sanctification?

Sanctification is the continuous operation of the Holy Spirit in believers, making us holy by conforming our character, affections, and behavior to the image of Christ. Justification is a one-time *event;* sanctification is an ongoing *process.* Justification frees us from the *guilt* of sin, sanctification from the *pollution* of sin. As we are seeing, one is as much a necessary part of God's saving work as the other.

Note this crucial distinction: At justification we surrender the *principle* of sin and self-rule. In sanctification we relinquish the *practice* of specific sins as we mature in Christ. Total surrender to Christ's lordship does not mean that we make all of life's decisions as a prerequisite to conversion (cf. *SGS* 49). It does not demand that we give up all our sins before we can be justified. It is not "the commitment of the years of one's life on earth" (*SGS* 118, cf. 106–7, 120, 123). It means that when we trust Christ for salvation we settle the issue of who is in charge. At salvation we surrender to Christ in principle, but as Christians we will surrender in practice again and again. This practical outworking of His lordship is the process of sanctification.

There *is* an immediate aspect of sanctification that is simultaneous with justification: "Such were some of you; but you were washed, but you were sanctified, but you were justified in the name of the Lord Jesus Christ, and in the Spirit of our God" (1 Cor. 6:11). This once-for-all aspect of sanctification is undoubtedly what the apostle had in view when he addressed the Corinthians as "those who *have been* sanctified"

(1:2). This initial, immediate aspect is sometimes referred to as "positional sanctification" (*SGS* 151).

But sanctification, unlike justification, is not a one-time, legal declaration. It is an experiential separation from sin that begins at salvation and continues in increasing degrees of practical holiness in one's life and behavior. Sanctification may be observable in greater or lesser degrees from believer to believer. But it is not optional, nor is it separable from the other aspects of our salvation.

Perhaps the writer to the Hebrews stated the necessity of practical sanctification most succinctly: "Pursue peace with all men, and the sanctification without which no one will see the Lord" (Heb. 12:14). The context shows that verse is speaking of holy behavior, practical righteousness, not just a positional or forensic holiness (vv. 11, 12, 13, 15, 16).

To Work, or Not to Work?

In Romans 4:5 ("But to the one who does not work, but believes in Him who justifies the ungodly, his faith is reckoned as righteousness") Paul's point was that God's righteousness is reckoned to people who believe, not to people who try to earn divine favor by religious ritual or self-righteous works. He was *not* suggesting, as many do today, that a believer who has been declared righteous might fail to produce good works. In no way does this verse erect a barrier—or even suggest a separation—between justification and sanctification.

In fact, following the progression of Paul's argument in Romans 3–8, we find he deals with precisely this issue. As we noted in chapter 6, Romans 3 and 4 describe the legal aspect of justification, God's reckoning by which a believing sinner is declared fully righteous. Romans 5 explains how guilt or righteousness can be imputed to one person because of the obedience or disobedience of another.

In Romans 6 the apostle turns to the practical aspect of God's righteousness—sanctification. He is teaching that God's righteousness, granted by faith to every believer, has both judicial and practical implications. There are not two *kinds* of righteousness—only two *aspects* of divine righteousness. Righteousness is a single package; God does not declare someone righteous whom He does not also make righteous. Having begun the process, He will continue it to ultimate glorification (Rom. 8:29–30; cf. Phil. 1:6).

Dr. B. B. Warfield saw this as the whole point of Romans 6:

> The whole sixth chapter of Romans . . . . was written for no other purpose than to assert and demonstrate that justification and sanctification are indissolubly bound together; that we cannot have the one without having the other; that, to use its own figurative language, dying with Christ and living with Christ are integral elements in one indisintegrable salvation. To wrest these two things apart and make separable gifts of grace of them evinces a confusion in the conception of Christ's salvation which is nothing less than portentous. It forces from us the astonished cry, Is Christ divided? And it compels us to point afresh to the primary truth that we do not obtain the benefits of Christ apart from, but only in and with His Person; and that when we have Him we have all.[5]

Sanctification is so much an essential part of salvation that the term is commonly used in Scripture as a synonym for salvation (cf. Acts 20:32; 26:18; 1 Cor. 1:2, 30; 6:11; 2 Thess. 2:13; Heb. 2:11; 10:14; 1 Pet. 1:2).

A Closer Look at Romans 6

As Paul finished his discussion of justification, he extolled the grace of God. "The Law came in that the transgression might increase; but where sin increased, grace abounded all the more, that, as sin reigned in death, even so grace might reign through righteousness to eternal life through Jesus Christ our Lord" (Rom. 5:20–21). If the increased presence of sin means grace abounds all the more, an obvious question comes to mind: "Are we to continue in sin that grace might increase?" (6:1). After all, if justification means we are instantly declared perfectly righteous, what real difference does it make whether we sin or not? If our sin only accents the grace of God, why not sin even more?

---

[5]Benjamin B. Warfield, *Perfectionism* (Philadelphia: Presbyterian & Reformed, 1958), 356–57. Warfield went on to say: "This crass separation of sanctification from justification, as if it was merely an additional gift of grace to be sought and obtained for itself—instead of, as it is, an inseparable component part of the one salvation that belongs to all believers—lays the foundation, of course, for that circle of ideas which are summed up in the phrase, 'the Second Blessing.' These are far from wholesome. Among them may be mentioned, for example, the creation of two different kinds of Christians, a lower and a higher variety" (ibid., 357–58). Of course, the two-classes-of-Christians error underlies all no-lordship teaching. See further discussion of this in chapter 8.

Paul anticipated that such questions would be raised. He answers them in depth by making several key points about how sanctification operates.

Sanctification is inseparably linked to justification. Paul attacks the notion that justification is the sum of God's work in salvation: "What shall we say then? Are we to continue in sin that grace might increase? May it never be! How shall we who died to sin still live in it? Or do you not know that all of us who have been baptized into Christ Jesus have been baptized into His death? Therefore we have been buried with Him through baptism into death, in order that as Christ was raised from the dead through the glory of the Father, so we too might walk in newness of life" (Romans 6:1–4).

Evidently Paul had already encountered considerable opposition to the doctrine of justification by faith. Certainly his Jewish audiences would have been unable to conceive of pleasing God by any means other than strict adherence to the rabbinic law. In their system, legalism epitomized godliness (cf. Acts 15:1–29). To legalistic Jews, justification by faith sounded like antinomianism. To teach that salvation is God's work, not ours, was an affront to their haughty egos. The notion that God's grace abounds where sin thrives hit at the heart of their system (cf. Luke 18:11–12). Because they didn't understand grace, they could think of only one alternative to legalism: antinomianism. They reasoned that if salvation is all by grace, and grace glorifies God, and God delights in justifying the ungodly, then why not sin more? After all, ungodliness only allows God to demonstrate His grace in greater measures.

That, by the way, was precisely the theology of Rasputin, religious adviser to the ruling family of Russia nearly a hundred years ago. He taught that man's sin glorifies God. The greater man's sin, the more God is glorified in giving grace. Therefore he encouraged people to sin with abandon. Those who suppress their sin suppress God's ability to show His glory, according to Rasputin. His teaching contributed to the downfall of Russia.

In the mid-seventeenth century an English sect known as the Ranters taught a similar doctrine. They encouraged immorality and indulgence, believing God is glorified by showing grace. Puritan Richard Baxter opposed their teaching.

Paul himself had already confronted similar ideas. In Romans 3:5–6 he cited the argument of those who claimed God was unrighteous to punish sin since our unrighteousness demonstrates His righteousness. Then he condemned those who had accused the apostles of teaching pragmatic antinomianism ("Let us do evil that good may come" [Rom. 3:8]).

We see that antinomianism has been a threat from the earliest days of the church. Jude wrote, "Certain persons have crept in unnoticed, those who were long beforehand marked out for this condemnation, ungodly persons who turn the grace of our God into licentiousness and deny our only Master and Lord, Jesus Christ" (Jude 4). Jude was describing early antinomians.

In Romans 6, Paul says justification by faith makes no place for antinomianism. He attacks the antinomians without yielding an inch of ground to the legalists. He would neither abandon God's grace to accommodate legalism nor abandon God's righteousness to accommodate libertinism. According to Paul, true holiness is as much a gift of God as is the new birth and the spiritual life it brings. The life that is void of holiness has no claim to justification.

"Are we to continue in sin that grace might increase?" The Greek word translated "continue" speaks of habitual persistence. Paul was not asking whether believers might fall into sin; he was ruling out intentional, willful, constant sinning as a routine of life.

Put in theological terms, this is the summary question: Can justification truly exist apart from sanctification? Paul's answer is emphatically no.

To be alive in Christ is to be dead to sin. "May it never be!" (6:2) is an accurate translation. But the King James Version captures the force of Paul's exclamation: "God forbid!" The very suggestion that sin in the Christian's life might in any way glorify God was abhorrent to Paul. "How shall we who died to sin still live in it?"

Christians have died to sin. It is therefore inconceivable to Paul that we might continue to live in the sin from which we were delivered by death. Only a corrupt mind using perverted logic could argue that continuing in sin magnifies God's grace. It is self-evident that death terminates life; it is equally obvious that death to sin must end a life of unbroken transgression.

"Died to sin" (Gk., *apothnēskō*) speaks of a historical fact referring to our death in the death of Christ. Because we are "in Christ" (6:11; 8:1), and He died in our place (5:6–8), we are counted dead with Him. We are therefore dead to sin's penalty and dominion. Death is permanent. Death and life are incompatible. So the person who has died to sin cannot continue living in iniquity. Certainly we can commit sins, but we do not live anymore in the dimension of sin and under sin's rule (cf. 8:2–4). Sin is contrary to our new disposition. "No one who is born of

God practices sin," according to John, "because His seed abides in him; and he cannot sin, because he is born of God" (1 John 3:9). It is not merely that we *should not* continue to live in unbroken sin but that we *cannot.*

Dying to sin implies an abrupt, irreversible, wholesale break with the power of sin. This schism with sin is the immediate, once-for-all aspect of sanctification we spoke of earlier. It is the past tense of sanctification out of which all practical holiness proceeds.

The phrase "we who died to sin" does not describe an advanced class of Christians. Paul is speaking here of all believers. His point is that a justified life must be a sanctified life. Practical holiness is as much God's work as any other element of redemption. When we are born again, God not only declares us righteous, but He also begins to cultivate righteousness in our lives. Thus salvation is not only a forensic declaration; it is a miracle of conversion, of transformation. There is no such thing as a true convert to Christ who is justified but who is not being sanctified. There is no gap between justification and sanctification. Dr. Donald Grey Barnhouse wrote,

> Although justification is not sanctification, justification is intended to produce sanctification. Holiness is to be the touchstone of the Christian life. Christ came in order to save his people from their sins (Matt. 1:21); they were not to be saved in the midst of their sins and then lie down in them again. Though men seek to pervert the gospel, the Christian must not be drawn aside to any position other than that which demands holiness and which leads to holiness. . . .
>
> Justification and sanctification are as inseparable as a torso and a head. You can't have one without the other. God does not give "gratuitous righteousness" apart from newness of life. While justification, in its action, has nothing to do with sanctification, it does not follow that sanctification is not necessary. "Without holiness no man shall see the Lord" (Heb. 12:14). Holiness starts where justification finishes, and if holiness does not start, we have the right to suspect that justification never started either.[6]

As the sinful, unregenerate person cannot help manifesting his or her true character, neither can the regenerate person.

So it is impossible to be alive in Christ and still be alive to sin.

---

[6]Donald G. Barnhouse, *Romans,* 4 vols. (Grand Rapids, Mich.: Eerdmans, 1961), 3:2:10–12.

Our union with Christ guarantees a changed life. Death to sin is a result of the believer's union with Christ. "Do you not know that all of us who have been baptized into Christ Jesus have been baptized into His death? Therefore we have been buried with Him through baptism into death, in order that as Christ was raised from the dead through the glory of the Father, so we too might walk in newness of life. For if we have become *united with Him* in the likeness of His death, certainly we shall be also in the likeness of His resurrection" (vv. 3–5, emphasis added).

Elsewhere Paul says we become new creatures "in Christ" (2 Cor. 5:17). He means that our union with Christ is the basis of our sanctification. It spells both the end of the old and the start of the new.

"In Christ" is one of Paul's favorite phrases (cf. Rom. 8:1; 12:5; 16:7; 1 Cor. 1:2; Col. 1:28). Because we are "in Christ Jesus" He has become to us "wisdom from God, and righteousness and sanctification, and redemption" (1 Cor. 1:30). Our life is hid with Christ in God (Col. 3:3). We are buried with Him by baptism into death (Rom. 6:4; Col. 2:12). We are one body in Him (Rom. 12:5). Christ is our life (Col. 3:4). Christ is in us, the hope of glory (Col. 1:27). Those verses describe the absolute identification with Christ that is the essential characteristic of the elect. We are indivisibly linked in a spiritual sphere of new life.

That unfathomable truth is why Paul so strongly rebuked the sexual immorality of some in the Corinthian church: "Do you not know that your bodies are members of Christ? Shall I then take away the members of Christ and make them members of a harlot? May it never be!" (1 Cor. 6:15).

To be "in Christ" is not only to believe some truths *about* Him, but rather to be united *to* Him inseparably as the source of our eternal life, as both the "author *and perfecter* of faith" (Heb. 12:2, emphasis added). To be "in Him" is to be in the process of sanctification.

We are united with Christ specifically in His death and resurrection (Rom. 6:3–10). This truth is far too wonderful for us to comprehend fully, but the main idea Paul wants to convey here is that we died with Christ so that we might have life through Him and live like Him. Paul's stress is not on the *immorality* of continuing to live the way we did before we were saved, but on the *impossibility* of it. The whole purpose of our union in Christ's death and resurrection with Christ is so that "we too might walk in newness of life" (v. 4). How could we continue in the realm of sin?

So the certain consequence of our union in Christ's death to sin and His resurrection to life is that we will share in His holy walk. "If we have become united with Him in the likeness of His death, certainly we shall be also in the likeness of His resurrection." As our old self died, a new creation was born (cf. 2 Cor. 5:17). Bishop Handley Moule wrote, "It is a thing not to be thought of that the sinner should accept justification—and live to himself. It is a moral contradiction of the very deepest kind, and cannot be entertained without betraying an initial error in the man's whole spiritual creed."[7]

In Christ we are not the same people we were before salvation. "Our old self was crucified with Him, that our body of sin might be done away with, that we should no longer be slaves to sin" (Rom. 6:6). Elsewhere Paul wrote, "I have been crucified with Christ; and it is no longer I who live, but Christ lives in me; and the life which I now live in the flesh I live by faith in the Son of God, who loved me, and delivered Himself up for me" (Gal. 2:20). Our new life as Christians is not an amended old life but a divinely bestowed new life that is of the same nature as Christ's very own. It is what our Lord spoke of when He promised abundant life (John 10:10).

Nor is Paul describing a dualistic, schizophrenic Christian. The old man—the unregenerate person that was "in Adam" (cf. 1 Cor. 15:22; Rom. 5:14–15)—is dead. We are to "lay aside" that crucified, dead, and corrupt old self (Eph. 4:22), and "put on the new self, which in the likeness of God has been created in righteousness and holiness of the truth" (v. 24). It is true of every genuine believer that our old self is dead. "Those who belong to Christ Jesus have crucified the flesh with its passions and desires" (Gal. 5:24). If the old self *isn't* dead, conversion hasn't occurred. Paul reminded the Colossians that they had *already* "laid aside the old self with its evil practices, and . . . put on the new self who is being renewed to a true knowledge according to the image of the One who created him" (Col. 3:9–10).

As we shall note in chapter 8, Christians sin because of the vestiges of sinful flesh, not because they have the same old active sinful nature. Certainly we sin, but when we sin it is contrary to our nature, not because we have two dispositions—one sinful and one not. "Our old self was crucified with Him, that our body of sin might be done away with" (Rom. 6:6).

---

[7]Handley Moule, *The Epistle to the Romans* (London: Pickering & Inglis, n.d.), 160–61.

That does not mean our sinful tendencies are annihilated. The Greek word translated "done away with" literally means "to render inoperative, invalidate." Sin has lost its dominating control over us. Obviously we all struggle with sinful propensities. Death to the sinful self does not mean death to the flesh and its corrupted inclinations. Because of the pleasures of sin and the weakness of our remaining flesh, we often yield to sin.

The tyranny and penalty of sin have been nullified, but sin's potential for expression has not yet been fully removed. Our human weaknesses and instincts make us capable of succumbing to temptation (as we shall see in chapter 8 when we study Romans 7:14–25). We are, in short, new creations—holy and redeemed but wrapped in grave clothes of unredeemed flesh. We are like Lazarus, who came forth from the grave still wrapped from head to foot in his burial garments. Jesus instructed those standing nearby to "unbind him, and let him go" (John 11:44).

So the apostle admonishes believers, "we should no longer be slaves to sin" (Rom. 6:6). The translation leaves the meaning somewhat ambiguous. Is Paul suggesting that it is optional as to whether we live as slaves to sin or not? Is he implying that we have a choice—that Christians can still be enslaved to sin? Verses 17–18 answer that question with no ambiguity: "Though you were slaves of sin, you *became obedient* from the heart to that form of teaching to which you were committed, and having *been freed* from sin, you *became slaves of righteousness*" (emphasis added). Every verb in those two verses underscores the truth that our slavery to sin is already broken by Christ and is henceforth a thing of the past. Verse 22 confirms it: "Having been freed from sin and enslaved to God, you derive your benefit [lit., "fruit"], resulting in sanctification, and the outcome, eternal life."

So in verse 6, the phrase "should no longer be slaves of sin" clearly means that believers *can* no longer be slaves of sin. No genuine Christian lives in bondage to sin. Those who have died in Christ are free from such slavery (v. 7). Paul even uses the analogy of marriage (Rom. 7:1–4), making the point that the first husband has died, so we are no longer obligated to him, but we have been freed and joined to a new husband, namely Christ, "that we might bear fruit for God" (v. 4).

Peter taught precisely the same thing: "Therefore, since Christ has suffered in the flesh arm yourselves also with the same purpose, because he who has suffered in the flesh has ceased from sin, so as to live the rest of the time in the flesh no longer for the lusts of men, but for the will of God" (1 Pet. 4:1–2).

Faith is the means by which we conquer sin. The series of verbs in Romans 6—"know" (vv. 3, 6, 9), "reckon" (v. 11, KJV), and "yield" (v. 13 KJV)—speak of faith. In fact, they perfectly parallel the three essential elements of faith we listed in chapter 3: know (*notitia*), reckon (*assensus*), and yield (*fiducia*). Paul is challenging the Romans to apply their faith more diligently, to take off the old grave clothes and live the new life to the fullness of Christ's righteousness and glory: "Consider yourselves to be dead to sin, but alive to God in Christ Jesus. Therefore do not let sin reign in your mortal body that you should obey its lusts, and do not go on presenting the members of your body to sin as instruments of unrighteousness; but present yourselves to God as those alive from the dead, and your members as instruments of righteousness to God. For sin shall not be master over you, for you are not under law, but under grace" (6:11–14). That sums up the life of faith.

Our spiritual death to sin and resurrection into new life with Christ are the underpinning of our sanctification. We need to know and believe that we are not what we used to be. We must see that we are not remodeled sinners but reborn saints. We must grasp the truth that we are no longer under sin's tyranny. The dawn of faith is *knowledge* of these spiritual realities. "My people are destroyed for lack of knowledge. Because you have rejected knowledge, I also will reject you" (Hos. 4:6).

Reckoning takes the believer's response one step further: "Consider yourselves to be dead to sin, but alive to God in Christ Jesus" (Rom. 6:11). "Consider," or "reckon" (KJV), in that verse comes from the same Greek term, *logizomai,* which we saw in Romans 4:3 ("Abraham believed God, and it was *reckoned* to him as righteousness"). It is an accounting term meaning "calculate," or "figure." In this context it takes the believer's faith beyond mere knowledge. To "reckon" here means to have unreserved confidence, to affirm a truth from the heart, as opposed to knowing it intellectually.

Yielding goes even beyond that and involves the believer's will. Paul writes, "Do not let sin reign in your mortal body that you should obey its lusts, and do not go on presenting the members of your body to sin as instruments of unrighteousness; but *present* [*yield,* KJV] yourselves to God as those alive from the dead, and your members as instruments of righteousness to God" (Rom. 6:12–13).

Sin is still a powerful force, but it is no longer master over the Christian. Sin is like a deposed but angry monarch, determined to reign again in our lives. It still occupies some territory, but not the capital city. Paul says we are not to yield to sin, but we must yield instead to God.

This is an act of trust. "This is the victory that has overcome the world—our faith" (1 John 5:4). So even our sanctification is by faith.

Grace guarantees victory over sin. Because salvation is forever, our immortal souls are eternally beyond sin's reach. But sin *can* attack Christians in their mortal bodies. Even our bodies will someday be glorified and forever be out of sin's reach, but as long as this life lasts we are subject to corruption and death. "This perishable must put on the imperishable, and this mortal must put on immortality" (1 Cor. 15:53). Until then our mortal bodies are still subject to sin. That is why "we . . . groan within ourselves, waiting eagerly for our adoption as sons, the redemption of our body" (Rom. 8:23).

Therefore Paul says, "Do not go on presenting the members of your body to sin as instruments of unrighteousness; but present yourselves to God as those alive from the dead, and your members as instruments of righteousness to God" (Rom. 6:13). This parallels Romans 12:1: "I urge you therefore, brethren, by the mercies of God, to present your *bodies* a living and holy sacrifice, acceptable to God, which is your spiritual service of worship" (Rom. 12:1, emphasis added), and "I buffet my *body* and make it my slave, lest possibly, after I have preached to others, I myself should be disqualified" (1 Cor. 9:27, emphasis added).

Many interpreters have been tripped up by the verb tenses in Romans 6:12–13. "Do not let sin reign" and "do not go on presenting" are present active imperative verbs. They are contrasted with an aorist imperative, "but present yourselves to God." At first glance it seems the apostle could be saying "*Stop* letting sin reign and *stop* yielding your members to sin, but submit yourselves to God" implying that these people were Christians who had never surrendered to Christ's lordship.

But the context clearly indicates otherwise. Paul also reminds them, "you became obedient from the heart" (v. 17); "you became slaves of righteousness" (v. 18); and "[you were] freed from sin and enslaved to God." These are not people who have never surrendered. Here, and in Romans 12:1–2, Paul was simply encouraging them to keep surrendering in practice what they had already surrendered in principle. He was calling for decisive, deliberate surrender in their lives right now.

Is the outcome in doubt? Certainly not. In verse 14 Paul offers these assuring words: "Sin shall not be master over you, for you are not under law, but under grace." The Christian is no longer under the condemning power of God's law but is now under the redeeming power of His grace. It is in the power of that grace, by faith, that the Lord now calls him to live.

Freedom from sin enslaves us to righteousness. Paul returns to the question of antinomianism:

> What then? Shall we sin because we are not under law but under grace? May it never be! Do you not know that when you present yourselves to someone as slaves for obedience, you are slaves of the one whom you obey, either of sin resulting in death, or of obedience resulting in righteousness? But thanks be to God that though you were slaves of sin, you became obedient from the heart to that form of teaching to which you were committed, and having been freed from sin, you became slaves of righteousness.
>
> Romans 6:15–18

Freedom from the law means freedom from sin's bondage and freedom from the law's penalty—not freedom from moral restraint. Grace does not mean we have permission to do as we please; it means we have the power to do what pleases God. The mere suggestion that God's grace gives us license to sin is self-contradictory, for the very purpose of grace is to free us from sin. How can we who are the recipients of grace continue in sin?

"May it never be!" is the same powerful and unequivocal denial Paul gave in verse 2. This truth needs no proof; it is self-evident: "Do you not know?" implies that *everyone* should understand something so basic. What could be more obvious? When you present yourselves to someone as slaves for obedience, you are slaves of the one whom you obey! There are only two choices. If our lives are characterized by sin, then we are sin's slaves. If we are characterized by obedience, then we are slaves of righteousness (vv. 16–18). Either way, we are not our own masters.

It is equally true that "no one can serve two masters; for either he will hate the one and love the other, or he will hold to one and despise the other. You cannot serve God and mammon" (Matt. 6:24). You cannot serve God and sin. Those who think they are Christians but are enslaved to sin are sadly deceived. We cannot have two contradictory natures at the same time. We cannot live in two opposing spiritual domains simultaneously. We cannot serve two masters. We are either slaves of sin by natural birth, or slaves of righteousness by regeneration. We can't be both in the Spirit and in the flesh (cf. Rom. 8:5–9).

Paul is not teaching the Romans that they *ought to be* slaves of righteousness. He is reminding them that they *are* slaves of righteousness. He told the Colossians the same thing: "Although you were formerly alienated and hostile in mind, engaged in evil deeds, yet He has now reconciled you in His fleshly body through death, in order to present you before Him holy and blameless and beyond reproach" (Col. 1:21–22). For the Christian, the life of unrighteousness and hostility toward God is in the *past.* No true believer will continue indefinitely in disobedience, because sin is diametrically opposed to our new and holy nature. Real Christians cannot endure perpetually sinful living.

Paul thus reminds the Romans that they are no longer enslaved to sin: "Thanks be to God that though you were slaves of sin, you became obedient from the heart to that form of teaching to which you were committed," (v. 17). Paul is not speaking about a legalistic or mechanical show of righteousness: "You became obedient from the heart." Grace transforms a person's innermost being. A person whose heart has not been changed is not saved. The hallmark of grace is an obedient heart.

Again, we must be clear: Obedience does not produce or maintain salvation, but it is the inevitable characteristic of those who are saved. The desire to know and obey God's truth is one of the surest marks of genuine salvation. Jesus made it clear that those who obey His word are the true believers (cf. John 8:31; 14:21, 23, 24; 15:10).

Slaves of sin—unbelievers—are free from righteousness (Rom. 6:20). Christians, on the other hand, are free from sin and enslaved to God through faith in Jesus Christ (v. 22). The inevitable benefit is sanctification, and the ultimate outcome is eternal life (v. 22). This promise sums up the whole point of Romans 6: God not only frees us from sin's penalty (justification), but He frees us from sin's tyranny as well (sanctification).

Nevertheless, though we are no longer subject to sin's dominion, all of us struggle desperately with sin in our lives. How that can be and what we can do about it is the subject of chapter 8.

8

The Death Struggle
with Sin

> The form that sanctification takes is conflict with the
> indwelling sin that constantly assaults us. The conflict, which
> is lifelong, involves both resistance to sin's assaults and the
> counterattack of mortification, whereby we seek to drain the
> life out of this troublesome enemy.
>
> J. I. Packer[1]

A man who has long championed no-lordship doctrine wrote me to
object to my teaching on the gospel. I invited him to lunch, thinking a
personal conversation might help us understand one another better. He
was a fellow pastor in a large church, and I believed we would have
much in common, even though we disagreed at this very basic level.

We met, and I felt our dialogue was beneficial. Though neither of
us changed our views on the gospel, we were able to clarify misunder-
standings on both sides.

Several months after our lunch meeting I was saddened to read a
news report disclosing that his church had asked him to step down because he was guilty of sexual immorality. He had been living a double
life for more than ten years, and now his sin and unfaithfulness were
shamefully exposed.

Was his tolerance of that sin solely the result of his theology? Perhaps not. Certainly other pastors who do not espouse the no-lordship

---

[1] J. I. Packer, *Hot Tub Religion* (Wheaton: Tyndale, 1987), 172.

view have morally disqualified themselves. Conversely, many who hold the no-lordship view manage to avoid falling into sordid sin.

But turn the question around: Was his theology an accommodation to his sinful lifestyle? It surely might have been. This much is certain: No-lordship theology would have a soothing effect on a professing Christian trying to rationalize long-term immorality. Instead of subjecting conscience and behavior to the most intense self-examination, he could find reassurance in the idea that, after all, many Christians are permanently "carnal." Surely the belief that repentance is optional would encourage someone who wants to claim Christ while justifying a life of unrepentant sin. Certainly preaching that constantly touts "grace" but never features law could help someone like that find comfort while sinning. No-lordship doctrine is a perfect fit for anyone trying to justify cold-hearted religion.

By no means do I intend to imply that everyone who holds the no-lordship view lives an immoral life. Obviously that is not the case. Nor am I saying that these people *advocate* unrighteous living. I do not know of a single no-lordship teacher who would openly condone sinful behavior. In fact, the opposite is true: No-lordship preachers often feature strong appeals for holiness. One of the main goals of no-lordship preaching is to convince "carnal believers" to become "spiritual believers." So appeals for obedience and surrender are quite common in no-lordship preaching, except in evangelistic messages. Fortunately, most no-lordship teachers live a better theology than they say they believe.

But I do believe that many people who purposefully allow unrepentant and unconfessed sin in their lives also adopt no-lordship doctrine because it allows them to have the solace of "assurance" in the midst of sinful rebellion.

And I do believe that no-lordship theology tends to undermine holiness, even though this is not the intent of no-lordship teachers. It does so by offering salvation from hell but not salvation from sin. It does so by removing the moral ramifications from faith and repentance. It does so by making obedience to God optional. It does so by promising assurance even to people who live in perpetual carnality.

The Myth of the Carnal Christian

Almost all no-lordship theology leans heavily on the notion that there are three classes of humanity: unsaved people, spiritual Christians, and carnal Christians. This was one of the planks in the no-lordship platform that was laid by Lewis Sperry Chafer. Chafer popularized the carnal-Christian idea in his 1918 book, *He That Is Spiritual*.[2] Chafer's friend C. I. Scofield included a similar scheme in one of the notes in *The Scofield Reference Bible*.

In recent years the idea of the carnal Christian has been disseminated through a series of tracts and booklets published by Campus Crusade for Christ. The Campus Crusade literature features a diagram with three circles representing the three classes of humanity. At the center of each circle is a throne. The non-Christian has self on the throne with Christ outside the circle. The carnal Christian has "invited" Christ into the circle but keeps self enthroned. The spiritual Christian puts Christ on the throne, with self at the foot of the throne. The tract challenges carnal Christians to become spiritual. Millions of these pamphlets have been distributed worldwide over the past thirty years or so. They are undoubtedly the most widely read single bit of no-lordship literature and have helped influence multitudes to accept the carnal-spiritual Christian dichotomy as biblical.

But the whole idea is based on a misunderstanding of 1 Corinthians 2:14–3:3:

> A natural man does not accept the things of the Spirit of God; for they are foolishness to him, and he cannot understand them, because they are spiritually appraised. But he who is spiritual appraises all things, yet he himself is appraised by no man. For who has known the mind of the Lord, that he should instruct Him? But we have the mind of Christ.
>
> And I, brethren, could not speak to you as to spiritual men, but as to men of flesh, as to babes in Christ. I gave you milk to drink, not solid food; for you were not yet able to receive it. Indeed, even now you are not yet able, for you are still fleshly. For since there is jealousy and strife among you, are you not fleshly, and are you not walking like mere men?

In that passage the apostle Paul was rebuking the Corinthians for their unchristlike behavior. The church was dividing into factions, some saying

---

[2]Lewis Sperry Chafer, *He That Is Spiritual* (New York: Our Hope, 1918). In *The Gospel According to Jesus* I described Chafer's book and B. B. Warfield's critique of it. Warfield's review in *The Princeton Theological Review* (April 1919): 322–27, was full of sound reason and biblical insight. It reads like a thorough critique of modern no-lordship theology. If Chafer and those who were influenced by him had interacted seriously with Warfield on these issues, perhaps twentieth-century American evangelicalism might have been spared a lot of confusion and false teaching.

"I am of Paul," and others, "I am of Apollos" (1 Cor. 3:4). Paul told them their divisive behavior was unworthy of Christians: "You are still fleshly [Gk. *sarkikos,* 'pertaining to the flesh, carnal']. For since there is jealousy and strife among you, are you not fleshly, and are you not walking like mere men?"

Clearly Paul was accusing the Corinthians of behaving like non-Christians. Factions were not the only problem at Corinth. The believers there were tolerating an incestuous relationship that a "so-called brother" (5:11) was carrying on with his father's wife. Some were drunk and disorderly in the communion service (11:17–22). Christians were taking one another to court (6:1–8). They were abusing the gift of tongues (14:23), and women were being unruly in their corporate worship services (14:33).

But in 1 Corinthians 2:14–3:3 Paul was most certainly *not* defining two classes of Christians, or three classes of humanity. Paul clearly distinguished between "the natural man" and "he who is spiritual" (2:14–15)—between the unsaved person and the Christian. He recognized that all Christians are capable of carnal behavior. But never in any of his epistles did the apostle address two classes of believers.

In Romans 8, Paul's contrast was between "the mind set on the flesh" (non-Christians) and "the mind set on the Spirit" (v. 6) (Christians); between "those who are in the flesh" (v. 8—non-Christians) and those who are "in the Spirit" (v. 9—Christians). His meaning is unmistakable, for he spells it out explicitly in verse 9: "You are not in the flesh but in the Spirit, if indeed the Spirit of God dwells in you. But if anyone does not have the Spirit of Christ, he does not belong to Him."

So according to Paul, *all* Christians are spiritual. As we shall see, Paul also recognized that all believers behave carnally at times. That is what he was rebuking the Corinthians for.

These Corinthian Christians were obviously immature; that's why Paul called them "babes in Christ" (3:1). But, unlike many so-called carnal Christians today, they were not indifferent to spiritual things. In fact, their allegiance to particular leaders and their abuse of the gifts reflected a misplaced zeal. These Christians clearly had spiritual desires, no matter how imperfectly they pursued them.

Note also that Paul did not urge the Corinthians to seek some second-level experience. He did not counsel them to "make Christ Lord" or dedicate themselves once and for all. On the contrary, he told them, "You are not lacking in any gift, awaiting eagerly the revelation of our Lord Jesus Christ, who shall also confirm you to the end, blameless in the day of our Lord Jesus Christ" (1:7–8).

Still, Paul had no tolerance for those willfully acting carnally. When he learned of the incestuous man's sin, for example, he instructed the Corinthians "to deliver such a one to Satan for the destruction of his flesh, that his spirit may be saved in the day of the Lord Jesus" (5:5). Note how the apostle spoke of those in the church who are immoral, covetous, idolaters, revilers, drunkards, or swindlers. He did not call them *carnal Christians* but *so-called brothers* (5:11). He instructed the Corinthians not even to eat with such people. Clearly he knew such sins—persistent, willful, inveterate sins of lifestyle—called one's profession of faith into question. Paul corrected the church's lenient attitude toward this sinning man and others of his ilk. Evidently the Corinthians routinely accepted such people, perhaps as second-class Christians—just as evangelicals today accept them. Paul, however, commanded the church to discipline them (5:9–13), which would provide insight into whether they were natural, unredeemed people associating with believers, or spiritual people behaving carnally.

How Far Can Christians Go in Sinning?

I recently read a book about Christians and sin that began with an unusual account. The author of this book was acquainted with a pastor who had been sent to prison for robbing fourteen banks to finance his dalliances with prostitutes! The author was fully convinced the bank-robbing Lothario was a true Christian, and so he wrote a book to explore how such a thing could be possible.

Call me old-fashioned, but I think it is fair to raise the question of whether someone who regularly robs banks to pay for illicit sex is truly saved! That man's sin was secretly his lifestyle. There is every reason to believe that he would still be committing his crimes today if he had not been caught. Can we concede that this "so-called brother" is a genuine Christian, just because he was once an evangelical pastor?

True, we cannot judge the man's heart, but we *must* judge his behavior (1 Cor. 5:12). "Or do you not know that the unrighteous shall not inherit the kingdom of God? Do not be deceived; neither fornicators, nor idolaters, nor adulterers, nor effeminate, nor homosexuals, nor thieves, nor the covetous, nor drunkards, nor revilers, nor swindlers, shall inherit the kingdom of God" (1 Cor. 6:9–11). In those verses the apostle Paul was describing sins of chronic behavior, sins that color one's whole character. A predilection for such sins reflects an unregenerate heart. Paul reminded the Corinthians, "Such *were* some of you; *but you were washed, but you were sanctified, but you were justified* in the name of the Lord Jesus Christ, and in the Spirit of our God" (v. 12, emphasis added).

But wait. Doesn't Scripture include examples of believers who committed gross sin? Didn't David commit murder and adultery and allow his sin to go unconfessed for at least a year? Wasn't Lot characterized by worldly compromise in the midst of heinous sin? Yes, those examples prove that genuine believers are capable of the worst imaginable sins. But David and Lot cannot be made to serve as examples of "carnal" believers, whose whole lifestyle and appetites are no different from unregenerate people.

David, for example, *did* repent thoroughly of his sin when Nathan confronted him, and he willingly accepted the Lord's discipline (2 Sam. 12:1–23). Psalm 51 is an expression of David's deep repentance at the end of this sordid episode in his life. The point, after all, is that this was merely one episode in David's life. He was certainly not predisposed to that kind of sin. In fact, 1 Kings 15:5 says, "David did what was right in the sight of the Lord, and had not turned aside from anything that He commanded him all the days of his life, *except in the case of Uriah the Hittite*" (emphasis added).

Lot is a different case. Not much is known about him from the Old Testament account, but what *is* recorded about him is disappointing. He was a pathetic example of compromise and disobedience. On the eve of Sodom's destruction when he should have fled the city, "he hesitated" (Gen. 19:16). The angelic messengers had to seize his hand and put him outside the city. Near the end of his life, his two daughters got him drunk and committed incest with him (Gen. 19:30–38). Lot certainly *did* seem to have a proclivity for sins of compromise and worldliness.

Yet the inspired New Testament writer tells us Lot was "oppressed by the sensual conduct of unprincipled men (for by what he saw and heard that righteous man, while living among them, felt his righteous soul tormented day after day with their lawless deeds)" (2 Pet. 2:8). He hated sin and desired righteousness. He had respect for holy angels—evidence of his fear of God (Gen. 19:1–14). He obeyed God by not looking back at Sodom when God's judgment rained down (cf. v. 26).

Lot was certainly not "carnal" in the sense that he lacked spiritual desires. Though he lived in a wicked place, he was not wicked himself. His soul was "tormented," vexed, grieved, tortured with severe pain at the sight of the evil all around him. Evidently his conscience did not become seared; he "felt his righteous soul tormented day after day" with the evil deeds of those around him. Though he lived in Sodom, he never became a Sodomite. Those who use him as an illustration of someone who is saved but utterly carnal miss the point of 2 Peter 2:8.

What is the lesson of Lot's life as Peter saw it? Verse 9 sums it up: "The Lord knows how to rescue the godly from temptation, and to keep the unrighteous under punishment for the day of judgment."

In Lot's case, one means the Lord used to rescue him from temptation was severe chastisement. Lot lost his home; his wife was killed by divine judgment; and his own daughters disgraced and debased him. He paid a terrible price for his sin, being "tormented day after day." If Lot proves anything, it is that true believers cannot sin with impunity.

God always chastens and disciplines His children who sin. If they do *not* experience chastening, they are not truly His children, but spiritual bastards. Hebrews 12:7–8 explicitly states this: "What son is there whom his father does not discipline? But if you are without discipline, of which all have become partakers, then you are illegitimate children and not sons." The specific purpose for which He disciplines us is "for our good, that we may share His holiness" (Heb. 12:10).

All of that flies in the face of the notion that millions of Christians live in a state of unbroken carnality. If these people are true children of God, why are they not constantly under His discipline?

Chief of Sinners

Perhaps the classic example of a sinning believer is the apostle Paul.

Paul? Yes. The more he matured in Christ, the more the apostle became aware of his own sinfulness. When he wrote his first epistle to the Corinthians, he referred to himself as "the least of the apostles . . . not fit to be called an apostle, because I persecuted the church of God" (1 Cor. 15:9). A few years later, when he wrote to Ephesus, he called himself "the very least of all saints" (Eph. 3:8). Near the end of his life, when he wrote to Timothy, Paul spoke of himself as "foremost of all [sinners]" (1 Tim. 1:15).

This was not clever posturing on Paul's part. He was extremely sensitive to sin in his life and painfully honest about his own struggle with sin. He grieved over his sin and battled against it constantly. Yet he was one of the greatest saints who ever lived.

How can that be? Wouldn't you think that someone of Paul's stature would be an example of victory over sin? He was. Yet he called himself a "wretched man" and "chief of sinners"? Yes. Can both things be true at once? Absolutely. In fact, the more saintly we become, the more sensitive to sin we become.

Martin Luther noted the paradox of sin in every believer's life and coined a Latin expression: *simul justus et peccator* ("just and sinful at the same time"). Every true believer wrestles with this dilemma. Our justification is complete and perfect; therefore our standing before God is faultless. But our sanctification will not be perfect until we are glorified. It is the prize of our high calling in Christ (Phil. 3:14). Paul wrote, "Not that I have already obtained it, or have already become perfect, but I press on in order that I may lay hold of that for which also I was laid hold of by Christ Jesus" (v. 12). Here on earth, our practice will never match our position, no matter how earnestly we pursue sanctification.

But pursue it we will if we are truly born again, for God Himself guarantees our perseverance in righteousness: "May the God of peace Himself sanctify you entirely; and may your spirit and soul and body be preserved complete, without blame at the coming of our Lord Jesus Christ" (1 Thess. 5:23). He "is able to keep you from stumbling, and to make you stand in the presence of His glory blameless with great joy" (Jude 24).

The classic passage on Paul's personal struggle against sin is Romans 7:14–25:

> We know that the Law is spiritual; but I am of flesh, sold into bondage to sin. For that which I am doing, I do not understand; for I am not practicing what I would like to do, but I am doing the very thing I hate. But if I do the very thing I do not wish to do, I agree with the Law, confessing that it is good. So now, no longer am I the one doing it, but sin which indwells me. For I know that nothing good dwells in me, that is, in my flesh; for the wishing is present in me, but the doing of the good is not. For the good that I wish, I do not do; but I practice the very evil that I do not wish. But if I am doing the very thing I do not wish, I am no longer the one doing it, but sin which dwells in me. I find then the principle that evil is present in me, the one who wishes to do good. For I joyfully concur with the law of God in the inner man, but I see a different law in the members of my body, waging war against the law of my mind, and making me a prisoner of the law of sin which is in my members. Wretched man that I am! Who will set me free from the body of this death? Thanks be to God through Jesus Christ our Lord! So then, on the one hand I myself with my mind am serving the law of God, but on the other, with my flesh the law of sin.

Wretched Man That I Am!

Many expositors have wondered how that passage can logically follow the great declarations in Romans 6 that believers are dead to sin (Rom. 6:2), crucified with Christ so that our body of sin might be done away with (v. 6), freed from sin (v. 7), not under law, but under grace (v. 14), and slaves of righteousness (v. 18).

Some have proposed that in Romans 7 Paul was describing his life *before Christ*. They suggest that verse 14 is the key: "I am carnal, sold under sin."

Others believe Paul was describing his life *as a carnal Christian*, before he surrendered to Christ's lordship. They point out that Paul says, "I joyfully concur with the law of God in the inner man, but I see a different law in the members of my body." They believe Paul's frequent use of the personal pronoun here reveals that this is the internal conflict of a selfish, self-righteous person, someone who is trying to become righteous in the power of his own flesh. Often "deeper life" teachers will cite this passage, urging Christians to "get out of Romans 7 and into Romans 8" in their experience with God.

But a study of the text reveals that this is neither the experience of an unbeliever nor the expression of a "carnal" Christian.[3] It was Paul's experience at the time he wrote it. Though he was one of the most spiritual saints who ever lived, he struggled with personal sin the same as all of us. Though he was used mightily of God, he battled sin and temptation. "Therefore let him who thinks he stands take heed lest he fall. No temptation has overtaken you but such as is common to man" (1 Cor. 10:12–13).

How do we know Paul was saved when he experienced what this passage describes? The change in verb tenses between verses 13 and 14 provides the first clue. In Romans 7:7–13 Paul was recounting his life

---

[3]"The best commentators in every era of the church have almost invariably applied the seventh chapter of Romans to advanced believers. The commentators who do not take this view have been, with a few bright exceptions, the Romanists, the Socinians and the Arminians. Against them is arrayed the judgement of almost all the Reformers, almost all the Puritans and the best modern evangelical divines. . . . While I ask no man to call the Reformers and Puritans 'masters,' I do ask people to read what they say on this subject, and answer their arguments, if they can. This has not been done yet! . . . Let us remember that there is a great fact which cannot be got over: on one side stand the opinions and interpretation of Reformers and Puritans, and on the other the opinions and interpretation of Romanists, Socinians and Arminians. Let that be distinctly understood." J. C. Ryle, *Holiness* (reprint, Durham, England: Evangelical Press, 1979), xxii.

before conversion and remembering the conviction he felt when he stood face-to-face with the law of God. The verbs in those verses are all in the past tense. In verses 14–25, however, the verbs are in the present tense. These verses describe the battle with sin that was Paul's present experience.

Furthermore, Paul writes, "I delight in the law of God after the inward man" (Rom. 7:22). In verse 25 he adds, "I myself with my mind am serving the law of God." No non-Christian could make that claim. "The mind set on the flesh is hostile toward God; for it does not subject itself to the law of God, for it is not even able to do so" (Rom. 8:7).

Paul further describes his often-thwarted desire to obey God: "I am not practicing what I would like to do, but I am doing the very thing I hate. . . . The wishing is present in me, but the doing of the good is not. For the good that I wish, I do not do. . . . I find then the principle that evil is present in me, the one who wishes to do good" (7:15, 18–19, 21). But back in Romans 3 Paul said that the unsaved person has no such longing to do the will of God: "There is none who understands, there is none who seeks for God. . . . There is none who does good, there is not even one. . . . There is no fear of God before their eyes" (vv. 11–12, 18). The person described in Romans 7:14–25 can only be a redeemed person.

This is no carnal Christian or someone with a low degree of sanctification. Paul's repeated use of the personal pronoun in this context emphasizes that this was his own personal experience. The verb tenses show that he did not consider himself past this stage. The conflict he describes here was one he knew well—even as an advanced Christian. God's sanctifying work in his heart is clearly evident. He says he hates sin (v. 15). He loves righteousness (vv. 19, 21). He delights in the law of God from his heart (v. 22). He thanks God for the deliverance that is his in Christ (v. 25). Those are all responses of a mature Christian, in this case a seasoned apostle; not someone floundering in the throes of a desperate state of established carnality. In fact, it is the description of a godly man whose occasional sin feels like a constant thing when set against the backdrop of his holy longings.

Romans 7:14–25 thus describes the human side of the sanctifying process. We must not set it against Romans 8, as some do, imagining that these chapters describe two separate stages of Christian growth. They simply give two different perspectives on sanctification. Romans 7 is the human perspective; Romans 8 is the divine perspective. Romans 7 is Paul's own testimony of how it is to live as a Spirit-controlled, spiritually grounded believer. He loved the holy law of God with his whole heart, yet he found himself wrapped in human flesh and unable to fulfill it the way his heart wanted to. Are there Christians anywhere who are so spiritual that they can testify to a life lived above this level? Or so carnal that they live below the level of Romans 8?

All true believers should be living at precisely this level, struggling with the tension Paul describes between an ever-increasing hunger for righteousness on the one hand, and a growing sensitivity to sin on the other. Though the degree of sin will vary depending on one's level of spiritual maturity, sin in the genuine believer should always make him or her feel the conflict Paul describes in these verses.

Though some *have* tried to claim they live above Romans 7, they only reveal their own insensitivity to the pervasive effects of sin in the flesh. If they would honestly measure themselves against God's standards of righteousness, they would realize how far they fall short. The closer we get to God, the more we see our own sin. Only immature, fleshly, and legalistic persons can live under the illusion that they measure up well by God's standards. The level of spiritual insight, brokenness, contrition, and humility that characterize the person depicted in Romans 7 are marks of a spiritual and mature believer, who before God has no trust in his own goodness and achievements.

So Romans 7 is not the cry of a carnal Christian who cares not for righteousness, but the lament of a godly Christian who, at the height of spiritual maturity, nevertheless find⌐ himself unable to live up to the holy standard. It is also the experience of every genuine believer at every stage of spiritual development.

I am fleshly, but the law is good. Look closely at Paul's lament: "We know that the Law is spiritual; but I am of flesh, sold into bondage to sin. For that which I am doing, I do not understand; for I am not practicing what I would like to do, but I am doing the very thing I hate. But if I do the very thing I do not wish to do, I agree with the Law, confessing that it is good. So now, no longer am I the one doing it, but sin which indwells me" (Rom. 7:14–17).

Justification by faith apart from the works of the law in no way implies that the law is evil. The law is spiritual. It comes from the Spirit of God. It is a reflection of His "holy and righteous and good" nature (v. 12).

But there is a barrier that prevents every believer from always obeying God's law: our carnal or fleshly nature. Note that Paul says, "I am *of* flesh"; he doesn't say he is "*in* the flesh." Here the *flesh* (Gk., *sarx*) is not a reference to the physical body, or even a "part" of our person like the body, but the principle of human frailty—especially our sinful selfishness—which remains with us after salvation until we are ultimately glorified. "Those who are in the flesh cannot please God" (8:8). "In the flesh" is descriptive of an unregenerate condition (7:5). Christians are not "in the flesh."

Nevertheless, the flesh is still in us. We are made "of flesh"; that is, we are human. And that is the problem: "I know that nothing good dwells in me, that is, in my flesh. . . . On the one hand I myself with my mind am serving the law of God, but on the other, with my flesh the law of sin" (7:18, 25). *Flesh*, used in this context, refers to our fallenness. It taints all the facets of the total person—including our mind, emotions, and body. This residual fallenness—the flesh—is what drags us repeatedly into sin, although we hate and despise sin.

That is what Paul meant in verse 14 when he said, "I am of flesh, sold into bondage to sin." That phrase "sold into bondage to sin" at first seems to pose a problem, as does a similar phrase in verse 23: "prisoner of the law of sin which is in my members." Is Paul contradicting what he said in Romans 6:14: "Sin shall not be master over you, for you are not under law, but under grace"? No, "sold into bondage to sin" doesn't mean Paul actively committed himself to sinning. He was only acknowledging that his flesh kept dragging him back into committing the very sins he hated.

This is the state of every true believer. We are no longer related to our former father, the devil (John 8:44); we no longer love the world (1 John 2:15); and we are no longer sin's slaves—but our flesh is still subject to sin's deceit and still attracted by many of its allurements. Yet as Christians we cannot be happy with our sin, because it is contrary to who we are in Christ and we know it grieves our Lord.

Sin grieves the Holy Spirit (Eph. 4:30), dishonors God (1 Cor. 6:19–20), keeps our prayers from being answered (1 Pet. 3:12), causes good things from God to be withheld (Jer. 5:25), robs us of the joy of our salvation (Ps. 51:12), inhibits spiritual growth (1 Cor. 3:1), brings chastisement from the Lord (Heb. 12:5–7), prevents us from being fit vessels for the Lord to use (2 Tim. 2:21), pollutes Christian fellowship (1 Cor. 10:21), and can even endanger our physical life and health (1 Cor. 11:29–30). No wonder true Christians hate sin.

One unbeliever, upon hearing the truth of justification by faith, commented, "If I believed that salvation is free through faith alone, I would believe and then take my fill of sin." The person witnessing to him wisely replied, "How much sin do you think it would take to fill a true Christian to satisfaction?" A person who has not lost any of his appetite for sin—and acquired instead a hunger for the things of God—has not been truly converted. "What are our tastes and choices and likings and inclinations? This is the great testing question."[4]

Here Paul confirms that the appetites and desires of the true believer's inner man are governed by the law of God: "I joyfully concur with the law of God in the inner man, but I see a different law in the members of my body, waging war against the law of my mind, and making me a prisoner of the law of sin which is in my members" (7:22–23).

The wishing is present in me, but the doing of the good is not. Every true Christian can echo Paul's lament. We concur that God's law is good. We desire to obey it. Yet we cannot rid ourselves of sin. We are bound hand and foot by our own human frailty. Sin is in our very members. Self-righteous people deceive themselves into thinking they are moral and good, but Romans 7 shows that a true Christian led by the Spirit will not. The more spiritual Christian is all the more aware of indwelling sin. The sin in our members cannot win all the time—and it will ultimately fail to defeat us—but it perpetually frustrates our attempts to obey God perfectly.

Paul says, "Nothing good dwells in me, that is, in my flesh" (v. 18). There's a big difference between surviving sin and reigning sin: Sin no longer reigns in us (6:18–19), but it does survive in us (7:20). Galatians 5:17 says, "The flesh sets its desire against the Spirit, and the Spirit against the flesh; for these are in opposition to one another, so that you may not do the things that you please." Romans 7 simply describes that battle in its hideous detail. But Galatians 5:16 tells us how to win: "Walk by the Spirit, and you will not carry out the desire of the flesh." The Holy Spirit gives us victory.

But that victory seems to come with frustrating languor. In verses 18–19 Paul writes, "The wishing is present in me, but the doing of the good is not. For the good that I wish, I do not do; but I practice the very evil that I do not wish." He is not saying he is incapable of doing *anything* right. He is saying that his *desire* to obey is always greater than his own *ability* to obey. This is the pattern of spiritual growth: As our hatred for sin increases and our capacity for victory over sin is enlarged, our frustration with the remnants of sin in the flesh is also intensified. In other words, our sensitivity to indwelling sin is inversely proportional to our experience of victory. The more we defeat sin in our lives, the more aware of its presence we become.

---

[4]Ryle, *Holiness,* 30.

Here is the crucial point: Paul was not saying he had a bent toward sinning. Just the opposite is true. His inclination was toward righteousness. He was simply frustrated by the pull of his sinful flesh.

Again, this is not the testimony of a someone living in a carelessly "carnal" state. In his heart Paul longed for righteousness, hungered to obey God, loved the law of God, and wanted to do good. That is the direction of every true Christian, regardless of where we are in the sanctifying process.

I joyfully concur with the law. "I find then the principle that evil is present in me, the one who wishes to do good. For I joyfully concur with the law of God in the inner man, but I see a different law in the members of my body, waging war against the law of my mind, and making me a prisoner of the law of sin which is in my members" (vv. 21–23).

It was not Paul's conscience that was bothering him. He was not lamenting some unforgiven sin or describing a defiant refusal to follow the Lord. What troubled him was his inner man, recreated in the likeness of Christ and indwelt by His Spirit. That inner person, having seen something of the true holiness, goodness, and glory of God's law, was grieved at the least infraction or falling short of it. In glaring contrast to his preconversion self-satisfaction (cf. Phil. 3:6), Paul now realized how wretchedly short of God's perfect law he lived, even as a Spirit-indwelt believer and an apostle of Jesus Christ.

That spirit of humble contrition is a mark of every true disciple of Christ, who cries out, "Lord, I can't be all you want me to be. I am unable to fulfill your perfect, holy, and glorious law." In great frustration and remorse we must sorrowfully confess with Paul, "I am not always practicing what I would like to do."

Paul delighted in God's law. The phrase "in the inner man" could be translated, "from the bottom of my heart." Emanating from the depths of his soul, Paul had a great love for the law of God. His inner man, the part that "is being renewed day by day" (2 Cor. 4:16) and "strengthened with power through [God's] Spirit" (Eph. 3:16), resonated with God's law. The source of his problems was the principle of frailty and fallenness that is inherent in human nature.

The author of Psalm 119 experienced the same conflict Paul did. His psalm reflects his deep longing for the things of God. Here are some sample expressions of the psalmist's desire for God's law:

- Verses 81–83: "My soul languishes for Thy salvation; I wait for Thy word. My eyes fail with longing for Thy

word, while I say, "When wilt Thou comfort me?"
Though I have become like a wineskin in the smoke, I
do not forget Thy statutes."

- Verse 92: "If Thy law had not been my delight, then I
would have perished in my affliction."
- Verse 97: "O how I love Thy law! It is my meditation all
the day."
- Verse 113: "I hate those who are double-minded, but I
love Thy law."
- Verse 131: "I opened my mouth wide and panted, for I
longed for Thy commandments."
- Verse 143: "Trouble and anguish have come upon me;
yet Thy commandments are my delight."
- Verse 163: "I hate and despise falsehood, but I love Thy
law."
- Verse 165: "Those who love Thy law have great peace,
and nothing causes them to stumble."
- Verse 174: "I long for Thy salvation, O Lord, and Thy
law is my delight."

The measure of spirituality the psalmist expresses is intimidating.
Clearly he was captivated by an overwhelming love for the things of
God. That is why the last verse in Psalm 119 is so surprising: "I have
gone astray like a lost sheep; seek Thy servant, for I do not forget Thy
commandments" (v. 176). You might think that a person with such an
intense love for God's law would not experience the failure of going
astray spiritually. But that is the conflict all believers experience.

Why do we sin? Because God didn't do a good enough job when He
saved us? Because He gave us a new nature that isn't complete yet? Because we're not prepared for heaven yet and still need to earn our way in?

No, because sin is still present in our flesh.

On the one hand . . . but on the other . . . "Wretched man
that I am! Who will set me free from the body of this death? Thanks be
to God through Jesus Christ our Lord! So then, on the one hand I
myself with my mind am serving the law of God, but on the other, with
my flesh the law of sin" (Rom. 7:24–25).

Paul thus lets out a final wail of distress and frustration. Again, he
echoes the psalmist: "Out of the depths I have cried to Thee, O Lord.
Lord, hear my voice! Let Thine ears be attentive to the voice of my

supplications. If Thou, Lord, shouldst mark iniquities, O Lord, who could stand? But there is forgiveness with Thee, that Thou mayest be feared. I wait for the Lord, my soul does wait, and in His word do I hope" (Ps. 130:1–5).

Paul was surely in a similar frame of mind when he said, "Who will set me free from the body of this death?" But Paul answers his own question: "I thank God through Jesus Christ, our Lord" (v. 25). Paul was assured of ultimate triumph over the sin in his own flesh: "I consider that the sufferings of this present time are not worthy to be compared with the glory that is to be revealed to us. For the anxious longing of the creation waits eagerly for the revealing of the sons of God" (8:18–19). The final phase of our salvation is guaranteed: "Whom He justified, these He also glorified" (8:30). "This perishable must put on the imperishable, and this mortal must put on immortality. . . . But thanks be to God, who gives us the victory through our Lord Jesus Christ" (1 Cor. 15:53, 57). "Indeed while we are in this tent, we groan, being burdened, because we do not want to be unclothed, but to be clothed, in order that what is mortal may be swallowed up by life" (2 Cor. 5:4). "We eagerly wait for a Savior, the Lord Jesus Christ; who will transform the body of our humble state into conformity with the body of His glory" (Phil. 3:20–21). Ours is a triumphant hope!

Yet for now the battle goes on. Full deliverance awaits glorification. Victory here and now is only possible bit by bit as we mortify the deeds of the body through the power of the Holy Spirit: "Therefore consider the members of your earthly body as dead to immorality, impurity, passion, evil desire, and greed, which amounts to idolatry" (Col. 3:5). "For if you are living according to the flesh, you must die; but if by the Spirit you are putting to death the deeds of the body, you will live" (Rom. 8:13).

We are bound to be frustrated by our inability to experience holiness to the degree we desire. That is the inevitable experience of every true saint of God. Because of our flesh we can never in this life achieve the level of holiness to which we aspire. "We ourselves, having the first fruits of the Spirit, even we ourselves groan within ourselves, waiting eagerly for our adoption as sons, the redemption of our body" (Rom. 8:23). But that hope only further inflames our aspirations to holiness.

"Beloved, now we are children of God, and it has not appeared as yet what we shall be. We know that, when He appears, we shall be like Him, because we shall see Him just as He is. Everyone who has this hope fixed on Him purifies himself, just as He is pure" (1 John 3:2–3).

9

The Faith That *Doesn't* Work

> Sanctification . . . is the invariable result of that vital union with Christ which true faith gives to a Christian. "He that abideth in Me, and I in him, the same bringeth forth much fruit" (John 15:5). The branch which bears no fruit is no living branch of the vine. The union with Christ which produces no effect on heart and life is a mere formal union, which is worthless before God. The faith which has not a sanctifying influence on the character is no better than the faith of devils. It is a "dead faith, because it is alone." It is not the gift of God. It is not the faith of God's elect. In short, where there is no sanctification of life, there is no real faith in Christ. True faith worketh by love. It constrains a man to live unto the Lord from a deep sense of gratitude for redemption. It makes him feel that he can never do too much for Him that died for him. Being much forgiven, he loves much. He whom the blood cleanses walks in the light. He who has real lively hope in Christ purifieth himself even as He is pure (James 2:17–20; Titus 1:1; Gal. 5:6; 1 John 1:7; 3:3).
>
> J. C. Ryle[1]

A tract written by one of the most extreme defenders of no-lordship salvation seeks to explain redemption: "Even at your best, you can never earn or deserve a relationship with God. Only the object of your faith,

---

[1]J. C. Ryle, *Holiness* (reprint, Durham, England: Evangelical Press, 1979), 17.

Jesus Christ, has the merit." I agree with that. It is the clear teaching of Scripture (Titus 3:5–7).

But the same tract also says, "Your personal sins are not an issue to God." When the author attempts to explain *faith* in practical terms, he says this: "You respond to God the Father by simply forming the words privately in your mind, 'I believe in Christ.'"[2]

All of that adds up to a notion of faith that is little more than a mental gambit. The "faith" that tract describes is not much more than a cursory nod of the head. It is bare *intellectual assent.*

As I noted in chapter 3, many no-lordship apologists resent being accused of portraying faith as mere mental acquiescence. Dr. Ryrie, for example, calls it a straw-man argument.

> Being convinced of something or putting one's trust in the Gospel could hardly be said to be a casual acceptance of something. When a person gives credence to the historical facts that Christ died and rose from the dead and the doctrinal fact that this was for his sins, he is trusting his eternal destiny to the reliability of those truths. . . . Make no mistake, non-lordship people do *not* say what [this] straw man . . . alleges they say (*SGS* 30).

But many no-lordship people *do* say precisely what Ryrie denies they say. Zane Hodges, for example, practically concedes that "intellectual assent" adequately describes his idea of faith. He is uncomfortable with that phrase's "prejudicial connotation," but he doggedly defends its gist. *Assent,* he points out, simply means "meaningful agreement." The negative undertone, Hodges suggests, is caused by modifiers like *mental* or *intellectual.* Though they mean "nothing more than 'of or pertaining to the intellect,'" he says, they are often taken to imply "detachment and personal disinterest" (*AF* 30). "In this context we should discard words like mental or intellectual altogether," Hodges adds. "The Bible knows nothing about an intellectual faith as over against some other kind of faith (like emotional or volitional). What the Bible does recognize is the obvious distinction between faith and unbelief!" (*AF* 30).

How does Hodges describe faith? "What faith really is, in biblical language, is receiving the testimony of God. It is the *inward conviction*

---

[2] R. B. Thieme, Jr., "A Matter of Life [and] Death: The Gospel of Jesus Christ" (Houston: Thieme Bible Ministries, 1990), 10–12.

that what God says to us in the gospel is true. That—and that alone—is saving faith" (*AF* 31, emphasis in original).[3]

Is that an adequate characterization of what it means to believe? Is faith totally passive? Is it true that people know intuitively whether their faith is real? Do all genuinely saved people have full assurance? Cannot someone be deceived into thinking he is a believer when in fact he is not? Can a person *think* he believes yet not truly believe? Is there no such thing as spurious faith?

Scripture plainly and repeatedly answers those questions. The apostles saw counterfeit faith as a very real danger. Many of the epistles, though addressed to churches, contain warnings that reveal the apostles' concern over church members they suspected were not genuine believers. Paul, for example, wrote to the Corinthian church, "Test yourselves to see if you are in the faith; examine yourselves! Or do you not recognize this about yourselves, that Jesus Christ is in you—unless indeed you fail the test?" (2 Cor. 13:5). Peter wrote, "Therefore, brethren, be all the more diligent to make certain about His calling and choosing you; for as long as you practice these things, you will never stumble" (2 Pet. 1:10).

Evidently there were some in the very early church who flirted with the notion that faith could be some kind of static, inert, inanimate assent to facts.[4] The Book of James, probably the earliest New Testament epistle, specifically confronts this error. James sounds almost as if he were writing to twentieth-century no-lordship advocates. He says people *can* be deluded into thinking they believe when in fact they do not, and he says the single factor that distinguishes bogus faith from the real thing is the righteous behavior inevitably produced by authentic faith.

These are the questions the lordship debate must ultimately answer: Is it enough to know and understand and assent to the facts of the gospel—even holding the "*inward conviction*" that these truths apply to me personally—and yet *never* shun sin or submit to the Lord Jesus? Is a

---

[3]By emphasizing the words "inward conviction" and underscoring them with the phrase "that—and that alone," Hodges is explicitly rejecting the concept that faith inevitably produces righteous behavior. In contrast, the Reformers had a saying: "Faith alone saves, but the faith that saves is *never* alone."

[4]"Probably as a reaction from justification by works of the law a fallacy had sprung up among the Jewish Christians that faith in Christ existing as an inactive principle, a mere speculative belief, would suffice without works. St. James shows what an impossible position this is." Arthur Carr, "The General Epistle of St. James," *Cambridge Greek Testament for Schools and Colleges* (Cambridge: Cambridge University Press, 1896), 35.

person who holds that kind of belief guaranteed eternal life? Does such a hope constitute faith in the sense Scripture uses the term? James is expressly teaching that it does not. Real faith, he says, will no doubt produce righteous behavior. The true character of saving faith may be examined in light of the believer's works. This is consistent with all Old Testament and New Testament soteriology. One enters into salvation by grace through faith (Eph. 2:8–9). Faith is by nature turned and toned toward obedience (Acts 5:32; Rom. 1:5, 2:8, 16:26), so good works are inevitable in the life of one who truly believes. These works have no part in bringing about salvation (Eph. 2:9; Rom. 3:20, 24; 4:5; Titus 3:5), but they show that salvation is indeed present (Eph. 2:10; 5:9; 1 John 2:5).

"It is evident that there is faith and FAITH," Roy Aldrich wrote in reference to James 2. "There is nominal faith and real faith. There is intellectual faith and heart faith. There is sensual faith and there is spiritual faith. There is dead faith and there is vital faith. There is traditional faith which may fall short of transforming personal faith. There is a faith that may be commended as orthodox and yet have no more saving value than the faith of demons."[5] James attacks all brands of "faith" that fall short of the biblical standard. What I and others have sometimes termed "mental acquiescence" or "intellectual assent," James characterizes as mere hearing, empty profession, demonic orthodoxy, and dead faith.

Mere Hearing

James wrote, "Prove yourselves doers of the word, and not merely hearers who delude themselves" (1:22). James uses a substantive (*pōietai*) "doers of the word," or "Word-doers" instead of a straightforward imperative ("do the word"). He is describing characteristic behavior, not occasional activity. It is one thing to fight; it is something else to be a soldier. It is one thing to build a shed; it is something else to be a builder. James is not merely challenging his readers to *do the Word;* he is telling them real Christians are *doers of the Word.* That describes the basic disposition of those who believe unto salvation.

Hearing is important, as James has emphasized in 1:19–21. Faith comes by hearing (Rom. 10:17). However, actual faith must be something *more* than mere hearing. Hearing is a means, not an end. The end is faith, which results in obedience.

---

[5]Roy L. Aldrich, "Some Simple Difficulties of Salvation," *Bibliotheca Sacra* 111/442 (April-June 1954): 167.

True believers cannot be hearers only. The Greek word for "hearer" (v. 22) is *akroatēs,* a term used to describe students who audited a class. An auditor usually listens to the lectures, but is permitted to treat assignments and exams as optional. Many people in the church today approach spiritual truth with an auditor's mentality, receiving God's Word only passively. But James' point, shown by his illustrations in verses 23–27, is that merely hearing God's Word results in worthless religion (v. 26). In other words, mere hearing is no better than unbelief or outright rejection. In fact, it's worse! The hearer-only is enlightened but unregenerate. James is reiterating truth he undoubtedly heard first-hand from the Lord Himself. Jesus warned powerfully against the error of hearing without doing (Matt. 7:21–27), as did the apostle Paul (Rom. 2:13–25).

James says hearing without obeying is self-deception (v. 22). The Greek term for "delude" (*paralogizomai*) means "to reason against." It speaks of skewed logic. Those who believe it is enough to hear the Word without obeying make a gross miscalculation. They deceive themselves. Robert Johnstone wrote,

> Knowing that the study of divine truth, through reading the Bible, giving attendance on the public ordinances of grace, and otherwise, is a most important duty,is, indeed, the road leading toward the gate of everlasting life,they allow themselves, through man's natural aversion to all genuine spirituality, to be persuaded by the wicked one that this is the sum of all Christian duty, and itself the gate of life, so that in mere "hearing" they enter in, and all is well with them. To rest satisfied with the means of grace, without yielding up our hearts to their power as means, so as to receive the grace and exhibit its working in our lives, is manifestly folly of the same class as that of a workman who should content himself with possessing tools, without using them,madness of the same class as that of a man perishing with hunger, who should exult in having bread in his hands, without eating it,but folly and madness as immeasurably greater than these, as the "work of God" (John vi. 29) transcends in importance the work of an earthly artisan, and "life with Christ in God" the perishable existence of earth.[6]

James gives two illustrations that contrast hearers-only with obedient hearers.

---

[6]Robert Johnstone, *Lectures Exegetical and Practical on the Epistle of James* (reprint, Minneapolis: Klock & Klock, 1978), 144.

The mirror. "For if anyone is a hearer of the word and not a doer, he is like a man who looks at his natural face in a mirror; for once he has looked at himself and gone away, he has immediately forgotten what kind of person he was. But one who looks intently at the perfect law, the law of liberty, and abides by it, not having become a forgetful hearer but an effectual doer, this man shall be blessed in what he does" (1:23–25).

"Not a doer" is literally "a not-doer," or someone whose disposition is to hear without doing. Contrary to some commentators, "looks . . . in a mirror" does not describe a hasty or casual glance. The verb (*katanoeō*) means "to look carefully, cautiously, observantly." "The man carefully studies his face and becomes thoroughly familiar with its features. [He] listens to the Word, apparently not momentarily but at length, so that he understands what he hears. He knows what God expects him to do. Any failure to respond cannot be blamed on lack of understanding."[7] James' point is not that this man failed to look long enough, or intently enough, or sincerely enough—but that he turned away without taking any action. "He has immediately forgotten what kind of person he was" (v. 24). This passage is reminiscent of the unproductive soils in Matthew 13. The person who hears the Word does not have the proper heart response. Therefore that which has been sown cannot bear fruit.

The point is twofold. First, James is illustrating *the urgency of actively obeying the Word*. If you don't deal with what you see while you are looking into the mirror, you will forget about it later. By Monday morning you may forget the impact of Sunday's sermon. By this afternoon, this morning's readings might be a dim memory. If you do not make the necessary responses while God is convicting your heart, you will probably not get around to it. The image reflected in the mirror of God's Word will soon fade.

Second, and more pointedly, James is illustrating *the utter uselessness of passively receiving the Word*. Verse 21 spoke of how we are to receive the Word: "Therefore putting aside all filthiness and all that remains of wickedness, in humility receive the word implanted, which is able to save your souls." The conjunction *but* at the beginning of verse 22 is equivalent to *moreover,* or *now,* implying that what follows is not a contrast but an amplification of the command in verse 21. In other words, James is saying it is wonderful to be receptive to the Word—to hear with approval and agreement—but that is not enough.

---

[7] Donald W. Burdick, "James," in *The Expositor's Bible Commentary,* ed. Frank E. Gaebelein (Grand Rapids, Mich.: Zondervan, 1981), 11:175.

We must receive it as those who would be doers. Non-doers are not true believers.

James gives a contrasting example. This is the effectual doer: "one who looks intently at the perfect law, the law of liberty, and abides by it, not having become a forgetful hearer but an effectual doer, this man shall be blessed in what he does" (1:25). The word translated "looks intently" is *parakuptō*, the same word used in John 20:5, 11 to describe how John stooped to peer into Jesus' empty tomb. The word is also used in 1 Peter 1:12 of the angels who long to look into things concerning the gospel. It speaks of a deep and absorbing look, as when someone stoops for a closer examination. Hiebert says the word "pictures the man as bending over the mirror on the table in order to examine more minutely what is revealed therein."[8] Implied is a longing to understand for reasons that go beyond the academic.

This is a description of the true believer. In contrast to the hearer-only, "he bent over the mirror, and, gripped by what he saw, he continued looking and obeying its precepts. This feature marks his crucial difference to the first man."[9] This man is gazing into "the perfect law, the law of liberty" (v. 25). That refers to the gospel in its fullest sense— the whole counsel of God, the implanted word that saves (v. 21). Burdick writes,

> It is not merely the OT law, nor is it the Mosaic law perverted to become a legalistic system for earning salvation by good works. When James calls it the "perfect law," he has in mind the sum total of God's revealed truth—not merely the preliminary portion found in the OT, but also the final revelation made through Christ and his Apostles that was soon to be inscripturated in the NT. Thus it is complete, in contrast to that which is preliminary and preparatory. Furthermore, it is the "law of liberty" (Gr.), by which James means that it does not enslave. It is not forced by external compulsion. Instead, it is freely accepted and fulfilled with glad devotion under the enablements of the Spirit of God (Gal. 5:22-23).[10]

James is not speaking of law in contrast to gospel. "The perfect law of liberty" *is* the implanted Word (v. 21). Those who understand the phrase "the perfect law of liberty" to mean something separate from the

---

[8]D. Edmond Hiebert, *The Epistle of James* (Chicago: Moody, 1979), 135–36.
[9]Ibid.
[10]Burdick, "James," 176.

gospel miss James' point. In describing the man who looks at the Word, continues in it, and is blessed, he is portraying the effect of true conversion.[11]

Does this mean all true believers are doers of the Word? Yes. Do they *always* put the Word into practice? No—or a pastor's task would be relatively simple. Believers do fail, and they sometimes fail in appalling ways. But even when they fail, true believers will not altogether cease having the disposition and motivation of one who is a doer. James, then, offers these words as both a reminder to the true believer (the "effectual doer," v. 25), and a challenge to unbelievers who have identified with the truth but are not obedient to it (the "forgetful hearer[s]").

The unbridled tongue. James further illustrates the deceptive nature of hearing without obeying: "If anyone thinks himself to be religious, and yet does not bridle his tongue but deceives his own heart, this man's religion is worthless. This is pure and undefiled religion in the sight of our God and Father, to visit orphans and widows in their distress, and to keep oneself unstained by the world" (1:26–27).

The word translated "religious" in verse 26 is *thrēskos,* a word often used in reference to ceremonial public worship. It is the word Josephus used, for example, when he described the worship of the Temple. *Thrēskeia* ("religion," vv. 26–27) is the same word Paul used in Acts 26:5 to refer to the tradition of the Pharisees. It emphasizes the externals of ceremony, ritual, liturgy, and so on. James is saying that all such things, when divorced from meaningful obedience, are worthless.

All of us struggle to control our tongues. It was James who wrote, "For we all stumble in many ways. If anyone does not stumble in what he says, he is a perfect man, able to bridle the whole body as well" (3:2). But this man's tongue is like an unbridled horse. He lets it run wild while deceiving his own heart (1:26). He is not battling a transitory lapse in tongue control. He is dominated by a pattern that characterizes his very nature. Though he professes to be religious, his character is out of sync with his claim. While he undoubtedly thinks of himself as righteous, he is misled about the efficacy of his own religion.

Despite this man's external religion, his constantly unbridled and out-of-control tongue demonstrates a deceived and unholy heart, for "the things that proceed out of the mouth come from the heart" (Matt.

---

[11]James' statement that the Word-doer will be blessed parallels Jesus' own words in John 13:17: "If you know these things, you are blessed if you do them," and Luke 11:28: "Blessed are those who hear the word of God, and observe it." The "blessing" these verses speak of is the birthright of all who are redeemed.

15:18). "The good man out of the good treasure of his heart brings forth what is good; and the evil man out of the evil treasure brings forth what is evil; for his mouth speaks from that which fills his heart" (Luke 6:45). Our Lord warned, "By your words you shall be justified, and by your words you shall be condemned" (Matt. 12:37).

Kistemaker notes the significance of the expression "deceiving his own heart":

> This is the third time that James tells his readers not to deceive themselves (1:16, 22, 26). As a pastor he is fully aware of counterfeit religion that is nothing more than external formalism. He knows that many people merely go through the motions of serving God, but their speech gives them away. Their religion has a hollow ring. And although they do not realize it, by their words and by their actions—or lack of them—they deceive themselves. Their heart is not right with God and their fellow man, and their attempt to hide this lack of love only heightens their self-deception. Their religion is worthless.[12]

This worthless religion contrasts sharply with the true religion that is "pure and undefiled . . . in the sight of our God and Father, to visit orphans and widows in their distress, and to keep oneself unstained by the world" (v. 27). James is not here attempting to define religion, but rather to set forth a concrete illustration of the principle he began with: that true religion involves more than mere hearing. True saving faith will inevitably bear the fruit of good works.

Empty Profession

The first thirteen verses of James 2 continue to expand on James' contention that believers are by disposition doers of the Word, not mere hearers. He confronts the problem of favoritism, which evidently had arisen in the church or churches James was writing to. Bearing in mind that this is the context, we move ahead to James 2:14. Here, after warning his readers that they were facing judgment for their unholy and unmerciful behavior (v. 13), James turns to the heart of the matter: their apparent misconception that faith is an inert ingredient in the salvation formula. His challenge could not be clearer:

> What use is it, my brethren, *if a man says he has faith, but he has no works? Can that faith save him?* If a brother or sister is without

---

[12]Simon J. Kistemaker, *Exposition of the Epistle of James* (Grand Rapids, Mich.: Baker, 1986), 64.

clothing and in need of daily food, and one of you says to them, "Go in peace, be warmed and be filled," and yet you do not give them what is necessary for their body, what use is that? Even so *faith, if it has no works, is dead, being by itself.* But someone may well say, "You have faith, and I have works; show me your faith without the works, and I will show you my faith by my works." You believe that God is one. You do well; the demons also believe, and shudder. But are you willing to recognize, you foolish fellow, that *faith without works is useless?* Was not Abraham our father justified by works, when he offered up Isaac his son on the altar? You see that faith was working with his works, and as a result of the works, faith was perfected; and the Scripture was fulfilled which says, "And Abraham believed God, and it was reckoned to him as righteousness," and he was called the friend of God. You see that *a man is justified by works, and not by faith alone.* And in the same way was not Rahab the harlot also justified by works, when she received the messengers and sent them out by another way? For just as the body without the spirit is dead, so also *faith without works is dead.*

James 2:14–26, emphasis added

No less than five times in that passage (vv. 14, 17, 20, 24, 26), James reiterates his thesis: passive faith is not efficacious faith. It is a frontal attack on the empty profession of those whose hope is in a dormant faith.

Reicke writes, "It must be noted that the discussion is about a person who only asserts that he has faith. This person has no real faith, since his faith does not find expression in deeds. The author does not take issue with faith itself, but with a superficial conception of it which permits faith to be only a formal concession. He desires to point out that a Christianity of mere words does not lead to salvation."[13] Cranfield likewise observes, "The clue to the understanding of the section is the fact (very often ignored) that in verse 14 . . . the author has not said, 'if a man have faith,' but 'if a man say he hath faith.' This fact should be allowed to control our interpretation of the whole paragraph. . . . The burden of this section is not (as is often supposed) that we are saved through faith plus works, but that we are saved through genuine, as opposed to counterfeit, faith."[14]

James cannot be teaching that salvation is earned by works. He has already described salvation as a "good thing bestowed" and a "perfect

---

[13]Bo Reicke, "The Epistles of James, Peter and John" *The Anchor Bible* (Garden City, N.Y.: Doubleday, 1964), 37:32.

[14]C. E. B. Cranfield, "The Message of James," *The Scottish Journal of Theology* 18/3 (September 1965): 338.

gift" given when "in the exercise of His will [God] brought us forth by the word of truth, so that we might be, as it were, the first fruits among His creatures" (1:17–18). Faith is part and parcel of that perfect gift. It is supernaturally bestowed by God, not independently conceived in the mind or will of the individual believer.

As we noted in chapter 3, faith is not a wistful longing, or a blind confidence, or even *"inward conviction."* It is a supernatural certainty, an understanding of spiritual realities "which eye has not seen and ear has not heard, and which have not entered the heart of man, all that God has prepared for those who love Him. For to us God revealed them through the Spirit; for the Spirit searches all things, even the depths of God" (1 Cor. 2:9–10). Faith is a gift of God, not something conjured up by human effort, so no one can boast—not even about his faith (cf. Eph. 2:8–9).

In the phrase "if a man says he has faith, but he has no works" (v. 14), the verbs are present tense. They describe someone who routinely claims to be a believer yet continuously lacks any external evidence of faith. The question "Can that faith save him?" employs the Greek negative particle *mē,* indicating that a negative reply is assumed. It might literally be rendered, "That faith cannot save him, can it?" James, like the apostle John, challenges the authenticity of a profession of faith that produces no fruit (cf. 1 John 2:4, 5, 9). The context indicates that the "works" he speaks of are not anyone's bid to earn eternal life. These are acts of compassion (v. 15).

Faith in this context is clearly *saving* faith (v. 1). James is speaking of eternal salvation. He has referred to "the word implanted, which is able to save your souls" in 1:21. Here he has the same salvation in view. He is not disputing whether faith saves. Rather, he is opposing the notion that faith can be a passive, fruitless, intellectual exercise and still save. Where there are no works, we must assume no faith exists either. On this matter James merely echoes Jesus, who said, "You will know them by their fruits. Grapes are not gathered from thorn bushes, nor figs from thistles, are they? Even so, every good tree bears good fruit; but the bad tree bears bad fruit. A good tree cannot produce bad fruit, nor can a bad tree produce good fruit" (Matt. 7:16–18). No works, no faith. Real faith *inevitably* produces faith-works.

Here even Charles Ryrie sounds like an advocate of "lordship salvation":

> Can a non-working, dead, spurious faith save a person? James is not saying that we are saved by works, but that a faith that does not produce good works is a dead faith. . . .

> Unproductive faith cannot save, because it is not genuine faith. Faith and works are like a two-coupon ticket to heaven. The coupon of works is not good for passage, and the coupon of faith is not valid if detached from works.[15]

James follows with an illustration comparing faith without works to phony compassion, words without action: "If a brother or sister is without clothing and in need of daily food, and one of you says to them, 'Go in peace, be warmed and be filled,' and yet you do not give them what is necessary for their body, what use is that?" (2:15–16). The faith of a false professor is similarly useless: "Even so faith, if it has no works, is dead, being by itself" (v. 17).

James concludes with a challenge to those whose profession is suspect: "But someone may well say, 'You have faith, and I have works; show me your faith without the works, and I will show you my faith by my works'" (v. 18). Commentators disagree on whether "someone" refers to an objector and how much of the discourse that follows is to be attributed to this "someone" as opposed to James himself.[16] However one reads it, the essential point James is making is clear: The only possible evidence of faith is works. How can anyone show faith without works? It cannot be done.

Barnes distills the sense of the passage:

> James was not arguing against real and genuine faith, nor against its importance in justification, but against the supposition that mere faith was all that was necessary to save a man, whether it was accompanied by good works or not. *He* maintains that if there is genuine faith it will always be accompanied by good works, and that it is only *that* faith which can justify and save. If it leads to no practical holiness of life . . . it is of no value whatever.[17]

Demonic Orthodoxy

James continues his assault on passive faith with this shocking statement: "You believe that God is one. You do well; the demons also

---

[15]Charles C. Ryrie, ed., *The Ryrie Study Bible* (Chicago: Moody, 1978), 1859–60.

[16]Hiebert, *The Epistle of James*, 182–85; see also Zane C. Hodges, "Light on James Two," *Bibliotheca Sacra* 120/480 (October-December 1963): 341–50.

[17]Albert Barnes, *Notes on the New Testament* (reprint, Grand Rapids, Mich.: Baker, 1983), 13:50.

believe, and shudder" (v. 19). Orthodox doctrine by itself is no proof of saving faith. Demons affirm the oneness of God and tremble at its implications, but they are not redeemed. Matthew 8:29 tells of a group of demons who recognized Jesus as the Son of God. They even exhibited fear. Demons often acknowledge the existence and authority of Christ (Matt. 8:29–30; Mark 5:7), His deity (Luke 4:41), and even His resurrection (Acts 19:15), but their diabolical nature is not changed by what they know and believe. Their fearful affirmation of orthodox doctrine is not the same as saving faith.

James implies that demonic faith is greater than the fraudulent faith of a false professor, for demonic faith produces fear, whereas unsaved men have "no fear of God before their eyes" (Rom. 3:18). If the demons believe, tremble, and are not saved, what does that say about those who profess to believe and don't even tremble? (cf. Isa. 66:2, 5).[18]

Puritan Thomas Manton perfectly sums up the subtly deceptive nature of the sterile orthodoxy that constitutes demonic faith:

> [It is] a simple and naked assent to such things as are propounded in the word of God, and maketh men more knowing but not better, not more holy or heavenly. They that have it may believe the promises, the doctrines, the precepts as well as the histories . . . but yet, lively saving faith it is not, for he who hath that, findeth his heart engaged to Christ, and doth so believe the promises of the gospel concerning pardon of sins and life eternal that he seeketh after them as his happiness, and doth so believe the mysteries of our redemption by Christ that all his hope and peace and confidence is drawn from thence, and doth so believe the threatenings, whether of temporal plagues or eternal damnation, as that, in comparison with them, all the frightful things of the world are nothing.[19]

---

[18]Lenski writes, "'Thou doest well!' is certainly irony since it is followed by: 'Even the demons believe it and—shudder!' The verb denotes terror which makes one's hair stand on end. This comes like a thunderclap. No more stunning illustration of dead faith has ever been presented. Yes, even the demons have faith. Will this 'someone' tell them that is enough? Will he intimate that the demons are saved by their faith; that the Christian to whom he says: 'Thou hast [professed] faith,' needs no better faith?" R. C. H. Lenski, *The Interpretation of the Epistle to the Hebrews and the Epistle of James* (Minneapolis: Augsburg, 1966), 585.

[19]Thomas Manton, *The Complete Works of Thomas Manton* (London: Nisbet, 1874), 17:113–14.

Dead Faith

James utters his strongest rebuke so far: "Are you willing to recognize, you foolish fellow, that faith without works is useless?" (2:20). He labels the objector "foolish," meaning "empty, defective." The man is hollow, because he lacks a living faith; his claim that he believes is fraudulent; his faith is a sham.

Hiebert writes, "'Wilt thou know' (*theleis gnōnai*), 'are you willing to know,' implies an unwillingness by the objector to face the issue. His unwillingness to agree with the truth set forth is not due to any obscurity of the subject but to his reluctance to acknowledge the truth. The aorist infinitive rendered 'know' also can mean 'recognize' or 'acknowledge' and calls for a definite act of acknowledgment by the objector. His refusal to do so would imply inner perversity of will."[20]

Both "faith" and "works" in verse 20 carry definite articles in the Greek ("the faith without the works"). "Useless" is *argē*, meaning "barren, unproductive." The sense seems to be that it is unproductive for salvation. The King James Version uses the word *dead*. Certainly that is the sense conveyed here (cf. vv. 17, 26). Dead orthodoxy has no power to save. It may in fact even be a hindrance to true and living faith. So James is not contrasting two methods of salvation (faith versus works). His contrast is between two kinds of faith: one that saves and one that doesn't.

James is simply affirming the truth of 1 John 3:7–10: "Little children, let no one deceive you; the one who practices righteousness is righteous, just as He is righteous; the one who practices sin is of the devil; for the devil has sinned from the beginning. The Son of God appeared for this purpose, that He might destroy the works of the devil. By this the children of God and the children of the devil are obvious: anyone who does not practice righteousness is not of God, nor the one who does not love his brother." Righteous behavior is an inevitable result of spiritual life. Faith that fails to produce such behavior is dead.

For brevity's sake, we must forego looking closely at the examples of living faith from the lives of Abraham and Rahab (2:21–25).[21] Nonetheless, here is an abridged statement of the point James is making: Abraham and Rahab, though they came from opposite ends of the

---

[20]Hiebert, *The Epistle of James*, 188.

[21]These verses are covered in detail in John MacArthur, Jr., *True Faith* (Chicago: Moody, 1989), 123–31.

social and religious spectrum, both had an attitude of willingness to sacrifice what mattered most to them because of their faith. That submission was proof their faith was real.

The most serious problem these verses pose is the question of what verse 24 means: "You see that a man is justified by works, and not by faith alone." Some imagine that this contradicts Paul in Romans 3:28: "For we maintain that a man is justified by faith apart from works of the Law." John Calvin explained this apparent difficulty:

> It appears certain that [James] is speaking of the manifestation, not of the imputation of righteousness, as if he had said, Those who are justified by faith prove their justification by obedience and good works, not by a bare and imaginary semblance of faith. In one word, he is not discussing the mode of justification, but requiring that the justification of all believers shall be operative. And as Paul contends that men are justified without the aid of works, so James will not allow any to be regarded as Justified who are destitute of good works. . . . Let them twist the words of James as they may, they will never extract out of them more than two propositions: That an empty phantom of faith does not justify, and that the believer, not contented with such an imagination, manifests his justification by good works.[22]

James is not at odds with Paul. "They are not antagonists facing each other with crossed swords; they stand back to back, confronting different foes of the gospel."[23] As we have seen, in 1:17–18, James affirmed that salvation is a gift bestowed according to the sovereign will of God. Now he is stressing the importance of faith's fruit—the righteous behavior that genuine faith always produces. Paul, too, saw righteous works as the necessary proof of faith.

Those who imagine a discrepancy between James and Paul rarely observe that it was Paul who wrote, "Shall we sin because we are not under law but under grace? May it never be!" (Rom. 6:15); and "Having been freed from sin, you became slaves of righteousness" (v. 18). Thus Paul condemns the same error James is exposing here. Paul never advocated any concept of dormant faith.

---

[22]John Calvin, *Institutes of the Christian Religion,* trans. Henry Beveridge, 3:17:12 (reprint, Grand Rapids, Mich.: Eerdmans, 1966), 2:115.

[23]Alexander Ross, "The Epistles of James and John," *The New International Commentary on the New Testament* (Grand Rapids, Mich.: Eerdmans, 1954), 53.

When Paul writes, "by the works of the Law no flesh will be justified in His sight," (Rom. 3:20), he

> is combatting a Jewish legalism which insisted upon the need for works to be justified; James insists upon the need for works in the lives of those who have been justified by faith. Paul insists that no man can ever win justification through his own efforts. . . . James demands that a man who already claims to stand in right relationship with God through faith must by a life of good works demonstrate that he has become a new creature in Christ. With this Paul thoroughly agreed. Paul was rooting out 'works' that excluded and destroyed saving faith; James was stimulating a sluggish faith that minimized the results of saving faith in daily life.[24]

James and Paul both echo Jesus' preaching. Paul's emphasis resounds with the spirit of Matthew 5:3: "Blessed are the poor in spirit, for theirs is the kingdom of heaven." James' teaching has the ring of Matthew 7:21: "Not everyone who says to Me, 'Lord, Lord,' will enter the kingdom of heaven; but he who does the will of My Father who is in heaven." Paul represents the beginning of the Sermon on the Mount; James the end of it. Paul declares that we are saved by faith *without the deeds of the law*. James declares that we are saved by faith, *which shows itself in works*. Both James and Paul view good works as the proof of faith—not the path to salvation.

James could not be more explicit. He is confronting the concept of a passive, false "faith," which is devoid of the fruits of salvation. He is not arguing for works in addition to or apart from faith. He is showing why and how true, living faith always works. He is fighting against dead orthodoxy and its tendency to abuse grace.

The error James assails closely parallels the teaching of no-lordship salvation. It is faith without works; justification without sanctification; salvation without new life.

Again, James echoes the Master Himself, who insisted on a theology of lordship that involved obedience, not lip-service. Jesus chided the disobedient ones who had attached themselves to Him in name only: "Why do you call Me, 'Lord, Lord,' and do not do what I say?" (Luke 6:46). Verbal allegiance, He said, will get no one to heaven (Matt. 7:21).

---

[24]Hiebert, *The Epistle of James,* 175.

That is in perfect harmony with James: "Prove yourselves doers of the word, and not merely hearers who delude themselves" (1:22); for "faith, if it has no works, is dead, being by itself" (2:17).[25]

---

[25]It is worth noting that Zane Hodges has published a pamphlet on James 2 that challenges more than four centuries of Protestant scholarship. Acknowledging that his views are unusual, he suggests that *all* the conventional interpretations of James 2 are fundamentally in error and proposes in a thirty-two-page tract to straighten them out. Hodges writes, "Not only is there no commonly accepted interpretation of James 2:14–26 in post-Reformation Protestantism, but indeed all of the major ways of reading this text are wrong. *And not simply wrong, but seriously so.* So incorrect are these views, that if James himself had heard them, he would have been both astonished and appalled!" Zane C. Hodges, *Dead Faith: What Is It?* (Dallas: Redención Viva, 1987), 7, emphasis in original. Another professor assesses Hodges' claim with skepticism: "Perhaps one of the most intriguing—and disturbing—features of Zane C. Hodges's book . . . is that to the best of my knowledge not one significant interpreter of Scripture in the entire history of the church has held to Hodges' interpretation of the passages he treats. That does not necessarily mean Hodges is wrong; but it certainly means he is probably wrong, and it probably means he has not reflected seriously enough on the array of fallacies connected with [reading one's own presuppositions into the biblical text]." D. A. Carson, *Exegetical Fallacies* (Grand Rapids, Mich.: Baker, 1984), 137. Because Professor Hodges' voice is so influential among those who are persuaded of the no-lordship position, I mention his booklet. I have responded to it in a journal article: "Faith According to the Apostle James," *Journal of the Evangelical Theological Society* 33/1 (March 1990): 13–34. Much of this chapter was adapted from that article.

10

A Foretaste of Glory

Believers cannot lose the habits, the seeds, the root of grace; yet they may lose assurance, which is the beauty and fragrancy, the crown and glory of grace, 1 John 3. 9; 1 Peter 1. 5. These two lovers, grace and assurance, are not by God so nearly joined together but that they may by sin on our side, and justice on God's, be put asunder. The keeping of these two lovers, grace and assurance, together, will yield the soul two heavens, a heaven of joy and peace here, and a heaven of happiness and blessedness hereafter; but the putting these two lovers asunder will put the soul into a hell here, though it escape a hell hereafter. This Chrysostom knew well, when he professed that the want of the enjoyment of God would be a far greater hell to him than the feeling of any punishment.

Thomas Brooks[1]

*I*s it possible to have full assurance of one's salvation? Can Christians rest in the firm and settled confidence that they are redeemed and bound for eternal heaven?

Scripture categorically answers yes. Not only does the Bible teach that assurance is *possible* for Christians in this life, but the apostle Peter also gave this command: "[Be] diligent to make certain about His calling and choosing you" (2 Pet. 1:10). Assurance is not only a privilege;

---

[1]Thomas Brooks, *Heaven on Earth: A Treatise on Christian Assurance* (reprint, Edinburgh: Banner of Truth, 1982), 49.

it is the birthright and sacred trust of every true child of God. We are commanded to *cultivate* assurance, not take it for granted. True assurance is a taste of heaven on earth. Fanny Crosby expressed that truth in a well-known hymn:

> Blessed assurance, Jesus is Mine!
> O what a foretaste of glory divine!

Puritan Thomas Brooks observed the same reality and entitled his book on assurance *Heaven on Earth*. To possess genuine assurance is to experience a bit of divine bliss this side of heaven. The greater our sense of assurance, the more we can savor that glory in this earthly life.

Critics often allege that lordship salvation renders personal assurance impossible. That is not true, but the lordship controversy certainly does have serious implications for the matter of assurance. Accordingly, assurance has emerged as one of the principal issues in the discussion. Although I barely touched on the subject in my earlier book,[2] the subsequent dialogue has seemed inevitably to converge on the question of whether and how Christians can be certain they are in the faith.

This is a good direction for the discussion to take, I am convinced. In contemporary Christianity assurance is too often either ignored, or claimed by people who have no right to it. Too many people believe they are saved merely because someone told them so. They do not examine themselves; they do not test their assurance by God's Word; they are taught that doubts about their salvation can only be detrimental to spiritual health and growth. Yet multitudes of these people give no evidence of any spiritual health or growth whatsoever.

---

[2]One editor published a "review" of *The Gospel According to Jesus* that began: "MacArthur's book hits four main issues: assurance, faith, repentance, and the relationship between salvation and discipleship." But there were no such divisions in my book. Assurance certainly was *not* a major issue; I mentioned *false assurance* only incidentally and three or four times at most. Nevertheless, this review continued, "While he never says it in so many words, MacArthur does not believe in assurance." Of course that is nonsense, and it is also a good example of why so many people do not understand what the lordship debate is all about. The review in question was published in the newsletter of an organization that exists to advocate no-lordship theology. The review contained several other gross inaccuracies and outright falsehoods. The editor did not respond to letters asking him to correct his distortions.

Assurance in the Reformation

Once again, the modern lordship controversy touches an issue that was at the heart of the Protestant Reformation. The Roman Catholic Church denied—and denies to this day—that anyone on earth can have assurance of salvation. Because Catholic theology sees salvation as a joint effort between God and the sinner, the outcome must be in doubt right up to the end. If a person fails spiritually before salvation is complete, that person forfeits eternal life. Since no one can know with certainty whether he or she will have the strength to endure to the end, no one can really be certain of heaven.[3]

The Reformers, by contrast, taught that believers can and should be fully assured of their salvation. The early Reformers went so far as to define faith in a way that included assurance. Calvin's definition of faith is often quoted: "It is a firm and sure knowledge of the divine favour toward us, founded on the truth of a free promise in Christ, and revealed to our minds, and sealed on our hearts, by the Holy Spirit."[4] Calvin emphasized faith as *knowledge,* in contrast to the Catholic Scholastics' idea that faith is a naive trust antithetical to knowledge. He thus built assurance into his definition of faith.

In other words, Calvin taught that *assurance is of the essence of faith.* That means the moment someone trusts Christ for salvation, that person will have *some* sense of assurance. As we noted in chapter 3, Hebrews 11:1 says, "Faith is the assurance of things hoped for, the conviction of things not seen." Thus it seems clear from Scripture that a measure of assurance *is* inherent in believing.

Often, however, the assurance of faith is darkened by doubt. Calvin also recognized that self-doubt can coexist with true belief. He wrote, "When we say that faith must be certain and secure, we certainly speak not of an assurance which is never affected by doubt, nor a security which anxiety never assails, we rather maintain that believers have a perpetual struggle with their own distrust, and are thus far from thinking that their consciences possess a placid quiet, uninterrupted by perturbation [distress]."[5]

---

[3]Obviously, a similar problem exists in Wesleyan and Arminian theology, and any other system of belief that makes room for Christians to fall away and lose their salvation.

[4]John Calvin, *Institutes of the Christian Religion,* trans. Henry Beveridge, 3:2:7 (reprint, Grand Rapids, Mich.: Eerdmans, 1966), 1:475.

[5]Ibid., 1:484.

Scripture is clearly on Calvin's side here. Some assurance belongs to the essence of faith, but believing does not necessarily bring *full* assurance. "I do believe; help my unbelief" (Mark 9:24) is a sincere expression of every new believer's heart. Even the apostles pleaded with Jesus, "Increase our faith!" (Luke 17:5).

Later Reformed theologians, recognizing that genuine Christians often lack assurance, denied that *any* assurance is implicit in believing. On this issue they were in disagreement with Calvin. Calvin, arguing against Rome, was eager to emphasize the possibility of immediate assurance. The later Reformers, battling antinomian tendencies in their movement, wanted to emphasize the importance of practical evidences in the lives of believers.

The Westminster Confession of Faith, drawn up in 1646, distinguished faith from assurance. The Confession included this:

> [CHAPTER 18] SECTION III.—This infallible assurance *doth not so belong to the essence of faith, but that a true believer may wait long, and conflict with many difficulties before he be partaker of it:* yet, being enabled by the Spirit to know the things which are freely given him of God, he may, without extraordinary revelation, in the right use of ordinary means, attain thereunto. And therefore it is the duty of every one to give all diligence to make his calling and election sure (emphasis added).

In other words, the Confession taught that assurance is something distinct from faith. A person can thus become a genuine believer yet remain unsure of salvation. To the Westminster divines, assurance was possible—even highly desirable—but not automatic. They believed some Christians need to "wait long" and wrestle with God before He grants them assurance. Most of the *Puritans* (seventeenth-century English Reformers) shared this view on assurance.

So on the one hand, Calvin tended to make the grounds for assurance wholly *objective,* urging believers to look to the promises of Scripture to gain a sense of personal assurance. On the other hand the Puritans tended to emphasize *subjective* means of establishing assurance, counseling people to examine their lives and behavior for evidences of their election.[6]

---

[6]Zane Hodges sees great significance in this divergence between Calvin and those who came after him. Hodges even tries to enlist Calvin in support of the no-lordship position! (*AF* 207–9, 214–15). Hodges, however, goes miles beyond Calvin on this issue, making assurance the sum and substance of saving faith (*AF* 50–51) and denying any

In fact, some of the Puritans carried their teaching on assurance to implausible extremes. They tended to become mystical on the issue, implying that assurance was something God grants supernaturally in His time and in special measures for select saints—almost like a heavenly vision one could be zapped with, or an added work of grace. Most of the Puritans taught that believers could not expect assurance until long after conversion, and only after a life of extended faithfulness.[7] They tended to make assurance dependent on the believer's ability to live at an almost unattainable level of personal holiness. I have profited greatly from reading their works, but I often wonder how many of them were able to live up to their own standards.

As we might expect, the Puritans' demanding preaching led to a widespread *lack* of assurance among their flocks. Christians became obsessed with whether they were truly elect, and many lapsed into morbid introspection and utter despair. That explains why so much of the Puritan literature is written for people struggling with the question of assurance.

By contrast, today assurance is rarely made an issue. Few professing Christians seem to lack assurance because evangelistic preaching is usually devoid of any call to holy living. Evangelists and counselors normally seek to dispel doubts about salvation by pronouncing them groundless, or by teaching converts to view all doubt as an attack by the enemy. Preachers are so fearful of shattering anyone's confidence that they seem to forget *false* assurance is a more serious problem than *no* assurance (cf. Matt. 7:21–23).

---

need for self-examination in the matter of assurance (*AF* 174–75). According to Hodges assurance *is* faith and vice versa. No other evidence of regeneration is necessary. He assumes the great Reformer taught the same thing.

But whatever Calvin's views on faith and assurance, it is clear that he would have been no supporter of Hodges' brand of no-lordship soteriology. Calvin wrote: "We must take care not to separate what the Lord perpetually conjoins. What then? Let men be taught that it is impossible they can be regarded as righteous by the merit of Christ, without being renewed by his Spirit unto a holy life . . . *God receives none into favour who are not also made truly righteous.*" Henry Beveridge and Jules Bonnet, eds., *Selected Works of John Calvin*, 7 vols. (reprint, Grand Rapids, Mich.: Baker, 1983), 3:246 (emphasis added).

Calvin added, "[Faith] is not a bare knowledge which flutters in the mind, [but] it carries along with it a lively affection, which has its seat in the heart." Ibid., 250.

[7]John Owen's writings on assurance are a refreshing exception to this rule. Cf. Sinclair B. Ferguson, *John Owen on the Christian Life* (Edinburgh: Banner of Truth, 1987), 99–124.

Surely there is a middle ground. Scripture encourages *true believers* with the promise of full assurance, while making *false professors* uncomfortable by seeking to destroy their false sense of security. A true believer's sense of assurance should not rise and fall with the emotions; assurance is meant to be an anchor even in the midst of life's difficulties. But a false professor has no right to assurance. Aren't those the twin emphases our preaching should reflect? Can we recover a biblical understanding of assurance?

We must. This is where the lordship debate touches almost every Christian at the most practical level. If we confuse the issue of assurance, we will have multitudes, on the one hand, whose spiritual lives are crippled by doubt, and multitudes, on the other, who expect to be ushered into heaven but will one day be devastated to hear the Lord say, "I never knew you; depart from Me" (Matt. 7:23).

Is Assurance Objective or Subjective?

The difference between Calvin and the Puritans raises a question that goes to the heart of the lordship debate: Should Christians seek assurance through clinging only to the *objective* promises of Scripture, or through *subjective* self-examination? If we opt for the objective promises only, those who profess faith in Christ while denying Him by their deeds (cf. Titus 1:16) can claim an assurance they have no entitlement to. But if we say assurance is available only through subjective self-examination we render full assurance practically impossible and make assurance a wholly mystical affair.

Those who argue for a subjective approach will point out that Scripture clearly calls for self-examination. We are commanded to examine ourselves regularly—at least as often as we participate in the Lord's Supper (1 Cor. 11:28). Paul also issued this challenge to the church at Corinth: "Test yourselves to see if you are in the faith; examine yourselves! Or do you not recognize this about yourselves, that Jesus Christ is in you—unless indeed you fail the test?" (2 Cor. 13:5). Clearly Paul was dealing here with the matter of assurance. The Corinthians were to test themselves *to see if they were "in the faith."*

But what kind of self-examination was Paul calling for? What was the "test" the Corinthians needed to pass? Was the apostle counseling them to look within themselves and anchor their assurance on their own goodness? Was he challenging them to think back and remember some moment of faith on which they could fix their hopes? Or was he suggesting that they should look to their works and place confidence in their spiritual accomplishments?

None of those suggestions answers the matter adequately. Works alone can no more guarantee genuine assurance than they can be the basis for our eternal salvation. After all, external works can be performed even by non-Christians. On the other hand, as we have seen, even the most spiritual Christians discover sin when they look within. So no one's works measure up to God's standard of perfection. In this regard, no-lordship teachers are correct: Those who only look within themselves to establish their assurance merely set themselves up for a life of frustration. Settled assurance cannot be found in any amount of works. If we must base our assurance solely on something in ourselves or our experience, our confidence will be resting on an inadequate foundation.[8] That approach to assurance is *too subjective.*

But no-lordship teaching offers this alternative:

> The promises of God are sufficient for assurance. While one's works can have a confirmatory value, they are not essential for assurance. Any believer can have 100% certainty of his salvation if he but looks to the promises in God's Word to the believer.
>
> One can have firm assurance of salvation and yet walk in sin. Sin, while a grievous thing, does not necessarily weaken assurance. Only if sin results in a person taking his eyes off God's promises can sin weaken assurance.[9]

So according to no-lordship teaching, as long as a person clings to the *objective promises* of God's Word, no amount of sin can trouble that person's assurance. Someone who chooses to "walk in sin" can do so with full assurance of faith.[10]

---

[8]"Faith totters if it pays attention to works, since no one, even the most holy, will find there anything on which to rely." John Calvin, *Institutes of the Christian Religion,* trans. Ford Lewis Battles (Philadelphia: Westminster, 1960), 3:11:11.

[9]Bob Wilkin, "Putting the Gospel Debate in Sharper Focus," *The Grace Evangelical Society News* (May 1991): 1.

[10]Assurance apart from sanctification is the essence of antinomianism. And antinomianism is often the result of an extreme emphasis on assurance as the essence of faith. Even in the early 1800s Charles Hodge noted that tendency: "Those who make assurance the essence of faith, generally reduce faith to a mere intellectual assent. They are often censorious, refusing to recognize as brethren those who do not agree with them; and sometimes they are antinomian." Charles Hodge, *Systematic Theology* (reprint, Grand Rapids, Mich.: Eerdmans, 1989), 3:106–7.

Berkhof, while recognizing the danger of antinomianism, nevertheless saw that one can hold the position that assurance is of the essence of faith yet keep that view in balance. He wrote, "Over against Rome the position must be maintained that this sure knowledge belongs to the essence of faith; and in opposition to [antinomian]

But that extreme cannot be supported practically *or* biblically. Hebrews 10:22 specifically says that to possess "full assurance of faith" we must have "our hearts sprinkled clean from an evil conscience." Second Peter 1:5–10 lists several spiritual virtues that are essential to salvation: faith, moral excellence, knowledge, self-control, perseverance, godliness, brotherly kindness, and love. The person who lacks these virtues will also lack assurance according to Peter: "He who lacks these qualities is blind or short-sighted, *having forgotten his purification from his former sins*" (v. 9, emphasis added).

Those who "walk in sin" may be convinced in their *minds* that their salvation is secure, but unless their heart and conscience are utterly seared, they will have to admit that sin ruins their assurance. The no-lordship approach to assurance is *too objective.*

What Are Biblical Grounds for Assurance?

The Bible suggests that a well-grounded assurance has both objective and subjective support.[11] The objective ground is *the finished work of Christ on our behalf,* including the promises of Scripture, which have their yea and amen in Him (2 Cor. 1:20). The subjective ground is *the ongoing work of the Holy Spirit in our lives,* including His convicting and sanctifying ministries. Romans 15:4 mentions both aspects of assurance: "Whatever was written in earlier times was written for our instruction, that through *perseverance* [subjective] *and the encouragement of the Scriptures* [objective] we might have hope."

Both the objective and subjective grounds for our assurance are applied to us by the Holy Spirit, who "bears witness with our spirit that we are children of God" (Rom. 8:16).

The objective basis for our assurance includes the truth of justification by faith, the promise that Christ will never leave us or forsake us (Heb. 13:5), the guarantee of our security in Christ (Rom. 8:38–39),

---

theologians such as Sandeman, Wardlaw, Alexander, Chalmers, and others, that a mere intellectual acceptance of truth is not the whole of faith." Louis Berkhof, *Systematic Theology* (Grand Rapids, Mich.: Eerdmans, 1939), 503.

[11]"In its NT context, the word [*assurance*] has both objective and subjective references. As objective, it denotes the ground of the believer's confidence and certainty. . . . As subjective, assurance has reference to the experience of the believer. . . . Inward assurance must be checked by moral and spiritual tests (cf. e.g., 1 Cor. 6:9; Eph. 4:17; 1 John 2:3–5, etc) by which we know we are of the truth and that our hearts are assured before God (1 John 3:19)." H. D. McDonald, "Assurance," *The New International Dictionary of the Christian Church* (Grand Rapids, Mich.: Zondervan, 1978), 79.

and all the objective truths of God's Word on which our faith is founded. The objective question asks, "Do you believe?" If you *truly* believe, you can be sure you are saved (John 3:16; Acts 16:31). The subjective question asks, "Is your faith real?" That is the question Paul was asking in 2 Corinthians 13:5.

Here we return to a question we raised earlier but have not yet answered: What *kind* of self-examination was Paul calling for in that verse? We know that he was not suggesting Christians may find assurance in themselves or in their works. What then is the test we must pass?

Paul had hinted at the answer several chapters earlier in the same epistle. In 2 Corinthians 3:18 he wrote, "We all, with unveiled face beholding as in a mirror the glory of the Lord, are being transformed into the same image from glory to glory, just as from the Lord, the Spirit." As true Christians look into the mirror of God's Word (cf. James 1:23), they should see the glory of the Lord reflected back. To be sure, it is a dim reflection. "Now we see in a mirror dimly, but then face to face; now I know in part, but then I shall know fully just as I also have been fully known" (1 Cor. 13:12). But it is that dim reflection of *His* glory—not anything inherent in us—that is the subjective basis for our assurance.

Even Calvin recognized a subjective ground for assurance, though it was not a major emphasis in his teaching. While emphasizing that all works are nonmeritorious, Calvin said believers' good works are "divine gifts, in which [believers] recognise [God's] goodness and signs of calling, in which they discern their election."[12] They are *God's* work in us, not our own accomplishments. In this same context Calvin quotes a prayer of Augustine: "'I commend not the works of my hands, for I fear that when thou examinest them thou wilt find more faults than merits. This only I say, this ask, this desire, Despise not the works of thy hands. See in me thy work, not mine. If thou seest mine, thou condemnest; if thou seest thine own, thou crownest. Whatever good works I have are of thee' (August. in Ps. cxxxvii)."[13]

God's glory—albeit a dim reflection of that glory—is what we will see in the mirror if we are true believers. This is the test Paul laid before the Corinthians: Can you see Christ's glory reflected in you—even dimly? "Test yourselves to see if you are in the faith; examine yourselves! Or *do you not recognize this about yourselves, that Jesus Christ is in you—*

---

[12]Calvin, *Institutes of the Christian Religion* [Beveridge], 3:14:20, 2:87.

[13]Ibid., 88.

unless indeed you fail the test?" (2 Cor. 13:5). The image of Christ in us thus provides the subjective ground of our assurance. In other words, Christ in you is the hope of glory (cf. Col. 1:27).

In Order That You May Know

The New Testament epistles are filled with enough material on assurance to fill volumes of commentary. It is not possible in a book of this nature to give a full overview of the New Testament doctrine of assurance. Even the little epistle of 1 John, written to deal with precisely the issue of assurance, is so rich with material that we cannot do full justice to it in these few pages. But I do want to underscore some of the highlights of this treasured epistle and its clear teaching on this subject. Surely no other passage of Scripture confronts no-lordship theology with more force than this brief but potent letter.

John's purpose statement is explicit in 1 John 5:13: "These things I have written to you who believe in the name of the Son of God, *in order that you may know that you have eternal life*" (emphasis added). There the apostle spells out his intention. He is not trying to make believers *doubt;* he wants them to have full assurance. What he has to say will not shake genuine believers; though it should certainly alarm those with a false sense of assurance.

Note that the apostle presupposes faith in Christ as the bedrock of all assurance: "I have written to you who believe . . ." There is no place for self-examination outside of faith in Christ. So everything John says about assurance is predicated on faith in Christ and the promises of Scripture.[14]

Throughout this epistle the apostle John maintains a careful balance between the objective and subjective grounds of assurance. The objective evidence constitutes a *doctrinal* test. The subjective evidence is not a works test, but a *moral* test. John moves in and out between the two kinds of tests. Here are the proofs he says will be evident in every genuine believer:

True believers walk in the light. "If we say that we have fellowship with Him and yet walk in the darkness, we lie and do not practice the truth; but if we walk in the light as He Himself is in the light, we

---

[14]"The grounds of assurance are more objective than subjective; they are not so much within us as without us. Hence the basis of assurance must rest on sufficient objective evidence." Robert F. Boyd, "Assurance," *Baker's Dictionary of Theology* (Grand Rapids, Mich.: Baker, 1960), 70.

have fellowship with one another, and the blood of Jesus His Son cleanses us from all sin" (1 John 1:6–7). Throughout Scripture, light is used as a metaphor for truth—both intellectual and moral truth.

Psalm 119:105 says, "Thy word is a lamp to my feet, and a light to my path." Verse 130 adds, "The unfolding of Thy words gives light; it gives understanding to the simple." Proverbs 6:23 says, "For the commandment is a lamp, and the teaching is light." Those verses all speak of truth as something that may be *known* and *obeyed*. It is both doctrinal and moral. The light of all truth is embodied in Christ, who said, "I am the light of the world; he who follows Me shall not walk in the darkness, but shall have the light of life" (John 8:12).

Walking in darkness is the antithesis of following Christ. All unsaved people walk in darkness; Christians have been delivered into the light: "You were formerly darkness, but now you are light in the Lord; walk as children of light" (Eph. 5:8). "You, brethren, are not in darkness" (1 Thess. 5:4). To "walk in the light" means to live in the realm of truth. So all true believers are walking in the light—even when we sin. When we sin, "The blood of Jesus . . . cleanses us" (1 John 1:7). The verb tense there indicates that Christ's blood *continually* cleanses us. When we sin, we are already being cleansed, so that no darkness ever clouds the light in which we dwell (cf. 1 Pet. 2:9).

"Walk[ing] in the light" describes both positional and practical reality for the believer. To trust Jesus Christ is to walk in the light. To walk in the light is to heed the light and live accordingly. So in this first test the apostle points us to both the *objective* and *subjective* grounds of assurance. To determine if we walk in the light we must answer the objective question, "Do I believe?" as well as the subjective question, "Is my faith real?"

True believers confess their sin. "If we say that we have no sin, we are deceiving ourselves, and the truth is not in us. If we confess our sins, He is faithful and righteous to forgive us our sins and to cleanse us from all unrighteousness. If we say that we have not sinned, we make Him a liar, and His word is not in us. My little children, I am writing these things to you that you may not sin. If anyone sins, we have an Advocate with the Father, Jesus Christ the righteous" (1 John 1:8–2:1).

The word for "confess" (Gk., *homologeō*) means "to say the same thing." To "confess our sins" means to agree with God about them. This is a characteristic of all true Christians. They agree with God about their sin. That means they hate their sin; they don't love it. They acknowledge that they are sinful, and yet they know they are forgiven and that they have an Advocate with the Father (2:1).

Here it seems the apostle is suggesting an *objective* test of assurance: "Do you believe?" Specifically, "Do you agree with what God has said about your sin?"

True assurance of salvation always goes hand in hand with an awareness of our own sinfulness. In fact, the more certain we are of salvation, the deeper our awareness of our sin becomes. John Owen wrote, "A man, then, may have a deep sense of sin all his days, walk under the sense of it continually, abhor himself for his ingratitude, unbelief, and rebellion against God, without any impeachment of his assurance."[15] That may sound paradoxical, but it is the very thing that keeps Christians from falling into utter despair. We *know* we are sinners. We agree with God about that. We're not surprised to discover sin in our lives, but nevertheless we hate it. We know we are forgiven and cleansed and that Christ is our Advocate. Far from using that knowledge to justify our sin, however, we see it as a motivation to mortify sin all the more: "I am writing these things to you *that you may not sin*" (2:1, emphasis added).

True believers keep His commandments. "And by this we know that we have come to know Him, if we keep His commandments. The one who says, 'I have come to know Him,' and does not keep His commandments, is a liar, and the truth is not in him" (2:3–4). "By this we know that we love the children of God, when we love God and observe His commandments. For this is the love of God, that we keep His commandments; and His commandments are not burdensome" (5:2–3).

Here the apostle focuses on the *subjective* ground for assurance. He is prodding us to ask the question, "Is my faith real?" Here's how we can be sure if we have come to know Him: We keep His commandments. This is a test of obedience. The Greek word translated "keep" in 2:3–4 conveys the idea of a watchful, observant obedience. It is not an obedience that is only the result of external pressure. It is the eager obedience of one who "keeps" the divine commandments as if they were something precious to guard.

In other words, this speaks of an obedience motivated by love. Verse 5 spells it out: "Whoever keeps His word, in him the love of God has truly been perfected. By this we know that we are in Him."

Those who claim to know God yet despise His commandments are liars (v. 4). "They profess to know God, but by their deeds they deny Him, being detestable and disobedient, and worthless for any good deed" (Titus 1:16).

---

[15]John Owen, *The Works of John Owen*, 16 vols. (reprint, London: Banner of Truth, 1966), 6:549.

True believers love the brethren. This test and the previous one are closely related: "By this the children of God and the children of the devil are obvious: anyone who does not practice righteousness is not of God, nor the one who does not love his brother" (1 John 3:10). "The one who says he is in the light and yet hates his brother is in the darkness until now. The one who loves his brother abides in the light and there is no cause for stumbling in him. But the one who hates his brother is in the darkness and walks in the darkness, and does not know where he is going because the darkness has blinded his eyes" (2:9–11). "We know that we have passed out of death into life, because we love the brethren. He who does not love abides in death. Everyone who hates his brother is a murderer; and you know that no murderer has eternal life abiding in him" (3:14–15). "By this we know that we love the children of God, when we love God and observe His commandments" (5:2).

The reason these two tests are so closely related is that love perfectly fulfills the law. "He who loves his neighbor has fulfilled the law" (Rom. 13:8). To love God and to love one's neighbor fulfills the whole moral law. Jesus said, "'You shall love the Lord your God with all your heart, and with all your soul, and with all your mind.' This is the great and foremost commandment. The second is like it, 'You shall love your neighbor as yourself.' On these two commandments depend the whole Law and the Prophets" (Matt. 22:37–40).

Love for fellow believers is a particularly important evidence of genuine faith. The point is not that love is intrinsic to us, or something that rises out of our own goodness. "Beloved, let us love one another, for *love is from God;* and everyone who loves is born of God and knows God" (1 John 4:7, emphasis added). The love that is evidence of true faith is *God's* love, which is being perfected in us: "If we love one another, God abides in us, and His love is perfected in us" (4:12). Once again, it is that dim reflection of divine glory in us that provides the subjective ground of our assurance.

True believers affirm sound doctrine. Here we return to the objective ground: "You have an anointing from the Holy One, and you all know. I have not written to you because you do not know the truth, but because you do know it, and because no lie is of the truth. Who is the liar but the one who denies that Jesus is the Christ? This is the antichrist, the one who denies the Father and the Son" (2:20–23). "Whoever denies the Son does not have the Father; the one who confesses the Son has the Father also. By this you know the Spirit of God: every spirit that confesses that Jesus Christ has come in the flesh is from

God. . . . We are from God; he who knows God listens to us; he who is not from God does not listen to us. By this we know the spirit of truth and the spirit of error" (4:2, 6).

John was writing in opposition to an early form of the gnostic heresy, which denied that Jesus Christ is fully God and fully man. He is saying that no one who truly is saved can fall into serious, Christ-denying error or heresy. Why? Because "you have an anointing from the Holy One, [and] the anointing which you received from Him abides in you, and you have no need for anyone to teach you; but as His anointing teaches you about all things, and is true and is not a lie, and just as it has taught you, you abide in Him" (2:20, 27). Again, it is the divine work in us, not our own skill or achievements, that provide a sound basis for our assurance.

What about those who depart completely from sound doctrine? John answers that question explicitly: "They went out from us, but they were not really of us; for if they had been of us, they would have remained with us; but they went out, in order that it might be shown that they all are not of us" (2:19). No-lordship teaching at this point rather blatantly contradicts Scripture (cf. *SGS* 141, *AF* 111). Those who fall away and deny Christ only prove that their faith was never genuine to begin with. We shall examine this idea closely in chapter 11.

True believers follow after holiness. "If you know that He is righteous, you know that everyone also who practices righteousness is born of Him" (2:29). "And everyone who has this hope fixed on Him purifies himself, just as He is pure. Everyone who practices sin also practices lawlessness; and sin is lawlessness" (3:3–4). "No one who abides in Him sins; no one who sins has seen Him or knows Him. Little children, let no one deceive you; the one who practices righteousness is righteous, just as He is righteous; the one who practices sin is of the devil; for the devil has sinned from the beginning. The Son of God appeared for this purpose, that He might destroy the works of the devil. No one who is born of God practices sin, because His seed abides in him; and he cannot sin, because he is born of God" (3:6–9).

Those verses have tripped many people up. The key to their meaning is the definition of sin in 3:4: "Sin is lawlessness." The Greek word for "lawlessness" is *anomia*. It literally means, "without law," and it describes those who live immoral, ungodly, unrighteous lives as a matter of continuous practice. They hate God's righteousness and perpetually live as if they were sovereign over God's law. This cannot be true of a genuine Christian.

The apostle is clearly *not* making sinless perfection a test of salvation. After all, he began his epistle by saying, "If we say that we have no sin, we are deceiving ourselves, and the truth is not in us" (1:8). Nor is he making an issue about the frequency, duration, or magnitude of one's sins. As we noted in chapter 8, all Christians sin, and true believers are capable even of prolonged and heinous sin. The issue John is raising here has to do with our attitude toward sin and righteousness, our heart's response when we *do* sin, and the overall direction of our walk.

The test is this: What is the object of your affections—sin or righteousness? If your chief love is sin, then you are "of the devil" (3:8, 10). If you love righteousness and practice righteousness, you are born of God (2:29). What is the direction of your affection? As John Owen aptly wrote, "Your state is not at all to be measured by the opposition that sin makes to you, but by the opposition you make to it."[16]

Those who cling to the *promise* of eternal life but care nothing for Christ's holiness have nothing to be assured of. Such people do not really believe. Either their professed "faith" in Christ is an utter sham, or they are simply deluded. If they did truly have their hope fixed on Christ, they would purify themselves, just as He is pure (3:3).

True believers have the Holy Spirit. This is the overarching test that sums up all the others: Does the Holy Spirit reside in you?[17] John writes, "By this we know that we abide in Him and He in us, because He has given us of His Spirit" (4:13). "The one who believes in the Son of God has the witness in himself; the one who does not believe God has made Him a liar, because he has not believed in the witness that God has borne concerning His Son. And the witness is this, that God has given us eternal life, and this life is in His Son" (5:10–11).

There is an echo of Pauline theology in these verses. Paul wrote, "The Spirit Himself bears witness with our spirit that we are children of God" (Rom. 8:16). Scripture says, "On the evidence of two or three witnesses a matter shall be confirmed" (Deut. 19:15; cf. Matt. 18:16; 2 Cor. 13:1). Romans 8:16 is saying that the Holy Spirit adds His testimony to the witness of our spirit, thereby confirming our assurance.

This utterly dispels the notion that self-examination is tantamount to placing one's faith in one's own works. The evidence we

---

[16]Ibid., 6:605.

[17]The test John is suggesting here is virtually identical to the self-examination Paul was calling for in 2 Corinthians 13:5: Does Jesus Christ live in you?

seek through self-examination is nothing other than the fruit of the Spirit (Gal. 5:22–23), the proof that He resides within. It is on that testimony that our assurance is confirmed.

The Danger of False Assurance

Before we move on to another chapter, we must deal briefly with the issue of false assurance. Throughout 1 John the apostle attacks the false profession of those who have no right to assurance: "The one who says, 'I have come to know Him,' and does not keep His commandments, is a liar, and the truth is not in him" (2:4). "The one who hates his brother is in the darkness and walks in the darkness, and does not know where he is going because the darkness has blinded his eyes" (2:11). "Whoever denies the Son does not have the Father" (2:23). "The one who practices sin is of the devil" (3:8). "Everyone who hates his brother is a murderer; and you know that no murderer has eternal life abiding in him" (3:15). "The one who does not love does not know God" (4:8). "If someone says, 'I love God,' and hates his brother, he is a liar; for the one who does not love his brother whom he has seen, cannot love God whom he has not seen" (4:20).

One of the dangers of radical no-lordship teaching is that it ignores the danger of false assurance. How? First of all, this view sees assurance and saving faith as virtually synonymous: "Simply put, [the gospel] message brings with it the assurance of salvation. . . . When a person believes, that person has assurance of life eternal. How could it be otherwise? . . . To doubt the guarantee of eternal life is to doubt the message itself. In short, if I do not believe that I am saved, I do not believe the offer that God has made to me. . . . A person who has *never been sure* of eternal life has *never believed* the saving message of God" (*AF* 50–51).

In effect, then, according to this view, a conviction of assurance in one's mind is the best evidence of salvation. "People know whether they believe something or not, and that is the real issue where God is concerned" (*AF* 31). Obviously, there is no room in such a view for *false* assurance. Everyone who professes to trust Christ is encouraged to claim "100 percent assurance." Everyone who professes assurance is accepted as a genuine believer, even if that person's lifestyle opposes everything Christ stands for.

The conscience screams against such a doctrine! It promises an "assurance" that the heart will never affirm. It offers no real peace to the soul. Instead it makes assurance a wholly intellectual property.

No-lordship doctrine is therefore forced to deny the subjective ground of assurance, because self-examination would immediately reveal the emptiness of every false professor's ungrounded hope. Laying half a foundation, no-lordship doctrine declares the building complete. The objective test is all they can endure. If the mind is convinced, there is no need to involve the conscience. That is the epitome of false assurance.

John Owen called false assurance a "notional apprehension of the pardon of sin."[18] The effect of such assurance, Owen believed, is that "it rather secretly insinuates into the soul encouragements unto a continuance in [sin]." "There are none in the world that deal worse with God than those who have an ungrounded persuasion of forgiveness. . . . Carnal boldness, formality, and despising of God, are the common issues of such a notion and persuasion."[19] "Where conscience accuses, [false assurance] must supply the defect."[20] Owen was not afraid to point out that those who turn the grace of our God into licentiousness are, after all, ungodly (Jude 4). "Let them profess what they will," Owen wrote, "they are ungodly men."[21]

No-lordship theology tells obstinately ungodly people that they can rest secure in the hope of heaven. That is not genuine assurance. Real assurance springs from faith that works, allowing us to look in the mirror and see beyond our sinful selves a reflection of *God's* glory that is dim but growing brighter in ever-increasing waves: "We all, with unveiled face beholding as in a mirror the glory of the Lord, are being transformed into the same image from glory to glory, just as from the Lord, the Spirit" (2 Cor. 3:18).[22]

---

[18]Owen, *The Works of John Owen*, 6:397.

[19]Ibid., 6:396.

[20]Ibid., 6:398.

[21]Ibid., 6:397

[22]For a fuller discussion about assurance, see John MacArthur, *Saved Without a Doubt* (Wheaton, Ill.: Victor, 1992).

11

Kept by the Power of God

In order to place the doctrine of perseverance in proper light we need to know what it is not. It does not mean that every one who professes faith in Christ and who is accepted as a believer in the fellowship of the saints is secure for eternity and may entertain the assurance of eternal salvation. Our Lord himself warned his followers in the days of his flesh when he said to those Jews who believed on him, "If ye continue in my word, then are ye truly my disciples, and ye shall know the truth, and the truth shall make you free" (John 8:31, 32). He set up a criterion by which true disciples might be distinguished, and that criterion is continuance in Jesus' Word.

John Murray[1]

If any New Testament character was ever prone to failure, it was Simon Peter. Judging from the biblical record, none of our Lord's disciples—excluding Judas the betrayer—stumbled more often or more miserably than he. Peter was the disciple with the foot-shaped mouth. He seemed to have a knack for saying the worst possible thing at the most inappropriate time. He was impetuous, erratic, vacillating—sometimes cowardly, sometimes weak, sometimes hotheaded. On several occasions he merited strong rebukes from the Lord, none more severe than that recorded in Matthew 16:23: "Get behind Me, Satan! You are a stumbling

---

[1]John Murray, *Redemption Accomplished and Applied* (Grand Rapids, Mich.: Eerdmans, 1955), 151–52.

block to Me; for you are not setting your mind on God's interests, but man's." *That* occurred almost immediately after the high point in Peter's experience with Christ, when Peter confessed, "Thou art the Christ, the Son of the living God" (Matt. 16:16).

Peter's life is proof that a true believer's spiritual experience is often filled with ups and downs.

But Peter illustrates another, more significant, biblical truth: the keeping power of God. On the night Jesus was betrayed, He gave Peter an insight into the behind-the-scenes spiritual battle over Peter's soul: "Simon, Simon, behold, Satan has demanded permission to sift you like wheat; but *I have prayed for you,* that your faith may not fail" (Luke 22:31–32, emphasis added).

Peter was confident of his willingness to stand with Jesus whatever the cost. He told the Lord, "Lord, with You I am ready to go both to prison and to death!" (v. 33).

But Jesus knew the truth and sadly told Peter, "The cock will not crow today until you have denied three times that you know Me" (v. 34).

Did Peter fail? Miserably. Was his faith overthrown? Never. Jesus Himself was interceding on Peter's behalf, and His prayers did not go unanswered.

Did you know that our Lord intercedes like that for all genuine believers? We get a glimpse of how He prays in John 17:11: "I am no more in the world; and yet they themselves are in the world, and I come to Thee. Holy Father, *keep them in Thy name,* the name which Thou hast given Me, that they may be one, even as We are" (emphasis added). He continues:

> I do not ask Thee to take them out of the world, but to *keep them from the evil one.* They are not of the world, even as I am not of the world. *Sanctify them in the truth;* Thy word is truth. As Thou didst send Me into the world, I also have sent them into the world. And *for their sakes I sanctify Myself, that they themselves also may be sanctified in truth.* I do not ask in behalf of these alone, but for those also who believe in Me through their word; that they may all be one; even as Thou, Father, art in Me, and I in Thee, that they also may be in Us; that the world may believe that Thou didst send Me. And *the glory which Thou hast given Me I have given to them;* that they may be one, just as We are one; I in them, and Thou in Me, *that they may be perfected in unity,* that the world may know that Thou didst send Me, and didst love them, even as Thou didst love Me.
>
> John 17:15–23, emphasis added

Notice what our Lord was praying for: that believers would be kept from the power of evil; that they would be sanctified by the Word; that they would share His sanctification and glory; and that they would be perfected in their union with Christ and one another. He was praying that they would persevere in the faith.

Was our Lord praying for the eleven faithful disciples only? No, He explicitly includes every believer in all succeeding generations: "I do not ask in behalf of these alone, but for those also who believe in Me through their word" (v. 20). That includes all true Christians even in our own day!

Moreover, the Lord Himself is continuing His intercessory ministry for believers even as you read this. "He is able to save forever those who draw near to God through Him, since He always lives to make intercession for them" (Heb. 7:25). The King James Version translates that verse like this: "He is able also to *save them to the uttermost* that come unto God by him, seeing he ever liveth to make intercession for them" (emphasis added).

Saved to the Uttermost

All true believers will be saved to the uttermost. Christ's high priestly ministry guarantees it. We have been justified, we are being sanctified, and we shall be glorified. No true believer will miss out on any stage of the process, though in this life we all find ourselves at different points along the way. This truth has been known historically as *the perseverance of the saints.*

No doctrine has been more savaged by no-lordship theology. That is to be expected, because the doctrine of perseverance is antithetical to the entire no-lordship system. In fact, what they have pejoratively labeled "lordship salvation" is nothing but this very doctrine!

Perseverance means that "those who have true faith can lose that faith neither totally nor finally."[2] It echoes God's promise through Jeremiah: "I will make an everlasting covenant with them that I will not turn away from them, to do them good; *and I will put the fear of Me in their hearts so that they will not turn away from Me*" (32:40, emphasis added).

That flatly contradicts the no-lordship notion of faith that can evaporate, leaving "believers" who no longer believe (cf. *SGS* 141). It stands in opposition to the radical no-lordship teaching that genuine

---

[2]Anthony A. Hoekema, *Saved by Grace* (Grand Rapids, Mich.: Eerdmans, 1989), 234.

Christians can choose to "drop out" of the spiritual growth process (*AF* 79–88) and "cease to confess Christianity" (*AF* 111). It is the polar opposite of the brand of theology that makes faith a "historical moment," a one-time "act" that secures heaven but offers no guarantee that the "believer's" earthly life will be changed (*AF* 63–64). Perseverance was defined by the Westminster Confession of Faith this way: "They whom God hath accepted in His Beloved, effectually called and sanctified by his Spirit, can neither totally nor finally fall away from the state of grace; but shall certainly persevere therein to the end, and be eternally saved" (chapter 17, section 1).

This truth does not deny the possibility of miserable failings in one's Christian experience. The Confession also stated:

> Nevertheless [believers] may, through the temptations of Satan and of the world, the prevalency of corruption remaining in them, and the neglect of the means of their preservation, fall into grievous sins; and for a time continue therein; whereby they incur God's displeasure, and grieve his Holy Spirit: come to be deprived of some measure of their graces and comforts; have their hearts hardened, and their consciences wounded; hurt and scandalize others, and bring temporal judgments upon themselves (section 3).

In chapter 8 we dealt with the reality of sin in the believer's experience, so it should be clear that lordship theology does not include the idea of perfectionism. Nevertheless, people steeped in no-lordship teaching often misunderstand the issue with regard to perseverance.

One Christian layman who has embraced no-lordship teaching wrote me a very graciously worded seventeen-page letter explaining why he rejects lordship doctrine. His complaint is that lordship theology "does not seem to allow for anything but highly successful Christian living."

Zane Hodges makes a similar charge:

> The belief that every Christian will live a basically successful life until the end is an illusion. It is not supported by the instruction and warnings of the New Testament. . . . It is not surprising that those who do not perceive this aspect of New Testament revelation have impoverished their ability to motivate both themselves and other believers. Tragically, they often fall back on the technique of questioning the salvation of those whose lives seem not to meet Biblical standards. But in the process they undermine the grounds for a

believer's assurance and take part—however unwittingly—in the siege of the Gospel.[3]

No advocate of lordship salvation I am aware of teaches "that every Christian will live a basically successful life until the end." Professor Hodges is quite right in saying the New Testament does not support such a view.

John Murray, defending the doctrine of perseverance, acknowledged the difficulties it poses: "Experience, observation, biblical history, and certain Scripture passages would appear to provide very strong arguments against the doctrine. . . . Is not the biblical record as well as the history of the church strewn with examples of those who have made shipwreck of the faith?"[4]

Certainly Scripture seems to be filled with warnings to people in the church lest they should fall away (cf. Heb. 6:4–8; 1 Tim. 1:18–19; 2 Tim. 2:16–19). Zane Hodges suggests such warnings prove Christians can fall away: "If anyone supposes that no true Christian could quit, or would quit, they have not been paying attention to the Bible. They need to re-read their New Testament, this time, with their eyes open" (*AF* 83).

But God does not contradict Himself. The warning passages do not negate the many promises that believers will persevere: "Whoever drinks of the water that I shall give him *shall never thirst; but the water that I shall give him shall become in him a well of water springing up to eternal life*" (John 4:14, emphasis added).[5] "I am the bread of life; he who comes to Me shall not hunger, and he who believes in Me shall never thirst" (6:35). "You are not lacking in any gift, awaiting eagerly the revelation of our Lord Jesus Christ, *who shall also confirm you to the end, blameless in the day of our Lord Jesus Christ. God is faithful,* through whom you were called into fellowship with His Son, Jesus Christ our Lord" (1 Cor. 1:7–9, emphasis added). "May the God of peace Himself sanctify you entirely; and *may your spirit and soul and body be preserved complete, without blame* at the coming of our Lord Jesus Christ. Faithful is He who calls you, and *He also will bring it to pass*" (1 Thess. 5:23–24, emphasis added). "They went out from us,

---

[3]Zane Hodges, *The Gospel Under Siege* (Dallas: Redención Viva, 1981), 113.

[4]Murray, *Redemption Accomplished and Applied*, 151.

[5]Ironically, Zane Hodges builds his entire system on Jesus' words to the woman at the well in John 4, but Hodges neglects the truth of perseverance that is included in this promise.

but they were not really of us; for *if they had been of us, they would have remained with us;* but they went out, in order that it might be shown that they all are not of us" (1 John 2:19, emphasis added). "Now unto *him that is able to keep you from falling, and to present you faultless before the presence of his glory with exceeding joy,* to the only wise God our Saviour, be glory and majesty, dominion and power, both now and for ever. Amen" (Jude 24–25 KJV, emphasis added).

Charles Horne observed, "It is noteworthy that when Jude exhorts us to keep ourselves in the love of God (v. 21), he concludes with a doxology for Him who is able to keep us from falling and who will present us without blemish before the presence of His glory (v. 24). The warning passages are *means* which God uses in our life to accomplish His purpose in grace."[6]

And, it might be added, the warning passages like Jude 21 reveal that the writers of Scripture were very keen to alert those whose hope of salvation might be grounded in a spurious faith. Obviously the apostolic authors were not laboring under the illusion that every person in the churches they were writing to was genuinely converted (cf. *AF* 98).

Once Saved, Always Saved?

It is crucial that we understand what the biblical doctrine of perseverance does *not* mean. It does not mean that people who "accept Christ" can then live any way they please without fear of hell. The expression "eternal security" is often used in this sense, as is "once saved, always saved." R. T. Kendall, arguing for the latter phrase, defines its meaning thus: *"Whoever once truly believes that Jesus was raised from the dead, and confesses that Jesus is Lord, will go to heaven when he dies. But I will not stop there. Such a person will go to heaven when he dies no matter what work (or lack of work) may accompany such faith."*[7] Kendall states, "I hope no one will take this as an attack on the Westminster Confession. It is not that."[8] But it is *precisely* that! Kendall is expressly

---

[6]Charles Horne, *Salvation* (Chicago: Moody, 1971), 95.

[7]R. T. Kendall, *Once Saved, Always Saved* (Chicago: Moody, 1983), 19 (emphasis in original). Kendall later expands that: "I therefore state categorically that the person who is saved—who confesses that Jesus is Lord and believes in his heart that God raised Him from the dead—*will go to heaven when he dies no matter what work (or lack of work) may accompany such faith.* In other words, no matter what sin (or absence of Christian obedience) may accompany such faith." Ibid., 52–53.

[8]Ibid., 22.

arguing against Westminster's assertion that faith cannot fail. Kendall believes faith is best characterized as a single look: "One need only *see* the Sin Bearer once to be saved."[9] This is a full-scale assault against the doctrine of perseverance affirmed in the Westminster Confession. Worse, it subverts Scripture itself. Unfortunately, it is a view that has come to be widely believed by Christians today.

John Murray, noting this trend nearly forty years ago, defended the expression "Perseverance of the saints":

> It is not in the best interests of the doctrine involved to substitute the designation, "The Security of the Believer," not because the latter is wrong in itself but because the other formula is much more carefully and inclusively framed. . . . It is not true that the believer is secure however much he may fall into sin and unfaithfulness. Why is this not true? It is not true because it sets up an impossible combination. It is true that a believer sins; he may fall into grievous sin and backslide for lengthy periods. But it is also true that a believer cannot abandon himself to sin; he cannot come under the dominion of sin; he cannot be guilty of certain kinds of unfaithfulness. And therefore it is utterly wrong to say that a believer is secure quite irrespective of his subsequent life of sin and unfaithfulness. The truth is that the faith of Jesus Christ is *always respective* of the life of holiness and fidelity. And so it is never proper to think of a believer irrespective of the fruits in faith and holiness. To say that a believer is secure whatever may be the extent of his addiction to sin in his subsequent life is to abstract faith in Christ from its very definition and it ministers to that abuse which turns the grace of God into lasciviousness. The doctrine of perseverance is the doctrine that believers *persevere.* . . . It is not at all that they will be saved irrespective of their perseverance or their continuance, but that they will assuredly persevere. Consequently the security that is theirs is inseparable from their perseverance. Is this not what Jesus said? "He that endureth to the end, the same shall be saved."
>
> Let us not then take refuge in our sloth or encouragement in our lust from the abused doctrine of the security of the believer. But let us appreciate the doctrine of the perseverance of the saints and recognize that we may entertain the faith of our security in Christ only as we persevere in faith and holiness to the end.[10]

---

[9]Ibid., 23. Hodges' similar rhetoric on this same issue is patently offensive: "People are not saved by staring at Christ. They are saved by looking at Him in faith" (*AF* 107).

[10]Murray, *Redemption Accomplished and Applied,* 154–55.

Any doctrine of eternal security that leaves out perseverance distorts the doctrine of salvation itself. Heaven without holiness ignores the whole purpose for which God chose and redeemed us:

> God elected us for this very purpose. "He chose us in him [Christ] before the creation of the world to be holy and blameless in his sight" (Eph. 1:4). We were predestinated to be conformed to the image of Christ in all His spotless purity (*Rom. 8.29*). This divine choice makes it certain that we shall be like Him when He appears (*I John 3:2*). From this fact, John deduces that everyone who has this hope in him purifies himself just as Christ is pure (*I John 3:3*). His use of the word "everyone" makes it quite certain that those who do not purify themselves will not see Christ, nor be like Him. By their lack of holiness they prove that they were not so predestinated. The apostle thus deals a crushing blow to Antinomianism.[11]

God's own holiness thus *requires* that we persevere. "God's grace insures our persevering—but this does not make it any less *our* persevering."[12] We cannot acquire "the prize of the upward call of God in Christ Jesus" unless we "press on toward the goal" (Phil. 3:14). But as we "work out [our] salvation with fear and trembling" (Phil. 2:12), we find that "it is God who is at work in [us], both to will and to work for His good pleasure" (v. 23).

The Outcome of Your Faith

Perhaps no apostle understood better than Peter the keeping power of God in the life of an inconsistent believer. God had preserved him and matured him through every kind of faux pas and failure, including severe sin and compromise—even repeated denials of the Lord accompanied by cursing and swearing! (Matt. 26:69–75). Yet Peter was kept in faith by the power of God despite his own failures. It is therefore appropriate that he was the instrument the Holy Spirit used to pen this glorious promise:

> Blessed be the God and Father of our Lord Jesus Christ, who according to His great mercy has caused us to be born again to a living

---

[11]Richard Alderson, *No Holiness, No Heaven!* (Edinburgh: Banner of Truth, 1986), 88.

[12]Horne, *Salvation,* 95.

hope through the resurrection of Jesus Christ from the dead, to obtain an inheritance which is imperishable and undefiled and will not fade away, reserved in heaven for you, who are protected by the power of God through faith for a salvation ready to be revealed in the last time. In this you greatly rejoice, even though now for a little while, if necessary, you have been distressed by various trials, that the proof of your faith, being more precious than gold which is perishable, even though tested by fire, may be found to result in praise and glory and honor at the revelation of Jesus Christ; and though you have not seen Him, you love Him, and though you do not see Him now, but believe in Him, you greatly rejoice with joy inexpressible and full of glory, obtaining as the outcome of your faith the salvation of your souls.

1 Peter 1:3–9

Peter was writing to scattered believers living in Asia Minor. They were facing a horrible persecution that had begun at Rome and was spreading through the Roman Empire. After the city of Rome burned, Nero blamed Christians for the disaster. Suddenly, believers everywhere had become targets of tremendous persecution. These people feared for their lives, and they feared they would fail if their faith were put to the test.

Peter wrote this epistle to encourage them. He reminded them that they were aliens in this world, citizens of heaven, a royal aristocracy, children of God, residents of an unearthly kingdom, living stones, a holy priesthood, and a people for God's own possession. Peter told them they were not to fear the threats, they were not to be intimidated, they were not to be troubled by the world's animosity, and they were not to be afraid when they suffered.

Why? Because Christians are "protected by the power of God through faith." Instead of giving them doses of sympathy and commiseration, Peter pointed them to their absolute security as believers. He knew they might be losing all their earthly possessions and even their lives, but he wanted them to know they would never lose what they had in Christ. Their heavenly inheritance was guaranteed. They were being kept by divine power. Their faith would endure through anything. They would persevere through their trials and be found worthy at the end. Their love for Christ would remain intact. Even now, in the midst of their difficulties, God would provide the spiritual deliverance they needed, according to His eternal plan. Those six means of perseverance sum up how God sustains every Christian.

We are born again to a living hope. "God . . . has caused us to be born again to a living hope through the resurrection of Jesus Christ from the dead to obtain an inheritance which is imperishable and undefiled and will not fade away, reserved in heaven for you" (vv. 3–4). Every Christian is born again to a *living hope*—that is, a hope that is perpetually alive, a hope that cannot die. Peter seems to be making a contrast to mere human hope, which is always a dying or a dead hope. Human hopes and dreams inevitably fade and ultimately disappoint. That's why Paul told the Corinthians, "If we have hoped in Christ in this life only, we are of all men most to be pitied" (1 Cor. 15:19). This living hope in Christ cannot die. God guarantees that it will finally come to a complete and total, glorious eternal fulfillment. "This hope we have as an anchor of the soul, a hope both sure and steadfast" (Heb. 6:19).

That has clear implications beyond the antinomian concept of eternal security. Again, the point is not only that Christians are saved forever and safe from hell "no matter what." It means more than that: Our *hope* doesn't die. Our *faith* won't fail. That is the heart of the doctrine of perseverance.

But this passage *does* teach eternal security as well. We are guaranteed "an inheritance which is imperishable and undefiled and will not fade away, reserved in heaven" (v. 4). Unlike everything in this life, which may be corrupted, decay, grow old, rust, corrode, be stolen, or lose its value, our heavenly inheritance is reserved for us where it remains incorruptible, undefiled, and unfading. Our full inheritance will one day be the culmination of our living hope. It is "reserved in heaven"—"not like a hotel reservation which may be unexpectedly cancelled, but permanently and unchangeably."[13]

Did you realize that we have already received part of that inheritance? Ephesians 1:13–14 says, "[Having] believed, you were sealed in Him with the Holy Spirit of promise, who is given as a pledge of our inheritance, with a view to the redemption of God's own possession, to the praise of His glory" (cf. 2 Cor. 1:22; 5:5). "Pledge" in verse 14 comes from the Greek word *arrabōn*, which means "down payment." When a person first believes, the Holy Spirit Himself moves into that person's heart. He is the security deposit on our eternal salvation. He is an advance on the Christian's inheritance. He is the guarantee that God will finish the work He has started. "And do not grieve the Holy Spirit

---

[13]Hoekema, *Saved by Grace,* 244.

of God, by whom you were *sealed for the day of redemption*" (Eph. 4:30, emphasis added).

We are kept by God's own power. "[We are] protected by the power of God through faith for a salvation ready to be revealed in the last time" (v. 5). That is a rich statement, guaranteeing the consummation of every believer's eternal salvation. The phrase, "a salvation ready to be revealed in the last time," speaks of our full, final salvation—from the curse of the law, the power and presence of sin, all decay, every stain of iniquity, all temptation, all grief, all pain, all death, all punishment, all judgment, and all wrath. God has begun this work in us already, and He will thoroughly complete it (cf. Phil 1:6).

Working our way carefully through that sentence, we note this phrase: "you . . . are protected by the power of God through faith." We are *protected* by the power of a supreme, omnipotent, sovereign, omniscient, almighty God. The verb tense speaks of continuous action. Even now we are *being protected.* "Neither death, nor life, nor angels, nor principalities, nor things present, nor things to come, nor powers, nor height, nor depth, nor any other created thing, shall be able to separate us from the love of God, which is in Christ Jesus our Lord" (Rom. 8:38–39). "If God be for us, who can be against us?" (Rom. 8:31 KJV). "[He] is able to keep you from stumbling, and to make you stand in the presence of His glory blameless with great joy" (Jude 24).

Furthermore, we are protected *through faith.* Our continued faith in Christ is the instrument of God's sustaining work. God didn't save us apart from faith, and He doesn't keep us apart from faith. Our faith is God's gift, and through His protecting power He preserves it and nurtures it. The maintenance of our faith is as much His work as every other aspect of salvation. Our faith is kindled and driven and maintained and fortified by God's grace.

But to say that faith is God's gracious gift, which He maintains, is not to say that faith operates apart from the human will. It is *our* faith. We believe. We remain steadfast. We are not passive in the process. The means by which God maintains our faith involves our full participation. We cannot persevere apart from faith; only *through* faith.

We are strengthened by the testing of our faith. "In this you greatly rejoice, even though now for a little while, if necessary, you have been distressed by various trials, that the proof of your faith, being more precious than gold which is perishable, even though tested by fire, may be found to result in praise and glory and honor at the revelation of

Jesus Christ" (1 Peter 1:5–6). Here we discover the chief means by which God maintains our faith: He subjects it to trials.

The little phrase "you greatly rejoice" may catch the unsuspecting reader off guard. Remember, the recipients of this epistle were facing life-threatening persecutions. They were fearful of the future. Yet Peter says, "you greatly rejoice." How could they be rejoicing?

Trials produce joy because the testing strengthens our faith. James said exactly the same thing: "Consider it all joy, my brethren, when you encounter various trials, knowing that the testing of your faith produces endurance" (James 1:2–3). Temptations (same word in the Greek) and tests don't weaken or shatter real faith—just the opposite. They strengthen it. People who lose their faith in a trial only show that they never had real faith to begin with. Real faith emerges from trials stronger than ever.

Trials themselves are anything but joyful, and Peter recognizes this: "though now for a little while, if necessary, you have been distressed by various trials" (v. 6). They come like fire to burn the dross off metal. But that's the point. The faith that emerges is that much more glorious. When the fire has done its burning, what is left is purer, brighter, stronger faith.

For whom does God test our faith? For His own sake? Is He wanting to find out whether our faith is real? Of course not. He knows. He tests us for our own benefit, so we will know if our faith is genuine. He tests our faith in order to refine it, strengthen it, bring it to maturity. What emerges from the crucible is "more precious than gold" (v. 7). Unlike gold, proven faith has eternal value. Mere gold may survive the refiner's fire, but it does not pass the test of eternity.

Peter wasn't giving these Christians empty platitudes. He had tasted the joy that accrues from a trial of persecution. Acts 5:41 says the apostles "went on their way from the presence of the [Sanhedrin] Council, *rejoicing that they had been considered worthy to suffer shame for His name*" (emphasis added). May I add that they must have gone on their way with a stronger faith, too? They had suffered, but their faith had passed the test. The great confidence of the believer is to know that his faith is real. Thus trials produce that mature faith by which God preserves us.

We are preserved by God for ultimate glory. "The proof of your faith . . . may be found to result in praise and glory and honor at the revelation of Jesus Christ" (v. 7). Here is an astonishing promise. The ultimate result of our proven faith will be praise, glory, and honor at Christ's appearing. The direction of this praise is from God to the believer, not vice versa! Peter is not talking about our praising, glorifying and honoring God, but His approval directed to us.

First Peter 2:20 says, "If when you do what is right and suffer for it you patiently endure it, this finds favor with God." Like the master of the faithful servant, God will say, "Well done, good and faithful slave . . . enter into the joy of your master" (Matt. 25:21, 23). Romans 2:29 says, "He is a Jew who is one inwardly; and circumcision is that which is of the heart, by the Spirit, not by the letter; *and his praise is not from men, but from God*" (emphasis added). True faith, tested and proved, receives praise from God.

Notice 1 Peter 1:13. Peter writes, "Therefore, gird your minds for action, keep sober in spirit, fix your hope completely on the grace to be brought to you at the revelation of Jesus Christ." What is that grace? "Praise and glory and honor." In 4:13 he says, "To the degree that you share the sufferings of Christ, keep on rejoicing; so that also at the revelation of His glory, you may rejoice with exultation." Paul says, "I consider that the sufferings of this present time are not worthy to be compared with the glory that is to be revealed to us" (Rom. 8:18).

Some people misunderstand 1 Peter 1:7 and think it is saying that our faith has to wait for the Second Coming to be found genuine. "That the proof of your faith . . . may be found [worthy] *at the revelation of Jesus Christ*"—as if the outcome were uncertain until that day. But the verse actually says that our faith, already tested and proved genuine, is awaiting its eternal reward. There's no insecurity in this. In fact, the opposite is true. We can be certain of the final outcome, because God Himself is preserving us through faith until that day.

We are motivated by love for the Savior. "Though you have not seen Him, you love Him, and though you do not see Him now, but believe in Him, you greatly rejoice with joy inexpressible and full of glory" (v. 8). That is a profound statement about the character of genuine faith. I am convinced beyond equivocation that the two key factors that guarantee our perseverance from the human side are love for and trust in the Savior. Peter knew this better than anyone.

After he denied Christ, Peter had to face Jesus Christ and have his love questioned. Jesus asked him three times, "Do you love Me?" and Peter was deeply grieved (John 21:17). Of course he *did* love Christ, and that is why he returned to Him and was restored. Peter's own faith was purified by that trial. I see here in 1 Peter a beautiful humility. Peter commends these suffering believers and says to them, "You've never seen Him and you love Him and you don't see Him now but you believe in Him." He might have been remembering that when he denied Christ he was standing close enough for their eyes to meet (Luke 22:60–61). Surely the pain of his own failure was still very real in his heart, even after many years.

A normal relationship involves love and trust for someone you can know face-to-face. But Christians love Someone they cannot see, hear, or touch. It is a supernatural, God-given love. "We love him, because he first loved us" (1 John 4:19 KJV).

There is no such thing as a Christian who lacks this love. Peter is saying categorically that the essence of what it means to be a Christian is to love Jesus Christ. In fact, there may be no better way to describe the essential expression of the new nature than to say it is *continual love for Christ*. The King James Version translates 1 Peter 2:7 like this: "Unto you therefore which believe he is precious." Note what Paul said in the very last verse of Ephesians: "Grace be with all those who love our Lord Jesus Christ with a love incorruptible" (6:24). Romans 8:28, one of the most familiar passages in all of Scripture, refers to believers as "those who love God." But Paul makes his strongest statement on this matter in 1 Corinthians 16:22: "If anyone does not love the Lord, let him be accursed."

No-lordship theology ignores this vital truth. Consequently, many people today who utterly lack any love for the Lord Jesus Christ are being given a false hope of heaven. True Christians love Christ. His love for us, producing our love for Him (1 John 4:19), is one of the guarantees that we will persevere to the end (Rom. 8:33–39). Jesus said, "If you love Me, you will keep My commandments." "He who has My commandments and keeps them, he it is who loves Me" (v. 21). Conversely, "He who does not love Me does not keep My words" (v. 24).

Those who are devoted to Christ long to promote His glory. They long to serve Him with heart and soul and mind and strength. They delight in His beauty. They love to talk about Him, read about Him, fellowship with Him. They desire to know Him better and to know Him deeper. They are compelled in their hearts to want to be like Him. Like Peter, they may stumble frequently and fail in pathetic ways as sinful flesh assaults holy longings. But like Peter, all true believers *will* persevere until the goal is ultimately reached.[14] "Beloved, now we are

---

[14]This is not to suggest that all believers will experience the same degree of spiritual success, only that none of them will turn away from Christ by giving in to settled unbelief.

children of God, and it has not appeared as yet what we shall be. We know that, when He appears, we shall be like Him, because we shall see Him just as He is" (1 John 3:2).

Robert Leighton, writing in 1853 in a wonderful commentary on 1 Peter, said this:

> *Believe, and you shall love; believe much, and you shall love much;* labour for strong and deep persuasions of the glorious things which are spoken of Christ, and this will command love. Certainly, did men indeed believe his worth, they would accordingly love him; for the reasonable creature cannot but affect that most which it firmly believes to be worthiest of affection. Oh! this mischievous unbelief is that which makes the heart cold and dead towards God. Seek then to believe Christ's excellency in himself, and his love to us, and our interest in him, and this will kindle such a fire in the heart, as will make it ascend in a sacrifice of love to him.[15]

So our love for Christ is another of the means God uses to assure our perseverance. That love and the faith that accompanies it are a source of inexpressible joy, full of glory (1 Peter 1:8).

We are saved through a working faith. ". . . obtaining as the outcome of your faith the salvation of your souls" (1:9). Here Peter is speaking of a present deliverance. "Obtaining" is a present-tense verb, middle voice. The word could be literally translated, "Presently receiving for yourselves . . ." This present salvation is "the outcome" of our faith—a working faith. In practical terms, it means a present-tense deliverance from sin, guilt, condemnation, wrath, ignorance, distress, confusion, hopelessness—everything that defiles. This is not speaking of the perfect consummation of salvation Peter mentioned in verse 5.

The salvation in view here in verse 9 is a constant, present-tense salvation. Sin no longer has dominion over us (Rom. 6:14). There is no way we can fail to persevere. We will certainly falter at times. We won't always be successful. In fact, some people may seem to experience more failure than success. But no true believer can fall into settled unbelief or permanent reprobation. To allow for such a possibility is a disastrous misunderstanding of God's keeping power in the lives of His chosen ones.

Thus Peter opens his first epistle. At the end of this same epistle he returns again to the theme of perseverance. There he writes, "After you have suffered for a little while, the God of all grace, who called you to

---

[15]Robert Leighton, *Commentary on First Peter* (reprint, Grand Rapids, Mich.: Kregel, 1972), 55.

His eternal glory in Christ, will Himself perfect, confirm, strengthen and establish you" (5:10).

Can you grasp the magnitude of that promise? *God Himself* perfects, confirms, strengthens, and establishes His children. Though His purposes for the future involve some pain in the present, He will nevertheless give us grace to endure and persevere. Even while we are being personally attacked by the enemy, we are being personally perfected by God. He Himself is doing it. He will accomplish His purposes in us, bringing us to wholeness, setting us on solid ground, making us strong, and establishing us on a firm foundation. All those terms speak of strength, resoluteness.

The Problem of Quantification

Inevitably, the question is raised, "How faithfully must one persevere?" Charles Ryrie wrote,

> So we read a statement like this: "A moment of failure does not invalidate a disciple's credentials." My immediate reaction to such a statement is to want to ask if two moments would? Or a week of defection, or a month, or a year? Or two? How serious a failure and for how long before we must conclude that such a person was in fact not saved? Lordship teaching recognizes that "no one will obey perfectly," but the crucial question is simply how imperfectly can one obey and yet be sure that he "believed"? . . .
>
> . . . A moment of defection, we have been told, is not an invalidation. Or "the true disciple will never turn away completely." Could he turn away almost completely? Or ninety percent? Or fifty percent and still be sure he was saved? . . .
>
> *Frankly, all this relativity would leave me in confusion and uncertainty. Every defection, especially if it continued, would make me unsure of my salvation.* Any serious sin or unwillingness would do the same. If I come to a fork in the road of my Christian experience and choose the wrong branch and continue on it, does that mean I was never on the Christian road to begin with? For how long can I be fruitless without having a lordship advocate conclude that I was never really saved? (*SGS* 48–49, emphasis added).

Ryrie suggests that if we cannot state precisely *how much* failure is possible for a Christian, true assurance becomes impossible. He wants the terms to be quantified: "Could he turn away almost completely? Or ninety percent? Or fifty percent?" To put it another way, Ryrie is suggesting that the doctrines of perseverance and assurance are incompatible. Astonishingly,

he wants a doctrine of assurance that allows those who have defected from
Christ to be confident of their salvation.

There are no quantifiable answers to the questions Ryrie raises.
Indeed, some Christians persist in sin for extended periods of time. But
those who do, forfeit their right to genuine assurance. "Serious sin or
unwillingness" certainly *should* cause someone to contemplate carefully
the question of whether he or she really loves the Lord. Those who turn
away completely (not *almost* completely, or 90 percent, or 50 percent)
demonstrate that they never had true faith.

Quantification poses a dilemma for no-lordship teaching, too.
Zane Hodges speaks of faith as a "historical moment." How brief
may that moment be? Someone listening to a debate between a
Christian and an atheist might believe for an instant while the Christian is speaking, but immediately be led back into doubt or agnosti-
cism by the atheist's arguments. Would we classify such a person as
a believer? One suspects some no-lordship advocates would answer
yes, although that view goes against everything God's word teaches
about faith.

Jesus never quantified the terms of His demands; He always made
them *absolute.* "So therefore, no one of you can be My disciple who
does not give up all his own possessions" (Luke 14:33); "He who loves
father or mother more than Me is not worthy of Me; and he who loves
son or daughter more than Me is not worthy of Me" (Matt. 10:37);
"He who loves his life loses it; and he who hates his life in this world
shall keep it to life eternal" (John 12:25). Those conditions are *impossible* in human terms (Matt. 19:26).[16] That does not alter or mitigate the
truth of the gospel. It certainly is no excuse for going to the other extreme and doing away with any necessity for commitment to Christ.

Ryrie's comments raise another issue that is worth considering.
It is the question of whether lordship teaching is inherently judgmental: "How long can I be fruitless without having a lordship advocate conclude that I was never really saved?" Zane Hodges has made
similar comments: "Lordship teaching reserves to itself the right to
strip professing Christians of their claims to faith and to consign such
people to the ranks of the lost" (*AF* 19).

Certainly no individual can judge another's heart. It is one thing
to challenge people to examine themselves (2 Cor. 13:5); it is entirely
another matter to set oneself up as another Christian's judge (Rom.
14:4, 13; James 4:11).

---

[16]Even those who want to make these statements of Christ apply to a postconversion
step of discipleship don't solve the dilemma of their absoluteness.

But while individual Christians must never be judgmental, the church body as a whole very definitely has a responsibility to maintain purity by exposing and excommunicating those who live in continual sin or defection from the faith. Our Lord gave very explicit instructions on how to handle a fellow believer who falls into such sin. We are to go to the brother (or sister) privately first (Matt. 18:15). If he or she refuses to hear, we are to go again with one or two more people (v. 16). Then if he or she refuses to hear, we are to "tell it to the church" (v. 17). If the sinning one still fails to repent, "let him be to you as a Gentile and a tax-gatherer" (v. 17). In other words, pursue that person for Christ evangelistically as if he or she were utterly unsaved.

This process of discipline is how Christ mediates His rule in the church. He went on to say, "Truly I say to you, whatever you shall bind on earth shall be bound in heaven; and whatever you loose on earth shall be loosed in heaven. Again I say to you, that if two of you agree on earth about anything that they may ask, it shall be done for them by My Father who is in heaven" (Matt. 18:18–19). The context shows this is not talking about "binding Satan" or about praying in general. Our Lord was dealing with the matter of sin and forgiveness among Christians (cf. v. 21ff). The verb tenses in verse 18 literally mean, "Whatever you bind on earth shall have been bound in heaven; and whatever you loose on earth shall have been loosed in heaven." Our Lord is saying that He Himself works personally in the discipline process: "For where two or three have gathered together in My name, there I am in their midst" (v. 20).

Thus the process of church discipline, properly followed, answers all of Dr. Ryrie's questions. How long can a person continue in sin before we "conclude that [he or she] was never really saved?" All the way through the discipline process. Once the matter has been told to the church, if the person still refuses to repent, we have instructions from the Lord Himself to regard the sinning one "as a Gentile and a tax-gatherer."

The church discipline process our Lord outlined in Matthew 18 is predicated on the doctrine of perseverance. Those who remain hardened in sin only demonstrate their lack of true faith. Those who respond to the rebuke and return to the Lord give the best possible evidence that their salvation is genuine. They can be sure that if their faith is real it will endure to the end—because God Himself guarantees it.

"I am confident of this very thing, that He who began a good work in you will perfect it until the day of Christ Jesus (Phil. 1:6). "I know whom I have believed and I am convinced that He is able to guard what I have entrusted to Him until that day" (2 Tim. 1:12).

12

What Must I Do to Be Saved?

> If one were to suggest that the time would come when a group of evangelical Christians would be arguing for a salvation without repentance, without a change of behavior or lifestyle, without a real avowal of the lordship and authority of Christ, without perseverance, without discipleship, and a salvation which does not necessarily result in obedience and works, and with a regeneration which does not necessarily change one's life, most believers of several decades ago would have felt such would be an absolute impossibility. But believe it or not, the hour has come.
>
> Richard P. Belcher[1]

What is the gospel? Here we get practical. The real question we are asking is, "How should I evangelize my friends, family, and neighbors?" For parents an even more important question is, "How should I present the gospel to my children?"

Twentieth-century Christianity has tended to take a minimalist approach to the gospel. Unfortunately, the legitimate desire to express the heart of the gospel clearly has given way to a less wholesome endeavor. It is a campaign to distill the essentials of the message to the barest possible terms. The glorious gospel of Christ—which Paul called "the power of God for salvation to everyone who believes" (Rom. 1:16)—

---

[1]Richard P. Belcher, *A Layman's Guide to the Lordship Controversy* (Southbridge, Mass.: Crowne, 1990), 71.

includes *all* the truth about Christ. But American evangelicalism tends
to regard the gospel as a "plan of salvation." We have reduced the message to a list of facts stated in the fewest possible words—and getting
fewer all the time. You've probably seen these prepackaged "plans of
salvation": "Six Steps to Peace with God"; "Five Things God Wants
You to Know"; "Four Spiritual Laws"; "Three Truths You Can't Live
Without"; "Two Issues You Must Settle"; or "One Way to Heaven."

Christians today are often cautioned not to say *too much* to the lost.
Certain spiritual issues are labeled taboo when speaking to the
unconverted: God's law, Christ's lordship, turning from sin, surrender,
obedience, judgment, and hell. Such things are not to be mentioned,
lest we "add something to the offer of God's free gift." Proponents of
no-lordship evangelism take the reductionist trend to its furthest extreme. Wrongly applying the Reformed doctrine of *sola fide* ("faith
alone"), they make faith the only permissible topic when speaking to
non-Christians about their duty before God. Then they render faith utterly meaningless by stripping it of everything but its notional aspects.

This, some believe, preserves the purity of the gospel.

What it actually has done is emasculate the message of salvation. It
has also populated the church with "converts" whose faith is counterfeit
and whose hope hangs on a bogus promise. Numbly saying they "accept
Christ as Savior," they brazenly reject His rightful claim as Lord. Paying
Him glib lip service, they utterly scorn Him with their hearts (Mark
7:6). Casually affirming Him with their mouths, they deliberately deny
Him with their deeds (Titus 1:16). Addressing Him superficially as
"Lord, Lord," they stubbornly decline to do His bidding (Luke 6:46).
Such people fit the tragic description of the "many" in Matthew 7 who
will one day be stunned to hear Him say, "I never knew you; depart
from Me, *you who practice lawlessness*" (v. 23, emphasis added).

The gospel is not primarily news about a "plan," but a call to
trust in a *Person*. It is not a formula that must be prescribed to sinners
in a series of steps. It does not call for a mere decision of the mind, but
a surrender of the heart, mind, and will—the whole person—to Christ.
It is not a message that can be capsulized, abridged, and shrink-
wrapped, then offered as a generic remedy for every kind of sinner.
Ignorant sinners need to be instructed about who He is and why He
has the right to demand their obedience. *Self-righteous* sinners need to
have their sin exposed by the demands of God's law. *Careless* sinners
need to be confronted with the reality of God's impending judgment.
Fearful sinners need to hear that God in His mercy has provided a way
of deliverance. *All* sinners must understand how utterly holy God is.

They must comprehend the basic truths of Christ's sacrificial death and the triumph of His resurrection. They need to be confronted with God's demand that they turn from their sin to embrace Christ as Lord and Savior.

The *form* of the message will vary in each case. But the *content* must always drive home the reality of God's holiness and the sinner's helpless condition. *Then* it points sinners to Christ as a sovereign but merciful Lord who has purchased full atonement for all who will turn to Him in faith.

Twentieth-century evangelicalism seems obsessed with the idea that unsaved people should never be told they have any duty other than believing. Lewis Sperry Chafer, for example, suggested that "in all gospel preaching every reference to the life to be lived beyond regeneration should be avoided as far as possible."[2] He claimed it was faulty evangelism to tell sinners they must "repent and believe," "believe and confess Christ," "believe and be baptized," "believe and surrender to God," or "believe and confess sin."[3] Yet Scripture employs *all* those expressions! Jesus Himself preached, "*Repent and believe* in the gospel" (Mark 1:15). Paul wrote, "If you *confess* with your mouth Jesus as Lord, *and believe* in your heart that God raised Him from the dead, you shall be saved" (Rom. 10:9). At Pentecost, Peter preached, "*Repent, and let each of you be baptized* in the name of Jesus Christ for the forgiveness of your sins; and you shall receive the gift of the Holy Spirit" (Acts 2:38). John wrote, "He who does not *obey* the Son shall not see life, but the wrath of God abides on him" (John 3:36). The writer to the Hebrews said that Christ "became to all those who *obey* Him the source of eternal salvation" (Heb. 5:9). James wrote, "*Submit* therefore to God. Resist the devil and he will flee from you. Draw near to God and He will draw near to you. *Cleanse your hands, you sinners;* and *purify your hearts, you double-minded*" (James 4:7, emphasis added). Jesus responded by preaching law and lordship to a man who asked Him how he might obtain eternal life! (Matt. 19:16–22).

Are we to believe that the inspired Scripture constitutes poorly worded theology?

I agree that terminology is important, and we dare not confuse the gospel message or add anything to the biblical terms for salvation. But it should be obvious that Jesus and the apostles certainly did not fuss

---

[2]Lewis Sperry Chafer, *Systematic Theology,* 8 vols. (Dallas: Seminary Press, 1948), 3:387.

[3]Ibid., 3:371–93.

about the phraseology of evangelistic invitations the way many Christians today do. Nor did they avoid mentioning God's law. On the contrary, the law is where they began! (cf. Rom. 1:16–3:20). The law reveals our sin (Rom. 3:20) and is a tutor to lead us to Christ (Gal. 3:24). It is the means God uses to make sinners see their own helplessness. Clearly, Paul saw a key place for the law in evangelistic contexts. Yet many today believe the law, with its inflexible demand for holiness and obedience, is contrary to and incompatible with the gospel.

Why should we make such distinctions where Scripture does not? If *Scripture* cautioned against preaching repentance, obedience, righteousness, or judgment to unbelievers, that would be one thing. But Scripture contains no such warnings. The opposite is true. If we want to follow a biblical model, we cannot ignore those issues. "Sin, righteousness, and judgment" are the very matters about which the Holy Spirit convicts the unsaved (John 16:8). Can we omit them from the message and still call it the gospel? Apostolic evangelism inevitably culminated in a call for repentance (Acts 2:38; 3:19; 17:30; 26:20). Can we tell sinners they *don't* have to turn from their sin, and then call that evangelism? Paul ministered to unbelievers by "declaring . . . that they should repent and turn to God, performing deeds appropriate to repentance" (Acts 26:20). Can we reduce the message to simply, "accept Christ" and still believe we are ministering biblically?

Furthermore, in all the instances where Jesus and the apostles evangelized—whether they were ministering to individuals or crowds—there are no two incidents where they presented the message in precisely the same terminology. They knew that salvation is a sovereign work of God. Their role was to preach truth; God Himself would apply it individually to the hearts of His elect.

The new birth is a sovereign work of the Holy Spirit. "That which is born of the flesh is flesh, and that which is born of the Spirit is spirit" (John 3:6). The Spirit sovereignly chooses where, how, and on whom He will work: "The wind blows where it wishes and you hear the sound of it, but do not know where it comes from and where it is going; so is everyone who is born of the Spirit" (John 3:8).

Clear proclamation of truth is the means through which the Spirit works—not inventive methodology or human charm (1 Cor. 1:21; 2:1–5).

Decisionism and Easy-Believism

Two fallacies—*decisionism* and *easy-believism*—taint much of what is labeled evangelism in contemporary Christianity. Decisionism is the idea that eternal salvation may be secured by the sinner's own movement toward Christ. A "decision for Christ" is usually signified by some physical or verbal act—raising a hand, walking an aisle, repeating a prayer, signing a card, reciting a pledge, or something similar. If the sinner performs the prescribed activity, he or she is usually pronounced saved and told to claim assurance. The "moment of decision" becomes the ground of the person's assurance.

Decisionism is often employed in evangelizing children. Youngsters in large groups are asked to raise a hand, stand, come forward, ask Jesus into their hearts, or make some similar gesture. Those things are supposed to indicate a positive response to the gospel. But because children are so susceptible to suggestion, so sensitive to peer pressure, and so desirous of gaining their leaders' approval, it is very easy to get large groups of children to profess faith in Christ through such means, even if they are utterly oblivious to the message. Unfortunately, many people go through life caring nothing for Christ but believing they are Christians only because they responded with a childhood "decision." Their hope of heaven hangs solely on the memory of that event. I'm afraid that in many cases it is a vain and damning hope.

Here is a familiar technique for counseling people who are unsure of their salvation: "Decide for Christ here and now, note the date, then drive a stake in your backyard and write the date on it. Whenever you doubt your salvation, go out and look at the stake. It will be a reminder of the decision you have made." But that is tantamount to telling people they should have faith in their own decision. Dr. Chafer even went so far as to give this advice to people struggling with a lack of assurance:

> The only cure for this uncertainty is to end it with certainty. Let such an one face his own utter sinfulness and meritlessness with the revelations of the cross and discover, as he must, no hope in himself, and then and there, once for all, appropriate the provisions of divine grace for every need of a sin-cursed soul. If need be, note the very day and hour of such a decision and *then believe in the decision itself* enough to thank God for His saving grace and faithfulness, and in every thought, act and word thereafter treat the decision as final and real.[4]

Ironically, Chafer simultaneously denounced trends in mass evangelism that were based on the same decisionist presuppositions reflected in that paragraph. In another book, he criticized the evangelists of his day for requiring converts to "come forward" publicly as an outward act of

---

[4]Lewis Sperry Chafer, *Salvation* (Philadelphia: Sunday School Times, 1917), 80 (emphasis added).

receiving Christ: "Such acts, if urged at all, should be so presented that they could not be thought of by any individual as forming a part of the one condition of salvation."[5] He believed that such methods could lead to false assurance: "If questioned carefully, the basis of assurance with all such converts will be found to be no more than a consciousness that they have acted out the program prescribed for them."[6] That is precisely the problem with decisionism. It offers a false hope based on a wrong premise. Salvation cannot be obtained by following any prescribed course of outward action. "For by grace you have been saved through faith; and that not of yourselves, it is the gift of God; not as a result of works, that no one should boast" (Eph. 2:8–9).

Decisionism and no-lordship doctrine do not always go hand in hand. In fact, the most aggressive advocates of modern no-lordship teaching nearly all recognize the fallacy of overt decisionism. They would affirm with us that no one is saved because of raising a hand, walking an aisle, praying a prayer, or any other physical act.

Most nevertheless believe saving faith hinges on human initiative. In their system, faith begins with a human response, not the work of God in the believer. Therefore they must scale back the definition of faith to make believing something depraved sinners are capable of. This is *easy-believism.*

Even those who are willing to grant that faith is a gift of God sometimes fall into easy-believism. Dr. Chafer, for example, seemed confused at this point. On the one hand, he roundly condemned those who tell sinners they must "believe and surrender." That places an undue demand on sinners, he argued. If unbelievers are dead in trespasses and sins, how can they surrender to God? "To impose a need to surrender the life to God as an added condition of salvation is most unreasonable," he wrote.[7]

On the other hand, Chafer evidently realized that if unsaved people are dead in trespasses and sins, they cannot even *believe* apart from God's initiative. Oddly, Chafer made this observation in the very same paragraph as the sentence I just quoted: "Saving faith is not a possession of all men but is imparted specifically to those who do believe (Eph. 2:8)."[8] Chafer rightly saw that only God can provoke faith in an unbelieving heart. But for some reason Chafer could not accept the idea that the

---

[5]Lewis Sperry Chafer, *True Evangelism* (Grand Rapids, Mich.: Zondervan, 1919), 13.

[6]Ibid., 15.

[7]Chafer, *Systematic Theology,* 3:385.

[8]Ibid.

faith God imparts comes with a built-in attitude of surrender and self-abandonment. So he defined faith in terms that posed no challenge to human depravity. At its heart, easy-believism is a misunderstanding of the depth of human sinfulness. If ungodly, depraved, spiritually dead sinners are capable of believing solely on their own initiative, then faith must be something that makes no moral or spiritual demands. That is precisely why no-lordship theology has unsanctified the act of believing and made faith a nonmoral exercise. That is easy-believism.

The rationale of easy-believism is expressed most clearly in a newspaper clipping I received from a radio listener. A pastor had published a column criticizing me for my stand against easy-believism. He wrote, "I think God intended for the act of salvation to be easy. . . . *God made it easy for us to receive him because he knew in our sinful state that easy was the only way we would be saved.*"[9]

But that is faulty and unbiblical theology. Believing isn't *easy*.[10] It isn't even *hard*.[11] It is *impossible* in human terms. Jesus Himself acknowledged this (Matt. 19:26). No one can come to Christ unless it has been granted by the Father (John 6:65). The unregenerate do not accept the things of the Spirit of God; spiritual things are foolishness to them. They cannot even begin to understand them, much less believe (1 Cor. 2:14). Only God can open the heart and initiate faith (cf. Acts 13:48; 16:14; 18:27).

The faith God grants trembles before Him (Luke 18:13). It is a faith that provokes obedience from the heart and makes the sinner a slave to righteousness (Rom. 6:17–18). It is a faith that works though love (Gal. 5:6). It has nothing to do with the sterile faith of easy-believism.

How Should We Call People to Faith?

There are many helpful books on how to witness offering practical advice and how-tos.[12] In this brief chapter, I want to focus on some crucial

---

[9]Stephen Kern, "It Is Easy to Receive Salvation from God," *The Idaho Statesman*, 29 June 1991, 3D (emphasis added).

[10]Hodges seems to be arguing that, after all, believing is supposed to be easy. Responding to the phrase "easy-believism," he writes: "Presumably the opposite would be 'hard believism.' And if any system of thought teaches 'hard believism,' lordship salvation certainly does. . . . But salvation really *is* simple and, in that sense, it is easy! After all, what could be simpler than to 'take of the water of life freely'?" (*AF* 30).

[11]Ryrie includes a chapter titled, "It's Not Easy to Believe" (*SGS* 117–23).

issues relating to the *content* of the message we are called to share with unbelievers. Specifically, if we want to articulate the gospel as precisely as possible, what are the points we need to make clear?

Teach them about God's holiness. "The fear of the Lord is the
beginning of wisdom" (Ps. 111:10, cf. Job 28:28; Prov. 1:7; 9:10;
15:33; Mic. 6:9). No-lordship theology misses this point entirely. In
fact, much of contemporary evangelism aims to arouse anything *but* fear
of God. "God loves you and has a wonderful plan for your life," is the
opening line of the typical evangelistic appeal today. No-lordship theology takes it a step further: God loves you and will save you from hell no
matter *whose* plan you choose for your life.

The remedy for such thinking is the biblical truth of God's holiness. *God is utterly holy, and His law therefore demands perfect holiness:*
"I am the Lord your God. Consecrate yourselves therefore, and be
holy; for I am holy. . . . You shall be holy for I am holy" (Lev.
11:44–45). "You will not be able to serve the Lord, for He is a holy
God. He is a jealous God; He will not forgive your transgression or
your sins" (Josh. 24:19). "There is no one holy like the Lord, indeed,
there is no one besides Thee, Nor is there any rock like our God" (1
Sam. 2:2). "Who is able to stand before the Lord, this holy God?"
(6:20).

Even the gospel requires this holiness: "You shall be holy, for I am
holy" (1 Pet. 1:16). "Without [holiness] no one will see the Lord"
(Heb. 12:14).

Because He is holy, God hates sin: "I, the Lord your God, am a jealous God, visiting the iniquity of the fathers on the children, on the third
and the fourth generations of those who hate Me" (Exod. 20:5). *Sinners
cannot stand before Him:* "The wicked will not stand in the judgment,
nor sinners in the assembly of the righteous" (Ps. 1:5).

Show them their sin. Gospel means "good news." What makes
it truly good news is not just that heaven is free, but that sin has been
conquered by God's Son. Sadly, it has become stylish to present the
gospel as something other than a remedy for sin. "Salvation" is offered
as an escape from punishment, God's plan for a wonderful life, a
means of fulfillment, an answer to life's problems, and a promise of

---

[12]One particularly helpful resource is by Will Metzger, *Tell the Truth,* 2d ed. (Downers
Grove, Ill.: InterVarsity, 1984). Along with very practical information, Metzger also
decries the reductionist trend in evangelism I have described, and he includes a very
insightful section contrasting God-centered evangelism with man-centered evangelism.
A helpful tract is "Who Do You Think I Am?" (Valencia, Calif.: Grace to You, 1991).

free forgiveness. All those things are true, but they are byproducts of redemption, not the main issue. When sin is left unaddressed, such promises of divine blessings cheapen the message.

Some no-lordship teachers go so far as to say that sin is not an issue in the gospel invitation. Sin, they believe, is a postsalvation concern. Others believe it is optional whether we confront unbelievers with their sin. One man who edits a no-lordship newsletter replied to a reader's question: "No, I do not believe that one *must* recognize that he is a sinner to be saved. The key word is *must*. It is conceivable that a person could be ignorant of the fact that he is a sinner and yet know that he was bound for hell and could only be saved by trusting in Christ alone. Some small children might fall into this category."[13]

He did not attempt to explain why people with no understanding of their own sinfulness would believe they are headed for hell. But one wonders what sort of salvation is available to those who don't even recognize their sin. Didn't Jesus say, "It is not those who are healthy who need a physician, but those who are sick; I did not come to call the righteous, but sinners" (Mark 2:17)? To offer salvation to someone who doesn't even understand the gravity of sin is to fulfill Jeremiah 6:14: "They have healed the brokenness of My people superficially, Saying, 'Peace, peace,' But there is no peace."

Sin is what makes true peace impossible for unbelievers: "The wicked are like the tossing sea, for it cannot be quiet, and its waters toss up refuse and mud. 'There is no peace,' says my God, 'for the wicked'" (Isa. 57:20–21).

All have sinned:

> There is none righteous, not even one; there is none who understands, there is none who seeks for God; all have turned aside, together they have become useless; there is none who does good, there is not even one. Their throat is an open grave, with their tongues they keep deceiving, the poison of asps is under their lips; whose mouth is full of cursing and bitterness; their feet are swift to shed blood, destruction and misery are in their paths, and the path of peace have they not known. There is no fear of God before their eyes (Rom. 3:10–18).

Sin makes the sinner worthy of death: "When sin is accomplished, it brings forth death" (James 1:15). "For the wages of sin is death" (Rom. 6:23).

---

[13]Bob Wilkin, "Letters to the Editor," *The Grace Evangelical Society News* (August 1990): 3.

Sinners can do nothing to earn salvation: "For all of us have become like one who is unclean, and all our righteous deeds are like a filthy garment; and all of us wither like a leaf, and our iniquities, like the wind, take us away" (Isa. 64:6). "By the works of the Law no flesh will be justified in His sight" (Rom. 3:20). "A man is not justified by the works of the Law . . . by the works of the Law shall no flesh be justified" (Gal. 2:16).

Sinners are therefore in a helpless state: "It is appointed for men to die once and after this comes judgment" (Heb. 9:27). "There is nothing covered up that will not be revealed, and hidden that will not be known" (Luke 12:2). "God will judge the secrets of men through Christ Jesus" (Rom. 2:16). "The cowardly and unbelieving and abominable and murderers and immoral persons and sorcerers and idolaters and all liars, their part will be in the lake that burns with fire and brimstone, which is the second death" (Rev. 21:8).

Instruct them about Christ and what He has done. The gospel is good news about who Christ is and what He has done for sinners. No-lordship doctrine tends to emphasize His *work* and de-emphasize His *Person,* particularly the aspect of His divine authority. But Scripture never presents Jesus as something less than Lord in salvation. The notion that His Lordship is an addendum to the gospel is utterly foreign to Scripture.

He is eternally God: "In the beginning was the Word, and the Word was with God, and the Word was God. He was in the beginning with God. All things came into being by Him, and apart from Him nothing came into being that has come into being. . . . And the Word became flesh, and dwelt among us, and we beheld His glory, glory as of the only begotten from the Father, full of grace and truth" (John 1:1–3, 14). "In Him all the fulness of Deity dwells in bodily form" (Col. 2:9).

He is Lord of all: "He is Lord of lords and King of kings, and those who are with Him are the called and chosen and faithful" (Rev. 17:14). "God highly exalted Him, and bestowed on Him the name which is above every name, that at the name of Jesus every knee should bow, of those who are in heaven, and on earth, and under the earth, and that every tongue should confess that Jesus Christ is Lord, to the glory of God the Father" (Phil. 2:9–11). "He is Lord of all" (Acts 10:36).

He became man: "Although He existed in the form of God, [He] did not regard equality with God a thing to be grasped, but emptied Himself, taking the form of a bond-servant, and being made in the likeness of men" (Phil. 2:6–7).

He is utterly pure and sinless: "[He was] tempted in all things as we are, yet without sin" (Heb. 4:15). He "committed no sin, nor was any deceit found in His mouth; and while being reviled, He did not revile in return; while suffering, He uttered no threats, but kept entrusting Himself to Him who judges righteously" (1 Pet. 2:22–23). "He appeared in order to take away sins; and in Him there is no sin" (1 John 3:5).

The sinless one became a sacrifice for our sin: "He made Him who knew no sin to be sin on our behalf, that we might become the righteousness of God in Him" (2 Cor. 5:21). He "gave Himself for us, that He might redeem us from every lawless deed and purify for Himself a people for His own possession, zealous for good deeds" (Titus 2:14). *He shed His own blood as an atonement for sin:* "In Him we have redemption through His blood, the forgiveness of our trespasses, according to the riches of His grace which He lavished upon us" (Eph. 1:7–8). "[He] loves us, and released us from our sins by His blood" (Rev. 1:5). *He died on the cross to provide a way of salvation for sinners:* "He Himself bore our sins in His body on the cross, that we might die to sin and live to righteousness; for by His wounds you were healed" (1 Pet. 2:24). "Through Him to reconcile all things to Himself, having made peace through the blood of His cross" (Col. 1:20).

He rose triumphantly from the dead: Christ "was declared the Son of God with power by the resurrection from the dead" (Rom. 1:4). "[He] was delivered up because of our transgressions, and was raised because of our justification" (4:25). "I delivered to you as of first importance what I also received, that Christ died for our sins according to the Scriptures, and that He was buried, and that He was raised on the third day according to the Scriptures" (1 Cor. 15:3–4).

Tell them what God demands of them. Repentant faith is the requirement. It is not merely a "decision" to trust Christ for eternal life, but a wholesale forsaking of everything else we trust, and a turning to Jesus Christ as Lord and Savior.

Repent: "Repent and turn away from all your transgressions" (Ezek. 18:30). "'I have no pleasure in the death of anyone who dies,' declares the Lord GOD. 'Therefore, repent and live'" (v. 32). "God is now declaring to men that all everywhere should repent" (Acts 17:30). "Repent and turn to God, performing deeds appropriate to repentance" (Acts 26:20).

Turn your heart from all that you know dishonors God: "[Turn] to God from idols to serve a living and true God" (1 Thess. 1:9). *Follow Jesus:* "If anyone wishes to come after Me, let him deny himself, and take up his cross daily, and follow Me" (Luke 9:23). "No one, after putting his hand to the plow and looking back, is fit for the kingdom of God" (v. 62). "If anyone serves Me, let him follow Me; and where I am, there shall My servant also be; if anyone serves Me, the Father will honor him" (John 12:26).

Trust Him as Lord and Savior: "Believe in the Lord Jesus, and you shall be saved" (Acts 16:31). "If you confess with your mouth Jesus as Lord, and believe in your heart that God raised Him from the dead, you shall be saved" (Rom. 10:9).

Advise them to count the cost thoughtfully. Salvation *is* absolutely free. So is joining the army. You don't have to buy your way in. Everything you will need is provided. But there is a sense in which following Christ—like joining the army—will cost you dearly. It can cost freedom, family, friends, autonomy, and possibly even your life. The job of the evangelist—like that of the army recruiter—is to tell potential inductees the full story. That is exactly why Jesus' message was often so full of hard demands:

> If anyone comes to Me, and does not hate his own father and mother and wife and children and brothers and sisters, yes, and even his own life, he cannot be My disciple. Whoever does not carry his own cross and come after Me cannot be My disciple. For which one of you, when he wants to build a tower, does not first sit down and calculate the cost, to see if he has enough to complete it? Otherwise, when he has laid a foundation, and is not able to finish, all who observe it begin to ridicule him, saying, "This man began to build and was not able to finish." Or what king, when he sets out to meet another king in battle, will not first sit down and take counsel whether he is strong enough with ten thousand men to encounter the one coming against him with twenty thousand? Or else, while the other is still far away, he sends a delegation and asks terms of peace. So therefore, no one of you can be My disciple who does not give up all his own possessions.
>
> Luke 14:26–33
>
> Do not think that I came to bring peace on the earth; I did not come to bring peace, but a sword. For I came to set a man against his father, and a daughter against her mother, and a daughter-in-law against her mother-in-law; and a man's enemies will be the members of his household. He who loves father or mother more than Me is not worthy of Me; and he who loves son or daughter more than Me is not worthy of Me. And he who does not take his cross and follow after Me is not worthy of Me.
>
> Matthew 10:34–38

The free-costly, death-life enigma is expressed in the clearest possible terms by John 12:24–25: "Truly, truly, I say to you, unless a grain of wheat falls into the earth and dies, it remains by itself alone; but if it dies, it bears much fruit. He who loves his life loses it; and he who hates his life in this world shall keep it to life eternal."
The cross is central to the gospel precisely because of its graphic message, including the awfulness of sin, the profundity of God's wrath against sin, and the efficacy of Jesus' work in crucifying the old man (Rom. 6:6). A. W. Tozer wrote,

> The cross is the most revolutionary thing ever to appear among men.
> The cross of Roman times knew no compromise; it never made concessions. It won all its arguments by killing its opponent and silencing him for good. It spared not Christ, but slew Him the same as the rest. He was alive when they hung Him on that cross and completely dead when they took Him down six hours later. That was the cross the first time it appeared in Christian history. . . .
> The cross effects its ends by destroying one established pattern, the victim's, and creating another pattern, its own. Thus it always has its way. It wins by defeating its opponent and imposing its will upon him. It always dominates. It never compromises, never dickers nor confers, never surrenders a point for the sake of peace. It cares not for peace; it cares only to end its opposition as fast as possible.
> With perfect knowledge of all this, Christ said, "If any man will come after me, let him deny himself, and take up his cross, and follow me." So the cross not only brings Christ's life to an end, it ends also the first life, the old life, of every one of His true followers. It destroys the old pattern, the Adam pattern, in the believer's life, and brings it to an end. Then the God who raised Christ from the dead raises the believer and a new life begins.
> This, and nothing less, is true Christianity. . . .
> We must do something about the cross, and one of two things only we can do—flee it or die upon it.[14]

"For whoever wishes to save his life shall lose it; but whoever loses his life for My sake and the gospel's shall save it. For what does it profit a man to gain the whole world, and forfeit his soul? For what shall a man give in exchange for his soul?" (Mark 8:35–37).

---

[14]A. W. Tozer, *The Root of the Righteous* (Harrisburg, Pa.: Christian Publications, 1955), 61–63.

Urge them to trust Christ. "Knowing the fear of the Lord, we persuade men" (2 Cor. 5:11). "[God] reconciled us to Himself through Christ, and gave us the ministry of reconciliation, namely, that God was in Christ reconciling the world to Himself, not counting their trespasses against them, and He has committed to us the word of reconciliation. Therefore, we are ambassadors for Christ, as though God were entreating through us; we beg you on behalf of Christ, be reconciled to God" (2 Cor. 5:20).

"Seek the Lord while He may be found; Call upon Him while He is near. Let the wicked forsake his way, and the unrighteous man his thoughts; and let him return to the Lord, and He will have compassion on him; and to our God, for He will abundantly pardon" (Isa. 55:7). "If you confess with your mouth Jesus as Lord, and believe in your heart that God raised Him from the dead, you shall be saved; for with the heart man believes, resulting in righteousness, and with the mouth he confesses, resulting in salvation" (Rom. 10:9–10).

Where Do Good Works Fit?

Nowhere in either the Old or New Testaments do we find an invitation for sinners to believe now, obey later. The call to trust and obey is a single summons. The word *obey* is sometimes even used to describe the conversion experience: "He became to all those who obey Him the source of eternal salvation" (Heb. 5:9).

Does anyone really suppose it is possible to *believe,* to really fathom everything that Jesus did in suffering and dying for sin, to accept the offer of forgiveness from His hand—and then turn away, not exalt Him with one's life, and even grow to despise and reject and disbelieve Him exactly like those who put Him to death? That kind of theology is grotesque.

The truth is, our surrender to Christ is never purer than at the moment we are born again. In that sacred moment we are wholly under the sovereign control of the Holy Spirit, united to Christ, and recipients of a new heart. Then more than ever, obedience is not negotiable, nor would any genuine convert desire it to be (cf. Rom. 6:17).

The apostle Paul's conversion furnishes the archetypical illustration. In Paul's conversion, the issue was clearly Jesus' lordship. What were Paul's first words as a believer? "What shall I do, Lord?" (Acts 22:10). Years later Paul wrote about all that he gave up on the road to Damascus:

> Though I might also have confidence in the flesh. If any other
> man thinketh that he hath whereof he might trust in the flesh, I

more: Circumcised the eighth day, of the stock of Israel, of the tribe of Benjamin, an Hebrew of the Hebrews; as touching the law, a Pharisee; concerning zeal, persecuting the church; touching the righteousness which is in the law, blameless. *But what things were gain to me, those I counted loss for Christ. Yea doubtless, and I count all things but loss for the excellency of the knowledge of Christ Jesus my Lord: for whom I have suffered the loss of all things, and do count them but dung,* that I may win Christ, and be found in him, not having mine own righteousness, which is of the law, but that which is through the faith of Christ, the righteousness which is of God by faith.

Philippians 3:4–9 KJV, emphasis added

Can we honestly look at Paul's conversion, life, and ministry, and believe that he ever espoused a gospel that taught people they could be saved without surrender to Christ's authority?

Lordship salvation is often caricatured as teaching people that they must change their lives in order to be saved.[15] But no advocate of lordship theology I know of has ever taught such a thing. There is not a legitimate teacher of the lordship doctrine anywhere who would ever tell any unbeliever he needs to "'prove' he qualifies for salvation."[16] As we have seen time and time again in our study, meritorious works have no place in salvation.

But *faith works* have everything to do with *why* we are saved. God's whole purpose in choosing us is "that He might redeem us from every lawless deed and purify for Himself a people for His own possession, *zealous for good deeds*" (Titus 2:14, emphasis added). This is God's purpose from eternity past: "We are His workmanship, created in Christ Jesus for *good works, which God prepared beforehand, that we should walk in them*" (Eph. 2:10, emphasis added).

The first command for every Christian is baptism. I mentioned earlier that the apostles sometimes included baptism in the call to faith (Acts 2:38; cf. Mark 16:16). Baptism is not a condition of salvation but an initial step of obedience for the Christian. Conversion is complete before baptism occurs; baptism is only an external sign that testifies to what has occurred in the sinner's heart. Baptism is a ritual, and

---

[15]J. Dwight Pentecost, "A Christian Perspective," *Kindred Spirit* (Winter 1988): 3.

[16]Ibid. This is a prime example of how lordship salvation is often exaggerated, parodied, and made into a caricature easy to debunk. Unfortunately it confuses and prejudices people while failing to address any real issues.

it is precisely the kind of "work" Paul states cannot be meritorious (cf. Rom. 4:10–11).[17]

Nevertheless, one can hardly read the New Testament without noticing the heavy stress the early church placed on baptism. They simply *assumed* that every genuine believer would embark on a life of obedience and discipleship. That was nonnegotiable. Therefore they viewed baptism as the turning point. Only those who were baptized were considered Christians. That is why the Ethiopian eunuch was so eager to be baptized (Acts 8:36–39).

Unfortunately, the church today takes baptism more casually. It is not unusual to meet people who have been professing Christians for years but have never been baptized. That was unheard of in the New Testament church. Unfortunately, we have lost the focus on initial obedience.

Spurgeon wrote, "If the professed convert distinctly and deliberately declares that he knows the Lord's will, but does not mean to attend to it, you are not to pamper his presumptions, but it is your duty to assure him that he is not saved."[18]

How Shall We Witness to Children?

Should we streamline or abbreviate the message when we teach children the gospel? There is no biblical warrant for that. Certainly we need to use terminology they can grasp and be clear and patient in communicating the message. But when Scripture talks about teaching children spiritual truth, the emphasis is on *thoroughness:* "And these words, which I am commanding you today, shall be on your heart; and you shall teach them diligently to your sons and shall talk of them when you sit in your house and when you walk by the way and when you lie down and when you rise up" (Deut. 6:6–7). Oversimplification is a greater danger, it seems, than giving too much detail.

Children cannot be saved before they are old enough to understand the gospel clearly and can embrace it with genuine faith. They must therefore be mature enough to understand good and evil, sin and punishment, and repentance and faith. Certainly they need to be old

---

[17]If baptism were necessary for salvation, Paul certainly would not have written, "I thank God that I baptized none of you except Crispus and Gaius . . . for Christ did not send me to baptize, but to preach the gospel" (1 Cor. 1:14, 17).

[18]Charles Haddon Spurgeon, *The Soul Winner* (reprint, Grand Rapids, Mich.: Eerdmans, 1963), 38.

enough to understand the gravity of sin and the nature of God's holiness. What is that age? Surely it varies from child to child. Children mature at different times. Part of our task in teaching them is to help them come to a developed understanding of these very issues.

Don't soften the parts of the message that sound unpleasant. Christ's blood, the cross, and atonement for sins are at the heart of the message. If we bypass such topics, we're not giving the full gospel. Don't tone down the demand for surrender. Christ's lordship is not too difficult for children to understand. Any child who is old enough to understand the basic gospel is also able by God's grace to trust Him completely and respond with the purest, most sincere kind of surrender. Jesus "called a child to Himself and set him before them, and said, 'Truly I say to you, unless you are converted and become like children, you shall not enter the kingdom of heaven. Whoever then humbles himself as this child, he is the greatest in the kingdom of heaven'" (Matt. 18:2–4).

Remember that the primary factor in any person's coming to Christ is not *how much doctrine* he or she knows. The real issue is the extent of God's work in the heart. Even the most mature believer does not comprehend all of God's truth. We can only begin to fathom the riches of God's Word in this present life. Full understanding of every aspect of the gospel certainly is not required for salvation. After all, the thief on the cross next to Jesus knew only that he himself was guilty and that Jesus, who was Lord and the true Messiah, had done nothing wrong (Luke 23:40–42). How did he know that much? As Jesus said to Peter, "Flesh and blood did not reveal this . . . but My Father who is in heaven" (Matt. 16:17). The thief's appeal was simple: "Jesus, remember me when You come in Your kingdom!" (v. 42). But despite the meager amount of doctrine he knew, our Lord assured him, "Truly I say to you, today you shall be with Me in Paradise" (v. 43).

It is the Holy Spirit's task, not ours, to offer assurance (Rom. 8:14–16). So don't overemphasize objective assurance with children. As I noted earlier, too many people whose hearts are utterly cold to the things of the Lord believe they are going to heaven simply because they responded positively as children to an evangelistic invitation. Having "asked Jesus to come into their hearts," they were then taught never to examine themselves and never to entertain any doubt about their salvation.

Certainly we cannot assume that every profession of faith reflects a genuine work of God in the heart, and this is particularly true of children. Children often respond positively to gospel invitations for a host of reasons. Many of these reasons are unrelated to any awareness of sin and are apart from any real understanding of spiritual truth. If we prod children to "faith" by external pressure, their "conversion" will prove to be spurious. Only those who understand and are prompted to believe by the Spirit are truly born again (John 3:6).

Remember, an early childhood response does not necessarily guarantee that the question of eternal salvation is settled forever. While many people *do* make a genuine commitment to Christ when young, many others—perhaps most—don't come to an adequate realization of the meaning of the gospel until their teenage years. Others who profess Christ in childhood turn away. That is exactly why we must eschew the quick, easy response and teach our children patiently, consistently, faithfully over all their developing years. Encourage every step of faith as they grow.

We must take extreme care lest we inoculate children against any real commitment to Christ when they do come to an age of full spiritual understanding. Teach children the gospel—all of it—but understand that you may be planting the seeds for a harvest that may not be mature for many years. If you mow a field as soon as it sprouts you will never be able to reap a full harvest.

A Final Word

The first creed of the early church was "Jesus is Lord" (cf. Rom. 10:9–10; 1 Cor. 12:3). The lordship of Christ permeated apostolic preaching, and it permeates the New Testament. In the very first apostolic sermon, Peter's message at Pentecost, this was the pinnacle:

> This Jesus God raised up again, to which we are all witnesses. Therefore having been exalted to the right hand of God, and having received from the Father the promise of the Holy Spirit, He has poured forth this which you both see and hear. For it was not David who ascended into heaven, but he himself says: "The Lord said to my Lord, 'Sit at My right hand, until I make Thine enemies a footstool for Thy feet.'" Therefore let all the house of Israel know for certain that *God has made Him both Lord and Christ*—this Jesus whom you crucified."
>
> Acts 2:32–36, emphasis added

The context leaves no doubt about Peter's meaning. This was a message about Christ's absolute authority as the blessed and only Sovereign, the King of kings and Lord of lords (cf. 1 Tim. 6:15–16).

Throughout the Book of Acts Jesus' absolute lordship is a recurring theme. When Peter opened the gospel ministry to Gentiles at the house of Cornelius, he again declared, "He is Lord of all" (Acts 10:36). In the Book of Acts alone, the title "Lord" is used of Jesus fifty times as often as "Savior." The truth of His lordship was the key to apostolic preaching. Christ's lordship *is* the gospel according to the apostles.

T. Alan Chrisope, in his wonderful book, *Jesus Is Lord*, writes, "There is no element of apostolic preaching more prominent than the resurrection, exaltation and lordship of Jesus."[19] He adds,

> The confession "Jesus is Lord" is the single most predominant Christian confession in the New Testament. Not only does it occur in several passages which emphasize its singular character as *the* Christian confession (e. g., Phil. 2:9–11; Rom. 10:9; 1 Cor. 12:3; 8:5–6; cf. Eph. 4:5), but it also occurs numerous times in a variant form in the phrase "our Lord," a designation of Jesus which was so widely used that it became the distinctive and universally recognized Christian confession, known and acknowledged by all believers.[20]

"All the basic facts of the gospel story are implicit in the single brief confession, 'Jesus is Lord.'"[21]

The apostle Paul said, "We do not preach ourselves but Christ Jesus as Lord" (2 Cor. 4:5). Jesus' lordship *is* the apostolic message.

I closed my earlier book on the gospel with these words, which make a fitting conclusion for this work as well:

> [Jesus] is Lord, and those who refuse Him as Lord cannot use Him as Savior. Everyone who receives Him must surrender to His authority, for to say we receive Christ when in fact we reject His right to reign over us is utter absurdity. It is a futile attempt to hold onto sin with one hand and take Jesus with the other. What kind of salvation is it if we are left in bondage to sin?
>
> This, then is the gospel we are to proclaim: That Jesus Christ, who is God incarnate, humbled Himself to die on our behalf. Thus He became the sinless sacrifice to pay the penalty of our guilt. He rose from the dead to declare with power that He is Lord over all,

---

[19]T. Alan Chrisope, *Jesus Is Lord* (Hertfordshire, England: Evangelical Press, 1982), 57.

[20]Ibid., 61.

[21]Ibid., 63.

and He offers eternal life freely to sinners who will surrender to Him in humble, repentant faith. This gospel promises nothing to the haughty rebel, but for broken, penitent sinners, it graciously offers everything that pertains to life and godliness (2 Peter 1:3).[22]

---

[22]John MacArthur, Jr., *The Gospel According to Jesus* (Grand Rapids, Mich.: Zondervan, 1988), 210.

Appendix 1

A Comparison of Three Views

The chart on the following pages is a side-by-side comparison of positions on the major issues of the lordship controversy. Refer to chapter 2 (pages 23-29) for documentation.

Readers interested in a further analysis of the key issues in the lordship controversy will benefit much from Robert Lescelius's superb book *Lordship Salvation: Some Crucial Questions and Answers* (Asheville, N.C.: Revival Literature, 1992). Another very helpful resource is Richard P. Belcher's *A Layman's Guide to the Lordship Controversy* (Southbridge, Mass.: Crowne Publications, 1990).

	Lordship	No-lordship	Radical No-lordship
The cross	Christ's death on the cross paid the full penalty for our sins and purchased eternal salvation. His atoning sacrifice enables God to justify sinners freely without compromising the perfection of divine righteousness. His resurrection from the dead declares His victory over sin and death.	Agree.	Agree.
Justification by faith	Salvation is by grace through faith in the Lord Jesus Christ alone—plus and minus nothing.	Agree.	Agree.
Good works	Sinners cannot earn salvation or favor with God.	Agree.	Agree.
Prerequisites for salvation	God requires of those who are saved no preparatory works or prerequisite self-improvement.	Agree.	Agree.
Eternal life	Eternal life is a gift of God.	Agree.	Agree.
Immediate justification	Believers are saved and fully justified before their faith ever produces a single righteous work.	Agree.	Agree.
Believers and sin	Christians can and do sin. Even the strongest Christians wage a constant and intense struggle against sin in the flesh. Genuine believers sometimes commit heinous sins.	Agree.	Agree.

	Lordship	No-lordship	Radical No-lordship
Repentance	The gospel calls sinners to faith joined in oneness with repentance. Repentance is turning from sin. It is not a work but a divinely bestowed grace. Repentance is a change of heart, but genuine repentance will effect a change of behavior as well.	Repentance is a change of mind about Christ. In the context of the gospel invitation, *repentance* is just a synonym for *faith*. No turning from sin is required for salvation.	Repentance is not essential to the gospel message. In no sense is repentance related to saving faith.
Faith	Salvation is all God's work. Those who believe are saved utterly apart from any effort on their own. Even faith is a gift of God, not a work of man. Real faith therefore cannot be defective or short-lived but endures forever.	The whole of salvation, including faith, is a gift of God. But faith might not last. A true Christian can completely cease believing.	Faith is a human act, not a gift from God. It occurs in a decisive moment but does not necessarily continue. True faith can be subverted, be overthrown, collapse, or even turn to unbelief.
Faith's object	The object of faith is Christ Himself, not only a creed or a promise. Faith therefore involves personal commitment to Christ. In other words, all true believers follow Jesus.	Saving faith is simply being convinced or giving credence to the truth of the gospel. It is confidence that Christ can remove guilt and give eternal life, not a personal commitment to *Him*.	To "believe" unto salvation is to believe the *facts* of the gospel. "Trusting Jesus" means believing the "saving facts" about Him, and to believe those facts is to appropriate the gift of eternal life. Those who add any suggestion of commitment have departed from the New Testament idea of salvation.
Faith's effects	Real faith inevitably produces a changed life. Salvation includes a transformation of the inner person. The nature of the Christian is different, new. The unbroken pattern of sin and enmity with God will not continue when a person is born again.	*Some* spiritual fruit is inevitable in every Christian's experience. The fruit, however, might not be visible to others. Christians can even lapse into a state of permanent spiritual barrenness.	Spiritual fruit is not guaranteed in the Christian life. Some Christians spend their lives in a barren wasteland of defeat, confusion, and every kind of evil.

	Lordship	No-lordship	Radical No-lordship
Salvation's extent	The "gift of God," eternal life, includes all that pertains to life and godliness, not just a ticket to heaven.	Only the *judicial* aspects of salvation—such as justification, adoption, imputed righteousness, and positional sanctification—are guaranteed for believers in this life. *Practical* sanctification and growth in grace require a postconversion act of dedication.	Heaven is guaranteed to believers but Christian victory is not. One could even say "the saved" still need salvation. Christ offers a whole range of postconversion deliverance experiences to supply what Christians lack. But these other "salvations" all require the addition of human works, such as obedience, submission, and confession of Jesus as Lord. Thus God is dependent to some degree on human effort in achieving deliverance from sin in this life.
Christ's lordship	Jesus is Lord of all, and the faith He demands involves unconditional surrender. He does not bestow eternal life on those whose hearts remain set against Him.	Submission to Christ's supreme authority as Lord is not germane to the saving transaction. Neither dedication nor *willingness* to be dedicated to Christ are issues in salvation. The news that Christ died for our sins and rose from the dead is the *complete* gospel. Nothing else must be believed for salvation.	Submission is not in any sense a condition for eternal life. "Calling on the Lord" means *appealing* to Him, not *submitting* to Him.
Holy desires	Those who truly believe will love Christ. They will therefore long to obey Him.	Christians may fall into a state of lifelong carnality. A whole category of "carnal Christians"—born-again people who continuously live like the unsaved—exists in the church.	Nothing guarantees that a true Christian will love God. Salvation does not necessarily even place the sinner in a right relationship of harmonious fellowship with God.

	Lordship	No-lordship	Radical No-lordship
Assurance	Behavior is an important test of faith. Obedience is evidence that one's faith is real. On the other hand, the person who remains utterly unwilling to obey Christ does not evidence true faith.	Disobedience and prolonged sin are no reason to doubt the reality of one's faith.	If people are sure they believe, their faith *must* be genuine. *All* who claim Christ by faith as Savior—even those involved in serious or prolonged sin—should be assured that they belong to God come what may. It is dangerous and destructive to question the salvation of professing Christians. The New Testament writers *never* questioned the reality of their readers' faith.
Perseverance	Genuine believers may stumble and fall, but they *will* persevere in the faith. Those who later turn completely away from the Lord show that they were never truly born again.	A believer may utterly forsake Christ and come to the point of not believing. God has guaranteed that He will not disown those who thus abandon the faith. Those who have once believed are secure forever, even if they turn away.	It is possible to experience a moment of faith that guarantees heaven for eternity, then to turn away permanently and live a life that is utterly barren of any spiritual fruit. Genuine believers might even cease to name the name of Christ or confess Christianity.

Appendix 2

What Is Dispensationalism and What Does It Have to Do with Lordship Salvation?

One of the most confusing elements of the entire lordship controversy involves dispensationalism. Some have supposed that my attack on no-lordship theology is an all-out assault against dispensationalism. That is not the case. It may surprise some readers to know that the issue of dispensationalism is one area where Charles Ryrie, Zane Hodges, and I share some common ground. We are all dispensationalists.

Many people are understandably confused by the term *dispensationalism*. I've met seminary graduates and many in Christian leadership who haven't the slightest idea how to define dispensationalism. How does it differ from covenant theology? What does it have to do with lordship salvation? Perhaps we can answer those questions simply and without a lot of theological jargon.

Dispensationalism is a system of biblical interpretation that sees a distinction between God's program for Israel and His dealings with the church. It's really as simple as that.

A *dispensation* is the plan of God by which He administers His rule within a given era in His eternal program. Dispensations are not periods of *time*, but different *administrations* in the eternal outworking of God's purpose. It is especially crucial to note that the way of salvation—by grace through faith—is the same in every dispensation. God's redemptive plan remains unchanged, but the way He administers it will vary from one dispensation to another. Dispensationalists note that Israel was the focus of God's redemptive plan in one dispensation. The church, consisting of redeemed people including Jews and Gentiles, is the focus in another. All dispensationalists believe at least one dispensation is still future—during the thousand-year reign of Christ on earth, known as the millennium, in which Israel will once again play a pivotal role.

Dispensationalism teaches that all God's remaining covenant promises to Israel will be literally fulfilled—including the promises of earthly blessings and an earthly messianic kingdom. God promised Israel, for example, that they would possess the promised land forever (Gen. 13:14–17; Exod. 32:13). Scripture declares that Messiah will rule over the kingdoms of the earth from Jerusalem (Zech. 14:9–11). Old Testament prophecy says that all Israel will one day be restored to the promised land (Amos 9:14–15); the temple will be rebuilt (Ezek. 37:26–28); and the people of Israel will be redeemed (Jer. 23:6; Rom. 11:26–27). Dispensationalists believe all those promised blessings will come to pass as literally as did the promised curses.

Covenant theology, on the other hand, usually views such prophecies as *already* fulfilled allegorically or symbolically. Covenant theologians believe that the church, not literal Israel, is the recipient of the covenant promises. They believe the church has superseded Israel in God's eternal program. God's promises to Israel are therefore fulfilled in spiritual blessings realized by Christians.[1] Since their system does not allow for literal fulfillment of promised blessings to the Jewish nation, covenant theologians allegorize or spiritualize those prophetic passages of God's Word.

I am a dispensationalist because dispensationalism generally understands and applies Scripture—particularly prophetic Scripture—in a way that is more consistent with the normal, literal approach I believe is God's design for interpreting Scripture.[2] For example, dispensationalists can take at face value Zechariah 12–14, Romans 11:25–29, and Revelation 20:1–6. The covenant theologian, on the other hand, cannot.

So I am convinced that the dispensationalist distinction between the church and Israel is an accurate understanding of God's eternal plan

---

[1]Here is the main inconsistency I see in the covenant approach: We all acknowledge that the promises of *judgment* on Israel were fulfilled literally. But covenant theology makes the church the recipient of the promised *blessings,* which then must be spiritualized to apply to the church. It seems to me that consistency would require that if the promises of judgment were fulfilled literally, the blessings should have a literal fulfillment as well.

[2]See the chapter "How Should We Interpret the Bible?" in my book *Charismatic Chaos* (Grand Rapids, Mich.: Zondervan, 1992), 85–105.

as revealed in Scripture. I have not abandoned dispensationalism, nor do I intend to.

Note, by the way, that Dr. Ryrie's description of dispensationalism and his reasons for embracing the system are very similar to what I have written here. Some years ago he wrote, "The essence of dispensationalism, then, is the distinction between Israel and the church. This grows out of the dispensationalist's consistent employment of normal or plain interpretation."[3] On these matters, it seems, Dr. Ryrie and I are in fundamental agreement. It is in the practical outworking of our dispensationalism that we differ. Dr. Ryrie's system turns out to be somewhat more complex than his own definition might suggest.

The lordship debate has had a devastating effect on dispensationalism. Because no-lordship theology is so closely associated with dispensationalism, many have imagined a cause-and-effect relationship between the two. In *The Gospel According to Jesus,* I made the point that some early dispensationalists had laid the foundation for no-lordship teaching. I disagreed with dispensational extremists who relegate whole sections of Scripture—including the Sermon on the Mount and the Lord's Prayer—to a yet-future kingdom era. I was critical of the way some dispensationalists have handled the preaching and teaching of Jesus in a way that erases the evangelistic intent from some of His most important invitations. I decried the methodology of dispensationalists who want to isolate salvation from repentance, justification from sanctification, faith from works, and Christ's lordship from His role as Savior, in a way that breaks asunder what God has joined together.

Several outspoken anti-dispensationalists hailed the book as a major blow to dispensationalism. They wanted to declare the system dead and hold a celebratory funeral.

Frankly, some mongrel species of dispensationalism ought to die, and I will be happy to join the cortege. But it is wrong to write off dispensationalism as altogether invalid. My purpose is not to attack the roots of dispensationalism, but rather to plead for a purer, more biblical application of the literal, historical, grammatical principle of interpretation. The hermeneutic method that underlies dispensationalism is fundamentally sound and must not be abandoned. That is *not* the point of the lordship debate.

Who are dispensationalists? Virtually all dispensationalists are theologically conservative evangelicals. Our view of Scripture is typically very high; our method of interpretation is consistently literal; and our zeal for

---

[3]Charles C. Ryrie, *Dispensationalism Today* (Chicago: Moody, 1965), 47.

spiritual things is inflamed by our conviction that we are living in the last days.

How does dispensationalism influence our overall theological perspective? Obviously, the central issue in any dispensationalist system is *eschatology*, or the study of prophecy. All dispensationalists are *premillennialists*. That is, they believe in a future earthly thousand-year reign of Christ. That's what a literal approach to prophecy mandates (cf. Rev. 20:1–10). Dispensationalists may disagree on the timing of the rapture, the number of dispensations, or other details, but their position on the earthly millennial kingdom is settled by their mode of biblical interpretation.

Dispensationalism also carries implications for *ecclesiology*, or the doctrine of the church, because of the differentiation between the church and Israel. Many dispensationalists, myself included, agree that there is some continuity between the Old and New Testament people of God in that we share a common salvation purchased by Jesus Christ and appropriated by grace through faith. But dispensationalists do not accept covenant theology's teaching that the church is spiritual Israel. Covenant theology sees continuity between Jewish ritual and the New Testament sacraments, for example. In their system, baptism and circumcision have similar significance. In fact, many covenant theologians use the analogy of circumcision to argue for infant baptism. Dispensationalists, on the other hand, tend to view baptism as a sacrament for believers only, distinct from the Jewish rite.

So dispensationalism shapes one's *eschatology* and *ecclesiology*. That is the extent of it. Pure dispensationalism has no ramifications for the doctrines of God, man, sin, or sanctification. More significantly, true dispensationalism makes no relevant contribution to *soteriology*, or the doctrine of salvation. In other words, nothing in a legitimate dispensational approach to Scripture mandates that we define the gospel in any unique or different way. In fact, if the same zealous concern for literal hermeneutics that yields a distinction between Israel and the church were followed consistently in the salvation issue, there would be no such thing as no-lordship soteriology.

What Is the Connection Between Dispensationalism and No-lordship Doctrine?

Yet the fact remains that virtually all the champions of no-lordship doctrine are dispensationalists. No covenant theologian defends the no-lordship gospel. Why?

Understand, first of all, that dispensationalism has not always been well represented by its most enthusiastic advocates. As I have noted, the uniqueness of dispensationalism is that we see a distinction in Scripture between Israel and the church. That singular perspective, common to all dispensationalists, sets us apart from nondispensationalists. It is, by the way, the only element of traditional dispensationalist teaching that is yielded as a result of literal interpretation of biblical texts. It also is the only tenet virtually all dispensationalists hold in common. That is why I have singled it out as the characteristic that defines dispensationalism. When I speak of "pure" dispensationalism, I'm referring to this one common denominator—the Israel-church distinction.

Admittedly, however, most dispensationalists carry far more baggage in their systems than that one feature. Early dispensationalists often packaged their doctrine in complex and esoteric systems illustrated by intricate diagrams. They loaded their repertoire with extraneous ideas and novel teachings, some of which endure today in various strains of dispensationalism. Dispensationalism's earliest influential spokesmen included J. N. Darby, founder of the Plymouth Brethren and considered by many the father of modern dispensationalism; Cyrus I. Scofield, author of the *Scofield Reference Bible;* Clarence Larkin, whose book of dispensational charts has been in print and selling briskly since 1918; and Ethelbert W. Bullinger, an Anglican clergyman who took dispensationalism to an unprecedented extreme usually called *ultradispensationalism.*[4] Many of these men were self-taught in theology and were professionals in secular occupations. Darby and Scofield, for example, were attorneys, and Larkin was a mechanical draftsman. They were laymen whose teachings gained enormous popularity largely through grass-roots enthusiasm.

Unfortunately some of these early framers of dispensationalism were not as precise or discriminating as they might have been had they had the benefit of a more complete theological education. C. I. Scofield, for example, included a note in his reference Bible that contrasted "legal obedience as the condition of [Old Testament] salvation" with "acceptance . . . of Christ" as the condition of salvation in the current dispensation.[5] Nondispensationalist critics have often attacked dispensationalism for teaching that the conditions for salvation differ from dispensation to dispensation. Here, at least, Scofield left himself open to

---

[4]Ultradispensationalism is disowned by most dispensationalists (cf. ibid., 192–205).

[5]*The Scofield Reference Bible* (New York: Oxford, 1917), 1115.

that criticism, though he seemed to acknowledge in other contexts that the law was never a means of salvation for Old Testament saints.[6] The maturing of dispensationalism, then, has mainly been a process of refining, distilling, clarifying, paring down, and cutting away what is extraneous or erroneous. Later dispensationalists, including Donald Grey Barnhouse, Wilbur Smith, Allan MacRae, and H. A. Ironside, were increasingly wary of the fallacies that peppered much early dispensationalist teaching. Ironside's written works show his determination to confront error within the movement. He attacked Bullinger's ultradispensationalism.[7] He criticized teaching that relegated repentance to some other era.[8] He condemned the "carnal Christian" theology that helped pave the way for today's radical no-lordship teaching.[9] Ironside's writings are replete with warnings against antinomianism.[10]

Nondispensationalists have tended to caricature dispensationalism by emphasizing its excesses, and frankly the movement has produced more than its share of abominable teaching. Dispensationalists have often been forced to acknowledge that some of their critics' points have been valid.[11] The biblical distinction between Israel and the church remains unassailed, however, as the essence of pure dispensationalism.

In recent years, dispensationalism has been hit with a blistering onslaught of criticism, mostly focusing on dispensationalism's love affair with the no-lordship gospel. Evidence of this may be seen in John Gerstner's *Wrongly Dividing the Word of Truth: A Critique of Dispensationalism*.[12] Gerstner rightly attacks elements of antinomianism and

---

[6]In a note at Exodus 19:3, where Moses was being given the law, Scofield wrote, "The law is not proposed as a means of life, but as a means by which Israel might become 'a peculiar treasure' and a 'kingdom of priests'" (ibid., 93).

[7] *Wrongly Dividing the Word of Truth* (New York: Loizeaux, n.d.)

[8] *Except Ye Repent* (Grand Rapids, Mich.: Zondervan, 1937).

[9] *Eternal Security of Believers* (New York: Loizeaux, 1934).

[10]See, for example, *Full Assurance* (Chicago: Moody, 1937), 64, 77–87; also *Holiness: The False and the True* (Neptune, N.J.: Loizeaux, 1912), 121–26.

[11]Ryrie, for example, conceded in *Dispensationalism Today* that Scofield had made "unguarded statements" about dispensationalist soteriology and that dispensationalists often give a wrong impression about the role of grace during the Old Testament era (112, 117).

[12]Brentwood, Tenn.: Wolgemuth & Hyatt, 1991. Cf. Richard L. Mayhue, "Who Is Wrong? A Review of John Gerstner's *Wrongly Dividing the Word of Truth*," *Master's Seminary Journal* 3:1 (Spring 1992): 73–94.

no-lordship soteriology in some dispensationalists' teaching. He wrongly assumes, however, that those things are inherent in all dispensationalism. He dismisses the movement altogether because of the shoddy theology he finds in the teaching of several prominent dispensationalists.

It is a gross misunderstanding to assume that antinomianism is at the heart of dispensationalist doctrine. Moreover, it is unfair to portray all dispensationalists as unsophisticated or careless theologians. Many skilled and discerning students of Scripture have embraced dispensationalism and managed to avoid antinomianism, extremism, and other errors. The men who taught me in seminary were all dispensationalists. Yet none of them would have defended no-lordship teaching.[13]

Nevertheless, no one can deny that dispensationalism and antinomianism have often been advocated by the same people. All the recent arguments that have been put forth in defense of no-lordship theology are rooted in ideas made popular by dispensationalists. The leading proponents of contemporary no-lordship theology are all dispensationalists. The lordship controversy is merely a bubbling to the surface of tensions that have always existed in and around the dispensationalist community. That point is essential to a clear understanding of the whole controversy.

Thus to appreciate some of the key tenets of the no-lordship gospel, we must comprehend their relationship to the dispensationalist tradition.

Tritely Dividing the Word?

For some dispensationalists, the Israel-church distinction is only a starting point. Their theology is laden with similar contrasts: church and kingdom, believers and disciples, old and new natures, faith and repentance. Obviously, there are many important and legitimate distinctions found in Scripture and sound theology: Old and New Covenants, law and grace, faith and works, justification and sanctification. But dispensationalists often tend to take even the legitimate contrasts too far. Most dispensationalists who have bought into no-lordship doctrine imagine, for example, that law and grace are mutually exclusive opposites, or that faith and works are somehow incompatible.

---

[13]Moreover, everyone on The Master's Seminary faculty is a dispensationalist. None of us holds any of the antinomian views Dr. Gerstner claims are common to all dispensationalists.

Some dispensationalists apply 2 Timothy 2:15 ("Study to show thyself approved unto God, a workman that needeth not to be ashamed, *rightly dividing the word of truth*"—KJV, emphasis added) as if the key word were *dividing* rather than *rightly*. The dispensationalist tendency to divide and contrast has led to some rather inventive exegesis. Some dispensationalists teach, for example, that "the kingdom of heaven" and "the kingdom of God" speak of different domains.[14] The terms are clearly synonymous in Scripture, however, as a comparison of Matthew and Luke shows (Matt. 5:3 // Luke 6:20; Matt. 10:7 // Luke 10:9; Matt. 11:11 // Luke 7:28; Matt. 11:12 // Luke 16:16; Matt. 13:11 // Luke 8:10; Matt. 13:31–33 // Luke 13:18–21; Matt. 18:4 // Luke 18:17; Matt. 19:23 // Luke 18:24). Matthew is the only book in the entire Bible that ever uses the expression "kingdom of heaven." Matthew, writing to a mostly Jewish audience, understood their sensitivity to the use of God's name. He simply employed the common euphemism *heaven*. Thus the kingdom of heaven *is* the kingdom of God.

This tendency to set parallel truths against each other is at the heart of no-lordship theology. Jesus' lordship and His role as Savior are isolated from one another, making it possible to claim Him as Savior while refusing Him as Lord. Justification is severed from sanctification, legitimizing the notion of salvation without transformation. Mere believers are segregated from disciples, making two classes of Christians, carnal and spiritual. Faith is pitted against obedience, nullifying the moral aspect of believing. Grace becomes the antithesis of law, providing the basis for a system that is inherently antinomian.

The grace-law dichotomy is worth a closer look. Many early dispensationalist systems were unclear on the role of grace in the Mosaic economy and the place of law in the current dispensation. As I noted, Scofield left the unfortunate impression that Old Testament saints were saved by keeping the law. Scofield's best-known student was Lewis Sperry Chafer, co-founder of Dallas Theological Seminary. Chafer, a prolific author, wrote dispensationalism's first unabridged systematic theology. Chafer's system became the standard for several generations of dispensationalists trained at Dallas. Yet Chafer repeated Scofield's error. In his summary on *justification,* he wrote,

> According to the Old Testament men were just because they were true and faithful in keeping the Mosaic Law. Micah defines such a life after this manner: "He hath shewed thee, O man, what is good;

---

[14]Scofield, *The Scofield Reference Bible,* 1003.

and what doth the LORD require of thee, but to do justly, and to love mercy, and to walk humbly with thy God?" (6:8). *Men were therefore just because of their own works for God, whereas New Testament justification is God's work for man in answer to faith* (Rom. 5:1).[15]

Though Chafer elsewhere denied that he taught multiple ways of salvation, it is clear that he fixed a great gulf between grace and law. He believed the Old Testament law imposed "an obligation to gain merit" with God.[16] On the other hand, Chafer believed grace delivers the child of God "from every aspect of the law—as a rule of life, as an obligation to make himself acceptable to God, and as a dependence on impotent flesh."[17] "Grace teachings are not *laws;* they are *suggestions.* They are not *demands;* they are *beseechings,*" he wrote.[18]

In Chafer's system, God seems to fluctuate between dispensations of law and dispensations of grace. Grace was the rule of life from Adam to Moses. "Pure law" took over when a new dispensation began at Sinai. In the current dispensation, "pure grace" is the rule. The millennial kingdom will be another dispensation of "pure law." Chafer evidently believed grace and law could not coexist side by side, and so he seemed to eliminate one or the other from every dispensation. He wrote,

> Both the age before the cross and the age following the return of Christ represent the exercise of pure law; while the period between the two ages represents the exercise of pure grace. *It is imperative, therefore, that there shall be no careless co-mingling of these great age-characterizing elements,* else the preservation of the most important distinctions in the various relationships between God and man are lost, and the recognition of the true force of the death of Christ and His coming again is obscured.[19]

No one denies that Scripture clearly contrasts law and grace. John 1:17 says, "The Law was given through Moses; grace and truth were realized through Jesus Christ." Romans 6:4 says, "You are not under

---

[15]Lewis Sperry Chafer, *Systematic Theology,* 8 vols. (Dallas: Seminary Press, 1948), 7:219 (emphasis added).

[16]Ibid., 7:179.

[17]Lewis Sperry Chafer, *Grace* (Wheaton, Ill.: Van Kampen, 1922), 344.

[18]Ibid.

[19]Ibid., 124 (emphasis added).

law, but under grace." So the distinction between law and grace is obvious in Scripture.

But grace *and* law operate in every dispensation. Grace is and always has been the only means of eternal salvation. The whole point of Romans 4 is that Abraham, David, and all other Old Testament saints were justified by grace through faith, not because they kept the law.[20] Did the apostle Paul believe we can nullify the law in this age of pure grace? Paul's reply to that question was unequivocal: "May it never be! On the contrary, we establish the Law" (Rom. 3:31).

In fairness, it is important to note that when pressed on the issue, Chafer acknowledged that God's grace and Christ's blood were the only ground on which sinners in any age could be saved.[21] It must be stressed, however, that Chafer, Scofield, and others who have followed their lead have made too much of the differences between Old and New Testament dispensations. Wanting to avoid what he thought was "careless comingling" of law and grace, Chafer ended up with an "age of law" that is legalistic and an "age of grace" that smacks of antinomianism.

Chafer himself was a godly man, committed to holiness and high standards of Christian living. In practice, he would never have condoned carnality. But his dispensationalist system—with the hard dichotomies it introduced; its "grace teachings" that were "suggestions," not demands; and its concept of "pure" grace that stood in opposition to law of any kind—paved the way for a brand of Christianity that has legitimized careless and carnal behavior.

Chafer could rightly be called the father of twentieth-century no-lordship theology. He listed repentance and surrender as two of "the more common features of human responsibility which are too often erroneously added to the one requirement of *faith* or *belief*."[22] He wrote, "to impose a need to surrender the life to God as an added condition of salvation is most unreasonable. God's call to the unsaved is never said to be unto the Lordship of Christ; it is unto His saving grace."[23] "Next to

---

[20]Galatians 3 also makes clear that it was never God's intent that righteousness should come through the law or that salvation could be earned through obedience (see especially vv. 7, 11). The law acted as a tutor, to bring people to Christ (v. 24). Thus even in the Old Testament, people were saved because of faith, not because of obedience to the law (cf. Romans 3:19–20).

[21]Lewis Sperry Chafer, "Dispensational Distinctions Denounced," *Bibliotheca Sacra* (July 1944): 259.

[22]Chafer, *Systematic Theology*, 3:372.

[23]Ibid., 3:385.

sound doctrine itself, no more important obligation rests on the preacher than that of preaching the Lordship of Christ to Christians exclusively, and the Saviorhood of Christ to those who are unsaved."[24]

It is important to note that when Chafer wrote those things, he was arguing against the Oxford Movement, a popular but dangerous heresy that was steering Protestants back into the legalism and works-righteousness of Roman Catholicism. Chafer wrote,

> The error of imposing Christ's Lordship upon the unsaved is disastrous. . . . A destructive heresy is abroad under the name The Oxford Movement, which specializes in this blasting error, except that the promoters of the Movement omit altogether the idea of believing on Christ for salvation and promote exclusively the obligation to surrender to God. They substitute consecration for conversion, faithfulness for faith, and beauty of daily life for believing unto eternal life. As is easily seen, the plan of this movement is to ignore the need of Christ's death as the ground of regeneration and forgiveness, and to promote the wretched heresy that it matters nothing what one believes respecting the Saviorhood of Christ if only the daily life is dedicated to God's service. . . . The tragedy is that out of such a delusion those who embrace it are likely never to be delivered by a true faith in Christ as Savior. No more complete example could be found today of "the blind leading the blind" than what this Movement presents.[25]

But Chafer prescribed the wrong remedy for the false teachings of the Oxford Movement. To answer a movement that "omit[s] altogether the idea of believing on Christ for salvation and promote[s] exclusively the obligation to surrender to God," he devised a notion of faith that strips believing of any suggestion of surrender. Although the movement he opposed was indeed an insidious error, Chafer unfortunately laid the foundation for the opposite error, with equally devastating results.

The notion of faith with no repentance and no surrender fit well with Chafer's concept of an age of "pure grace," so it was absorbed and expanded by those who developed their theology after his model. It endures today as the basis of all no-lordship teaching.

One other particularly unfortunate outgrowth of Chafer's rigid partitioning of "the age of law" and "the age of grace" is its effect on Chafer's view of Scripture. Chafer believed that "The teachings of the

---

[24]Ibid., 3:387.

[25]Ibid., 3:385–86.

law, the teachings of grace, and the teachings of the kingdom are separate and complete systems of divine rule."[26] Accordingly, he consigned the Sermon on the Mount and the Lord's Prayer to the yet-future kingdom age, and concluded that the only Scriptures directly applicable to this age of grace are "portions of the Gospels, portions of the Book of Acts, and the Epistles of the New Testament"[27]—the "grace teachings." How does one know *which* portions of the Gospels and Acts are "grace teachings" meant for this age? Chafer was vague:

> The grace teachings are not, for convenience, isolated in the Sacred Text. The three economies appear in the four Gospels. The grace teachings are rather to be identified by their intrinsic character wherever they are found. Large portions of the New Testament are wholly revelatory of the doctrine of grace. The student, like Timothy, is enjoined to study to be one approved of God in the matter of rightly dividing the Scriptures.[28]

In other words, there is a lot of law and kingdom teaching mixed into the New Testament. It is not explicitly identified for us, but we can fall into error if we wrongly try to apply it to the present age. Scripture is therefore like a puzzle. We must discern and categorize which portions apply to this age and categorize them accordingly. We can do this only by "their intrinsic character."

Chafer was certain about one thing: much if not most of Christ's earthly teaching is *not* applicable to the Christian in this age:

> There is a dangerous and entirely baseless sentiment abroad which assumes that every teaching of Christ must be binding during this age simply because Christ said it. The fact is forgotten that Christ, while living under, keeping, and applying the Law of Moses, also taught the principles of His future kingdom, and, at the end of His ministry and in relation to His cross, He also anticipated the teachings of grace. If this threefold division of the teachings of Christ is not recognized, there can be nothing but confusion of mind and consequent contradiction of truth.[29]

---

[26]Ibid., 4:225.

[27]Ibid., 4:206.

[28]Ibid., 4:185.

[29]Ibid., 4:224.

Dispensationalists who follow Chafer at this point *wrongly* divide the Word of truth, assigning whole sections of the New Testament to some other dispensation, nullifying the force of major segments of the Gospels and our Lord's teaching for today.[30]

Which Gospel Should We Preach Today?

Not long ago I received a paper that has been circulated widely by a well-known dispensationalist. He wrote, "Dr. MacArthur was quite correct in titling his book *The Gospel According to Jesus.* The Gospel that Jesus taught in His pre-Cross humiliation, as Israel's Messiah and to covenant people under the law was, for all intents and purposes, Lordship salvation." But, he added, "Lordship salvation is based upon the Gospel according to Jesus, John the Baptist, and the early disciples. This Gospel is directed to the covenant nation of Israel. . . . The Lord Jesus' Kingdom Gospel had nothing whatsoever to do with Christians, or the Church."

The paper quotes heavily from Dr. Chafer's writings, attempting to demonstrate that Jesus' gospel "was on the level of the law and the earthly kingdom" and has nothing to do with grace or the current dispensation. The paper's author notes that I wrote, "On a disturbing number of fronts, the message being proclaimed today is not the gospel according to Jesus." To that he replies, "How blessedly true! Today we are to minister Paul's 'by grace are ye saved through faith' Gospel . . . not the Lord Jesus' Gospel relating to the law-oriented theocratic kingdom."

He continues, "The convert via the Gospel according to Jesus became a child of the kingdom [not a Christian]. And divine authority will ever be the driving force in his heart—the indwelling Spirit writing the law upon his heart to enable him to surrender to the theocratic kingdom law, under his King. . . . [But the Christian] is not under authority, he is not seeking to obey—unless he is under law as described in Romans Seven. For him to live is Christ, and that life is not under authority. . . . Paul was offering an altogether different salvation."

---

[30]Ultradispensationalists take Chafer's methodology even a step further. Noting that the apostle Paul called the church a mystery "which in other generations was not made known to the sons of men, as it has now been revealed to His holy apostles and prophets in the Spirit" (Eph. 3:5), they conclude that the church age did not begin until this point in Paul's ministry. Thus they abrogate all the New Testament except for Paul's prison epistles.

There, as clearly as can be stated, are all the follies that have ever defiled dispensationalism, synthesized into a single system. Blatant antinomianism: "the Christian . . . is not under authority, he is not seeking to obey"; multiple ways of salvation: "Paul was offering an altogether different salvation"; a fragmented approach to Scripture: "the Lord Jesus' Kingdom Gospel had nothing whatsoever to do with Christians, or the Church"; and the tendency to divide and disconnect related ideas: "Today we are to minister Paul's [Gospel] . . . not the Lord Jesus' Gospel."

Note carefully: This man acknowledges that Jesus' gospel demanded surrender to His lordship. His point is that Jesus' message has no relevance to this present age. He believes Christians today ought to proclaim a different gospel than the one Jesus preached. He imagines that Jesus' invitation to sinners was of a different nature than the message the church is called to proclaim. He believes we should be preaching a different gospel.

None of those ideas is new or unusual within the dispensationalist community. All of them can be traced to one or more of dispensationalism's early spokesmen. But it is about time all of them were abandoned.

In fairness, we should note that the paper I have quoted expresses some rather extreme views. Most of the principal defenders of no-lordship evangelism would probably not agree with that man's brand of dispensationalism. But the no-lordship doctrine they defend is the product of precisely that kind of teaching. It is not enough to abandon the rigid forms of extreme dispensationalism; we must abandon the antinomian tendencies as well.

The careful discipline that has marked so much of our post-Reformation theological tradition must be carefully guarded. Defenders of no-lordship salvation lean too heavily on the assumptions of a predetermined theological system. They often draw their support from presupposed dispensationalist distinctions (salvation/discipleship, carnal/spiritual believers, gospel of the kingdom/gospel of grace, faith/repentance). They become entangled in "what-ifs" and illustrations. They tend to fall back on rational, rather than biblical, analysis. When they deal with Scripture, they are too willing to allow their theological system to dictate their understanding of the text. As a result, they regularly adopt novel interpretations of Scripture in order to make it conform to their theology.

A reminder is in order: Our theology must be biblical before it can be systematic. We must start with a proper interpretation of Scripture and build our theology from there, not read into God's Word unwarranted presuppositions. Scripture is the only appropriate gauge by which we may ultimately measure the correctness of our doctrine.

Dispensationalism is at a crossroads. The lordship controversy represents a signpost where the road forks. One arrow marks the road of biblical orthodoxy. The other arrow, labeled "no-lordship," points the way to a sub-Christian antinomianism. Dispensationalists who are considering that path would do well to pause and check the map again.

The only reliable map is Scripture, not someone's dispensational diagrams. Dispensationalism as a movement must arrive at a consensus based solely on God's Word. We cannot go on preaching different gospels to an already-confused world.

Appendix 3

Voices from the Past

Zane Hodges claims lordship salvation is propelling the church backward into the dark ages. He makes this allegation:

> It may even be said that lordship salvation throws a veil of obscurity over the entire New Testament revelation. In the process, the marvelous truth of justification by faith, apart from works, recedes into shadows not unlike those which darkened the days before the Reformation. What replaces this doctrine is a kind of faith/works synthesis which differs only insignificantly from official Roman Catholic dogma (*AF* 19–20).

Elsewhere Hodges writes, "Let it be said clearly: *lordship salvation holds a doctrine of saving faith that is in conflict with that of Luther and Calvin and, most importantly, in conflict with God's Word*" (*AF* 209, emphasis in original).

No-lordship teachers often claim that they are the true heirs of the Reformation. Many have echoed the tired charge that lordship salvation "is paving the road back to Rome." They selectively quote from the great Reformers on the issues of faith and assurance, then make the preposterous suggestion that no-lordship theology is "comfortably aligned with both Calvin and Luther and many of their successors."[1]

---

[1]Thomas G. Llewellen, "Has Lordship Salvation Been Taught throughout Church History? *Bibliotheca Sacra* (January-March 1990): 59.

It is extremely difficult to understand how anyone at all familiar with the literature of the Reformation could ever make such a claim. The writings of Luther and Calvin are filled with material that argues explicitly against many of the same errors no-lordship theology has embraced. Nowhere in their writings do we find any support for the idea that someone who is justified can remain unsanctified. That is a topic about which the Reformers had much to say.

Why not let them speak for themselves?

Luther on Justification by Faith

Martin Luther's discovery of the biblical truth about justification by faith launched the Reformation. Note how Luther contends against the notion that true faith might coexist with an unbroken pattern of unholy living:

> True faith, of which we speak, cannot be manufactured by our own thoughts, for it is solely a work of God in us, without any assistance on our part. As Paul says to the Romans, it is God's gift and grace, obtained by one man, Christ. *Therefore, faith is something very powerful, active, restless, effective, which at once renews a person and again regenerates him, and leads him altogether into a new manner and character of life, so that it is impossible not to do good without ceasing.*
>
> For just as natural as it is for the tree to produce fruit, so natural is it for faith to produce good works. And just as it is quite unnecessary to command the tree to bear fruit, so there is no command given to the believer, as Paul says [1 Thess. 4:9], nor is urging necessary for him to do good, for he does it of himself, freely and unconstrained; just as he of himself without command sleeps, eats, drinks, puts on his clothes, hears, speaks, goes and comes.
>
> Whoever has not this faith talks but vainly about faith and works, and does not himself know what he says or whither it tends. He has not received it. He juggles with lies and applies the Scriptures where they speak of faith and works to his own dreams and false thoughts, which is purely a human work, whereas the Scriptures attribute both faith and good works not to ourselves, but to God alone.
>
> Is not this a perverted and blind people? They teach we cannot do a good deed of ourselves, and then in their presumption go to work and arrogate to themselves the highest of all the works of God, namely faith, to manufacture it themselves out of their own perverted thoughts. Wherefore I have said that we should despair of ourselves and pray to God for faith as the apostles did in Luke

17:5. When we have faith, we need nothing more; for it brings with it the Holy Spirit, who then teaches us not only all things, but also establishes us firmly in it, and leads us through death and hell to heaven.

Now observe, we have given these answers, that the Scriptures have such passages concerning works, on account of such dreamers and self-invented faith; *not that man should become good by works, but that man should thereby prove and see the difference between false and true faith. For wherever faith is right it does good. If it does no good, it is then certainly a dream and a false idea of faith.* So, just as the fruit on the tree does not make the tree good, but nevertheless outwardly proves and testifies that the tree is good, as Christ says, "By their fruits ye shall know them." Thus we should also learn to know faith by its fruits.

From this you see, there is a great difference between being good, and to be known as good; or to become good and to prove and show that you are good. *Faith makes good, but works prove the faith and goodness to be right.* Thus the Scriptures speak plainly, which prevails among the common people, as when a father says unto his son, "Go and be merciful, good and friendly to this or to that poor person." He does not command him to be merciful, good and friendly, but because he is already good and merciful, he requires that he should also show and prove it outwardly toward the poor by his act, in order that the goodness which he has in himself may also be known to others and be helpful to them.

You should explain all passages of Scripture referring to works, that God thereby desires to let the goodness received in faith express and prove itself, and become a benefit to others, so that false faith may become known and rooted out of the heart. *God gives no one His grace that it may remain inactive and accomplish nothing good, but in order that it may bear interest, and by being publicly known and proved externally, draw every one to God,* as Christ says: "Let your light so shine before men, that they may see your good works, and glorify your Father which is in heaven" (Matthew 5:16). Otherwise it would be but a buried treasure and a hidden light. But what profit is there in either? Yea, goodness does not only thereby become known to others, but we ourselves also become certain that we are honest, as Peter says: "Wherefore, brethren, give the more diligence to make your calling and election sure" (2 Peter 1:10). *Where works do not follow, a man cannot know whether his faith is right; yea, he may be certain that his faith is a dream, and not right as it should be.* Thus Abraham became certain of his faith, and that he feared God, when he offered up his son. As God by the angel said to Abraham: "Now I know, that is, it is manifest, that thou fearest

God, seeing thou hast not withheld thy son, thine only son, from me" (Genesis 22:12).

Then abide by the truth, that man is internally, in spirit before God, justified by faith alone without works, but externally and publicly before men and himself, he is justified by works, that he is at heart an honest believer and pious. The one you may call a public or outward justification, the other an inner justification, yet in the sense that the public or external justification is only the fruit, the result and proof of the justification in the heart, that a man does not become just thereby before God, but must previously be just before Him. So you may call the fruit of the tree the public or outward good of the tree, which is only the result and proof of its inner and natural goodness.

This is what James means when he says in his Epistle: "Faith without works is dead" (2:26). *That is, as the works do not follow, it is a sure sign that there is no faith there; but only an empty thought and dream, which they falsely call faith. . . .*

. . . Inasmuch as works naturally follow faith, as I said, it is not necessary to command them, for it is impossible for faith not to do them without being commanded, in order that we may learn to distinguish the false from the true faith.[2]

Calvin on the Nature of Faith

John Calvin defended himself vigorously against those who would "throw odium" on the doctrine of justification by faith by saying those who teach it "destroy good works, and give encouragement to sin."[3] He wrote, "We acknowledge that faith and works are necessarily connected."[4] Calvin debated a Catholic cardinal on this very issue:

If you would duly understand how inseparable faith and works are, look to Christ. . . . Where zeal for integrity and holiness is not vigor, there neither is the Spirit of Christ nor Christ Himself; and wherever Christ is not, there is no righteousness, nay, there is no faith; for faith cannot apprehend Christ for righteousness without the Spirit of sanctification.[5]

---

[2]Martin Luther, "Justification by Faith," in *Classic Sermons on Faith and Doubt,* ed. Warren W. Wiersbe (Grand Rapids, Mich.: Kregel, 1985), 78–83 (emphasis added).

[3]John Calvin, *Institutes of the Christian Religion,* trans. Henry Beveridge, 3:16:1 (reprint, Grand Rapids, Mich.: Eerdmans, 1966), 2:98.

[4]Ibid.

[5]John C. Olin, ed., *A Reformation Debate* (Grand Rapids, Mich.: Baker, 1966), 68.

Calvin attacked the Scholastic movement of the Roman Catholic Church over their definition of faith. The Scholastics taught that there is a kind of "faith" that has no transforming effect on the affections or behavior of those who "believe." This "faith," they taught, exists in people who have no desire for holiness and no love for God. Calvin was clearly offended by this suggestion. Listen to his diatribe against this error:

I must refute the nugatory distinction of the Schoolmen as to formed and unformed faith. For *they imagine that persons who have no fear of God, and no sense of piety, may believe all that is necessary to be known for salvation;* as if the Holy Spirit were not the witness of our adoption by enlightening our hearts unto faith. Still, however, though the whole Scripture is against them, *they dogmatically give the name of faith to a persuasion devoid of the fear of God.* It is unnecessary to go farther in refuting their definition, than simply to state the nature of faith as declared in the word of God. From this it will clearly appear how unskillfully and absurdly they babble, rather than discourse, on this subject. I have already done this in part, and will afterwards add the remainder in its proper place. At present, I say that nothing can be imagined more absurd than their fiction. *They insist that faith is an assent with which any despiser of God may receive what is delivered by Scripture.* But we must first see whether any one can by his own strength acquire faith, or whether the Holy Spirit, by means of it, becomes the witness of adoption. Hence it is childish trifling in them to inquire whether the faith formed by the supervening quality of love be the same, or a different and new faith. By talking in this style, they show plainly that they have never thought of the special gift of the Spirit; since *one of the first elements of faith is reconciliation implied in man's drawing near to God. Did they duly ponder the saying of Paul, "With the heart man believeth unto righteousness" (Rom. x. 10), they would cease to dream of that frigid quality.* There is one consideration which ought at once to put an end to the debate—viz. that assent itself (as I have already observed, and will afterwards more fully illustrate) is more a matter of the heart than the head, of the affection than the intellect. . . . Assent itself, such at least as the Scripture describes, consists in pious affection. But we are furnished with a still clearer argument. *Since faith embraces Christ as he is offered by the Father, and he is offered not only for justification, for forgiveness of sins and peace, but also for sanctification, as the fountain of living waters, it is certain that no man will ever know him aright without at the same time receiving the sanctification of the Spirit; or, to express the matter more plainly, faith consists*

*in the knowledge of Christ; Christ cannot be known without the sanc-
tification of his Spirit:* therefore faith cannot possibly be disjoined
from pious affection.

. . . Although, in discoursing of faith, we admit that it has a
variety of forms; yet, when our object is to show what knowledge of
God the wicked possess, *we hold and maintain, in accordance with
Scripture, that the pious only have faith.*

. . . Simon Magus is said to have believed, though he soon
after gave proof of his unbelief (Acts viii, 13–18). In regard to the
faith attributed to him, we do not understand with some, that he
merely pretended a belief which had no existence in his heart: we
rather think that, overcome by the majesty of the Gospel, he
yielded some kind of assent, and so far acknowledged Christ to be
the author of life and salvation, as willingly to assume his name. In
like manner, in the Gospel of Luke, those in whom the seed of the
word is choked before it brings forth fruit, or in whom, from having no depth of earth, it soon withereth away, are said to believe
for a time. Such, we doubt not, eagerly receive the word with a
kind of relish, and have some feeling of its divine power, so as not
only to impose upon men by a false semblance of faith, but even to
impose upon themselves. They imagine that the reverence which
they give to the word is genuine piety, because they have no idea
of any impiety but that which consists in open and avowed contempt. But whatever that assent may be, it by no means penetrates
to the heart, so as to have a fixed seat there. Although it sometimes seems to have planted its roots, these have no life in them.
The human heart has so many recesses for vanity, so many lurking
places for falsehood, is so shrouded by fraud and hypocrisy, that it
often deceives itself. *Let those who glory in such semblances of faith
know that, in this respect, they are not a whit superior to devils.*

. . . Meanwhile, *believers are taught to examine themselves
carefully and humbly, lest carnal security creep in and take the place
of assurance of faith.* We may add, that the reprobate never have any
other than a confused sense of grace laying hold of the shadow
rather than the substance, because the Spirit properly seals the forgiveness of sins in the elect only, applying it by special faith to their
use. Still it is correctly said, that the reprobate believe God to be
propitious to them, inasmuch as they accept the gift of reconciliation, though confusedly and without due discernment; not that they
are partakers of the same faith or regeneration with the children of
God; but because, under a covering of hypocrisy, they seem to have
a principle of faith in common with them. Nor do I even deny that
God illumines their minds to this extent, that they recognise his

grace; *but that conviction he distinguishes from the peculiar testimony which he gives to his elect in this respect, that the reprobate never obtain to the full result or to fruition.* When he shows himself propitious to them, it is not as if he had truly rescued them from death and taken them under his protection. He only gives them a manifestation of his present mercy. *In the elect alone he implants the living root of faith, so that they persevere even to the end.*[6]

The Puritans and Reformation Theology

Zane Hodges believes the English Reformers altered and corrupted the doctrine of justification by faith. They did this, he says, by expanding the early Reformers' definition of faith. He calls Puritan teaching on faith and assurance "a tragic blemish on the history of the Christian church" (*AF* 32). Puritan teaching, he says, is the basis of "lordship salvation": "In the English-speaking world, this radically altered concept of saving faith can with considerable fairness be described as Puritan theology. Lordship salvation, in its best known contemporary form, simply popularizes the Puritanism to which it is heir" (*AF* 33).

In a note at that point, Hodges points out that a catalog of quotations I included as an appendix in *The Gospel According to Jesus* drew heavily from Puritan sources. He repeats his charge that "Puritan theology, especially in the area of faith and assurance, did not at all reflect the doctrine of John Calvin himself and is a distinct departure from Reformation thought" (*AF* 208).

But as I have suggested elsewhere (see chapter 10, footnote 6) Hodges is making far too much of the difference between Calvin and the Puritans. No group of theologians ever defended justification by faith more doggedly than the English Reformers. As the quotations I have cited above prove, no one was more convinced than Luther and Calvin that genuine faith works.

While Luther, Calvin, and the Puritans might have differed somewhat on how to describe faith and how to obtain assurance, they all agreed that sanctification inevitably follows justification. None of them would have tolerated the notion that true believers might fail to persevere in righteousness, or that genuine faith might lapse into inactivity or permanent unbelief. On this point the proponents of modern no-lordship theology are rather seriously deluded.

---

[6]Calvin, *Institutes* [Beveridge], 3:2:8–11, 1:475–79 (emphasis added).

J. C. Ryle on Justification and Sanctification

Bishop J. C. Ryle was an English churchman in the Puritan tradition (though he lived in the nineteenth century). He recognized in his day all the incipient trends that have led to no-lordship theology in our time. His landmark 1879 work, *Holiness,* is his response to those trends. It stands today as an effective answer to the no-lordship error and is in many ways the definitive work on the issue.

Ryle, in harmony with all Puritan and Reformed theology, despised the notion that justification and sanctification could be disjoined or that sanctification might be optional in a true believer's experience. He saw justification and sanctification as distinct but inseparable. He wrote:

In what, then, are justification and sanctification alike?

a. Both proceed originally from the free grace of God. It is of His gift alone that believers are justified or sanctified at all.

b. Both are part of that great work of salvation which Christ, in the eternal covenant, has undertaken on behalf of His people. Christ is the fountain of life, from which pardon and holiness both flow. The root of each is Christ.

c. Both are to be found in the same persons. Those who are justified are always sanctified, and those who are sanctified are always justified. God has joined them together, and they cannot be put asunder.

d. Both begin at the same time. The moment a person begins to be a justified person, he also begins to be a sanctified person. He may not feel it, but it is a fact.

e. Both are alike necessary to salvation. No one ever reached heaven without a renewed heart as well as forgiveness, without the Spirit's grace as well as the blood of Christ, without a meetness for eternal glory as well as a title. The one is just as necessary as the other.

Such are the points on which justification and sanctification agree. Let us now reverse the picture, and see wherein they differ.

a. Justification is the reckoning and counting a man to be righteous for the sake of another, even Jesus Christ the Lord. Sanctification is the actual making a man inwardly righteous, though it may be in a very feeble degree.

b. The righteousness we have by our justification is not our own, but the everlasting perfect righteousness of our great Mediator Christ, imputed to us, and made our own by faith. The righteousness we have by sanctification is our own righteousness, imparted, inherent and wrought in us by the Holy Spirit, but mingled with much infirmity and imperfection.

c. In justification our own works have no place at all and simple faith in Christ is the one thing needful. In sanctification our own works are of vast importance, and God bids us fight and watch and pray and strive and take pains and labour.

d. Justification is a finished and complete work, and a man is perfectly justified the moment he believes. Sanctification is an imperfect work, comparatively, and will never be perfected until we reach heaven.

e. Justification admits of no growth or increase: a man is as much justified the hour he first comes to Christ by faith as he will be to all eternity. Sanctification is eminently a progressive work, and admits of continual growth and enlargement so long as a man lives.

f. Justification has special reference to our persons, our standing in God's sight, and our deliverance from guilt. Sanctification has special reference to our natures, and the moral renewal of our hearts.

g. Justification gives us our title to heaven, and boldness to enter in. Sanctification gives us our meetness for heaven, and prepares us to enjoy it when we dwell there.

h. Justification is the act of God about us, and is not easily discerned by others. Sanctification is the work of God within us, and cannot be hid in its outward manifestation from the eyes of men.

I commend these distinctions to the attention of all my readers, and I ask them to ponder them well. I am persuaded that one great cause of the darkness and uncomfortable feelings of many well-meaning people in the matter of religion is their habit of confounding, and not distinguishing, justification and sanctification. It can never be too strongly impressed on our minds that they are two separate things. No doubt they cannot be divided, and every one that is a partaker of either is a partaker of both. But never, never ought they to be confounded, and never ought the distinction between them to be forgotten.[7]

Charles Spurgeon on Holiness

Charles Spurgeon was an English Baptist in the Puritan tradition. No one preached more powerfully than he against the concept of "accepting Christ as Savior" while spurning His lordship. "Verily I say unto

[7] J. C. Ryle, *Holiness* (reprint, Durham, England: Evangelical Press, 1979), 29–30.

you, you cannot have Christ for your Savior unless you also have him as Lord," Spurgeon said.[8] Pages of material could be adduced from Spurgeon's preaching to debunk no-lordship teaching.

Spurgeon stands with all the Puritans and Reformers on the question of whether practical sanctification is an essential evidence of justification. Preaching on Matthew 22:11–14, for example, Spurgeon said,

> Holiness is always present in those who are loyal guests of the great King, for "without holiness no man shall see the Lord." Too many professors pacify themselves with the idea that they possess imputed righteousness, while they are indifferent to the sanctifying work of the Spirit. They refuse to put on the garment of obedience, they reject the white linen which is the righteousness of the saints. They thus reveal their self-will, their enmity to God, and their non-submission to his Son. Such men may talk what they will about justification by faith, and salvation by grace, but they are rebels at heart, they have not on the wedding dress any more than the self-righteous, whom they so eagerly condemn. The fact is, if we wish for the blessings of grace, we must in our hearts submit to the rules of grace without picking and choosing.[9]

In another context, Spurgeon said,

> Christ Jesus did not come in order that you might continue in sin and escape the penalty of it; he did not come to prevent the disease being mortal, but to take the disease itself away. Many people think that when we preach salvation, we mean salvation from going to hell. We do mean [only] *that,* but we mean a great deal more; we preach salvation *from sin;* we say that Christ is able to save a man; and we mean by that that he is able to save him from sin and to make him holy; to make him a new man. No person has any right to say, "I am saved," while he continues in sin as he did before. How can you be saved from sin while you are living in it? A man that is drowning cannot say he is saved from the water while he is sinking in it; a man that is frost-bitten cannot say, with any truth, that he is saved from the cold while he is stiffened in the wintry blast. No, man, Christ did not come to save thee *in* thy sins, but to save thee *from* thy sins; not to make the disease so that it should not kill thee,

---

[8]C. H. Spurgeon, *The Metropolitan Tabernacle Pulpit,* vol. 47 (reprint, Pasadena, Tex.: Pilgrim, 1986), 570.

[9]C. H. Spurgeon, *The Metropolitan Tabernacle Pulpit,* vol. 17 (London: Passmore & Alabaster, 1894), 99.

but to let it remain in itself mortal, and, nevertheless, to remove it from thee, and thee from it. Christ Jesus came then to heal us from the plague of sin, to touch us with his hand and say, "I will, be thou clean."[10]

Spurgeon attacked an incipient variety of no-lordship doctrine in an 1872 sermon:

There are some who seem willing to accept Christ as Saviour who will not receive him as Lord. They will not often state the case quite as plainly as that; but, as actions speak more plainly than words, that is what their conduct practically says. How sad it is that some talk about their faith in Christ, yet their faith is not proved by their works! Some even speak as if they understood what we mean by the covenant of grace; yet, alas! there is no good evidence of grace in their lives, but very clear proof of sin (not grace) abounding. I cannot conceive it possible for anyone truly to receive Christ as Saviour and yet not to receive him as Lord. One of the first instincts of a redeemed soul is to fall at the feet of the Saviour, and gratefully and adoringly to cry, "Blessed Master, bought with thy precious blood, I own that I am thine,—thine only, thine wholly, thine for ever. Lord, what wilt thou have me to do?" A man who is really saved by grace does not need to be told that he is under solemn obligations to serve Christ; the new life within him tells him *that*. Instead of regarding it as a burden, he gladly surrenders himself—body, soul, and spirit, to the Lord who has redeemed him, reckoning this to be his reasonable service. Speaking for myself, I can truthfully say that, the moment I knew that Christ was my Saviour, I was ready to say to him,—

I am thine, and thine alone,
This I gladly, fully own;
And, in all my works and ways,
Only now would seek thy praise.

Help me to confess thy name,
Bear with joy thy cross and shame,
Only seek to follow thee,
Though reproach my portion be.

It is not possible for us to accept Christ as our Saviour unless he also becomes our King, for a very large part of salvation consists in our being saved from sin's dominion over us, and the only way in

[10]C. H. Spurgeon, *The Metropolitan Tabernacle Pulpit*, vol. 11 (reprint, Pasadena, Tex.: Pilgrim, 1979), 138.

which we can be delivered from the mastery of Satan is by becoming subject to the mastery of Christ. . . . If it were possible for sin to be forgiven, and yet for the sinner to live just as he lived before, he would not really be saved.[11]

American Evangelicalism and No-lordship Theology

I stated in chapter 2 my conviction that the contemporary no-lordship movement is a chiefly American phenomenon. Yet I would also add that no-lordship theology is a radical *departure* from historic fundamentalist and evangelical belief in America. American Protestant belief has its roots, of course, in the English Puritan movement. The great evangelical awakenings of the eighteenth and nineteenth centuries, the Methodist movement, and the rise of revivalism at the beginning of this century all featured Christ's lordship at the heart of the gospel they proclaimed. Jonathan Edwards, perhaps the greatest theological mind America has ever produced, wrote,

> As to that question, Whether closing with Christ in his kingly office be of the essence of justifying faith? I would say: 1. That accepting Christ in his kingly office, is doubtless the proper condition of having an interest in Christ's kingly office, and so the condition of that salvation which he bestows in the execution of that office; as much as accepting the forgiveness of sins, is the proper condition of the forgiveness of sin. Christ, in his kingly office, bestows salvation; and therefore, accepting him in his kingly office, by a disposition to sell all and suffer all in duty to Christ, and giving proper respect and honor to him, is the condition of salvation. This is manifest by Heb v.9 "And being made perfect, he became the author of eternal salvation to all them that obey him."[12]

Of course the strong Reformed tradition of Princeton Seminary, which produced Charles Hodge, B. B. Warfield, and J. Gresham Machen, featured a clear lordship message. Hodge wrote,

> That good works are the certain effects of faith is included in the doctrine that we are sanctified by faith. For it is impossible that there

---

[11]C. H. Spurgeon, *The Metropolitan Tabernacle Pulpit,* vol. 56 (reprint, Pasadena, Tex.: Pilgrim, 1979), 617.

[12]Cited in John Gerstner, *The Rational Biblical Theology of Jonathan Edwards* (Orlando: Ligonier, 1991), 301.

should be inward holiness, love, spirituality, brotherly kindness, and zeal, without an external manifestation of these graces in the whole outward life. Faith, therefore, without works, is dead. We are saved by faith. But salvation includes deliverance from sin. If, therefore, our faith does not deliver us from sin, it does not save us. Antinomianism involves a contradiction in terms.[13]

Only one strand of American evangelicalism has embraced and propagated no-lordship theology, and that is the branch of dispensationalism I described in Appendix 2.

D. L. Moody on Repentance

D. L. Moody, evangelist and founder of Moody Bible Institute, featured a clear call to repentance in his preaching:

There is a good deal of trouble among people about what repentance really is. If you ask people what it is, they will tell you "It is feeling sorry." If you ask a man if he repents, he will tell you: "Oh, yes; I generally feel sorry for my sins." That is not repentance. It is something more than feeling sorry. Repentance is turning right about, and forsaking sin. I wanted to speak Sunday about that verse in Isaiah, which says: "Let the guilty forsake his way, and the unrighteous man his thoughts." That is what it is. If a man don't turn from his sin, he won't be accepted of God; and if righteousness don't produce a turning about—a turning from bad to good—it isn't true righteousness.[14]

Moody stated,

We do not walk in the same way as before we were converted. A man or a woman who professes Christianity and yet goes on in the same old way has not been born again. When we are born again, we are born in a new way; and Christ is that new way himself. We give up our old way, and take his. The old way leads to death, the new way to life everlasting. In the old way, Satan leads us; in the new way the Son of God leads us. We are led by Him, not into bondage and darkness, but into the way of peace and joy.[15]

---

[13]Charles Hodge, *Systematic Theology* (reprint, Grand Rapids, Mich.: Eerdmans, 1989), 3:110.

[14]D. L. Moody, "True Repentance," in *The Gospel Awakening* (Chicago: Fairbanks, Palmer, 1883), 417.

[15]"Signs of the New Birth," ibid., 658.

R. A. Torrey on Lordship

R. A. Torrey, first president of Moody Bible Institute, instructed students on leading people to Christ:

> Show them Jesus as Lord.
>
> It is not enough to know Jesus as a Saviour, we must know Him as Lord also. A good verse for this purpose is Acts 2:36:
>
> > "Therefore let all the house of Israel know assuredly, that *God hath made that same Jesus,* whom ye have crucified, *both Lord and Christ.*"
>
> When the inquirer has read the verse, ask him what God hath made Jesus, and hold him to it until he replies, "Both Lord and Christ." Then say to him, "Are you willing to accept Him as your Divine Lord, the one to whom you will surrender your heart, your every thought, and word, and act?"
>
> Another good verse for this purpose is Rom. 10:9:
>
> > "That if thou shalt confess with thy mouth *the Lord* Jesus, and shalt believe in thine heart that God hath raised him from the dead, thou shalt be saved."
>
> When the inquirer has read the verse, ask him what we are to confess Jesus as. He should reply, "Lord." If he does not so reply, ask him other questions until he does answer in this way. Then ask him, "Do you really believe that Jesus is Lord, that He is Lord of all, that He is rightfully the absolute Lord and Master of your life and person?" Perhaps it will be well to use Acts 10:36 as throwing additional light upon this point:
>
> > "The word which God sent unto the children of Israel, preaching peace by Jesus Christ: (*he is Lord of all*)."[16]

James M. Gray on Salvation

James M. Gray, second president of Moody Bible Institute, wrote,

> The design of the atonement is stated in the words: "*That we being dead to sins, should live unto righteousness,*" a two-fold design, as we see. The thought of God was not only punitive but remedial. He gave His Son not only to take away our guilt but to change our lives. . . .

---

[16] R. A. Torrey, *How to Work for Christ* (Old Tappan, N.J.: Revell, n.d.), 37–38.

The moment we receive Christ by faith, we do also receive the Holy Spirit to dwell within us, regenerating us, creating within us a clean heart and renewing within us a right spirit, so that we become "dead to sins" not only in the judicial or imputed sense . . . but in the actual and experimental sense as well. That is not to say that sin becomes eradicated from our hearts and no longer dwells even latently within us (1 John 1:8); but that its power over us is broken. We do really come to hate the sins we used to love and to love the holiness we used to hate.

. . . Christ died not merely that we should be dead to sins judicially and experimentally but that we might *"live unto righteousness."* As our substitute and representative He both died *and rose again.* . . .

Now Paul tells us also in the sixth chapter of Romans already quoted that if we are united with Christ in the likeness of His death, we are also in the likeness of His resurrection. If we died with Him we also live with Him.

This is not merely that we *shall* live with Him by and by in a physical state of resurrection glory, but that we live with Him now in a spiritual state of resurrection glory. The death He died He died unto sin once, but the life He liveth, He liveth unto God. He liveth it unto God now. Even so we are to reckon ourselves not only to be dead indeed unto sin as we have already considered, but alive unto God in Christ Jesus (6:11), alive *now.* . . .

Nor is it *only* in an imputed sense that this is true; but, as in the other half of this declaration, in an experimental sense as well. As we have just seen, the Holy Spirit within the regenerated man, not only enables him to hate sin but to love holiness and follow after it. No longer yields he his "members (as) servants to uncleanness and to iniquity unto iniquity," but as "servants to righteousness unto holiness." He crucifies the flesh with its affections and lust. He not only puts off all these: "Anger, wrath, malice, railing, shameful speaking out of his mouth"; but he puts on, as the elect of God, "a heart of compassion, kindness, humility, meekness, long-suffering, and above all these, love, which is the bond of perfection."

It is thus that *"by His stripes we are healed."* Perfectly healed. God having begun the good work in us perfects it until the day of Jesus Christ (Philippians 1:6). The man who receives Christ as his Saviour, and confesses Him as his Lord, need not fear as to whether he shall be "able to hold out."[17]

---

[17]James M. Gray, *Salvation from Start to Finish* (Chicago: Moody, n.d.), 39–44.

W. H. Griffith Thomas on Surrender

W. H. Griffith Thomas, co-founder of Dallas Theological Seminary, wrote,

God says "Here I am" to man, and then man welcomes this and responds with "Here am I" to God.

The words imply *Surrender*. When the believer says "Here am I" to God, he places himself at God's disposal. This wholehearted response is the natural outcome of the reception of God's revelation to the soul. We can see this truth on every page of the New Testament. God comes to the soul, enters the heart and life, and then man yields himself entirely to God as belonging to Him. "Ye are not your own, ye are bought." This is the meaning of St. Paul's great word translated "yield" in Rom. vi. 13, 19, and "present" in ch. xii. 1. In the latter passage the Apostle bases his exhortation on the "mercies of God," on the revelation of God saying "Here I am" to man, and after urging his readers to "present" their bodies as a sacrifice to God he speaks of this surrender as their "logical service," the rational, logical, necessary outcome of their acceptance of "the mercies of God." The Gospel does not come to the soul simply for personal enjoyment, it comes to awaken in it a sense of its true life and marvelous possibilities. Consequently, when God says to the believer, "I am thine," the believer responds, "I am Thine" (Psalm cxix. 94), "I am the Lord's" (Isa. xliv. 5). This was one part of the purpose of our Lord's redemption work, "that He might be Lord" and now, "we are the Lord's" (Rom. xiv. 8 and 9). This whole-hearted response should be made from the first moment of acceptance in and of Christ. "Christ is all" to us from the outset; and we should be "all to Him." There should be no *hiatus,* no gap, no interval, between the acceptance of Christ as Saviour and the surrender to Him as Lord. His full title is "Jesus Christ our Lord"; and the full extent of its meaning (though of course not its full depth) is intended to be realised from our very first experience of His saving presence and power. . . .

This initial act of surrender, however, is but the beginning of a life of surrender. The act must develop into an attitude. This has been recognised by God's true children in all ages as their "bounden duty and service."[18]

---

[18]W. H. Griffith Thomas, *The Christian Life and How to Live It* (Chicago: Moody, 1919), 46–49.

H. A. Ironside on Assurance

Dr. H. A. Ironside, pastor of Moody Memorial Church in Chicago, wrote,

> Perhaps some one may ask, "But does it make no difference to God what I am myself? May I live on in my sins and still be saved?" No, assuredly not! But this brings in another line of truth. The moment one believes the gospel, he is born again and receives a new life and nature—a nature that hates sin and loves holiness. If you have come to Jesus and trusted Him, do you not realize the truth of this? Do you not now hate and detest the wicked things that once gave you a certain degree of delight? Do you not find within yourself a new craving for goodness, a longing after holiness, and a thirst for righteousness? All this is the evidence of a new nature. And as you walk with God you will find that daily the power of the indwelling Holy Spirit will give you practical deliverance from the dominion of sin.[19]

Regarding 1 John 3:9, Ironside wrote,

> See how the two families, the unregenerated and the regenerated, are here depicted. Unsaved men practice sin. Whatever fine things there may be in their characters, as judged by the world's standards, they delight in having their own way. This is the essence of sin. "Sin is lawlessness." All careful scholars agree that this is a more correct translation than "Sin is the transgression of the law." We are told that "until the law sin was in the world," and although sin was not imputed as transgression because no written standard had yet been given, nevertheless sin manifested itself as self-will, or lawlessness, and was seen everywhere among fallen mankind. Lawlessness is the refusal of a person to submit his will to Another, even to God Himself, who has the right to claim his full obedience. In this the children of the devil show plainly the family to which they belong.
>
> But with the believer it is otherwise. Turning to Christ he is born from above, as we have seen, and thus possesses a new nature. This new nature abominates sin, and henceforth dominates his desires and his thinking. Sin becomes detestable. He loathes himself for the follies and iniquities of his past, and he yearns after holiness. Energized by the Holy Spirit, his life-trend is changed. He practices righteousness. Though ofttimes conscious of failure, the whole trend of his life is altered. The will of God is his joy and delight. And

---

[19]H. A. Ironside, *Full Assurance* (Chicago: Moody, 1937), 33.

as he learns more and more the preciousness of abiding in Christ, he grows in grace and in knowledge, and realizes that divine power is given him to walk in the path of obedience. His new nature finds joy in surrendering to Jesus as Lord, and so sin ceases to be character-istic of his life and character.[20]

A. W. Tozer on Following Christ

A. W. Tozer wrote much on the lordship issue. He began to see the dangers of a no-lordship gospel nearly half a century ago, and he sounded many warning blasts to the church. Here are a few excerpts:

Allowing the expression "Accept Christ" to stand as an honest effort to say in short what could not be so well said any other way, let us see what we mean or should mean when we use it.

To accept Christ is to form an attachment to the Person of our Lord Jesus altogether unique in human experience. The attachment is intellectual, volitional and emotional. The believer is intellectually convinced that Jesus is both Lord and Christ; he has set his will to follow Him at any cost and soon his heart is enjoying the exquisite sweetness of His fellowship.

This attachment is all-inclusive in that it joyfully accepts Christ for all that He is. There is no craven division of offices whereby we may acknowledge His Saviourhood today and withhold decision on His Lordship till tomorrow. The true believer owns Christ as his All in All without reservation. He also includes all of himself, leaving no part of his being unaffected by the revolutionary transaction.

Further, his attachment to Christ is all-exclusive. The Lord becomes to him not one of several rival interests, but the one exclu-sive attraction forever. He orbits around Christ as the earth around the sun, held in thrall by the magnetism of His love, drawing all his life and light and warmth from Him. In this happy state he is given other interests, it is true, but these are all determined by his relation to his Lord.

That we accept Christ in this all-inclusive, all-exclusive way is a divine imperative. Here faith makes its leap into God through the Person and work of Christ, but it never divides the work from the Person. It never tries to believe on the blood apart from Christ Himself, or the cross or the "finished work." It believes on the Lord Jesus Christ, the whole Christ without modification or reservation, and thus it receives and enjoys all that He did in His work of

---

[20]Ibid., 82–83.

redemption, all that He is now doing in heaven for His own and all that He does in and through them.

To accept Christ is to know the meaning of the words "as he is, so are we in this world" (I John 4:17). We accept His friends as our friends, His enemies as our enemies, His ways as our ways, His rejection as our rejection, His cross as our cross, His life as our life and His future as our future.

If this is what we mean when we advise the seeker to accept Christ we had better explain it to him. He may get into deep spiritual trouble unless we do.[21]

Tozer wrote, "The Christian is saved from his past sins. With these he simply has nothing more to do; they are among the things to be forgotten as the night is forgotten at the dawning of the day."[22]

This essay hits several themes that Tozer emphasized again and again:

We are under constant temptation these days to substitute another Christ for the Christ of the New Testament. The whole drift of modern religion is toward such a substitution.

To avoid this we must hold steadfastly to the concept of Christ as set forth so clearly and plainly in the Scriptures of truth. Though an angel from heaven should preach anything less than the Christ of the apostles let him be forthrightly and fearlessly rejected.

The mighty, revolutionary message of the Early Church was that a man named Jesus who had been crucified was now raised from the dead and exalted to the right hand of God. "Therefore let all the house of Israel know assuredly, that God hath made that same Jesus, whom ye have crucified, both Lord and Christ." . . .

Salvation comes not by "accepting the finished work" or "deciding for Christ." It comes by believing on the Lord Jesus Christ, the whole, living, victorious Lord who, as God and man, fought our fight and won it, accepted our debt as His own and paid it, took our sins and died under them and rose again to set us free. This is the true Christ, and nothing less will do.

But something less is among us, nevertheless, and we do well to identify it so that we may repudiate it. That something is a poetic fiction, a product of the romantic imagination and maudlin religious fancy. It is a Jesus, gentle, dreamy, shy, sweet, almost effeminate,

---

[21]A. W. Tozer, *That Incredible Christian* (Harrisburg, Pa.: Christian Publications, 1964), 18–19.

[22]Ibid., 44.

and marvelously adaptable to whatever society He may find Himself in. He is cooed over by women disappointed in love, patronized by pro tem celebrities and recommended by psychiatrists as a model of a well-integrated personality. He is used as a means to almost any carnal end, but He is never acknowledged as Lord. These quasi Christians follow a quasi Christ. They want His help but not His interference. They will flatter Him but never obey Him.[23]

Tozer called no-lordship teaching a "discredited doctrine" that divides Christ. He described the teaching he opposed:

It goes like this: Christ is both Saviour and Lord. A sinner may be saved by accepting Him as Saviour without yielding to Him as Lord. The practical outworking of this doctrine is that the evangelist presents and the seeker accepts a divided Christ. . . .

Now, it seems odd that none of these teachers ever noticed that the only true object of saving faith is none other than Christ Himself; not the "saviourhood" of Christ nor the "lordship" of Christ, but Christ Himself. God does not offer salvation to the one who will believe on one of the offices of Christ, nor is an office of Christ ever presented as an object of faith. Neither are we exhorted to believe on the atonement, nor on the cross, nor on the priesthood of the Saviour. All of these are embodied in the person of Christ, but they are never separated nor is one ever isolated from the rest. Much less are we permitted to accept one of Christ's offices and reject another. The notion that we are so permitted is a modern day heresy, I repeat, and like every heresy it has had evil consequences among Christians. No heresy is ever entertained with impunity. We pay in practical failure for our theoretical errors.

It is altogether doubtful whether any man can be saved who comes to Christ for His help but with no intention to obey Him. Christ's saviourhood is forever united to His lordship. Look at the Scriptures: "If thou shalt confess with thy mouth the Lord Jesus, and shalt believe in thine heart that God hath raised him from the dead, thou shalt be saved . . . for the same Lord over all is rich unto all that call upon him. For whosoever shall call upon the name of the Lord shall be saved" (Rom. 10:9–13). There the *Lord is* the object of faith for salvation. And when the Philippian jailer asked the way to be saved, Paul replied, "Believe on the Lord Jesus Christ, and thou shalt be saved" (Acts 16:31). He did not tell him

---

[23]A. W. Tozer, *Man: The Dwelling Place of God* (Camp Hill, Pa.: Christian Publications, 1966), 140–43.

to believe on the Saviour with the thought that he could later take up the matter of His lordship and settle it at his own convenience. To Paul there could be no division of offices. Christ must be Lord or He will not be Saviour.[24]

This penetrating analysis on faith shows how deeply Tozer had thought about the dangers of no-lordship doctrine:

For a number of years my heart has been troubled over the doctrine of faith as it is received and taught among evangelical Christians everywhere. Great emphasis is laid upon faith in orthodox circles, and that is good; but still I am troubled. Specifically, my fear is that the modern conception of faith is not the Biblical one; that when the teachers of our day use the word they do not mean what Bible writers meant when they used it.

The causes of my uneasiness are these:

1. The lack of spiritual fruit in the lives of so many who claim to have faith.

2. The rarity of a radical change in the conduct and general outlook of persons professing their new faith in Christ as their personal Saviour.

3. The failure of our teachers to define or even describe the thing to which the word *faith* is supposed to refer.

4. The heartbreaking failure of multitudes of seekers, be they ever so earnest, to make anything out of the doctrine or to receive any satisfying experience through it.

5. The real danger that a doctrine that is parroted so widely and received so uncritically by so many is false as understood by them.

6. I have seen faith put forward as a substitute for obedience, an escape from reality, a refuge from the necessity of hard thinking, a hiding place for weak character. I have known people to miscall by the name of faith high animal spirits, natural optimism, emotional thrills and nervous tics.

7. Plain horse sense ought to tell us that anything that makes no change in the man who professes it makes no difference to God either, and it is an easily observable fact that for countless numbers of persons the change from no-faith to faith makes no actual difference in the life. . . .

---

[24]A. W. Tozer, *The Root of the Righteous* (Harrisburg, Pa.: Christian Publications, 1955), 84–86.

Any professed faith in Christ as personal Saviour that does not bring the life under plenary obedience to Christ as lord is inadequate and must betray its victim at the last.

The man that believes will obey; failure to obey is convincing proof that there is not true faith present. To attempt the impossible God must give faith or there will be none, and He gives faith to the obedient heart, only. Where real repentance is, there is obedience; for repentance is not only sorrow for past failures and sins, it is a determination to begin now to do the will of God as He reveals it to us.[25]

Arthur Pink on No-lordship Evangelism

Arthur W. Pink was a largely self-taught classic Reformed theologian. He wrote and distributed short studies on theological and biblical topics through a monthly magazine, *Studies in the Scriptures*. His understanding of Scripture and ability to express himself in writing are legendary.

Pink often wrote with an acid pen, however, and he reserved some of his harshest criticism for those whom he saw corrupting the gospel message with easy-believism. It is fair to say that he held no-lordship doctrine in utter contempt. "The evangelism of the day is not only superficial to the last degree, but it is *radically defective*," Pink wrote.[26]

As early as the 1930s, decades before the lordship debate became a familiar issue, Pink clearly saw major problems with emerging no-lordship doctrine:

Saving faith consists of the complete surrender of my whole being and life to the claims of God upon me: "But first gave their own selves to the Lord" (2 Cor. 8:5).

It is the unreserved acceptance of Christ as my absolute Lord, bowing to His will and receiving His yoke. Possibly someone may object, Then why are Christians exhorted as they are in Romans 12:1? We answer, All such exhortations are simply a calling on them to *continue as they began:* "As ye have therefore received Christ Jesus the Lord, so walk ye in Him" (Col. 2:6). Yes, mark it well that Christ is "received" as *Lord*. Oh, how far, far below the New Testament standard is this modern way of begging sinners to receive Christ as their own personal "Saviour." If the reader will consult his

---

[25]Tozer, *Man: The Dwelling Place of God,* 30–33.

[26]Arthur Pink, *Studies on Saving Faith* (Swengel, Pa.: Reiner, n.d.), 5.

concordance, he will find that in *every passage* where the two titles are found together it is *always* "Lord and Saviour, and never vice versa: see Luke 1:46, 47; 2 Peter 1:11; 2:20; 3:18.[27]

He decried the disaster he saw happening as no-lordship evangelism grew more and more popular:

> The terrible thing is that so many preachers today, under the pretence of magnifying the grace of God, have represented Christ as the Minister of *sin;* as One who has, through His atoning sacrifice, procured an indulgence for men to continue gratifying their fleshly and worldly lusts. Provided a man professes to believe in the virgin birth and vicarious death of Christ and claims to be resting upon Him alone for salvation, he may pass for a real Christian almost anywhere today, even though his daily life may be no different from that of the moral worldling who makes no profession at all. The Devil is chloroforming thousands into hell by this very delusion. The Lord Jesus asks, "Why call ye Me, Lord, Lord, and *do not* the things which I say?" (Luke 6:46); and insists, "Not every one that saith unto Me, Lord, Lord, shall enter into the kingdom of heaven; but he that *doeth* the will of My Father which is in heaven" (Matt. 7:21).[28]

Pink gave this advice on how to deal with the purveyors of the doctrine he saw corrupting the church:

> It is the bounden duty of every Christian to have no dealings with the "evangelistic" monstrosity of the day: to *withhold* all moral and financial support of the same, to attend none of their meetings, to circulate none of their tracts. Those preachers who tell sinners they may be saved *without* forsaking their idols, *without* repenting, without-surrendering to the Lordship of Christ are as erroneous and dangerous as others who insist that salvation is by works and that Heaven must be earned by our own efforts.[29]

Startling words. But Pink felt the seriousness of the no-lordship error called for the strongest possible warning. One wonders what his reaction would have been if he had seen the radical no-lordship doctrine that has emerged in recent years.

---

[27]Arthur Pink, *Practical Christianity* (Grand Rapids, Mich.: Baker, 1974), 20.
[28]Ibid., 24–25.

Summary

No-lordship soteriology departs from the mainstream of evangelical orthodoxy. The fact remains that prior to this century and the rise of Chafer-Scofield dispensationalism, no prominent theologians or pastors ever embraced the tenets of no-lordship doctrine.[30]

The church as a whole needs to study this issue very carefully. None of us enjoys controversy, but the issues we are dealing with here are more important than mere matters of preference. It is the *gospel* that is at stake. We must get the message right. It is no mere academic question. These are the very issues many great men of God in the past have given their lives for.

We cannot continue to compromise and tolerate and sweep the error under the rug. That kind of response to the controversy has only contributed to the decline of the biblical gospel. It has decimated the church of our generation:

> Today's "Christianity" is in a state of disarray and decay, and the condition is deteriorating year by year. The truth of God's Word has been watered down and compromised to reach a common denominator that will appeal to and accommodate the largest number of participants. The result is a hybrid Christianity which is essentially man-centered, materialistic and worldly, and shamefully dishonouring to the Lord Jesus Christ. This shameful degeneracy is due in large part to the erroneous gospel that is presented by many today around the world.[31]

Let us search the Scriptures, ask the hard questions, and come to accord on the gospel.

---

[29]Pink, *Studies on Saving Faith,* 14.

[30]It might be possible, through selective quotations, to find comments from dependable theologians that appear to support some of the *ideas* advanced by various no-lordship teachers. But you will find no leading figures in the Reformation, Post-Reformation, or evangelical movements who ever endorsed the *system* of no-lordship soteriology Dr. Ryrie defends, much less the more extreme variety Professor Hodges espouses.

The true historical forerunners of no-lordship teaching include the Sandemanian antinomians (also known as "Glasites") in eighteenth-century Scotland. That movement was roundly denounced by the Puritans. D. Martyn Lloyd-Jones gives an overview of the Sandemanian sect and their doctrine in *The Puritans: Their Origins and Successors* (Edinburgh: Banner of Truth, 1987), 170–90.

[31]Jeffrey E. Wilson, "The Authentic Gospel" (Edinburgh: Banner of Truth, 1990), 1.

Glossary

antinomianism: the idea that behavior is unrelated to faith, or that Christians are not bound by any moral law. Antinomianism radically separates justification and sanctification, making practical holiness elective.

assensus: see *assent.*

assent (assensus): one of three elements of true faith; the settled confidence and affirmation that Christ's salvation is applicable to one's own soul (see *knowledge* and *trust*).

cheap grace: self-imparted grace that promises forgiveness without the need for repentance; pseudograce, which makes no change in the recipient's character.

common grace: divine grace bestowed to mankind in general. Common grace restrains sin, mitigates sin's destructive effects in human society, and imparts blessings of all kinds to all peoples. This grace is not redemptive (see *special grace*).

conversion: turning to God in repentance and faith.

decisionism: the idea that eternal salvation may be secured by the sinner's own movement toward Christ, a "decision for Christ" that is usually signified by some physical or verbal act—raising a hand, walking an aisle, reciting a prayer, signing a card, repeating a pledge, or something similar.

dispensation: the plan of God by which He adminsters His rule within a given era in His eternal program.

dispensationalism: a system of biblical interpretation that sees a distinction between God's program for Israel and His dealings with the church.

easy-believism: the view that saving faith is a solely human act. Those who adopt such a view must then scale back the definition of faith so that believing is something depraved sinners are capable of.

ecclesiology: the doctrine of the church.

efficacious grace: grace that is certain to produce the desired effect. God's grace is always efficacious.

eschatology: the doctrine of future things; prophecy.

faith: see *saving faith.*

fiducia: see *trust.*

flesh: the principle of human frailty—especially our sinful selfishness —which remains with us after salvation until we are ultimately glorified.

grace: the free and benevolent influence of a holy God operating sovereignly in the lives of undeserving sinners.

irresistible grace: grace that transforms the heart and thus makes the believer wholly willing to trust and obey. Saving grace is always irresistible.

justification: an act of God's grace whereby He declares that all the demands of the law are fulfilled on behalf of the believing sinner through the righteousness of Jesus Christ. Justification is the reversal of God's attitude toward the sinner. Whereas He formerly condemned, He now vindicates—not because of any good thing found in the sinner himself, but because of the imputed righteousness of Christ. Because of justification believers not only are perfectly free from any charge of guilt, but also have the full merit of Christ reckoned to their personal account. Justification and sanctification are both essential elements of salvation (see *sanctification*).

knowledge (notitia): one of three elements of true faith; a recognition and understanding of the truth that Christ saves (see *assent* and *trust*).

legalism: the teaching that people can earn favor with God by doing certain things. Some legalists teach that salvation must be earned by works. Others practice extreme ritualism or live by rigid codes of conduct. Even Christians can fall into legalism if they focus too much on externals and neglect to cultivate the right heart attitudes (cf. Rom. 2:29).

lordship salvation: the belief that the gospel call to faith presupposes that sinners must repent and yield to Christ's authority.

meritorious works: ritual or conduct that earns merit with God or is worthy of His rewards or honor. Scripture is clear that human works can *never* be meritorious (Isa. 64:6; Rom. 6:23; 8:8; Titus 3:5). No works of merit are necessary for salvation, but grace will produce works through faith as manifestations of God's saving work in every believer's life.

notitia: see *knowledge.*

ordo salutis: the order of salvation, a logical arrangement of various aspects of saving grace. A typical *ordo salutis* in Reformed theology would be: election, calling, regeneration, conversion, repentance, faith, justification, sanctification, perseverance, and glorification. Obviously, the part of the sequence from regeneration through sanctification is logical, not chronological. These events all happen in the same moment.

penance: an activity performed to try to atone for one's own sins.

premillennialism: the belief that Christ will come again, then inaugurate a thousand-year reign on earth.

Puritans: seventeenth-century English Reformers.

regeneration: the new birth—the work of the Holy Spirit that imparts new life to the sinner.

repentance: a change of heart involving turning from sin to embrace Jesus Christ. Repentance and *faith* are distinguishable elements that blend in one composite work by God's gracious moving in genuine *conversion.*

sanctification: the continuous operation of the Holy Spirit in believers, making us holy by conforming our character, affections, and behavior to the image of Christ.

saving faith: The soul's appropriation of and surrender to the Lord Jesus Christ as the solitary hope for eternal life and deliverance from sin. This faith is a work of God in the heart of the believing sinner.

saving grace: see *special grace.*

special grace: the irresistible work of God that frees men and women from the penalty and power of sin, renewing the inner person and sanctifying the sinner through the operation of the Holy Spirit. Also called *saving grace* and *irresistible grace.*

soteriology: doctrine of salvation.

spurious faith: counterfeit or defective faith. Radical no-lordship teaching denies the possibility of spurious faith in Christ as Savior. That view asserts that if the *object* of faith is trustworthy, the character of the faith itself is not to be challenged.

total depravity: corruption by sin in every aspect of being. Unredeem-ed sinners are totally depraved; that is, they are spiritually dead, unable to respond to or please God, and in total need of God's gracious inclining.

trust (fiducia): one of three elements of true faith; a personal commitment to and appropriation of Christ as the only hope for eternal salvation (see *assent* and *knowledge*).

ultradispensationalism: an extreme brand of dispensationalism that places the beginning of the church at varying points later than Acts 2. Many ultradispensationalists reject water baptism and the Lord's Supper as ordinances intended for another age, and they believe the only Scripture directly applicable for this age is contained in the Pauline epistles.

Scripture Index

Subject Index

Abraham, 51, 52, 92, 99–103, 118,
148, 152, 228, 237
accepting Christ, 73, 75, 196–99,
246, 252–53
affections. *See* desires
Alderson, Richard, 182
Aldrich, Roy L., on faith, 142
antinomianism, 93–96, 98, 112–13,
120, 160, 163–64, 182, 224–25,
228, 232–33, 247, 259
appetites. *See* desires
assent, 44–45, 47, 49–50, 259
assurance, 157–73, 217
faith and, 41–42
false, 41, 124, 161–64, 166, 172–
73
lordship salvation and, 158, 217
objective and subjective aspects of,
160, 162–72

baptism, 55, 62, 69, 83, 102, 112,
115, 207–8, 222, 262
Barnhouse, Donald Grey
on dispensationalism, 224
on justification and sanctification,
114
Belcher, Richard P., 193
belief. *See* faith
Berkhof, Louis
on antinomianism, 163–64
on elements of faith, 44–45, 49
on grace, 57
on repentance, 75, 77
Bonhoeffer, Dietrich 55–56
Boyd, Robert F., 166
Brooks, Thomas, 157–58
Bullinger, Ethelbert W., 223–24
Butcher, J. Kevin, 94

Calvin, John
on assurance, 159, 161, 163, 165

on faith, 44, 161, 163
on James and justification by works,
153
on justification and sanctification,
92–93, 238–41
Campus Crusade for Christ, 125, 194
carnality, 95, 116, 124–27, 131, 216,
260
Catholicism
on assurance, 159
on justification, 87–88, 90–91
Chafer, Lewis Sperry
on assurance, 197
on carnality, 124–25
dispensationalism of, 226–31
on evangelism, 195, 197–98
no-lordship theology of, 35, 228
on repentance and John's gospel,
79
Chantry, Walter, 73
chastisement. *See* discipline
children, witnessing to, 197, 208–10
Chrisope, T. Alan, 211
commitment, spiritual, 43–45, 74,
107–8
consecration. *See* commitment
conversion, 33–34, 108, 134–35, 259,
261
covenant theology, vs.
dispensationalism, 219–22
cross, demanding nature of the, 205

Darby, J. N., 223
David, sin of King, 128
debates, limitation of, 14–15
decisionism, 196–99, 259
dedication. *See* commitment
"deeper life" theology, 106–9
demons, faith of, 150–51
depravity, total, 62–66, 261
desires, holy, 135, 216

THE
VANISHING
CONSCIENCE

JOHN F. MacARTHUR, JR.

THE VANISHING CONSCIENCE

Library of Congress Cataloging-in-Publication Data

MacArthur, John, 1939–
    The vanishing conscience / John F. MacArthur, Jr.
      p. cm.
    Includes bibliographical references.
    ISBN 0–8499–0842–6 (hardcover)
         0–8499–3595–4 (special edition)
         0–8499–3678–0 (trade paper)
    1. Sin. 2. Conscience—Religious aspects—Christianity.
  3. Guilt—Religious aspects—Christianity. 4. Church and the world. I. Title.
    BT715.M126   1994
    241'.3—dc20   93—47503
                                         CIP

Printed in the United States of America

6 7 8 9   QBP   9 8 7 6 5 4 3 2

To Al Sanders

*with gratitude for half a century
of loyal service to the Savior
and thanks for many years
as a wise and generous friend.*

Contents

Contents

Preface

We live in a culture that has elevated pride to the status of a virtue. Self-esteem, positive feelings, and personal dignity are what our society encourages people to seek. At the same time, moral responsibility is being replaced by victimism, which teaches people to blame someone else for their personal failures and iniquities. Frankly, the biblical teachings about human depravity, sin, guilt, repentance, and humility are not compatible with any of those ideas.

The church has been far too willing to embrace the fads of worldly opinion—particularly in the area of psychology and self-esteem. Christians often merely echo worldly thinking on the psychology of guilt and the importance of feeling good about oneself. The adverse effect on the life of the church can hardly be underestimated.

Nowhere has the damage registered more than in the way professing Christians deal with their own sin. In speaking to Christians around the country, I have seen a disheartening trend developing for at least two decades. The church as a whole is growing less concerned with sin, and more obsessed with self-exoneration and self-esteem. Christians are rapidly losing sight of sin as the root of all human woes. And many Christians are explicitly denying that their own sin can be the cause of their personal anguish. More and more are attempting to explain the human dilemma in wholly unbiblical terms: temperament, addiction, dysfunctional families, the child within, codependency, and a host of other irresponsible escape mechanisms promoted by secular psychology.

The potential impact of such a drift is frightening. Remove the reality of sin, and you take away the possibility of repentance. Abolish the doctrine of human depravity and you void the divine plan of salvation. Erase the notion of personal guilt and you eliminate the need for a Savior. Obliterate the human conscience, and you will raise an amoral and unredeemable generation. The church cannot join hands with the world in such a grossly satanic enterprise. To do so is to overthrow the very gospel we are called to proclaim.

This book is not merely a lament about society's deplorable moral state or the damage we see caused by sin all around us. Nor is it an attempt to stir Christians up to tackle the impossible task of reconstructing society. Awakening the *church* to the awful reality of sin is my only point of concern. That alone would have a positive effect on the world.

Is social reconstruction even an appropriate way for Christians to spend their energies? I recently mentioned to a friend that I was working on a book dealing with sin and our culture's declining moral climate. He immediately said, "Be sure you urge Christians to get actively involved in reclaiming society. The main problem is that Christians haven't acquired enough influence in politics, art, and the entertainment industry to turn things around for good." That, I acknowledge, is a common view held by many Christians. But I'm afraid I don't agree. The weakness of the church is not that we're too uninvolved in the politics or administration of our society, but that we too easily absorb the false values of an unbelieving world. The problem is not too little activism, but too much assimilation. As I noted in a recent book, the church is fast becoming like the world in several respects. Those most active in the social and political realms are often the *first* to absorb the world's values. Social and political activists cannot have any worthwhile impact on society if their own consciences are not clear and strong.

"Reclaiming" the culture is a pointless, futile exercise. I am convinced we are living in a post-Christian society—a civilization that exists under God's judgment. As we will note in an early chapter of this book, abundant evidence suggests that God has abandoned this culture to its own depravity. Certainly He is not interested in superficial moral reform for an unregenerate society. God's purpose in this world—and the church's only legitimate commission—is the proclamation of the message of sin and salvation to individuals, whom God sovereignly redeems and calls *out* of the world. God's purpose is to save those who will repent of their sins and believe the gospel—not to work for external corrections in a morally bankrupt culture.

If that sounds the least bit pessimistic or cynical to you, it isn't. Scripture predicted times exactly like these:

In the last days difficult times will come. For men will be lovers of self, lovers of money, boastful, arrogant, revilers, disobedient to parents, ungrateful, unholy, unloving, irreconcilable, malicious gossips, without self-control, brutal, haters of good, treacherous, reckless, conceited, lovers of pleasure rather than lovers of God; holding to a form of godliness, although they have denied its power. . . . [And] evil men and impostors will proceed from bad to worse, deceiving and being deceived (2 Tim. 3:1–5, 13).

God's purposes *are* being fulfilled, no matter how vainly people strive against Him. Titus 2:11 assures us that God's grace appears, bringing salvation in the midst of the lowest human depravity, teaching us to live "sensibly, righteously and godly in the present age" (v. 12).

There is great hope, even in the midst of a wicked and perverse generation, for those who love God. Remember, He will build His church and "the gates of hades will not prevail against it" (Matt. 16:18). He also is able to make all things work together for the good of His elect (Rom. 8:28). Christ Himself intercedes for His chosen ones, people who are not of this world, even as He is not of this world (Jn. 17:14). What is His prayer? "I do not ask Thee to take them out of the world, but to keep them from the evil one. . . . Sanctify them in the truth; Thy word is truth" (vv. 15, 17).

As believers, then, our duty with regard to sin is not to try to purge all society's ills, but to apply ourselves diligently to the work of our own sanctification. The sin we need to be most concerned with is the sin in our own lives. Only as the church becomes holy can it begin to have a true, powerful effect on the outside world—and it won't be an external effect, but a changing of hearts. That is the focus of this book. This is a message for believers—Christians who are aliens and strangers in a hostile world (1 Pet. 2:11). It is an appeal that we commit ourselves to *biblical* thinking, that we see ourselves as God sees us, and that we deal honestly with our own sin.

To understand how to deal honestly with our own sin, we must first fully understand the problem. Part I of this book describes the decadent state of contemporary society, how sin has been treated, and consequently how the conscience has been affected. Part II examines the nature of sin. Part III provides practical solutions to gaining victory over sin. Three appendixes provide additional treatments of topics that are central in this book. Appendix 1 looks at the apostle Paul's instructions for gaining victory over sin as outlined in Romans 6. Appendixes 2 and 3 provide modern renderings of sermons in the seventeenth-century by Richard Sibbes and in the eighteenth-century by Jonathan Edwards. The sermon by Sibbes examines 1 Peter 3:21, and particularly the phrase "an appeal to God for a good conscience." It also highlights the advantages of a pure conscience. The sermon by Edwards examines why we may live in sin without knowing it and suggests ways to search our conscience to identify and arrest sin. These two sermons are included for two reasons. First, they offer helpful advice to Christians who want to deal seriously with sin and sharpen their consciences. Second, they reveal in a graphic way how differently the church once regarded sin—and thus how far contemporary Christianity has sunk. The church desperately needs to recover some of our ancestor's holy dread of sin—or we will enter the twenty-first century severely crippled.

My prayer is that this book will help to prompt evangelicals to turn again with new appreciation to the biblical doctrines of human depravity, sin, and the role of the conscience, leading to personal holiness. My prayer also is that it will help stem the tide of spiritual apathy, carelessness, shamelessness, and self-centeredness that worldly thinking has begun to breed among Bible-believing Christians. My most earnest prayer is that individual Christians who read it will be encouraged to reject such worldly values, and instead nurture "love from a pure heart and a good conscience and a sincere faith" (1 Tim. 1:5).

Part I

A Sinful Society

Modern society is full of sin, decadence, and devastating spiritual catastrophe. It can be seen at every turn. Part I isolates the causes in a sinful world where consciences have been silenced by sin.

Chapter 1, "Whatever Happened to Sin?," singles out society's tolerant notions about guilt and sin. It shows numerous examples of how society has treated every human failing as some kind of disease and created a "disease-model therapy" that only compounds the problem. It shows how victimism has taken the place of traditional morality, even in the church.

Chapter 2, "The Soul's Automatic Warning System," introduces the book's key concept of the vanishing conscience, which warns the soul about the presence of sin. It discusses how the conscience can be cleansed and strengthened.

Chapter 3, "How Sin Silences the Conscience," examines society's continuing downward spiral into sin because of secularism, lack of common sense, corrupt religion, uncontrolled lust, and sexual perversion. It parallels the decadence of Rome with today's moral decline and highlights the desperate need for revival.

1
Whatever Happened to Sin?

In all of the laments and reproaches made by our seers and prophets, one misses any mention of "sin," a word which used to be a veritable watchword of prophets. It was a word once in everyone's mind, but now rarely if ever heard. Does that mean that no sin is involved in all our troubles—sin with an "I" in the middle? Is no one any longer guilty of anything? Guilty perhaps of a sin that could be repented and repaired or atoned for? Is it only that someone may be stupid or sick or criminal—or asleep? Wrong things are being done, we know; tares are being sown in the wheat field at night. But is no one responsible, no one answerable for these acts? Anxiety and depression we all acknowledge, and even vague guilt feelings; but has no one committed any sins?

Where, indeed, did sin go? What became of it?

Dr. Karl Menninger[1]

Katherine Power was a fugitive for more than twenty-three years. In 1970, during the heyday of student radicalism, she participated in a Boston bank robbery in which a city policeman, the father of nine children, was shot in the back and killed. Pursued by federal authorities for murder, Ms. Power went into hiding. For fourteen years she was one of the FBI's Ten Most Wanted Fugitives. Finally, in late 1993, she surrendered to authorities.

In a statement she read to the press, Katherine Power characterized her actions in the bank robbery as "naive and unthinking." What motivated her to surrender? "I know that I must answer this accusation from the past, in order to live with full authenticity in the present."

Power's husband explained further: "*She did not return out of guilt.* She wanted her life back. She wants to be whole."

In a perceptive piece about Katherine Power's surrender, commentator Charles Krauthammer wrote,

> Her surrender—for the sake of "full authenticity"—was a form of therapy, indeed the final therapeutic step toward regaining her sense of self.
>
> Allan Bloom once described a man who had just gotten out of prison, where he had undergone "therapy." "He said that he had found his identity and learned to like himself," writes Bloom. "A generation ago he would have found God and learned to despise himself as a sinner."
>
> In an age where the word sin has become quaint—reserved for such offenses against hygiene as smoking and drinking (which alone merit "sin taxes")—surrendering to the authorities for armed robbery and manslaughter is not an act of repentance but of personal growth. Explains Jane Alpert, another '60s radical who served time (for her part in a series of bombings that injured twenty-one people): "Ultimately, I spent many years in therapy, learning to understand, to tolerate and forgive both others and myself."
>
> Learning to forgive oneself. Very important nowadays for revolutionaries with a criminal bent.[2]

Indeed, it is not at all uncommon these days to hear all kinds of people talking about learning to forgive themselves. But the terminology is misleading. "Forgiveness" presupposes an acknowledgement of guilt. Most people nowadays who speak of forgiving themselves explicitly repudiate the notion of personal guilt. Katherine Power is a typical example. Her husband denied that guilt had been a factor in her surrender. She only wanted to feel better about herself, to "answer [an] accusation from the past"—to be whole.

An admission of guilt today clearly is considered incompatible with the popular notion of "wholeness" and the need to protect the fantasy of a good self.

Guilt Bashing

Our culture has declared war on guilt. The very concept is considered medieval, obsolete, unproductive. People who trouble themselves with feelings of personal guilt are usually referred to therapists, whose task it is to boost their self-image. No one, after all, is supposed to feel guilty. Guilt is not conducive to dignity and self-esteem. Society encourages sin, but it will not tolerate the guilt sin produces.

Dr. Wayne Dyer, author of the 1976 mega-bestseller, *Your Erroneous Zones*, seems to have been one of the first influential voices to decry guilt altogether. He named guilt as "the most useless of all erroneous zone behaviors." According to Dr. Dyer, guilt is nothing but a neurosis. "Guilt zones," he wrote, "must be exterminated, spray-cleaned and sterilized forever."[3]

Society encourages sin, but it will not tolerate the guilt sin produces.

How do we spray-clean and sterilize our guilt zones? By renouncing the sinful behavior that makes us feel guilty? By repenting and seeking forgiveness? Not according to Dr. Dyer. In fact, his remedy for guilt is about as far from the biblical concept of repentance as it is possible to get. Here is his advice to readers suffering from guilt: "Do something which you know is bound to result in feelings of guilt. . . . Take a week to be alone if you've always wanted to do so, despite the guilt-engendering protestations from other members of your family. These kinds of behavior will help you to tackle that omnipresent guilt."[4] In other words, defy your guilt. If necessary, spurn your own spouse and children. Attack that sense of self-disapproval head on. Do something that is sure to make you feel guilty, then refuse to heed the cries of conscience, the duties of family responsibility, or even the appeal of your own loved ones. You owe it to yourself.

Guilt is rarely treated seriously anymore. It is usually portrayed as a mere annoyance, a nuisance, one of life's little aggravations. Our local newspaper recently ran a feature article on guilt. It was a light-hearted piece, dealing mostly with small, secret indulgences like rich food and French fries, sleeping late, and other "guilty pleasures," as the article called them. It quoted several psychiatrists and other mind experts. All of them characterized guilt as a usually groundless emotion that has the potential of taking all the fun out of life.

The library's periodical catalog lists these recent magazine articles under the heading *Guilt*: "How to Stop Being So Tough on Yourself," "Guilt Can Drive You Crazy," "Guilt Mongering," "Getting Rid of the Guilts," "Stop Pleading Guilty," "Guilt: Letting Go," "Don't Feed the Guilt Monster"—and a host of similar titles.

The headline of an advice column caught my eye. It summed up the universal counsel of our generation: "IT'S NOT YOUR FAULT." A woman had written to say she had tried every form of therapy she knew and still could not break a self-destructive habit.

"The first step you must take," the columnist responded, "is to stop blaming yourself. Your compulsive behavior is *not* your fault; refuse to accept blame—and above all, do not blame yourself—for what you cannot control. Heaping guilt on yourself only adds to your stress, low self-esteem, worry, depression, feelings of inadequacy, and dependence on others. Let go of your guilt feelings."

Nearly every kind of guilt can now be off-loaded. We live in a no-fault society. Even Ann Landers has written,

> One of the most painful, self-mutilating, time- and energy-consuming exercises in the human experience is guilt. . . . It can ruin your day—or your week or your life—if you let it. It turns up like a bad penny when you do something dishonest, hurtful, tacky, selfish, or rotten. . . . Never mind that it was the result of ignorance, stupidity, laziness, thoughtlessness, weak

flesh, or clay feet. You did wrong and the guilt is killing you. Too bad. But be assured, the agony you feel is normal. . . . Remember guilt is a pollutant and we don't need any more of it in the world.[5]

In other words, you shouldn't let yourself feel bad "when you do something dishonest, hurtful, tacky, selfish, or rotten." Think of yourself as good. Ignorant, stupid, lazy, thoughtless, or weak, perhaps— but *good*. Don't pollute your mind with the debilitating thought that you might actually be guilty of something.

No Guilt, No Sin

That kind of thinking has all but driven words like *sin, repentance, contrition, atonement, restitution,* and *redemption* out of public discourse. If no one is supposed to feel guilty, how could anyone be a sinner? Modern culture has the answer: people are *victims*. Victims are not responsible for what they do; they are casualties of what happens to them. So every human failing must be described in terms of how the perpetrator has been victimized. We are all supposed to be "sensitive" and "compassionate" enough to see that the very behaviors we used to label "sin" are actually evidence of victimization.

Victimism has gained so much influence that as far as society is concerned, there is practically no such thing as sin anymore. Anyone can escape responsibility for his or her wrongdoing simply by claiming the status of a victim. It has radically changed the way our society looks at human behavior.

Anyone can escape responsibility for his or her wrongdoing simply by claiming the status of a victim.

A man who was shot and paralyzed while committing a burglary in New York recovered damages from the store owner who shot him. His attorney told a jury the man was first of all a victim of society, driven to crime by economic disadvantages. Now, the lawyer said, he is a victim of the insensitivity of the man who shot him. Because of that man's callous disregard of the thief's plight as a victim, the poor criminal will be confined to a wheelchair for the rest of his life. He deserves some redress. The jury agreed. The store owner paid a large settlement. Several months later, the same man, still in his wheelchair, was arrested while committing another armed robbery.

Bernard McCummings parlayed a similar victimism into wealth. After mugging and brutally beating an elderly New York man in the subway, McCummings was shot while fleeing the scene. Permanently paralyzed, he sued and won $4.8 million in compensation from the New York Transit Authority. The man he mugged, a cancer patient, is still paying doctor bills. McCummings, the mugger—whom the courts deemed the greater victim—is now a multimillionaire.[6]

In two separate cases in England, a barmaid who stabbed another woman to death in a barroom brawl, and a woman who angrily drove her car into her lover were both acquitted of murder after they claimed acute pre-menstrual syndrome (PMS) addled their thinking and caused them to act in ways they could not control. Both received therapy rather than punishment.[7]

A San Francisco city supervisor claimed he murdered a fellow supervisor and Mayor George Moscone because too much junk food—especially Hostess Twinkies—made him act irrationally. Thus the famous "Twinkie" defense was born. "A lenient jury bought the line and produced a verdict of voluntary manslaughter rather than murder."[8] They ruled that the junk food resulted in "diminished mental capacity," which mitigated the killer's guilt. He was out of prison before the mayor's next term would have been complete.

Rioting gang members in Los Angeles beat truck driver Reginald Denny almost to death before live television cameras. A jury acquitted them of all but the most minor charges, deciding that they were caught up in the mayhem of the moment and therefore not responsible for their actions.

It is theoretically possible today in America to commit the most monstrous crimes and get off scot-free, simply by blaming some imaginative mental or emotional disorder, or by inventing some affliction to explain why you are not responsible for what you have done.

A drug dealer and cocaine addict from the Bronx was acquitted of murder after killing eight children and two women whom he shot in the head at point-blank range. His crime was the largest mass killing in the New York area since 1949. But jurors decided that drugs and stress "were a reasonable explanation for his actions." They said the man "had acted under extreme emotional distress and the influence of drugs"—so they found him guilty on a lesser charge that brought only a light sentence.[9]

But it isn't only career criminals who are using such excuses to shift blame for their wrongdoing. Millions of people from the top of society to the bottom are using similar tactics to excuse themselves for the evil things they do.

Michael Deaver, Ronald Reagan's deputy chief of staff, pleaded not guilty to perjury, claiming alcoholism and drug use had impaired his memory. He admitted "he was secretly drinking up to a quart of Scotch a day" while working in the White House.[10] The judge was at least partly swayed by the argument and gave Deaver a suspended sentence.[11]

Richard Berendzen, president of American University in Washington, D. C., was caught making obscene telephone calls to women. Claiming he was a victim of childhood abuse, Berendzen received a suspended sentence and negotiated a million-dollar severance package from the university. He has now written a book about his ordeal in which he explains that the obscene calls were his method of "data gathering." The book was given rave reviews in the *Washington Post* and *USA Today*. [12]

The Sin-as-Disease Model

Perhaps the most prevalent means of escaping blame is by classifying every human failing as some kind of disease. Drunkards and drug addicts can check into clinics for treatment of their "chemical dependencies." Children who habitually defy authority can escape condemnation by being labeled "hyperactive"or having ADD (attention deficiency disorder). Gluttons are no longer blameworthy; they suffer from an "eating disorder." Even the man who throws away his family's livelihood to pay for prostitutes is supposed to be an object of compassionate understanding; he is "addicted to sex."

An FBI agent was fired after he embezzled two thousand dollars, then gambled it away in a single afternoon at a casino. Later he sued, arguing that his gambling addiction was a disability, so his firing was an act of illegal discrimination. He won the case! Moreover, his therapy for the gambling addiction had to be funded under his employer's health-care insurance, just as if he had been suffering from appendicitis or an ingrown toenail.[13]

These days *everything* wrong with humanity is likely to be explained as an illness. What we used to call sin is more easily diagnosed as a whole array of disabilities. All kinds of immorality and evil conduct are now identified as symptoms of this or that psychological illness. Criminal behavior, various perverse passions, and every imaginable addiction have all been made excusable by the crusade to label them medical afflictions. Even commonplace problems, such as emotional weakness, depression, and anxiety are also almost universally defined as quasi-medical, rather than spiritual, afflictions.

The American Psychiatric Association publishes a thick book to help therapists in the diagnosis of these new diseases. *The Diagnostic and Statistical Manual of Mental Disorders* (Third Edition, Revised)—or DSM-III-R, as it is popularly labeled—lists the following "disorders":

- *Conduct Disorder*—"a persistent pattern of conduct in which the basic rights of others and major age-appropriate societal norms or rules are violated."
- *Oppositional Defiant Disorder*—"a pattern of negativistic, hostile, and defiant behavior."
- *Histrionic Personality Disorder*—"a pervasive pattern of excessive emotionality and attention-seeking."
- *Antisocial Personality Disorder*—"a pattern of irresponsible and antisocial behavior beginning in childhood or early adolescence and continuing into adulthood."

And there are dozens more like those. Multitudes of parents, influenced by such diagnoses, refuse to punish their children for misbehavior. Instead, they seek therapy for ODD, or HDP, or whatever new diagnosis fits the unruly child's behavior.

In the words of one author, the disease-model approach to human behavior has so overwhelmed us as a society that we have gone haywire. We want to pass laws to excuse compulsive gamblers when they embezzle money to gamble and to force insurance companies to pay to treat them. We want to treat people who can't find love and who instead (when they are women) go after dopey, superficial men or (when they are men) pursue endless sexual liaisons without finding true happiness. And we want to call all these things—and many, many more—addictions.

. . . .

> What is this new addiction industry meant to accomplish? More and more addictions are being discovered, and new addicts are being identified, until all of us will be locked into our own little addictive worlds with other addicts like ourselves, defined by the special interests of our neuroses. What a repugnant world to imagine, as well as a hopeless one. Meanwhile, *all of the addictions we define are increasing.*[14]

Worse yet, the number of people who suffer from such newly identified "sicknesses" is increasing even faster. The therapy industry is clearly *not* solving the problem of what Scripture calls sin. Instead it merely convinces multitudes that they are desperately sick and therefore not really responsible for their wrong behavior. It gives them permission to think of themselves as patients, not malefactors. And it encourages them to undergo extensive—and expensive— treatment that lasts for years, or better yet, for a lifetime. These new diseases, it seems, are ailments from which no one is ever expected to recover completely.

The sin-as-disease model has proved to be a boon to the multibillion-dollar counseling industry, and the shift toward long-term or even permanent therapy promises a bright economic future for professional therapists. One psychologist who has analyzed this trend suggests there is a clear strategy to the way therapists market their services:

1. Continue the psychologization of life;
2. Make problems out of difficulties and spread the alarm;
3. Make it acceptable to have the problem and be unable to resolve it on one's own;
4. Offer salvation [psychological, not spiritual].[15]

He notes that many therapists purposely extend their treatments over periods of many years, even after the original problem that provoked the client to seek counseling has been solved or forgotten. "They go on for so long and the client becomes so dependent on the therapist that a special period of time—sometimes extending to six months or more—is required to get the client ready to leave."[16]

Even commonplace problems, such as emotional weakness, depression, and anxiety are also almost universally defined as quasi-medical, rather than spiritual, afflictions.

"Recovery," the code-word for programs modeled after Alcoholics Anonymous, is explicitly marketed as a lifelong program. We've grown accustomed to the image of a person who has been sober for forty years standing up in an AA meeting and saying, "I'm Bill, and I'm an alcoholic." Now all "addicts" are using the same approach—including sex addicts, gambling addicts, nicotine addicts, anger addicts, wife-beating addicts, child-molesting addicts, debt addicts, self-abuse addicts, envy addicts, failure addicts, overeating addicts, or whatever. People suffering from such maladies are taught to speak of themselves as "recovering," never "recovered." Those who dare to think of themselves as delivered from their affliction are told they are living in denial.

The Wrong Prescription

Disease-model therapy therefore feeds the very problem it is supposed to treat. It alleviates any sense of guilt, while making people feel they are victims, helplessly bound for life to their affliction. Is it any wonder that such a diagnosis so often becomes a self-fulfilling prophecy?

Misdiagnosis means *any* prescribed treatment will be utterly ineffective. The care indicated for conditions labeled pathological usually involves long-term therapy, self-acceptance, a recovery program, or all of the above—perhaps even with some other psychological gimmick such as self-hypnosis thrown in to complete the elixir. "In place of evil, therapeutic society has substituted 'illness'; in place of consequence, it urges therapy and understanding; in place of responsibility, it argues for a personality driven by impulses. The illness excuse has become almost routine in cases of public misconduct."[17]

But assume for the moment that the problem *is* sin rather than sickness. The only true remedy involves humble repentance, confession (the recognition that you deserve the chastening of God because you alone are responsible for your sin)—then restitution, and growth through the spiritual disciplines of prayer, Bible study, communion with God, fellowship with other believers, and dependence on Christ. In other words, if the problem is in fact spiritual, labeling it a clinical issue will only exacerbate the problem and will offer no real deliverance from the sin. That is precisely what we see happening everywhere.

The sad truth is that disease-model treatment is disastrously counterproductive. By casting the sinner in the role of a victim, it ignores or minimizes the personal guilt inherent in the misbehavior. "I am sick" is much easier to say than, "I have sinned." But it doesn't deal with the fact that one's transgression is a serious offense against a holy, omniscient, omnipotent God. Personal guilt is for that very reason at the heart of what must be confronted when dealing with one's sin. But the disease-model remedy cannot address the problem of guilt without explaining it away. And by explaining guilt away, disease-model therapy does untold violence to the human conscience. It is therefore no remedy at all, but a disastrous prescription for escalating wickedness and eternal damnation.

The Victimization of Society

The obvious ineffectiveness of disease-model therapy has been no obstacle to its acceptance by society. After all, people want sin without guilt, and this philosophy promises just that. The trend has resulted in what author Charles J. Sykes calls "A Nation of Victims." Sykes is troubled by the rush to embrace victimism, which he suggests is badly eroding the moral character of American society. "The politics of victimization has taken the place of more traditional expressions of morality and equity," he writes.[18]

Victimism has so infected our culture that one might even say the victim has become the very symbol—the mascot—of modern society. Sykes observes,

> Whatever the future of the American mind—and the omens are not propitious—the destiny of the American character is perhaps even more alarming. . . .
> The National Anthem has become The Whine.
> Increasingly, Americans act as if they had received a lifelong indemnification from misfortune and a contractual release from personal responsibility. The British *Economist* noted with bemusement that in the United States, "If you lose your job you can sue for the mental distress of being fired. If your bank goes broke, the government has insured your deposits. . . . If you drive drunk and crash you can sue somebody for failing to warn you to stop drinking. *There is always somebody else to blame.*" [Emphasis added.]
> Unfortunately, that is a formula for social gridlock: the irresistible search for someone or something to blame colliding with the unmovable unwillingness to accept responsibility. Now enshrined in law and jurisprudence, victimism is reshaping the fabric of society, including employment policies, criminal justice, education, urban politics, and, in an increasingly Orwellian emphasis on "sensitivity" in language. A community of interdependent citizens has been displaced by a society of resentful, competing, and self-interested individuals who have dressed their private annoyances in the garb of victimism.[19]

Those who define themselves as victims claim entitlements and shun responsibility. They thus jettison any obligation they might have toward others or toward society as a whole. Once upon a time, when society affirmed the concept of personal responsibility, citizens were expected to contribute to society. They were encouraged to ask not what their country could do for them but what they could do for their country. Now that everyone is a victim, however, people think they have every right to demand society's benevolence without giving anything in return.

---

*Victimism has so infected our culture
that one might even say the victim
has become the very symbol—
the mascot—of modern society.*

Moreover, if everyone is a victim, no one needs to accept personal responsibility for wrong behavior or toxic attitudes. After all, victims are entitled to self-pity; they shouldn't be saddled with guilt feelings. Thus victimism obviates the conscience.

And if nobody shoulders any blame for society's ills, where *does* the guilt lie? With God? That would be the implication—if our culture even acknowledged God's existence. But in a society of victims there is no room for the concept of a benevolent, holy God.

Disease-Model Therapy Invades the Church

One might think that victimism and disease-model therapy are so obviously contrary to biblical truth that Bible-believing Christians would rise up *en masse* and expose the error of such thinking. But tragically, that has not been the case. Victimism has become almost as influential within the evangelical church as it is in the unbelieving world, thanks to self-esteem theology and the church's fascination with worldly psychology.

These days, when sinners seek help from churches and other Christian agencies, they are likely to be told that their problem is some emotional disorder or psychological syndrome. They might be encouraged to forgive themselves and told they ought to have more self-love and self-esteem. They are not as likely to hear that they must repent and humbly seek God's forgiveness in Christ. That is such an extraordinary change of direction for the church that even secular observers have noticed it.

Wendy Kaminer, for example, does not purport to be a Christian. If anything, she seems hostile to the church. She describes herself as "a skeptical, secular humanist, Jewish, feminist, intellectual lawyer."[20] But she has seen the change of direction within evangelicalism, and she describes it with uncanny precision. She notes that religion and psychology have always more or less deemed one another incompatible. Now she sees "not just a truce but a remarkable accommodation."[21] Even from her perspective as an unbeliever, she can see that this accommodation has meant a wholesale alteration of the fundamental message about sin and salvation. She writes:

> Christian codependency books, like those produced by the Minirth-Meier clinic in Texas, are practically indistinguishable from codependency books published by secular writers. . . . Religious writers justify their reliance on psychology by praising it for "catching up" to some eternal truths, but they've also found a way to make the temporal truths of psychology palatable. Religious leaders once condemned psychoanalysis for its moral neutrality. . . . Now popular religious literature equates illness with sin.[22]

Some of the criticism Kaminer levels against evangelicals is unwarranted or misguided, but in this respect, she is right on target: the inevitable result of Christians' embracing secular psychology has been the abandonment of any coherent concept of sin. And that has inevitably clouded the message we proclaim.

Describing the prevailing spirit of our age, Kaminer writes, "No matter how bad you've been in the narcissistic 1970s and the acquisitive 1980s, no matter how many drugs you've ingested, or sex acts performed, or how much corruption enjoyed, you're still essentially innocent: the divine child inside you is always untouched by the worst of your sins."[23] Elsewhere, she says,

> Inner children are always good—innocent and pure—like the most sentimentalized Dickens characters, which means that people are essentially good. . . . Even Ted Bundy had a child within. Evil is merely a mask—a dysfunction.
>
> The therapeutic view of evil as sickness, not sin, is strong in co-dependency theory—it's not a fire and brimstone theology. "Shaming" children, calling them bad, is considered a primary form of abuse. Both guilt and shame "are not useful as a way of life," Melody Beattie writes earnestly in *Codependent No More.* "Guilt makes *everything* harder. . . . We need to forgive ourselves" [(New York: Harper & Row, 1989), pp. 114–115]. Someone should

remind Beattie that there's a name for people who lack guilt and shame: sociopaths. We ought to be grateful if guilt makes things like murder and moral corruption "harder."[24]

Victimism has become almost as influential within the evangelical church as it is in the unbelieving world.

Ms. Kaminer suggests that evangelicalism has been infiltrated by this new anthropology-psychology-theology, and that it is antithetical to what we ought to believe and teach about sin. In that regard she surely understands more than the horde of evangelical writers who continue to echo themes from the secular self-esteem cult.

This is a serious matter. Whether you deny sin overtly and openly and totally, or covertly and by implication, any tampering with the biblical concept of sin makes chaos of the Christian faith.

Those ubiquitous phone-in counseling programs on Christian radio may provide one of the best barometers of popular Christianity's trends. When was the last time you heard an on-the-air counselor tell someone suffering from conscience pangs, "Your guilt is valid; you are sinful and must seek full repentance before God"?

Recently I listened to a talk show on a local religious radio station. This daily program features a man who bills himself as a Christian psychologist. On the day I listened he was talking about the importance of overcoming our sense of guilt. Self-blame, he told his audience, is usually irrational and therefore potentially very harmful. He gave a long lecture about the importance of forgiving oneself. The whole discourse was an echo of the world's wisdom: Guilt is a virtual mental defect. Don't let it ruin your self-image. And so on. He never mentioned repentance or restitution as prerequisites for self-forgiveness, and he never cited a single passage of Scripture.

That kind of counsel is as deadly as it is unbiblical. Guilt feelings may not always be rational, but they are nearly always a reliable signal that something is wrong somewhere, and we had better come to grips with whatever it is and make it right. Guilt functions in the spiritual realm like pain in the material realm. Pain tells us there is a physical problem that must be dealt with or the body will suffer harm. Guilt is a spiritual pain in the soul that tells us something is evil and needs to be confronted and cleansed.

To deny personal guilt is to sacrifice the soul for the sake of the ego. Besides, disavowal doesn't really deal with guilt, as we all know intuitively. Far from having beneficial results, it destroys the conscience, and thereby weakens a person's ability to avoid destructive sin. Furthermore, it actually renders a healthy self-image altogether unattainable. "How can we have self-respect if we are not responsible for what we are?"[25] More important, how can we have true self-respect without hearty approval from a healthy conscience?

The Futility of Denying Our Guilt

Twenty years ago psychiatrist Karl Menninger wrote a landmark book titled *Whatever Became of Sin?* [26] Menninger, who is no evangelical, nevertheless saw clearly the folly of treating social and behavioral problems as if their causes were all utterly nonmoral. He pointed out that modern psychology's approach—making guilt an aberration and treating self-blame as a fallacy—in effect absolves people from any moral responsibility for their behavior. That, Menninger said, eats at the fabric of the soul and society. He added that we desperately need to recover the conviction that certain behavior is *sinful*. After twenty years, the book still has the ring of a voice crying in the wilderness. But the message is needed more urgently than ever today.

Some of Menninger's views we might not entirely agree with. But his central thesis is right on target. He clearly understands that *mental* health is contingent upon, if not synonymous with, *moral* health. He therefore sees that the first step to any truly effective remedy for all mental and emotional afflictions is an honest assessment of one's own sin and the acceptance of complete responsibility for one's own moral failings. Most important, he knows there is ultimately no help for those who deny responsibility for their own behavior.

That single premise, if appreciated and applied throughout the massive counseling industry, would have an immediate beneficial effect on all society.

But as we have seen, most of the counseling being dispensed today takes precisely the opposite tack. When guilt feelings are derided as useless and unproductive, when shame is thought to be unwholesome, and when professional counselors encourage people to forgive themselves without repenting, what do we expect to become of the conscience?

What is evident is that people in our culture are becoming very good at blame-shifting—making scapegoats of parents, childhood disappointments, and other dysfunctions beyond their control. No matter what problem you suffer from—whether you are a cannibalizing serial murderer or just someone struggling with emotional distress—you can easily find someone who will explain to you why your failing is not your fault, and teach you how to silence a troubled conscience.

But from a *practical* perspective alone, that approach clearly is not working. More people than ever feel they are in need of professional counseling. Many are even becoming addicted to such therapy. Unable to cope with their own feelings, they become dependent on a therapist who must continually stoke their sense of self-worth with counsel like, "Don't be so hard on yourself"; "You mustn't blame yourself"; "You need to pamper your inner child"; "Stop punishing yourself"; "Let go of your guilt"; "You're not such a bad person"; and so on.

No matter what problem you suffer from—whether you are a cannibalizing serial murderer or just someone struggling with emotional distress— you can easily find someone who will explain to you why your failing is not your fault, and teach you how to silence a troubled conscience.

From a *biblical* perspective, that kind of counsel can be spiritually destructive. It fails to address the real problem of human sinfulness. It feeds the worst tendencies of human nature. It engenders the most catastrophic form of denial—denial of one's own guilt. And for most, who can't really shake the guilt, it adds more guilt for blaming someone who isn't really to blame at all.

Disavowing our personal culpability can never free us from a sense of guilt. On the contrary, those who refuse to acknowledge their sinfulness actually place themselves in bondage to their own guilt. "He that covereth his sins shall not prosper: but whoso confesseth and forsaketh them shall have mercy" (Prov. 28:13, KJV). "If we say that we have no sin, we are deceiving ourselves, and the truth is not in us. [But] if we confess our sins, He is faithful and righteous to forgive us our sins and to cleanse us from all unrighteousness" (1 Jn. 1:8–9).

Jesus Christ came into the world to save sinners! Jesus specifically said He had *not* come to save those who want to exonerate themselves (Mk. 2:17). Where there is no recognition of sin and guilt, when the conscience has been abused into silence, there can be no salvation, no sanctification, and therefore no real emancipation from sin's ruthless power.

2

The Soul's Automatic Warning System

An educated, sensitive conscience is God's monitor. It alerts us to the moral quality of what we do or plan to do, forbids lawlessness and irresponsibility, and makes us feel guilt, shame, and fear of the future retribution that it tells us we deserve, when we have allowed ourselves to defy its restraints. Satan's strategy is to corrupt, desensitize, and if possible kill our consciences. The relativism, materialism, narcissism, secularism, and hedonism of today's western world help him mightily toward his goal. His task is made yet simpler by the way in which the world's moral weaknesses have been taken into the contemporary church.

J. I Packer[1]

In 1984 an Avianca Airlines jet crashed in Spain. Investigators studying the accident made an eerie discovery. The "black box" cockpit recorders revealed that several minutes before impact a shrill, computer-synthesized voice from the plane's automatic warning system told the crew repeatedly in English, "Pull up! Pull up!"

The pilot, evidently thinking the system was malfunctioning, snapped, "Shut up, Gringo!" and switched the system off. Minutes later the plane plowed into the side of a mountain. Everyone on board died.

When I saw that tragic story on the news shortly after it happened, it struck me as a perfect parable of the way modern people treat the warning messages of their consciences.

As we noted in the previous chapter, the wisdom of our age says guilt feelings are nearly always erroneous or hurtful; therefore we should switch them off. But is that good advice? What, after all, is the conscience—this sense of guilt we all seem to feel? How much heed should we pay to the pangs of a grieved conscience? The conscience is not infallible, is it? So how do we know whether the guilt we feel is legitimate or whether we're simply burdened with an excess of angst? What role does the conscience play in the life of a Christian who wants to pursue sanctification according to biblical means?

What Is the Conscience?

The conscience is generally seen by the modern world as a defect that robs people of their self-esteem. Far from being a defect or a disorder, however, our ability to sense our own guilt is a tremendous gift from God. He designed the conscience into the very framework of the human soul. It is the automatic warning system that tells us, "Pull up! Pull up!" before we crash and burn.

The conscience, Puritan Richard Sibbes wrote in the seventeenth century, is *the soul reflecting upon itself.*[2] Conscience is at the heart of what distinguishes the human creature. People, unlike animals, can contemplate their own actions and make moral self-evaluations. That is the very function of conscience.

The conscience is an innate ability to sense right and wrong. Everyone, even the most unspiritual heathen, has a conscience: "When Gentiles who do not have the Law do instinctively the things of the Law, these, not having the Law, are a law to themselves, in that they show the work of the Law written in their hearts, *their conscience bearing witness*, and their thoughts alternately accusing or else defending them" (Rom. 2:14–15, emphasis added).

The conscience entreats us to do what we believe is right and restrains us from doing what we believe is wrong. The conscience is not to be equated with the voice of God or the law of God. It is a human faculty that judges our actions and thoughts by the light of the highest standard we perceive. When we violate our conscience, it condemns us, triggering feelings of shame, anguish, regret, consternation, anxiety, disgrace, and even fear. When we follow our conscience, it commends us, bringing joy, serenity, self-respect, well-being, and gladness.

The word *conscience* is a combination of the Latin words *scire* ("to know") and *con* ("together"). The Greek word for "conscience" is found more than thirty times in the New Testament—*suneidēsis*, which also literally means "co-knowledge." Conscience is knowledge together with oneself; that is, conscience knows our inner motives and true thoughts. Conscience is above reason and beyond intellect. We may rationalize, trying to justify ourselves in our own minds, but a violated conscience will not be easily convinced.

Multitudes today respond to their conscience by attempting to suppress it, overrule it, or silence it.

The Hebrew word for conscience is *leb*, usually translated "heart" in the Old Testament. The conscience is so much at the core of the human soul that the Hebrew mind did not draw a distinction between conscience and the rest of the inner person. Thus when Moses recorded that Pharaoh "hardened his heart" (Exod. 8:15), he was saying that Pharaoh had steeled his conscience against God's will. When Scripture speaks of a tender heart (cf. 2 Chr. 34:27), it refers to a sensitive conscience. The "upright in heart" (Ps. 7:10) are those with pure consciences. And when David prayed, "Create in me a clean heart, O God" (Ps. 51:10), he was seeking to have his life and his conscience cleansed.

As we noted in chapter 1, multitudes today respond to their conscience by attempting to suppress it, overrule it, or silence it. They conclude that the real blame for their wrong behavior lies in some childhood trauma, the way their parents raised them, societal pressures, or other causes beyond their control. Or they convince themselves that their sin is a clinical problem, not a moral one—and therefore define their alcoholism, sexual perversion, immorality, or other vices as "diseases." To respond to the conscience with such arguments is tantamount to telling the conscience, "Shut up, Gringo!"

It is possible virtually to nullify the conscience through repeated abuse. Paul spoke of people whose consciences were so convoluted that their "glory is in their shame" (Phil. 3:19; cf. Rom. 1:32). Both the mind and the conscience can become so defiled that they cease making distinctions between what is pure and what is impure (cf. Tit. 1:15). After so much violation, the conscience finally falls silent. Morally, those with defiled consciences are left flying blind. The annoying warning signals may be gone, but the danger certainly is not; *in fact, the danger is greater than ever*.

Furthermore, even the most defiled conscience will not remain silent forever. When we stand in judgment, every person's conscience will side with God, the righteous judge. The worst sin-hardened evildoer will discover before the throne of God that he has a conscience which testifies against him.

The conscience, however, is *not* infallible. Nor is it a source of revelation about right and wrong. Its role is not to teach us moral and ethical ideals, but to hold us accountable to the highest standards of right and wrong we know. The conscience is informed by tradition as well as by truth, so the standards it holds us to are not necessarily biblical ones (1 Cor. 8:6–9). The conscience can be needlessly condemning in areas where there is no biblical issue. In fact, it can try to hold us to the very thing the Lord is trying to release us from (Rom. 14:14, 20–23). The conscience, to operate fully and in accord with true holiness, must be informed by the Word of God. So even when guilt feelings don't have a biblical basis, they are an important spiritual distress sign. If they're only signaling a weak conscience, that should spur us to seek the spiritual growth that would bring our conscience more in harmony with God's Word.

The conscience reacts to the convictions of the mind and therefore can be encouraged and sharpened in accordance with God's Word. The wise Christian wants to master biblical truth so that the conscience is completely informed and judges right because it is responding to God's Word. A regular diet of Scripture will strengthen a weak conscience or restrain an overactive one. Conversely, error, human wisdom, and wrong moral influences filling the mind will corrupt or cripple the conscience.

In other words, the conscience functions like a skylight, not a light bulb. It lets light into the soul; it does not produce its own. Its effectiveness is determined by the amount of pure light we expose it to, and by how clean we keep it. Cover it or put it in total darkness and it ceases to function. That's why the apostle Paul spoke of the importance of a clear conscience (1 Tim. 3:9) and warned against anything that would defile or muddy the conscience (1 Cor. 8:7; Tit. 1:15).

Or, to switch metaphors, our conscience is like the nerve endings in our fingertips. Its sensitivity to external stimuli can be damaged by the buildup of callouses or even wounded so badly as to be virtually impervious to any feeling. Paul also wrote of the dangers of a calloused conscience (1 Cor. 8:10), a wounded conscience (v. 12), and a seared conscience (1 Tim. 4:2).

The conscience is privy to all our secret thoughts and motives. It is therefore a more accurate and more formidable witness in the soul's courtroom than any external observer.

Psychopaths, serial killers, pathological liars, and other people who seem to lack any moral sense are extreme examples of people who have ruined or desensitized their consciences. Can such people really sin without remorse or scruples? If so, it is only because they have ravaged their own consciences through relentless immorality and lawlessness. They certainly weren't born devoid of any conscience. The conscience is an inextricable part of the human soul. Though it may be hardened, cauterized, or numbed into apparent dormancy, the conscience continues to store up evidence that will one day be used as testimony to condemn the guilty soul.

The Conscience Holds Court

Richard Sibbes pictured the conscience as a court in the council of the human heart. In Sibbes's imagery, the conscience itself assumes every role in the courtroom drama. It is a *register* to record what we have done in exact detail (Jer. 17:1). It is the *accuser* that lodges a complaint against us when we are guilty, and a *defender* to side with us in our innocence (Rom. 2:15). It acts as a *witness*, giving testimony for or against us (2 Cor. 1:12). It is the *judge*, condemning or vindicating us (1 Jn. 3:20–21). And it is the *executioner*, smiting us with grief when our guilt is discovered (1 Sam. 24:5). Sibbes compared the chastisement of a violated conscience to "a flash of hell."[3]

The conscience is privy to all our secret thoughts and motives. It is therefore a more accurate and more formidable witness in the soul's courtroom than any external observer. Those who gloss over an accusing conscience in favor of a human counselor's reassurances are playing a deadly game. Ill thoughts and motives may escape the eye of a human counselor, but they will not escape the eye of conscience. Nor will they escape the eye of an all-knowing God. When such people are summoned to final judgment, their own conscience will be fully informed of every violation and will step forward as an eternally tormenting witness against them.

That, Sibbes wrote, ought to discourage us from secret sins:

> We should not sin in hope of concealment. What if thou conceal it from all others, canst thou conceal [it from] thy own conscience? As one saith well, What good is it for thee that none knows what is done, when thou knowest it thyself? What profit is it for him that hath a conscience that will accuse him, that he hath no man to accuse him but himself? He is a thousand witnesses to himself. *Conscience is not a private witness.* It is a thousand witnesses. Therefore, never sin in hope to have it concealed. It were better that all men should know it than that

thyself should know it. All will be one day written in thy forehead. *Conscience will be a blab.* If it cannot speak the truth now, though it be bribed in this life, it will have power and efficacy in the life to come. . . . We have the witness in us; and, as Isaiah saith, 'Our sins witness against us.' It is in vain to look for secrecy. Conscience will discover all.[4]

How the Conscience Is Cleansed

One aspect of the miracle of salvation is the cleansing and rejuvenating effect the new birth has on the conscience. At salvation, the believer's heart is "sprinkled clean from an evil conscience" (Heb. 10:22). The means through which the conscience is cleansed is the blood of Christ (Heb. 9:14). That does not mean, of course, that Jesus' actual blood has some mystical or magical potency as a conscience-cleansing agent. What does it mean?

The theological concepts involved here are simple but quite profound. The Old Testament Law required blood sacrifices to atone for sin. But Old Testament sacrifices could do nothing for the conscience. Hebrews 9:9–10 says, "Gifts and sacrifices [under the Levitical system] could not make the worshiper perfect in conscience, since they relate only to food and drink and various washings, regulations for the body imposed until a time of reformation." Those sacrifices had no actual efficacy in atoning for sin, "for it is impossible for the blood of bulls and goats to take away sins" (Heb. 10:4). They simply demonstrated the faith and obedience of the worshiper while foreshadowing the death of Christ, who would shed His blood as the once for-all perfect sacrifice for sin.

---

*Christ's atonement fully satisfied
the demands of God's righteousness,
so forgiveness and mercy are guaranteed
to those who receive
Christ in humble, repentant faith.*

Christ's sacrifice on the cross therefore accomplished what the blood of goats and bulls and the ashes of heifers could only symbolize: "He Himself bore our sins in His body on the cross" (1 Pet. 2:24). Our sins were imputed to Him, and He paid the penalty for them. Conversely, His perfect righteousness is imputed to us who believe (Rom. 4:22–24; Phil. 3:9). Since the guilt of all our sins was entirely erased by His death, and since His unblemished righteousness is credited to our account, God declares us not guilty and receives us as fully righteous. That is the doctrine known as *justification*.

When God's own verdict is "Not guilty; wholly righteous" how can anyone else accuse us? "Who will bring a charge against God's elect? God is the one who justifies; who is the one who condemns? Christ Jesus is He who died, yes, rather who was raised, who is at the right hand of God, who also intercedes for us" (Rom. 8:33–34). In other words, when Satan, "the accuser of our brethren . . . , who accuses them before our God day and night" (Rev. 12:10), brings an allegation against us, the blood of Christ speaks of mercy. When our own sins cry out against us, the blood of Christ speaks on our behalf. Thus the blood of Christ "speaks better than the blood of Abel" (Heb. 12:24).

Most important, whenever our own conscience would mercilessly condemn us, the blood of Christ cries for forgiveness. Christ's atonement fully satisfied the demands of God's righteousness, so forgiveness and mercy are guaranteed to those who receive Christ in humble, repentant faith. We accept the responsibility for our sin, and also believe God that in the death of Christ sin is forgiven. We confess our sin so that the Lord can cleanse our conscience and give us joy (1 Jn. 1:9). That is how "the blood of Christ, who through the eternal Spirit offered Himself without blemish to God, cleanse[s] your conscience from dead works to serve the living God" (Heb. 9:14). In other words, our faith communicates to our conscience that we are pardoned through the precious blood of Christ.

Does that mean believers can persist in sinning and yet enjoy a clear conscience? Certainly not. "How shall we who died to sin still live in it?" (Rom. 6:2). The new birth entails a complete overhaul of the human soul (2 Cor. 5:17). A washed and rejuvenated conscience is only one evidence that such a transformation has taken place (cf. 1 Pet. 3:21). Love of righteousness and hatred of sin is another evidence (1 Jn. 3:3, 8). Believers whose behavior contradicts their faith cause their consciences to be defiled (1 Cor. 8:7). And those who profess Christ but ultimately reject faith and a good conscience suffer shipwreck spiritually (1 Tim. 1:19)—that is, they prove they never truly believed in the first place (cf. 1 Jn. 2:19).

A sound conscience therefore goes hand in hand with assurance of salvation (Heb. 10:22). The steadfast believer must maintain the proper focus of faith in order to have a conscience that is perpetually being cleansed from guilt: "If we confess our sins, He is faithful and righteous to forgive us our sins and to [keep on cleansing] us from all unrighteousness" (1 Jn. 1:9).

What a gift it is to be cleansed from a defiled conscience! In the same way that a grieved conscience is a flash of hell, so a pure conscience is a foretaste of glory.

It is the Christian's high and holy duty to guard the purity of his regenerated conscience. Paul had much to say about this. Note how he spoke of the conscience in the following verses (emphasis added):

- "Paul, looking intently at the Council, said, 'Brethren, I have lived my life with *a perfectly good conscience* before God up to this day'" (Acts 23:1).
- "In view of this, I also do my best to maintain always *a blameless conscience* both before God and before men" (Acts 24:16).
- "The goal of our instruction is love from a pure heart and *a good conscience* and a sincere faith" (1 Tim. 1:5).
- "Fight the good fight, keeping faith and *a good conscience*" (1 Tim. 1:18–19).
- "I serve [God] with *a clear conscience* the way my forefathers did" (2 Tim. 1:3).

One of the basic qualifications for deacons, Paul told Timothy, is "holding to the mystery of the faith with *a clear conscience*" (1 Tim. 3:9).

Ironically, a weak conscience is more likely to accuse than a strong conscience. Scripture calls this a weak conscience because it is too easily wounded.

A pure conscience is essential not only for what it does for oneself, but for what it says to others. A sound conscience marks the life that is a strong testimony for Christ. Paul frequently pointed to his conscience as a witness: "For our proud confidence is this, the testimony of our conscience, that in holiness and godly sincerity, not in fleshly wisdom but in the grace of God, we have conducted ourselves in the world, and especially toward you" (2 Cor. 1:12). "We have renounced the things hidden because of shame, not walking in craftiness or adulterating the word of God, but by the manifestation of truth commending ourselves to every man's conscience in the sight of God" (2 Cor. 4:2). Peter wrote, "Keep a good conscience so that in the thing in which you are slandered, those who revile your good behavior in Christ may be put to shame" (1 Pet. 3:16).

Overcoming a Weak Conscience

As we noted briefly earlier, Scripture indicates that some Christians have weak consciences. A weak conscience is not the same as a seared conscience. A seared conscience becomes inactive, silent, rarely accusing, insensitive to sin. But the weakened conscience usually is hypersensitive and overactive about issues that are not sins. Ironically, a weak conscience is more likely to accuse than a strong conscience. Scripture calls this a weak conscience because it is *too easily wounded*. People with weak consciences tend to fret about things that should provoke no guilt in a mature Christian who knows God's truth.

A weak conscience results from an immature or fragile faith not yet weaned from worldly influences and not yet saturated in the Word of God. Weak believers are to be accepted with love and not judged because their consciences are too tender. Paul instructed the Romans, "Now accept the one who is weak in faith, but not for the purpose of passing judgment on his opinions. One man has faith that he may eat all things, but he who is weak eats vegetables only" (Rom. 14:1–2). We see from Paul's comment that the weak believer is likely to be overscrupulous, legalistic, troubled by his conscience in an unhealthy way. And as we shall note, a weak conscience is often the companion of legalism.

Repeatedly Paul admonished the early church that those with strong consciences were not to be judgmental (Rom. 14:3), and above all they must not encourage those who are weak to violate their consciences. Weak believers must not learn to overrule conscience. If that becomes a habit—if they condition themselves to reject all the promptings of conscience—they will thus forfeit one of the most important means of sanctification.

In fact, Paul instructed those who were strong to defer whenever possible to the qualms of the weaker brother's conscience. To encourage an immature believer to wound his own conscience is to lead him into sin: "He who doubts [on account of a weak conscience] is condemned if he eats, because his eating is not from faith; and whatever is not from faith is sin" (Rom. 14:23).

The Corinthian church was torn by a disagreement over whether it was sinful to eat food offered to idols. Corinth, a pagan city, was filled with temples where food was sacrificed to heathen gods and goddesses. Food would be prepared, then laid on the altar by a worshiper. Obviously, the idol could not consume the food, so the pagan priests and priestesses would take whatever was offered and sell it at a discount. That was how such people earned their livelihood. Food offered to idols could therefore be obtained in Corinth at prices considerably cheaper than in the regular food shops.

Some Christians believed such food was defiled and therefore sinful to eat. Others, knowing that idols are nothing, could eat the food without qualms. Corinthian believers were beginning to split into factions over the issue, so they asked Paul to instruct them.

Paul's advice illuminates the question of how Christians should respond to their consciences. First of all, he told them, an idol is nothing. "There is no such thing as an idol in the world, and . . . there is no God but one" (1 Cor. 8:4). "For us there is but one God" (v. 6). Idols are imaginary gods. They do not exist. As believers we do not even acknowledge them. How can a non-existent god defile otherwise edible food? Therefore to eat food offered to idols is *not* inherently sinful. The question of what foods are edible is a matter of complete liberty for a Christian. "Food will not commend us to God; we are neither the worse if we do not eat, nor the better if we do eat" (v. 8).

But, Paul pointed out, not everyone's faith was strong enough to embrace that truth. Many of the Corinthians had recently been saved out of idolatry. They had spent their whole lives developing a mindset of fear and worship directed toward these false gods. The associations and memories of the old life of darkness were too strong. Food offered on a heathen altar was more than their consciences could bear (1 Cor. 8:7).

No believer, Paul told the Corinthians, has a right to violate his or her conscience. More significant, no believer has a right to urge fellow Christians to sin by violating their consciences—even if their consciences are merely weak and condemning them for something they are legally and morally free to do. Liberty in Christ is thus accompanied by an uncompromising accountability to our own consciences, and by a still higher responsibility to the whole body of believers:

> Take care lest this liberty of yours somehow become a stumbling block to the weak. For if someone sees you, who have knowledge, dining in an idol's temple, will not his conscience, if he is weak, be strengthened to eat things sacrificed to idols? For through your knowledge he who is weak is ruined, the brother for whose sake Christ died. And thus, by sinning against the brethren and wounding their conscience when it is weak, you sin against Christ (vv. 9–12).

A weak and constantly accusing conscience is a spiritual liability, not a strength. Many people with especially tender consciences tend to display their overscrupulousness as if it were proof of deep spirituality. It is precisely the opposite.

The point is this: If your faith is strong and your conscience healthy, you may enjoy your own freedom in Christ without making any effort to arouse more intense scrutiny from your own conscience: "Eat anything that is sold in the meat market, without asking questions for conscience' sake" (1 Cor. 10:25). But if you have reason to think that someone watching you might be wounded in conscience by your exercise of freedom, abstain. Guard the other person's tender conscience. Paul gave this example: "If anyone should say to you, 'This is meat sacrificed to idols,' do not eat it, for the sake of the one who informed you, and *for conscience' sake; I mean not your own conscience, but the other man's*" (vv. 28–29, emphasis added). Don't put a stumbling block or an occasion to fall in someone else's way (Rom. 14:13).

A weak and constantly accusing conscience is a spiritual liability, not a strength. Many people with especially tender consciences tend to display their overscrupulousness as if it were proof of deep spirituality. It is precisely the opposite. Those with weak consciences tend to be too easily offended and stumble frequently (cf. 1 Cor. 8:13). They are often overly critical of others (Rom. 14:3–4). They are too susceptible to the lure of legalism (Rom. 14:20; cf. Gal. 3:2–5). Their thoughts and hearts are soon defiled (Tit. 1:15).

Throughout Paul's discussion of those with weak consciences (Rom. 14; 1 Cor. 8–10), he treats the condition as a state of spiritual immaturity—a lack of knowledge (1 Cor. 8:7) and a lack of faith (Rom. 14:1, 23). Paul clearly expected that those with weak consciences would grow out of that immature state, like children inevitably outgrow their fear of the dark. Those who choose instead to live in such a state—particularly those who point to a too-tender conscience as something to boast about—have a warped sense of what it means to be mature in the faith. True spiritual growth enlightens the mind and strengthens the heart in faith. It is ultimately the only way to overcome a weak conscience.

Keeping a Pure Conscience

How can we keep our consciences pure? What is the proper response to guilt feelings? Those questions will be the focus of much of this book, but for now here are some simple principles to remember involving confession, forgiveness, restitution, procrastination, and education.

Confess and forsake known sin. Examine your guilt feelings in light of Scripture. Deal with the sin God's Word reveals. Proverbs 28:13 says, "He who conceals his transgressions will not prosper, but

he who confesses and forsakes them will find compassion." First
John 1 speaks of confession of sin as an ongoing characteristic of the
Christian life: "If we confess our sins, He is faithful and righteous to
forgive us our sins and to cleanse us from all unrighteousness" (v. 9).
We should certainly confess to those we have wronged: "Therefore,
confess your sins to one another, and pray for one another, so that
you may be healed" (Jas. 5:16). But above all, we should confess to
the One whom sin offends most. As David wrote, "I acknowledged my
sin to Thee, and my iniquity I did not hide; I said, 'I will confess
my transgressions to the Lord'; and Thou didst forgive the guilt of my
sin" (Ps. 32:5).

Ask forgiveness and be reconciled to anyone you have wronged.
Jesus instructed us, "If therefore you are presenting your offering at
the altar, and there remember that your brother has something
against you, leave your offering there before the altar, and go your
way; first be reconciled to your brother, and then come and present
your offering" (Matt. 5:23–24). "If you forgive men for their transgressions, your heavenly Father will also forgive you. But if you do
not forgive men, then your Father will not forgive your transgressions" (Matt. 6:14–15).

Make restitution. God told Moses: "Speak to the sons of Israel,
'When a man or woman commits any of the sins of mankind, acting
unfaithfully against the Lord, and that person is guilty, then he shall
confess his sins which he has committed, and he shall make restitution in full for his wrong, and add to it one-fifth of it, and give it to
him whom he has wronged'" (Num. 5:6–7). The principle behind
this law is binding on believers living in the New Testament era as
well (cf. Philem. 19; Lk. 19:8).

Don't procrastinate in clearing your wounded conscience. Paul
said he did his best "to maintain always a blameless conscience both
before God and before men" (Acts 24:16). Some people put off dealing with their guilt, thinking their conscience will clear itself in
time. It won't. Procrastination allows the guilt feelings to fester. That
in turn generates depression, anxiety, and other emotional problems. Guilt feelings may persist long after the offense is forgotten,
often spilling over to other areas of our lives. That's one reason

people often feel guilty and are not sure why. Such confused guilt may be a symptom that something is terribly wrong spiritually. Paul may have had that in mind when he wrote, "To those who are defiled and unbelieving, nothing is pure, but both their mind and their conscience are defiled" (Tit. 1:15).

Dealing with a wounded conscience immediately by heart-searching prayer before God is the only way to keep it clear and sensitive. Putting off dealing with guilt inevitably compounds the problems.

Educate your conscience. As we saw earlier, a weak, easily grieved conscience results from a lack of spiritual knowledge (1 Cor. 8:7). If your conscience is too easily wounded, don't violate it; to do so is to train yourself to override conviction, and that will lead to overriding true conviction about real sin. Moreover, violating the conscience is a sin in itself (v. 12, cf. Rom. 14:23). Instead, immerse your conscience in God's Word so it can begin to function with reliable data.

An important aspect of educating the conscience is teaching it to focus on the right object—divinely revealed truth. If the conscience looks only to personal feelings, it can accuse us wrongfully. We are certainly not to order our lives according to our feelings. A conscience fixed on feelings becomes unreliable. Individuals subject to depression and melancholy especially should not allow their conscience to be informed by their feelings. Despondent feelings will provoke unnecessary doubts and fears in the soul when not kept in check by a well-advised conscience. The conscience must be persuaded by God's Word, not by our feelings.

Furthermore, conscience errs when the mind focuses wholly on our faltering in sin and ignores the triumphs of God's grace in us. True Christians experience both realities. Conscience must be allowed to weigh the fruit of the Spirit in our lives as well as the remnants of our sinful flesh. It must see our faith as well as our failings. Otherwise the conscience will become overly accusing, prone to unwholesome doubts about our standing before God.

We must subject our conscience to the truth of God and the teaching of Scripture. As we do that, the conscience will be more clearly focused and better able to give us reliable feedback. A trustworthy conscience becomes a powerful aid to spiritual growth and stability.

Recovering the Doctrine of the Conscience

The conscience may be the most underappreciated and least understood attribute of humanity. Psychology, as we have noted, is usually less concerned with understanding the conscience than with attempting to silence it. The influx of popular psychology into evangelicalism has had the disastrous effect of undermining a biblical appreciation of the role of the conscience. It is bad enough that secular society's collective conscience has been vanishing for years. But now the don't-blame-yourself philosophy is having a similar effect in the church.

But as we have seen, Scripture never suggests that we should respond to our conscience by repudiating guilt. On the contrary, the Bible reveals that most of us are far more guilty than our own hearts tell us. Paul wrote, "I am conscious of nothing against myself, yet I am not by this acquitted; but the one who examines me is the Lord" (1 Cor. 4:4).

Rather than discarding or silencing a condemning conscience, we who know Christ must educate our consciences carefully with the pure Word of God, listen to them, and learn to understand them. Above all, we must keep our consciences undefiled. That is crucial to our testimony before an ungodly world.

We must not permit the message we proclaim to become infected with worldly notions that minimize guilt and seek only to make people feel good about themselves. The popular gospel of our generation usually leaves the impression that Jesus is a Savior from trouble, sadness, loneliness, despair, pain, and suffering. Scripture says He came to save people from *sin*. Therefore one of the fundamental truths of the gospel is that all of us are contemptible sinners (Rom. 3:10–23). The only way to find real forgiveness and freedom from our sin is through humble, contrite repentance. We can't escape guilt by telling ourselves we are really not that bad. We must come face to face with the exceeding sinfulness of our sin. Isn't that the whole point of this familiar parable?

Two men went up into the temple to pray, one a Pharisee, and the other a tax-gatherer. The Pharisee stood and was praying thus to himself, "God, I thank Thee that I am not like other people: swindlers, unjust, adulterers, or even like this tax-gatherer. I fast twice a week; I pay tithes of all that I get." But the tax-gatherer, standing some distance away, was even unwilling to lift up his eyes to heaven, but was beating his breast, saying, "God, be merciful to me, the sinner!" I tell you, this man went down to his house justified rather than the other; for everyone who exalts himself shall be humbled, but he who humbles himself shall be exalted (Lk. 18:10–14).

The gospel thus speaks directly through the Holy Spirit to the human conscience. Before it ever offers salvation, it must bring the sinner face to face with his or her own desperate sinfulness. Those who are conditioned to disavow their consciences in small matters certainly will not respond to a message that convicts them of sin so heinous as to warrant eternal condemnation. The attack on the conscience is therefore hardening people against the truth of the gospel.

Some Christians, sensing this effect, have concluded that the gospel message needs updating. They have removed the idea of sin altogether from the message. They offer Christ as a Savior from meaninglessness, as a means to personal fulfillment, as a solution to self-image problems, or as an answer to emotional needs. The gospel they extend to unbelievers makes no appeal to the conscience, no mention of sin. It is therefore an impotent and spurious message.

How can anyone genuinely repent who has no sense of personal responsibility for sin? Thus the contemporary tendency to devalue the conscience actually undermines the gospel itself.

Others, instead of eliminating sin from the message completely, treat the subject as briefly or as mildly as possible. They might stress the universality of sin but never explain the seriousness of it: "Of course you've sinned. We all have!"—as if it were sufficient to concede the notion of universal sinfulness without really feeling any personal guilt in one's own conscience. But how can anyone genuinely repent who has no sense of personal responsibility for sin? Thus the contemporary tendency to devalue the conscience actually undermines the gospel itself.

The vanishing conscience has a detrimental effect on Christian living as well. The conscience is an important key to joy and victory in the Christian life. The benefits of a pure conscience comprise some of the greatest blessings of the Christian life. As we have noted, the apostle Paul frequently appealed to his blameless conscience in the midst of the afflictions and persecutions he suffered (e.g., Acts 23:1; 24:16; 2 Cor. 1:12). Through those trials the knowledge that his heart was unimpeachable supplied him with the strength and confidence to endure. Paul carefully guarded his heart and conscience lest he lose that source of assurance. He also treasured his pure conscience as a thing of joy in and of itself.

A pure conscience is more to be sought than the world's approval. The very process of spiritual maturity is learning to subject one's conscience to Scripture, then live accordingly, regardless of popular opinion.

Charles Wesley wrote this hymn about the conscience:

> I want a principle within
> Of watchful, godly fear,
> A sensibility of sin,
> A pain to feel it near.
> Help me the first approach to feel
> Of pride or wrong desire;
> To catch the wandering of my will,
> And quench the kindling fire.
>
> From Thee that I no more may stray,
> No more Thy goodness grieve,
> Grant me the filial awe, I pray,
> The tender conscience give.
> Quick as the apple of an eye,
> O God, my conscience make!
> Awake my soul when sin is nigh,
> And keep it still awake.

That hymn is rarely sung these days. The church as a whole seems to have forgotten the spiritual importance of a sound conscience. I am convinced that is one of the chief reasons so many Christians seem to live in sorrow and defeat. They are not taught to respond correctly to their consciences. They treat their consciences flippantly. They have not learned the importance of keeping the conscience clear and healthy. Instead they dispute what their own conscience tells them. They treat any sense of guilt or self-blame as a liability or a threat. They expend too much of their spiritual energy in a vain attempt to deal with feelings spawned by an accusing conscience—without a corresponding willingness to deal with the sin that offended the conscience in the first place.

That is spiritual suicide. Paul wrote of those who by rejecting their consciences "suffered shipwreck in regard to their faith" (1 Tim. 1:19). They are like a pilot who turns off his warning system.

We *must* pay attention to our consciences. The cost of switching them off is frightfully high. It will inevitably result in a devastating spiritual catastrophe. Of all people, we who are committed to the truth of Scripture cannot relinquish the importance of a sound conscience. We must recover and apply the biblical truth about the conscience, or we will be left with nothing whatsoever to say to a sinful world.

3

How Sin Silences the Conscience

This myth [that mankind is basically good] deludes people into thinking that they are always victims, never villains; always deprived, never depraved. It dismisses responsibility as the teaching of a darker age. It can excuse any crime, because it can always blame something else—a sickness of our society or a sickness of the mind.

One writer called the modern age "the golden age of exoneration." When guilt is dismissed as the illusion of narrow minds, then no one is accountable, even to his conscience.

The irony is that this should come alive in this century, of all centuries, with its gulags and death camps and killing fields. As G. K. Chesterton once said, the doctrine of original sin is the only philosophy empirically validated by centuries of recorded human history.

Charles W. Colson[1]

The legacy of the age of psychology is disastrous, pervasive wickedness. Sin has hardly ever been as heinous as it is in our age. Drugs, prostitution, pornography, sexual perversion, and crime are rampant in our cities. Gang violence has turned our streets into war zones. Criminals are getting younger and bolder all the time. The prison system is overcrowded and ineffective.

Such problems are not new, someone will say. Similar evils have plagued mankind since the earliest times. And indeed they have. But unlike previous generations, ours fails to see even the grossest wickedness for what it is—a transgression against the immutable moral law of a supremely holy God. Modern society seems to miss the point that such behavior is actually *sinful*.

Bob Vernon, former Assistant Chief of the Los Angeles Police Department, warns of the increasing number of what he terms "moral flatliners"—young people who choose crime as a career and who can commit the most heinous acts with no apparent remorse. He describes one such youth, a gang member known as "Cool Aid." Cool Aid unleashed a barrage of gunshots on a float carrying the queen's court in a high-school homecoming parade. Several young girls were wounded, one critically. The crime was carried out in broad daylight, and scores of eyewitnesses immediately fingered Cool Aid as the perpetrator. In the interrogation room after his arrest, Cool Aid explained to Chief Vernon his motives for the shooting. He needed to do some prison time because he knew he would get free medical treatment behind bars. He had a case of venereal disease that required treatment and some teeth that needed filling. He also planned to spend the time in prison getting "buffed out" by lifting weights. But before he went in, he had to acquire a "rep"—a reputation. "I'll be known as the enforcer," he proudly told police officers.[2]

Vernon writes,

> What we see so clearly in Cool Aid's case is [one of the root problems] destroying our society and families: the loss of conscience. The trend is to no longer be ashamed of our darker side. This shocking trend is ravaging our culture. It's becoming a badge of honor to not only violate social norms, but even to flaunt that behavior. . . . The behaviors have always been there, even those we've recognized as harmful to society. The significant change is in how we react to those actions.

Today it's not uncommon to literally applaud a person who discloses what in the past has been looked upon as a weakness [or a sin]. The "Phil Donahue" show is an obvious example of this trend. People get on nationwide TV, admit to breaking their marriage vows, and boast of a determination to continue the practice. Others talk of purposely bringing a baby into the world with no family to support it. Some flaunt the lies and deception that have brought them wealth, and many brag about cheating the government on their tax returns. Usually the audience cheers the speaker's "courage" in publicly going against the social norms.[3]

> *Today it's not uncommon to literally applaud a person who discloses what in the past has been looked upon as a weakness [or a sin]. (Bob Vernon)*

Is society becoming incapable of even thinking in terms of good and evil? Has the relativism of a humanistic culture rendered modern society wholly amoral?

Hardened by the Deceitfulness of Sin

The most ominous aspect of our culture's moral slide is that the problem tends to feed itself. Sin denied dulls the conscience. The writer of Hebrews warned about the danger of being "hardened by the deceitfulness of sin" (3:13). Sin defies and deceives the human conscience, and thereby hardens the human heart. A sin-hardened heart grows ever more susceptible to temptation, pride, and every kind of evil. Unconfessed sin therefore becomes a cycle that desensitizes and corrupts the conscience and drags people deeper and deeper into bondage.

On the cultural level, for example, we can see that as conviction of sin is silenced and the community conscience vanishes, society becomes more corrupt and more tolerant of worse debauchery.

The rapid erosion of social standards regarding obscenity and moral propriety provides abundant evidence of this phenomenon. What was shocking and unacceptable only a decade ago is now standard fare on network television. Lewd humor that would have been judged inappropriate outside the locker room not so long ago is now the main attraction in children's entertainment. And things are steadily growing worse. Just when "The Simpsons" seemed to be plumbing the depths of moral nihilism in animated cartoons, MTV introduced a couple of characters who make Bart Simpson look like a choirboy. Beavis, and his friend whose name is too crude to mention, epitomize the degeneracy of modern culture. Everything that is vulgar, disrespectful, or illegal, they consider "cool"—and all that is good or sacred, they ridicule.

Beavis and his buddy are the heroes of the next generation. That is an appalling thought. How low can the culture sink?

Evidence of serious moral decline is all around. Look at the tabloids lining the supermarket checkout stands. The headlines scream news of people's perversions, adultery, gluttony, extravagance, arrogance, selfishness, drunkenness, immorality, anger, and all kinds of vice. Worst of all, as Chief Vernon pointed out, these vices are brandished almost like badges of honor! Have you noticed the proliferation of T-shirts and bumper stickers that are printed with the most unspeakable profanities to be displayed shamelessly in public? Our society takes pleasure in its own wickedness. People are not ashamed of their sin; they boast about it. They go on televised talk shows just to glory in their own depravity. And the audiences love it. As the apostle Paul wrote, "Although they know the ordinance of God, that those who practice such things are worthy of death, they not only do the same, but also give hearty approval to those who practice them" (Rom. 1:32).

Paul made that comment at the end of Romans 1, concluding a discourse about the downward spiral of sin. His words throughout the second half of that chapter are strikingly applicable to the predicament of contemporary society. Here the apostle shows how and why the human conscience vanishes. He reveals that those who ignore or suppress their conscience risk a dreadful judgment: God ultimately abandons such people to the devastating effects of their own sin. That is exactly what we see happening in our nation. It is also the record of human history—nation after nation being abandoned by God after they first abandoned Him and became hopelessly enthralled with their own sin.

First the Bad News . . .

Romans 1:16 begins an extended, systematic treatment of the gospel that continues throughout the epistle. Paul crowned his introduction and greeting to the Roman believers with these words: "I am not ashamed of the gospel, for it is the power of God for salvation to everyone who believes, to the Jew first and also to the Greek. For in it the righteousness of God is revealed from faith to faith; as it is written, 'But the righteous man shall live by faith'" (Rom. 1:16–17).

There can be no salvation for those who aren't convinced of the seriousness of their sin.

Right there, just when it seemed Paul was going to begin talking about the *good news* and the power of God unto salvation, he unleashed this thunderbolt: "For the wrath of God is revealed from heaven against all ungodliness and unrighteousness of men, who suppress the truth in unrighteousness" (1:18). About this verse and the passage that follows, D. Martyn Lloyd-Jones wrote, "It is a terrible [terrifying] passage. Melancthon described the eighteenth verse as 'an exordium terrible as lightning.' And it has not only the terrifying quality of lightning, but also its illuminating power."[4]

It turns out that the good news about salvation starts with the bad news about sin. As Jesus said, "It is not those who are healthy who need a physician, but those who are sick; I did not come to call the righteous, but sinners" (Mk. 2:17). Paul knew that those who underestimate the enormity and gravity of human sinfulness—especially those who do not see their own depravity—cannot apply the only effective remedy to their problems. That, after all, is precisely the issue we are addressing in this book.

There can be no salvation for those who aren't convinced of the seriousness of their sin. There can be no word of reconciliation for sinners who remain oblivious to their estrangement from God. True fear of God cannot grip those who are blind to the depth of their sinfulness. And no mercy is available for those who do not tremble at God's holy threats.

In other words, to attempt to eradicate the human conscience is one of the most spiritually destructive pursuits any individual or society can engage in. It results in God's wrath—not yet ultimate wrath (hell) or eschatalogical wrath (the Day of the Lord), but temporal wrath. That is, He removes restraining grace and turns a person or a society over to the cycle of sin without the mitigating deterrent of conscience. This is the very judgment Paul spoke of at Lystra, when he said that God "in the generations gone by . . . permitted all the nations to go their own ways" (Acts 14:16).

That is Paul's main point in Romans 1:18–32. There he describes the judgment of God that results in humanity's decline into wanton sin. Notice that the most dramatic feature of his narrative is not the ghastly sins he names—although he chronicles some pretty gross practices. But the singular feature that marks each step of mankind's descent under God's wrath involves the hardening and decimation of the conscience.

The Conscience Evident Within

Paul says God's wrath is revealed because people "suppress the truth in unrighteousness" (Rom. 1:18). He is referring to sinners who have successfully hushed their own consciences. "The truth" they suppress is innately-known truth about the character of God, a sense of good and bad, and a basic knowledge of right and wrong. These things are universally known to all, "evident within them, for God made it evident to them" (v. 19). In other words, God manifests Himself in the most basic sense within every human conscience.

That internal knowledge about God is further augmented by evidences of His power and deity in the natural order of creation—"His invisible attributes, His eternal power and divine nature have been clearly seen, being understood through what has been made" (v. 20). The truth thus revealed is not cryptic or ambiguous—it is "clearly seen." Nor is it observable only by a few specially gifted souls. "The heavens are telling of the glory of God; and their expanse is declaring the work of His hands" (Ps. 19:1). They testify to a universal audience.

In other words, these truths—that God exists, that He is powerful, that He is good, and that He is glorious—are evident to believers and non-believers, Christians and pagans, Jews and Gentiles. No one can plead ignorance. Even the most unenlightened pagan knows more truth than he is willing to accept. Those who suppress that truth—those who abrogate their consciences—"are without excuse" (v. 20).

The Downward Spiral

Paul traces the wrath of God through humanity's descent into deeper and more pervasive sin. He outlines the steps of that descent, and they read as if they had been taken from the front pages of our newspapers. The more modern society reaches into the abyss of unbelief and wantonness, the more the truth of Scripture is fulfilled. Notice how the issues Paul outlined nearly two-thousand years ago describe precisely the sins most popular today. They appear in the following areas: secularism, lack of common sense, corrupt religion, uncontrolled lust, and sexual perversion.

Notice how the issues Paul outlined nearly two-thousand years ago describe precisely the sins most popular today.

Foolish speculations. "Even though they knew God, they did not honor Him as God, or give thanks; but they became futile in their speculations, and their foolish heart was darkened" (Rom. 1:21).

Once a person begins to suppress the truth in unrighteousness, that person looses all spiritual moorings. Reject the light, and you are left in darkness. That is precisely what has happened to the human race throughout history.

Modern society is no exception to the rule. If anything, we have greater access to truth than any other previous generation. Yet unbelief may be more widespread now than ever before.

As science advances, we learn more and more about the intricacy and complexities of the universe. Modern science has discovered, for example, that the molecular world is far more elaborate than anyone imagined a hundred years ago. We are able to identify subatomic particles. We know that a single drop of water contains innumerable billions of particles. A single drop of pond water also contains a whole community of tiny, marvelous living creatures unimaginable before the advent of microscopes. At the opposite end of the spectrum, we now realize that the edges of our own galaxy are far broader and the universe more complex than our grandparents ever could have realized. We understand more than ever about how it all fits together, about how nature is delicately balanced.

We ought to be more certain than any of our forebears about the infinite power and wisdom of the Creator. Science has uncovered whole wondrous worlds in nature that previous generations never knew existed. The more we see of creation, the more it reveals the order and the wisdom and the goodness of the One who designed it all and spoke it into existence. Yet at the same time science is learning all of this, scientific theory is becoming increasingly atheistic. Incredibly, as the power, sophistication, and harmony of the universe come more and more to light, many modern scientists try all the more desperately to explain away the notion of a divine Creator who rules the universe.

Could such an ordered, systematic creation be the result of mere chance? No more than shaking a paper bag filled with watch parts might produce an accurate timepiece. But evolutionary atheism is nothing more than "futile speculation," explanations devised by people who want to suppress the truth about God from their own consciences. Thus, their foolish hearts are darkened (v. 21).

The human race is devolving, not evolving. Instead of ascending into freedom and enlightenment, mankind, having rejected the true God, is receding into the bondage and gloom of its own sin and unbelief. When men and women refuse God, they become enslaved to sin, enveloped in darkness, entrapped by futility. Forsaking God, they forsake truth, light, and eternal life. They spurn the basis of all morality and start on the downward spiral Paul describes in these verses.

Spiritual darkness inevitably accompanies moral corruption. People who reject God necessarily forfeit righteousness. Godlessness inescapably leads to moral perversion—and vice versa. Unbelief and immorality are thus inextricably woven together.

The death of common sense. "Professing to be wise, they became fools" (Rom. 1:22). Those who refuse to honor God lack spiritual understanding. Even their rational faculties are corrupted by their unbelief. Their thinking is especially twisted with regard to spiritual matters, because their sin is spiritual rebellion. They have no means of discerning between truth and falsehood, right and wrong. Having rejected God, they have no hope of reasoning their way to spiritual truth. They are fools in the most profound sense of the word: "The fool has said in his heart, 'There is no God.' They are corrupt, they have committed abominable deeds; there is no one who does good" (Ps. 14:1; cf. 53:1).

The foolishness that verse describes is a comprehensive spiritual blindness. It is the worst foolishness of all. It corrupts the conscience and leaves the unbeliever incapable of right thinking about any spiritual matters.

Our society is shot through with spiritual foolishness. It seems moral judgment has been completely overturned. Public schools cannot teach the Bible or even morality but are encouraged to instruct children in sexual technique, then supply them with free condoms. School nurses are not supposed to dispense aspirin without parental consent, but they may send young girls to abortion clinics without informing anyone in authority. Baby whales and baby seals have more legal rights than unborn infants. Courts are more concerned to protect criminals' rights than victims' rights.

Common sense rarely figures into public policy or society's sense of morality. Professing wisdom, our culture has enshrined its foolishness proudly for all to see.

Corrupt religion. Moral foolishness inevitably corrupts spirituality. In fact, all the religions humanity has ever devised are the fruit of blind spiritual foolishness. They "[exchange] the glory of the incorruptible God for an image in the form of corruptible man and of birds and four-footed animals and crawling creatures" (Rom. 1:23).

Contrary to the notions of modern anthropology, human religion has not followed an upward evolutionary path. Religion did not begin with paganism and mature over time into monotheism. The exact opposite is true. All human religion, according to Scripture, moves in a direction away from the truth, away from the true God, tending always toward idolatry ("an image in the form of corruptible man"), then animism ("of birds and four-footed animals and crawling creatures").

> ## *Contrary to the notions of modern anthropology, human religion has not followed an upward evolutionary path.*

After the Fall, Scripture says, "men began to call upon the name of the Lord" (Gen. 4:26). From the Fall to the Flood, there is no record of any idolatry. God destroyed the world in the Flood because "the wickedness of man was great on the earth, and . . . every intent of the thoughts of his heart was only evil continually" (Gen. 6:5). But nothing in Scripture states that people had devised false gods to worship.

Sometime after the Flood, idolatry began to predominate. Abraham was called out of an idolatrous family (Josh. 24:2). Egypt was overrun with idolatry by the time of Moses. And when Israel returned to the Promised Land, they discovered forms of idolatry among the Canaanites that were even more hideous than anything they had seen in Egypt. When they failed to wipe out all the Canaanites, those people's false religions became a perpetual snare to the succeeding generations of Israelites.

Ancient history confirms that religion has *de*volved and descended into polytheism and animism. Herodotus, writing in the fifth century B.C., said early Persia had no pagan temples or idols.[5] Augustine cites a first-century Roman historian, Varro, who said "the old Romans were a hundred threescore and ten years without idols."[6] That means it was not until 170 years *after* Rome was founded that the Romans adopted polytheism and idolatry. Lucian, a second-century Greek writer, made a similar observation about ancient Greece and Egypt.[7]

People are by nature inclined to turn from the glory of God to idols, to "[exchange] the truth of God for a lie, and [worship and serve] the creature rather than the Creator" (Rom. 1:25). The human conscience demands God, but people tend to choose a diety of their own making. That is why the First Commandment is, "You shall have no other gods before Me. You shall not make for yourself an idol, or any likeness of what is in heaven above or on the earth beneath or in the water under the earth. You shall not worship them or serve them" (Ex. 20:3–5). But even while Moses was receiving that commandment from the Lord, Aaron and the Israelites were making a golden calf to worship (32:1–6).

Is our society any different from the Romans 1 description? Certainly not. People in modern culture tend to have materialistic idols—money, prestige, success, philosophy, health, pleasure, sports, entertainment, possessions, and other such things. Those things become idols when we give them the love and dedication we owe to God. The problem is the same—worshiping the creation rather than the Creator.

But don't get the idea that the idolatry in our society is somehow more sophisticated than the idolatry of primitive paganism. Consider the changes that have taken place in religion in America in the past fifty years or so. The New Age movement has popularized Hinduism. Astrology, spiritism, and other occult religions have enjoyed unprecedented popularity. Native American religions, Voodoo, Santeria, Druidism, Wicca (witchcraft), and other ancient pagan beliefs have been revived. Now Satan worship, a thing unheard of in our nation two generations ago, is one of the fastest growing cults in the nation—and is especially conspicuous in the youth culture. I recently heard a news report that in Orange County, California, alone more than five hundred cases of ritual animal sacrifice involving stolen pets have been recorded over the past decade.

Now people in our culture are worshiping the elements, spotted owls, or dolphins and whales. Earth- and creature- worship seem at their apex in this society, which has no place for the Creator God. Mother Earth is preferred to Father God.

Far from being humanity's highest attainment, religion is one of the most obvious manifestations of the debauchery of our race.

The vilest sin of all is blaspheming God by having other gods before Him. So sinners who reject the true God are often extremely religious. Manmade religion is not evidence of human nobility; it is proof of human depravity. False religion is humanity at its lowest. It is not humanity ascended to the heights, but people lost and groping in the muck of godlessness. All the trends in modern religion and modern materialism underscore that fact.

Uncontrolled lust. Another step in humanity's downward spiral occurs when people become enslaved to their own passions: "God gave them over in the lusts of their hearts to impurity, that their bodies might be dishonored among them" (Rom. 1:24).

Nothing characterizes contemporary Western society more than lust. The size and power of the modern entertainment industry testifies eloquently to how thoroughly given over to lust our society is. Greed, gluttony, and sexual desire are the primary tools of the advertizing industry. Lust is big business in our culture.

A dozen or so daily televised talk shows appeal shamelessly to people's prurient interests.

As people's lusts are fed and encouraged, society grows more and more tolerant of immorality, indecency, obscenity, pornography, profanity, and other forms of smut. We noted earlier how standards in the entertainment industry have declined dramatically in the past few years. Gratuitous obscenities and sex scenes are routinely included even in films promoted as children's fare. Music videos thrive on sex and sleaze. What the television networks are willing to broadcast into our living rooms becomes more explicit each season.

A dozen or so daily televised talk shows appeal shamelessly to people's prurient interests. Every conceivable lewd and perverted practice is paraded before daytime audiences. The only moral values viewers are expected to maintain, it seems, are tolerance and an open mind toward any kind of behavior.

Sinful lust comes in various forms. The Greek word for lust is *epithumia*, which simply means "desire." Sinful desires include an insatiable hunger for pleasure, profits, power, prestige, and sex. In short, lust is a desire for anything God forbids. Such sinful cravings Scripture calls fleshly lusts (cf. Rom. 13:14; Eph. 2:3; 2 Pet. 2:18; 1 Jn. 2:16). We are explicitly commanded to "abstain from fleshly lusts, which wage war against the soul" (1 Pet. 2:11).

Those who feed their lusts are judged accordingly: "God gave them over . . . to impurity" (Rom. 1:24). The expression "gave them over" (Gk., *paradidōmi*) is a word sometimes used of putting someone in prison (Mk. 1:14; Acts 8:3). It speaks of a judicial act of God whereby He withdraws His restraining hand from an individual whose conscience is hardened. That person becomes enslaved to his or her own lusts. In other words, God allows the consequences of that person's sin to run their catastrophic course. That course, driven by uncontrolled lust, inevitably reverts to the worst forms of sexual promiscuity: "Their bodies [are] dishonored among them" (Rom. 1:24).

Sexual perversion. Free from the deterrent of a healthy conscience and without God's gracious restraint, runaway lusts inevitably lead to the most debased and perverted kinds of sexual sin. Fleshly desires deteriorate to become "degrading passions": "For this reason God gave them over to degrading passions; for their women exchanged the natural function for that which is unnatural, and in the same way also the men abandoned the natural function of the woman and burned in their desire toward one another, men with men committing indecent acts and receiving in their own persons the due penalty of their error" (Rom. 1:26–27).

That is precisely the course our society has taken. Sexual practices that were almost universally viewed as hideously perverted a few decades ago are now flaunted and celebrated in our streets. Homosexuals have become bold—even arrogant—in demanding society's approval for their wickedness. Nonbiblical thinking has so corrupted society's collective conscience that the consensus is fast growing sympathetic with the homosexual movement. Having abandoned Scripture as a standard, our culture has no authority to declare homosexuality immoral. A few consciences are still struck with horror at the thought of such iniquity. But extreme pressure is brought to bear upon such people to try to make them feel they should be broad-minded, accepting, permissive, and even supportive of such perversions. Those who are not fully committed to Scripture have no line of defense against the tide of public opinion. And so society's collective conscience erodes even further, hastening the downward spiral.

How tolerant has our society become of homosexual practices? Many large cities now sponsor annual "Gay Pride" celebrations, featuring parades with floats and marching groups that exalt the homosexual lifestyle. The news reports you see about "Gay Pride" parades do not tell the full story. They couldn't. Much of what goes on in those parades is so explicit and so debauched that to capture the images and put them on television news would constitute the grossest kind of pornography. Such parades have become rallying points for the homosexual community in their bid to gain political influence and thereby impose their deviant and deadly value system on the rest of society. In that pursuit they have had remarkable success over the past few years.

New York City, for example, opened the nation's first high school for homosexuals—Harvey Milk School, named for a murdered San Francisco city supervisor who was also a homosexual rights activist.[8] The school meets, incongruously enough, in the parish house of a Methodist church. Some of the school's students are transvestites, and some are male prostitutes.

Gay advocacy groups abound and have grown more militant in recent years. With names such as Queer Nation, GLAAD ("Gay and Lesbian Alliance Against Defamation"), ACT-UP ("AIDS Coalition To Unleash Power"), SQUISH ("Strong Queers United In Stopping Heterosexism"), Dykes on Bikes, and Fighting Fairies, these groups practice a kind of in-your-face activism designed to shock, defy, and intimidate anyone who dares suggest that their lifestyle is sinful.

Politically, the gay rights movement has made substantial gains. In his first year as president, Bill Clinton appointed at least seventeen homosexuals and lesbians to public office—then invited them all to a breakfast reception to celebrate. "For the first time in the history of mankind a president has sought to break this barrier, this taboo," one of the appointees said triumphantly. "For that, Bill Clinton is going to go down in history."[9]

Government agencies and the courts are now adding their clout to the effort to recognize homosexuality as a legitimate lifestyle. In

Wisconsin, two young female students advertised for a third room-mate to share their private residence. Because they rejected an applicant who had told them she was a lesbian, they were forced by the state Human Rights Commission to pay the lesbian applicant $1,500 for having caused her distress. The Commission also demanded a public letter of apology and required the two girls to attend a "re-education class" taught by homosexuals.

Such government-sponsored moral indoctrination is becoming more and more common. Homosexual rights laws have forced groups such as Big Brothers to advertize in homosexual newspapers for men whom they match up with fatherless boys for companionship and role modeling. The organization once excluded homosexual applicants, but they have changed their policy under government pressure. The same kind of pressure has been levied against the Boy Scouts to accept homosexuals as scoutmasters.

The rhetoric of gay-rights activism portrays homosexuality in wholly non-moral terms: it is an "alternate lifestyle," a matter of one's "sexual orientation." At the heart of the argument is the notion that one's sexual behavior is not a matter of choice. Homosexual tendencies are determined by genetic, not environmental causes— or so the argument goes—and therefore homosexuality cannot be inherently immoral. But in the first place, researchers have not been able to establish that homosexual tendencies have any genetic causes. Even if such a cause could be established, however, would that alter the fact that God's Word declares homosexuality to be immoral? Humanistic psychopathology has been attempting for years to blame all sorts of sinful behavior—alcoholism, drug addiction, habitual criminality, and sexual perversion—on genetic causes. That whole line of argument misses the obvious point that Scripture clearly teaches we are all born utterly sinful. Everyone has an inborn tendency to sin. That does not release us from the guilt of sinful actions.

And what is the next "alternate lifestyle" or "sexual orientation" to be legitimized? Sadomasochism—sex mixed with brutality? Bestiality—sex with animals? Necrophilia—sex with corpses? Or perhaps pedophilia—sex with children?

You might be shocked to know that homosexual pedophiles already have an advocacy group: NAMBLA—"National American Man Boy Love Association." NAMBLA's slogan is "Sex by eight, before it's too late." The organization, which operates openly under constitutional protection, even publishes a newsletter for members all across the country. The publisher of that paper is a schoolteacher!

Others believe incest should be legalized and encouraged. The Sex Information and Education Council of the United States (SEICUS) has circulated a paper suggesting that "moral and religious pronouncements with respect to incest" are all wrong. Guilt about breaking the taboo is actually more harmful than the practice itself, the paper says. It complains that the incest taboo "has prevented scientific investigation," and calls for those with "the guts to find out what is really happening" to launch an aggressive program of incest research.[10] SEICUS, by the way, is the same group that has been so influential in setting the sex-education agenda for public schools nationwide.

What is most distressing is that many churches and denominations are now ordaining practicing homosexuals to the ministry.

Society has become so tolerant that no behavior, it seems, is too perverted to be openly advocated. All of this is frightening evidence that God has abandoned our sinful society to its own degrading passions. Humanism has dehumanized our culture.

What is most distressing is that many churches and denominations are now ordaining practicing homosexuals to the ministry. The homosexual community even has its own denominations, some of which profess to be evangelical. More and more people within the evangelical community are voicing the opinion that homosexuality may not really be sinful after all. Many church leaders seem reluctant to take an uncompromising biblical stand.

But Scripture is clear. The Bible condemns homosexuality in explicit and undeniable terms. The Old Testament law grouped homosexuality with incest, bestiality, and other perversions, and the penalty for its practice was death (Lev. 20:13, cf. vv. 11–16). In Romans 1, Paul clearly teaches that homosexual practices are "indecent acts" (v. 27), driven by "degrading passions" (v. 26). The apostle listed homosexuality with the lowest forms of human degradation: "those who are lawless and rebellious . . . , the ungodly and sinners . . . , the unholy and profane . . . , those who kill their fathers or mothers . . . , murderers and immoral men and *homosexuals* and kidnappers and liars and perjurers, and whatever else is contrary to sound teaching" (1 Tim. 1:9–10, emphasis added). He wrote, "Do you not know that the unrighteous shall not inherit the kingdom of God? Do not be deceived; neither fornicators, nor idolaters, nor adulterers, nor effeminate, nor *homosexuals*, nor thieves, nor the covetous, nor drunkards, nor revilers, nor swindlers, shall inherit the kingdom of God" (1 Cor. 6:9–10, emphasis added).

Is there no hope for homosexuals? Thankfully, there *is* hope. Those who repent and are reborn in Christ can be freed from the sins that would otherwise destroy them. Immediately after giving that long list of the kinds of people who will not inherit the kingdom, Paul wrote to the Corinthian believers, "*Such were some of you*; but you were washed, but you were sanctified, but you were justified in the name of the Lord Jesus Christ, and in the Spirit of our God" (v. 11, emphasis added).

Unrepentant homosexuals, according to Scripture, "receiv[e] in their own persons the due penalty of their error" (Rom. 1:27). And the society that tolerates such sins is judged as well. What is "the due penalty of their error"? The consequences of their sin. AIDS is certainly one aspect of that. But an even worse judgment, the final temporal blow from the hand of a righteous God, is when He "[gives] them over to a depraved mind" (v. 28). They bottom out spiritually as well as morally. The conscience seems to vanish completely. They can indulge themselves in the evil acts they so love—"those things which are not proper"—until they fill themselves up with unrighteousness.

The Death of the Conscience

It is unsettling to see how precisely the decline of our society parallels Paul's description of the downward spiral of sin. Maurice Roberts has written,

71

The wheel of history has come full-circle. We are, as a civilization, rotating back to the state of affairs depicted by the apostle Paul in the first chapter of the Epistle to the Romans. . . .

The time was when Bible commentators expounded Romans chapter 1 more or less from the standpoint of the first century of the Roman world only. But that day has gone forever. The modern Christian in the West can now see himself as much in the arena of a reprobate society as did the apostles. The state of modern religion and morals exactly parallels that of the apostolic age and it is summed up in the one word: *Decadence.* Pagan Rome could teach modern man very little that he does not know already about sophisticated wickedness. Pagan Greece, pagan Egypt, and pagan Babylon might even learn a thing or two from this generation about how to shun gospel-light and add to the mountains of man's provocation.

What makes the Bible-reader saddest of all is to see that society today has learnt nothing from the past or from two thousand years of Bible production and printing, but is repeating the very vices which always provoke God to give the world over to its own sensuality and self-destruction.[11]

Perhaps even more distressing is the realization that we have already reached that final stage. Conscience has been silenced. Nothing is left to instruct people's behavior but their own depraved minds. The mind becomes a tool of lust unrestrained:

Just as they did not see fit to acknowledge God any longer, God gave them over to a depraved mind, to do those things which are not proper, being filled with all unrighteousness, wickedness, greed, evil; full of envy, murder, strife, deceit, malice; they are gossips, slanderers, haters of God, insolent, arrogant, boastful, inventors of evil, disobedient to parents, without understanding, untrustworthy, unloving, unmerciful; and, although they know the ordinance of God, that those who practice such things are worthy of death, they not only do the same, but also give hearty approval to those who practice them (Rom. 1:28–32).

For the third time in the space of five verses, Paul has used the word *paradidōmi,* "gave them over." First he said, "God gave them over . . . to impurity" (v. 24); then, "God gave them over to degrading passions" (v. 26); and now, "God gave them over to a depraved mind" (v. 28). Notice the downward progression. Again, it exactly parallels the decline of contemporary society over the past three or four decades. Who can read those verses and deny that they describe our own society right now with an uncanny precision? The mind is morally useless. It cannot discern right from wrong, good from evil. We might assume that someone would figure out that a biblical moral standard would correct much that is wrong with our society, but that simple, rational idea escapes the reprobate mind. Confirmed sinners cannot think logically about moral issues. The conscience itself is victimized!

In a final act of temporal judgment, God has utterly abandoned people to the wickedness they love so much: "unrighteousness, wickedness, greed, evil; full of envy, murder, strife, deceit, [and] malice," so that society is filled with "gossips, slanderers, haters of God, insolent, arrogant, boastful, inventors of evil, disobedient to parents, without understanding, untrustworthy, unloving, unmerciful" (vv. 29–31).

The word translated "unloving" in that list is *astorgos*, literally meaning "without natural affection"—and it is so translated in the King James Version. It speaks of those who lack instinctive love for their own families—such as mothers who abandon their children, husbands who beat their wives, children who despise their parents, fathers who molest their children, or brothers and sisters who loathe one another. Our society is rife with such wrongdoing; perhaps no other description would better characterize contemporary culture than to say people lack natural affection.

The other items in Paul's list—such as greed, envy, murder, strife, deceit, gossip, slander, insolence, arrogance, pride, inventive evildoing, disobedience to parents, mercilessness, and hatred of God—perfectly catalog the most visible traits of modern society. Not that previous generations have been free of such evils. But unlike our ancestors, people in our day openly exhibit such sins with a shameless arrogance. "They not only do [those things], but also give hearty approval to those who practice them" (v. 32). Something is seriously, desperately wrong with our culture.

People who follow the culture rather than obey God's Word are utterly without excuse. "They know the ordinance of God, that those who practice such things are worthy of death," Paul writes (v. 32). Their own consciences witness against them. They may suppress their sense of guilt now, but when they must give account to God, their own consciences will stand against them.

Civilization as we know it has reached the deepest level of corruption and abides under a sentence of divine condemnation.

Those who deal falsely with their own consciences place themselves under God's holy wrath even in this life. "God [gives] them over to a depraved mind" (v. 28). In other words, it turns out that the damage they do to their own consciences *is* God's immediate judgment against them. "This is the judgment," Jesus said, "that the light is come into the world, and men loved the darkness rather than the light; for their deeds were evil" (Jn. 3:19). Those who reject the light are condemned to live in darkness. God gives them over to their own depravity, and their conscience ceases to function correctly.

It is a wretched and horrifying state of affairs. Our society openly condones and defends the worst kinds of evil. Civilization as we know it has reached the deepest level of corruption and abides under a sentence of divine condemnation. People's consciences have been seared, debased, obstructed, repressed, and overturned. Without a functioning conscience, people are destined only to sink deeper and deeper into wickedness. Humanity is merely storing up wrath against the day of wrath (cf. Rom. 2:5).

Is there hope? For those willing to repent and follow Christ, there is. They can "be saved from this perverse generation" (Acts 2:40). Their consciences can be renewed and cleansed (Heb. 9:14). They can become new creatures (2 Cor. 5:17).

Can society itself be saved? Certainly not without full-scale revival. Unless multitudes turn to Christ, the downward spiral is certain to continue. With so many dampened consciences and hardened hearts, it would take a revival of unprecedented proportions to reverse the downward direction of our culture. The problems are spiritual and cannot be solved through politics or education. Christians who believe political activism can reverse the trends in our society do not understand the nature of the problem. True believers must realize that the state of our society is the result of the righteous judgment of God. God has not commissioned His people to reconstruct society. We are not called to expend our energies for moral reform. We are salt—a preservative for a decaying generation (Matt. 5:13). And we are lights designed to shine in a way that enables people who see our good works to glorify our heavenly Father (vv. 14–16). In other words, our primary task is to preach the truth of God's Word, live in obedience to that truth, and to keep ourselves unstained by the world (Jas. 1:27). Our influence on society must be the fruit of that kind of living, not the product of fleshly energy or political clout.

What we can do, and *must* do, is keep our own consciences pure. We must saturate our minds and hearts with the truth of Scripture, and refuse to yield to the spirit of our age. To do that, we must understand our own sinfulness and know how to deal with our sins. That will be the focus of the following chapters.

Part II

The Nature of Sin

We must understand the nature of sin—specifically our own sinfulness—before we can know how to deal with it, without and within. If we are to rejuvenate our vanishing consciences, we must first understand the nature of sin. Once we understand the enemy, we will be able to employ the biblical strategy to gain real victory over sin (the focus of Part III). Part II specifically provides this understanding by showing how and why the conscience is silenced by sin.

Chapter 4, "What Do You Mean, Totally Depraved?" explains the doctrine of total depravity as explained by Paul in Romans 1-3. It also introduces the self-esteem credo of modern psychology as a major stumbling block to people's understanding the depth of their own sinfulness. It shows society's focus on self, not God.

Chapter 5, "Sin and Its Cure," examines the character of sin and how we attempt to justify it. It explores the theological problem of where sin and evil come from and how they fit in God's providence. It then turns to the liberation from sin through union with Christ and the new birth.

Chapter 6, "The Conquered Enemy Within," examines some misguided religious attempts to deal with sin. It exposes the dangers of perfectionism and examines several perfectionist groups in church history. It shows the importance of keeping the proper relationship between sanctification and justification. It treats what it means to be "freed from sin."

4
What Do You Mean, "Totally Depraved"?

The blind man can see no difference between a master-piece of Titian or Raphael and the queen's head on a village signboard. The deaf man cannot distinguish between a penny whistle and a cathedral organ. The very animals whose smell is most offensive to us have no idea that they are offensive and are not offensive to one another. And man, fallen man, I believe, can have no just idea what a vile thing sin is in the sight of that God whose handiwork is absolutely perfect.

J. C. Ryle[1]

No concept is more important to the gurus of modern psychology than self-esteem. According to the self-esteem credo, there are no bad people—only people who think badly of themselves.

For years, educational experts, psychologists, and a growing number of Christian leaders have championed self-esteem as a panacea for all sorts of human miseries. According to the purveyors of this doctrine, if people feel good about themselves, they will behave better, have fewer emotional problems, and achieve more. People with high self-esteem, we are told, are less likely to commit crimes, act immorally, fail academically, or have problems in their relationships with others.

The Blind Faith of Self-Esteem

Advocates of self-esteem have been remarkably successful in convincing people that self-esteem is the solution to whatever ails anyone. One survey revealed that a majority of people view self-esteem as the single most important motivator for hard work and success. In fact, self-esteem ranked several points higher than a sense of responsibility or fear of failure.[2]

But does self-esteem really work? Does it, for example, promote higher achievement? There is plenty of evidence to suggest it does not. In a recent study, a standardized math test was given to teenagers from six different nations. Besides the math questions, the test asked the youngsters to respond yes or no to the question, "I am good at mathematics." American students scored lowest on the math questions, far behind Korean students, who had the top scores. Ironically, more than three-fourths of the Korean students had answered *no* to the "I am good at math" question. In stark contrast, however, 68 percent of the American students believed their math skills were just fine.[3] Our kids may be failing math, but they obviously feel pretty good about how they are doing.

Morally, our culture is in precisely the same boat. Empirical evidence strongly suggests, as we have seen, that society is at an all-time moral low. We might expect people's self-esteem to be suffering as well. But statistics show Americans are feeling better about themselves than ever. In a survey conducted in 1940, 11 percent of women and 20 percent of men agreed with the statement, "I am an important person." In the 1990s, those figures jumped to 66 percent of women and 62 percent of men.[4] Ninety percent of people surveyed in a recent Gallup Poll say their own sense of self-esteem is robust and healthy.[5] Incredibly, while the moral fabric of society continues to unravel, self-esteem is thriving. All the positive thinking about ourselves seems not to be doing anything to elevate the culture or motivate people to live better lives.

Can it really be that low self-esteem is what is wrong with people today? Does anyone seriously believe that making people feel better about themselves has helped the problems of crime, moral decay, divorce, child abuse, juvenile delinquency, drug addiction, and all the other evils that have dragged society down? Could so much still be wrong in our culture if the assumptions of self-esteem theory were true? Do we really imagine that more self-esteem will finally solve society's problems? Is there even a shred of evidence that would support such a belief?

Absolutely none. A report in *Newsweek* suggested that "the case for self-esteem . . . is a matter less of scientific pedagogy than of faith—faith that positive thoughts can make manifest the inherent goodness in anyone."[6] In other words, the notion that self-esteem makes people better is simply a matter of blind religious faith. Not only that, it is a religion that is antithetical to Christianity, because it is predicated on the unbiblical presupposition that people are basically good and need to recognize their own goodness.

The Church and the Self-Esteem Cult

Nevertheless, the most persuasive proponents of self-esteem religion have always included clergymen. Norman Vincent Peale's "positive thinking" doctrine, which was popular a generation ago, was simply an early self-esteem model. Peale wrote *The Power of Positive Thinking* in 1952.[7] The book opened with these words: "Believe in yourself! Have faith in your abilities!" In the introduction, Peale called the book a "personal-improvement manual . . . written with the sole objective of helping the reader achieve a happy, satisfying, and worthwhile life."[8] The book was marketed as motivational therapy, not theology. But in Peale's estimation the whole system was merely "applied Christianity; a simple yet scientific system of practical techniques of successful living that works."[9]

Evangelicals for the most part were slow to embrace a system that called people to faith in themselves rather than faith in Jesus Christ. Self-esteem as Norman Vincent Peale outlined it was the offspring of theological liberalism married to neo-orthodoxy.

The most persuasive proponents of self-esteem religion have always included clergymen.

Time has evidently worn away evangelicals' resistance to such doctrine. Now many of the hottest-selling books in evangelical bookstores promote self-esteem and positive thinking. Even *Newsweek* has commented on the trend. Noting that self-esteem is considered "religiously correct" nowadays, the magazine observed:

> The notion [of self-esteem] may put off anyone old enough to remember when "Christian" as an adjective was often followed by "humility." But American churches, which once did not shrink from calling their congregants wretches, have moved toward a more congenial view of human nature . . . . Chastising sinners is considered counterproductive: it makes them feel worse about themselves.[10]

Surely the most influential voice selling self-esteem to evangelicals is Norman Vincent Peale's best-known disciple, Dr. Robert Schuller. Broadcasting weekly to millions of people worldwide, Schuller's "Hour of Power" telecast relentlessly promotes the "theology" of self-esteem. More than any other source, this weekly media exposure has advocated and normalized self-esteem for the church in our day. It has bred an effective movement by creating an appetite to receive this teaching. Indeed, that is its intent.

Unlike Peale, who until recent years made no pretense of being evangelical, Schuller has always framed his teaching in the terminology of traditional, conservative, Reformed theology. He speaks of conversion, calls unbelievers to be born again, and affirms the need for a personal relationship with Jesus Christ. But Schuller's actual teaching owes far more to neo-orthodoxy than to evangelicalism. In fact, his self-esteem doctrines reflect *secular humanism*, a non-religious system of thought that places human beings, their values, and their needs above the glory of God.

If this teaching is seriously in error, as I am convinced it is, it must be refuted and the church needs to be warned of the danger (Tit. 1:9, ff.).

J. C. Ryle decried the tendency of his own age to tolerate seriously aberrant theology under the rubric of magnanimity and charity:

> The tendency of modern thought is to reject dogmas, creeds and every kind of bounds in religion. It is thought grand and wise to condemn no opinion whatsoever, and to pronounce all earnest and clever teachers to be trustworthy, however heterogeneous and mutually destructive their opinions may be. Everything, forsooth, is true and nothing is false! Everybody is right and nobody is wrong! Everybody is likely to be saved and nobody is to be lost![11]

Christian love demands that we walk in truth (2 Jn. 6), and that we not turn a blind eye to error. Because I preach and publish, I must be held accountable to the Word of God for what I teach. So must all preachers. Please understand that my criticism of Dr. Schuller's teaching is by no means an attack on his personal character. My concerns are altogether doctrinal, not personal. Because of the aggressive influence of his teaching on the contemporary church worldwide, it is imperative that we let him speak for himself, then measure what he says by the pure Word of God.

The Sanctification of Human Pride?

Robert Schuller says "the 'will to self-love' is the deepest of all human desires."[12] Far from being a sin, he says, people's lust for self-love is a good thing that should be encouraged, fostered, and fed. He labels the church's historic aversion to pride "neurotic"; and he contends that people should be taught not to fear human pride.[13] *"The cross sanctifies the ego trip,"* he has written.[14] Amplifying that statement on a televised talk show, he declared, "Jesus had an ego. He said, 'I, if I be lifted up, will draw all men unto me.' *Wow, what an ego trip He was on!*"[15]

According to Schuller, "sin is psychological self-abuse."[16] More specifically, "Sin is any act or thought that robs myself or another human being of his or her self-esteem," and hell is simply the loss of pride that follows such an act.[17]

Can such statements be reconciled with the biblical teaching that pride itself was the first sin, which resulted in Satan's fall (cf. Isa. 14:12–14) as well as Adam's (Gen. 3)? Can they be harmonized with Jesus' words about the publican who lamented his own unworthiness? Jesus held that man up as an example of true repentance (Lk. 18:13–14).

Far from being a sin, he says, people's lust for self-love is a good thing that should be encouraged, fostered, and fed.

In self-esteem theology, however, "a profoundly deep sense of unworthiness" is no virtue; it is unbelief.[18] Moreover, according to this doctrine, "The most serious sin is the one that causes me to say, 'I am unworthy. I may have no claim to divine sonship if you examine me at my worst.' For once a person believes he is an 'unworthy sinner,' it is doubtful if he can really honestly accept the saving grace God offers in Jesus Christ."[19] Dr. Schuller even suggests that "too many prayers of confession of sin and repentance have been destructive to the emotional health of Christians by feeding their sense of nonworth."[20]

Those who take the whole Bible at face value are likely to surmise differently. David prayed, "The sacrifices of God are a broken spirit; a broken and a contrite heart, O God, Thou wilt not despise" (Ps. 51:17). In the first of His beatitudes Jesus said, "Blessed are the poor in spirit: for theirs is the kingdom of heaven" (Matt. 5:3). James wrote, "Cleanse your hands, you sinners; and purify your hearts, you double-minded. Be miserable and mourn and weep; let your laughter be turned into mourning, and your joy to gloom. Humble yourselves in the presence of the Lord, and He will exalt you" (Jas. 4:8–10). Scripture also says, "Before destruction the heart of man is haughty, but humility goes before honor" (Prov. 18:12; cf. Prov. 15:33). "God is opposed to the proud, but gives grace to the humble. Humble yourselves, therefore, under the mighty hand of God, that He may exalt you at the proper time" (1 Pet. 5:5–6). "Whosoever shall exalt himself shall be abased; and he that shall humble himself shall be exalted" (Matt. 23:12, KJV).

On a recent radio interview Dr. Schuller was asked how he reconciles his teaching with Scriptures like those. In his reply he stated, "Just because it's in the Bible doesn't mean you should preach it."[21] Borrowing a rudimentary error from neo-orthodoxy, he downplays the authority of Scripture, setting up a false dichotomy between Christ's authority and the authority of His Word ("Christ is the Lord over the Scriptures; the Scriptures are not Lord over Christ. . . . The Bible must not compete with the Lord for the seat of glory").[22] He echoes the common neo-orthodox notion that Jesus' words are "safer ground" on which to build one's ministry than the writings of the apostle Paul.[23] Schuller is particularly averse to expressions like "the wrath of God": "I'll *never* use that language," he told a talk-show host. "I'm interested in attracting people, not driving them farther away. . . . There are times when if we are wise, there's language we will not use."[24] Why? Because according to Dr. Schuller, "the gospel message is not only faulty but potentially dangerous if it has to put a person down before it attempts to lift him up."[25]

In fact, Schuller states that the "basic defect" of contemporary Christianity is our "failure to proclaim the gospel in a way that can satisfy every person's deepest need—one's spiritual hunger for glory."[26] He says the church should glorify the human being and reinterpret sin in a way that does not assault a person's self-esteem.[27] "What we need," he declares, "is a theology of salvation that begins and ends with a recognition of every person's hunger for glory."[28]

What about *God's* glory? According to the new self-esteem theology, that is the wrong starting point: "Classical theology has erred in its insistence that theology be 'God-centered,' not 'man-centered.'"[29] "This is part of the reason the church is in the predicament it is in today," Dr. Schuller alleges.[30] In his estimation "Reformation theology [also] failed to make clear that the core of sin is a lack of self-esteem."[31] Thus he calls for a fresh starting point for our faith—other than Scripture, other than the doctrine of God. That new starting point, he suggests, must be an emphasis on the glory of humanity. "The 'Dignity of the Person,'" Schuller writes, "will then be the new theological bench mark!"[32] "And the result will be a faith that will bring glory to the human race."[33]

What Is Man, That Thou Art Mindful of Him?

But is human glory a worthy goal? God says, "I am the Lord, that is My name; I will not give My glory to another" (Isa. 42:8). God has said, "For the sake of My name I delay My wrath, and for My praise I restrain it for you, in order not to cut you off. Behold, I have refined you, but not as silver; I have tested you in the furnace of affliction. For My own sake, for My own sake, I will act; for how can My name be profaned? And *My glory I will not give to another*" (Isa. 48:9–11, emphasis added). In other words, God extends His longsuffering, grace, and mercy to mankind not because we are worthy of it, but for His own name's sake—for His own glory, not ours. "O Lord, *what is man*, that Thou dost take knowledge of him? Or the son of man, that Thou dost think of him? Man is like a mere breath; His days are like a passing shadow" (Ps. 144:3–4, emphasis added; cf. Job 7:17; 15:14; Ps. 8:4; Heb. 2:6).

> *In other words, God extends His longsuffering, grace, and mercy to mankind not because we are worthy of it, but for His own name's sake— for His own glory, not ours.*

On the other hand, the gospel according to self-esteem theology says, "We must tell people everywhere that God wants them to feel good about themselves!"[34]

Does God really want all people to feel good about themselves? Or does He first call sinners to recognize the utter helplessness of their own estate? The answer is obvious to those who let Scripture speak for itself.

Self-esteem theology is forced to redefine sin in a way that minimizes the offense to God: "The core of sin is a negative self-image."[35] In other words, sin—according to the self-esteem gospel—is an offense against *human* glory. It is a transgression against ourselves, our own dignity—not necessarily an offense against God or His law. In fact, classical theology's definition of sin as rebellion against God is now deemed "shallow and insulting."[36]

Robert Schuller goes so far as to deny that fallen human nature is truly evil: "By nature we are fearful, not bad. . . . Label it a 'negative self-image,' but do not say that the central core of the human soul is wickedness. If this were so, then truly, the human being is totally depraved."[37]

Understanding the Doctrine of Total Depravity

Scripture, of course, teaches from beginning to end that all humanity *is* totally depraved. Paul says unredeemed people are "dead in . . . trespasses and sins" (Eph. 2:1). Apart from salvation, all people walk in worldliness and disobedience (v. 2). We who know and love the Lord once "lived in the lusts of our flesh, indulging the desires of the flesh and of the mind, and were by nature children of wrath, even as the rest" (v. 3). We were "separate from Christ, excluded from the commonwealth of Israel, and strangers to the covenants of promise, having no hope and without God in the world" (v. 12).

Scripture, of course, teaches from beginning to end that all humanity is totally depraved.

In those passages Paul describes the state of unbelievers as estrangement from God. Paul's words cannot be twisted to support Dr. Schuller's assertion that the human problem is fearfulness rather than depravity. In fact, Paul says, "There is no fear of God" in the unregenerate person (Rom. 3:18). Before our salvation, we were actually God's enemies (Rom. 5:8, 10). We were "alienated and hostile in mind, engaged in evil deeds" (Col. 1:21). Sinful passions, inflamed by our hatred of God's law, motivated all our living (Rom. 7:5). We were tainted by sin in every part of our being. We were corrupt, evil, thoroughly sinful.

Theologians refer to this doctrine as "total depravity." It does not mean that unbelieving sinners are always as bad as they could be (cf. Lk. 6:33; Rom. 2:14). It does not mean that the expression of sinful human nature is always lived out to the fullest. It does not mean that unbelievers are incapable of acts of kindness, benevolence, goodwill, or human altruism. It certainly does not mean that non-Christians cannot appreciate goodness, beauty, honesty, decency, or excellence. It *does* mean that none of this has any merit with God.

Depravity also means that evil has contaminated every aspect of our humanity—our heart, mind, personality, emotions, conscience, motives, and will (cf. Jer. 17:9; Jn. 8:44). Unredeemed sinners are therefore incapable of doing anything to please God (Isa. 64:6). They are incapable of truly loving the God who reveals Himself in Scripture. They are incapable of obedience from the heart, with righteous motives. They are incapable of understanding spiritual truth. They are incapable of genuine faith. And that means they are incapable of pleasing God or truly seeking Him (Heb. 11:1).

Total depravity means sinners have no ability to do spiritual good or work for their own salvation from sin. They are so completely disinclined to love righteousness, so thoroughly dead in sin, that they are not able to save themselves or even to fit themselves for God's salvation. Unbelieving humanity has no capacity to desire, understand, believe, or apply spiritual truth: "A natural man does not accept the things of the Spirit of God; for they are foolishness to him, and he cannot understand them, because they are spiritually appraised" (1 Cor. 2:14). In spite of all this, people are *proud* of themselves! Lack of self-esteem is not the issue.

Because of Adam's sin, this state of spiritual death called total depravity has passed to all mankind. Another term for this is "original sin." Scripture explains it this way: "Through one man sin entered into the world, and death through sin, and so death spread to all men, because all sinned (Rom. 5:12). When, as head of the human race, Adam sinned, the whole race was corrupted. "Through the one man's disobedience the many were made sinners" (Rom. 5:19). How such a thing could happen has been the subject of much theological discussion for centuries. For our purposes, however, it is sufficient to affirm that Scripture clearly teaches that Adam's sin brought guilt upon the entire race. We were "in Adam" when he sinned, and therefore the guilt of sin and the sentence of death passed upon all of us: "In Adam all die" (1 Cor. 15:22).

We might be tempted to think, *If I'm sinful by birth and never had a morally neutral nature, how can I be held responsible for being a sinner?* But our corrupt nature is precisely why our guilt is such a serious matter. Sin flows from the very soul of our being. It is because of our sinful nature that we commit sinful acts: "For from within, out of the heart of men, proceed the evil thoughts, fornications, thefts, murders, adulteries, deeds of coveting and wickedness, as well as deceit, sensuality, envy, slander, pride and foolishness. All these evil things proceed from within and defile the man" (Mk. 7:21–23). We are "by nature children of wrath" (Eph. 2:3). Original sin—including all the corrupt tendencies and sinful passions of the soul —is as deserving of punishment as all our voluntary acts of sin. What is sin, after all, but *anomia*—"lawlessness" (1 Jn. 3:4)? Or as the Westminster Shorter Catechism says, "Sin is any want of conformity to, or transgression of, the law of God" (q. 14). Far from being an excuse, original sin itself is at the heart of *why* we are guilty. And original sin itself is sufficient grounds for our condemnation before God.

Moreover, original sin with its resulting depravity is the *reason* we commit voluntary acts of sin. D. Martyn Lloyd-Jones wrote,

> Why is it that man ever chooses to sin? The answer is that man has fallen away from God, and as a result, his whole nature has become perverted and sinful. Man's whole bias is away from God. By nature he hates God and feels that God is opposed to him. His god is himself, his own abilities and powers, his own desires. He objects to the whole idea of God and the demands which God makes upon him. . . . Furthermore, man likes and covets the things which God prohibits, and dislikes the things and the kind of life to which God calls him. These are no mere dogmatic statements. They are facts. . . . They alone explain the moral muddle and the ugliness that characterise life to such an extent to-day.[38]

Salvation from original sin is only through the cross of Christ: "As through the one man's disobedience [Adam's sin] the many were made sinners, even so through the obedience of the One [Jesus Christ] the many will be made righteous" (Rom. 5:19). We are born in sin (Ps. 51:5), and if we are to become children of God and enter God's kingdom, we must be born again by God's Spirit (Jn. 3:3–8).

In other words, contrary to what most people think—contrary to the presuppositions of self-esteem doctrine—men and women are not naturally good. Just the opposite is true. We are by nature enemies of God, sinners, lovers of ourselves, and in bondage to our own sin. We are blind, deaf, and dead to spiritual matters, unable even to believe apart from God's gracious intervention. Yet we are relentlessly proud! In fact, nothing is more illustrative of human wickedness than the desire for self-esteem. And the first step to a proper self-image is a recognition that these things are true.

> *We are by nature enemies of God,*
> *sinners, lovers of ourselves,*
> *and in bondage to our own sin.*

That's why Jesus *commended* the tax-gatherer—rather than rebuking him for his low self-esteem—when the man pounded his chest and pleaded, "God, be merciful to me, the sinner!" (Lk. 18:13). The man had finally come to the point where he saw himself for what he was and he was so overcome that his emotion released in acts of self-condemnation. The truth is, his self-image had never been more sound than at that moment. Rid of pride and pretense, he now saw there was nothing he could ever do to earn God's favor. Instead, he pleaded with God for mercy. And therefore he "went down to his house justified"—exalted by God because he had humbled himself (v. 14). For the first time ever he was in a position to realize true joy, peace with God, and a new sense of self-worth that is granted by God's grace to those He adopts as His children (Rom. 8:15).

All Have Sinned and Fall Short

Deep in our hearts, we all know something is desperately wrong with us. Our conscience constantly confronts us with our own sinfulness. Try as we might to blame others or seek psychological explanations for how we feel, we cannot escape reality. We cannot ultimately deny our own consciences. We all feel our guilt, and we all know the horrible truth about who we are on the inside.

We *feel* guilty because we *are* guilty. Only the cross of Christ can answer sin in a way that frees us from our own shame. Psychology might mask some of the pain of our guilt. Self-esteem might sweep it under the rug for a time. Other things—such as seeking comfort in relationships, or blaming our problems on someone else—might make us feel better, but the relief is only superficial. And it is dangerous. In fact, it often intensifies the guilt, because it adds dishonesty and pride to the sin that originally wounded the conscience.

We feel *guilty because we* are *guilty.*
Only the cross of Christ can
answer sin in a way that
frees us from our own shame.

True guilt has only one cause, and that is sin. Until sin is dealt with, the conscience will fight to accuse. And sin—not low self-esteem—is the very thing the gospel is given to conquer. That is why, as we saw in chapter 3, the apostle Paul began his presentation of the gospel to the Romans with a lengthy discourse about sin. Total depravity is the first gospel truth he introduced, and he spent nearly three full chapters on the subject. Romans 1:18–32 demonstrates the guilt of the pagans. Romans 2:1–16 proves the guilt of the moralist, who violates the very standard by which he judges others. And Romans 2:17–3:8 establishes the guilt of the Jews, who had access to all the benefits of divine grace but as a whole rejected God's righteousness nonetheless.

Since Romans 1 Paul has argued eloquently, citing evidence from nature, history, sound reason, and conscience to prove utter sinfulness of all humanity. And in verses 9–20 of chapter 3, he sums it all up. Paul reasons like an attorney giving his final summation. He reviews his arguments like a prosecutor who has made an iron-clad case against all humanity. It is a powerful and compelling presentation, replete with a charge, convincing proof, and the inexcapable verdict.

The charge. "What then? Are we better than they? Not at all; for we have already charged that both Jews and Greeks are all under sin" (Rom. 3:9). Paul's indictment thus begins with two questions: What then? or, "Is there any need of further testimony?" And, Are we better than they? or, "Can anyone honestly claim to live above the level of human nature I have been describing?"

"*Not at all,*" he answers. Everyone from the most degenerate, perverted sinners (Rom. 1:28–32) to the most rigidly legalistic Jews falls into the same category of total depravity. In other words, the entire human race, without exception, is arraigned in the divine courtroom and charged with being "under sin"—wholly subjugated to the power of sin. All unredeemed people, Paul is saying, are subservient to sin, in thrall to it, taken captive to sin's authority.

Paul's Jewish readers would have found this truth every bit as shocking and unbelievable as it must be to those weaned on modern self-esteem doctrine. His Jewish readers believed they were acceptable to God by birth and that only Gentiles were sinners by nature. Jews were, after all, God's chosen people. The idea that all Jews were sinners was contrary to the beliefs of the Pharisees. They taught that only derelicts, beggars, and Gentiles were born in sin (cf. Jn. 9:34). But Scripture clearly pronounces otherwise. Even David said, "I was brought forth in iniquity, and in sin my mother conceived me" (Ps. 51:5) "The whole world lies in the power of the evil one" (1 Jn. 5:19). Modern humanity, weaned on self-esteem psychology, also finds it shocking to learn that all of us are by nature sinful and unworthy creatures.

The proof. Paul, continuing his courtroom summation, goes on to prove from the Old Testament Scriptures the universality of human depravity:

> As it is written, "There is none righteous, not even one; there is none who understands, there is none who seeks for God; all have turned aside, together they have become useless; there is none who does good, there is not even one." "Their throat is an open grave, with their tongues they keep deceiving," "The poison of asps is under their lips"; "Whose mouth is full of cursing and bitterness"; "Their feet are swift to shed blood, destruction and misery are in their paths, and the path of peace have they not known" (Rom. 3:10–17).

Notice how Paul underscores the universality of sin. In those few verses, he says "none" or "not even one" six times. No person escapes the accusation. "The Scripture has shut up all men under sin" (Gal. 3:22).

Paul's argument is constructed in three parts: how sin corrupts the character (Rom. 3:10–12), how sin defiles the conversation (vv. 13–14), and how sin perverts the conduct (vv. 15–17). First he proves *how sin corrupts the character*: "There is none righteous . . . there is none who does good, there is not even one" (Rom. 3:10–12). Here Paul makes six charges. He says that because of their innate depravity, people are universally evil ("none righteous"), spiritually ignorant ("none who understands"), rebellious ("none who seeks for God"), wayward ("all have turned aside"), spiritually useless ("together they have become useless"), and morally corrupt ("there is none who does good").

The verse Paul is quoting is Psalm 14:1: "The fool has said in his heart, 'There is no God.' They are corrupt, they have committed abominable deeds; there is no one who does good." The words at the end of Romans 3:12, "not even one," are an editorial comment from Paul, added to make the truth inescapable for someone who might otherwise think of himself as an exception to the rule—as is the common attitude of self-justifying sinners.

Notice Paul does not suggest that some sinners might be prone to think worse of themselves than they ought to. The very opposite is true: "I say to every man among you not to think more highly of himself than he ought to think" (Rom. 12:3). Undue pride is the typical and expected response of sinners. Modern self-esteem teaching, in fact, is the expression of that very pride. Making a savage feel good about himself only increases his deadliness.

Again, the utter depravity Paul is describing certainly does not mean that all people play out the expression of their sin to the ultimate degree. There are certainly some people who are "good" in a relative sense. They may have characteristics of compassion, generosity, kindness, integrity, decency, thoughtfulness, and so on. But even those characteristics are imperfect and sullied with human sin and weakness. No one—"not even one"—comes close to true righteousness. God's standard, after all, is absolute perfection: "You are to be perfect, as your heavenly Father is perfect" (Matt. 5:48). In other words, no one who falls short of the touchstone of perfection is acceptable to God! What does that do to self-esteem theology? How does one feel good about oneself when God Himself declares us worthy of His wrath?

There *is* an answer to the dilemma, of course. God justifies the ungodly by faith (Rom. 4:5). Christ's own perfect righteousness is imputed to our account, so by faith we can stand before God clothed in a perfect righteousness that is not our own (Phil. 3:9). This does not speak of external works we do. It is a superior righteousness, the totality of Christ's own righteousness, credited to our account. Christ on our behalf has already fulfilled the requirement of being as perfect as our heavenly Father is perfect. His virtue is assigned to our account, so God regards us as fully righteous.

But we're jumping ahead of the apostle's carefully arranged evidence. He adds a paraphrase also from Psalm 14: "The Lord has looked down from heaven upon the sons of men, to see if there are any who understand, who seek after God" (v. 2; cf. 53:3). Ignorance and depravity go hand in hand. But people are not sinful and enemies of God because of their spiritual ignorance; rather they are spiritually ignorant because of their sinfulness and their adversarial disposition toward God. They are "darkened in their understanding, excluded from the life of God, because of the ignorance that is in them, *because of the hardness of their heart*" (Eph. 4:18, emphasis added). In other words, because of their hatred of God and their love for their own sin, they reject the witness of God in creation and the testimony of their conscience (Rom. 1:19–20). That, as we noted in chapter 3, hardens the heart and darkens the mind.

The hard heart and darkened mind refuse to seek for God: "There is *none* who seeks for God." That again echoes Psalm 14:2. God invites the seeker, and promises that those who seek Him with all their hearts will find Him (Jer. 29:13). Jesus also promised that everyone who seeks Him will find Him (Matt. 7:8). But the sinful heart is inclined away from God and does not seek Him. Without God's gracious, sovereign intervention, seeking and drawing sinners to Himself first, no one would seek and be saved. Jesus Himself said, "No one can come to Me, unless the Father who sent Me draws him" (Jn. 6:44).

Without God's gracious, sovereign intervention, seeking and drawing sinners to Himself first, no one would be saved.

Rather than seeking God, sinners inevitably go their own way. Still using the 14th Psalm, Paul cites verse 3: "They have all turned aside"—or as Romans 3:12 has it, "All have turned aside." This is reminiscent of Isaiah 53:6: "All of us like sheep have gone astray, each of us has turned to his own way." Sinners are naturally wayward. Inherent in human depravity is an inescapable drift away from truth and righteousness. Sinners always lose their way: "There is a way which seems right to a man, but its end is the way of death" (Prov. 14:12).

The taint of sin further renders the sinner "useless" (v. 12)—translating a Greek word used to describe spoiled milk or contaminated food to be thrown out. Unredeemed people are unfit for any spiritual good, useless for righteousness, fit only to be thrown into the fire and burned (Jn. 15:6). Their great need is not self-esteem or positive thinking, but redemption from their prideful sin.

In the next few verses Paul presents his second proof concerning *how sin defiles the conversation*: "Their throat is an open grave, with their tongues they keep deceiving, the poison of asps is under their lips; whose mouth is full of cursing and bitterness" (3:13–14). One's true character inevitably becomes apparent in conversation. Scripture is filled with affirmation of this truth:

- "The mouth speaks out of that which fills the heart. The good man out of his good treasure brings forth what is good; and the evil man out of his evil treasure brings forth what is evil" (Matt. 12:34–35).
- "The things that proceed out of the mouth come from the heart" (15:18).
- "The mouth of the righteous flows with wisdom, but the perverted tongue will be cut out. The lips of the righteous bring forth what is acceptable, but the mouth of the wicked, what is perverted" (Prov. 10:31–32).
- "The tongue of the wise makes knowledge acceptable, but the mouth of fools spouts folly. . . . The heart of the righteous ponders how to answer, but the mouth of the wicked pours out evil things" (Prov. 15:2, 28).
- "Your iniquities have made a separation between you and your God, and your sins have hidden His face from you, so that He does not hear. For your hands are defiled with blood, and your fingers with iniquity; your lips have spoken falsehood, your tongue mutters wickedness" (Isa. 59:2–3).
- "They bend their tongue like their bow; lies and not truth prevail in the land. . . . Every neighbor goes about as a slanderer. And everyone deceives his neighbor, and does not speak the truth; they have taught their tongue to speak lies" (Jer. 9:3–5).

Paul chooses more passages from the psalms to underscore the point:

- "Poison of a viper is under their lips" (Ps. 140:3).
- "There is nothing reliable in what they say; their inward part is destruction itself; their throat is an open grave; they flatter with their tongue" (Ps. 5:9).
- "His mouth is full of curses and deceit and oppression; under his tongue is mischief and wickedness" (Ps. 10:7).

Those verses, all written to condemn "the wicked," Paul applies to everyone. He is making the point that human depravity is universal. *All* are wicked. *Everyone* is guilty. *No one* can claim exemption from the charges Paul levels.

Moreover, he is illustrating how thoroughly sin pervades and permeates every aspect of our humanity. Note how completely sin contaminates the conversation: it defiles the "throat," corrupts the "tongue," poisons the "lips," and pollutes the "mouth." Evil speech, an expression of the wickedness of the heart, thus defiles every organ it touches as it "proceeds out of the mouth," defiling the whole person (Matt. 15:11).

Third, Paul concludes his proof by quoting several verses to show *how sin perverts the conduct*: "Their feet are swift to shed blood, destruction and misery are in their paths, and the path of peace have they not known" (Rom. 3:15–17). Here Paul is quoting a passage from Isaiah. This is significant, because in these verses Isaiah was excoriating Israel for their sins against Jehovah. This was no denunciation of wicked pagans, but an indictment of religious people who believed in God: "Their feet run to evil, and they hasten to shed innocent blood; their thoughts are thoughts of iniquity; devastation and destruction are in their highways. They do not know the way of peace, and there is no justice in their tracks; they have made their paths crooked; whoever treads on them does not know peace" (Isa. 59:7–8).

In some of our larger cities, as many as two hundred murders will occur in a typical week.

The phrase "their feet are swift to shed blood" describes sinful humanity's penchant for murder. Remember, Jesus taught that hatred is the moral equivalent of murder (Matt. 5:21–22). The seed of hatred ripens and matures, and the fruit it bears is the shedding of blood. Sinners are naturally attracted to hatred and its violent offspring. People are "swift" in their advance toward such acts. We see this very clearly in our own society. An article in *Newsweek,* for example, recently reported that "a twelve-year-old boy turn[ed] without a word and [shot] dead a seven-year-old girl because she 'diss'ed' him by standing on his shadow."[39]

97

In some of our larger cities, as many as two hundred murders will occur in a typical week. Drive-by shootings, drunken brawls, gang violence, family strife, and other crimes all contribute to the body count. If lack of self-esteem is the problem of the human heart, why, we must ask, is the murder rate on the rise so dramatically in a society where self-esteem is also growing? The answer is that low self-esteem is not the problem. On the contrary, pride itself is the very problem that leads to all sin, including hate, hostility, and killing. A love for bloodshed festers in the heart of sinful humanity. Remove the moral restraints from society, and the inevitable result will be an escalation of murder and violence—no matter how good people feel about themselves.

"Destruction and misery" further characterize the tendencies of depraved humanity. Again, no one familiar with the trends of modern society can deny the truth of Scripture on this point. The lid is off, and we can see clearly the true nature of the human heart. What else could explain our culture—where people are robbed, beaten, raped, or murdered for no reason other than sheer enjoyment? Wanton destruction is so much a part of society that we have become inured to much of it.

"Gangsta rap"—music that glorifies murder, rape, and drug use—now accounts for many of the hottest-selling albums on the record charts. The lyrics of most gangsta rap are indescribably vile. They mix violence, sexual imagery, and unimaginable profanity in a way that is repulsive and purposely offensive. Worse, they openly incite young people to join gangs, kill policemen, rape women, riot, and commit other acts of wanton destruction. Gangsta rap is big business. These recordings are not sold secretly out of the back of some hoodlum's car, but marketed openly in retail stores everywhere—with slick ad campaigns designed by executives in companies like Capitol Records. And the prime target for such products are kids younger than eighteen. A whole generation is being indoctrinated with these vices. Destruction and misery *are* in their path. And woe to those unfortunate enough to cross their path! In recent months several nationally-known rap artists have been charged with violent crimes, including murder and gang rape.

Why is it that misery and despair are so characteristic of this modern age, even though humanity has made such remarkable advances in technology, psychology, and medicine? It is because depravity is at the very heart of the human soul. All these problems are so bound up in the human heart that no amount of learning and no measure of self-esteem will ever erase them. As science advances, people only become more sophisticated in their use of evil means. The destruction and misery wrought by human sin does not diminish; it accelerates. The history of this century, filled with world wars, holocausts, serial killers, escalating crime, and bloody revolutions, is graphic proof of that. Depravity is bound up in the human heart.

In other words, "the path of peace" is unknown to sinful humanity (Rom. 3:17). Though we hear much talk these days of "peace, peace," there is no peace (cf. Jer. 6:14).

Paul sums up the evidence for human depravity: "There is no fear of God before their eyes" (Rom. 3:18). There he returns to the psalms for a final quotation. Psalm 36:1 says, "Transgression speaks to the ungodly within his heart; there is no fear of God before his eyes." Human sinfulness is a defect of the human heart itself. Evil commands the heart of man. People's hearts are naturally attuned to wickedness. They have no native fear of God.

We don't hear much about fearing God these days. Even many Christians seem to feel the language of fear is somehow too harsh or too negative.

Fear of the Lord, of course, is the primary prerequisite to spiritual wisdom (Prov. 9:10). Moses commanded Israel, "You shall fear only the Lord your God; and you shall worship Him, and swear by His name" (Deut. 6:13). In fact, as Moses summed up the responsibilities of the Israelites, this is what he said: "And now, Israel, what does the Lord your God require from you, but to *fear* the Lord your God, to walk in all His ways and love Him, and to serve the Lord your God with all your heart and with all your soul, and to keep the Lord's commandments and His statutes which I am commanding you today for your good?" (Deut. 10:12–13, emphasis added). We in the New Testament era are likewise commanded to "cleanse ourselves from all defilement of flesh and spirit, perfecting holiness in the fear of God" (2 Cor. 7:1). We are to "honor all men; love the brotherhood, *fear God*, honor the king" (1 Pet. 2:17, emphasis added; cf. Rev. 14:7).

"The fear of the Lord is the instruction for wisdom" (Prov. 15:33). "By the fear of the Lord one keeps away from evil" (Prov. 16:6). "The fear of the Lord is a fountain of life, that one may avoid the snares of death" (Prov. 14:27).

We don't hear much about fearing God these days. Even many Christians seem to feel the language of fear is somehow too harsh or too negative. How much easier it is to speak of God's love and infinite mercy. But longsuffering, kindness, and such attributes aren't the truths that are missing from most people's concept of God. The problem is that most people don't think of God as Someone to be *feared*. They don't realize that He hates the proud and punishes evildoers. They presume on His grace. They fear what people think more than they care what God thinks. They seek their own pleasure, unmindful of God's displeasure. Their conscience is defiled and in danger of vanishing. "There is no fear of God before their eyes."

The fear of God, by the way, is a concept diametrically opposed to the doctrine of self-esteem. How can we encourage fear of the Lord in people and at the same time be obsessed with boosting their self-esteem? Which is the more biblical pursuit? The Scriptures speak for themselves.

The verdict. Having presented a convincing case for total depravity, Paul makes the verdict clear: "Now we know that what things soever the law saith, it saith to them who are under the law: *that every mouth may be stopped, and all the world may become guilty before God*" (Rom. 3:19, KJV, emphasis added).

Here Paul blasts the assumption of those who believed that merely *having* the law of God somehow made the Jews morally superior to pagan Gentiles. The law carried its own condemnation against those who did not keep it perfectly: "Cursed is he who does not confirm the words of this law by doing them" (Deut. 27:26; cf. Gal. 3:10). "Whoever keeps the whole law and yet stumbles in one point, he has become guilty of all" (Jas. 2:10). Merely having the law did not make the Jews any better than the rest of humanity.

The Gentiles, on the other hand, were accountable to the law written on their own consciences (Rom. 2:11–15). Both groups are proven in violation of the law they possessed. The prosecution rests. There can be no defense. Every mouth must be stopped. The case is closed. Unredeemed humanity is guilty of all charges. There are no grounds for acquittal. The whole world stands guilty before God.

Self-esteem is no solution to human depravity. It aggravates it! The problems of our culture—especially the anguish that wracks individual human hearts—will not be solved by the deception of getting people to think better of themselves. People really *are* sinful to the core. The guilt and shame we all feel as sinners is legitimate, natural, and even appropriate. It has the beneficial purpose of letting us know the depth of our own sinfulness. We dare not whisk it aside for the faulty teachings of humanistic self-esteem.

Self-esteem is no solution to human depravity.

I recently read an unusually clear-sighted article dealing with the myth of human goodness from a non-Christian perspective. The author, a Jewish social critic, writes,

> To believe that people are basically good after Auschwitz, the Gulag and the other horrors of our century, is a statement of irrational faith, as irrational as any [fanatical] religious belief. Whenever I meet people—especially Jews, victims of the most concentrated evil in history—who persist in believing in the essential goodness of people, I know that I have met people for whom evidence is irrelevant. How many evils would human beings have to commit in order to shake a Jew's faith in humanity? How many more innocent people have to be murdered and tortured? How many more women need to be raped?[40]

This article lists five consequences of the people-are-basically-good myth. Notice how they all contribute to the destruction of the conscience:

The first such consequence is, quite logically, the attribution of all evil to causes outside of people. Since people are basically good, the bad that they do must be caused by some external force. Depending on who is doing the blaming, that outside force could be the social environment, economic circumstances, parents, schools, television violence, handguns, racism, the devil, government cutbacks, or even corrupt politicians (as expressed by this frequently heard foolishness: "How can we expect our children to be honest when the government isn't?").

People are therefore not responsible for the evil they commit. It's not my fault that I mug old women, or that I cheat much of the time—something (chosen from the previous list) made me do it.

A second terrible consequence is the denial of evil. If good is natural, then bad must be unnatural, or "sick." Moral categories have been replaced by psychological ones. There is no longer good and evil, only "normal" and "sick."

Third, neither parents nor schools take the need to teach children goodness seriously—why teach what comes naturally? Only those who recognize that people are not basically good recognize the need to teach goodness.

Fourth, since much of society believes that evil comes from outside of people, it has ceased trying to change people's values and concentrates instead on changing outside forces. People commit crimes? It is not values and character development that we need to be concerned with; we need to change the socioeconomic environment that "produces" rapists and murderers. Irresponsible men impregnate irresponsible women? It is not better values they need, but better sex education and better access to condoms and abortions.

Fifth, and most destructive of all, those who believe that people are basically good conclude that people do not need to feel accountable of their behavior to God and to a religion, only to themselves.[41]

That author, oddly enough, denies human depravity as well as human goodness. He believes people are neither good *nor* bad but choose their way in life. (At the outset of his article, however, he quotes Genesis 8:21: "The intent of man's heart is evil from his youth.")

Despite this inconsistency in the author's position, the article shows very clearly the dangers of the myth of human goodness.

The church must safeguard sound doctrine by recovering the doctrine of human depravity. As J. C. Ryle wrote nearly a century ago,

> A scriptural view of sin is one of the best antidotes to that vague, dim, misty, hazy kind of theology which is so painfully current in the present age. It is vain to shut our eyes to the fact that there is a vast quantity of so-called Christianity nowadays which you cannot declare positively unsound, but which, nevertheless, is not full measure, good weight and sixteen ounces to the pound. It is a Christianity in which there is undeniably "something about Christ and something about grace and something about faith and something about repentance and something about holiness," but it is not the real "thing as it is" in the Bible. Things are out of place and out of proportion. As old Latimer would have said, it is a kind of "mingle-mangle," and does no good. It neither exercises influence on daily conduct, nor comforts in life, nor gives peace in death; and those who hold it often wake too late to find that they have got nothing solid under their feet. Now I believe that the likeliest way to cure and mend this defective kind of religion is to bring forward more prominently the old scriptural truth about the sinfulness of sin.[42]

"To believe that people are basically good after Auschwitz, the Gulag and the other horrors of our century, is a statement of irrational faith, as irrational as any [fanatical] religious belief." (Dennis Prager)

You may be asking, on the other hand, *Does God want us to wallow in shame and self-condemnation permanently?* Not at all. God offers freedom from sin and shame through faith in Jesus Christ. If we are willing to acknowledge our sinfulness and seek His grace, He will wonderfully deliver us from our sin and all its effects. "There is therefore now no condemnation for those who are in Christ Jesus. For the law of the Spirit of life in Christ Jesus has set you free from the law of sin and of death" (Rom. 8:1–2). The liberation from sin those verses describe is the only basis on which we can really feel good about ourselves. And it is to that process that we now turn our attention.

5

Sin and Its Cure

Man's very nature is fallen. Man is wrong at the centre of his being, and therefore everything is wrong. He cannot be improved, for, finally, nothing will suffice but a radical change, a new nature. Man loves the darkness and hates the light. What can be done for him? Can he change himself? Can he renew his nature? "Can the Ethiopian change his skin or the leopard his spots?" Can man change the whole bias of his life? Give him new clothing, provide him with a new house in new surroundings, entertain him with all that is best and most elevating, educate him and train his mind, enrich his soul with frequent doses of the finest culture ever known, do all and more, but still he will remain the same essential man, and his desires and innermost life will be unchanged.

D. Martyn Lloyd-Jones[1]

Tom Wolfe's 1987 blockbuster novel *The Bonfire of the Vanities*[2] told the story of a fictional young Wall Street tycoon, Sherman McCoy, who is caught in the vortex of a scandal after he and his mistress inadvertently take a wrong exit on a Bronx expressway. Lost in the wrong part of town, they are threatened by some thugs who try to block their car. One of the young attackers is seriously injured when the car strikes him as McCoy and his lover are fleeing the scene. The boy lies in a coma for more than a year before dying. Meanwhile, the case becomes a political *cause célèbre*, with McCoy at the mercy of a ruthless press and inept criminal justice system. The book tells the story of how his world slowly and painfully unravels.

Though innocent of most of the charges against him, McCoy is by no means guiltless. His troubles begin because he is trying to conceal his adultery. He compounds his own guilt with a series of lies in an attempt to cover up. His own duplicity ultimately draws him deeper and deeper into trouble. In the end, he loses his career, his family, his fortune, and all his friends—and seems headed for a lengthy trial probably followed by a prison term.

Wolfe's book anticipated with remarkable accuracy a string of celebrity scandals that characterized the second half of the 1980s. Jim and Tammy Bakker, Gary Hart, Jimmy Swaggart, Michael Milken, and a host of others all saw their lives disintegrate in a manner reminiscent of Sherman McCoy. What all these cases demonstrate so graphically is the destructive, catastrophic effects of sin. Sin once begun will eat like gangrene at the human soul. It will dishonor the sinner, expose him, scandalize him, and ultimately destroy his life. "Be sure your sin will find you out" (Num. 32:23).

The Scandal of Sin

Sin rules every human heart, and if it had its way, it would damn every human soul. If we do not understand our own sinfulness or see our sin as God sees it, we cannot understand or make use of sin's remedy. Those who want to deny their guilt or hide their own sinfulness cannot discover sin's cure. Those who try to justify their sin forfeit the justification of God. Until we understand what an utterly abhorrent thing our sin is, we can never even know God.

> ## *If we do not understand our own sinfulness or see our sin as God sees it, we cannot understand or make use of sin's remedy.*

Sin is abominable to God. He hates it (cf. Deut. 12:31). His eyes "are too pure to approve evil, and [He cannot] look on wickedness with favor" (Hab. 1:13). Sin is contrary to His very nature (Isa. 6:3; 1 Jn. 1:5). The ultimate penalty—death—is exacted for every infraction against the divine law (Ezek. 18:4, 20; Rom. 6:23). Even the very smallest transgression is worthy of the same severe penalty: "For whoever keeps the whole law and yet stumbles in one point, he has become guilty of all" (Jas. 2:10).

Sin stains the soul. It degrades a person's nobility. It darkens the mind. It makes us worse than animals, for animals cannot sin. Sin pollutes, defiles, stains. All sin is gross, disgusting, loathsome, revolting in God's sight. Scripture calls it "filthiness" (Prov. 30:12; Ezek. 24:13; Jas. 1:21). Sin is compared to vomit, and sinners are the dogs who lick it up (Prov. 26:11; 2 Pet. 2:22). Sin is called mire, and sinners are the swine who love to wallow in it (Ps. 69:2; 2 Pet. 2:22). Sin is likened to a putrefying corpse, and sinners are the tombs that contain the stench and foulness (Matt. 23:27). Sin has turned humanity into a polluted, befouled race.

The terrifying consequences of sin include hell, of which Jesus said, "If your right eye makes you stumble, tear it out, and throw it from you; for it is better for you that one of the parts of your body perish, than for your whole body to be thrown into hell" (Matt. 5:30). Scripture describes hell as a dreadful, hideous place where sinners are "tormented with fire and brimstone. . . . And the smoke of their torment goes up forever and ever; and they have no rest day and night" (Rev. 14:10–11). Those truths become all the more alarming when we realize that they are part of the inspired Word of an infinitely merciful and gracious God.

God wants us to understand the exceeding sinfulness of sin (Rom. 7:13). We dare not take it lightly or dismiss our own guilt frivolously. When we really see sin for what it is, we must hate it.

Scripture goes even further than that: "You will remember your ways and all your deeds, with which you have defiled yourselves; and *you will loathe yourselves* in your own sight for all the evil things that you have done" (Ezek. 20:43, emphasis added). In other words, when we truly see what sin is, far from achieving self-esteem, we will despise ourselves.

Nature of Human Depravity

Sin pervades our innermost beings. As we saw in the previous chapter, sin is at the very core of the human soul. "Out of the heart come evil thoughts, murders, adulteries, fornications, thefts, false witness, slanders. These are the things which defile the man" (Matt. 15:19–20). "The evil man out of the evil treasure [of his heart] brings forth what is evil; for his mouth speaks from that which fills his heart" (Lk. 6:45).

Yet sin is not a weakness or flaw for which we cannot be held responsible. It is an energetic, purposeful antagonism to God. Sinners freely and gladly choose sin. It is human nature to love sin and hate God. "The carnal mind is enmity against God" (Rom. 8:7, KJV).

Yet sin is not a weakness or flaw for which we cannot be held responsible. It is an energetic, purposeful antagonism to God.

In other words, sin is rebellion against God. Sinners reason in their hearts, "With our tongue we will prevail; our lips are our own; *who is lord over us?*" (Ps. 12:4, emphasis added). Isaiah 57:4 characterizes sinners as rebellious children who open wide their mouths and stick out their tongues against God. Sin would dethrone God, depose Him, usurp Him, and set self in His rightful place. All sin is ultimately an act of pride, which says, "Move over, God; I'm in charge." That's why all sin at its core is blasphemy.

We initially love our sin; we delight in it; we seek opportunities to act it out. Yet because we know instinctively that we are guilty before God, we inevitably attempt to camouflage or disavow our own sinfulness. There are many ways we do this, as we have noted in previous chapters. They can be summarized in roughly three categories: covering up, justifying ourselves, and being oblivious to our own sins.

First, *we try to cover up.* Adam and Eve did this in the Garden, after the first sin: "The eyes of both of them were opened, and they knew that they were naked; and they sewed fig leaves together and made themselves loin coverings" (Gen. 3:7)—then they hid themselves from the presence of the Lord (v. 8). King David tried in futility to cover his guilt when he sinned against Uriah. He had committed adultery with Uriah's wife, Bathsheba. When she became pregnant, David first plotted to try to make it seem as if Uriah was the father of the baby (2 Sam. 11:5–13). When that didn't work, he schemed to have Uriah killed (vv. 14–17). That only compounded his sin. For all the months of Bathsheba's pregnancy, David continued to cover his sin (2 Sam. 11:27). Later, when David was confronted with his sin and repented, he confessed, "When I kept silent about my sin, my body wasted away through my groaning all day long. For day and night Thy hand was heavy upon me; my vitality was drained away as with the fever heat of summer" (Ps. 32:3–4).

Second, *we attempt to justify ourselves.* Sin is always someone else's fault. Adam blamed Eve, whom he described as "the woman whom *Thou* gavest to be with me" (Gen. 3:12, emphasis added). That shows he was blaming God as well. He didn't even know what a woman was, until he woke up married to one! God, he reasoned, was responsible for the woman who victimized him. We likewise try to excuse our wrongdoing because we think it is someone else's fault. Or we argue that we think we have a valid reason. We convince ourselves that it is OK to return evil for evil (cf. Prov. 24:29; 1 Thess. 5:15; 1 Pet. 3:9). Or we reason that if our ultimate motives are good, evil can be justified—the perversion of thinking the end justifies any means (cf. Rom. 3:8). We call sin sickness, label ourselves victims, or deny that what we have done is really wrong. The human mind is endlessly creative when it comes to finding ways to justify evil.

Third, *we are oblivious to our own sin.* We do often sin in ignorance or presumption. That's why David prayed, "Who can discern his errors? Acquit me of hidden faults. Also keep back Thy servant from presumptuous sins" (Ps. 19:12–13). Jesus warned against the folly of tolerating a log in our own eye while being concerned about a tiny speck in someone else's (Matt. 7:3). Because sin is so pervasive, we naturally tend to be insensitive to our own sin, just as a skunk is impervious to its own odor. Even a highly sensitive conscience can't know everything (cf. 1 Cor. 4:4).

Sin does not necessarily express itself in overt acts. Sinful attitudes, sinful dispositions, sinful desires, and a sinful state of heart are just as reprehensible as the actions they produce. Jesus said anger is as sinful as murder, and lust is tantamount to adultery (Matt. 5:21–28).

Sin is deceitful in a way that hardens the sinner against its own enormity (Heb. 3:13). We naturally want to minimize our sin, as if it were not really any big deal. After all, we tell ourselves, God is merciful and loving, is He not? He understands our sin and can't be so hard on us, can He? But to reason that way is to be deceived by sin's cunning.

Sin, according to Scripture, "is the transgression of the law" (1 Jn. 3:4, KJV). In other words, "Everyone who practices sin also practices lawlessness; and sin is lawlessness" (NASB). Sin, therefore, is any lack of conformity to the perfect moral standard of God. The central demand of God's law is that we love Him: "You shall love the Lord your God with all your heart, and with all your soul, and with all your strength, and with all your mind" (Lk. 10:27). Hence, lack of love for God is the epitome of all sin.

But "the carnal mind . . . is not subject to the law of God, neither indeed can be" (Rom. 8:7, KJV). Our natural hatred of the law is such that even knowing what the law demands stirs up in us an urge to disobey. Paul wrote, "The sinful passions [are] aroused by the Law. . . . I would not have come to know sin except through the Law; for I would not have known about coveting if the Law had not said, 'You shall not covet.' But sin, taking opportunity through the commandment, produced in me coveting of every kind" (Rom. 7:5, 7). Such is the sinner's penchant for sin that it controls him. He is in bondage to it. But he nevertheless pursues it with an insatiable appetite, and with all the passion in his heart.

The Theological Problem Posed by Evil

Where did sin come from? We know that God created everything in the universe and saw that it was very good (Gen. 1:31). "All things came into being by Him, and apart from Him nothing came into being that has come into being" (Jn. 1:3). That raises the obvious question of whether God is responsible for evil. If He isn't, who is? Didn't God have the power to keep sin from spoiling His perfect creation?

It is helpful to see that sin is not a separate substance that exists independently of moral agents. Evil is not a created thing. It is not an element. Sin is an ethical and moral reality, not a physical one. Sin is a defect in something good. Nobody *created* it; it is a loss of perfection in beings whom God created perfectly.

Nobody created it; sin is a loss of perfection in beings whom God created perfectly.

But that doesn't really resolve the question of how sin happened. How could perfect beings rebel? How could angels who were made perfect turn against God? How could humans, created in God's own image, choose to sin? And if God could have stopped it, why didn't He? Is He somehow to blame for the existence of evil?

Attempts to resolve the problem of sin's origin in a way that vindicates God's goodness are called "theodicies". The theodicy of Christian Scientists is simple; they flatly deny the reality of evil. According to their system, all sin, badness, disease, and other negative effects of evil are simply figments of the imagination, or as they would say, the errors of mortal thinking. Jay Adams answers the Christian Science theodicy: "They implode their own belief by this internally-inconsistent, self-contradictory explanation. If there is no such thing as evil, if God is all, and all is God (as they also teach), then, this all-knowing god of which every human being is a part, cannot err, and there is no such thing as a mortal mind."[3] The Christian Science theodicy is no answer to the problem of evil.

Another theodicy suggests that God was not able to control

the entrance of evil into the world. Having created creatures who enjoyed free will, He could not control their use of their moral freedom or overrule their choices. God, according to this view, has no command over circumstances that occur in His universe. He is at the mercy of circumstances. God, like people, is a "victim" of sin and evil. That is essentially the view expressed in Rabbi Harold Kushner's bestselling book, *When Bad Things Happen to Good People.*[4]

The problem with that view is that it denies God's sovereignty. Scripture clearly teaches that God is utterly sovereign over all things. Or, as the Westminster Confession says, "God from all eternity did, by the most wise and holy Counsel of His own will, freely and unchangeably ordain whatsoever comes to pass" (Chap. 3, sec. 1). He "works all things after the counsel of His will" (Eph. 1:11). "From Him and through Him and to Him are all things" (Rom. 11:36). His purposes are unchangeable (Heb. 6:17). His plan is eternal (Eph. 3:11). And with God "there is no variation, or shifting shadow" (Jas. 1:17). All His works were determined according to His purposes in eternity past.

In fact, Scripture clearly teaches that God is sovereign over every circumstance, situation, and event:

He controls so-called random happenings. "The lot is cast into the lap, but its every decision is from the Lord" (Prov. 16:33). "Are not two sparrows sold for a cent? And yet not one of them will fall to the ground apart from your Father" (Matt. 10:29).

He is sovereign over the free actions of all moral agents. "The king's heart is like channels of water in the hand of the Lord; He turns it wherever He wishes" (Prov. 21:1). "We are His workmanship, created in Christ Jesus for good works, which God prepared beforehand, that we should walk in them" (Eph. 2:10). "It is God who is at work in you, both to will and to work for His good pleasure" (Phil. 2:13).

He determines even the most evil acts of sinners. Peter told the crowd who had demanded Christ's crucifixion, "This Man, delivered up *by the predetermined plan and foreknowledge of God,* you nailed to a cross by the hands of godless men and put Him to death. And God raised Him up again, putting an end to the agony of death, since it was impossible for Him to be held in its power" (Acts 2:23–24, emphasis added). The companions of Peter and John prayed, "Truly in this city there were gathered together against Thy holy servant Jesus, whom Thou didst anoint, both Herod and Pontius Pilate, along with the Gentiles and the peoples of Israel, *to do whatever Thy hand and Thy purpose predestined to occur*" (Acts 4:27–28, emphasis added). Joseph told his brothers, "Now do not be grieved or angry with yourselves, because you sold me here; for God sent me before you to preserve life" (Gen. 45:5). And Isaiah 10:5 says God used the wicked nation of Assyria as the rod of His anger.

He appoints the powers that oversee the evil world system. Pontius Pilate said to Jesus, "Do You not know that I have authority to re-lease You, and I have authority to crucify You?" Jesus replied, "You would have no authority over Me, unless it had been given you from above" (Jn. 19:10–11). Truly "there is no authority except from God, and those which exist are established by God" (Rom. 13:1).

Indeed, the whole course of all events and circumstances is ordained in the divine decree, from the most profound milestone of the divine plan to the most trivial detail. God even determines the number of hairs on our heads (Matt. 10:30).

Ultimately, we must concede that sin is something God *meant* to happen. He planned for it, ordained it—or, in the words of the Westminster Confession, He decreed it. Sin is not something that sneaked in and took Him by surprise, caught Him off guard, or spoiled His plans. The reality of sin figured into His changeless pur-poses from eternity past. Thus evil and all its consequences were included in God's eternal decree before the foundation of the world.

Ultimately, we must concede that sin is something God meant to happen.

Yet by the same token God cannot be considered the author, or originator, of sin. "God cannot be tempted by evil, and He Himself does not tempt anyone" (Jas. 1:13). "God is light, and in Him there is no darkness at all" (1 Jn. 1:5).

God in no sense *causes* sin, *incites* it, *condones* it, *authorizes* it, *approves* it, or otherwise *consents to* it. God is never the cause or the agent of sin. He only *permits* evil agents to do their deeds, then over-rules the evil for His own wise and holy ends. God's purposes in permitting evil are always good. That is why Joseph could say to his brothers, who had sold him into slavery, "You meant evil against me, but God meant it for good in order to bring about this present result, to preserve many people alive" (Gen. 50:20).

Scripture also tells us that God permitted evil so that He could "demonstrate His wrath and . . . make His power known" (Rom. 9:22). In other words, He allowed sin to enter His perfect creation so that He could display His hatred of evil and destroy it forever. Why did He not wipe out all evil immediately the moment it first appeared? Scrip-ture suggests an answer for that as well. He "endured [it] with pa-tience . . . in order that He might make known the riches of His glory upon vessels of mercy, which He prepared beforehand for glory" (Rom. 9:22–23). That means He allows evil to continue even now so that He can display His mercy and grace fully through the redemp-tion of sinners. Sin thus allows God to reveal His glory in forgiveness.

Ultimately, however, Scripture does not undertake any elabo-rate philosophical argument to vindicate God for the existence of evil. It simply declares that He is "holy, holy, holy" (Isa. 6:3; Rev. 4:8). It reveals that He hates evil (Ps. 11:5; Zech. 8:17; Lk. 16:15). And it makes clear that the existence of sin does not in any way dampen God's glory or taint His impeccable character: "Far be it from God to do wickedness, and from the Almighty to do wrong" (Job 34:10). "Ascribe greatness to our God! The Rock! His work is perfect, for all His ways are just; a God of faithfulness and without injustice, righteous and upright is He" (Deut. 32:3–4). "The Lord is upright; He is my rock, and there is no unrighteousness in Him" (Ps. 92:15). "Thou art not a God who takes pleasure in wickedness; no evil dwells with Thee" (Ps. 5:4).

The most satisfying theodicy is implied in the cross of Christ. As R. L. Dabney wrote, "The doctrine of Christ's sacrifice, coupled with His proper divinity, enables us to complete our 'theodicy' of the permission of evil. . . . For had there been in God the least defect of [holiness or benevolence], He certainly would never have found it in His heart to send His infinite Son, more great and important than all worlds, to redeem anyone."[5]

Sin and the Cross of Christ

In fact, the cross is proof of both the immense love of God and the profound wickedness of sin. Do you want to see God's love at its pinnacle and sin's vileness at its nadir? Look at the passion of our Lord Jesus Christ. See Him hanging on the cross—the sinless, spotless, Lamb of God, bearing the sins of the world (cf. Jn. 1:29). Hear Him cry in agony, "Eli, Eli, lama sabachthani?"—that is, "My God, My God, why hast Thou forsaken Me?" (Matt. 27:46). Realize that nothing short of the shed blood of the eternal, beloved Son of God Himself could have atoned for sin. The weight of our guilt must have been infinitely heavy and the heinousness of our sin indescribably black to require such a sacrifice! And God's love must have been inexpressibly rich to allow it!

The cross is proof of both the immense love of God and the profound wickedness of sin.

Sin is a horrible malignancy for which there is no other cure. "Weighed down with iniquity, offspring of evildoers, sons who act corruptly! They have abandoned the Lord, they have despised the Holy One of Israel, they have turned away from Him. . . . The whole head is sick, and the whole heart is faint. From the sole of the foot even to the head there is nothing sound in it, only bruises, welts, and raw wounds, not pressed out or bandaged, nor softened with oil" (Isa. 1:4–6). That pictures sin as an incurable leprosy of the soul. We are sick with sin from top to bottom, within and without.

Sinners cannot improve their own condition. Jeremiah 13:23 says, "Can the Ethiopian change his skin or the leopard his spots? Then you also can do good who are accustomed to doing evil." Sin is so much a part of our nature and we love it so much that we are unable to break away from its domination over our lives. We love darkness rather than light (Jn. 3:19). The unregenerate mind is naturally "hostile toward God; for it does not subject itself to the law of God, for *it is not even able to do so*; and those who are in the flesh *cannot please God*" (Rom. 8:7–8, emphasis added). Unredeemed sinners are slaves of their sin (Jn. 8:34; Rom. 6:20). As Job asked, "Who can make the clean out of the unclean? No one!" (Job 14:4). "The bad tree bears bad fruit . . . nor can a bad tree produce good fruit" (Matt. 7:17–18).

No amount of tears can atone for sin. No number of good deeds can make amends for wrong we have done against God. No quantity of prayer or personal devotion can extenuate our guilt or cover it in any way. Even everlasting burning in hell will not purify the soul from sin. In the human realm there is nothing in time or eternity that can free us from the guilt of our sin. Those who seek a do-it-yourself solution to the problem of sin only shackle themselves all the more securely to their guilt.

Moreover, the smallest sin is so exceedingly vile that God—despite His infinite mercy, grace, and forgiveness—will not and cannot overlook even one sin without exacting its full penalty.

There has to be a solution. There must be a way God can satisfy His perfect righteousness yet enable Him to display His rich mercy toward sinners. The cross of Christ provided the way by enabling the only Perfect Sacrifice to atone for human sin once for all.

The offering for sin had to be perfect, spotless, untainted by sin. Jesus lived a sinless, holy life in perfect obedience to God's law. "We do not have a high priest who cannot sympathize with our weaknesses, but One who has been tempted in all things as we are, yet without sin" (Heb. 4:15). He is "holy, innocent, undefiled, separated from sinners and exalted above the heavens" (Heb. 7:26).

Our Lord, the sinless One, was the Lamb of God to be offered up as a sacrifice for our sin (Jn. 1:29). That is the very purpose for which He came. "You know that He appeared in order to take away sins; and in Him there is no sin" (1 Jn. 3:5). As He hung on the cross, He carried the guilt of *our* sin. "Surely *our* griefs He Himself bore, and *our* sorrows He carried. . . . He was pierced through for *our* transgressions, He was crushed for *our* iniquities; the chastening for *our* well-being fell upon Him" (Isa. 53:4–5, emphasis added). He "offered Himself without blemish to God" to cleanse *our* consciences (Heb. 9:14). He paid the penalty to the fullest on *our* behalf. And in the same way that our sins were imputed to Him, so His righteousness is reckoned to us who believe: "[God] made Him who knew no sin to be sin on our behalf, that we might become the righteousness of God in Him" (2 Cor. 5:21). He rose from the dead to declare His victory over sin. "[He] was delivered up because of our transgressions, and was raised because of our justification" (Rom. 4:25).

> *Our Lord, the sinless One, was the Lamb of God to be offered up as a sacrifice for our sin (Jn. 1:29).*

"He Himself bore our sins in His body on the cross, that we might die to sin and live to righteousness; for *by His wounds you were healed*" (1 Pet. 2:24, emphasis added). That is the only possible remedy for our sin. It is the only way God can be both "just and the justifier of the one who has faith in Jesus" (Rom. 3:26).

God's healing for sin involves more than forgiveness and justification. God transforms the very nature of the sinner. He makes us partakers of His own nature (2 Pet. 1:4). Martyn Lloyd-Jones wrote,

> Man needs a new nature. Whence can he obtain it? Again, there is but one answer, in Jesus Christ the Son of God. He came from Heaven and took upon Him human nature perfect and whole. He is God and man. In Him alone are the divine and the human united. And He offers to give us His own nature. He desires to make of us new men. He is "the first-born among many brethren." All who believe on Him, and receive Him, obtain this new nature, and as the result all things become different. Those who hated God now love Him and desire to know more and more about Him. Their supreme desire now is to please Him and to honour and to glorify Him. The things which formerly delighted them they now hate and detest, and the ways of God are the ways they desire.[6]

That is God's gracious answer to our sin. He redeems those who believe and makes them new creatures (2 Cor. 5:17). He gives them an entirely new nature, including a love for righteousness and an aversion to sin. As we shall see in subsequent chapters, the residue of sin still remains in believers until they are finally glorified, but they are no longer enslaved to sin or incapable of pleasing God.

God So Loved the World

As much as God hates sin, He loves sinners. Set against the dark background of our sin, the grace of God becomes all the more wondrous. The most familiar passage in all Scripture is John 3:16. Without an understanding of the wickedness of sin, however, we cannot grasp the tremendous significance of this verse: "For God so loved the world, that He gave His only begotten Son, that whoever believes in Him should not perish, but have eternal life."

"For God so loved the world, that He gave His only begotten Son, that whoever believes in Him should not perish, but have eternal life." (John 3:16)

"God so loved . . ." Why would God love me despite my sin?

"God so loved the world . . ." Why would God love a whole world of sinners?

"God so loved the world, that He gave His only begotten Son . . ." Why would God's love for sinners be so compelling as to make Him sacrifice His beloved Son in such agony and humiliation?

"God so loved the world, that He gave His only begotten Son, that whoever believes in Him . . ." Why would God make salvation so simple for sinners, requiring only faith of us, and having done all the necessary expiatory work Himself?

"God so loved the world, that He gave His only begotten Son, that whoever believes in Him should not perish . . ." Why would God want to exempt sinners from the judgment they themselves deserve, even to the point of allowing His only begotten Son to accept that judgment on behalf of those who do not deserve His mercy?

"God so loved the world, that He gave His only begotten Son, that whoever believes in Him should not perish, but have eternal life." Why would God want to give everlasting life in His presence to sinners who have done nothing but oppose Him and hate Him?

The answer is found in *God's grace.* "God, being rich in mercy, because of His great love with which He loved us, even when we were dead in our transgressions, made us alive together with Christ (by grace you have been saved)" (Eph. 2:4–5). "The wages of sin is death, but the free gift of God is eternal life in Christ Jesus our Lord" (Rom. 6:23). "Blessed are those whose lawless deeds have been forgiven, and whose sins have been covered. Blessed is the man whose sin the Lord will not take into account" (Rom. 4:7–8).

You Must Be Born Again

How does a sinner obtain forgiveness and acquire the perfect righteousness of Christ? How can someone who is sinful by nature become a partaker in the divine nature?

As Jesus told a Pharisee named Nicodemus, "You must be born again" (Jn. 3:3). Nicodemus saw that as an impossible demand: "How can a man be born when he is old?" (v. 4). Jesus simply reiterated, "Truly, truly, I say to you, unless one is born of water and the Spirit, he cannot enter into the kingdom of God. That which is born of the flesh is flesh, and that which is born of the Spirit is spirit. Do not marvel that I said to you, 'You must be born again'" (vv. 5–7).

Jesus was talking about a spiritual rebirth, a regenerative act of God. Nicodemus was right in suggesting that the new birth is not something a sinner can accomplish for himself. It is a sovereign work of the Spirit of God, which cannot be controlled by human means: "The wind blows where it wishes and you hear the sound of it, but do not know where it comes from and where it is going; so is everyone who is born of the Spirit" (v. 8). Salvation is wholly God's work.

If you're reading this as an unbeliever or as someone who is unsure whether you have ever been born again, you might be tempted to despair. If the Spirit works sovereignly when and where and in whom He will, aren't we in an impossible dilemma? You might ask with the people who heard Peter at Pentecost, "What shall we do?" (Acts 2:37)—or like the Philippian jailer, "What must I do to be saved?" (Acts 16:30). If that is the plea of your own heart, the Spirit of God is *already* working within. God has established a time for you, and *now* is that time: "Behold, now is 'the acceptable time,' behold, now is 'the day of salvation'" (2 Cor. 6:2). "The Holy Spirit says, 'Today if you hear His voice, do not harden your hearts'" (Heb. 3:7–8).

Nicodemus was right in suggesting that the new birth is not something a sinner can accomplish for himself. It is a sovereign work of the Spirit of God, which cannot be controlled by human means.

The Spirit was working in Nicodemus's heart too. And Jesus told him what God required of him: "As Moses lifted up the serpent in the wilderness, even so must the Son of Man be lifted up; that whoever believes may in Him have eternal life" (Jn. 3:14–15). Our Lord was recalling an incident from the Old Testament, when the Israelites had sinned against God by grumbling about Moses, complaining that the journey through the wilderness was too difficult, and protesting that food and water were too scarce (Num. 21:5). God punished them by sending a plague of poisonous serpents among them. Many were bitten and dying, and Moses interceded with God on their behalf. The Lord instructed Moses, "Make a fiery serpent, and set it on a standard; and it shall come about, that everyone who is bitten, when he looks at it, he shall live" (Num. 21:8). Moses made a bronze serpent and put it on a pole as God had commanded. The sinning Israelites only had to look at the snake and they were instantly healed. Jesus would also be lifted up, He told Nicodemus, and whoever believed in Him would be saved.

Nicodemus could not have understood every aspect of what Jesus was telling him. Surely it did not occur to him that the way Jesus would be "lifted up" would be on a cross of crucifixion. But Nicodemus, as an Old Testament scholar, was entirely familiar with Moses' account of the bronze serpent. He knew this much: that the ones who had to look at the snake were the rebellious Israelites who had sinned, and that those who looked were healed solely by God's miraculous grace—not because of any medicine they took, not because of anything they did to earn God's favor, but simply because they had enough faith to look and trust God for the cure.

As a spiritual leader over all Israel, Nicodemus undoubtedly identified with Moses whenever he read the account of the bronze serpent. Jesus was suggesting that he should take his place with the sinning Israelites instead. In other words, he was confronting Nicodemus with his sinfulness. He was urging Nicodemus to repent. And He was calling Nicodemus to believe in Him as the Savior who would be lifted up so that whoever believes might be saved.

In other words, "Repent and believe in the gospel" (Mk. 1:15) was Jesus' appeal to Nicodemus. That is God's message to all sinners, and He graciously makes the invitation broad enough so that "*whoever* believes in Him should not perish, but have eternal life" (Jn. 3:16, emphasis added). As you read this, if you are unsure of your spiritual condition, or longing to be free from your sin, this is also the Lord's message to you: "There is no God else beside me; a just God and a Saviour; there is none beside me. *Look unto me, and be ye saved*, all the ends of the earth: for I am God, and there is none else" (Isa. 45:21–22, KJV, emphasis added). Or as contemporary translations render the verse, "Turn to Me, and be saved" (NASB).

Repent. The turning that passage calls for is *repentance* toward Christlikeness. It is not merely a positive "decision for Christ." We cannot simply add Christ to a sin-laden life, then go on loving sin, as if giving lip-service to Him somehow sanctifies all our wickedness. Repentance means turning from our love of sin, and turning to Jesus Christ for salvation: "Repent ye therefore, and be converted" (Acts 3:19).

Specifically, repentance means "turn[ing] away from all your transgressions" (Ezek. 18:30). It means confessing and forsaking your iniquities (Prov. 28:13). It means abhorring your sin, being full of indignation against it (2 Cor. 7:11).

Repentance certainly does not mean you must do works of penance or correct your behavior *before* you can turn to Christ. Turn to the Savior *now*, and in turning to Him, you will turn your heart from all that dishonors him (cf. 1 Thess. 1:9). *He* will begin a good work in you that He Himself will see through to completion (Phil. 1:6).

"Repent and turn to God," and you will discover that changed behavior is the inevitable fruit (Acts 26:20; Lk. 3:8; Matt. 7:20).

Turn to Him today, while it is still today (Heb. 3:13). "Seek the Lord while He may be found; call upon Him while He is near. Let the wicked forsake his way, and the unrighteous man his thoughts; and let him return to the Lord, and He will have compassion on him; and to our God, for He will abundantly pardon" (Isa. 55:7). Do not despise or take for granted the riches of His kindness, forbearance, and patience, for "the kindness of God leads you to repentance" (Rom. 2:4). God does not delight in the death of the wicked, "but rather that the wicked turn from his way and live" (Ezek. 33:11).

These truths apply to *you*. The call to repent is universal: "God is now declaring to men that all everywhere should repent" (Acts 17:30). "The Lord . . . is patient toward you, not wishing for any to perish but for all to come to repentance" (2 Pet. 3:9). "Therefore, repent and live" (Ezek. 18:32).

Repentance means you turn now and follow Jesus. Jesus issued this open invitation: "If anyone wishes to come after Me, let him . . . follow Me" (Matt. 16:24). "If anyone serves Me, let him follow Me" (Jn. 12:26).

But you cannot follow Him halfheartedly. The full invitation is this: "If anyone wishes to come after Me, let him *deny himself, and take up his cross daily*, and follow Me" (Lk. 9:23, emphasis added). "No one, after putting his hand to the plow and looking back, is fit for the kingdom of God" (v. 62). "He who loves father or mother more than Me is not worthy of Me; and he who loves son or daughter more than Me is not worthy of Me. And he who does not take his cross and follow after Me is not worthy of Me" (Matt. 10:37–38). "If anyone comes to Me, and does not hate his own father and mother and wife and children and brothers and sisters, yes, and even his own life, he cannot be My disciple. Whoever does not carry his own cross and come after Me cannot be My disciple" (Lk. 14:26–27).

Jesus cautions you to count the cost carefully (Lk. 14:28–33). "For whoever wishes to save his life shall lose it; but whoever loses his life for My sake and the gospel's shall save it. For what does it profit a man to gain the whole world, and forfeit his soul? For what shall a man give in exchange for his soul?" (Mk. 8:35–37).

Our Lord even pictured repentance as a kind of death: "Unless a grain of wheat falls into the earth and dies, it remains by itself alone; but if it dies, it bears much fruit" (Jn. 12:24).

Believe. Repentance and faith go hand in hand. If repentance stresses our turning *away from* sin and self, believing emphasizes what our hearts turn *toward*. "Believe in the Lord Jesus, and you shall be saved" (Acts 16:31). "If you confess with your mouth Jesus as Lord, and believe in your heart that God raised Him from the dead, you shall be saved" (Rom. 10:9). Repentance without faith would be no good, for righteousness comes not by sorrowing over sin. "Righteousness . . . comes from God on the basis of faith" (Phil. 3:9). Our penitence does not save us; only Christ can do that. Good resolutions cannot win God's favor; we must lay hold of Christ by faith. "There is salvation in no one else; for there is no other name under heaven that has been given among men, by which we must be saved" (Acts 4:12).

> *Repentance and faith go hand in hand. If repentance stresses our turning away from sin and self, believing emphasizes what our hearts turn toward.*

You must believe in the Christ of Scripture. He is both Savior and Lord (cf. Lk. 2:11). "I, even I, am the Lord; and there is no savior besides Me" (Isa. 43:11). You must welcome Him as your Lord, not as Savior only (Col. 2:6). You must receive Him on His own terms; you cannot have His pardon without also accepting His right to rule over you.

And you cannot lay hold of Christ while still clinging to your sin. He came to save His people from their sins (Matt. 1:21)—not to offer heaven to sinners still revelling in their wickedness. The salvation He offers is not merely an escape from the flames of hell, but it is first of all a glorious liberation from the dominion of sin.

Having seen the awful reality of sin, why would anyone want a salvation that stops short of delivering the sinner from sin's bondage? When you understand the exceeding sinfulness of sin, when you realize its power over you, and when you know the dreadful hazards it poses to your soul, you should be driven to Christ as your refuge.

What is truly wonderful is that He promises to receive those who come to Him (Jn. 6:37).

What is truly wonderful is that He promises to receive those who come to Him (Jn. 6:37). More than that, He bids them come: "Come to Me, all who are weary and heavy-laden, and I will give you rest. Take My yoke upon you, and learn from Me, for I am gentle and humble in heart; and you shall find rest for your souls. For My yoke is easy, and My load is light" (Matt. 11:28–30).

Recognition of sin is the necessary first step on the only path to Christ and the salvation He offers.

6

The Conquered Enemy Within

Let me put it very plainly in this way: there is no point in our saying that we believe that Christ has died for us, and that we believe our sins are forgiven, unless we can also say that for us old things are passed away and that all things are become new; that our outlook towards the world and its method of living is entirely changed. It is not that we are sinless, nor that we are perfect, but that we have finished with that way of life. We have seen it for what it is, and we are new creatures for whom everything has become new.

D. Martyn Lloyd-Jones[1]

Nobody's perfect. That truth, which ought to make us tremble before a God who is holy, holy, holy, is usually invoked instead to excuse sinful behavior, to make us feel better. How often do we hear people brush aside their own wrongdoing with the casual words, "Well, after all, nobody's perfect"? People claim they're not perfect to boost their self-esteem, but it is another evidence of a vanishing conscience. There is accuracy in the claim, but it should be a timid confession, not a flippant means of justifying sin.

Scripture recognizes that we are not perfect. Even the apostle Paul wrote, *"Not that I have already obtained it, or have already become perfect,* but I press on in order that I may lay hold of that for which also I was laid hold of by Christ Jesus. Brethren, *I do not regard myself as having laid hold of it yet*; but one thing I do: forgetting what lies behind and reaching forward to what lies ahead, I press on toward the goal for the prize of the upward call of God in Christ Jesus" (Phil. 3:12–14, emphasis added).

It is folly to think that being imperfect somehow provides us with a legitimate excuse to exempt us from God's perfect standard.

We all fall short of perfection—way short. Paul teaches us that our own imperfection should only spur us on toward the goal of complete Christlikeness. When we begin to use our human frailty as an excuse from guilt, we are walking on dangerous ground. We must continue to press on toward the goal: "Therefore you are to be perfect, as your heavenly Father is perfect" (Matt. 5:48). "You shall be holy, for I am holy" (1 Pet. 1:16). It is folly to think that being imperfect somehow provides us with a legitimate excuse to exempt us from God's perfect standard.

The Danger of Perfectionism

Ironic as it may seem, however, it is equally dangerous—or

surely even more so—to think spiritual perfection is something attainable by Christians in this lifetime. Church history is littered with examples of sects and factions who taught various versions of Christian perfectionism. Nearly all these groups have either made utter shipwreck of the faith or been forced to modify their perfectionism to accommodate human imperfection. Every perfectionist inevitably comes face-to-face with clear and abundant empirical evidence that the residue of sin remains in the flesh and troubles even the most spiritual Christians throughout their earthly lives. In order to hang onto perfectionist doctrine, they must redefine sin or diminish the standard of holiness. Too often they do this at the expense of their own consciences.

One perfectionist group, the Oneida Community, founded by John Humphrey Noyes, flourished in New York from 1849 to 1879. Based on a notion of perfectionism that had much in common with the teaching of Charles Finney (Noyes was a convert of Finney's), the Oneida Community was the best known of about fifty utopian communes that operated in New York state in the second half of the nineteenth century. Oneida members (about three hundred of them) lived in a commune whose centerpiece was a huge stone mansion. They started a tableware company that still thrives today. They worked together, worshiped together, and fashioned a communal lifestyle that was widely hailed in its day as a model of Christian brotherhood and holiness.

What the outside world did not fully understand until after the commune was dissolved in 1879 is that the Oneida Community also practiced communal marriage. Every woman was considered married to every man, and all were at liberty to have sex with anyone else in the community they chose. Worse, children were expected to be sexually active as soon as they were old enough. Noyes himself usually initiated the young girls as soon as they reached puberty.[2]

Noyes, like all too many perfectionists, simply adapted moral standards to suit his own preferences. Rather than acknowledge that sexual desire outside of marriage is sin and accept the corollary that his own lust proved he was not yet perfect, he devised a doctrine that permitted him and the others at Oneida to indulge their fleshly passions and still claim they had attained sinlessness.

The Oneida Community was certainly one of the more heinous examples of how perfectionism is abused. But in all types of perfectionism the same tendency exists. Ultimately all perfectionists are forced to devise down-scaled definitions of sin, holiness, and perfection that can accommodate the *im*perfections of human carnality.

Most who hold this view believe "entire sanctification" is obtained all at once through a second work of grace.

The Holiness movement is a more typical variety of perfectionism than the fanatical extremes of Oneida. So-called "Holiness doctrine" is rooted in Wesleyan theology and may be found in traditional Methodism (but not necessarily in the liberal branch of the denomination), the Salvation Army, the Church of the Nazarene, and many charismatic denominations. Most who hold this view believe "entire sanctification" is obtained all at once through a second work of grace. The believer is thereby elevated to a position of "perfect" holiness in which he or she no longer sins—at least not consciously or intentionally. Ordinary failings are called "mistakes," or "temptations," not sins. Only deliberate, premeditated, and grotesque acts are labeled sin. Sin is thus externalized. Evils clearly named as *sin* in Scripture are reduced to misdemeanors. And conscience must be dampened in order to cope with the doctrine.

H. A. Ironside, former pastor of Moody Church, Chicago, wrote a book about his struggle with perfectionist doctrine as a young Salvation Army officer. Ironside ultimately left the organization and abandoned his belief in perfectionism. He described perfectionism as a conscience-shattering doctrine:

> The teaching of holiness in the flesh [perfectionism] tends to harden the conscience and to cause the one who professes it to lower the standard to his own poor experience. Any who move much among those in this profession will soon begin to realize how greatly prevalent are the conditions I have described. Holiness professors are frequently cutting, censorious, uncharitable

and harsh in their judgment of others. Exaggerations, amounting to downright dishonesty, are unconsciously encouraged by and often indulged in in their "testimony" meetings.

. . . .

Holiness advocates have all the little unpleasant ways that are so trying in many of us: they are no more free from penuriousness, tattling, evil-speaking, selfishness, and kindred weaknesses, than their neighbors.

And as to downright wickedness and uncleanness, I regret to have to record that sins of a positively immoral character are, I fear, far more frequently met with in holiness churches . . . than the outsider would think possible. I know whereof I speak; and only a desire to save others from the bitter disappointments I had to meet leads me to write as I do.[3]

All perfectionism is essentially a disastrous misunderstanding of how God works in *sanctification*. Sanctification is a process by which God—working in believers through the Holy Spirit—gradually moves them toward Christlikeness (2 Cor. 3:18). The process of sanctification hones the believer's conscience and keeps it from vanishing. That the transformation is gradual, not instantaneous—and never complete in this lifetime—is confirmed by many verses of Scripture.

As we noted at the outset of this chapter, for example, the apostle Paul wrote near the end of his ministry that he was not yet perfect (Phil. 3:12). He told the Romans, "Be [constantly being] transformed by the renewing of your mind" (Rom. 12:2). And to the Galatians he wrote that he labored with them "until Christ is formed in you" (Gal. 4:19). Sanctification will not end "until we all attain to the unity of the faith, and of the knowledge of the Son of God, to a mature man, to the measure of the stature which belongs to the fulness of Christ" (Eph. 4:13). He urged the Ephesians to stop being children, susceptible to error and trends. How were they to do that? By seeking a sudden experience? No, he wrote, "*grow up* in all aspects into Him, who is the head, even Christ" (4:14–15, emphasis added).

Likewise Peter instructed believers to "grow in the grace and knowledge of our Lord and Savior Jesus Christ" (2 Pet. 3:18). He wrote, "like newborn babes, long for the pure milk of the word, that by it you may grow in respect to salvation" (1 Pet. 2:2).

> *All perfectionism is essentially a
> disastrous misunderstanding of
> how God works in sanctification.
> Sanctification is a process by which
> God—working in believers through the
> Holy Spirit—gradually moves them
> toward Christlikeness (2 Cor. 3:18).*

The Bible clearly teaches that Christians can never attain sinless perfection in this life. "Who can say, 'I have cleansed my heart, I am pure from my sin'?" (Prov. 20:9). "For we all stumble in many ways. If anyone does not stumble in what he says, he is a perfect man, able to bridle the whole body as well" (Jas. 3:2). "For the flesh sets its desire against the Spirit, and the Spirit against the flesh; for these are in opposition to one another, so that you may not do the things that you please" (Gal. 5:17). "If we say that we have no sin, we are deceiving ourselves, and the truth is not in us" (1 Jn. 1:8).

Sanctification is therefore never complete in this lifetime. In heaven alone are the spirits of righteous people made perfect (Heb. 12:23). And at the return of Christ, "when He appears, we shall be like Him, because we shall see Him just as He is" (1 Jn. 3:2). "We ourselves groan within ourselves, waiting eagerly for our adoption as sons, the redemption of our body" (Rom. 8:23). Those verses describe *glorification*, the immediate and instantaneous completion of our sanctification.

In his masterful work against perfectionism, B. B. Warfield characterized perfectionists as "impatient souls" who "tolerate more readily the idea of an imperfect perfection than the admission of lagging perfecting. They must at all costs have all that is coming to them at once."[4] In other words, perfectionists reject the idea that sanctification is a lifelong process. They insist it is something God does all at once. And so they are forced by sheer reality to conclude that God's work in sanctifying must stop short of true conformity to the perfect likeness of Christ. They give up the pursuit of authentic biblical sanctification in exchange for a quick and dirty substitute. And in order to do so, they must inevitably tone down their consciences.

Perfectionism's Key Error

Warfield explains the common theological roots of all modern perfectionism:

> It was John Wesley who infected the modern Protestant world with this notion of "entire instantaneous sanctification." In saying this we are not bringing a railing accusation against him. There was no element of his teaching which afforded him himself greater satisfaction. There is no element of it which is more lauded by his followers, or upon their own possession of which they more felicitate themselves. . . . As wave after wave of the "holiness movement" has broken over us during the past century, each has brought, no doubt, something distinctive of itself. But a common fundamental character has informed them all, and this common fundamental character has been communicated to them by the Wesleyan doctrine. The essential elements of that doctrine repeat themselves in all these movements, and form their characteristic features. *In all of them alike justification and sanctification are divided from one another as two separate gifts of God.* In all of them alike sanctification is represented as obtained, just like justification, by an act of simple faith, but not by the same act of faith by which justification is obtained, but by a new and separate act of faith, exercised for this specific purpose. In all of them alike the sanctification which comes on this [second] act of faith, comes immediately on believing, and all at once, and in all of them alike this sanctification, thus received, is complete sanctification. In all of them alike, however, it is added, that this complete sanctification does not bring freedom from all sin; but only, say, freedom from sinning; or only freedom from conscious sinning; or from the commission of "known sins." And in all of them alike this sanctification is not a stable condition into which we enter once for all by faith, but a momentary attainment, which must be maintained moment by moment, and which may readily be lost and often is lost, but may also be repeatedly instantaneously recovered.[5]

The error Warfield describes—this tendency to make a radical separation between sanctification and justification—is the key mistake of perfectionism. Virtually all perfectionists treat sanctification as if it were a second conversion experience. Under this scheme, holiness must be obtained by a separate act of faith that occurs sometime after initial salvation—a "second blessing," as it is often called.

Biblically, as we shall see, sanctification begins immediately at justification and continues its work—despite our frequent failings—all the way to the end of life. In my book, *Faith Works*, I examined this very issue from a totally different perspective.[6] In that book I was answering the error of those who say sanctification is optional. Here, however, my purpose is to examine *how* the process of sanctification works in the lives of believers as they wage their lifelong battle against the sin in their own flesh. Interestingly, the issues are virtually identical. That is because the key to sound doctrine in the matter of sanctification is a correct understanding of the close relationship between sanctification and justification.

Contrary to the perfectionists, contrary to the so-called "deeper-life" teachers, and contrary to the prevailing notion of what it means to be Spirit-filled, sanctification is not something that begins with a crisis experience sometime after conversion. Sanctification begins at the very moment of conversion and continues throughout the Christian's earthly life. As Dr. Warfield was suggesting in the above quotation, sanctification is obtained by the very same act of faith with which we lay hold of justification. Jesus Christ becomes to all who believe, "wisdom from God, and *righteousness and sanctification, and redemption*" (1 Cor. 1:30, emphasis added). If sanctification did not occur at the moment of salvation, it could not be said of all believers, "you were washed . . . you were sanctified . . . you were justified" (1 Cor. 6:11).

---

*Biblically, as we shall see, sanctification
begins immediately
at justification and continues its work
—despite our frequent failings—
all the way to the end of life.*

This is not doctrine for advanced Christians only. Nothing in the Christian life is more practical than a right understanding of how the Holy Spirit works to conform us to Christ's image. Conversely, it is hard to imagine anything that undermines spiritually healthy Christian living more disastrously than a *mis*understanding of sanctification.

How Does Sanctification Work?

The word *sanctify* in Scripture comes from Hebrew and Greek words that mean "set apart." To be sanctified is to be set apart from sin. At conversion, all believers are disengaged from sin's bondage, released from sin's captivity—set apart unto God, or sanctified. Yet the process of separation from sin is only begun at that moment. As we grow in Christ, we become more separated from sin and more consecrated to God. Thus the sanctification that occurs at conversion only initiates a lifelong process whereby we are set apart more and more from sin and brought more and more into conformity with Christ—separated from sin, and separated unto God.

Maturing Christians never become self-justifying, smug, or satisfied with their progress. They do not pursue self-esteem; they seek instead to deal with their sin. And the more we become like Christ, the more sensitive we are to the remaining corruptions of the flesh. As we mature in godliness our sins become more painful and more obvious to ourselves. The more we put away sin, the more we notice sinful tendencies that still need to be put away. This is the paradox of sanctification: the holier we become, the more frustrated we are by the stubborn remnants of our sin. The apostle Paul vividly described his own anguish over this reality in Romans 7:21–24:

> I find then the principle that evil is present in me, the one who wishes to do good. For I joyfully concur with the law of God in the inner man, but I see a different law in the members of my body, waging war against the law of my mind, and making me a prisoner of the law of sin which is in my members. Wretched man that I am! Who will set me free from the body of this death?

Romans 7 poses a number of difficult challenges for Bible interpreters, but surely the most difficult question of all is how Paul could say those things *after* he wrote in chapter 6, "Our old self was crucified with Him, that our body of sin might be done away with, that we should no longer be slaves to sin; for he who has died is freed from sin" (Rom. 6:6–7).

These are vital truths for the Christian to understand. They hold the formula for a healthy spiritual walk, and they give much practical insight into how we should battle sin in our own lives. In order to understand them better, we must go back into Romans 6. According to Dr. Warfield, Romans 6 "was written for no other purpose than to assert and demonstrate that justification and sanctification are indissolubly bound together."[7] Or, in Paul's own imagery, dying with Christ (justification) and living with Christ (sanctification) are both necessary results of true faith. Those who think grace makes holiness optional are tragically deceived. Those who think they have experienced all the sanctification they need are equally deluded. Those who think self-esteem is more important than holiness are blind to the truth. If we would know God's principles for dealing with sin, we must understand that it is a life-and-death struggle to the end. To be content with good feelings about oneself is to be content with sin.

Shall We Continue in Sin?

God's grace does not mean holiness is optional. There have always been people who abuse God's grace by assuming it grants leeway for sin. Paraphrasing that philosophy, Paul writes, "What shall we say then? Are we to continue in sin that grace might increase?" (6:1). If grace abounds most where sin is worst (Rom. 5:20–21), then doesn't our sin only magnify the grace of God? Should we continue in sin so that God's grace can be magnified?

---

*God's grace does not mean
holiness is optional.*

"May it never be!" Paul answers in a phrase so emphatic that the King James Version renders it "God forbid!" The notion that anyone would use such an argument to condone sin was clearly offensive to Paul. "How shall we who died to sin still live in it?" (Rom. 6:3).

Paul wrote elsewhere, "I have been crucified with Christ; and it is no longer I who live, but Christ lives in me" (Gal. 2:20).

But in what sense are we dead to sin? All honest Christians will testify that we are still tempted, we still fall, we are still guilty of sin all the time. What does Paul mean by saying believers have "died to sin"?

He is talking about our union with Christ. All believers are joined to Christ by faith:

> Do you not know that all of us who have been baptized into Christ Jesus have been baptized into His death? Therefore we have been buried with Him through baptism into death, in order that as Christ was raised from the dead through the glory of the Father, so we too might walk in newness of life. For if we have become united with Him in the likeness of His death, certainly we shall be also in the likeness of His resurrection (Rom. 6:3–5).

The phrase "baptized into Christ Jesus . . . baptized into His death" has nothing to do with water baptism. Paul is using the expression *baptizō* in the same way he employed it in 1 Corinthians 10:2, where he spoke of the Israelites as having been "baptized into Moses." *Baptized into* in that sense means "identified with," "linked to." In Galatians 3:27, Paul says, "All of you who were baptized into Christ have clothed yourselves with Christ" (Gal. 3:27). Again, he is speaking of *union with Christ*: "The one who joins himself to the Lord is one spirit with Him" (1 Cor. 6:17).

Our union with Christ is the premise on which justification, sanctification, and every other aspect of God's saving work hinge. If we would understand our salvation, we must first grasp what it means to be united with Christ. About this doctrine, Martyn Lloyd-Jones wrote,

> We are actually in union with Christ and to him. You cannot have read the New Testament even cursorily without noticing this constantly repeated phrase—"in Christ"—"in Christ Jesus." The apostles go on repeating it and it is one of the most significant and glorious statements in the entire realm and range of truth. It means that we are joined to the Lord Jesus Christ; we have become a part of him. We are in him. We belong to him. We are members of his body.

And the teaching is that God regards us as such; and this, of course, means that now, *in this relationship, we are sharers in, and partakers of, everything that is true of the Lord Jesus Christ himself.*[8]

"As in Adam all die, so also in Christ all shall be made alive" (1 Cor. 15:22). "In Adam" describes the state of the unregenerate person still in bondage to sin, dying, unable to please God in any way. But "in Christ" describes precisely the opposite state, the position of every true believer in Christ. We are free from sin's tyranny, able to love and obey God from the heart, partakers in all the blessedness of Christ Himself, the objects of God's loving favor, destined for a glorious eternity. "There is therefore now no condemnation for those who are in Christ Jesus" (Rom. 8:1).

Our union with Christ results in some very dramatic changes. First of all, we are justified. Justification takes place in the court of God. It is a divine "not guilty" verdict. The term *justification* does not describe the actual change in the sinner's character; it describes the change in his or her standing before God.

Our union with Christ is the premise on which justification, sanctification, and every other aspect of God's saving work hinge.

But because we are united with Christ, changes in our very nature occur as well. *Regeneration, conversion,* and *sanctification* are the words that describe that change. We are born again—*regenerated*—given a new heart, a new spirit, and a new love for God (Ezek. 36:26; 1 Jn. 4:19–20). We become partakers of the divine nature (2 Pet. 1:3–4). We are raised to walk in newness of life (Rom. 6:4). And the old sinful self is put to death: "Knowing this, that our old self was crucified with Him, that our body of sin might be done away with, that we should no longer be slaves to sin; for he who has died is freed from sin" (Rom. 6:6–7).

Freed from Sin—Or Are We?

Here is precisely where the challenge in understanding Romans 6 and 7 comes in. What is this "old self" that is said to be crucified? If the old self is done away, why do we still struggle so much with sin? And if "He who has died [in Christ] is freed from sin" (Rom. 6:7), why does Paul later write, "Wretched man that I am! Who will set me free from the body of this death?" (Rom. 7:24).

It helps to understand the terms Paul is using here. *"The old self"* refers to the unregenerate nature, who we were when we were "in Adam." It is not the dark side of a Jekyll-Hyde disposition. It is not half of a dual temperament unique to Christians. It is not an "old nature" that battles with our new nature for control of our wills. It is simply who we used to be before we were born again. The old self is no more. It has been crucified, slain, put off, laid aside. All of those expressions are used in Scripture.

For example, Paul told the Ephesians: "In reference to your former manner of life . . . lay aside the old self, which is being corrupted in accordance with the lusts of deceit, and . . . be renewed in the spirit of your mind (Eph. 4:22–23, emphasis added). The Greek verb tenses there are infinitives, not imperatives. They could be translated "you have laid aside" and "you are renewed"—not as commands, but as statements of fact. That seems to make better sense of what Paul is saying. Certainly it is the only way we can possibly read the parallel passage, Colossians 3:9–10: "Do not lie to one another, since *you laid aside the old self* with its evil practices, and *have put on the new self* who *is being renewed* to a true knowledge according to the image of the One who created him," (emphasis added). Taking all these verses together, it becomes very clear that the old self—the old unregenerate "I"—is "crucified with Christ; and it is no longer I who live, but Christ lives in me" (Gal. 2:20).

The flesh (Rom. 6:19; 7:18) is like the corpse of the old self. Though dead, it continues to influence and infect all it touches with decay, filthiness, rottenness, the stench of death, and a putrefying contamination.

When I was a small boy living in Philadelphia, a family friend died. As the custom was, his body remained in the living room of his house for several days. This was to be a tribute to him and allow the family and friends to ease the separation. I thought it was bizarre—a dead man in the living room of a small house! His presence influenced everything. He was dead, but he was still there exercising influence over all the activities.

When Paul speaks of "the flesh," he is referring to the remains of our sinfulness: our mortal weakness, our selfishness, and our tendency to sin and failure. These will not be eradicated until we are finally glorified.

But we are not entirely at sin's mercy, as was the case under our former bondage. "Walk by the Spirit, and you will not carry out the desire of the flesh. For the flesh sets its desire against the Spirit, and the Spirit against the flesh; for these are in opposition to one another, so that you may not do the things that you please" (Gal. 5:16–17).

"Flesh" in such contexts does not refer to the physical body. Nor does it describe a specific part of our being. Paul is not setting up a dualism between the material and the immaterial part of humanity, or between the body and the soul. "Spirit" in those verses refers to the Holy Spirit. "Flesh" refers to the sinfulness that remains in us while we are on this earth. It is a corruption that permeates and influences every aspect of our being—body, mind, emotions, and will. It is what makes us susceptible to sin even after we are made partakers in the divine nature (cf. 2 Pet. 1:4). Though sin does not *reign* in us, it nevertheless *remains* in us. It is *dethroned*, but not *destroyed*.

"The flesh," then, is not the body, or the soul, or any other *part* of our beings. It is a *principle* that works in us. It is the source and stimulus of our sin. Though deprived of its dominion, it has not been divested of its potency, passions, or persuasive ability. The flesh wages battle against our godly desires with the fervor of a deposed monarch seeking to regain his throne.

Unbelievers are said to be "in the flesh" (cf. Rom. 8:8–9). Christians are no longer *in* the flesh. We are in the Spirit. But we are still "of flesh" (1 Cor. 3:1)—that is, we are still fallen humans. Paul even says, "I am of flesh, sold into bondage to sin" (Rom. 7:14).

That verse underscores the dilemma between Romans 6 and 7. As we have noted, Paul has already stated explicitly that believers are "freed from sin" (6:7). Now he seems to be stating the opposite. This has made many commentators assume that Romans 7 describes Paul's life before his salvation. But as usual, the context makes very clear his meaning. Romans 7:23 shows what kind of "bondage" he has in mind in this chapter: "I see a different law in the members of my body, waging war against the law of my mind, and making me a prisoner of the law of sin which is in my members." This speaks not of the fatal soul-bondage to sin Paul referred to in 6:7. Here he is speaking of a persistent spiritual weakness in his "members"—his body, mouth, mind, emotions, imagination, and so on. This "bondage" is a persistent snare that keeps tripping him up and pulling him back into the sin he hates. This is the experience of all Christians.

In what sense, then, are believers "freed from sin" (Rom. 6:7)? What does Paul mean when he says our old self is crucified so that "our body of sin might be done away with" (v. 6)? "Done away with" almost sounds as if he were saying sin is eradicated, wiped out, "destroyed" (KJV), annihilated. But the Greek word (*katargeō*) literally means "to render inoperative," "nullify" (cf. Rom. 3:3, 31; 4:14). The word for "freed" in 6:7 is *dikaioō*, the word usually translated "justified." In other words, believers are delivered from the dreadful penalty and condemnation of sin. Because they are justified—declared not guilty and covered with the perfect righteousness of Christ—sin and death have no claim over them.

Moreover, because they have been justified from sin's penalty, they are also sanctified—liberated from sin's absolute tyranny. The old self is crucified and the body of sin nullified. That speaks of the change of character that is wrought in regeneration. Believers are emancipated from the total corruption of their natures that rendered them unable to do anything *but* sin. They are free to love and obey God.

Believers are emancipated from the total corruption of their natures that rendered them unable to do anything but sin. They are free to love and obey God.

But they are *not* yet totally free from sin's reach. They are still prone to sin's seductive power. They are unable to break free of sin's presence. They are still vulnerable to sin's enchantment. They still carry in their corrupt flesh a tendency to sin.

It Is No Longer I Who Sin

One comment of Paul's is frequently misunderstood. In Romans 7 he writes,

> For that which I am doing, I do not understand; for I am not practicing what I would like to do, but I am doing the very thing I hate. But if I do the very thing I do not wish to do, I agree with the Law, confessing that it is good. So now, *no longer am I the one doing it, but sin which indwells me.* For I know that nothing good dwells in me, that is, in my flesh; for the wishing is present in me, but the doing of the good is not. For the good that I wish, I do not do; but I practice the very evil that I do not wish. But if I am doing the very thing I do not wish, *I am no longer the one doing it, but sin which dwells in me* (vv. 15–20, emphasis added).

It is important to understand that Paul was not disclaiming responsibility for his sin. He was not using a dualistic argument—ascribing all his sin to an "old nature" or a wicked alter ego. Above all, he was not trying to evade the blame for his own sin.

He was simply saying that sin is contrary to the impulses of his new disposition as a believer. Before salvation, we are all defined by our sinfulness. We are enemies of God, in bondage to sin, in love with sin, incapable of anything *but* sin, sinful to the very core of our beings. But when we become believers that old self dies. We are born again with a new nature that loves God and desires to do righteousness. We "agree with the Law." "The wishing [to obey] is present" in us. Sin no longer defines our character; it is "the very thing [we] hate." Our new "I" (cf. Gal. 2:20) craves righteousness and abhors sin.

When we sin, therefore, it is a contradiction of everything we stand for as believers. It is no longer "I" that sins—meaning sin is no longer an expression of our true character.

Why do we sin? Because the corrupt principle of the flesh remains in us. And that is what drags us into disobedience. We are certainly responsible for our sins. But when we sin, it is no longer because of *what we are*. It is because of the stubborn flesh-principle that remains in us and exerts its continual influence until we are transformed to heavenly glory. As Paul says, "I find then the principle that evil is present in me, the one who wishes to do good" (Rom. 7:21).

Both Scripture and experience prove that all Christians struggle with sinful weaknesses and carnal tendencies as long as they live. Sin's absolute tyranny has been broken; we are loosed from its clutches. But we still succumb to sin's temptations. We carry our own flesh—the sin-principle that remains in us ("the body of this death," Rom. 7:24)—like a ball and chain. We are wholly new creations, redeemed and empowered by the Holy Spirit, filled with all the fullness of God—yet incarcerated in sinful flesh. We "groan within ourselves, waiting eagerly for our adoption as sons, the redemption of our body" (Rom. 8:23).

The sin within ourselves, therefore, although a "conquered enemy," still must be vigorously opposed throughout our lives. We are freed from sin, but we must remain on guard. Perfectionism, moreover, only undoes the process of sanctification. We are not perfect. We are human. We still groan.

While we groan and wait for that glorious day, we must continue to wage battle against the defeated enemy within. Scripture gives clear instructions about how we are to carry on our campaign against sin in the flesh. In Part III, we turn to the practical means that are available to us to gain victory over sin in our daily walk.

Part III

Handling Sin

Part III provides many practical solutions to gaining victory over sin in our daily walk.

Chapter 7, "Hacking Agag to Pieces," describes the necessity and the "how-to" of continuously mortifying the sin in our lives, lest it keep sprouting up again to wound us.

Chapter 8, "Handling Temptation," examines society's glorification of the seven deadly sins. It suggests ways of overcoming temptation by looking at its means, nature, and extent. It shows how God sends not temptation but tests, which we can learn from and which are not beyond our endurance.

Chapter 9, "Keeping a Pure Mind," examines the dangers of a sinful thought life and gives suggestions for guarding against sins of thought by watching over our hearts and knowing how the mind sins.

Chapter 10, "Holding to the Mystery of Faith with a Clear Conscience," emphasizes how modern evangelicalism has forgotten the exceeding sinfulness of sin and instead preoccupied believers with the pursuit of "feeling good." It examines the Bible's stance on the intrinsic worth of individuals and modern psychology's hostility to the doctrine of sin. It concludes with showing specific and practical principles to assist our consciences to detect and cope with the presence of sin in our lives.

7
Hacking Agag to Pieces

Mortification abates [sin's] force, but doth not change its nature. Grace changeth the nature of man, but nothing can change the nature of sin. . . . Destroyed it may be, it shall be, but cured it cannot be. . . . If it be not overcome and destroyed, it will overcome and destroy the soul.

And herein lies no small part of its power. . . . It is never quiet, [whether it is] conquering [or] conquered.

. . . .

Do you mortify; do you make it your daily work; be always at it whilst you live; cease not a day from this work; be killing sin or it will be killing you.

John Owen[1]

If sin is a defeated enemy, how can it cause us so much trouble? If sin's dominion has been broken, why does sin so often seem to dominate us? Why have the forces of secular humanism, the new hedonism, the New Age, self-esteem teaching, and bad theology all made such an impact among *believers*? Why is the conscience seemingly vanishing even in the evangelical world?

Every honest Christian will testify that the tendency to sin is not erased by becoming a believer. We still derive pleasure from sin. We still struggle with sinful habits. Some of those habits are so deeply ingrained that we still battle them after years of spiritual warfare against them. We fall into appalling, shameful sins. The truth is, we sin daily. Our thoughts are not what they ought to be. Our time is often wasted on frivolous and worldly pursuits. From time to time our hearts grow cold to the things of God. Why does all this happen if sin's dominion is broken?

We fall into appalling, shameful sins.
The truth is, we sin daily.

This section of our book examines the biblical antidote to the influence of sin in the believer's life. Here we see that Scripture urges us to avoid any lackadasical approach to dealing with our sin. We must put to death sin and its influence throughout our lifetime. It is here that our study becomes most practical.

God's Anger Against Amalek

An Old Testament illustration may help to shed light on our relationship to sin. In 1 Samuel 15, we read that Samuel anointed Saul and solemnly gave him these instructions from the Lord: "Now go and strike Amalek and utterly destroy all that he has, and do not spare him; but put to death both man and woman, child and infant, ox and sheep, camel and donkey" (v. 3).

God's command was clear. Saul was to deal ruthlessly with the Amalekites, killing even their infant children and animals. Their whole tribe was to be utterly and mercilessly leveled—no hostages taken.

What would make a God of infinite love mete out such a severe judgment? The Amalekites were an ancient nomadic race, descendants of Esau (Gen. 36:12). They inhabited the southern part of Canaan and were perennial enemies of the Israelites. They were the same tribe that viciously attacked Israel at Rephidim shortly after the Exodus, in the famous battle when Aaron and Hur had to support Moses' arms (Exod. 17:8–13). They ambushed Israel from behind, massacring the stragglers who were most weary (Deut. 25:18). It was a cowardly attack by the most powerful and savage tribe in the whole region. God supernaturally delivered Israel that day, and the Amalekites fled into hiding. At the conclusion of that skirmish, God swore to Moses, "I will utterly blot out the memory of Amalek from under heaven" (v. 14). He actually made it a point of the Mosaic law that Israel was to destroy Amalek:

> Remember what Amalek did to you along the way when you came out from Egypt, how he met you along the way and attacked among you all the stragglers at your rear when you were faint and weary; and he did not fear God. Therefore it shall come about when the Lord your God has given you rest from all your surrounding enemies, in the land which the Lord your God gives you as an inheritance to possess, you shall blot out the memory of Amalek from under heaven; *you must not forget"* (Deut. 25:17–19, emphasis added).

The Amalekites were fearful warriors. Their intimidating presence was one of the reasons the Israelites disobeyed God and balked at entering the Promised Land at Kadesh-barnea (Num. 13:29).

God's anger burned against the Amalekites for their wickedness. He constrained even the corrupt prophet Balaam to prophecy their doom: "Amalek was the first of the nations, but his end shall be destruction" (Num. 24:20). The Amalekites used to harass Israel by coming into the land after crops had been sown and moving through the farmland with their tents and livestock, razing everything in their path (Judg. 6:3–5). They hated God, detested Israel, and seemed to delight in wicked and destructive acts.

God's instructions to Saul, therefore, fulfilled the vow He swore to Moses. Saul was to wipe out the tribe forever. He and his armies were the instrument through which a righteous God would carry out His holy judgment on a sinister people.

The Folly of Partial Obedience

But Saul's obedience was only partial. He won a crushing defeat against the Amalekites, routing them "from Havilah as you go to Shur, which is east of Egypt" (1 Sam. 15:7). As commanded, he killed all the people, but "he captured Agag the king of the Amalekites alive" (v. 8). "Saul and the people spared Agag and the best of the sheep, the oxen, the fatlings, the lambs, and all that was good, and were not willing to destroy them utterly; but everything despised and worthless, that they utterly destroyed" (v. 9). In other words, motivated by covetousness, they kept all the best possessions of the Amalekites, collecting the spoils of victory, willfully disobeying the Lord's instructions.

Why did Saul spare Agag? Perhaps he wanted to use the humiliated king of the Amalekites as a trophy to display his own power. Saul seemed motivated only by pride at this point; he even set up a monument to himself at Carmel (v. 12). Whatever his reasons, he disobeyed the clear command of God and allowed Agag to live.

The sin was so serious that God immediately deposed Saul and his descendants forever from the throne of Israel. Samuel told him, "Because you have rejected the word of the Lord, He has also rejected you from being king" (v. 23).

Then Samuel said, "Bring me Agag, the king of the Amalekites" (v. 32).

Agag, evidently thinking that his life had been spared and feeling pretty confident, "came to him cheerfully." "Surely the bitterness of death is past," he said.

But Samuel was not amused. He told Agag, "As your sword has made women childless, so shall your mother be childless among women." Scripture simply says, "And Samuel hewed Agag to pieces before the Lord at Gilgal" (v. 33).

Our minds instinctively recoil from what seems a merciless act. But it was *God* who commanded that this be done. This was an act of divine judgment to show the holy wrath of an indignant God against wanton sin. Unlike his countrymen and their king, Samuel was determined to carry out the Lord's command entirely. As it was, the battle that was supposed to exterminate the Amalekites forever ended before the goal was accomplished. Scripture records that only a few years later, the reinvigorated tribe raided the southern territory and took all the women and children captive—including David's family (1 Sam. 30:1–5).

When David found the marauding Amalekites, "Behold, they were spread over all the land, eating and drinking and dancing because of all the great spoil that they had taken from the land of the Philistines and from the land of Judah" (v. 16). He slaughtered them from twilight until the next evening, killing all but four hundred who escaped on camels (v. 17).

The Amalekites make an apt illustration of the sin that remains in the believer's life. That sin—already utterly defeated—must be dealt with ruthlessly and hacked to pieces, or it will revive and continue to plunder and pillage our hearts and sap our spiritual strength. We cannot be merciful with Agag, or he will turn and try to devour us. In fact, the remaining sin in us often becomes more fiercely determined after it has been overthrown by the gospel.

That sin—already utterly defeated—
must be dealt with ruthlessly and
hacked to pieces, or it will revive and
continue to plunder and pillage our
hearts and sap our spiritual strength.

Scripture commands us to deal with our sin by putting it to death: "Mortify therefore your members which are upon the earth; fornication, uncleanness, inordinate affection, evil concupiscence, and covetousness, which is idolatry: for which things' sake the wrath of God cometh on the children of disobedience" (Col. 3:5-6, KJV). We cannot obey partially or halfheartedly as we seek to eliminate sin from our lives. We cannot stop while the task remains incomplete. Sins, like Amalekites, have a way of escaping the slaughter, breeding, reviving, regrouping, and launching new and unexpected assaults on our most vulnerable areas.

Life in the Spirit

In Romans 8:13 Paul also wrote of "putting to death the deeds of the body." After declaring victory over sin in Romans 6, then describing the ongoing struggle with sin in chapter 7, he describes the triumphant experience of life in the Spirit throughout chapter 8. In the midst of that chapter, the apostle declares that the distinctive behavior of those who are led by the Spirit is that they continually put their evil deeds to death.

It is significant that the Holy Spirit is mentioned only once in the introduction to the epistle (1:4, "the spirit of holiness"), then not mentioned again until Romans 8:1. In Romans 8 alone there are at least twenty references to the Holy Spirit.

Romans 8 portrays the Holy Spirit as the divine agent who frees us from sin and death (vv. 2–3), enables us to live righteously (4–13), assures and comforts us in our affliction (14–19), preserves and sustains us in Christ (20–28), and guarantees our final victory in eternal glory (29–39). Right in the context of this profound teaching about the Holy Spirit's role in the Christian's life, Paul has some important things to say about mortifying sin. He begins by contrasting life in the Spirit with life in the flesh and under the law. It is important to understand these truths in their proper context:

> What the Law could not do, weak as it was through the flesh, God did: sending His own Son in the likeness of sinful flesh and as an offering for sin, He condemned sin in the flesh, in order that the requirement of the Law might be fulfilled in us, who do not walk according to the flesh, but according to the Spirit. Those who are according to the flesh set their minds on the things of the flesh, but those who are according to the Spirit, the things of the Spirit. For the mind set on the flesh is death, but the mind set on the Spirit is life and peace, because the mind set on the flesh is hostile toward God; for it does not subject itself to the law of God, for it is not even able to do so; and those who are in the flesh cannot please God. *However, you are not in the flesh but in the Spirit, if indeed the Spirit of God dwells in you.* But if anyone does not have the Spirit of Christ, he does not belong to Him. And if Christ is in you, though the body is dead because of sin, yet the spirit is

alive because of righteousness. But if the Spirit of Him who raised Jesus from the dead dwells in you, He who raised Christ Jesus from the dead will also give life to your mortal bodies through His Spirit who indwells you (vv. 3–11, emphasis added).

In other words, life in the Spirit is markedly different from the life of the unbeliever. *All* true Christians are "in the Spirit." They "do not walk according to the flesh, but according to the Spirit." Those who walk according to the flesh are unbelievers, and Paul is quite definite in making that clear: "If anyone does not have the Spirit of Christ, he does not belong to Him" (v. 9). Later he adds, "For all who are being led by the Spirit of God, these are sons of God" (v. 14).

The Holy Spirit changes our basic disposition when we are born again. He brings us into accord with Himself.

That means there are only two kinds of people in the world— those who are in accord with the flesh, and those who are in accord with the Spirit. Of course, there are in-the-Spirit people at many different levels of spiritual maturity. In-the-flesh people also come in varying degrees of wickedness. But everyone is either "in the flesh" (v. 8) or "in the Spirit" (v. 9). There is no category called "in between."

What Paul is suggesting is that the Holy Spirit changes our basic disposition when we are born again. He brings us into accord with Himself. He actually indwells us (vv. 9, 11). We become partakers of the divine nature (2 Pet. 1:4). Our orientation to God changes. Where there was enmity, there is now love (cf. Rom. 8:28). In the flesh we could not please God (v. 8) but now the righteous requirement of the law is fulfilled in us (v. 4). Central to all of this is the reality that our whole mind-set is new. Whereas the mind set on the flesh meant death, the mind set on the things of the Spirit results in life and peace (v. 6).

If your mind-set—the fundamental orientation of your understanding, its bent, its dispositions, its thought patterns—did not change when you made a profession of faith in Christ, something is seriously wrong. That is not to suggest that Christians cannot fall into old patterns and habits. But it *does* mean that our thoughts toward God, sin, and righteousness are radically different now that we are "in the Spirit" from when we were "in the flesh." We have new holy affections and longings for godliness. We have a love for God that transcends our attachment to this world (Jas. 4:4). We can no longer blithely "indulge the flesh in its corrupt desires" (2 Pet. 2:10). We no longer have anything in common with those "who set their minds on earthly things. For our citizenship is in heaven" (Phil. 3:19–20). And it is toward heaven that our minds are now inclined. We set our minds on the things of the Spirit (Rom. 8:5). Even when we fail or fall to earthly temptations, we "joyfully concur with the law of God in the inner man" (7:22). That is our basic orientation and mind set.

In contrast, "the mind set on the flesh is death" (v. 6). Paul does not say that the mind set on the flesh *causes* death. He declares that it *is* death. The state of mind that is dominated by fleshly desires is a condition of spiritual death. In other words, those whose thoughts and desires are altogether fleshly are *already* "dead in [their] trespasses and sins" (Eph. 2:1). This cannot be a description of the true believer in Christ.

As we noted in chapter 6, Christians are no longer "in the flesh": "You are not in the flesh but in the Spirit, if indeed the Spirit of God dwells in you. But if anyone does not have the Spirit of Christ, he does not belong to Him" (Rom. 8:9). The Greek word translated "dwells" is *oikeō*, which means "to inhabit." Paul is saying that the very Spirit of God indwells every person who trusts in Jesus Christ. The Spirit is in us, and we are "in the Spirit." We are not "in the flesh."

Death in the Physical Body

But we are still "of flesh," and therefore our physical bodies deteriorate and die. The germ of death inhabits us all. Because of the curse of sin, we begin to die as soon as we are born.

For the Christian, however, there is more to this earthly life than death: "If Christ is in you, though the body is dead because of sin, yet the spirit is alive because of righteousness" (Rom. 8:10). In other words, the human body is subject to death (and is already dying) because of sin, but the believer's spirit is already alive in Christ. Eternal life is our present possession. Though the body is dying, the spirit is already endowed with incorruptibility.

For the Christian, however, there is more to this earthly life than death.

Here the word "body" clearly refers to the actual physical body (not the flesh-principle), and the expression "dead" speaks of physical death. (See the discussion in Appendix 1 of how Paul often uses "flesh" and "body" to refer to the sin-tendency in believers.) Notice that verses 10 and 11 use the word "body" (*sōma*) instead of "flesh" (*sarx*)—the word Paul used throughout the first nine verses. By contrasting "the body" and "the spirit" in this way, he makes his meaning inescapable. In verse 10, "the spirit is alive" refers to the human spirit, the immaterial part of our being. The body may be dying because of sin, but the believer's spirit is fully alive and thriving "because of righteousness"—because we are justified and therefore already have "passed out of death into life" (Jn. 5:24). Paul is simply saying here what he also told the Corinthians, "Though our outer man is decaying, yet our inner man is being renewed day by day" (2 Cor. 4:16).

In fact, the indwelling Spirit also promises "life to [our] mortal bodies" in a future resurrection with a glorified body (Rom. 8:11).

Paul's point is that the body apart from the Spirit of God has no future. It is subject to death. Therefore we have no duty to the mortal side of our beings: "So then, brethren, we are under obligation, not to the flesh, to live according to the flesh—for if you are living according to the flesh, you must die; but if by the Spirit you are putting to death the deeds of the body, you will live" (Rom. 8:12–13). Here Paul uses the word *sarx* ("flesh") in the sense of "sin principle"—and equates it with "the deeds of the body." If you live in accord with the flesh—if you live in response to sinful impulses—you "must die."

Paul is once more drawing the line of distinction as clearly as possible between Christians and non-Christians. He is by no means warning believers that they might lose their salvation if they live according to the flesh. He has already made the point that true believers do not and *cannot* live in accord with the sin principle (vv. 4–9). Besides, Paul began chapter 8 with the statement, "There is therefore now no condemnation for those who are in Christ Jesus" (8:1). He will end it with the promise that nothing can separate us from the love of God in Christ Jesus (vv. 38–39). A warning of the possibility of falling away would contradict the very purpose for which he was writing.

Paul is simply reiterating what he says again and again throughout his New Testament epistles—that those whose lives and hearts are altogether fleshly are not true Christians. They are already spiritually dead (v. 6), and unless they repent they are headed for eternal death. Meanwhile, their earthly lives are a kind of abject bondage to sin. They are enslaved to their own flesh, constrained to cater to its sensual desires.

What Is Mortification?

Christians, on the other hand, have a different obligation—not to the flesh, but to the new principle of righteousness embodied in the Holy Spirit. Therefore they labor by the power of the Spirit to mortify sin in the flesh—to "[put] to death the deeds of the body." If you are doing this, he says, "you will live" (Rom. 8:13).

Nothing is more natural than for people "led by the Spirit of God" (v. 14) to mortify their sin.

Of course, Paul is not suggesting that anyone can obtain life or merit God's favor by the process of mortification. He is saying it is characteristic of true believers that they put to death the deeds of the body. Nothing is more natural than for people "led by the Spirit

154

of God" (v. 14) to mortify their sin. One of the proofs of our salvation is that we do this. It is expected of believers. It is the expression of the new nature.

In other words, the true believer is not like Saul, who wanted to pamper and preserve Agag, but like Samuel who hacked him to pieces without mercy and without delay. Saul may have wanted to make a lap dog of Agag, but Samuel knew that was utterly impossible. Similarly, we will never tame our flesh. We cannot molly-coddle our sin. We must deal with it quickly and severely.

It was Jesus who said,

> If your right eye makes you stumble, tear it out, and throw it from you; for it is better for you that one of the parts of your body perish, than for your whole body to be thrown into hell. And if your right hand makes you stumble, cut it off, and throw it from you; for it is better for you that one of the parts of your body perish, than for your whole body to go into hell (Matt. 5:29–30).

Jesus was not speaking in literal terms, of course, though many have misunderstood this passage. No less than the great theologian Origen had himself castrated in a misguided effort to fulfill this command literally. Jesus was *not* calling for self-mutilation, but for mortification of the deeds of the body. Mortification, in the words of Puritan John Owen, means that the flesh, "with [its] faculties, and properties, [its] wisdom, craft, subtlety, strength; this, says the apostle, must be killed, put to death, mortified,—that is, *have its power, life, vigour, and strength, to produce its effects, taken away by the Spirit.*"[2]

Romans 8:12–13, the verses where Paul introduces the idea of mortifying sin, signal a major turning point in the logical thread that runs through this chapter. Martyn Lloyd-Jones said,

> It is here for the first time, in this chapter, that we come to the realm of practical application. All we have had up to this point has been a general description of the Christian—his character, his position. But now the Apostle has really come explicitly to the doctrine of sanctification. *Here we are told exactly how, in practice, the Christian becomes sanctified.* Or, to state it differently, here we are told in detail and in practice how the Christian is to wage the battle against sin.[3]

Paul does not promise immediate freedom from sin's harassment. He does not describe a crisis-moment sanctification, where the believer is immediately made perfect. He does not tell the Romans to "let go and let God" take over while they sit idle. He does not suggest that a turning-point "decision" will solve the matter once and for all. On the contrary, he speaks of a continuous struggle with sin, where we are persistently, perpetually "putting to death the deeds of the body."

The language is often misunderstood. Paul is not calling for a life of self-flagellation. He is not saying believers should starve themselves, literally torture their bodies, or deprive themselves of life's basic needs. He is not telling them to mutilate themselves or live monastic lives or anything of the sort. The mortification Paul speaks of has nothing to do with external self-punishment. It is a spiritual process accomplished "by the Spirit."

Paul is describing a way of life where *we seek to throttle sin and crush it from our lives, sapping it of its strength, rooting it out, and depriving it of its influence.* That is what it means to mortify sin.

How Do We Mortify Sin?

Mortification involves the cultivation of new habits of godliness, combined with the elimination of old sinful habits from our behavior. It is a constant warfare that takes place within the believer. Although we should expect our triumph over sin to be ever-increasing, our mortification can never be wholly complete before we are glorified. We are to remain perpetually committed to the task. We must see sin as a sworn enemy, and commit ourselves to slaying it wherever and whenever it rears its head.

Obviously, mortification is the work of believers only. Unbelievers are called to repent and flee to Christ. Those still enslaved to sin have no means by which to put sin to death. The Holy Spirit— the agent of mortification—does not indwell them. Their only hope is the salvation that is offered to those who will trust Jesus Christ and entrust themselves to Him. No one can mortify sin who is not "in Christ" and "in the Spirit."

Scripture offers several practical means whereby believers can mortify their sin. Our growth in grace depends on our obedience to these duties. None of them are fleshly or mechanical formulas. They are not religious activities or rituals. John Owen observed that most of the Roman Catholic religious system consists of "mistaken ways and means of mortification. . . . Their vows, orders, fastings, penances, are all built on this ground; they are all for the mortifying of sin. Their preachings, sermons, and books of devotion, they look all this way.[4]

Although we should expect our triumph over sin to be ever-increasing, our mortification can never be wholly complete before we are glorified.

But sin cannot be annihilated through legalism, monasticism, pietism, asceticism, pharisaism, celibacy, self-flagellation, confessional booths, rosary beads, hail Marys, or any other external means. The instrument of mortification is the Holy Spirit, and His power is the energy that works in us to carry out the process. All the means of mortification are simple commands of Scripture that we are to obey. Some of the key commands are highlighted below:

Abstain from fleshly lusts. Peter wrote, "Beloved, I urge you as aliens and strangers to abstain from fleshly lusts, which wage war against the soul" (1 Pet. 2:11). In other words, stop lusting. Abstain from it. Stay away from it. "Flee immorality" (1 Cor. 6:18). What could be more direct?

Do you want to put to death the lusts in your heart? Then stop entertaining them. Peter does not prescribe a program of therapy. He does not suggest that such sin be treated as an addiction. He simply says abstain. Quit doing it. You have no business indulging such thoughts. Put them away at once. *You yourself* must do this; it cannot be done for you. There is no point waiting for some heavenly power to erase this sin automatically from your life. You are to stop it, and stop it immediately. Martyn Lloyd-Jones said,

> I do not know of a single scripture—and I speak advisedly—
> which tells me to take my sin, the particular thing that gets me

down, to God in prayer and ask him to deliver me from it and then trust in faith that he will.

Now that teaching is also often put like this: you must say to a man who is constantly defeated by a particular sin, "I think your only hope is to take it to Christ and Christ will take it from you." But what does Scripture say in Ephesians 4:28 to the man who finds himself constantly guilty of stealing, to a man who sees something he likes and takes it? What am I to tell such a man? Am I to say, "Take that sin to Christ and ask him to deliver you?" No, what the apostle Paul tells him is this: "Let him that stole, steal no more." Just that. Stop doing it. And if it is fornication or adultery or lustful thoughts, again: Stop doing it, says Paul. He does not say, "Go and pray to Christ to deliver you." No. You stop doing that, he says, as becomes children of God.[5]

Here is perhaps the most straightforward, obvious means of mortifying our sin: *stop doing it.* Too many people think they must wait for an extraordinary experience, a miracle from heaven, a sign from the Lord, or whatever. They think some special divine intervention is necessary to free them from a sinful practice or pattern of thinking. No, that is precisely the error Romans 6 refutes. You *are* free from sin; now stop doing it. You are dead to sin; now put to death the sin that remains. How? "Abstain." Reckon yourself dead to sin, and don't do it anymore. "Resist the devil and he will flee from you" (Jas. 4:7). It is as simple as that.

Make no provision for the flesh. In Romans 13:14 Paul writes, "Put on the Lord Jesus Christ, and make no provision for the flesh in regard to its lusts." In other words, simply refuse to accommodate fleshly lusts. If you struggle with gluttony, don't load up on junk food when you shop at the market. If you are tempted with sexual desire, don't fill your mind with images that feed your lust. If you don't want to fall, don't walk where it is slippery. Refuse to furnish your mind with the means to entertain evil thoughts. Make no preparations for the possibility of sin. Thus you can slay sin before it breeds.

Fix your heart on Christ. The apostle John wrote, "We know that, when He appears, we shall be like Him, because we shall see Him just as He is. And everyone who has this hope fixed on Him purifies himself, just as He is pure" (1 Jn. 3:2–3). It is an inexorable spiritual law that you become like the object of your worship. Psalm 135 says,

> The idols of the nations are but silver and gold, the work of man's hands. They have mouths, but they do not speak; they have eyes, but they do not see; they have ears, but they do not hear; nor is there any breath at all in their mouths. *Those who make them will be like them*, yes, everyone who trusts in them. (vv. 15–18, emphasis added).

If the heathen become like the lifeless gods they worship, how much more will we be made like Christ, who have the Holy Spirit in us working to accomplish that very goal? As we fix our hearts on Christ, we discover our worship has the effect of conforming us to His image: "But we all, with unveiled face beholding as in a mirror the glory of the Lord, are being transformed into the same image from glory to glory, just as from the Lord, the Spirit" (2 Cor. 3:18).

Meditate on God's Word. The psalmist wrote, "Thy word I have treasured in my heart, that I may not sin against Thee" (Ps. 119:11). The Lord told Joshua, "This book of the law shall not depart from your mouth, but you shall meditate on it day and night, so that you may be careful to do according to all that is written in it; for then you will make your way prosperous, and then you will have success" (Josh. 1:8). Do you want to have success in the battle against sin? Familiarize yourself with the Word of God. Meditate on it "day and night" (cf. Ps. 1:2). Let it be a lamp to your feet and a light to your path (Ps. 119:105). As the truth begins to penetrate your heart and mind, it will confront and attack sin.

Jesus prayed, "Sanctify them in the truth; thy word is truth" (Jn. 17:17). The truth of God's Word is the medium the Holy Spirit uses in our sanctification. Load your mind with it. Fill your heart with it. Ponder it carefully and let it direct your walk. "Whatever is true, whatever is honorable, whatever is right, whatever is pure, whatever is lovely, whatever is of good repute, if there is any excellence and if anything worthy of praise, let your mind dwell on these things" (Phil. 4:8). "Let the word of Christ richly dwell within you" (Col. 3:16). You will discover that "the sword of the Spirit, which is the word of God" (Eph. 6:17) is the most effective weapon for hacking the flesh to pieces.

Pray without ceasing. On the night Jesus was betrayed, He took His disciples with Him to Gethsemane and told them, "Pray that you may not enter into temptation" (Lk. 22:40). Later He found them sleeping and rebuked them for their prayerlessness. He told them, "Keep watching and praying, that you may not enter into temptation; the spirit is willing, but the flesh is weak" (Matt. 26:41).

Prayer must include confession and repentance if it is to be effective in mortifying our sin.

"Lead us not into temptation" was part of the model prayer He gave the disciples (Lk. 11:4). Prayer is an effective and necessary means for heading off sinful temptations *before* they can attack. Look at prayer as a preemptive strike against fleshliness. By drawing us near to the Lord and focusing our thoughts on Him, prayer both steels us against fleshly temptation, and weakens the temptations when they come.

Watch and pray. Identify the circumstances that lead you into sin, and pray specifically for strength to face those situations. Pray for a holy hatred of sin. Pray that God will show you the real state of your sinful heart. The psalmist prayed this prayer for sanctification:

> Who can discern his errors? Acquit me of hidden faults. Also keep back Thy servant from presumptuous sins; let them not rule over me; then I shall be blameless, and I shall be acquitted of great transgression. Let the words of my mouth and the meditation of my heart be acceptable in Thy sight, O Lord, my rock and my Redeemer (Ps. 19:12–14).

Prayer must include confession and repentance if it is to be effective in mortifying our sin. John wrote, "If we confess our sins, He is faithful and righteous to forgive us our sins and to cleanse us from all unrighteousness" (1 Jn. 1:9). And the writer of Hebrews says,

"Let us therefore draw near with confidence to the throne of grace, that we may receive mercy and may find grace to help in time of need" (Heb. 4:16).

Exercise self-control. Self-control is a fruit of the Spirit (Gal. 5:23)—and it is also one of the means through which the Spirit enables us to mortify the deeds of the body. Paul wrote,

> Everyone who competes in the games exercises self-control in all things. They then do it to receive a perishable wreath, but we an imperishable. Therefore I run in such a way, as not without aim; I box in such a way, as not beating the air; but I buffet my body and make it my slave, lest possibly, after I have preached to others, I myself should be disqualified (1 Cor. 9:25–27).

The word "buffet" in that passage is a translation of the Greek word *hupōpiazō*, meaning "to strike under the eye." Athletes discipline their bodies for mere earthly prizes. If they are willing to do that, shouldn't we also be willing to exercise a similar kind of self-control for the heavenly prize?

Paul is not speaking here of punishing the body through self-flagellation or neglect. He certainly is not advocating anything that would physically weaken or injure the body. No athlete would do such things.

I once met a man who wore a belt studded with nails that constantly tore at his flesh. He felt he was punishing his body and atoning for his own sins. Lots of misguided people over the ages have attempted similar means of dealing with the body. Martin Luther almost destroyed his body with excessive fasting as a young monk before he discovered that God's Word says, "The just shall live by faith" (Rom. 1:17, KJV). In the Philippines at Easter each year, there are men who actually have themselves crucified in a bloody ritual that they believe makes them holy.

That is not at all the spirit of what Scripture calls for. Self-control is a watchful discipline that refuses to pander to the appetites of the body at the soul's expense. Jesus said, "Be on guard, that your hearts may not be weighted down with dissipation and drunkenness and the worries of life, and [the Day of the Lord] come on you suddenly like a trap" (Lk. 21:34).

Be filled with the Holy Spirit. "Do not get drunk with wine, for that is dissipation," Paul wrote, "but be filled with the Spirit" (Eph. 5:18). To be Spirit-filled is to be controlled by the Holy Spirit, just as to be drunk is to be under the influence of alcohol. Believers are to be utterly yielded to the Spirit's control.

Now this brings us full circle to where we began in Romans 8:13. We mortify sin "by the Spirit." It is the Holy Spirit's power in us that actually does the work of mortification in those who are yielded to Him. I must emphasize again, however, that this does not mean we are passive in the process. As John Owen wrote,

> He doth not so work our mortification in us as not to keep it still an act of our *obedience*. The Holy Ghost works in us and upon us, as we are fit to be wrought in and upon; that is, so as to pre-serve our own liberty and free obedience. He works upon our understandings, wills, consciences, and affections, agreeably to their own natures; he works *in us* and *with us*, not *against us* or *without us*; so that his assistance is an encouragement as to the facilitating of the work, and no occasion of neglect as to the work itself.[6]

In other words, as we have noted repeatedly, we cannot abandon our own responsibility and passively wait for God to mortify sin on our behalf. The Spirit-filled life is an active, vigorous, working en-deavor, where we work out our own salvation with fear and trem-bling (Phil. 2:12). When we obey, we then discover it is actually God who is at work in us "both to will and to work for His good pleasure" (v. 13). In other words, God both molds our wills to obey and then gives us the energy to work according to whatever pleases Him. That is the Spirit-filled life.

In other words, God both molds our wills to obey and then gives us the energy to work according to whatever pleases Him. That is the Spirit-filled life.

There are many more duties related to mortifying sin—such as clothing oneself with humility (1 Pet. 5:5); having the mind of Christ (Phil. 2:5); putting away spiteful feelings toward others (Eph. 4:31–32); putting on the armor of God (Eph. 6:11–17); laying aside sinful attitudes (Col. 3:8–9); adding the graces of spiritual growth to one's life (2 Pet. 1:5–7); following the *know, reckon, yield, obey, serve* pattern of Romans 6 (see Appendix 1)—and many similar responsibilities the New Testament assigns to believers. These may *all* be subsumed under this basic category of being filled with the Spirit.

It is really as simple as this: "Walk by the Spirit, and you will not carry out the desire of the flesh" (Gal. 5:16). The fruit of the Spirit will overgrow and choke out the works of the flesh.

"Let us [therefore] cleanse ourselves from all defilement of flesh and spirit, perfecting holiness in the fear of God" (2 Cor. 7:1).

Strike Sin at Its Head

John Owen wrote, "He that is appointed to kill an enemy, if he leave striking before the other ceases living, doth but half his work."[7] We must be always at the task of mortifying sin. We may slaughter a whole tribe of Amalekites, but if we deliberately permit one Agag to escape, God will not be pleased with our efforts.

The flesh is very subtle and deceptive, as we know. A particular sin may leave us alone for awhile to make us think we are rid of it. But it can come back with a hellish fury if we are not on our guard. Sin perpetually stalks us; we must be continually mortifying it. This is a duty we cannot rest from until we rest in glory.

Give sin an inch, it will take a mile. If it can gain a footing in our lives, it will send forth roots and grow like kudzu. It will use us and abuse us and inflict as much disaster as possible. Owen wrote,

> Every unclean thought or glance would be adultery if it could; every covetous desire would be oppression, every thought of unbelief would be atheism, might it grow to its head. . . . It proceeds toward its height by degrees, making good the ground it hath got by hardness. . . . Now nothing can prevent this but mortification; that withers the root and strikes at the head of sin every hour, so that whatever it aims at it is crossed in. *There is*

not the best saint in the world but, if he should give over this duty,
would fall into as many cursed sins as ever did any of his kind.[8]

Later, he added, "Sin sets itself against every act of holiness, and against every degree we grow to. Let not that man think he makes any progress in holiness while he walks not over the bellies of his lusts."[9]

We are not ignorant of Satan's devices, the apostle declares (2 Cor. 2:11). Neither should we be naive about the subtleties of our own flesh. When Agag comes to us cheerfully, saying, "Surely the bitterness of death is past" (1 Sam. 15:32); when he wants to make friends and declare an end to hostilities—that is when it is most imperative that we turn on him and cut him ruthlessly to pieces before the Lord. Sin is not mortified when it is merely covered up, internalized, exchanged for another sin, or repressed. It is not mortified until the conscience has been appeased.

Sin is not mortified when it is merely covered up. You can obscure your sin from others' sight, but that is not the same as mortification. If a sin has simply been papered over with hypocrisy, what good is there in that? If conscience has only been daubed, we are in a much more dangerous state than before. "He who conceals his transgressions will not prosper, but he who confesses and forsakes them will find compassion" (Prov. 28:13). You have not done your duty with regard to your sin until you have confessed and forsaken it.

Sin is not mortified when it is only internalized. If you forsake the outward practice of some evil yet continue to ruminate on the memory of that sin's pleasures, beware. You may have moved your sin into the privacy of your imagination, where it is known only to you and to God. But that sin has not been mortified. If anything it has been made more deadly by being married to pretended righteousness. Jesus rebuked the Pharisees for this very thing. They avoided murder but tolerated hate. They refrained from fornication, but indulged in lustful thoughts. Jesus declared them worthy of eternal hell (Matt. 5:21–28).

Sin is not mortified when it is exchanged for another sin. What good is it to trade the lust of the flesh for the lust of the eyes? That lust has not been mortified; it has only changed form. Puritan Thomas Fuller said, "Some think themselves improved in piety, because they have left prodigality and reel into covetousness."[10] If you succumb to this tactic, your heart is in danger of being hardened by the deceitfulness of sin (Heb. 3:13).

Sin is not mortified until the conscience has been appeased. The goal is "love from a pure heart and a good conscience and a sincere faith" (1 Tim. 1:5). As long as the conscience remains defiled, it affects our testimony. "Sanctify Christ as Lord in your hearts, always being ready to make a defense to everyone who asks you to give an account for the hope that is in you, yet with gentleness and reverence; *and keep a good conscience* so that in the thing in which you are slandered, those who revile your good behavior in Christ may be put to shame" (1 Pet. 3:15–16, emphasis added).

Part of the process of mortification is working through the issue of our guilt. Those who attempt to evade the guilt have not properly confessed their sin; therefore they cannot be cleansed and fully forgiven.

If you want to mortify sin, John Owen wrote, *"Load thy conscience with the guilt of it."*[11] Contrary to the popular wisdom of our day, he believed the pangs of guilt were a natural and healthy consequence of wrongdoing. "Be ashamed," he wrote,[12] for he saw shame as an advantage in the mortification of sin. He correctly understood Paul's meaning in 2 Corinthians 7:10: "The sorrow that is according to the will of God produces a repentance without regret."

Those who give a nod of the head to their guilt, claim the promise of forgiveness, quickly reassure themselves, and then think no more of their wrongdoing are subjecting themselves to the heart-hardening deceit of sin—especially when the sin threatens to become a habit. Let sorrow do its full work in your heart to produce a deep, honest repentance, and those sins will be severely weakened.

Sin is not mortified when it is merely repressed. Some people use diversions to avoid dealing with their sin. They try to drown their conscience with alcohol or drown out their guilt with entertainment and other distractions. When temptation surfaces they do not give a biblical answer, as Jesus did (Matt. 4:4, 7, 10). Instead they seek a fleshly escape route. Of this tendency Martyn Lloyd-Jones said,

If you merely repress a temptation or this first motion of sin within you, it will probably come up again still more strongly. To that extent I agree with the modern psychology. Repression is always bad. "Well, what do you do?" asks someone. I answer: When you feel that first motion of sin, just pull yourself up and say, "Of course I am not having any dealings with this at all." Expose the thing and say, "This is evil, this is vileness, this is the thing that drove the first man out of Paradise." Pull it out, look at it, denounce it, hate it for what it is; then you have really dealt with it. You must not merely push it back in a spirit of fear, and in a timorous manner. Bring it out, expose it, and analyse it; and then denounce it for what it is until you hate it.[13]

That is sound advice. We should deal with our sin courageously, striking at its head. Subduing it a little bit is not enough. We need to exterminate it, hack it in pieces—seek by the means of grace and the power of the Spirit to wring the deadly life from it.

It is a lifelong task, in which our progress will always be only gradual. That may make the fight seem daunting at first. But as soon as we set ourselves to the work, we discover that sin shall *not* be master over us, for we are under grace (Rom. 6:14). That means it is God who is at work in us both to will and to work for His good pleasure (Phil. 2:13). And having begun His good work in us, He "will perfect it until the day of Christ Jesus" (1:6).

8

Handling Temptation

The Christian. . . knows that he cannot embrace that cross, or, more important, embrace the Christ who died on it and now lives for ever in the service of God, without renouncing all known sin. We cannot serve two masters—a crucified Christ who died for our sin, and sin for which he died. The more we rejoice in the way of salvation, therefore, the more we will mortify sin. That will not make us perfect, because there is no complete mortification in this life. But it will bring us joy in walking in the power of Christ and being delivered from the power of sin. This, in part, is the answer to our common perplexity: How can we keep our way pure?

Sinclair Ferguson[1]

At the beginning of this book, I noted that our culture seems to have abandoned the notion of sin. Recently, however, MTV aired a special program titled "The Seven Deadly Sins." I watched a videotape of the program, and it more than confirmed my worst fears about the state of contemporary culture, especially how it perceives traditional sources of temptation.

The seven deadly sins are pride, covetousness, lust, anger, envy, gluttony, and sloth. That is not a biblical list, but a classification of medieval theology. Some monastic theologians probably first set forth that grouping of sins, trying to systematize and identify all the *root* sins, not necessarily the most serious ones. The seven deadly sins, along with seven cardinal virtues (faith, hope, love, justice, prudence, temperance, and fortitude) receive much emphasis in Roman Catholic theology.

People love their sin. They will go to any lengths to rationalize it and defend it.

On MTV, however, the sins were portrayed as anything but deadly. Sound bites featuring celebrities, cartoon characters, excerpts from well-known movies, punk rockers, rappers, and interviews with people in the mall were all edited together to provide a running commentary on pop culture's attitude toward sin. Most of them described sin as a positive reality.

"Pride is a sin?" exclaimed rap singer Queen Latifah. "I wasn't aware of that."

Actress Kirstie Alley agreed: "I don't think pride is a sin, and I think some idiot made that up. Who made all these up?"

A rocker from the group Aerosmith stated, "Lust is what I live for. It's what I got into the band for—little girls in the front row."

Rapper Ice-T said of anger, "It's necessary. You have to release this tension because life brings tension. We release our anger when we do records. When we did 'Cop Killer,' we were angry—and the cops got angry back."

"Greed is good," says the Michael Douglas character from the movie *Wall Street*.

And of course there was the inevitable appeal to pop psychology to defend these sins as essential to one's self-esteem. Ice-T said, "Pride is mandatory. That's one of the problems of the inner city—kids don't have enough pride. I got into a gang because of pride."

A perceptive article in *U.S. News & World Report* summed up the program's flavor:

> Instead of the language of moderation and self-control, everybody seems to speak the therapized language of feelings and self-esteem. "Pride isn't a sin—you're supposed to feel good about yourself." "Envy makes you feel bad about yourself." When you have sex with a woman, one rocker says, "she makes you feel good about yourself, but I don't know if it saves you in the end." Even the repentant gay basher is totally committed to self-talk: "Forgiving myself has been the challenge of my life."
>
> There's a vague sense that sin, if it exists, is surely a problem of psychology. Kurt Loder, the narrator, tells us at the start of the program that we are dealing with compulsions: "The seven deadly sins are not evil acts but, rather, universal human compulsions that can be troubling and highly enjoyable." Discussion of gluttony quickly deteriorates into chatter about addictions. That's the way all habits and attachments are discussed in the pop therapies the MTV generation grew up on. "I'm addicted to my girlfriend," one male says about gluttony. Someone else says that the twelve-step self-help program is God's gift to the twenty-first century.[2]

"The repentant gay basher" referred to in the *U.S. News* article—a young man who had actually killed a homosexual—describes his feelings of remorse. He wonders if he can ever be forgiven. A chaplain has told him forgiveness is possible, but the only way the boy will know God has forgiven him is if he "feels" it someday. And so he lives each day hoping for a feeling!

Sin, it seems, is not defined as a matter of fixed morality, but instead is wholly subjective. The individual's own preferences determine the line between good and evil. The MTV program ends with an appeal for universal tolerance. The real danger of sin, according to MTV, is the damage it does to the human ego. One gets the clear idea that no sin is as evil as the killjoy attitude of those who think sin is offensive to a holy God.

The entire production reminded me that we live in a culture given over by God to its own evil lusts. People love their sin. They will go to any lengths to rationalize it and defend it.

For Christians, however, life cannot reflect our culture's values. We cannot try to excuse or tolerate sin. It was sin that put our blessed Savior on the cross to bleed and die. Sin was what set us at enmity with God. Now that that enmity has been broken, we want nothing to do with the old life. Now that we are freed from sin, we do not want to go back into bondage. And we don't have to! To choose to do so would be a denial of our Lord. As the beloved apostle wrote,

> No one who abides in Him sins; no one who sins has seen Him or knows Him. Little children, let no one deceive you; the one who practices righteousness is righteous, just as He is righteous; the one who practices sin is of the devil; for the devil has sinned from the beginning. The Son of God appeared for this purpose, that He might destroy the works of the devil. No one who is born of God practices sin, because His seed abides in him; and he cannot sin, because he is born of God. By this the children of God and the children of the devil are obvious: anyone who does not practice righteousness is not of God, nor the one who does not love his brother (1 Jn. 3:6–10).

Of course, John is speaking there about following sin as a practice. He is describing a lifestyle of unbroken, wanton sin—which no true believer is capable of.

Can We Really Overcome Temptation?

Nevertheless, even we who are Christians are besieged with constant temptation. It seems overwhelming at times. We might pose the question—is it really possible to overcome temptation in any meaningful sense? How can we be triumphant? With Satan, the world, and our own flesh against us, is there any hope for us to overcome sin's pull? Our enemies are so subtle and their strategies so sophisticated, how can we fight them? Aren't we sometimes confronted with temptations that are so effective that we frankly have no hope of defeating them? Isn't Satan so wily that we cannot possibly overcome some of his schemes? And isn't our own heart so deceitful and desperately wicked that it leaves us without a proper defense? Isn't it really folly for us to dream of victory over our sin?

Popular Christian fiction portrays the church as engaged in a fearsome satanic battle, orchestrated by a formidable conspiracy of visible and invisible evil forces that want to mow us down.

Take it a step further. With the steady stream of pastors and church leaders who have fallen into gross, disqualifying, scandalous sin, many Christians are asking if the church itself and her leaders in particular are being subjected to some level of assault for which they are no match. Indeed, several of the fallen televangelists have blamed demonic forces beyond their control for their personal moral collapse. Popular Christian fiction portrays the church as engaged in a fearsome satanic battle, orchestrated by a formidable conspiracy of visible and invisible evil forces that want to mow us down. And we know from Scripture that we *are* engaged in spiritual warfare with demons we cannot see (Eph. 6:12). If all the forces of hell are arrayed against us, are we any match for that? Or are we really just victims of overwhelming temptation that we do not have the resources to deal with?

Scripture clearly answers that question. In fact, it answers all those questions in one verse: "No temptation has overtaken you but such as is common to man; and God is faithful, who will not allow you to be tempted beyond what you are able, but with the temptation will provide the way of escape also, that you may be able to endure it" (1 Cor. 10:13).

That verse is surely one of the most welcome and comforting promises in all of Scripture. No temptation can be so overpowering that we are left helpless to resist. Satan is not so powerful; demons are not so effective; the evil conspiracy is not so cleverly devised; the flesh is not so weak; the human heart is not so deceitful—that we are left helpless to be victimized by temptation.

This verse contains principles that will help us understand how we can triumph over specific temptations through understanding more about the means by which they work, their nature, and their extent.

The Means of Temptation

First, we are told the means by which temptation works. It wants to overtake us, to ambush us when we are not prepared, and thus dominate us. It seeks control of us.

The word for "temptation" in the Greek text is *peirasmos*. It can be translated "test" or "temptation." Tests and temptations are two sides of the same thing. Life is full of trials, and each of them is a potential temptation.

An illustration might be helpful to show how this is so: A friend once told me about his new job with a very important company. After he had been on the job only a little while, one night after everyone else had left the office, he noticed that someone had left a large sum of money on his desk. He immediately took the money, put it in his briefcase and thought, *I'm going to have to return this.* He wrapped it up and the next morning walked into the boss's office, put the money on the boss's desk, and said, "Someone left this money on my desk and I don't know who it was or who will be missing it, but I wanted to turn it in as soon as I could so that no one would be distressed by its absence."

His boss looked him in the face and said, "I put the money there. It was a test. You passed."

Life offers us similar tests. Depending on how we respond, they can become temptations.

If my friend had taken the money home and counted it, and desired it, and thought through his options, he might have said to himself, *Hmm, nobody will know,* and begun to battle in his heart whether to turn it in or keep it for himself. Then the test would have become a temptation. When the heart is solicited to do evil, that is a temptation.

Life is full of tests that have the potential of becoming temptations. For example, when you are in the midst of a financial setback
and you say, "I'm going to trust God to meet my needs. I will cut back,
live frugally, budget carefully, and be faithful to my obligations. I will
live on less and trust the Lord to provide my needs"—you pass the
test. But if you say, "I can take money from the till and no one will
know. I can save money by cheating on my income tax. And I can cut
expenses by not paying what I owe"—you have moved from a test
into a temptation because your heart is being solicited to evil.

Or the test might be some personal disappointment. Perhaps
you had expectations of someone who did not fulfill your hopes.
You can either accept your circumstances with a trusting heart,
and love that person in spite of your disappointment—or you can
begin to feel animosity and bitterness in your heart. The moment
those evil thoughts petition your heart, your test becomes a temptation.

Or you might face the test of illness, injury, or unexpected disaster. Perhaps someone you love dies. Or your plans are thwarted.
Or you fail to accomplish something you had dreamed for a long
time. Maybe you will face a problem with no obvious solution. Or
perhaps a friend will urge you to do something you know is wrong.
These are the kind of tests that make up life. And when they begin
to entreat us to respond with evil they become temptations. Job had
to face *all* those tests at the same time.

James gives a very lucid explanation of how trials turn into
temptations. He writes, "Consider it all joy, my brethren, when you
encounter various trials, knowing that the testing of your faith produces endurance. And let endurance have its perfect result, that you
may be perfect and complete, lacking in nothing" (Jas. 1:2–4). Later,
he adds, "Blessed is a man who perseveres under trial; for once he
has been approved, he will receive the crown of life, which the Lord
has promised to those who love Him" (v. 12).

In other words, God has a beneficent purpose in allowing us to
go through trials. The trials perfect us, mold us to Christ's image,
give us endurance, and bring us to the point of spiritual complete-
ness. Peter said something similar: "After you have suffered for a
little while, the God of all grace, who called you to His eternal glory
in Christ, will Himself perfect, confirm, strengthen and establish
you" (1 Pet. 5:10).

God sends us tests but not temptations. James also said, "Let no one say when he is tempted, 'I am being tempted by God'; for God cannot be tempted by evil, and He Himself does not tempt anyone" (Jas. 1:13). God himself is never responsible for the solicitation to do evil.

God sends us tests but not temptations.

Then how does it happen? James 1 tells us: "Each one is tempted when he is carried away and enticed by his own lust. Then when lust has conceived, it gives birth to sin; and when sin is accomplished, it brings forth death" (vv. 14–15). It is *our own lust* that produces the solicitation to do evil. God only gives good gifts: "Do not be deceived, my beloved brethren. Every good thing bestowed and every perfect gift is from above, coming down from the Father of lights, with whom there is no variation, or shifting shadow" (vv. 16–17). God is perfect, unchanging, invariable. He is not responsible for our temptations, though He sends trials to test us.

Victory then begins with an understanding of how temptation comes. It comes when we respond wrongly to tests. It comes when we are drawn away by our own lusts. That plants the seeds for sin, and when sin bears fruit, that fruit is death. So we need to learn to respond correctly to tests.

The Nature of Temptation

We return to that wonderful promise in 1 Corinthians 10:13 to see the true nature of temptation: "No temptation has overtaken you but such as is common to man." In a word, temptation is *human*. It is not supernatural. It is not a force so powerful, so extraordinary that we are at a loss regarding how to deal with it. Temptation is common to humanity. The temptations you face are the very same ones everyone else faces. It is the same for all of us. The temptations that come to you are the same temptations that come to me. We may each have our peculiar besetting sins—areas where our habits or weaknesses frequently draw us into the same sins over and over. We may be particularly vulnerable or susceptible to different temptations. But we all get hit with the same basic temptations.

More encouraging yet, these are the very same temptations Jesus experienced. Hebrews 4:15 says Christ "has been tempted in all things as we are." Hebrews 2:17 says He was "made like His brethren in all things." He suffered all the very same temptations that are common to us. That is why He is such a faithful and merciful high priest. That is why He is touched with the feeling of our infirmities.

The Extent of Temptation

Moreover, there are limits to the amount or extent of temptation that God will allow us to face: "God is faithful who will not allow you to be tempted beyond what you are able." God knows your individual limitations. If you are a Christian, He has planned your life to guarantee your security in Christ eternally. He will never allow you to face any test that is more than you at any given point in your spiritual life can handle.

He will never allow you to face any test that is more than you at any given point in your spiritual life can handle.

We see an illustration of this principle in Jesus' dealings with the eleven disciples. On the night of His betrayal, Jesus told Peter, "Simon, Simon, behold, Satan has demanded permission to sift you like wheat; but I have prayed for you, that your faith may not fail" (Lk. 22:31–32). When Peter assured the Lord that he was ready to follow Him even to death, Jesus replied, "I say to you, Peter, the cock will not crow today until you have denied three times that you know Me" (v. 34). It happened just as Jesus prophesied. But did Peter's faith fail? No, Jesus' prayer for him was answered, and Peter was ultimately restored to full fellowship and even leadership in the early church.

On that same evening of Jesus' betrayal, while our Lord was praying in the garden, He prayed for His disciples: "While I was with them, I was keeping them in Thy name which Thou hast given Me; and I guarded them, and not one of them perished but the son of perdition, that the Scripture might be fulfilled" (Jn. 17:12). In other words, the eleven had been perpetually guarded and upheld by Jesus' sovereign, gracious keeping power. Only Judas, who never was a true believer, was left to carry out his own evil purposes.

While Jesus was praying, the disciples fell asleep (Mk. 13:37–43). When soldiers arrived with Judas, "Jesus therefore, knowing all the things that were coming upon Him, went forth, and said to them, 'Whom do you seek?' They answered Him, 'Jesus the Nazarene.' He said to them, 'I am He'" (Jn. 18:4–5). His words had a profound effect on the soldiers: "They drew back, and fell to the ground"(v. 6).

He asked them again, "Whom do you seek?" And they said, "Jesus the Nazarene" (v. 7).

Scripture says, "Jesus answered, 'I told you that I am He; if therefore you seek Me, let these go their way'" (v. 8). He was protecting the disciples. Twice He made the soldiers state whom they had come for. Then He volunteered the information that He was the one they were seeking, and He urged the soldiers to let the others go. He wanted to insure that none of the eleven were arrested, so "that the word might be fulfilled which He spoke, 'Of those whom Thou hast given Me I lost not one'" (v. 9).

This implies that if any of the disciples had been taken captive, they would have been spiritually too weak to survive such a test and would have defaulted from the faith. Therefore Jesus made sure they never had to face such a test. Peter almost messed everything up, because he took out a weapon and sliced off the ear of the high priest's servant (vv. 10–11). But Jesus miraculously healed the ear and rebuked Peter, and the disciples were able to flee (Mk. 14:50).

Through it all, Jesus Himself orchestrated all the events to make sure the disciples were not tested beyond their ability to withstand. Peter, especially, was confronted with a severe test that night. And although he sinned greatly by denying the Lord three times and even sealing his denial with a curse, Peter's faith did not fail. He was forced to look into his own soul, and he learned some valuable lessons that night. But through it all the Lord sustained him and made sure he did not fall away.

Whatever level of spiritual growth we are at, our Lord never allows us to go through any temptation beyond our ability to handle. If we are true Christians we cannot fall away. Our Lord Himself sees to that.

Furthermore, Christ prays for all true believers just as He prayed for the eleven in the garden. Hebrews 7:25 says, "He is able to save forever those who draw near to God through Him, since *He always lives to make intercession for them*" (emphasis added). He also puts limits on the extent of temptation we can undergo. He is faithful. He will not allow you to be tempted beyond your ability.

The Escape from Temptation

Best of all, when God allows us to be tested, He always provides a way out. There is always a path to victory. There is always an escape hatch. *Ekbasis* is the Greek word for "escape" in 1 Corinthians 10:13. It literally means "an exit."

Best of all, when God allows us to be tested, He always provides a way out. There is always a path to victory.

Here is a truth you may never have noticed in this verse— Paul tells us exactly what the way of escape is: God "with the temptation will provide the way of escape also, that you may be able to endure it." *The way out is through.* The way out of the temptation is to endure it as a trial and never let it become a solicitation to evil. You have been wronged. You have been falsely accused. You have been maligned or treated unkindly or dealt with unjustly. So what? Accept it. Endure it with joy (Jas. 1:2); that is the way of escape. Usually we look for a quick and easy escape route. God's plan for us is different. He wants us to count it all joy, "and let endurance have its perfect result, that [we] may be perfect and complete, lacking in nothing" (v. 4). God is using our trials to bring us to maturity.

How can we endure? There are several practical answers. I will mention only a few.

First, *meditate on the Word*: "Thy word I have treasured in my heart, that I may not sin against Thee" (Ps. 119:11). Second, *pray*: "Do not lead us into temptation, but deliver us from evil" (Matt. 6:13). In other words, ask God to keep the test from becoming a temptation. Third, *resist Satan and yield to God*: "Submit therefore to God. Resist the devil and he will flee from you" (Jas. 4:7).

There are many more I could mention, but do these begin to look familiar? They are precisely the same means of mortifying the deeds of the flesh we listed in chapter 8. The way to endure temptation *is* to be mortifying the deeds of the flesh.

There is one more key to endurance that I want to focus on, and that is faith. Hebrews 11 talks about the great heroes of faith, and their common characteristic is that they endured faithfully to the end. Of Moses, the writer of Hebrews says, "By faith he left Egypt, not fearing the wrath of the king; for he *endured*, as seeing Him who is unseen" (11:27, emphasis added). Abel, Enoch, Noah, Abraham, Sarah, Isaac, Jacob, Joseph, and Rahab all ran the race that was set before them *with endurance* (12:1). The writer of Hebrews summarizes:

> What more shall I say? For time will fail me if I tell of Gideon, Barak, Samson, Jephthah, of David and Samuel and the prophets, who by faith conquered kingdoms, performed acts of righteousness, obtained promises, shut the mouths of lions, quenched the power of fire, escaped the edge of the sword, from weakness were made strong, became mighty in war, put foreign armies to flight. Women received back their dead by resurrection; and others were tortured, not accepting their release, in order that they might obtain a better resurrection; and *others experienced mockings and scourgings, yes, also chains and imprisonment. They were stoned, they were sawn in two, they were tempted, they were put to death with the sword; they went about in sheepskins, in goatskins, being destitute, afflicted, ill-treated (men of whom the world was not worthy), wandering in deserts and mountains and caves and holes in the ground* (11:32–39, emphasis added).

Most of the heroes of faith endured incredible trials. If *our* faith is genuine, it will enable us to withstand whatever trials the Lord permits *us* to encounter. If you think your own trials are particularly severe, the writer of Hebrews reminds us, "You have not yet resisted to the point of shedding [your own] blood in your striving against sin" (Heb. 12:4).

By now we know these truths. When testing comes we must apply them. What an encouragement to our faith it is to know that no test can come to us that is more than we can bear!

Meanwhile, we must continually, faithfully mortify our sin. We must pray and ask God to deliver us from evil temptations. We must refuse to heed the lustful hankerings of our own flesh. And we must pursue God's whole purpose in allowing us to be tested—the perfecting of our faith unto endurance and spiritual maturity.

Through it all, we must look to Christ and lean on Him, our merciful and faithful High Priest, who is touched by the feeling of our infirmities, who can sympathize with our weaknesses because He was tempted in all points like we are—yet without sin (Heb. 4:15).

How can we "run with endurance the race that is set before us"? (Heb. 12:1). By "fixing our eyes on Jesus, the author and perfecter of faith, who for the joy set before Him endured the cross, despising the shame, and has sat down at the right hand of the throne of God. For consider Him who has endured such hostility by sinners against Himself, so that you may not grow weary and lose heart" (Heb. 12:2–3).

We live in a culture that is filled with temptation. Our society glorifies sin and despises God. It is certainly not an easy age in which to live. But neither was the first century. Remember, we have not yet resisted to the point of shedding blood.

Someday He may test us in a way that requires us to endure physical harm or death in our striving against sin. If that day comes, we are assured that He will sustain us through it. In the meantime, our trials are strengthening us, drawing us closer to Him, building our endurance, and conforming us to His image. What an encouragement to know that He personally insures that our temptations will not be too great for us! He sustains us so that we will not fall away. And "He Himself has said, 'I will never desert you, nor will I ever forsake you,' so that we confidently say, 'The Lord is my helper, I will not be afraid. What shall man do to me?'" (Heb. 13:5–6).

9

Keeping a Pure Mind

Seeing that sin is so sinful, it is evil even to be a thinking sinner, or a sinner though only in thought. It is too commonly said that thoughts are free. They are indeed free in respect of men, who cannot judge us for them, but God can and will. Many people who seem to be modest and sparing as to evil words and deeds will still make bold with thoughts and, as the saying is, pay it with thinking. Such are speculative, contemplative sinners.

Ralph Venning[1]

No sin is more destructive to the conscience than the sin that takes place in the arena of the mind. Sins of the mind assault the conscience like no other sins, because the conscience is their only deterrent. After all, who but God and the sinner ever knows about them? "Who among men knows the thoughts of a man except the spirit of the man, which is in him?" (1 Cor. 2:11). Many people who will not do evil deeds are nevertheless boldly evil in their thoughts. A man who abstains from fornication for fear of getting caught might convince himself it is all right to indulge in salacious fantasies because he thinks no one else will ever discover such a private sin. The sins he deliberately entertains in his mind may be a thousand times more evil than anything he would ever think of doing before others. Scripture says his guilt is the same as if he acted out his fantasies.

> *No sin is more destructive to the conscience than the sin that takes place in the arena of the mind.*

To indulge in sins of thought, therefore, is to molest the conscience directly. Those whose thoughts are impure *cannot* have pure consciences; the guilt is inherent in the evil thought. When the thoughts are defiled, the conscience immediately is, too. That is why nothing is more characteristic of unbelief than an impure mind combined with a defiled conscience: "To the pure, all things are pure; but to those who are defiled and unbelieving, nothing is pure, but *both their mind and their conscience are defiled*" (Tit. 1:15, emphasis added). In fact, nothing damages the conscience more than the habit of indulging in evil thoughts. Unfortunately, once begun, the practice becomes all too easy. This is a sin that does not have to wait for an opportunity; the mind can sin anytime, anywhere, under any circumstances. So the habit is quickly and easily established.

The Danger of a Sinful Thought Life

By engaging the inner faculties—mind, emotions, desire, memory, and imagination—thought-sins work directly on the soul to bias it toward evil. Sow a thought, reap an act. Sow an act, reap a habit. Sow a habit, reap a character. Sow a character, reap a destiny. Evil thoughts thus underlie and lay the groundwork for all other sins.

By engaging the inner faculties—
mind, emotions, desire, memory, and
imagination—thought-sins work directly
on the soul to bias it toward evil.

No one ever "falls" into adultery. The adulterer's heart is always shaped and prepared by lustful thoughts before the actual deed occurs. Likewise, the heart of the thief is bent by covetousness. And murder is the product of anger and hatred. All sin is first incubated in the mind.

Jesus taught this truth to His disciples: "The things that proceed out of the mouth *come from the heart*, and those defile the man. For *out of the heart* come evil thoughts, murders, adulteries, fornications, thefts, false witness, slanders. *These are the things which defile the man*; but to eat with unwashed hands does not defile the man" (Matt. 15:18–19, emphasis added).

Jesus was teaching that the real point of the Mosaic Law was the moral truth embodied in the external ceremonial requirements. He downplayed the symbolic aspects of washing and abstaining from what is legally declared unclean. Instead He emphasized the moral requirement of the law. Defilement, He suggested, is not primarily a ceremonial or external problem; what is truly defiling in the spiritual sense is the wickedness that emanates from the heart. In the New Testament, "the heart" is the seat of the whole person— mind, imagination, affections, conscience, and will. "Heart" is often used as a synonym for "mind." In these verses, therefore, our Lord was condemning the wickedness of an impure thought life.

Again and again Christ rebuked the Pharisees for their fastidious observance of the external, ceremonial law and their wanton neglect of the law's moral requirements. They were utterly preoccupied with appearing to be righteous. Yet they were willing to tolerate the grossest sins of the heart. They thought no one else could ever discover what was really inside them. But our Lord knew what was in their hearts (Matt. 9:4; 12:25). He compared them to elegant crypts, beautiful on the outside but full of defilement and death on the inside:

> Woe to you, scribes and Pharisees, hypocrites! For you clean the outside of the cup and of the dish, but inside they are full of robbery and self-indulgence. You blind Pharisee, first clean the inside of the cup and of the dish, so that the outside of it may become clean also. Woe to you, scribes and Pharisees, hypocrites! For you are like whitewashed tombs which on the outside appear beautiful, but inside they are full of dead men's bones and all uncleanness. Even so you too outwardly appear righteous to men, but inwardly you are full of hypocrisy and lawlessness (Matt. 23:25–28).

The Pharisees' teaching had so inculcated this notion into people that it was commonly believed evil thoughts were not really sinful, as long as they did not become acts. That is precisely why our Lord targeted sins of the heart in His Sermon on the Mount:

> You have heard that the ancients were told, "You shall not commit murder" and "Whoever commits murder shall be liable to the court." But I say to you that everyone who is angry with his brother shall be guilty before the court. . . . You have heard that it was said, "You shall not commit adultery"; but I say to you, that everyone who looks on a woman to lust for her has committed adultery with her already in his heart (Matt. 5:21–22, 27–28).

What *should* take place in our minds and hearts? What *should* be the deepest secret of our souls? Worship to God:

> When you give alms, do not let your left hand know what your right hand is doing that your alms may be in secret; and your Father who sees in secret will repay you. And when you pray, you are not to be as the hypocrites; for they love to

stand and pray in the synagogues and on the street corners, in order to be seen by men. Truly I say to you, they have their reward in full. But you, when you pray, go into your inner room, and when you have shut your door, pray to your Father who is in secret, and your Father who sees in secret will repay you (Matt. 6:3–6).

To sin in the mind, therefore, is to desecrate the very sanctuary where our highest and best worship should be taking place.

Watch over Your Heart

It is relatively easy to confess and forsake deeds of sin, sins of omission, and unintentional sin. But the sins of our thought life are soul-coloring sins, character-damaging sins. Because they work so directly against the conscience and will, dealing with them honestly and thoroughly is one of the most difficult aspects of mortifying our sin. If we ever want to see real progress in sanctification, however, this is an area where we must attack and destroy our sinful habits with a vengeance. If we allow our thoughts to be influenced by the values of the world, our conscience will surely be dulled. Listening to and entertaining the claims of bad theologies or the self-esteem credo of modern psychology will surely deaden the conscience. Not only thoughts about lust, envy, and the other traditional sins, but also thoughts about the myriad false values and idols of an unbelieving world can be devastating obstacles to a pure mind.

The Old Testament sage wrote, "Watch over your heart with all diligence, for from it flow the springs of life" (Prov. 4:23).

God knows our hearts (Acts 15:8). "God is greater than our heart, and knows all things" (1 Jn. 3:20). David wrote, "Thou dost understand my thought from afar. . . . and art intimately acquainted with all my ways. Even before there is a word on my tongue, behold, O Lord, Thou dost know it all" (Ps. 139:2–4). Why, then, would we ever feel free to indulge in gross sins in our imagination—sins we would never act out before others—when we know that God is the audience to our thoughts? "Would not God find this out? For He knows the secrets of the heart" (Ps. 44:21).

Because they work so directly against the conscience and will, dealing with them honestly and thoroughly is one of the most difficult aspects of mortifying our sin.

Jesus told the Pharisees, "You are those who justify yourselves in the sight of men, but God knows your hearts; for that which is highly esteemed among men is detestable in the sight of God" (Lk. 16:15). Is not what we do in the sight of God infinitely more important than what we do in the sight of others?

Moreover, the thoughts of our heart are the real litmus test of our character: "As he thinks within himself, so he is" (Prov. 23:7). "A worthless person, a wicked man, is the one . . . who with perversity in his heart devises evil continually" (Prov. 6:12–14). Do you want to know who you really are? Take a hard look at your thought life. For "as in water face reflects face, so the heart of man reflects man" (27:19). External behavior is not an accurate mirror of your character; the thoughts of your heart reveal the truth. Only your conscience and God can assess the real truth about you.

Job's "comforters" falsely accused him of an impure thought life. Zophar was sure he understood Job's real problem: "Evil is sweet in his mouth, and he hides it under his tongue, though he desires it and will not let it go, but holds it in his mouth" (Job 20:12–13). The picture he painted of the evil thinker is vividly true-to-life. Evil thoughts are like candy to them. They derive great satisfaction from their imaginary sins. They savor their evil fantasies. They relish them like a choice morsel of sweetness under the tongue. They roll them around in their imagination. They return to the same wicked musings from which they can glean illicit pleasure over and over again. They mull them over like an animal chewing the cud, bringing up their favorite evil thoughts time and time again to re-enact them anew in the mind.

But Zophar misjudged Job. Job had carefully guarded himself against wicked and lustful thoughts: "I have made a covenant with my eyes; how then could I gaze at a virgin?" (Job 31:1). He knew God was audience to his thoughts: "Does He not see my ways, and number all my steps? If I have walked with falsehood, and my foot has hastened after deceit, let Him weigh me with accurate scales, and let God know my integrity" (vv. 4–6). Job denied that his heart had followed his eyes (v. 7). He denied that his heart had been enticed by another woman (v. 9). "That would be a lustful crime . . . an iniquity punishable by judges," he acknowledged (v. 11). To hide iniquity in the bosom, he said, would be to cover one's transgression like Adam (v. 33). The very thought appalled his righteous mind.

Moreover, the thoughts of our heart are the real litmus test of our character.

Clearly, Job was well aware of the danger of sinful thoughts. He had consciously, deliberately set a guard in his heart to avoid any such sin. He even offered special sacrifices to God just in case his children sinned in *their* hearts: "When the days of feasting had completed their cycle, that Job would send and consecrate them, rising up early in the morning and offering burnt offerings according to the number of them all; for Job said, 'Perhaps my sons have sinned and cursed God in their hearts.' *Thus Job did continually*" (1:5, emphasis added). Job's careful safeguarding of his thought life seems to have been the very reason God singled him out for unique blessing. "There is no one like him on the earth," the Lord told Satan. "[He is] a blameless and upright man, fearing God and turning away from evil" (1:8).

How the Mind Sins

Job understood what the Pharisees stubbornly refused to see: that just because you don't act out an evil deed, that doesn't excuse the secret desire. Lust itself is sinful. Greed alone is wicked. Covetousness, anger, pride, concupiscence, envy, discontent, hatred, and all evil thoughts are just as bad as the behavior they produce. To treasure such thoughts in the heart and relish the thought of them is an especially grievous sin against God, because it adds hypocrisy to the original evil thought. There are at least three ways the mind engages in this sin: remembering, scheming, and imagining.

Sins of remembering. One way is to cherish the memories of sins past. To bring back a lurid memory of a bygone sin is to repeat the sin all over again. Can someone who is truly repentant about a sin still harvest pleasure from the memory of that deed? The answer is yes, because of the deceitfulness of our own hearts and the sinful tendencies of our flesh.

Not long ago I baptized a man who was a former homosexual transformed by Christ. His life was changed. His circle of friends was different. And he had removed himself as much as possible from a lifestyle that would hold any temptation to return to his former sins. But he admitted to me that the most difficult problem he faced was that his own mind was filled with memories that became temptations to him every time he thought of them. He had entertained himself with many vile kinds of sexual relationships and activities, and those memories were so embedded in his brain that he would never forget them. Even though he was transformed as a Christian, Satan would bring back the memory of his former life. If he allowed himself to dwell on such thoughts, he would discover that his flesh was trying to draw him back into the sin. All his senses were stirred up easily by the memories, and the memories could be recalled unexpectedly by his senses. Some sound or smell or sight would provoke a memory in his mind, and he would find himself battling temptation.

The truth is, we all know what that is like. Sin has a way of impressing itself on our memories with vivid sensations we cannot shake off. As adults we can still remember the sins of our youth as if they occurred only yesterday. Perhaps it was just such thoughts that prompted David to pray, "Do not remember the sins of my youth or my transgressions" (Ps. 25:7). David himself remembered them all too graphically.

Don't think this problem is unique to sexual sins. Some people like to rehearse memories of the time they got angry and poured out vengeance on someone. Some enjoy thoughts of the time they lied and got away with it. All kinds of tempting memories lodge themselves in us and become new sins every time we remember them with pleasure.

Satan will take all the garbage out of your past and try to drag it back through your mind so that you relive it.

Savoring memories of one's past sin is a particularly heinous form of sin. In Ezekiel 23, the Lord condemned Israel by comparing the nation to a harlot named Oholibah. This was His charge against her: "She multiplied her harlotries, remembering the days of her youth, when she played the harlot in the land of Egypt" (v. 19).

And the spiritual devastation this practice leaves in its wake is tremendous. It hardens the conscience. It corrupts the character. It can even destroy relationships. I have talked to young couples who lived a life of fornication before they came to Christ. They become Christians and get married. Then they find it very difficult to be singly devoted to each other because they struggle with constant thoughts about all the fornication and sinful relationships they indulged in before they knew the Lord.

Satan will take all the garbage out of your past and try to drag it back through your mind so that you relive it. That is precisely why pornography is so spiritually destructive. Once you implant a lurid image in your thoughts, you cannot take it away. But it isn't only hard-core pornography that has this effect. Many of the films and television programs produced for the mass market routinely include images, themes, and story lines that tempt people to sinful thought patterns. Once the suggestive pictures and thoughts are planted in the mind, they reside there as potential temptations anytime we think of them. We would all do well to emulate Job's example, and refuse to expose our eyes to anything that might provoke such thoughts.

Sins of scheming. A second way the mind can sin is by plotting sins of the future. Scripture is full of strong condemnations of those whose minds are engaged in this kind of activity:

- "Transgression speaks to the ungodly within his heart; there is no fear of God before his eyes. For it flatters him in his own eyes, concerning the discovery of his iniquity and the hatred of it. The words of his mouth are wickedness and deceit; he has ceased to be wise and to do good. He plans wickedness upon his bed; He sets himself on a path that is not good; He does not despise evil" (Ps. 36:1–4).

- "Hide me from the secret counsel of evildoers, from the tumult of those who do iniquity, who have sharpened their tongue like a sword. They aimed bitter speech as their arrow, to shoot from concealment at the blameless; suddenly they shoot at him, and do not fear. They hold fast to themselves an evil purpose; they talk of laying snares secretly; they say, 'Who can see them?' They devise injustices, saying, 'We are ready with a well-conceived plot'; for the inward thought and the heart of a man are deep. But God will shoot at them with an arrow; suddenly they will be wounded" (Ps. 64:2–7).

- "A good man will obtain favor from the Lord, But He will condemn a man who devises evil" (Prov. 12:2).

- "Deceit is in the heart of those who devise evil" (Prov. 12:20).

- "Will they not go astray who devise evil? But kindness and truth will be to those who devise good" (Prov. 14:22).

- "Evil plans are an abomination to the Lord, But pleasant words are pure" (Prov. 15:26).

- "The Lord hates . . . a heart that devises wicked plans (Prov. 6:16–18).

- Do not be envious of evil men, nor desire to be with them; for their minds devise violence, and their lips talk of trouble" (Prov. 24:1–2).

- "He who plans to do evil, men will call him a schemer. The devising of folly is sin, and the scoffer is an abomination to men" (Prov. 24:8–9).

- For a fool speaks nonsense, and his heart inclines toward wickedness, to practice ungodliness and to speak error against the Lord, to keep the hungry person unsatisfied and to withhold drink from the thirsty. As for a rogue, his weapons are evil; he devises wicked schemes to destroy the afflicted with slander, even though the needy one speaks what is right. But the noble man devises noble plans; and by noble plans he stands (Isa. 32:6–8).

Some people love to dream of sins they will commit, evil they long to do, and sinister plots they want to hatch. Their thoughts vent their anger, hatred, lust, greed, envy, pride, and every evil desire. Their minds and hearts are full of wickedness, and God condemns them for it.

But even Christians can fall into this habit if they are not careful. This is what Paul was warning against when he wrote, "Put on the Lord Jesus Christ, and make no provision for the flesh in regard to its lusts" (Rom. 13:14). We are not to make plans that will cater to our fleshly desires. We are not to devise evil plans in our minds.

Sins of imagining. A third kind of sin that takes place in the mind is the purely imaginary sin. This is what Jesus referred to when he said, "Everyone who looks on a woman to lust for her has committed adultery with her already in his heart" (Matt. 5:28). You may have no intention of ever performing the deed, but Jesus says if you even imagine it, you are guilty.

That sets the standard extremely high—but this is the level of purity we must maintain if we are to have a clear conscience. Every imagined sin offends the healthy conscience. Those who tolerate this kind of sin in their hearts as a habit give irrefutable evidence of a defiled and hardened conscience. It is here that our self-examination becomes most convicting. But it is here that we must train our consciences to be most sensitive.

People fantasize about sins they long to commit. They imagine what it would be like to indulge their favorite lusts, or wreak revenge on a despised enemy, or hurt someone they loathe. They act out a robbery in their minds, or fantasize about an illicit relationship, or visualize killing someone.

But many imaginary sins are not so heinous. People dream covetous thoughts about winning the lottery. They imagine themselves with great power, wealth, or prestige. They daydream about what it would be like to be married to someone else, or muse about a luxury vacation, or indulge their gluttony in an imaginary binge. Modern society is filled with temptations to those kinds of sins. The entire advertizing industry thrives on appealing to such lusts. And most of the entertainment industry is focused on creating those kinds of images. The result is that literally millions of people live in a fantasy world of sin.

Are such sins really that disastrous? Yes, they defile us (Matt. 15:18–20). They are an abomination to God: "The thought of foolishness is sin" (Prov. 24:9, KJV). Any thought that is not God-honoring, Christ-exalting, and representative of full obedience to the Word of God is sin. Covetousness, the basis of most of our evil fantasies, is expressly forbidden by the Tenth Commandment.

We dare not think of these thought-sins as mere peccadillos. They open the door to actual deeds of sin. James 1:15 says, "When lust [evil desire] has conceived, it gives birth to sin." Puritan Ralph Venning wrote in 1669:

> Evil deeds are the offspring and children of evil thoughts, the branches and fruit which grow out of this root. Thoughts are the first-born of the soul; words and actions are only younger brothers. They are the oil that feeds and maintains the wick, which would otherwise go out; life-sins receive their juice and nourishment from thought-sins. St. James speaks as if our thoughts were the belly and womb where sin is conceived (Jas. 1:15). . . . As Job [cursed] the day and place of [his] birth, the womb that bore [him]; so should you curse sin even in the very womb that bore it, laying the axe to the root of this tree.
>
> The wickedness of men's lives is charged upon their thoughts, that it has its root and rise there: murders, adulteries, etc., all come out of the heart, as out of the belly of a Trojan horse (Gen. 6:5; Mat. 12:35; 15:19). One would wonder (as we do at some birds, where they nest all winter) to see so many flocks and herds of wickedness. One would wonder from what corner of the world they come. Why, they all come out of the heart, the rendezvous of wickedness, the inn where lodge all the thieves and travelling lusts that are in the world and that do so much mischief in it. All the unclean streams flow from this unclean fountain, this ocean and sea of sin.[2]

That is why David cried out for God to help him at the very front line of defense: "Create in me a clean heart, O God" (Ps. 51:10). It was an appeal for a sound conscience arising from a pure mind.

Discerning the Thoughts and Intents of the Heart

Do you realize that the difference between a sincere, Spirit-controlled, devoted, godly, obedient Christian and a defeated, weak, struggling Christian is what takes place in the mind? They may be attending the same church, active in the same ministries, and externally doing the same things, but one is defeated and the other lives a spiritually fruitful life. The difference is the thought life.

Do you realize that the difference between a sincere, Spirit-controlled, devoted, godly, obedient Christian and a defeated, weak, struggling Christian is what takes place in the mind?

One day the difference will be made manifest. Paul told the Corinthians that when the Lord comes, He "will both bring to light the things hidden in the darkness and disclose the motives of men's hearts" (1 Cor. 4:5). Jesus said something similar: "Nothing is hidden that shall not become evident, nor anything secret that shall not be known and come to light" (Lk. 8:17). And, "Beware of the leaven of the Pharisees, which is hypocrisy. But there is nothing covered up that will not be revealed, and hidden that will not be known" (Lk. 12:1–2).

I urge you to look deeply into the mirror of God's Word (Jas. 1:23–24), which is a powerful "discerner of the thoughts and intents of the heart" (Heb. 4:12, KJV). As Jeremiah counseled Israel, "Wash your heart from evil, O Jerusalem, that you may be saved. How long will your wicked thoughts lodge within you?" (Jer. 4:14). And "let us cleanse ourselves from all defilement of flesh and spirit, perfecting holiness in the fear of God" (2 Cor. 7:1).

Taking Every Thought Captive to Obedience

How *can* we deal with the problem of evil thoughts? The process is like mortifying any other sin; it involves taking the following steps:

First confess and forsake the sin. "Let the wicked forsake his way, *and the unrighteous man his thoughts*; and let him return to the Lord, and He will have compassion on him; and to our God, for He will abundantly pardon" (Isa. 55:7, emphasis added). If your thought life harbors sins of immorality, sins of anger toward someone, sins of vengeance, sins of bitterness, sins of covetousness, or whatever—confess them to God. Repent and ask forgiveness. If we confess, He is faithful and just to forgive and keep on cleansing (1 Jn. 1:9).

Refuse to entertain those thoughts. Purpose to abandon your wrong thought patterns immediately and begin to build new, righteous habits. If you find yourself slipping into old ways of thinking, confess your sin and refuse once again to give place to evil thoughts. Consciously direct your mind to fix itself on pure things: "Whatever is true, whatever is honorable, whatever is right, whatever is pure, whatever is lovely, whatever is of good repute, if there is any excellence and if anything worthy of praise, let your mind dwell on these things" (Phil. 4:8). In other words, reprogram your mind with truth and righteousness.

Feed on the Word of God. "Thy word I have treasured in my heart, that I may not sin against Thee" (Ps. 119:11). The Word insulates the mind. It strengthens the heart. It occupies the soul and fortifies it against evil thoughts. Only as we use the sword of the Spirit skillfully can we mortify our fleshly imaginations (Eph. 6:17).

Avoid evil attractions. Don't expose yourself to activities, images, or conversation that provoke evil thoughts. Like Job, make a covenant with your eyes (Job 31:1)—or with your ears, or with whatever sensations lead you into evil thoughts. Refuse to feed any tendencies that draw your imagination into wickedness. This is what Jesus meant figuratively when He said, "If your right eye makes you stumble, tear it out, and throw it from you; for it is better for you that one of the parts of your body perish, than for your whole body to be thrown into hell. And if your right hand makes you stumble, cut it off, and throw it from you; for it is better for you that one of the parts of your body perish, than for your whole body to go into hell" (Matt. 5:29–30).

Cultivate the love of God. David said in Psalm 119:97, "O how I love Thy law! It is my meditation all the day." And then four verses later he said, "I have restrained my feet from every evil way." If we set our minds on things above, things on the earth will cease to hold the same fascination for us (Col. 3:2). "Where your treasure is, there will your heart be also" (Matt. 6:21)—and where your affections are set, your thoughts will be there as well.

David ended Psalm 19, his great paean to the sufficiency of Scripture, with these words:

> Who can discern his errors? Acquit me of hidden faults. Also keep back Thy servant from presumptuous sins; let them not rule over me; then I shall be blameless, and I shall be acquitted of great transgression. Let the words of my mouth and the meditation of my heart be acceptable in Thy sight, O Lord, my rock and my Redeemer (vv. 12–14).

That is the state of mind of every truly godly person. It is also the goal of biblical instruction: "love from a pure heart and a good conscience and a sincere faith" (1 Tim. 1:5).

How's *your* thought life?

10

Holding to the Mystery of Faith with a Clear Conscience

It is a very evil choice for any soul under heaven to choose the least sin rather than the greatest affliction. Better be under the greatest affliction than be under the guilt or power of any sin. . . . There is more evil in sin than in outward trouble in the world; more evil in sin than in all the miseries and torments of hell itself.

Jeremiah Burroughs[1]

One of the great tragedies of contemporary culture is that we have lost any concept of the exceeding sinfulness of sin. Puritan Jeremiah Burroughs wrote an entire book on the subject, titled, *The Evil of Evils*. Burroughs's thesis was that it is better to choose the sufferings of affliction than sin. The smallest sin, he pointed out, is more evil than the greatest affliction. Describing the horrors of hell, he suggested that one act of sin contains more evil than all the sufferings of eternal doom:

> Suppose that God should bring any of you to the brink of that bottomless gulf and open it to you, and there you should see those damned creatures sweltering under the wrath of the infinite God, and there you should hear the dreadful and hideous cries and shrieks of those who are under such soul-amazing and soul-sinking torments through the wrath of the Almighty. Yet, I say, there is more evil in one sinful thought than there is in all these everlasting burnings. . . . The truth is, that if it should come into competition whether we would endure all the torments that there are in hell to all eternity rather than to commit one sin, I say, if our spirits were as they should be, we would rather be willing to endure all these torments than commit the least sin.[2]

Sin, Burroughs pointed out, is contrary to the very character of God. Sin is the evil of all evils—the source from which emanates every affliction, pain, suffering, disease, and human misery. Unlike suffering, sin brings a curse from God. No one is condemned for affliction, but all are condemned for sin. Sin makes the sinner evil; affliction cannot—and so on. Burroughs argues eloquently and convincingly through sixty-seven chapters, examining the vileness of sin and showing it for what it is. His book is a masterpiece of Puritan literature, showing the depth and richness of the English Reformers' biblical mastery.

In stark contrast, today's church seems utterly to lack any notion of the profound evil of sin. We grieve over calamities. We are troubled by our miseries. The trials of life distress us. But are we equally disturbed by our sin? Do *we* believe that the least sin contains more evil than the least affliction? Few contemporary Christians, it seems, have ever entertained the thought that sin is *that* evil.

Sin and Shame

In fact, modern evangelicalism seems often to teach precisely the opposite. Today we are more concerned that people *feel* good than that they *do* good. Affliction, we believe, is to be avoided at all costs. Sin, on the other hand, is thought to be easily forgivable. Therefore to offend God is viewed as the lesser of evils when the other choice is to endure some kind of personal pain or affliction. We see *shame* as a worse evil than the *sin* that causes it. This is precisely the mentality behind the massive self-esteem movement.

Today's church seems utterly to lack any notion of the profound evil of sin.

At the opposite end of the spectrum from Burroughs's work is another book I recently read. This one was written by a modern seminary professor who is very well known for his popular books on human relationships, psychology, religion, and related topics. His latest book deals with the subject of human shame. He begins by recounting his saintly mother's death. As she lay dying she told him, "I'm so glad that the Lord forgives me all of my sins; I've been a great sinner, you know."

"Great sinner?" he writes incredously. "As far back as I can remember, she was on her knees scrubbing people's kitchen floors most days, up to her neck in the frets of five fussing children every evening, and, when late night fell, there she was on her knees again . . . asking the Lord for strength to do it again for one more day."[3]

His assessment was that his mother was inflicted with "a classic case of unhealthy shame." He writes, "It saddens me still that such a triumph of a woman should have to die feeling like a wretch. Her shame was totally out of touch with her reality. She did not deserve to be stuck with so much shame."[4]

Yet the professor acknowledges that in both her living and her dying, his mother was "wondrously serene. She was given a grace to turn her shame into peace with a life tougher than she deserved."[5]

Evidently her statements about being a "great sinner" reflected nothing but the godly response of a chastened and transformed heart. Her lament was only an echo of what we all should feel when we realize the nature and the profound depth of our sinfulness (Rom. 7:24). Why this man concluded his mother's shame was "unhealthy" and undeserved is not entirely clear.

After all, didn't even the apostle Paul describe himself as foremost of all sinners (1 Tim. 1:15)? Peter fell on his face before Christ and said, "Depart from me, for I am a sinful man, O Lord" (Lk. 5:8). Isaiah, the most godly man in all Israel, said, "Woe is me, for I am ruined! Because I am a man of unclean lips, and I live among a people of unclean lips" (Isa. 6:5). The greatest saints of history have all felt the same deep sense of shame.

But this professor suggests that we really are not so vile after all. In fact, he believes we are *worthy* of divine grace: "If grace heals all our shame, it must be a grace that tells us we are worthy to have it. We need, I believe, to recognize that we are accepted not only in spite of our undeserving but because of our worth."[6] He distinguishes between "deserving" and "worthy" like this: "If I deserve some good that comes my way, it is because I *did* something to earn it. If I am worthy, it is because I *am* somebody of enormous value."[7]

But does Scripture portray sinful humanity as inherently "worthy" of God's favor? Not at all. Nowhere in Scripture are we told we are "accepted . . . because of our worth." Grace is *grace* precisely because it comes to people who are utterly ineligible for any favor from God: "While we were still *helpless* . . . Christ died for the ungodly. . . . While we were yet *sinners*, Christ died for us. . . . While we were *enemies*, we were reconciled to God through the death of His Son" (Rom. 5:6, 8, 10, emphasis added). Paul's very point in those verses is to suggest the supreme marvel of God's grace—that it should be extended to helpless, sinful, undeserving, even loathsome, adversaries.

Look, for example, at Daniel's prayer of repentance: "Righteousness belongs to Thee, O Lord, but to us *open shame*, as it is this day—to the men of Judah, the inhabitants of Jerusalem, and all Israel, those who are nearby and those who are far away in all the countries to which Thou hast driven them, because of their unfaithful deeds which they have committed against Thee. *Open shame belongs to us, O Lord, to our kings, our princes, and our fathers, because we have sinned against Thee*" (Dan. 9:7–8, emphasis added). Daniel would hardly have been an advocate of self-esteem theology!

The reasons for God's grace to sinners are a mystery. We certainly are never told that God loves us because we are worthy.

The Bible simply does not speak of sinners as intrinsically worthy of God's grace. The Prodigal Son, Jesus' illustration of a repentant sinner, admitted his unworthiness (Lk. 15:21). Even John the Baptist—who by Jesus' own testimony was the greatest prophet who ever lived (Matt. 11:11)—said he was *unworthy* to carry the shoes of the Savior (3:11). "What is man, that Thou dost take thought of him? And the son of man, that Thou dost care for him?" (Ps. 8:4). The reasons for God's grace to sinners are a mystery. We certainly are never told that God loves us because we are worthy. That notion is simply an echo of worldly self-esteem doctrine.

The focus of Scripture is entirely on *God's* worth, *His* majesty, *His* glory, *His* holiness, and *His* grace and mercy. Our worth as Christians is a *product* of God's grace, certainly not the *reason* for it. If people were inherently worthy of salvation, God would be unrighteous not to save everyone.

As we noted in chapter 4, Adam's sin plunged the whole human race into sin, so we are born guilty. Shame is not an undeserved emotion, but an honest reflection of who we are. Human beings have felt shame ever since that first sin (cf. Gen. 2:25; 3:10). Sometimes our shame may be misplaced, irrational, or even emotionally unbalanced—but shame itself is certainly not undeserved. No one is "too good" to feel he or she is a miserable sinner. That is, after all, precisely what we are.

This doctrine is in serious decline these days, to the detriment of the church. We change the words of great hymns so that they don't refer to us as "wretches" or "worms." We buy into the self-esteem lie. We want to minimize our sin, eliminate our sense of shame, boost our ego, and feel good about ourselves. We want, in other words, all those things which deaden the conscience. We abhor shame, however justified. We abhor repentance because it is too hard. We avoid guilt. We want the easy street.

Sin and Psychology

The rush to embrace psychology has done much to contribute to these trends. Psychology itself is hostile to the biblical doctrine of sin, and the move to marry Scripture with psychotherapy has certainly not changed this. One well-known and widely used handbook of psychology for pastoral counselors included the following under the heading "original sin." Though it is rather lengthy I include the entire section entitled "Original Sin," because it shows how psychology can corrupt the biblical doctrine of sin:

No reputable psychologist would hold the ancient theological and anthropological theory that sin is passed on from generation to generation. The term "sin" is now reserved for conscious and deliberate acts of a person against accepted norms or mores of his society and the ideals associated with a moral God. Sin is thus a *responsible* misdemeanor. Original sin has, however, an element of psychological validity, viz., the fact that weaknesses of personality ingredients have a history beyond the pale of conscious responsibility.

Our inherited drives, for example, are our equipment. As such they are amoral. They function for biological purposes. When in conflict with standards of conduct they make for trouble and become easy predispositions to (deliberate) sin. Add to this the disorders provoked by early environment—beyond the will of the individual—and there is the picture of a handicap on the kind of social adjustment called "moral."

If it is true that all of us have genetically come out of the forest primeval with a long standing equipment to employ in the hard struggle for survival in a world not too easy (temperature changes, wild animals, floods, disease germs, etc.) and in the course of social development have attained a kind of set of interpersonal social relationships which call for softer dealings with others, then it is easy to see how difficult it is to adjust elemental drives useful for one kind of hardfisted world to another which demands their curbing. Biologically, elemental drives have a way of persisting in spite of an environment calling for their softening. "Original sin" is an unhappy term for the elemental failings of man to live as he ought to live in a social order where virtues of altruism are supposed to eliminate selfishness. But there is this truth in "original sin," viz., that man's long history has not been erased in spite of ideals emphasized in developing society. So long as there is this disparity (for which the individual person is not responsible) there is more than a myth in the doctrine that we are not easily made into saints.[8]

Notice how this passage absolves people from responsibility for all inherited drives, all evil desires, all sinful tendencies, all the "elemental failings of man"—and it even excuses us from original sin itself! The only things deemed sin are "conscious and deliberate acts of a person against accepted norms or mores of his society and the ideals associated with a moral God." How far that is from the biblical definition! But does anyone notice? Does anyone still know?

Sin and the Church

Martyn Lloyd-Jones suggested years ago that the doctrine of sin was fast disappearing from evangelical teaching and preaching. He said,

When we are dealing with the unconverted, we tend to say: "Ah, you need not worry about sin now, that will come later. All you need to do is to come to Christ, to give yourself to Christ. Do not worry your head about sin—of course you cannot understand that now. Do not worry either whether or not you have got a sense of sin or deep conviction, or whether you know these things. All you need to do is to come to Christ, to give yourself to Christ, and then you will be happy."

Then when we are dealing with those who have so come, our tendency, again, is to say to them, "Of course, you must not look at yourself, you must look to Christ. You must not be for ever analysing yourself. That is wrong, that is what you did before you were converted. You were thinking in terms of yourself and of what you had got to do. The only thing you must do is to keep looking to Christ and away from yourself." We imagine, therefore, that all that is needed by Christians is a certain amount of comfort and encouragement, of preaching about the love of God and about his general providence and perhaps a certain amount of moral and ethical exhortation. And so, you see, the doctrine of sin is, as it were, crowded out. We fail to emphasise it both before and after conversion, and the result is that we hear very little about it.[9]

Martyn Lloyd-Jones suggested years ago that the doctrine of sin was fast disappearing from evangelical teaching and preaching.

An entire generation of believers is now virtually ignorant about sin. When they hear *any* mention of sin, they think it is harsh, unloving, ungracious. The trends toward user-friendly churches and seeker-sensitive ministry have only heightened this problem.[10]

Sin and the Christian

We desperately need to recover a holy hatred of sin. We need to do this corporately as a church, but we also need to do it individually as believers. Sin is surely not a pleasant subject to study or preach on, but it is necessary. Here in the midst of an increasingly worldly church it is *critical*. We must see our sin for what it is. An inadequate view of one's own sinfulness is spiritually debilitating. Those who don't see themselves as despicably sinful will never take the necessary steps to lay sin aside.

We desperately need to recover a holy hatred of sin.

God has clearly indicted us for our own sin and assigned full responsibility to each individual sinner. The proof of that is the biblical doctrine of hell—the awful reality that each damned and unforgiven sinner will pay forever in hell the terrible price for his or her own sins. In no way can this guilt be escaped by blaming others. Clearly, God does not see us as a race of victims! If He saw us as victims, He would punish someone else. But every condemned sinner will pay the full price in eternal torment for his or her own deeds—because each one is fully responsible.

No one's conscience will be silent then. It will turn on the sinner with a fury, reminding him that he alone is responsible for the agonies he will suffer eternally. John Blanchard writes,

> Things will be very different in hell [for those who have numbed their consciences here on earth] . . . Their consciences will be their worst tormentors. Nor will there be any way in which they can be stifled or silenced. As John Flavel wrote in the seventeenth century, "Conscience, which should have been the sinner's curb here on earth, becomes the whip that must lash his soul in hell. Neither is there any faculty or power belonging to the soul of man so fit and able to do it as his own conscience. That which was the seat and centre of all guilt, now becomes the seat and centre of all torments."
>
> Conscience will make the sinner acutely aware that he deliberately, freely and gladly chose the lifestyle that led him to hell, that he is there because of his willfulness and obstinacy. In addition, it will force him to admit the truth of every charge it brings, and the justice of every pain he suffers, so that, in Flavel's words, "In all this misery, there is not one drop of injury or wrong." As if this were not horrifying enough, the castigation will be uninterrupted; the sinner will have "No rest day or night" (Rev. 14:11). As never before, he will discover the truth of God's words that "There is no peace . . . for the wicked" (Isa. 48:22).[11]

If you find your conscience vanishing, you must realize the seriousness of your condition and repent, beseech God for a clear, functioning conscience, and set yourself to the task of laying aside sin in your own life.

I want to leave you with a very practical list of principles that will assist you in that task. Many of these simply review and restate issues that we have seen throughout this book, but they are essential nevertheless. And perhaps this final checklist will give you a place to start as you seek to recover a healthy conscience:

Don't underestimate the seriousness of your sin. Surely this is the primary reason most people tolerate sin in their lives. If they saw their sin as God sees it, they could not continue indifferently in ways of known sin. Sin violates God's holiness, it brings His discipline, it destroys our joy, and it causes death. If we really understood, as Jeremiah Burroughs said, that the smallest sin contains more evil than all the torments of hell, we could not remain unconcerned about mortifying our sins. God gave the law precisely so that the exceeding sinfulness of sin would be evident (Rom. 7:13).

Purpose in your heart not to sin. Make a solemn vow to oppose all sin in your life. The psalmist did that: "I have sworn, and I will confirm it, that I will keep Thy righteous ordinances" (Ps. 119:106). Unless you have that kind of determination in your life, you will find you are easily entangled by sin. In fact, it is that kind of bold affirmation and earnest heart that is at the root of all holy living. Until you make that kind of conscious commitment to the Lord, you're going to battle the same things over and over—and be defeated.

That same psalm contains this wonderful verse: "I shall run the way of Thy commandments, for Thou wilt enlarge my heart" (v. 32). Distance runners' hearts are usually larger than average. The many miles running in training actually conditions the heart to enable it to pump blood more efficiently during long periods of exercise. David was saying that God would equip him spiritually with a heart that fit him to run the race he had committed himself to. In other words, God will honor your commitment to lay aside sin.

Be suspicious of your own spirituality. Paul said, "Let him who thinks he stands take heed lest he fall" (1 Cor. 10:12). "The heart is more deceitful than all else and is desperately sick; who can understand it?" (Jer. 17:9). The seducing subtlety of our own heart will sometimes ensnare us at the very moments of our greatest spiritual victories. We can all be deceived quite easily; except for the grace of God, we would fall into any and every sin. Learn to seek that grace and never become confident in your own flesh (Phil. 3:3).

We can all be deceived quite easily;
except for the grace of God,
we would fall into any and every sin.

Resist the first hint of evil desire. "When lust has conceived, it gives birth to sin; and when sin is accomplished, it brings forth death" (Jas. 1:15). The time to stop sin is at conception, not after it has been born and gets a life of its own. At the first suggestion of lust, exterminate the thought before it hatches and begins to bring forth its own diabolical offspring.

Meditate on the Word. "The mouth of the righteous utters wisdom, and his tongue speaks justice. *The law of his God is in his heart; his steps do not slip*" (Ps. 37:30, emphasis added). When the heart is controlled by the Word, the steps are sure and steady. The Word of God fills the mind and controls the thinking, and that strengthens the soul against temptation. Scripture acts as a powerful restraint in the heart given over to its truth.

Be instantly repentant over your lapses. When Peter sinned his great sin, denying Christ three times, Scripture says, "He went out and wept bitterly" (Matt. 26:75). We shudder at his sin, but we must admire him for the immediacy of his remorse. Unconfessed sin contaminates and hardens the conscience. "If we confess our sins, He is faithful and righteous to forgive us our sins and to cleanse us from all unrighteousness" (1 Jn. 1:9). And when you confess your sin, name it. Let your ear hear the specific sin you are repenting for. That's one way to develop a high degree of accountability to God and keep from falling into the same sins over and over again. If you hold back from naming your sin, it may be that you secretly want to do that same sin again.

Continually watch and pray. After all the armor of Ephesians 6 is itemized, Paul writes, "With all prayer and petition pray at all times in the Spirit, and with this in view, be on the alert" (Eph. 6:18). He told the Colossian believers, "Devote yourselves to prayer, keeping alert in it" (Col. 4:2). Jesus Himself said, "Keep watching and praying, that you may not enter into temptation; the spirit is willing, but the flesh is weak" (Matt. 26:41).

Be part of a church with other believers who hold you account-able. We all struggle with the same temptations (1 Cor. 10:13). That is why Paul told the Galatians, "Bear one another's burdens, and thus fulfill the law of Christ" (Gal. 6:2). We need each other. Can we keep each other from sinning? Not always. But we can encourage one another (Heb. 3:13; 1 Thess. 5:11). We can stimulate one another to love and good works (Heb. 10:24–25). And "even if a man is caught in any trespass, you who are spiritual, restore such a one in a spirit of gentleness; each one looking to yourself, lest you too be tempted" (Gal. 6:1).

This is a very important reason the church was instituted. We are to hold one another accountable, lovingly pursue those who sin (Matt. 18:15–17), love one another, and serve one another. All of this works corporately to help us as individuals mortify our sin.

Sin and God

Remember that God hates sin. Remember that it was sin that put His beloved Son on the cross. Remember that His eyes are too pure to approve evil (Hab. 1:13). And remember that His own perfect holiness is the standard He calls us to.

Will we reach that goal? Not in this lifetime, but He guarantees that we *will* reach it. "For whom He foreknew, He also predestined to become conformed to the image of His Son" (Rom. 8:29). We already "are being transformed into the same image from glory to glory, just as from the Lord, the Spirit" (2 Cor. 3:18). And "we know that, when He appears, we shall be like Him, because we shall see Him just as He is" (1 Jn. 3:2). "Whom He predestined, these He also called; and whom He called, these He also justified; and whom He justified, these He also glorified" (Rom. 8:30).

Meanwhile, we dare not become discouraged and give up the fight. We dare not yield an inch to sin and temptation. And above all, we must keep our conscience pure and undefiled.

"And the work of righteousness will be peace, and the service of righteousness, quietness and confidence forever" (Isa. 32:17).

Appendix 1

Gaining Victory over Sin—A Closer Look at Romans 6

We must never think that grace, wonderful as it is, either permits or encourages us to go on sinning. . . . "Shall we go on sinning so that grace may increase?" asked Paul. He answered, "By no means! We died to sin; how can we live in it any longer?" (Rom. 6:1–2).

This is why the ending of the story of Jesus and the woman trapped in adultery is so important, though it is often overlooked. [Having forgiven her, Jesus] added, "Go now and leave your life of sin." This always follows upon forgiveness. . . . If we are saved, we must stop sinning.

At the same time, we can be grateful that Jesus spoke as he did. For we notice that he did not say, "Leave your life of sin, and I will not condemn you." If he had said that, what hope for us could there be? Our problem is precisely that we do sin. There could be no forgiveness if forgiveness was based upon our ceasing to sin. Instead of that, Jesus actually spoke in the reverse order. First, he granted forgiveness freely, without any conceivable link to our performance. Forgiveness is granted only on the merit of his atoning death. But then, having forgiven us freely, Jesus tells us with equal force to stop sinning.

James M. Boice[1]

Lazarus had been dead four days when the Lord arrived at his grave. Although Jesus loved Lazarus and his family intensely, He had purposely delayed coming so that He might exhibit God's glory through an unprecedented miracle that would demonstrate His power over death. Mary and Martha, sisters of Lazarus, knew that if Jesus had come in time He could have healed Lazarus and kept him from dying (Jn. 11:21, 32). Jesus waited, however, because He wanted them to understand and believe the full scope of His power.

He went to Lazarus' tomb, a cave with a rock over the opening, and instructed the mourners to remove the stone. Martha, assuming the worst, warned Him, "Lord, by this time he stinketh: for he hath been dead four days" (Jn. 11:39, KJV).

Jesus nevertheless cried out with a loud voice, "Lazarus, come forth" (v. 43).

The sight that greeted the bewildered mourners might have been humorous if it were not so poignant. Lazarus, "bound hand and foot with wrappings; and his face . . . wrapped around with a cloth," waddled to the cave opening. There he stood, wrapped like a mummy, but alive!

"Unbind him, and let him go," Jesus commanded them (v. 44). As long as the grave clothes enshrouded Lazarus, the aura of death clung to him and hindered him from the full expression of his new life.

The story of Lazarus offers a particularly graphic illustration of our predicament as believers. We have been raised to walk in newness of life (Rom. 6:4). We "joyfully concur with the law of God in the inner man" (Rom. 7:22). Yet we cannot do what we desire (Gal. 5:17). "The wishing is present in [us], but the doing of the good is not" (Rom. 7:18). We are held prisoner by the remnants of the very fallenness from which we have been redeemed (7:22). It is as if we were still bound in our grave clothes. This appendix compares our situation and that of Lazarus in casting off the binding remnants of sin. It offers the apostle Paul's instructions (in Romans 6) for liberation, which involve knowing, reckoning, yielding, obeying, and serving.

We Being Raised Yet Stink

There is, however, an important difference between our situation and the raising of Lazarus. His mummy suit came off immediately. It was merely a linen shroud. Fortunately, the corruption of death—such as the awful stench Martha feared—did not follow Lazarus forth from the grave.

Our predicament, however, cannot be resolved so quickly. It is not just a linen shroud that fastens itself to us, but a full-fledged carcass—Paul calls it "the body of this death" (Rom. 7:24). It is the fleshly sin-principle that casts its pall over our glorious new lives throughout our earthly pilgrimage. It befouls our spiritual atmosphere, surrounding us with the fetid stink of sin. It no longer can dominate us like a ruthless tyrant, but it will plague us with temptation, torment, and grief until we are finally glorified.

That is precisely why we "groan within ourselves, waiting eagerly for our adoption as sons, the redemption of our body" (Rom. 8:23).

While we wait for that final glorious deliverance from sin's presence, we must not live as we did when sin was lord over us. Sin's mastery is broken. Our old self is crucified, so that "we should no longer be slaves to sin" (Rom. 6:6).

> *While we wait for that final glorious
> deliverance from sin's presence,
> we must not live as we did
> when sin was lord over us.*

Don't be confused by the language of that verse. "Should" there does not indicate that emancipation from sin's absolute control is a yet-future *possibility*. Paul is declaring that because our old self is dead, freedom from sin is already an accomplished *reality*. A few verses later, he makes it very clear that this is the present state of every true believer: "Thanks be to God that though you were slaves of sin, you became obedient from the heart to that form of teaching to which you were committed, *having been freed from sin, you became slaves of righteousness*" (Rom. 6:17–18; emphasis added). He reiterates the point once more in verse 22: "Now *having been freed from sin* and enslaved to God, you derive your benefit, resulting in sanctification, and the outcome, eternal life" (emphasis added). "He who has died"—that is, he who is joined with Christ in His death—"is freed from sin" (v. 7). The liberation he is describing is a *fait accompli.*

But as we have seen repeatedly, he is not suggesting that Christians are sinless—or even that they can be. Nor is he suggesting that sin is no longer the problem in Christians' lives. Paul is simply teaching that all believers are released from sin's absolute domination.

We can experience that liberation practically. We can live lives that reflect our new natures. We can shed ourselves of fleshly tendencies by mortifying the deeds of the flesh. Let's look a little more closely at Romans 6 as a way of summarizing and reviewing the practical means by which we can attack and mortify the remnants of sin in our lives.

Know

Fundamental to everything is sound knowledge. "Do you not *know* . . . ?" Paul asks at the outset of the whole discussion. Growth in righteousness and godly living are based on spiritual principles that must be *known* before they can do us any good.

Notice how many times in these verses Paul uses the word *know* and its cognates: "Do you not *know* that all of us who have been baptized into Christ Jesus have been baptized into His death?" (v. 3). "*Knowing* this, that our old self was crucified with Him, that our body of sin might be done away with, that we should no longer be slaves to sin" (v. 6). "*Knowing* that Christ, having been raised from the dead, is never to die again; death no longer is master over Him" (v. 9). "Do you not *know* that when you present yourselves to someone as slaves for obedience, you are slaves of the one whom you obey . . . ?" (v. 16). "Do you not *know*, brethren . . . that the law has jurisdiction over a person as long as he lives?" (7:1; cf. also vv. 7, 14, 18).

It is popular in some circles to denigrate knowledge and elevate passion, mysticism, brotherly love, blind faith, or whatever. Christian doctrine is often set against practical Christianity, as if the two were antithetical. Truth is ignored and harmony exalted. Knowledge is scorned while feeling is elevated. Reason is rejected and sentiment put in its place. Understanding is disdained and gullibility encouraged. That eats away at genuine spiritual maturity, which is always grounded in sound doctrine (cf. Tit. 1:6–9).

Knowledge alone is no virtue, of course. If someone "knows the right thing to do, and does not do it, to him it is sin" (Jas. 4:17). Knowledge without love corrupts the character: "Knowledge makes arrogant, but love edifies" (1 Cor. 8:1). Knowledge not mixed with obedience hardens the heart: "If we go on sinning willfully after receiving the knowledge of the truth, there no longer remains a sacrifice for sins" (Heb. 10:26). Knowledge can be destructive when not tempered with other virtues: "If someone sees you, who have knowledge, dining in an idol's temple, will not his conscience, if he is weak, be strengthened to eat things sacrificed to idols? For through your knowledge he who is weak is ruined, the brother for whose sake Christ died" (1 Cor. 8:10–11).

But *lack* of knowledge is even more deadly. Israel rejected Christ because they had zeal without knowledge (Rom. 10:2). Hosea recorded the Lord's complaint against Israel's spiritual leaders: "My people are destroyed for lack of knowledge. Because you have rejected knowledge, I also will reject you from being My priest. Since you have forgotten the law of your God, I also will forget your children" (Hos. 4:6). Isaiah recorded a similar indictment: "Israel does not know, My people do not understand" (Isa. 1:3).

All spiritual growth is based on *knowledge of truth*. Sound doctrine is crucial to a successful spiritual walk (Tit. 2:1, ff.). Paul told the Colossians that the new self is renewed to true knowledge (Col. 3:10). Knowledge is foundational to our new position in Christ. The entire Christian life is established on knowledge of divine principles, sound doctrine, and biblical truth. Those who repudiate knowledge in effect jettison the most basic means of spiritual growth and health, while leaving themselves vulnerable to a host of spiritual enemies.

And as Paul suggests in Romans 6, if we are to experience victory over sin, it must begin with knowledge. What, specifically, are we to know? Our position in Christ: "Knowing this, that our old self was crucified with Him, that our body of sin might be done away with, that we should no longer be slaves to sin; for he who has died is freed from sin" (Rom. 6:6–7). We must understand the very truths we have focused on throughout this book: that we are united with Christ in His death and resurrection and therefore free from our former enslavement to sin.

Reckon

Fine, you may be thinking to yourself. *Now I know those truths. But like Paul himself I still find myself unable to shake free of sin's influence. What do I do now?* Paul tells us, "Reckon . . . yourselves to be dead indeed unto sin, but alive unto God through Jesus Christ our Lord" (Rom. 6:11, KJV). The word translated "reckon" ("consider" in the NASB) is *logizomai*, which literally means "to calculate or number something." It is the same word Jesus used when He quoted Isaiah 53:12: "He was numbered with transgressors" (Lk. 22:37).

Reckoning in this sense goes beyond knowledge. It moves our faith out of the realm of the purely intellectual and makes it supremely practical. Paul is suggesting that our union with Christ ought to be something more than a theoretical truth. We are to count on it, deem it a reality, consider it done—and act accordingly. "Consider yourselves to be dead to sin, but alive to God in Christ Jesus [and] do not let sin reign in your mortal body that you should obey its lusts" (Rom. 6:11–12).

Reckoning our old self dead is certainly not an easy thing. So much in our experience seems to argue against the truth we know in our hearts. We may be free from sin's dominion, but our daily battle with sin often seems very much like the old slavery. Nevertheless, we must reckon ourselves dead to sin but alive to God. We cannot live as if the old self were still in control.

Nevertheless, we must reckon ourselves dead to sin but alive to God. We cannot live as if the old self were still in control.

It may seem at this point that Paul's advice has something in common with the ideology of the modern "positive thinking" and self-esteem cults. But Paul was not proposing that we play a mere mind game. He was not saying we should seek to convince ourselves of something that is not true. He was not suggesting that we should elevate ourselves in our own minds to a spiritual level we have not actually attained. He was not advising us to shut down our rational minds and dream of something that hasn't really occurred.

On the contrary, he was affirming the absolute truth of the believer's union with Christ, and assuring us that we can live our lives in light of that truth. Our old self *is* dead. God's Word declares it. We must regard it as true.

Too many Christians fail at this point. They think of themselves as hopelessly enslaved to sin. They have been taught that the old nature is still alive in all its fury. They do not understand that Christ has broken the power of sin. And therefore they cannot live victoriously. They do not consider themselves genuinely dead to sin.

That is precisely why I oppose the two-nature dualism that was popularized by *The Scofield Reference Bible*. Since this is probably the predominant view in American evangelicalism today, it is helpful to examine what is being taught.

Scofield believed all Christians have two active natures—"the old or Adamic nature, and the divine nature received through the new birth."[2] These, he taught, are equal but opposing realities that operate in every believer. The old Adamic nature—with its love for sin, its thoroughgoing depravity, all its evil propensities, and its inability to love God or do good—is still alive and powerful. The new divine nature is given only to believers, but once implanted within, it competes with the old nature for control of the will. Therefore, according to this view, every Christian still has the old sinful nature to contend with—but now has a new, godly nature as well. It is a kind of spiritual schizophrenia. It views conversion as not so much a *transformation* of the person but rather the *addition* of a new nature.

One writer who shared Scofield's views on the two natures wrote,

> When the "New Man" is born in the heart of the Believer the "Old Man" does not die. He is still there and very much alive. There are now two natures, diametrically opposed, fighting for the possession of the same body, like two tenants fighting for the possession of the same dwelling house. . . . We must remember that we cannot get rid of the "Old Nature" until the death of our body of "Flesh."[3]

The dualism of that view inevitably frustrates Christian growth. After all, if our old nature is just as alive and powerful as ever, how can we truly consider ourselves dead to sin but alive to God? In fact, it would seem rather dangerous to deem the old self dead if it is actually still "very much alive."

---

*Some people even use the two-nature
view as an excuse for their sin.
"It is only the old nature that sins,"
they claim—as if they personally
were not responsible.*

Indeed, those who hold to the two-nature view have a very hard time with Paul's instructions in Romans 6:11. Because they believe the old sinful self still lives on, by definition they *cannot* reckon themselves dead to sin. They *cannot* regard the old nature as crucified with Christ or believe that the body of sin has been nullified. This is obvious in their writings. The same author I quoted above wrote, "We must remember that while we may starve the Old Man, and he may become very feeble and cause little trouble, and we may reckon him dead, he is *not dead*, and if we begin to feed him again he will revive and recover his strength and give us trouble."[4] That quotation illustrates perfectly why those who hold the two-nature view of the Christian dare not reckon the old self dead. Their system tells them the old man is *not really* dead, and therefore those who *consider* him to be dead feel they may be actually placing themselves in a dangerous position of presumption.

Some people even use the two-nature view as an excuse for their sin. "It is only the old nature that sins," they claim—as if they personally were not responsible. Such a notion wreaks havoc on the conscience and seriously stunts spiritual growth. It disallows personal responsibility and thus dulls the conscience.

R. L. Dabney argued against an early form of the two-nature view more than a century ago. He noted the doctrine's "antinomian tendencies":

If one believes that he has two "real men," or "two natures" in him, he will be tempted to argue that the new man is in no way responsible for the perversity of the old. Here is a perilous deduction. . . . [And if] the old nature never loses any of its strength until death; then the presence, and even the flagrancy of indwelling sin need suggest to the believer no doubts whatever, whether his faith is spurious. How can it be denied that there is here terrible danger of carnal security in sin? How different this from the Bible which says Jas. ii:18, "Show me thy faith without thy works; and I will show thee my faith by my works." If then any professed believer finds the "old man" in undiminished strength, this is proof that he has never "put on the new man."[5]

Scripture does not support the dualistic view. Romans 6:6 clearly says that our old self was crucified with Christ. The person we were before we trusted Christ is no more. The tyranny of sin is nullified. Our nature is *changed*, transformed. We are new creations, not merely the same old creatures with a new side to our personalities. We have a new heart—not an added one, but a whole different one. This, after all, is the promise of the New Covenant: "I will give you a new heart and put a new spirit within you; and *I will remove the heart of stone* from your flesh and give you a heart of flesh" (Ezek. 36:26, emphasis added). This new heart has a *conscience*. It can take charge.

You can count on it. Reckon it to be so. Consider it accomplished.

Yield

"Yield" is the next key word in our quest for freedom from sin: "Let not sin therefore reign in your mortal body, that ye should obey it in the lusts thereof. Neither yield ye your members as instruments of unrighteousness unto sin: but *yield yourselves unto God*, as those that are alive from the dead, and your members as instruments of righteousness unto God" (Rom. 6:12–13, KJV, emphasis added).

As we have noted repeatedly, Christians are no longer dominated and controlled by sin. We are finally able to say no to sin's edicts. We are free from its absolute control. Before we were born again, we did not have that capability. But now sin has no authority to command us.

It can, however, beguile, tantalize, threaten, intimidate, and use every ploy it knows to tempt us. Although overthrown and defeated, it has not been eliminated. It still poses dangers. It does not give up easily. It taunts and torments us. It rages and storms. *But it no longer reigns over us.* And we do not have to yield to it.

Rather we must yield ourselves to a new Lord. "Present yourselves to God as those alive from the dead, and your members as instruments of righteousness to God" (v. 13). The surrender this calls for is a conscious, active submission of all our members to God as instruments of righteousness. In other words, we can use for God's glory the very faculties that sin once dominated.

Notice that Paul speaks of "your mortal body" (v. 12) and "the members of your body" (v. 13). But he has in mind not merely the corporeal body and its physical members. He is actually speaking more particularly of the soul's faculties, such as the mind, emotions, imagination, appetites, and will. Colossians 3:5 spells out precisely what he means: "Mortify therefore your members which are upon the earth; fornication, uncleanness, inordinate affection, evil concupiscence, and covetousness, which is idolatry" (Col. 3:5, KJV). "Members" in that verse clearly does not refer primarily to the physical extremities. It speaks instead of the faculties and activities of "the hidden person of the heart" (cf. 1 Pet. 3:4).

In our thinking, terms like *flesh, members,* and *body* tend to represent only the physical components of our beings. We contrast those terms with *heart, soul,* and *mind,* which we associate with the immaterial, or spiritual, part of our beings. But Scripture often refers to "the body" when it means the whole person—both the material and immaterial parts included—making no distinction between body and soul. James wrote, "The tongue . . . defiles the entire body" (Jas. 3:6)—that is, it debases the whole person. Jesus said, "The lamp of the body is the eye; if therefore your eye is clear, your whole body will be full of light. But if your eye is bad, your whole body will be full of darkness. If therefore the light that is in you is darkness, how great is the darkness!" (Matt. 6:22–23). "If therefore your whole body is full of light, with no dark part in it, it shall be wholly illumined, as when the lamp illumines you with its rays" (Lk. 11:36). In those verses, the expression "your whole body" refers to the entire mortal soul—the *complete person*—not the literal, tangible flesh and blood.

Likewise throughout Romans 6 and 7 Paul uses the terms *body* and *members* to describe the entire person who is yet unglorified—body, mind, emotions, and will—not just the physical side.

In places the wording can be hard to understand. Paul writes, for example, "I joyfully concur with the law of God in the inner man, but I see a different law in the members of my body, waging war against the law of my mind, and making me a prisoner of the law of sin which is in my members" (Rom. 7:22–23). There he seems to be contrasting the "inner man" with the physical body, as if he were suggesting that his flesh and blood wage war against his mind. Some readers wrongly assume this means the mind is good but the physical body is evil. That is the very kind of dualism the gnostic heretics preached. But that is not at all the point Paul was making. He was simply saying that his mortal members—including his body, his passions, his appetites, his emotions, and surely in some sense even his mind—were in conflict with his "inner man"—the new, immortal, vibrant, Spirit-wrought principle of righteousness that made him love and affirm the law of God. He was using the expressions "members of my body" and "inner man" as a convenient shorthand to contrast the flesh principle with the new person.

Our mortality—"the mortal body," as Paul uses the term—is the only ground on which sin can attack us. Sin cannot claim our eternal souls. One day our mortal selves—body and mind—will be "swallowed up by life" (2 Cor. 5:4). The perishable will put on imperishability (1 Cor. 15:53–54). That is what we wait eagerly for: "the redemption of our body" (Rom. 8:23). "The Lord Jesus Christ . . . will transform the body of our humble state into conformity with the body of His glory" (Phil. 3:20–21). Then, and only then, we will be forever out of sin's reach. But while we are still mortal, we are subject to corruption.

This "body of our humble state" and all its faculties are still susceptible to the lure of sin. We wage a continual warfare against sin in our mortal minds and bodies. We must not "go on presenting [our members] to sin as instruments of unrighteousness" (Rom. 6:13). Instead, we must "present [our] bodies a living and holy sacrifice, acceptable to God, which is [our] spiritual service of worship" (Rom. 12:1). We must "present [ourselves] to God as those alive from the dead, and [our] members as instruments of righteousness to God" (6:13).

"Sin shall not be master over you, for you are not under law, but under grace" (Rom. 6:14).

Paul inserts a glorious promise at this point: "Sin shall not be master over you, for you are not under law, but under grace" (v. 14). We are free from sin's condemnation because of our justification. But grace also frees us from sin's day-to-day domination, so that we can become "slaves of righteousness" (v. 18)—so that we can obey a new Lord.

Obey

The very purpose of grace is to free us from sin—"so we too might walk in newness of life" (v. 4). Grace is much more than mere forgiveness for our sins, or a free ride to heaven. Grace certainly does not leave us under sin's dominion. Saved by grace, "we are [God's own] workmanship, created in Christ Jesus for good works, which God prepared beforehand, that we should walk in them" (Eph. 2:10). Grace "[instructs] us to deny ungodliness and worldly desires and to live sensibly, righteously and godly in the present age" (Tit. 2:12). This is the very reason Christ gave Himself for us: "That He might redeem us from every lawless deed and purify for Himself a people for His own possession, zealous for good deeds" (v. 14).

Yet it seems there have always been those who have corrupted the grace of God by turning it into lasciviousness (cf. Jude 4). They characterize grace as total freedom, but they themselves are enslaved to corruption (2 Pet. 2:19). Thus they nullify the grace of God (cf. Gal. 2:21).

"The true grace of God" (cf. 1 Pet. 5:12) does not offer freedom from moral restraint. Grace is no sanction for sin. On the contrary, it grants the believer freedom *from* sin. It frees us from the law and from sin's penalty, but it also liberates us from sin's absolute control. It frees us to obey God.

Anticipating the thoughts of those who misunderstand God's grace, Paul echoes his query from Romans 6:1: "What then? Shall we sin because we are not under law but under grace?" (v. 15). And he answers once again emphatically, "May it never be!"

His argument against the objection is an appeal to common sense: "Do you not know that when you present yourselves to someone as slaves for obedience, you are slaves of the one whom you obey, either of sin resulting in death, or of obedience resulting in righteousness?" (v. 16). In other words, if you present yourself as a slave to do sin's bidding, you only demonstrate that you are still under sin's dominion. The clear implication is that those truly saved by grace would not willingly choose to return to the old slavery.

In fact, the phrase "present yourselves" suggests a conscious, active, willing *choice* of obedience. It pictures a soldier who presents himself with all his weapons to his commander, prepared to do the master's bidding. It is a voluntary, deliberate surrender of oneself and one's members to a life of service—either to "sin resulting in death, or [to] obedience resulting in righteousness." Here Paul is calling for a deliberate, willful, conscious choice of obedience. For unbelievers, there is no choice. They are enslaved to sin and cannot choose otherwise. Here Paul is suggesting that genuine Christians also have only one choice.

In other words, those who choose to serve sin as its slaves are in fact still enslaved to sin—they have never experienced God's grace. "When you present yourselves to someone as slaves for obedience, you are slaves of the one whom you obey." That at first may sound like a tautology, but a paraphrase may help explain the apostle's meaning: "When you voluntarily relinquish yourself to sin and its service, you give evidence that you were never freed from sin's dominion to begin with. Your pattern of life proves who your true master is—whether sin unto death, or obedience that results in righteousness." Or, as Peter wrote, "By what a man is overcome, by this he is enslaved" (2 Pet. 2:18–19).

In Romans 5 Paul made precisely the same point, only arguing in reverse. There he suggested that sin and death reign over all those in Adam (5:12); but grace, righteousness, and eternal life reign over the one who is in Christ (vv. 17–20).

In Romans 6, Paul suggests that everyone is a slave who has a master. Fallen man likes to declare that he is the master of his fate and the captain of his soul. But no one really is. All people are either under Satan's lordship and in bondage to sin, or they are under

Christ's lordship and servants of righteousness. There is no neutral ground, and no one can serve two masters (Matt. 6:24). "If we would know to which of these two families we belong, we must inquire to which of these two masters we yield our obedience."[6]

His point is that true Christians cannot be anything but slaves of righteousness.

Again, Paul is not telling the Romans that Christians *ought to be* slaves of righteousness. His point is that true Christians *cannot be anything but* slaves of righteousness. They were taken out of sin's servitude for precisely that purpose: "Thanks be to God that though you were slaves of sin, you became obedient from the heart to that form of teaching to which you were committed, and having been freed from sin, you became slaves of righteousness" (Rom. 6:17–18). That corresponds exactly to what the apostle John wrote: "No one who is born of God practices sin, because His seed abides in him; and he cannot sin, because he is born of God. By this the children of God and the children of the devil are obvious: anyone who does not practice righteousness is not of God" (1 Jn. 3:9–10).

For the Christian, the life of slavery to sin is *past*. Sin cannot continue to be the chief characteristic of our lives. Fleshly disobedience interrupts the new life frequently and we do sin. At times sin may *appear* to dominate a Christian's life completely (as was the case when David sinned). But all true believers still have a new and holy nature. They hate their sin and love righteousness. They cannot live in unbroken sin or hardened rebellion against God and enjoy it. That would be a contradiction of who they are (cf. 1 Jn. 3:9).

Serve

Paul makes very clear that the obedience he is calling for is a lifelong servitude to God:

> Just as you presented your members as slaves to impurity and to lawlessness, resulting in further lawlessness, so now present

your members as slaves to righteousness, resulting in sanctification. For when you were slaves of sin, you were free in regard to
righteousness. Therefore what benefit were you then deriving
from the things of which you are now ashamed? For the outcome of those things is death. But now having been freed from
sin and enslaved to God, you derive your benefit, resulting in
sanctification, and the outcome, eternal life (Rom. 6:19–22).

In other words, Christians should serve righteousness exactly like
we once served sin—as slaves.

Paul has moved from the issue of our position ("consider yourselves to be dead to sin," v. 11) to the matter of our practice ("now
present your members as slaves to righteousness," v. 19). Obviously,
our position ought to determine our practice.

In other words, Christians should serve righteousness exactly like we once served sin—as slaves.

Just as sin once led us into impurity and lawlessness, "resulting in further lawlessness" (v. 19), now righteousness results in
our ever-increasing progress in sanctification. Martyn Lloyd-Jones
wrote,

> As you go on living this righteous life, and practising it with all
> your might and energy, and all your time . . . you will find that
> the process that went on before, in which you went on from bad
> to worse and became viler and viler, is entirely reversed. You
> will become cleaner and cleaner, and purer and purer, and ho-
> lier and holier, and more and more conformed unto the image of
> the Son of God.[7]

It is impossible to stand still spiritually and morally. Everyone is
moving one way or the other—either sinking deeper into sin and
degradation, or gloriously progressing toward Christlikeness.

After all, life in Christ *should* be dramatically different from our lives before conversion: "When you were slaves of sin, you were free in regard to righteousness." If what you really desire now is freedom from moral restraint, you are no Christian. You are still a servant of sin.

True righteousness can neither command nor instruct those who are still captive to sin. They serve a different master. Though many of them put on a show of *self*-righteousness—as was true of Paul himself before his conversion—the works of the flesh have absolutely nothing to do with real righteousness. Scripture uses some of its strongest language to condemn such fleshly efforts. Isaiah wrote, "All our righteous deeds are like a filthy garment"—literally, "like a menstrual cloth" (Isa. 64:6). Paul called his pre-Christian self-righteousness "dung" (Phil. 3:8, KJV).

The real fruit of sin's mastery includes "immorality, impurity, sensuality, idolatry, sorcery, enmities, strife, jealousy, outbursts of anger, disputes, dissentions, factions, envying, drunkenness, carousing, and things like these." And the ultimate result is eternal condemnation: " . . . of which I forewarn you just as I have forewarned you that those who practice such things shall not inherit the kingdom of God" (Gal. 5:19–21). "Therefore what benefit were you then deriving from the things of which you are now ashamed? For the outcome of those things is death" (Rom. 6:21).

True faith bears exactly the opposite fruit. "Now having been freed from sin and enslaved to God, you derive your benefit, resulting in sanctification, and the outcome, eternal life" (v. 22).

"Freed from sin and enslaved to God" is as good a description of the Christian life as any I know. Of course it does not mean believers are incapable of sinning. But it *does* mean they are no longer enslaved to sin, no longer helpless to answer its attacks, no longer loving darkness rather than light.

What Paul has given us in this brief chapter is a courageous call to stand firm in the face of sin's onslaughts. Believers need to *know* that they are united with Christ in His death and resurrection, and therefore freed from sin's dominion. They need to *reckon* that their union with Christ means the old self is dead, nullified, no longer able to demand obedience to its sinful lusts. They need to *yield* themselves to God and surrender all their members—body, mind, emotions, and the whole person—to God as instruments of righteousness. They need to *obey* Him as their new Lord. And they need to *serve* Him with the same unquestioning obedience they once gave to sin.

Though sin is a defeated enemy, though we wage our battle against it from a position of victory, it is still a life-and-death struggle.

That is Paul's formula for victory. It calls for boldness, determination, and an intelligent, informed faith. It assumes that we love God and desire to see His righteousness working in our lives. It offers freedom from sin's absolute authority and the means to defeat sin in our daily walk.

But it does not assume that the process is easy or that glorious victory will always be our daily experience. Paul certainly was not suggesting that the Christian walk is never marked by defeat or failure. As we have noted throughout, all we need to do is read on to Romans 7, and it becomes evident that Paul's experience with his own sin was often deeply frustrating to him: "I am not practicing what I would like to do, but I am doing the very thing I hate" (v. 15). "That which I am doing, I do not understand . . . for I know that nothing good dwells in me, that is, in my flesh; for the wishing is present in me, but the doing of the good is not" (vv. 15, 18). "The good that I wish, I do not do; but I practice the very evil that I do not wish" (v. 19). "Evil is present in me, the one who wishes to do good" (v. 21). "Wretched man that I am! Who will set me free from the body of this death?" (v. 24).

The truth is, when we look into our own hearts, every one of us must echo those words of frustration. Though sin is a defeated enemy, though we wage our battle against it from a position of victory, it is still a life-and-death struggle. And it is a battle we must continue to take to the enemy as we mortify sin and attack its remaining influence in our lives.

Appendix 2

An Appeal for a Good Conscience

by Richard Sibbes[1]

And corresponding to that, baptism now saves you—not the removal of dirt from the flesh, but an appeal to God for a good conscience—through the resurrection of Jesus Christ (1 Pet. 3:21).

The context of these words from 1st Peter is this: the blessed apostle had just spoken of those who perished in the flood, and of Noah's salvation in the ark ("few, that is, eight persons, were brought safely through the water"). Then he mentions baptism ("corresponding to that, baptism now saves you").

Christ is the same yesterday, today, and forever (Heb. 13:8). He has always taken care to save His Noahs in the midst of destruction. Salvation is a work that He has carried since the beginning of the world. There were two cities prefigured in Cain and Abel. And God has always communicated Himself differently to the citizens of the two cities. "The Lord knows how to rescue the godly" (2 Pet. 2:9). All who were ever saved were saved by Christ, and all had different sacrifices that foreshadowed Christ.

For those who are not His, those of Cain's posterity, God communicates Himself in a contrary way to them: He destroys them.

But to come to the words "and corresponding to that, baptism now saves you. . . . " The saving of Noah in the ark was an illustration of baptism; for as baptism pictures Christ, so did the saving of Noah in the ark. They correspond to one another in many things.

First, as everyone who was not in the ark perished, so shall everyone perish who is not in Christ (those not engrafted into Him by faith). Baptism is an emblem of that engrafting.

Second, as the same water in the flood *preserved* Noah in the ark and *destroyed* all the old world, so the same blood and death of Christ kills all our spiritual enemies. They are all drowned in the Red Sea of Christ's blood, but it preserves His children. There were three main deluges in the Old Testament, which all prefigure Christ: the flood that drowned the old world; the passing through the Red Sea; and the waters of Jordan. In all these God's people were saved and the enemies of God's people destroyed. That is what Micah the prophet alludes when he says, "Thou wilt cast all their sins into the depths of the sea" (7:19). He alludes to Pharaoh and his host drowned in the bottom of the sea. They sunk as lead; so all our sins, which are our enemies if we be in Christ, they sink as lead.

Third, as Noah was mocked by the wretched world while he was making the ark, so all are derided who flee to Christ for salvation.

Yet Noah was thought a wise man when the flood came. Likewise when destruction comes, they are wise who have secured their standing in Christ before. There are many such resemblances between the ark and baptism. I name but a few, and move on.

Outward Ritual Is Not Enough

"Corresponding to that, baptism now saves you." Here, first of all, in a word, is a description of the means of salvation, how we are saved: "baptism now saves you."

Then he anticipates an objection: "—not the removal of dirt from the flesh," the outward part of baptism.

Then he sets down *how* baptism saves us: "but an appeal to God for a good conscience."

And then the ground of it: "through the resurrection of Jesus Christ."

All that I pass over, so that I may come to that which I specially intend. I come, therefore, to the anticipated objection, which I will not speak much of. But I will say something, because it is a useful point.

The ritual of baptism does not save. When he said that baptism saves us, he said it is *not* that baptism which is a removal of dirt from the flesh—insinuating that baptism has two parts. There is a double baptism: the outward, which is the washing of the body; the inward, which is the washing of the soul. The outward does not save without the inward. Therefore he deflects the notion, lest they should think that all who are baptized outwardly with water are saved by Christ.

The danger of looking too much to externals. The apostle knew that people are naturally prone to give too much to outward things. The devil is an extremist. He labors to bring people to extremes, to make the outward rituals idols, or to make them idle rituals. That is, he wants us to focus so intently on the external aspects of our faith (such as baptism and the Lord's Supper) that we make the ceremonies themselves objects of idolatry—or else get us to care so little for them that they mean nothing at all. The devil gets what he wants either way.

The apostle knew the disease of the times, especially in his time. People attributed too much to outward things. The apostle Paul, writing to the Galatians, twice repeats it: "Neither is circumcision anything, nor uncircumcision, but a new creation" (Gal. 6:15; cf. 5:6). You stand too much on outward things, he was saying. What counts with God is the "new creation."

Likewise in the Old Testament, when God prescribed both outward and inward worship, they attributed too much to the outward, and let the inward alone. As in Psalm 50:16–17, God complains how they served Him: "What right have you to tell of My statutes, and to take My covenant in your mouth? For you hate discipline, and you cast My words behind you." Also in Isaiah 1:13–14 and 66:3, we see God's decisive dealing with them: "Bring your worthless offerings no longer, incense is an abomination to Me. . . . I hate your new moon festivals and your appointed feasts." And, "He who kills an ox is like one who slays a man; he who sacrifices a lamb is like the one who breaks a dog's neck; he who offers a grain offering is like one who offers swine's blood; he who burns incense is like the one who blesses an idol"— yet these were sacrifices anointed by God Himself. What was the reason for this? They played the hypocrites with God, and gave Him only the shell. They brought Him outward performances. They attributed too much to that, and left the spiritual part that God most esteems.

Notice also how our Savior Christ rebukes the Pharisees: "Do not suppose that you can say to yourselves, 'We have Abraham for our father'" (Matt. 3:9). They boasted too much of their outward privileges. You see throughout the Scriptures that people who don't belong to God are especially apt to attribute too much to outward things. They ought to combine that with the inward, which they neglect.

Why people overemphasize external religion. There are always two parts of God's service, outward and inward. The inward aspect is hard for flesh and blood to lay hold of. As in baptism there are two parts, outward and inward washing; and hearing the Word involves both the outward man and the inward soul, bowing to hear what God says; so in the Lord's Supper, there is outward receiving of bread and wine, and inward making of a covenant with God. Now people give too much to the outward, and think that God owes them something for it. But they neglect the inward because they are protecting their own lust.

But more particularly, the reason is in corrupt nature.

First, because the outward part is easy and glorious to the eye of the world. Everyone can see the sacrament administered, everyone can see when one comes and hears the Word of God.

Second, people rest in the outward ritual because it does something to mollify the conscience, which would clamor if they did nothing religious, or if they were direct atheists. Therefore they say, *We will hear the Word, and perform the outward things.* But being loath to search into the bottom of their conscience, they stop with the outward things, and satisfy conscience by that. Those and similar reasons explain why so many people attend to external religion only.

Application. Let us take notice of this tendency to focus on externals; let us know that God does not regard the outward without the inward. More than that, He abhors it. If God can despise the worship that He Himself appointed, how much more must He loathe the empty devices and ceremonies of men's own devising? The liturgy of papal religion, for example, is but a barren external. They labor to *put off* God with the work done. Their doctrine is tailor-made for corrupt human nature. They teach that the sacrament administered confers grace regardless of the person's state of heart. In their system the elements themselves confer grace, as if grace could be transmitted through a lifeless substance. The whole process makes people dote too much on outward things. But our text shows that the outward part of baptism without the inward is nothing: "not the removal of dirt from the flesh, but an appeal to God for a good conscience," says Peter.

Let us labor, therefore, in all our services to God, to rivet our hearts especially on the spiritual part. As Samuel told Saul, "Behold, to obey is better than sacrifice, and to hearken than the fat of rams" (1 Sam. 15:22). And God said through the prophet Hosea, "I delight in loyalty rather than sacrifice, and in the knowledge of God rather than burnt offerings" (Hos. 6:6). Too many Christians are content to do the externals, which is the easy part of religion.

But what is not done in the heart is not truly done. "God is spirit, and those who worship Him must worship in spirit and truth" (Jn. 4:24). There is a kind of divine power necessary in all true worship that goes beyond anything the outward person can bring. In *hearing* divine truth a divine power is required to make a person hear as he or she should (1 Cor. 2:9–15). Similarly in *worship*, more is required than the outward man is able to supply. There is both form and power in all the parts of religion. Let us not rest in the form, but labor for the power.

We see what kind of persons those were in 2 Timothy 3:5: "Holding to a form of godliness, although they have denied its power." Paul names a catalogue of sins there: they were "lovers of pleasure rather than lovers of God." Nevertheless, these people wanted a form of religion, although they denied the power of it. But I hasten to the issue I want to dwell on.

Appealing to God for a Good Conscience

After removing people's false confidence in external religion, Peter positively sets down what it is that *does* save: It is "an appeal to God for a good conscience." The holy apostle might have said, "Not water baptism, but the baptism by the Spirit into Christ's Body" (1 Cor. 12:13). He might have said, "Not putting off the filth of the body, but putting off the filth of the soul." Instead he names the act of the soul that lays hold of God's gracious salvation—"an appeal to God for a good conscience." Of course he is speaking of *faith*.

God must be satisfied before conscience can be satisfied. God is satisfied with the death of the mediator; so when we are sprinkled with the blood of Christ—when the death of Christ is applied to us— our conscience is satisfied too. That is how "the blood of Christ, who through the eternal Spirit offered Himself without blemish to God, cleanse[s our] conscience from dead works to serve the living God" (Heb. 9:14).

The "appeal to God for a good conscience," then, is the same thing as faith. Peter is describing the attitude of those who engage themselves to believe and to live as Christians.

When we believe, our conscience is made good. If Satan lays anything to our charge, we can answer with a good conscience. "Who will bring a charge against God's elect? God is the one who justifies; who is the one who condemns? Christ Jesus is He who died, yes, rather who was raised, who is at the right hand of God, who also intercedes for us" (Rom. 8:33–34). We may, with a heart sprinkled with the blood of Christ, answer all objections, and triumph against all enemies. We may "draw near with confidence to the throne of grace, that we may receive mercy and may find grace to help in time of need" (Heb. 4:16).

"A good conscience" in the sense Peter employs the term, then, is a conscience cleansed from the defilement of sin, set free to serve God. Only true Christians have such a conscience. It is a conscience that looks to God and will ultimately answer to Him. How can we know if we are "in Christ," recipients of God's saving grace and favor? Conscience is set in us for this very purpose, to tell us what we are doing, and with what motives we are doing it, and what our standing is before God. If you want to test your spiritual health, ask simply whether your conscience is set toward God.

If you are righteous, honorable, and good because your conscience responds to God's commands, it is a good conscience. But if you are doing good works or religious ritual just so that others will see, those are not from a good conscience (Matt. 6:5–6, 16–18). A good conscience holds us accountable simply because God commands it. The conscience is God's deputy in the heart of a believer.

Therefore what we do from a good conscience we do from the heart. When we do something grudgingly, not out of love, and not from the heart, that is not from a good conscience. A healthy conscience looks not merely to *what* we do, but it examines *why* we do it as well—whether it is out of love for God and a desire to obey, or from a sense of resentful obligation.

A good conscience renounces and denies *all* sin. Those, therefore, who labor to feed their corruptions while thinking they are Christians contradict their profession of faith. Those who feed their eyes with vanity and their ears with filthy discourse; those who allow their feet to carry them to places where they infect their souls; those who, instead of renouncing their sins, maintain them—what shall we think of them? Can they think to be saved by Christ when they live with a defiled conscience?

David prayed, "Restore to me the joy of Thy salvation, and sustain me with a willing spirit" (Ps. 51:12). He lost that joy and willingness by sin. For when we deliberately sin against conscience, we stop the mouth of our prayers, so that we cannot go to God. We stop the mouth of conscience, so that we cannot go *boldly* to God. Let us labor to be pliable to the Spirit. Let us submit to God in all that we are exhorted to do. And let us yield the obedience of faith to all His promises. That is what it means to have a good conscience. Therefore let us resolve to take this course if we would attain a good conscience.

Let us examine ourselves carefully so that our consciences may be convinced of the sin that is in us. Let us put questions to ourselves: *Do I believe? Or have I merely placated my own heart without satisfying God? Do I obey? Do I willingly cast myself into the mold of God's Word and willingly obey all that I hear? Or am I deceiving myself?* Put those questions to your own heart. "For God is greater than our heart, and knows all things" (1 Jn. 3:20). If we answer God with reservations (*I will obey God in this, but not in that; I will go along with Christ as long as I don't have to give up a favorite sin*) that is not the answer of a good conscience. What is done for God must be done wholeheartedly and without reservation. If our hearts balk, we do not have a good conscience. Partial obedience is no obedience at all. To single out easy things that do not oppose our lusts or threaten our pride is not the obedience God calls for. Our obedience must be universal to all His commands. Therefore let us search ourselves, and propound searching questions to ourselves, whether we believe and obey or not, and what are our motives in doing so.

The life of many is nothing but a breach of their profession of faith. What will they have to look for at the hour of death, and in the day of judgment? Can they possibly hope that God should keep His promise with them to give them life everlasting, when they never had grace to keep any commitment to Him? How can they look for God's grace then, when they have spurned His grace here, and their whole life has been a satisfying of their base lusts? If your profession of faith is meaningless now, it will be meaningless at the judgment. Fetch that argument against sin when you are tempted.

On the other hand, when you fail, do not let Satan tempt you to discouragement, but come and cast yourself on Christ. Faith and repentance are not one-time acts; you must live your life believing and repenting.

The Advantage of a Pure Conscience

What a comfort to have a good conscience! It will uphold us in sickness, in death, and at the day of judgment. Let the devil object what he can; let our own unbelieving thoughts object what they can—if we have a renewed, sanctified conscience, it can answer all.

Though we be ever so vexed in this world, we are never truly overcome until our conscience is cracked. If our conscience stands upright, we conquer, and are more than conquerors.

Conscience is either the greatest friend or the greatest enemy in the world. When it knows we have obeyed God in all things, conscience is a friend that speaks to God on our behalf. Then again at the hour of death, what a comfort a good conscience will be! And especially at the day of judgment—a sincere heart, a conscience that has labored to obey the gospel—it can look God in the face.

A Christian that has the answer of a good conscience, has Christ to be his ark in all deluges. Christ saves us not only from hell and damnation, but in all the miseries of this life.

But for those who live in rebellion and thus defile their conscience, alas! What comfort can such as these have? Their conscience tells them that their lives do not witness for God, but they rebel against Him. Their hearts tell them they cannot look to heaven for comfort. They carry a hell in their bosom, a guilty conscience. Those that have their conscience thus stained, especially those who deliberately live in sin—they can look for nothing but vengeance from God.

In times of trouble, and at the hour of death it is shown that they are the wisest people who kept their conscience pure and kept their covenant with God. Their faith is not external ceremony only—it emanates from a pure heart and a clear conscience. Let us bind our consciences to closer obedience.

Appendix 3

Searching Your Conscience

by Jonathan Edwards[1]

Search me, O God, and know my heart: try me, and know my thoughts: and see if there be any wicked way in me, and lead me in the way everlasting (Ps. 139:23–24, KJV).

Psalm 139 is a meditation on the omniscience of God. God views and perfectly knows *everything*. The psalmist represents that perfect knowledge by affirming that God knows all our *actions* ("Thou dost know when I sit down and when I rise up," v. 2); all our *thoughts* ("Thou dost understand my thought from afar," v. 2); all our *words* ("Even before there is a word on my tongue, Behold, O Lord, Thou dost know it all," v. 4).

Then he illustrates the impossibility of fleeing from the divine presence:

> Where can I go from Thy Spirit? Or where can I flee from Thy presence? If I ascend to heaven, Thou art there; if I make my bed in Sheol, behold, Thou art there. If I take the wings of the dawn, if I dwell in the remotest part of the sea, even there Thy hand will lead me, and Thy right hand will lay hold of me. If I say, "Surely the darkness will overwhelm me, and the light around me will be night," even the darkness is not dark to Thee, and the night is as bright as the day. Darkness and light are alike to Thee (vv. 7–12).

Then he speaks of the knowledge God had of him before he was even born:

> Thou didst form my inward parts; thou didst weave me in my mother's womb. . . . My frame was not hidden from Thee, when I was made in secret, and skillfully wrought in the depths of the earth. Thine eyes have seen my unformed substance; and in Thy book they were all written, the days that were ordained for me, when as yet there was not one of them (vv. 13, 15–16).

After this the psalmist observes what must be inferred as a necessary consequence of God's omniscience: He will slay the wicked (v. 19).

Finally, the psalmist makes a practical application of his meditation on God's omniscience: he begs God to search and test him, and see if there is any wicked way in him, and lead him in the everlasting way.

Obviously, the psalmist was not imploring God to search him so that *God* could gain any information. The whole point of the psalm is to declare that God already knows everything. Therefore, the psalmist must be praying for God to search him so that *the psalmist himself* might see and be informed of the sin in his own heart.

David obviously had examined his own heart and ways, but he did not trust that. He was still fearful that there might be some unknown sin in him that had escaped his own searching, so he cried to God to examine him.

Elsewhere, David wrote, "Who can discern his errors? Acquit me of hidden faults" (Ps. 19:12). By "hidden faults" he meant sins that were secret to himself—those sins that were in him that he was not aware of.

All of us ought to be concerned to know whether we live in ways of sin without even knowing it. Whether we entertain some secret lust or neglect some spiritual duty, our hidden sins are just as offensive to God and just as dishonoring to Him as the open, flagrant, known sins. Since we are prone to sin anyway and our natural hearts are full of sin, we must take special care to avoid those sins that are presumptuous, unintentional, and done in ignorance.

Why People Live in Sin Without Knowing It

Our trouble in seeing whether there be any wicked way in us is not because we lack external light. God has certainly not failed to tell us plainly and abundantly what wicked ways are. He has given us ample commandments to show us what we ought to do or not do, and these are clearly set before us in His Word. So our difficulty in knowing our own hearts is *not* because we lack the proper guidelines.

How *can* people live in ways that displease God—yet seem completely insensitive and go on utterly oblivious to their own sin? Several factors contribute to this evil tendency of humanity:

The blinding, deceitful nature of sin. The human heart is full of sin and corruption, and corruption has a spiritually blinding effect. Sin always carries a degree of darkness with it. The more it prevails, the more it darkens and deludes the mind. It blinds us to the reality of what is in our own hearts. Again, the problem is not at all that we lack the light of God's truth. The light shines clearly enough around us, but the fault is in our own eyes; they are darkened and blinded by a deadly disability that results from sin.

Sin easily deceives because it controls the human will, and that colors the judgment. Where lust prevails, it disposes the mind to approve. Where sin influences our preferences, that sin seems pleasing and good. The mind is naturally prejudiced to think whatever is pleasing is right. Therefore when a sinful desire gains the will, it also prejudices the understanding. And the more a person walks in sin, the more that person's mind will probably be darkened and blinded. That is how sin gains its mastery of people.

Therefore when people are unaware of their own sin, it can be extremely difficult to make them see the wrongness of it. After all, the same evil desires that lead them into sin blind them in it. The more an angry person gives in to malice or envy, the more those sins blind the understanding to approve of them. The more a man hates his neighbor, the more he will be disposed to think that he has good cause to hate, and that the neighbor is hateful, and that he deserves to be hated, and that it is not his duty to love him. The more a man's impure lust prevails, the more sweet and pleasant the sin will appear, and the more he will be inclined to think there is no evil in it.

Likewise, the more a person covets material things, the more likely he is to think himself excusable in doing so. He will tell himself that he *needs* certain things and cannot do without them. If they are necessary, he reasons, it is no sin to desire them. All the lusts of the human heart can be justified in such a way. And the more they prevail, the more they blind the mind and influence the judgment to approve of them. That is why Scripture calls worldly appetites "lusts of deceit" (Eph. 4:22). Even godly people may for a time be blinded and deluded by lust, so that they live in a way which is displeasing to God.

Lusts also stir up the carnal mind to invent excuses for sinful practices. Human nature is very subtle when it comes to rationalizing sin. Some people are so strongly devoted to their wickedness that when conscience troubles them about it, they will rack their brains to find arguments to stop the mouth of conscience and make themselves believe they may proceed lawfully in a sinful practice.

Self-love also prejudices people to condone their own sin. People do not like to condemn themselves. They are naturally prejudiced in their own favor. So they will look for good names by which to call their sinful dispositions and practices. They will make them virtuous—or at least they will make them innocent. They label covetousness "prudence" or call greed "business savvy." If they rejoice at another's calamity, they pretend it is because they hope it will do the person good. If they drink too much, it is because their constitutions require it. If they backbite or talk against their neighbor, they claim it is only zeal against sin. If they get into a dispute, they call their stubbornness conscience, and categorize their petty disagreements as matters of principle. Thus they find good names for all their evil ways.

People tend to shape their principles according to their practices rather than vice versa. Rather than allowing their behavior to conform to their consciences, they will expend tremendous energy trying to get their consciences to conform to their behavior.

Because sin is so deceitful, and because we have so much sin dwelling in our hearts, it is difficult for us to judge our own ways and practices righteously. On this account we should make diligent self-examination and be much concerned to know whether there is any wicked way in us. "Take care, brethren, lest there should be in any one of you an evil, unbelieving heart, in falling away from the living God. But encourage one another day after day, as long as it is still called 'Today,' lest any one of you be hardened by the deceitfulness of sin" (Heb. 3:12–13).

People more easily see faults in others than in themselves. When they see others do wrong, they immediately condemn them—even while excusing themselves for the very same sin! (cf. Rom. 2:1). We all see the specks in others' eyes better than the beams in our own. "Every man's way is right in his own eyes" (Prov. 21:2). "The heart is more deceitful than all else and is desperately sick; who can understand it?" (Jer. 17:9). We cannot trust our own hearts in this matter. Instead, we must keep a protective eye on ourselves, interrogate our own hearts carefully, and cry to God that he will search us thoroughly. "He who trusts in his own heart is a fool" (Prov. 28:26).

The subtlety of Satan. The devil works hand in hand with our own deceitful lusts. He labors to blind us to our own faults. He continually endeavors to lead us into sin, then works with our carnal minds to flatter us with the idea we are better than we are. He thus blinds the conscience. He is the prince of darkness. Blinding and deceiving have been his work ever since he began it with our first parents.

The power of habit. Some people are oblivious to the sins they practice out of habit. Habitual sins often stupefy the mind, so that sins that once pricked the conscience begin to seem harmless.

The example of others. Some people become desensitized to their own sin because they let popular opinion dictate their standards. They look to the behavior of others to discern what is right and wrong. But society is so tolerant of sin that many sins have become destigmatized. Things that displease God and are abominations in His sight appear innocent when viewed through the eyes of popular opinion. Perhaps we see them practiced by those whom we esteem highly, by our superiors, and by those who are accounted wise. That greatly slants the mind in favor of them and diminishes the sense of their evil. It is especially dangerous when godly men, respected Christian leaders, are seen engaging in sinful practices. That especially tends to harden the observer's heart and blind the mind with respect to any evil habit.

Incomplete obedience. Those who obey God halfheartedly or incompletely are in great danger of living in undetected sin. Some professing Christians neglect half of their spiritual duties while concentrating on the other half. Perhaps their thoughts will be wholly taken up with secret prayer, Bible reading, public worship, meditation, and other religious duties—while ignoring moral duties, such as their responsibilities to their spouse, their children, or their neighbors.

They know they must not defraud their neighbor, lie, or fornicate. But they seem not to consider what an evil it is to talk against others lightly, to take up a reproach against a neighbor, to contend and quarrel with people, to live hypocritically before their families, or to neglect their children's spiritual instruction.

Such people may seem very conscientious in some things—those branches of their duty on which they keep their eye—but they may entirely neglect other important branches.

How to Discover the Unknown Sin Within

As we have observed, it is naturally very difficult to assess our own sin honestly. But if we are sufficiently concerned about it, and if we are strict and thorough in searching our own hearts, we can, for the most part, discover the sin within. Persons who want to please and obey God, with all the light we enjoy, certainly do not need to go on in the ways of sin through ignorance.

It is true that our hearts are exceedingly deceitful. But God, in His holy Word, has given sufficient light for the state of darkness we are in. By thorough care and inquiry, we may know our spiritual responsibilities, and we can know whether we are living in any sinful way. Everyone with any true love for God will be glad for biblical assistance in this inquiry. Such persons are deeply concerned to walk in all things as God would have them walk, so as to please and honor Him. If their lives are in any way offensive to God, they will be glad to know it and would by no means choose to have their own sin concealed from them.

Also, those who sincerely inquire, *What shall I do to be saved?* will want to identify the sin in their lives. For their sin is what keeps them from Christ.

There are two means by which we come to the knowledge of our own sin:

Knowledge of God's law. If you desire to know whether you live in some unknown sin, you must become thoroughly acquainted with what God requires of you. In Scripture God has given us a true and perfect guide by which we ought to walk. He has expressed His precepts clearly and abundantly, so that we might be able to know—despite our own spiritual darkness and disadvantages—precisely what He requires of us. What a full and abundant revelation of God's mind we have in the Scriptures! How plain it is in instructing us how to behave! How often the precepts are repeated! And how explicitly they are revealed in so many various forms so that we might fully understand them!

But what good is all that if we neglect God's revelation and make no effort to become acquainted with it? What good is it to have godly principles yet not know them? Why should God reveal His mind to us if we don't care enough to know what it is?

Yet the only way we can know whether we are sinning is by knowing His moral law: "By the law is the knowledge of sin" (Rom. 3:20). Therefore if we don't want to go on displeasing God, we ought to study diligently the principles of right and wrong He has revealed.

We ought to read and search the Holy Scriptures much. And we ought to do it with the intention of knowing our *whole* duty, so that the Word of God may be "a lamp unto our feet, and a light unto our paths" (Ps. 119:105).

That being so, it is clear that most people are very much guilty simply because of their negligence of spiritual duties. They are blameworthy first of all because they disregard God's Word and other resources that might inform them. They act as if such study were the work of ministers only. Such ignorance is often willful, deliberate carelessness. If they are unaware of what God demands of them, it is their own fault. They have enough opportunities to know, and they *could* know if they wanted to. Furthermore, they take pains to acquire other kinds of knowledge. They are well trained in whatever worldly interests strike their fancy. They learn whatever is necessary to earn a living in this world. But they will not expend any energy in spiritual pursuits that count for eternity.

Knowledge of ourselves. Second, if you desire to know whether you are harboring secret sin, you must examine *yourself*. Compare your life with God's law to see if you conform to the divine standard. That is the primary way we must discover our own character. This is an important difference between human beings and brute creatures: a human is capable of self-reflection, contemplating his own actions, and evaluating the nature and quality of them. Doubtless it was partly for this very reason that God gave us this power—so that we might know ourselves, and consider our own ways.

We must examine ourselves until we satisfactorily discover either agreement or disagreement with the principles of Scripture. This requires the utmost diligence, lest we overlook our own irregularities, or lest some evil way in us should lie hidden under disguise.

How to Examine Yourself

You might think we would already be better acquainted with ourselves than with anything else. After all, we are always present with ourselves. We are immediately conscious of our own actions. We instantly know about everything that happens within us and everything that we do.

But in some respects the true knowledge of ourselves is harder to obtain than almost anything else. We therefore must pry diligently into the secrets of our own hearts and examine carefully all our ways and practices. Here are some guidelines to help in this process:

Always join self-reflection with your reading and hearing of God's Word. When you read the Bible or hear sermons, reflect on yourself, comparing your own ways with what you read or hear. Ponder what agreement or disagreement there is between the Word and your ways. The Scriptures testify against all kinds of sin, and contain directions for every spiritual responsibility, as Paul wrote: "All Scripture is inspired by God and profitable for teaching, for reproof, for correction, for training in righteousness; that the man of God may be adequate, equipped for *every good work*" (2 Tim. 3:16–17, emphasis added). Therefore when you read the commandments given by Christ and His apostles, ask yourself, *Do I live according to this rule? Or do I live in any way contrary to it?*

When you read in the historical parts of Scripture about the sins others have been guilty of, reflect on yourself as you go along. Ask yourself whether you are guilty of similar sins. When you read how God reproved the sins of others and executed judgments on them for their sins, ask whether you deserve similar chastisement. When you read the examples of Christ and the saints, ask yourself whether you live in ways contrary to their example. When you read how God commended and rewarded His people for their virtues and good deeds, ask whether you deserve the same blessing. Make use of the Word as a mirror in which you carefully inspect yourself—and be a doer of the Word (Jas. 1:23–25).

How few are there who do this as they should! While the minister is testifying against sin, most are busy thinking how others fail to measure up. They may hear hundreds of things in sermons that properly apply to them; yet it never so much as comes into their minds that what the preacher is saying in any way concerns them. Their minds readily fix on other people whom the message seems to fit, but they never think whether they themselves need the message.

If you do things that are generally avoided by people who are discerning and mature, be especially careful to ask yourself if

such activities might actually be sinful. Perhaps you have argued with yourself that such and such a practice is lawful; you don't see any evil in it. But if the thing is generally condemned by godly people, it certainly looks suspicious. You may be wise to consider conscientiously whether it is actually displeasing to God. If a practice is generally disapproved of by those who in such cases are most likely to be right, you ought to consider all the more carefully whether the thing in question is lawful or unlawful.

Ask yourself whether on your deathbed you will have pleasant memories of the way you have lived. Healthy people often indulge in activities they would not dare do if they thought they would soon stand before the Lord. They think of death as something in the distance, so they find it much easier to still their consciences about what they are doing today. Yet if they thought they might soon die, they would not find it so comfortable to contemplate such activities. Conscience is not so easily blinded and muffled when the end of life appears imminent.

Ask yourself solemnly, therefore, whether you are doing anything now that might trouble you on your deathbed. Think over your ways and test yourself with the sobering expectation of soon going out of the world into eternity. Earnestly endeavor to judge impartially what things you will be glad for on a deathbed—as well as what you will disapprove of, and wish you had left alone.

Consider what others may say of you. Although people are blind to their own faults, they easily discover the faults of others—and are apt enough to speak of them. Sometimes people live in ways that are not at all appropriate, yet they are blind to it themselves. They do not see their own shortcomings, though the faults are perfectly plain and evident to others. They themselves cannot see their failings, yet others cannot shut their eyes or avoid seeing where they fall short.

Some people, for instance, are very proud without knowing it. But the problem appears notorious to others. Some are very worldly; yet they seem not to be aware of it themselves. Some are malicious and envious. Others see it, and to them it appears truly hateful. Yet the very ones with the problem do not reflect on it. There is no trusting our own hearts or our own eyes in such cases. So we must hear what others say of us, observe what they charge us with, heed what fault they find with us, and strictly examine whether there is some foundation for it.

If others charge us with being proud, worldly, or spiteful and malicious—or accuse us of any other ill temper or practice—we should ask ourselves honestly whether it is so. The accusation may seem to us to be altogether groundless, and we may think that the accuser's motives or spirit are wrong. But the discerning person will see it as an occasion for self-examination.

We should especially listen to what our *friends* say to us and about us. It is foolhardy, as well as unchristian, to take offense, and resent it, when we are thus told of our faults. "Faithful are the wounds of a friend, but deceitful are the kisses of an enemy" (Prov. 27:6). We should rejoice that we are shown our spots.

But also we should heed what our *enemies* accuse us of. If they reproach and revile us to our faces—even out of a wrong attitude— we should ponder it enough to reflect inwardly, and ask ourselves whether there is any truth in it. Even if what is said comes across in a reproachful, reviling manner, there may still be much truth in it. When people criticize others, even when their motives for criticizing are wrong, they are nevertheless likely to target real faults. In fact, our enemies are likely to attack us where we are weakest and most defective, and where we have given them most grounds to criticize. They are most prone to attack us where we can least defend ourselves. Those who revile us—though they do it from an unchristian spirit and in an unchristian manner—will usually identify the very areas where we are the most blameworthy.

So when we hear of others talking against us behind our backs, no matter what the spirit of the criticism, the right response is to reflect upon ourselves, and consider whether we indeed are guilty of the faults they lay to our charge. That is certainly a more godly response than to be in a rage, to revile in return, or to despise them for their evil-speaking. Thus we may get good out of evil, and it is the surest way to defeat the designs of our enemies who revile and backbite against us. They do it from wrong motives, wanting to injure us. But in this way we may turn it to our own good.

When you see others' faults, examine whether you have the same deficiencies in yourself. Too many people are ready to speak of others' faults when they have the very same shortcomings. Nothing is more common than for proud men to accuse others of pride. Likewise it is common for dishonest men to complain of being wronged by others. Evil traits and practices in others appear much more odious in others than they do in ourselves. We can easily see how contemptible this or that sin is in someone else. We see so readily in others what a hateful thing pride is, or how evil malice can be, or how pernicious other faults can be. But though we can easily see such imperfections in others, when we look at ourselves, those things are obscured by a mirror of deceit.

Therefore when you see others' faults, when you notice how someone else acts amiss, what an unkind attitude he shows, or how unsuitable her behavior is, when you hear others speak of it, or when you find fault with others in their dealings with you—reflect. Consider whether there is any similar shortcoming in your own conduct or attitude. Realize that these things are just as unbecoming and offensive in you as they are in others. Pride, or a haughty spirit and mannerisms, are as odious in you as they are in your neighbor. Your own malicious and revengeful spirit toward your neighbor is just as despicable as his malicious and revengeful spirit toward you. It is just as sinful for you to wrong or deceive your neighbor as it is for him to wrong or deceive you. It is just as destructive and unkind for you to talk against others behind their backs as it is for them to do the same to you.

Consider how others are blind to their own sins, and ask yourself if you suffer from the same kind of blindness. You know that others are blinded by their lusts. Could it be that some carnal appetite or lust of the mind has blinded you? You see how others are blinded by their worldliness. Ask whether your own attachment to this world might be blinding you in a way that causes you to justify things in your life that are not right. You are as prone to be blinded by sinful desires as others. You have the same deceitful and desperately wicked heart. "As in water face reflects face, so the heart of man reflects man" (Prov. 27:19).

Search Your Conscience for Secret Sins

Examine the secrets of your own heart. Do you live with some hidden sin? Do you neglect some duty only you and God know about? Do you indulge in some secret practice that is offensive to the all-seeing eye of God? Examine yourself concerning all your private responsibilities: Bible reading, meditation, secret prayer. Do you fulfill those duties at all? And if so, do you fulfill them in an unsteady and careless manner? What is your behavior like when you are hid from the eye of the world—when you have no restraints other than conscience? What does your own conscience tell you?

I will mention two matters in particular:

Ask yourself whether you neglect the reading of God's Word. The Bible was surely written to be read—not only by ministers, but by the people, too. It is not enough to have read the Bible once, or to read it once in a great while. The Scriptures were given to be with us continually, to act as our rule of life. Just as the craftsman must have his yardstick and the blind man his guide, just as he who walks in darkness carries a light, so the Bible was meant to be a lamp to our feet and a light to our path (Ps. 119:105).

Joshua 1:8 says, "This book of the law shall not depart from your mouth, but you shall meditate on it day and night, so that you may be careful to do according to all that is written in it; for then you will make your way prosperous, and then you will have success." Deuteronomy 6:6–9 commanded the Israelites,

> These words, which I am commanding you today, shall be on your heart; and you shall teach them diligently to your sons and shall talk of them when you sit in your house and when you walk by the way and when you lie down and when you rise up. And you shall bind them as a sign on your hand and they shall be as frontals on your forehead. And you shall write them on the doorposts of your house and on your gates.

In the same way Christ commands us to search the Scriptures (Jn. 5:39). These are mines in which we are to dig for hidden treasures. Do you neglect this duty?

Ask yourself whether you are secretly gratifying some sensual lust. There are many ways and degrees of gratifying our carnal lusts, but every one of them is provoking to a holy God. Even if you refrain from gross indulgences, do you in some way secretly from time to time gratify your lusts and allow yourself to taste the sweets of unlawful delight?

Do you realize that it is offensive to God even when we gratify a lust only in our thoughts and imagination? Are you guilty of this sin?

The Danger of Unforsaken Sin

You have had directions laid before you on how to examine yourself for sin you may be unaware of. How are things in your own life? Do you find that you are living in some sinful way? I'm not asking whether you find yourself clear from sin. That is not expected of you, for there is no one who does not sin (1 Ki. 8:46). But is there some way of sin in which you *live*, which is your *lifestyle* or *practice*? There are doubtless some who are clear in this matter, some "whose way is blameless, who walk in the law of the Lord. . . . who observe His testimonies, who seek Him with all their heart. They also do no unrighteousness; they walk in His ways" (Ps. 119:1–3).

Let your own conscience answer how you find your own life. Are you guilty? Do you practice some sin as a matter of habit? Have you *allowed* yourself to do so? If that is the case, consider the following things:

If you have been seeking salvation and not yet found it, some way of sin in your life may be the reason. You may have wondered what is the matter when you have long been concerned about your salvation—when you have sought it diligently—yet to no avail. You have many times cried to God, yet He does not regard you. Others obtain comfort, yet you remain in darkness. But is it any wonder at all, if you have held on to your sin for so long? Isn't this a sufficient reason why all your prayers and all your pleas have been blasted?

If you are trying to retain your sin while seeking the Savior, you are not seeking salvation the right way. The right way is to turn from your ungodliness. If there is one member that is corrupt and you don't cut it off, there is danger that it will carry you to hell (Matt. 5:29–30).

If grace seems to be languishing rather than flourishing in your soul, perhaps some way of sin is the cause. The way to grow in grace is to walk in obedience, and to be very thorough in doing so. Grace will flourish in the hearts of all who live in this manner. If you live in some way of sin, however, it will be like some secret disease eating at your vitals. Sin will thus keep you poor, weak, and languishing.

Just one sin practiced habitually will suppress your spiritual prosperity and will diminish the growth and strength of grace in your heart. It will grieve the Holy Spirit (Eph. 4:30). It will prevent the good influence of God's Word. As long as it remains it will be like an ulcer, keeping you weak and lean, though you be fed the most wholesome spiritual food.

If you have fallen into great sin, perhaps some way of sin in your life was the underlying root of your greater failure. A person who does not avoid every sin and is not meticulously obedient cannot be guarded against great sins. The sin in which he lives will always be an inlet, an open door, by which Satan will find entrance. It is like a breach in your fortress through which the enemy may get in and find his way to hurt you greatly. If you have fallen into some horrible sin, perhaps this is the reason.

Or if you allow some way of sin as an outlet for your own corruption, it will be like a breach in a dam, which if left alone will grow bigger and bigger until it cannot be stopped.

If you live very much in spiritual darkness, without sensing God's presence, it may be that some way of sin is the reason. If you complain that you have little sweet communion with God; if you feel God has deserted you; if God seems to hide His face from you and seldom shows you evidences of His glory and grace; or if you seem left to grope in darkness and wander in the wilderness—this may be the reason. Perhaps you have cried to God often. Perhaps you experience sleepless nights and sorrowful days. If you are living in some way of sin, it is very probable *that* is the cause, the root of your mischief, the Achan, the troubler that offends God and brings so many clouds of darkness over your soul. You are grieving the Holy Spirit, and that is why you have no comfort from Him.

Christ promised He would disclose Himself to His disciples. But it is on the condition that they keep His commands: "He who has My commandments and keeps them, he it is who loves Me; and he who loves Me shall be loved by My Father, and I will love him, and will disclose Myself to him" (Jn. 14:21). But if you habitually live in disobedience to any of His commandments, then it is no wonder He does not give you reassuring manifestations of Himself. The way to receive God's favor is to walk closely with Him.

If you have been doubting your salvation, perhaps some way of sin in your life has stoked those doubts. The best way to gain clear evidence of your salvation is by a close walk with God. This, as we have already observed, is also the way to have grace flourishing in the soul. And the more lively God's grace is in us, the more likely it is to be seen. When Christ is disclosing Himself to us, we have the reassurance of His love and favor.

But if you live in some way of sin, it is no wonder if that greatly diminishes your assurance. After all, it subdues the exercise of grace and hides the light of God's countenance. It may be that you will never know whether you are a true Christian or not until you have wholly forsaken the way of sin in which you live.

If you have met with the frowns of Providence, perhaps some way of sin in your life explains why. When you have received sore rebukes and chastisements, it is very probable that your practicing a sinful habit or tolerating an evil act is what has caused you the trouble. Sometimes God is exceedingly severe in His dealings with His own people for their sins in this world. Moses and Aaron were not permitted to enter Canaan because they disobeyed God and sinned with their lips at the waters of Meribah. And how terrible was God in His dealings with David! What affliction did He send upon him through his family! One of his sons raped his sister; another murdered his brother; and having expelled his father out of his own kingdom in the sight of all Israel, he defiled his father's concubines on the housetop in full view of everyone. In the end he met with a terrible demise that utterly broke his father's heart (2 Sam. 18:33). Immediately after that followed the rebellion of Sheba (2 Sam. 20). Then at the end of his life, David saw another of his sons usurping the crown.

How harshly did God deal with Eli for living in the sin of not restraining his children from wickedness! Both sons were killed in one day, and Eli himself died a violent death. The ark was taken into captivity (1 Sam. 4). Eli's house was cursed forever; God Himself swore that the iniquity of Eli's house would never be purged by sacrifice and offerings (1 Sam 3:13–14). The priesthood was taken from Eli and given to another line. And there never again was an old man in Eli's family (1 Sam. 12:31).

Is the way of sin in which you live the reason for the rebukes of Providence you have met with? True, it is not the proper business of your neighbors to judge you with respect to events of Providence, but you certainly ought to inquire yourself whether God is contending with you (Job 10:2).

If death is a fearful thought for you, perhaps it is because you are living in some way of sin. When you think of dying, do you find yourself shrinking back at the thought? When you have an illness, or when something threatens your life, are you frightened? Are thoughts of dying and going into eternity alarming to you, even though you profess to be a Christian?

If you are living in some sinful way, that is probably the foundation of your fears. Sin keeps your mind sensual and worldly and hinders a lively sense of heaven and heavenly enjoyments. Sin keeps grace low and prevents the anticipation of heavenly comforts you would otherwise have. Sin prevents your having the comforting sense of the divine favor and presence. Without that, no wonder you cannot look death in the face without terror.

Don't continue in any way of sin. If you have found in reading this that you *have* lived in a way of sin, consider that from this point on if you live in the same way, you will be living in *known* sin. Whether it was known sin in the past or not, you may have inadvertently been living in it. But now that you are aware of it, if you continue in it, your sin will not be a sin of *ignorance*, but you will show yourself to be one of those who willfully live in ways of known sin.

Notes

Chapter 1 — *"Whatever Happened to Sin?"*

1. Karl Menninger, *Whatever Became of Sin?* (New York: Hawthorn, 1973), 13.
2. Charles Krauthammer, "From People Power to Polenta," *Time* (4 October 1993), 94.
3. Wayne W. Dyer, *Your Erroneous Zones* (New York: Funk & Wagnalls, 1976), 90–91.
4. Ibid., 105–106.
5. *The Ann Landers Encyclopedia* (New York: Doubleday, 1978), 514–17.
6. Steve Lopez, "Thief Becomes a Millionaire over a Beating," *LA Daily News* (2 December 1993), 25.
7. Barbara Sommer, "PMS in the Courts: Are All Women on Trial?," *Psychology Today* (August 1984), 36.
8. "Bitter Legacy," *Time* (26 September 1983), 19.
9. J. Rangel, "Defendant in the Killing of 10 Is Guilty of Reduced Charge," *New York Times* (27 July 1985), 1, 27.
10. Amy Wilentz, "Pondering a High-Proof Defense," *Time* (2 November 1987), 60.
11. P. Shenon, "Deaver Is Sentenced to Suspended Term and $10,000 Fine," *New York Times* (24 September 1988), 1.
12. Andrew Ferguson, "Take Off the Kid Gloves," *National Review* (1 November 1993), 80.
13. "Compulsive Gambling May Be a Handicap, and a Shield from Firing," *Wall Street Journal* (21 June 1988), 1.
14. Stanton Peele, *Diseasing of America* (Lexington, Mass.: Lexington, 1989), 2–4 (emphasis in original).
15. Bernie Zilbergeld, *The Shrinking of America* (Boston: Little, Brown, 1983), 89.
16. Ibid., 167.

17. Charles J. Sykes, *A Nation of Victims: The Decay of the American Character* (New York: St. Martin's, 1992), 13.

18. Ibid., 16.

19. Ibid., 15.

20. Wendy Kaminer, *I'm Dysfunctional, You're Dysfunctional* (Reading, MA.: Addison-Wesley, 1992), 121.

21. Ibid., 124.

22. Ibid., 124–125.

23. Ibid., 20.

24. Ibid., 18.

25. Garth Wood, *The Myth of Neurosis* (New York: Harper & Row, 1986), 9.

26. Karl Menninger, *Whatever Became of Sin?* (New York: Hawthorn, 1973).

Chapter 2 — "The Soul's Automatic Warning System"

1. J. I. Packer, *Rediscovering Holiness* (Ann Arbor: Servant, 1992), 151.

2. Richard Sibbes, *Commentary on 2 Corinthians Chapter 1*, in Alexander B. Grosart, ed., *Works of Richard Sibbes*, 7 vols. (Edinburgh: Banner of Truth, 1981 reprint), 3:208.

3. Ibid., 210–211.

4. Ibid., 212 (emphasis added).

Chapter 3 — "How Sin Silences the Conscience"

1. Charles W. Colson, "The Enduring Revolution: 1993 Templeton Address," (pamphlet) "Sources, No. 4" (Washington: Wilberforce Forum, 1993), 4–5.

2. Robert L. Vernon, *L. A. Justice* (Colorado Springs: Focus on the Family, 1993), 209–212.

3. Ibid., 213.

4. D. Martyn Lloyd-Jones, *The Plight of Man and the Power of God* (Grand Rapids: Eerdmans, 1945), 14.

5. Herodotus, *The Histories*, 1:31.

6. Augustine, *The City of God*, 4:31.

7. Lucian, *The Syrian Goddess*, 34.
8. Dennis A. Williams and Susan Agrest, "A School for Homosexuals," *Newsweek* (17 June 1985), 93.
9. "Quotable," *Daily News* (3 November 1993), 6.
10. Benjamin DeMott, "The Pro-Incest Lobby," *Psychology Today* (March 1980), 11.
11. Maurice Roberts, "God Gave Them Up," *The Banner of Truth* (October 1993), 3–4.

Chapter 4—"What Do You Mean, 'Totally Depraved'?"

1. J. C. Ryle, *Holiness* (Durham, England: Evangelical Press, 1979 reprint), 6. (First published in 1879.)
2. Jerry Adler, Pat Wingert, Lynda Wright, Patrick Houston, Howard Manley, and Alden Cohen, "Hey, I'm Terrific," *Newsweek* (17 February 1992), 50.
3. Charles Krauthammer, "Education: Doing Bad and Feeling Good," *Time* (5 February 1990), 70.
4. Cheryl Russell, "Predictions for the Baby Boom," *The Boomer Report* (15 September 1993), 4.
5. Adler, 50.
6. Ibid.
7. Norman Vincent Peale, *The Power of Positive Thinking* (Englewood Cliffs, NJ: Prentice Hall, 1952).
8. Ibid., viii.
9. Ibid., ix.
10. Adler, 50.
11. Ryle, 16.
12. Robert Schuller, *Self-Esteem: The New Reformation* (Waco: Word, 1982), 33.
13. Ibid., 57.
14. Ibid., 75 (emphasis in original).
15. Robert Schuller, "The Phil Donahue Show," 12 August 1980.
16. Schuller, *Self-Esteem*, 99.
17. Ibid., 14.
18. Ibid., 15.
19. Ibid., 98.

20. Ibid., 104.
21. "A Special Interview with Dr. Robert Schuller," "The White Horse Inn" radio broadcast with Michael Horton, host (1 November 1992).
22. Schuller, *Self-Esteem*, 45.
23. Ibid., 39.
24. "A Special Interview."
25. Schuller, *Self-Esteem*, 127.
26. Ibid., 31.
27. Ibid.
28. Ibid., 26–27.
29. Ibid., 64.
30. Ibid., 36.
31. Ibid., 98.
32. Ibid., 37.
33. Ibid., 39.
34. Ibid., 58.
35. Ibid., 67.
36. Ibid., 65.
37. Ibid.
38. D. Martyn Lloyd-Jones, *The Plight of Man and the Power of God* (Grand Rapids: Eerdmans, 1945), 87.
39. George F. Will, "A Trickle-Down Culture," *Newsweek* (13 December 1993), 84.
40. Dennis Prager, "The Belief That People Are Basically Good," *Ultimate Issues* (January-March 1990), 15.
41. Ibid.
42. Ryle, 9–10.

Chapter 5 — "Sin and Its Cure"

1. D. Martyn Lloyd-Jones, *The Plight of Man and the Power of God* (Grand Rapids: Eerdmans, 1945), 147
2. Tom Wolfe, *The Bonfire of the Vanities* (New York: Farrar, Straus, Giroux, 1987).
3. Jay Adams, *The Grand Demonstration* (Santa Barbara: EastGate, 1991), 16.
4. Harold S. Kushner, *When Bad Things Happen to Good People* (New York: Schocken, 1981).

5. R. L. Dabney, *Systematic Theology* (Edinburgh: Banner of Truth, 1985 reprint of 1871 original), 537–38.
6. Lloyd-Jones, 89.

Chapter 6 — "The Conquered Enemy Within"

1. D. Martyn Lloyd-Jones, *Sanctified Through the Truth: The Assurance of Our Salvation* (Wheaton: Crossway, 1989), 120.
2. Spencer Klaw, *Without Sin: The Life and Death of the Oneida Community* (New York: Allen Lane, 1993), 3.
3. H. A. Ironside, *Holiness: The False and the True* (Neptune, NJ: Loizeaux, 1912), 36–37.
4. B. B. Warfield, *Perfectionism,* vol. 2 (Grand Rapids: Baker, 1981 reprint of 1932 original), 561.
5. Ibid., 562 (emphasis added).
6. John MacArthur, *Faith Works: The Gospel According to the Apostles* (Dallas: Word, 1993), 105–121.
7. Warfield, 568.
8. Lloyd-Jones, 116–17 (emphasis added).

Chapter 7 — "Hacking Agag to Pieces"

1. John Owen, *The Works of John Owen,* 16 vols. (Edinburgh: Banner of Truth, 1967 reprint of 1853 edition), 6:177, 6:9.
2. Ibid., 6: 8 (emphasis added).
3. D. Martyn Lloyd-Jones, *Romans: An Exposition of Chapter 8:5–17: The Sons of God* (Grand Rapids: Zondervan, 1974), 92 (emphasis added).
4. Owen, 6:16–17.
5. D. Martyn Lloyd-Jones, *Sanctified Through the Truth: The Assurance of Our Salvation* (Wheaton: Crossway, 1989), 54.
6. Owen, 6:20.
7. Ibid., 6:11.
8. Ibid., 6:12 (emphasis added).
9. Ibid., 6:14.
10. Cited in I.D.E. Thomas, *A Puritan Golden Treasury* (Edinburgh: Banner of Truth, 1977), 264.
11. Ibid., 6:56.
12. Ibid., 55.
13. Lloyd-Jones, *Romans 8:5–17,* 143.

Chapter 8 — "Handling Temptation"

1. Sinclair Ferguson, *Taking the Christian Life Seriously: A Study on Christian Maturity* (Grand Rapids: Zondervan, 1981), 84–85.
2. John Leo, "The Seven Video Sins," *U.S. News & World Report* (23 August 1993), 19.

Chapter 9 — "Keeping a Pure Mind"

1. Ralph Venning, *The Sinfulness of Sin* (Edinburgh: Banner of Truth, 1965 reprint of 1669 original), 224.
2. Ibid., 227.

Chapter 10 — "Holding to the Mystery of Faith with a Clear Conscience"

1. Jeremiah Burroughs, *The Evil of Evils* (Ligonier, PA: Soli Deo Gloria, 1992 reprint of 1654 original), 2–3.
2. Ibid., 3.
3. Lewis B. Smedes, *Shame and Grace: Healing the Shame We Don't Deserve* (San Francisco: HarperCollins, 1993), 3–4.
4. Ibid., 4.
5. Ibid.
6. Ibid., 119.
7. Ibid., 120.
8. Vergilius Ferm, *A Dictionary of Pastoral Psychology* (New York: Philosophical Library, 1955), 173–74.
9. D. Martyn Lloyd-Jones, *Sanctified Through the Truth: The Assurance of Our Salvation* (Wheaton: Crossway, 1989), 96–97.
10. My analysis of this movement is in John MacArthur, *Ashamed of the Gospel: When the Church Becomes Like the World* (Wheaton: Crossway, 1993).
11. John Blanchard, *Whatever Happened to Hell?* (Durham, England: Evangelical Press, 1993), 145.

Appendix 1 – "Gaining Victory Over Sin – A Closer Look at Romans 6"

1. James M. Boice, *Amazing Grace* (Wheaton: Tyndale, 1993), 41–42.
2. C. I. Scofield, *The Scofield Reference Bible* (New York: Oxford, 1917), 1200.
3. Clarence Larkin, *Rightly Dividing the Truth* (Philadelphia: Larkin Estate, n.d.), 210–211.
4. Ibid. (emphasis in original).
5. R. L. Dabney, *Systematic Theology* (Edinburgh: Banner of Truth, 1985 reprint of 1878 edition), 677.
6. Matthew Henry, *Commentary on the Whole Bible*, 6 vols. (Old Tappan, NJ: Revell, n.d.], 6:405.
7. D. Martyn Lloyd-Jones, *Romans: An Exposition of Chapter Six: The New Man* (Grand Rapids: Zondervan, 1972), 268–69.

Appendix 2 – "An Appeal for a Good Conscience"

1. Adapted into modern English and abridged from a sermon originally titled, "The Demand of a Good Conscience" first published in Sibbes's *Evangelical Sacrifices*, published in London in 1640.

Appendix 3 – "Searching Your Conscience"

1. Adapted and paraphrased into modern English from Edwards' tract "Christian Cautions: The Necessity of Self-Examination" (first printed 1788).

Scripture Index

Subject Index

Index

The God Who Loves

The God Who Loves

by

John MacArthur, Jr.

ISBN 0-8499-4274-8

To Patricia,

whom I love more than life itself
and whose love for me
is closer to heavenly perfection
than anything I have known on earth.

Contents

The God Who Loves

Contents

Introduction

A FEW YEARS AGO I had the opportunity to spend several days traveling with Bill and Gloria Gaither, the well-known gospel musicians. At one point I asked Bill what, in his estimation, were the greatest Christian lyrics ever written—aside from the inspired Psalms.

Without hesitation, he began quoting the words from F. M. Lehman's "The Love of God:"

> *The love of God is greater far*
> *Than tongue or pen can ever tell;*
> *It goes beyond the highest star,*
> *And reaches to the lowest hell.*
> *The guilty pair, bowed down with care,*
> *God gave His Son to win;*
> *His erring child He reconciled,*
> *And pardoned from his sin.*
>
> *When hoary time shall pass away,*
> *And earthly thrones and kingdoms fall,*
> *When men who here refuse to pray,*

The God Who Loves

On rocks and hills and mountains call,
God's love so sure, shall still endure,
All measureless and strong;
Redeeming grace to Adam's race—
The saints' and angels' song.

Could we with ink the ocean fill,
And were the skies of parchment made,
Were every stalk on earth a quill,
And every man a scribe by trade,
To write the love of God above
Would drain the ocean dry.
Nor could the scroll contain the whole,
Though stretched from sky to sky.

O love of God, how rich and pure!
How measureless and strong!
It shall forevermore endure—
The saints' and angels' song.

No lyrics in all hymnody surpass the third stanza of that song, he said.

Indeed, few rivals come to mind. The poetry alone is beautiful—but the meaning is profound.

As I pondered that song, my mind was flooded with echoes from Scripture. "God is love," the apostle John wrote (1 Jn. 4:8, 16). "His lovingkindness is everlasting" is the refrain for all twenty-six verses of Psalm 136. Those same words appear at least forty-one times in the Old Testament. God's lovingkindness is better than life itself, the psalmist reminds us (Ps. 63:3). God is "merciful and gracious, slow to anger and abundant in lovingkindness and truth (Ps. 86:15)." He "is good; His lovingkindness is everlasting" (Ps. 100:5).

Elsewhere the psalmist writes, "How precious is Thy lovingkindness, O God! And the children of men take refuge in the shadow of Thy wings" (Ps. 36:7). And "I will sing of the loving-kindess of the Lord forever. . . . Lovingkindness will be built up forever" (Ps. 89:1–2).

The New Testament unveils the ultimate proof of God's love: "But God demonstrates His own love toward us, in that while we were yet sinners, Christ died for us" (Rom. 5:8). "By this the love of God was manifested in us, that God has sent His only begotten Son into the world so that we might live through Him. In this is love, not that we loved God, but that He loved us and sent His Son to be the propitiation for our sins" (1 Jn. 4:9–10). "God, being rich in mercy, because of His great love with which He loved us . . . made us alive together with Christ (by grace you have been saved), and raised us up with Him, and seated us with Him in the heavenly places, in Christ Jesus" (Eph. 2:4–6).

And the most familiar verse of all says this: "For God so loved the world, that He gave His only begotten Son, that whoever believes in Him should not perish, but have eternal life" (Jn. 3:16).

No wonder the apostle exults, "See how great a love the Father has bestowed upon us. . . ." (1 Jn. 3:1).

Obviously, God's love and goodness are persistent themes in both the Old and New Testaments. If the amount of space the Bible gives the subject is any indication, hardly any truth about God is as important as His love. On almost every page of Scripture we see divine goodness, tender mercies, lovingkind-ness, patience, longsuffering, and grace. All those virtues are expressions of God's love.

The doctrine of God's love is by no means simple. It raises a host of philosophical and theological difficulties. For example, some of the most obvious questions it brings up are these: If God is so lov-ing, why does He send people to hell? Why does He allow sin and suffering and pain and sorrow? How can holocausts and natural disasters and other forms of mass destruction and human suffering exist in a universe designed by a God who is truly loving? Why did God allow the human race to be plunged into sin in the first place?

In all honesty we need to acknowledge the difficulty of questions like those. All of us have asked them. Many of us have been challenged with such questions from skeptics who ask us to provide satisfactory answers. If we're honest, we must admit that the answers are not easy. God Himself has not seen fit to reveal full answers to some of those questions. Instead, He reveals Himself as loving, all-wise, perfectly righteous, and supremely good—and He simply bids us trust Him.

That becomes easier the better we understand what Scripture teaches about the love of God. In this book we will grapple with some of those difficult questions about God's love, but not until we've laid a good foundation for understanding what Scripture means when it says, "God is love."

We must also note that several of the very worst corruptions of Christian truth are based on the notion that God can be understood solely in terms of His love. Those who hold such a perspective often refuse to acknowledge God's wrath against sin, because they believe He cannot be *both* loving *and* angry with sinners. Others, perhaps intending to dissociate God from the tragedies and terrors of human experience, reason that if God is truly loving, He can't possibly be all-powerful; otherwise, He would put a stop to all suffering.

On the other hand, some well-meaning Christians concerned with doctrinal orthodoxy are so cautious about overemphasizing God's love that they fear to speak of it at all. Our culture, after all, is "in love" with sin and self-love, and utterly dull to the wrath of God against sin. Isn't it counterproductive to preach the love of God in the midst of such an ungodly society? Some who reason thus tend to see every bad thing that happens as if it were a direct judgment from the hand of a severe Deity.

Both extremes paint a distorted picture of God and further confuse the issue of understanding God's love.

As long as we stay within the bounds of biblical truth about God's love, we can avoid both of these transgressions. As we examine what the Bible says about this subject, we will see how wonderfully God's love can be presented to sinners and how perfectly it fits with His hatred of sin. And the things hard to understand are made easier.

In our pursuit of understanding on this matter, however, we must be willing to shed a lot of popular, sentimental notions about divine love. Many of our favorite presuppositions about God need to be corrected. God's love and His holiness must be carefully understood in light of His wrath against sin. We must see love from the divine perspective before we can truly grasp the import of God's great love for us.

The remedy, as always, is an open-hearted embracing of all the biblical data. And it is my design in this book to try to highlight a broad, balanced cross-section of that data. As the songwriter pointed out, to cover the subject as it deserves to be covered would drain the oceans of ink and fill a galaxy of skies. And even after many eons, the preface would barely be written.

Eternity will be spent in just such a study, I am sure. That's why for me, the opportunity to write this book has been like a little slice of heaven. As you read, I hope you will sense something of the heavenly glory as well, and learn that all the sadness, pain, and sorrow of human life do not negate the love of God to humanity. On the contrary; it is only the knowledge of His love in the midst of such trials that enables us to endure and be strengthened by them.

We'll spend the first three chapters laying a foundation for understanding God's love. Beginning in chapter 4, we will return to deal with the hard questions we raised here, such as why God allows suffering. In the chapters that follow, we'll see how God's love defines who He is, how it applies to all humanity, and how it applies in a unique and special way to Christians.

My prayer for all who read this book is an echo of Paul's prayer for the Ephesians:

". . . that Christ may dwell in your hearts through faith; and that you, being rooted and grounded in love, may be able to comprehend with all the saints what is the breadth, and height and depth, and to know the love of Christ which surpasses knowledge, that you may be filled up to all the fulness of God" (Eph. 3:17–19).

God So Loved the World

God's Love in Recent Church History

God's Love and the Contemporary Church

God's Love for the Unbelieving World

Chapter 1

God So Loved the World

LOVE IS THE BEST KNOWN but least understood of all God's attributes. Almost everyone who believes in God these days believes that He is a God of love. I have even met agnostics who are quite certain that *if* God exists, He must be benevolent, compassionate, and loving.

All those things *are* infinitely true about God, of course, but not the way most people think. Because of the influence of modern liberal theology, many suppose that God's love and goodness ultimately nullify His righteousness, justice, and holy wrath. They envision God as a benign heavenly grandfather—tolerant, affable, lenient, permissive, devoid of any real displeasure over sin, who without consideration of His holiness will benignly pass over sin and accept people as they are.

God's Love in Recent Church History

PEOPLE IN PAST GENERATIONS often went to the opposite extreme. They tended to think of God as stern, demanding, cruel, even abusive. They so magnified God's wrath that they virtually

1

ignored His love. Little more than a hundred years ago, nearly all evangelistic preaching portrayed God only as a fierce Judge whose fury burned against sinners. History reveals that some dramatic shifts in how we think of God have taken place over the past three centuries.

Jonathan Edwards

PERHAPS THE MOST FAMOUS sermon ever preached in America was Jonathan Edwards's "Sinners in the Hands of an Angry God." Edwards was a pastor in colonial Massachusetts and a brilliant theological mind. He preached his most famous sermon as a guest speaker in a church at Enfield, Connecticut, on July 8, 1741. This sermon sparked one of the most dramatic episodes of revival in the Great Awakening. Here is an excerpt that shows the preacher's graphic and frightening bluntness in portraying God's dreadful wrath against sinners:

> The God that holds you over the pit of hell, much as one holds a spider, or some loathsome insect over the fire, abhors you, and is dreadfully provoked: his wrath towards you burns like fire; he looks upon you as worthy of nothing else, but to be cast into the fire; he is of purer eyes than to bear to have you in his sight; you are ten thousand times more abominable in his eyes, than the most hateful venomous serpent is in ours. You have offended him infinitely more than ever a stubborn rebel did his prince; and yet it is nothing but his hand that holds you from falling into the fire every moment. It is to be ascribed to nothing else, that you did not go to hell the last night; that you was suffered to awake again in this world, after you closed your eyes to sleep. And there is no other reason to be given, why you have not dropped into hell since you arose in the morning, but that God's hand has held you up. There is no other reason to be

given why you have not gone to hell, since you have sat here in the house of God, provoking his pure eyes by your sinful wicked manner of attending his solemn worship. Yea, there is nothing else that is to be given as a reason why you do not this very moment drop down into hell.

O sinner! Consider the fearful danger you are in: it is a great furnace of wrath, a wide and bottomless pit, full of the fire of wrath, that you are held over in the hand of that God, whose wrath is provoked and incensed as much against you, as against many of the damned in hell. You hang by a slender thread, with the flames of divine wrath flashing about it, and ready every moment to singe it, and burn it asunder; and you have no interest in any Mediator, and nothing to lay hold of to save yourself, nothing to keep off the flames of wrath, nothing of your own, nothing that you ever have done, nothing that you can do, to induce God to spare you one moment.

The language and imagery were so vivid that many people who heard Edwards trembled, some cried out for mercy, and others fainted.

Our generation—weaned on "Jesus loves me! this I know"— finds Edwards's famous sermon shocking for an altogether different reason. Most people today would be appalled that anyone would describe God in such terrifying terms.

But it is important that we understand the context of Edwards's sermon. Edwards was no fiery emotionalist; he appealed dispassionately to his hearers' sense of reason—even reading his message in a carefully controlled tone lest anyone be emotionally manipulated. His message ended with a tender appeal to flee to Christ for mercy. One observer who was present that evening recorded that "Several Souls were hopefully wrought upon [that] night, & oh ye cheerfulness and pleasantness of their countenances [that] receivd comfort—oh [that] God wd strengthen and confirm—we sung an hymn & prayd & dismissd ye Assembly."[1] So the overall tenor of that evening's service was decidedly uplifting. It signaled a time of great revival throughout New England.

Edwards has been falsely caricatured by some as a harsh and pitiless preacher who took great delight in frightening his congregations with colorful descriptions of the torments of hell. Nothing could be further from the truth. He was a warm and sensitive pastor as well as a meticulous theologian, and he stood on solid biblical ground when he characterized God as an angry Judge. Scripture tells us, "God judgeth the righteous, and God is angry with the wicked every day" (Ps. 7:11, KJV). Edwards's sermon that night was an exposition of Deuteronomy 32:35–36: "To me belongeth vengeance, and recompense; their foot shall slide in due time: for the day of their calamity is at hand, and the things that shall come upon them make haste. For the Lord shall judge his people" (KJV). Those are biblical truths that do need to be proclaimed. And when Jonathan Edwards preached them, he did so with a humble heart of loving compassion. A broader look at his ministry reveals that he also heavily emphasized the grace and love of God. This sermon alone does not give us the full picture of what his preaching was like.

Yet Edwards was not reluctant to preach the unvarnished truth of divine wrath. He saw conversion as the loving work of God in the human soul, and he knew the truth of Scripture was the means God uses to convert sinners. He believed his responsibility as a preacher was to declare both the positive and the negative aspects of that truth as plainly as possible.

Charles Finney

UNFORTUNATELY, A LATER GENERATION of preachers were not so balanced and careful in their approach to evangelism, and not so sound in their theology. Charles Finney, an early nineteenth-century lawyer-turned-revivalist, saw conversion as a *human* work. Finney declared that revival could virtually be manufactured if preachers would employ the right means. He wrote:

> There is nothing in religion beyond the ordinary powers of nature. It consists entirely in the *right exercise* of the powers of nature. It is just that, and nothing else. . . . A revival is not a miracle, nor dependent on a miracle, in any sense. It is a purely philosophical result of the right use of the constituted means—as much so as any other effect produced by the application of means.[2]

Finney even denied that the new birth is a sovereign work of the Holy Spirit (cf. Jn. 3:8). He taught instead that regeneration is something accomplished by the sinner: "The Spirit of God, by the truth, *influences* the sinner to change, and in this sense is the efficient Cause of the change. *But the sinner actually changes, and is therefore himself, in the most proper sense, the author of the change.* . . . A change of heart is *the sinner's own act.*"[3]

Finney believed that people could be psychologically manipulated into responding to the gospel. One of his favorite measures for heightening emotions was preaching passionately about the fiery threats of divine vengeance. By this he sought to intimidate people into responding to the gospel. Whereas Edwards had looked to the Holy Spirit to use the truth of Scripture to convert sinners, Finney believed it was the preacher's task to evoke the desirable response, through artful persuasion, browbeating, manipulation, or whatever means possible. He found that terrorizing people was a very effective method of arousing a response. His repertoire was filled with sermons designed to heighten the fears of unbelievers.

Preachers who adopted Finney's methods often carried them to preposterous extremes. Preaching about divine wrath was often merely theatrical. And the subject of God's wrath against sin began to be preached to the exclusion of God's love.

The God Who Loves

D. L. Moody

ALL THIS HAD A VERY PROFOUND IMPACT on the popular perception of God. The typical Christian of the mid-1800s would have been scandalized by the suggestion that God loves sinners. Even D. L. Moody, so well-known for his strong emphasis on God's love, wasn't always that way. In fact, he was disturbed the first time he heard another evangelist proclaim God's love for sinners.

The evangelist Moody heard was an unassuming British preacher, converted pickpocket Harry Moorhouse. In the winter of 1868 Moorhouse showed up unexpectedly in Chicago and offered to preach to Moody's congregation. Moody, just leaving for a few days' ministry in St. Louis, was uncertain about Moorhouse's preaching ability. But he had once met Moorhouse while in England, so he reluctantly arranged for the Englishman to speak to a midweek gathering in the church basement.

Returning on Saturday from his trip, Moody asked his wife about Moorhouse's preaching.

"He preaches a little different from you," she told Moody. "He preaches that God loves sinners."

"He is wrong," Moody replied.

Mrs. Moody advised her husband to withhold judgment until she had heard Moorhouse preach. "I think you will agree with him when you hear him, because he backs up everything he says with the Bible."

J. C. Pollock recounts what happened in the few days that followed:

> On Sunday morning Moody noticed his congregation were all carrying Bibles. He had never told them that persons in pews should bring Bibles. "It was something strange to see the people coming in with Bibles, and listen to the flutter of the leaves."
>
> Moorhouse announced his text: "John 3:16: God so loved the world that he gave his only begotten son, that

whosoever believeth in him should not perish but have everlasting life." Instead of dividing the text into firstly, secondly, thirdly in ministerial manner Moorhouse, Moody noted, "went from Genesis to Revelation giving proof that God loves the sinner, and before he got through, two or three of my sermons were spoiled. . . . I never knew up to that time that God loved us so much. This heart of mine began to thaw out; I could not keep back the tears." Fleming Revell remembered all his long life the sight of Moody drinking it in on that Sunday morning, February 8th, 1868, and how "on Sunday night little Harry Moorhouse stood swaying from one foot to another in his seeming awkwardness, but you forgot all about it as you heard the message coming from his lips." The text was the same, "God so loved the world . . ." unfolded once again from Genesis to Revelation, by a different route, his address not a sermon so much as a string of related texts or passages, briefly commented upon to form what came to be known, rather oddly, as a "Bible Reading."

At the end Moody jumped up. "Mr. Moorhouse will speak every night this week. Everybody come. Tell your friends to come."

Night after night Moorhouse announced, "God so loved the world . . ." and drew his hearers by a fresh line through the Bible: "My friends, for a whole week I have been trying to tell you how much God loves you, but I cannot do it with this poor stammering tongue. . . . "

Outside, in the sharp February air, Chicago life rolled on unawares. Merchants dined and wined, the poor huddled half-frozen round smoking stoves, sailors from iced-up ships lechered or boozed or brawled. At Illinois Street among that crowd of humble citizens and a few new immigrants and a sprinkle of the rich, the spirit of love ran unfettered. And D. L. Moody turned in his ways, to become from that time forth an apostle of the love of God.[4]

The God Who Loves

That event transformed D. L. Moody's evangelistic style. Moody was subsequently used by God to reach both Britain and America with the simple gospel of love and grace. To people almost utterly unaware of God's lovingkindness, he preached that God is a God of mercy and grace. To multitudes who had been conditioned to think of God only as a wrathful judge, he preached that God is "compassionate and gracious, slow to anger, and abounding in lovingkindness and truth" (Exod. 34:6; cf. 2 Chr. 30:9; Neh. 9:17, 31; Ps. 103:8; 111:4; 112:4; 116:5; Joel 2:13; Jonah 4:2). Moody was instrumental in recovering the truth of divine love from near obscurity.

Modern Liberalism

BUT WITH THE RISE OF LIBERAL THEOLOGY the pendulum swung too far. *Liberalism* (sometimes called *modernism*) was a corruption of Christianity, based on a wholesale denial of the authority and inspiration of Scripture. It was a growing trend throughout the nineteenth century, influenced strongly by trends in German theology. (Friedrich Schliermacher and Albrecht Ritschl were among the leading German theologians responsible for liberalism.) While retaining some of the moral teachings of Christianity, liberalism attacked the historic foundations of the faith. Liberals denied the deity of Christ, the historicity of the Bible, and the uniqueness of the Christian faith. Instead, they proclaimed the brotherhood of all humanity under the fatherhood of God—and consequently insisted that God's only attitude toward humanity was pure love.[5] In fact, the overarching interpretive principle for liberals became the theme of love. If a passage didn't reflect their definition of divine love, it was disallowed as Scripture.[6]

In the early part of this century liberalism took mainline Protestant churches by storm. It might be argued that the first half of the present century ushered in the most serious spiritual decline since the Protestant Reformation. Evangelicalism, which had dominated Protestant America since the days of the founding fathers, was virtually driven out of denominational schools and churches. Evangelicalism managed to survive and even thrive outside the denominations. But it never regained its influence in the mainline groups. Instead it has flourished chiefly in relatively small denominations and non-denominational churches. In a few decades, liberalism virtually destroyed the largest Protestant denominations in America and Europe.

Harry Emerson Fosdick

ONE OF THE MOST POPULAR SPOKESMEN for liberal Christianity was Harry Emerson Fosdick, pastor of the Riverside Church in New York City. Fosdick, while remaining strongly committed to liberal theology, nevertheless acknowledged that the new theology was undermining the concept of a holy God. Contrasting his age with that of Jonathan Edwards, Fosdick wrote:

> Jonathan Edwards' Enfield sermon pictured sinners held over the blazing abyss of hell in the hands of a wrathful deity who at any moment was likely to let go, and so terrific was that discourse in its delivery that women fainted and strong men clung in agony to the pillars of the church. *Obviously, we do not believe in that kind of God any more,* and as always in reaction we swing to the opposite extreme, so in the theology of these recent years we have taught a very mild, benignant sort of deity. . . . Indeed, the god of the new theology has not seemed to care acutely about sin; certainly he has not been warranted to punish heavily; he has been an indulgent parent and when we have sinned, a polite "Excuse me" has seemed more than adequate to make amends.[7]

Fosdick never spoke more truly. He correctly saw that liberalism had led to a warped and imbalanced concept of God. He could even see far enough ahead to realize that liberalism was taking society into a dangerous wasteland of amorality, where "man's sin, his greed, his selfishness, his rapacity roll up across the years an accumulating mass of consequence until at last in a mad collapse the whole earth crashes into ruin."[8]

Despite all that, Fosdick ultimately would not acknowledge the literal reality of God's wrath toward impenitent sinners. To him, "the wrath of God" was nothing more than a metaphor for the natural consequences of wrongdoing. Writing in the wake of World War I, Fosdick suggested that *the moral order of the world has been dipping us in hell.*[9] His theology would not tolerate a personal God whose righteous anger burned against sin. Moreover, to Fosdick, the threat of actual hellfire was only a relic of a barbaric age. *"Obviously, we do not believe in that kind of God any more."*

God's Love and the Contemporary Church

FOSDICK WROTE THOSE WORDS almost eighty years ago. Sadly, what was true of liberalism then is all too true of evangelicalism today. We have lost the reality of God's wrath. We have disregarded His hatred for sin. The God most evangelicals now describe is all-loving and not at all angry. We have forgotten that "It is a terrifying thing to fall into the hands of the living God" (Heb. 10:31). *We do not believe in that kind of God anymore.*

Ironically, this overemphasis on divine beneficence actually works against a sound understanding of God's love. Some theologians are so bent on this perception of God as all love, that when things go wrong they see it as evidence that God can't really control everything. They believe if God is truly loving, He can't be fully sovereign. This view makes God into a victim of evil.[10]

Multitudes have embraced the disastrous idea that God is impotent to deal with evil. They believe He is kindly but feeble, or

10

perhaps aloof, or simply unconcerned about human wickedness. Is it any wonder that people with such a concept of God defy His holiness, take His love for granted, and presume on His grace and mercy? Certainly no one would *fear* a deity like that.

Yet Scripture tells us repeatedly that *fear* of God is the very foundation of true wisdom (Job 28:28; Ps. 111:10; Prov. 1:7; 9:10; 15:33; Mic. 6:9). People often try to explain the sense of those verses away by saying that the "fear" called for is a devout sense of awe and reverence. Certainly the fear of God includes awe and reverence, but it does not *exclude* literal holy terror. "It is the Lord of hosts whom you should regard as holy. And He shall be your fear, and He shall be your dread" (Isa. 8:13).

We must recapture some of the holy terror that comes with a right understanding of God's righteous anger. We need to remember that God's wrath *does* burn against impenitent sinners (Ps. 38:1–3). That reality is the very thing that makes His love so amazing. We must therefore proclaim these truths with the same sense of conviction and fervency we employ when we declare the love of God. It is only against the backdrop of divine wrath that the full significance of God's love can be truly understood. That is precisely the message of the cross of Jesus Christ. After all, it was on the cross that God's love and His wrath converged in all their majestic fullness.

Only those who see themselves as sinners in the hands of an angry God can fully appreciate the magnitude and wonder of His love. In this regard our generation is surely at a greater disadvantage than any previous age. We have been force-fed the doctrines of self-esteem for so long that most people don't really view themselves as sinners worthy of divine wrath. On top of that, religious liberalism, humanism, evangelical compromise, and ignorance of the Scriptures have all worked against a right understanding of who God is. Ironically, in an age that conceives of God as wholly loving, altogether devoid of wrath, few people really understand what God's love is all about!

The God Who Loves

How we address the misconception of the present age is crucial. We must not respond to an overemphasis on divine love by denying that God is love. Our generation's imbalanced view of God cannot be corrected by an equal imbalance in the opposite direction. I am frankly fearful that this is a very real danger in some circles. One of the deep concerns that has prompted me to write this book is a growing trend I have noticed—particularly among people committed to the biblical truth of God's sovereignty and divine election. Some of them flatly deny that God in any sense loves those whom He has not chosen for salvation.

I am convinced from Scripture that God is absolutely sovereign in the salvation of sinners. Salvation "does not depend on the man who wills or the man who runs, but on God who has mercy" (Rom. 9:16). We are redeemed not because of anything good in us, but because God chose us unto salvation. He chose certain individuals and passed over others, and He made that choice in eternity past, before the foundation of the world (Eph. 1:4). Moreover, He chose without regard to anything He foresaw in the elect; simply "according to the good pleasure of his will [and] to the praise of the glory of his grace" (vv. 5–6, KJV). Election arises from the love of God. Those whom He chose, He "loved . . . with an everlasting love [and drew them to Himself] with lovingkindness" (Jer. 31:3).

But certainly we can affirm those truths without also concluding that God's attitude toward the non-elect is one of utter hatred.

I am troubled by the tendency of some—often young people newly infatuated with Reformed doctrine—who insist that God cannot possibly love those who never repent and believe. I encounter this view, it seems, with increasing frequency. The argument inevitably goes like this: Psalm 7:11 tells us "God is angry with the wicked every day." It seems reasonable to assume that if God loved everyone, He would have chosen everyone unto salvation. Therefore, God does not love the non-elect. Those who hold this view often go to great lengths to argue that John 3:16 cannot really mean God loves the whole world.

Perhaps the best-known argument for this view is found in the unabridged edition of an otherwise excellent book, *The Sovereignty of God,* by A. W. Pink.[11] Pink wrote, "God loves whom He chooses. He does not love everybody."[12] Later in the book, he added this:

> Is it true that God *loves* the one who is *despising* and rejecting His blessed Son? God is Light as well as Love, and therefore His love must be a *holy* love. To tell the Christ-rejecter that God loves him is to cauterize his conscience, as well as to afford him a sense of security in his sins. The fact is, that the love of God, is a truth for the saints only, and to present it to the enemies of God is to take the children's bread and cast it to the dogs. With the exception of John 3:16, not once in the four gospels do we read of the Lord Jesus—the perfect teacher—telling sinners that God loved them![13]

In an appendix to the unabridged edition, Pink argued that the word *world* in John 3:16 ("For God so loved the *world* . . . ") "refers to *the world of believers* (God's elect), in contradistinction from *'the world of the ungodly.'*"[14]

Pink was attempting to make the crucial point that God is sovereign in the exercise of His love. The gist of his argument is certainly valid: It is folly to think that God loves all alike, or that He is compelled by some rule of fairness to love everyone equally. Scripture teaches us that God loves because He chooses to love (cf. Deut. 7:6–7), because He is loving—because He *is* love (1 Jn. 4:8)—not because He is under some obligation to love everyone the same. Nothing but God's own sovereign good pleasure compels Him to love sinners. Nothing but His own sovereign will governs His love. This has to be true, since there is certainly nothing in any sinner worthy of even the smallest degree of divine love.

The God Who Loves

Unfortunately, Pink took the corollary too far. The fact that some sinners are not elected to salvation is no proof that God's attitude toward them is utterly devoid of sincere love. We know from Scripture that God is compassionate, kind, generous, and good even to the most stubborn sinners. Who can deny that these mercies flow out of God's boundless love? Yet it is evident that they are showered even on unrepentant sinners. According to Paul, for example, the knowledge of divine goodness and forbearance and patience ought to lead sinners to repentance (Rom. 2:4). Yet the apostle acknowledged that many who are the recipients of these expressions of divine love spurn them and thereby store up wrath for themselves in the day of wrath (v. 5). The hardness of the sinful human heart is the only reason people persist in their sin, despite God's goodness to them. Is God therefore insincere when He pours forth mercies calling them to repentance? And how can anyone conclude that God's real attitude toward those who reject His mercies is nothing but sheer hatred?

I want to acknowledge, however, that explaining God's love toward the reprobate is not as simple as most modern evangelicals want to make it. Clearly there is a sense in which the psalmist's expression, "I hate the assembly of evildoers" (Ps. 26:5) is a reflection of the mind of God. "Do I not hate those who hate Thee, O Lord? And do I not loathe those who rise up against Thee? I hate them with the utmost hatred; they have become my enemies" (Ps. 139:21–22). Such hatred as the psalmist expressed is a virtue, and we have every reason to conclude that it is a hatred God Himself shares. After all, He *did* say, "I have hated Esau" (Mal. 1:3; Rom. 9:13). The context reveals God was speaking of a *whole race* of wicked people. So there is a true and real sense in which Scripture teaches that God hates the wicked.

Many try to dodge the difficulty this poses by suggesting that God hates the sin, not the sinner. Why, then does God condemn the sinner and consign the person—not merely the sin—to eternal hell? Clearly we cannot sweep the severity of this truth away by denying God's hatred for the wicked. Nor should we imagine that such hatred is any kind of blemish on the character of God. It is a holy hatred. It is perfectly consistent with His spotless, unapproachable, incomprehensible holiness.

God's Love for the Unbelieving World

YET I AM CONVINCED from Scripture that God's hatred toward the wicked is not a hatred undiluted by compassion, mercy, or love. We know from human experience that love and hatred are not mutually exclusive. It is not the least bit unusual to have concurrent feelings of love and hatred directed at the same person. We often speak of people who have love-hate relationships. There is no reason to deny that in an infinitely purer and more noble sense, God's hatred toward the wicked is accompanied by a sincere, compassionate love for them as well.[15]

The fact that God will send to eternal hell all sinners who persist in sin and unbelief proves His hatred toward them. On the other hand, the fact that God promises to forgive and bring into His eternal glory all who trust Christ as Savior—and even pleads with sinners to repent—proves His love toward them.

We must understand that it is God's very nature to love. The reason our Lord commanded us to love our enemies is "in order that you may be sons of your Father who is in heaven; for He causes His sun to rise on the evil and the good, and sends rain on the righteous and the unrighteous" (Matt. 5:45, NASB). That passage and the verses in its immediate context refute Arthur Pink's claim that Jesus never told sinners God loved them. Here Jesus clearly characterized His Father as One who loves even those who purposefully set themselves at enmity against Him.

While we are all eager to ask why a loving God lets bad things happen to His children, surely we should also ask why a holy

God lets good things happen to bad people. The answer is that God is merciful even to those who are not His own.

At this point, however, an important distinction must be made: God loves believers with a particular love. It is a family love, the ultimate love of an eternal Father for His children. It is the consummate love of a Bridegroom for His bride. It is an eternal love that guarantees their salvation from sin and its ghastly penalty. That special love is reserved for believers alone. Limiting this saving, everlasting love to His chosen ones does not render God's compassion, mercy, goodness, and love for the rest of mankind insincere or meaningless. When God invites sinners to repent and receive forgiveness (Isa. 1:18; Matt. 11:28–30) His pleading is from a sincere heart of genuine love. "'As I live!' declares the Lord God, 'I take no pleasure in the death of the wicked, but rather that the wicked turn from his way and live. Turn back, turn back from your evil ways! Why then will you die, O house of Israel?'" (Ezek. 33:11). Clearly God *does* love even those who spurn His tender mercy, but it is a different quality of love, and different in degree from His love for His own.

A parallel in the human realm would be this: I love my neighbors. I am commanded by numerous Scriptures to love them as I love myself (e.g., Lev. 19:18; Matt. 22:39; Lk. 10:29–37). I also love my wife. That, too, is in accord with Scripture (Eph. 5:25–28; Col. 3:19). But clearly my love for my wife is superior, both in excellence and in degree, to my love for my neighbor. I chose my wife; I did not choose my neighbor. I willingly brought my wife into my family to live with me for the rest of our lives. There's no reason to conclude that since I do not afford the same privilege to my neighbors, my love for them is not a real and genuine love. Likewise it is with God. He loves the elect in a special way reserved only for them. But that does not make His love for the rest of humanity any less real.

Furthermore, even in the human realm, love for one's spouse and love for one's neighbor still don't exhaust the different varieties of love we share. I also love my children with the utmost fervency; yet again I love them with a different quality of love than my love for my wife. And I love my Christian neighbors in a way that rises above my love for my non-Christian neighbors. Obviously genuine love comes in varying kinds and degrees. Why is it difficult for us to conceive that God Himself loves different people differently and with different effects?

God's love for the elect is an infinite, eternal, saving love. We know from Scripture that this great love was the very cause of our election (Eph. 2:4). Such love clearly is not directed toward all of mankind indiscriminately, but is bestowed uniquely and individually on those whom God chose in eternity past.

But from that, it does not follow that God's attitude toward those He did not elect must be unmitigated hatred. Surely His pleading with the lost, His offers of mercy to the reprobate, and the call of the gospel to all who hear are all sincere expressions of the heart of a loving God. Remember, He has no pleasure in the death of the wicked, but tenderly calls sinners to turn from their evil ways and live. He freely offers the water of life to all (Isa. 55:1; Rev. 22:17). Those truths are not at all incompatible with the truth of divine sovereignty.

Reformed theology has historically been the branch of evangelicalism most strongly committed to the sovereignty of God. At the same time, the mainstream of Reformed theologians have always affirmed the love of God for all sinners. John Calvin himself wrote regarding John 3:16, "[Two] points are distinctly stated to us: namely, that faith in Christ brings life to all, and that Christ brought life, because the Father loves the human race, and wishes that they should not perish."[16] Calvin went on to add this:

> [In John 3:16 the evangelist] has employed the universal term *whosoever*, both to invite all indiscriminately to partake of life, and to cut off every excuse from unbelievers. Such is also the import of the term *world*, which he formerly used; for

though nothing will be found in *the world* that is worthy of the favor of God, yet he shows himself to be reconciled to the whole world, when he invites all without exception to the faith of Christ, which is nothing else than an entrance into life.

Let us remember, on the other hand, that while *life* is promised universally to *all who believe* in Christ, still faith is not common to all, but the elect alone are they whose eyes God opens, that they may seek him by faith.[17]

Calvin's comments are both balanced and biblical. He points out that both the gospel invitation and "the world" that God loves are by no means limited to the elect alone. But he also recognizes that God's electing, saving love is uniquely bestowed on His chosen ones.

These same truths have been vigorously defended by a host of Reformed stalwarts, including Thomas Boston, John Brown, Andrew Fuller, W. G. T. Shedd, R. L. Dabney, B. B. Warfield, John Murray, R. B. Kuiper, and many others.[18] In no sense does belief in divine sovereignty rule out the love of God for all humanity.

We're seeing today an almost unprecedented interest in the doctrines of the Reformation and the Puritan era. I'm very encouraged by this in most respects. A return to these historic truths is, I'm convinced, absolutely necessary if the church is to survive. Yet there is a danger when overzealous souls misuse a doctrine like divine sovereignty to deny God's sincere offer of mercy to all sinners.

We must maintain a carefully balanced perspective as we pursue our study of God's love. God's love cannot be isolated from His wrath and vice versa. Nor are His love and wrath in opposition to each other like some mystical yin-yang principle. Both attributes are constant, perfect, without ebb or flow. God Himself is immutable—unchanging. He is not loving one moment and wrathful the next. His wrath coexists with His love; therefore, the two never contradict. Such are the perfections of God that we can never begin to comprehend these things. Above all, we must not set them against one another, as if there were somehow a discrepancy in God. God is always true to Himself and true to His Word (Rom. 3:4; 2 Tim. 2:13).

Both God's wrath and His love work to the same ultimate end—His glory. God is glorified in the condemnation of the wicked, and He is glorified in the salvation of His people. The expression of His wrath and the expression of His love are both necessary to display His full glory. Since His glory is the great design of His eternal plan, and since all that He has revealed about Himself is essential to His glory, we must not ignore any aspect of His character. We cannot magnify His love to the exclusion of the other attributes.

Nevertheless, those who truly know God will testify that the deepest spiritual delights are derived from the knowledge of His love. His love is what drew us to Him in the first place: "We love him, because he first loved us" (1 Jn. 4:19, KJV). His love—certainly not anything worthy in us—is the reason He saved us and bestowed on us such rich spiritual privileges: "But God, being rich in mercy, *because of His great love with which He loved us,* even when we were dead in our transgressions, made us alive together with Christ (by grace you have been saved), and raised us up with Him, and seated us with Him in the heavenly places, in Christ Jesus" (Eph. 2:4–6, emphasis added).

We will return again and again to some of these same truths as we pursue our study in this book. My purpose is not to engage in polemics. My only design is to present God's love in such a fashion that the splendor of it will fill your heart. If you are a Christian, my prayer is that the glory and greatness of His love will deepen your love for Him, and that you will grasp the joys and pains of life with a correct understanding of God's love.

If you are not a believer, perhaps God is drawing you to Himself. We know from Scripture that He is calling you to repentance and offering you the water of life. My prayer is that as you read these pages, the wonder and privilege of divine love will be unfolded to you—and that you will therefore respond to the truth of God's Word with a humble and believing heart. I encourage you to drink in the mercy that Jesus offered in these tender words: "Come to Me, all who are weary and heavy-laden, and I will give you rest. Take My yoke upon you, and learn from Me, for I am gentle and humble in heart; and you shall find rest for your souls. For My yoke is easy, and My load is light" (Matt. 11:28–30).

But be warned: the knowledge of God's goodness and mercy will only deepen your condemnation if you spurn Him. "How shall we escape if we neglect so great a salvation?" (Heb. 2:3). God's love is a refuge for repentant sinners only. Those satisfied with their sin should take no solace from the knowledge that God is full of mercy and compassion. And impenitent sinners inclined to disregard the Savior's offer of mercy should first consider this crucial warning of Scripture: "If we go on sinning willfully after receiving the knowledge of the truth, there no longer remains a sacrifice for sins, but a certain terrifying expectation of judgment, and the fury of a fire which will consume the adversaries" (Heb. 10:26–27).

That "terrifying expectation of judgment, and the fury of a fire which will consume the adversaries" provide the only legitimate context in which anyone can justly apprehend God's love.

> I will extol Thee, my God, O King;
> And I will bless Thy name forever and ever.
> Every day I will bless Thee,
> And I will praise Thy name forever and ever.
> Great is the Lord, and highly to be praised;
> And His greatness is unsearchable.
> One generation shall praise Thy works to another,
> And shall declare Thy mighty acts.
> On the glorious splendor of Thy majesty,
> And on Thy wonderful works, I will meditate.
> And men shall speak of the power of Thine awesome acts;
> And I will tell of Thy greatness.

God So Loved the World

They shall eagerly utter the memory of Thine abundant goodness,
And shall shout joyfully of Thy righteousness.
The Lord is gracious and merciful;
Slow to anger and great in lovingkindness.
The Lord is good to all,
And His mercies are over all His works.
All Thy works shall give thanks to Thee, O Lord,
And Thy godly ones shall bless Thee.
They shall speak of the glory of Thy kingdom,
And talk of Thy power;
To make known to the sons of men Thy mighty acts,
And the glory of the majesty of Thy kingdom.
Thy kingdom is an everlasting kingdom,
And Thy dominion endures throughout all generations.
The Lord sustains all who fall,
And raises up all who are bowed down.
The eyes of all look to Thee,
And Thou dost give them their food in due time.
Thou dost open Thy hand,
And dost satisfy the desire of every living thing.
The Lord is righteous in all His ways,
And kind in all His deeds.
The Lord is near to all who call upon Him,
To all who call upon Him in truth.
He will fulfill the desire of those who fear Him;
He will also hear their cry and will save them.
The Lord keeps all who love Him;
But all the wicked, He will destroy.
My mouth will speak the praise of the Lord;
And all flesh will bless His holy name forever and ever.

—Psalm 145 (emphasis added)

"May the Lord direct your hearts into the love of God"
(2 Thess. 3:5).

God Is Love

Love Is at the Heart of God's Character

Everyone Who Loves Is Born of God and Knows God

The One Who Does Not Love Does Not Know God

The Cross Is the Consummate Proof of Divine Love

Chapter 2

God Is Love

ON A CROSS-COUNTRY DOMESTIC AIRLINER a few years ago, I plugged in the earphones and began to listen to the music program. I was amazed at how much of the music dealt with love. At the time I was preaching through 1 John 4, so the subject of love was very much on my mind. I couldn't help noticing how glib and shallow most of the lyrics were. "She Loves You, Yeah, Yeah, Yeah" is a classic by worldly standards. But few people would argue that its lyrics are truly profound.

I began to realize how easily our culture trivializes love by sentimentalizing it. The love we hear about in popular songs is almost always portrayed as a *feeling*—usually involving unfulfilled desire. Most love songs describe love as a longing, a passion, a craving that is never quite satisfied, a set of expectations that are never met. Unfortunately, that sort of love is devoid of any ultimate meaning. It is actually a tragic reflection of human lostness.

As I thought about it, I realized something else: Most love songs not only reduce love to an emotion, but they also make it an involuntary one. People "fall" in love. They get swept off their feet by love. They can't help themselves. They go crazy for love.

The God Who Loves

One song laments, "I'm hooked on a feeling," while another confesses, "I think I'm going out of my head."

It may seem a nice romantic sentiment to characterize love as uncontrollable passion, but those who think carefully about it will realize that such "love" is both selfish and irrational. It is far from the biblical concept of love. Love, according to Scripture, is not a helpless sensation of desire. Rather, it is a purposeful act of self-giving. The one who genuinely loves is deliberately devoted to the one loved. True love arises from the will—not from blind emotion. Consider, for example, this description of love from the pen of the apostle Paul:

> Love is patient, love is kind, and is not jealous; love does not brag and is not arrogant, does not act unbecomingly; it does not seek its own, is not provoked, does not take into account a wrong suffered, does not rejoice in unrighteousness, but rejoices with the truth; bears all things, believes all things, hopes all things, endures all things (1 Cor. 13:4–7).

That kind of love cannot possibly be an emotion that ebbs and flows involuntarily. It is not a mere feeling. All the attributes of love Paul lists involve the mind and volition. In other words, the love he describes is a thoughtful, willing commitment. Also, notice that genuine love "does not seek its own." That means if I truly love, I'm concerned not with having my desires filled, but with seeking the best for whoever is the object of my love.

So the mark of true love is not unbridled desire or wild passion; it is a giving of oneself. Jesus Himself underscored this when He told His disciples, "Greater love has no one than this, that one lay down his life for his friends" (Jn. 15:13). If love is a giving of oneself, then the greatest love is shown by laying down one's very life. And of course, such love was perfectly modeled by Christ.

God Is Love

Love Is at the Heart of God's Character

THE APOSTLE JOHN has been called "the apostle of love" because he wrote so much on the subject. He was fascinated by it, overwhelmed with the reality that he was loved by God. He often referred to himself in his gospel as "the disciple whom Jesus loved" (Jn. 21:20; cf. 13:23; 20:2; 21:7).

In his first epistle, John wrote, "God is love. By this the love of God was manifested in us, that God has sent His only begotten Son into the world so that we might live through Him" (1 Jn. 4:8–9). Those words are a clear echo of a familiar passage, John 3:16: "For God so loved the world, that He gave His only begotten Son, that whoever believes in Him should not perish, but have eternal life."

Look carefully, first of all, at this simple phrase from 1 John 4:8: "God is love."

In what sense is it true that God is love? There are many ways to *misunderstand* John's meaning. In fact, 1 John 4:8 seems a particular favorite of cultists. All kinds of false sects from Christian Science to the Children of God have misapplied this verse to support wildly heretical notions—the former using it to portray "God as divine Principle, Love, rather than personality";[1] and the latter using it to justify sexual promiscuity.[2] It is important that we understand and reject not only those doctrines, but also the false ideas on which they are based, lest we be led astray in our own thinking.

First, the expression "God is love" is not meant to depersonalize God or portray Him as a force, a sensation, a principle, or some sort of cosmic energy. He is a personal Being, with all the attributes of personality—volition, feeling, and intellect. In fact, what the apostle is saying is that God's love is the highest expression of His person. Therefore, to use this text to attempt to depersonalize God is to do great violence to the clear meaning of Scripture. Such an interpretation actually turns this text on its head.

Second, this verse by no means identifies God with everything our society labels love. Gordon Clark wrote, "John is not saying that all sorts of emotions called love are from God. The romanticism of Goethe, and much more the present sexual debauchery, are not from God."[3] In fact, those who cite this verse to attempt to legitimize illicit forms of "love" are about as far from the apostle's intent as it is possible to get. The love of which he speaks is a pure and holy love, consistent with all the divine attributes.

Third, this is not meant to be a definition of God or a summary of His attributes. Divine love in no way minimizes or nullifies God's other attributes—His omniscience, His omnipotence, His omnipresence, His immutability, His lordship, His righteousness, His wrath against sin, or any of His glorious perfections. Deny any one of them and you have denied the God of Scripture.

There is certainly more to God than love. Similar expressions elsewhere in Scripture demonstrate this. For example, the same apostle who penned these words also wrote, "God is Spirit" (Jn. 4:24). We have already noted that Scripture also says, "God is a consuming fire" (Deut. 4:24; Heb. 12:29). And Psalm 7:11 says, "God is a righteous judge, and a God who has indignation every day." The simple statement "God is love" obviously does not convey everything that can be known about God. We know from Scripture that He is also holy and righteous and true to His Word. God's love does not contradict His holiness; instead, it complements and magnifies it and gives it its deepest meaning. So we cannot isolate this one phrase from the rest of Scripture and attempt to make love represent the sum of what we know about God.

Notice, by the way, that this phrase "God is love" is not even the only such statement in John's first epistle

In the introduction to the epistle, at the very outset, John gave this shorthand statement of the message he wanted to declare: "That *God is light,* and in Him there is no darkness at all" (1 Jn. 1:5, emphasis added). When the apostle says, "God is light," he encompasses several ideas, including holiness, truth, and divine splendor. So as we read from this epistle, remember that these two statements, "God is light" and "God is love," must be kept in balance at all times. God *is* love, but having said that, we have not said everything that is true about God.

Nevertheless, we dare not minimize the force of this crucial text. By saying "God is love," the apostle is making a very strong statement about the character and the essence of God. It is God's very nature to love—love permeates who He is. Or, as John Stott has written, "God is love in His innermost being."[4] Stott calls the apostle's declaration that God is love "the most comprehensive and sublime of all biblical affirmations about God's being."[5]

This statement, "God is love," is so profound that no less than Augustine saw it as an important evidence for the doctrine of the Trinity. If God is love—that is, if love is intrinsic to His very nature—then He has always loved, even from eternity past, before there was any created object for His love. Augustine suggested that this love must have existed between the Persons of the Trinity, with the Father loving the Son, and so on. So according to Augustine, the very fact that God is love corroborates the doctrine of the Trinity.

Clearly the love this text describes is an eternal reality. It flows from the very nature of God and is not a response to anything outside the person of God. The apostle does not say, "God is *loving*," as if he were speaking of one of many divine attributes, but "God is *love*"—as if to say that love pervades and influences all His attributes.

For example, we know that God is holy, "undefiled, separated from sinners and exalted above the heavens," (Heb. 7:26). As a holy being, He would be perfectly righteous to view all sinners with the utmost contempt. But His is a loving holiness that reaches out to sinners with salvation for them—the antithesis of aloofness or indifference.

The God Who Loves

Love surely tempers even God's judgments. What a wonder it is that He who is a consuming fire, He who is unapproachable light, is also the personification of love! He postpones His judgments against sin while pleading with sinners to repent. He freely offers mercy to all who *will* repent. He shows longsuffering and goodness even to many who steel their hearts against Him. Divine love not only keeps divine wrath in check while God appeals to the sinner— but it also proves that God is just when He finally condemns.

And even when He condemns, "God is love." Our God therefore shows Himself to be not only glorious but also good; not only spotlessly holy, but also wondrously compassionate; not only righteous, but also a God of matchless love. And that love emanates from His very essence.

Everyone Who Loves Is Born of God and Knows God

FROM THE TRUTH that God is love, the apostle draws this corollary: "Love is from God" (1 Jn. 4:7). God is the source of all true love. Love is therefore the best evidence that a person truly knows God: "Everyone who loves is born of God and knows God. The one who does not love does not know God" (vv. 7–8). In other words, love is the proof of a regenerate heart. Only true Christians are capable of genuine love.

Clearly, the kind of love the apostle is speaking of is a higher, purer form of love than we commonly know from human experience. The love of which he speaks does not flow naturally from the human heart. It is not a carnal love, a romantic love, or even a familial love. It is a supernatural love that is peculiar to those who know God. It is *godly* love.

In fact, the apostle employed a Greek word for "love" that was highly unusual in first-century culture. The word was *agape,* not a common word until the New Testament made it so. When a typical first-century pagan thought of love, *agape* was not the word that would have come to mind. In fact, there were two other common Greek words for love: *phileo,* to describe brotherly love, and *eros,* to describe everything from romantic love to sexual passion.

Phileo is occasionally used as a synonym for *agape,* but generally the word *agape* is used as a more refined and elevated term. In the sense that John uses it here, *agape* is unique to God. He is the sole source of it.

Love for one's family, romantic love, and the love of good friends all fall into the category of what Scripture calls "natural affection" (Rom. 1:31; 2 Tim. 3:3, KJV). Even these expressions of "natural affection," or human love, can be marvelously rich. They fill life with color and joy. They are, however, merely pale reflections of the image of God in His creatures. His love is *perfect* love. It is that pure, holy, godly love which can be known only by those who are born of Him. It is the same unfathomable love that moved God to send "His only begotten Son into the world so that we might live through Him" (1 Jn. 4:9).

Donald W. Burdick gives three characteristics of this godly sort of love:

> *It is spontaneous.* There was nothing of value in the persons loved that called forth such sacrificial love. God of His own free will set His love on us in spite of our enmity and sin. [*Agape*] is love that is initiated by the lover because he wills to love, not because of the value or lovableness of the person loved. *It is self-giving.* [*Agape*] is not interested in what it can gain, but in what it can give. It is not bent on satisfying the lover, but on helping the one loved whatever the cost. *It is active.* [*Agape*] is not mere sentiment cherished in the heart. Nor is it mere words however eloquent. It does involve feeling and may express itself in words, but it is primarily an attitude toward another that moves the will to act in helping to meet the need of the one loved.[6]

The God Who Loves

All true believers have this love; and all who have it are true believers.

This kind of love cannot be conjured up by the human will. It is wrought in the hearts of believers by God Himself. "We love, because He first loved us" (1 Jn. 4:19). Love for God and love for fellow believers is an inevitable result of the new birth, by which we "become partakers of the divine nature" (2 Pet. 1:4). Just as it is God's nature to love, love is characteristic of His true children. "The love of God has been poured out within our hearts through the Holy Spirit who was given to us" (Rom. 5:5).

Godly love, therefore, is one of the most important tests of the reality of one's faith.

The One Who Does Not Love Does Not Know God

IT IS IMPORTANT to understand the context of John's first epistle. He is writing about assurance of salvation and outlining several practical and doctrinal tests that either demonstrate or disprove the genuineness of one's salvation.

John is writing to help struggling believers gain assurance. He says so in 1 John 5:13: "These things I have written to you who believe in the name of the Son of God, *in order that you may know that you have eternal life*" (emphasis added).

But along the way he has a secondary purpose, and that is to destroy the *false assurance* of those who may profess faith in Christ without really knowing Him. Therefore, he writes such things as, "If we say that we have fellowship with Him and yet walk in the darkness, we lie and do not practice the truth" (1:6). And, "The one who says, 'I have come to know Him,' and does not keep His commandments, is a liar, and the truth is not in him" (2:4). And, "The one who says he is in the light and yet hates his brother is in the darkness until now" (v. 9).

Here he makes godly love a kind of litmus test for the true

Christian: "The one who does not love does not know God, for God is love" (4:8). With regard to that statement, Martyn Lloyd-Jones observed,

> John does not put this merely as an exhortation. He puts it in such a way that it becomes a desperately serious matter, and I almost tremble as I proclaim this doctrine. There are people who are unloving, unkind, always criticizing, whispering, backbiting, pleased when they hear something against another Christian. Oh, my heart grieves and bleeds for them as I think of them; they are pronouncing and proclaiming that they are not born of God. They are outside the life of God; and I repeat, there is no hope for such people unless they repent and turn to Him.[7]

Sadly, most of us have encountered professing Christians whose hearts seem bereft of any genuine love. The apostle John's admonition is a solemn reminder that a mere pretension of faith in Christ is worthless. *Genuine* faith will inevitably be shown by love. After all, real faith works through love (Gal. 5:6).

This sort of God-given love is not easily counterfeited. Look at all that is involved: love for God Himself (1 Cor. 16:22); love for the brethren (1 Jn. 3:14); love of truth and righteousness (Rom. 6:17–18); love for the Word of God (Psa. 1:2); and even love for one's enemies! (Matt. 5:44). Such love is contrary to human nature. It is antithetical to our natural selfishness. The very thought of loving those things is odious to the sinful heart.

Later in this same chapter, the apostle writes, "God is love, and the one who abides in love abides in God, and God abides in him" (v. 16)—again making the godly kind of love the mark of genuine faith.

Martyn Lloyd-Jones listed ten simple, practical ways of knowing whether we abide in love.[8] I've paraphrased them here and added Scripture references to underscore each point:

❒ Is there a loss of the sense that God is against me? (Rom. 5:1; 8:31).

❒ Is there a loss of craven fear of God, and a corresponding increase in godly fear? (cf. 1 Jn. 4:18; Heb. 12:28).

❒ Do I sense the love of God for me? (1 Jn. 4:16).

❒ Do I know that my sins are forgiven? (Rom. 4:7–8).

❒ Do I have a sense of gratitude to God? (Col. 2:6–7).

❒ Do I have an increasing hatred for sin? (Rom. 7:15–16).

❒ Do I desire to please God and live a holy life? (Jn. 14:21; 1 Jn. 2:5–6).

❒ Is there a desire to know God better and draw near to Him? (Phil. 3:10).

❒ Is there a conscious regret that my love for Him is less than what it ought to be? (Phil. 1:9–10).

❒ Is there a sense of delight in hearing about God and the things of God? (Ps. 1:1–2).

Suppose you fail those tests. How can you know the love of God? In Lloyd-Jones's words, "You need not start traveling the mystic way, you need not try to work up feelings; there is only one thing for you to do: face God, see yourself and your sin, and see Christ as your Saviour."[9]

The Cross Is the Consummate Proof of Divine Love

LET'S NOW TAKE A FRESH LOOK at the text from which we drew the title of this chapter: "God is love. By this the love of God was manifested in us, that God has sent His only begotten Son into the world so that we might live through Him" (1 Jn. 4:8–9).

We would not be doing justice to this verse if we limited our discussion of divine love to abstract terms. The love of God is not merely a subjective noumenon. It is dynamic, active, vibrant, and powerful. God has "manifested" His love, or displayed it in a particular act that can be examined objectively.

In other words, Scripture does not merely say "God is love" and leave it to the individual to interpret subjectively what that means. There is a very important doctrinal context in which the love of God is explained and illustrated. To affirm that God is love while denying the doctrine underlying and defining that truth is to render the truth itself meaningless.

But that is precisely what many have done. For example, our adversaries, the theological liberals, are very keen to affirm that God is love; yet they often flatly deny the significance of Christ's substitutionary atonement. They suggest that because God is love, Christ did not actually need to die as a substitutionary sacrifice to turn away the divine wrath from sinners. They portray God as easy to mollify, and they characterize the death of Christ as an act of martyrdom or a moral example for believers—denying that it was God's own wrath that needed to be propitiated through a blood sacrifice, and denying that He purposely gave His Son in order to make such an atonement. Thus, they reject the consummate manifestation of God's love, even while attempting to make divine love the centerpiece of their system.

I commonly encounter people who think that because God is love, theology doesn't really matter. A young man recently wrote me a letter that said in part, "Do you really think God is concerned about all the points of doctrine that divide us Christians? How much better it would be if we forgot our doctrinal differences and just showed the world the love of God!"

But that position is untenable, because many who call themselves Christians are deceivers. For that reason the apostle John began the chapter from which our text is taken with these words:

"Beloved, do not believe every spirit, but test the spirits to see whether they are from God; because many false prophets have gone out into the world" (1 Jn. 4:1).

And since an important body of doctrine underlies what Scripture teaches about divine love, it is a fallacy to think of divine love and sound theology as in any way opposed to each other.

Martyn Lloyd-Jones wrote about this very thing:

> The great tendency in this present century has been to put up as antitheses the idea of God as a God of love on the one side, and theology or dogma or doctrine on the other. Now the average person has generally taken up such a position as follows: "You know, I am not interested in your doctrine. Surely the great mistake the church has made throughout the centuries is all this talk about dogma, all this doctrine of sin, and the doctrine of the Atonement, and this idea of justification and sanctification. Of course there are some people who may be interested in that kind of thing; they may enjoy reading and arguing about it, but as for myself," says this man, "there does not seem to be any truth in it; all I say is that God is love." So he puts up this idea of God as love over and against all these doctrines which the church has taught throughout the centuries.[10]

Indeed, such thinking has been the predominant mood both in popular thinking and in much of organized religion for the bulk of this century. That mindset in many ways has become the hallmark of the visible church in the twentieth century.

Lloyd-Jones points out that according to 1 John 4:9–10, "people who thus put up as opposites the idea of God as love and these basic, fundamental doctrines can, in the last analysis, *know nothing whatsoever about the love of God.*"[11]

Indeed, looking at these verses again, we discover that the apostle explains the love of God in terms of sacrifice, atonement for sin, and propitiation: "In this is love, not that we loved God, but that He loved us and sent His Son to be the *propitiation* for our sins" (1 Jn. 4:10, emphasis added). That word speaks of a sacrifice designed to turn away the wrath of an offended deity. What the apostle is saying is that God gave His Son as an offering for sin, to satisfy His own wrath and justice in the salvation of sinners.

This is the very heart of the gospel. The "good news" is not that God is willing to overlook sin and forgive sinners. That would compromise God's holiness. That would leave justice unfulfilled. That would trample on true righteousness. Furthermore, that would not be love on God's part, but apathy.

The *real* good news is that God Himself, through the sacrifice of His Son, paid the price of sin. He took the initiative ("not that we loved God, but that He loved us"). He was not responding to anything in sinners that made them worthy of His grace. On the contrary, His love was altogether undeserved by sinful humanity. The sinners for whom Christ died were worthy of nothing but His wrath. As Paul wrote, "Christ died for the *ungodly*. For one will hardly die for a righteous man; though perhaps for the good man someone would dare even to die. But God demonstrates His own love toward us, in that *while we were yet sinners,* Christ died for us" (Rom. 5:7–8, emphasis added).

Because God is righteous, He must punish sin; He cannot simply absolve guilt and leave justice unsatisfied. But the death of Christ totally satisfied God's justice, His righteousness, and His holy hatred of sin.

Some people recoil at the thought of an innocent victim making atonement for guilty sinners. They like the idea that people should pay for their own sins. But take away this doctrine of substitutionary atonement and you have no gospel at all. If the death of Christ was anything less than a guilt offering for sinners, no one could ever be saved.

But in Christ's death on the cross, there is the highest possible expression of divine love. He, who *is* love, sent His precious Son to die as an atonement for sin. If your sense of fair play is out-raged by that—good! It ought to be shocking. It ought to be astonishing. It ought to stagger you. Think it through, and you'll begin to get a picture of the enormity of the price God paid to manifest His love.

The cross of Christ also gives the most complete and accurate perspective on an issue we will revisit again and again in this book: the balance between God's love and His wrath.

At the cross His *love* is shown to sinful humanity—fallen crea-tures who have no rightful claim on His goodness, His mercy, or His love. And His *wrath* is poured out on His beloved Son, who had done nothing worthy of any kind of punishment.

If you're not awestruck by that, then you don't yet understand it.

If you do catch a glimpse of this truth, however, your thoughts of God as a loving Father will take on a whole new depth and richness. "God is love"—and He demonstrated His love for us in that while we were sinners in rebellion against Him, He gave His only Son to die on our behalf—and so that we might live through Him (Rom. 5:8; 1 Jn. 4:9–10). That is the very heart of the gospel, and it holds forth the only hope to those in bondage to their sin: "Believe in the Lord Jesus, and you shall be saved" (Acts 16:31).

Behold the Goodness . . .

Sin City

◼

A Reluctant Prophet and a Great Revival

◼

God's Gift of Repentance

Chapter 3

Behold the Goodness . . .

A. W. TOZER WROTE, "What comes into our minds when we think about God is the most important thing about us."[1] Tozer was right. A proper conception of God provides the foundation of all that is absolutely essential to spiritual life and health. On the other hand, for those with a seriously distorted concept of who God is, genuine faith is utterly impossible. Therefore, to misconstrue God's character can even be spiritually fatal.

That is the real danger posed by the contemporary misunderstanding of God's love. In spite of the clarity of Scripture on God's love, millions are kept in spiritual darkness by a notion of God that is completely out of balance. They want a God who is loving but not wrathful. The God of Scripture doesn't fit the bill. They therefore worship a god of their own making. Their thoughts about God constitute sheer idolatry.

For this very reason there is an inherent danger in focusing too intently on any one attribute of God, such as His love. The apostle Paul wrote, "Behold therefore the goodness *and* severity of God" (Rom. 11:22, KJV, emphasis added). It is crucial that we maintain the biblical balance in our thinking. While we study God's love, we must bear in mind that God is also holy, innocent, undefiled, separated from sinners, exalted above the heavens (Heb. 7:26); that He "is a righteous judge, and a God who has indignation every day" (Ps. 7:11); and that "if a man does not repent, He will sharpen His sword; He has bent His bow and made it ready. He has also prepared for Himself deadly weapons; He makes His arrows fiery shafts" (vv. 12–13). "For our God is a consuming fire" (Heb. 12:29). He is a jealous God, visiting the iniquity of the fathers on the children, on the third and the fourth generations of those who hate Him (Exod. 20:5; Deut. 5:9).

God's love, measureless as it is, does not negate any of those truths. We must not stress divine love to the extent that we distort these other equally crucial truths about God. Unfortunately, that is precisely the tragic path our culture as a whole has taken. God's wrath is virtually a taboo subject. Most people would be only too willing to relegate the notion of divine wrath to the scrap heap of outmoded or unsophisticated religious ideas. There is no room for an angry God in an "enlightened" age such as ours. Even some preachers who profess to believe Scripture, yet knowing how people feel about an angry God, are careful to avoid such themes in favor of a friendlier message. All of this has only intensified the problem.

One widespread misconception is that the angry-God concept is confined to the Old Testament. According to this view, Scripture reveals God to us progressively. The Old Testament portrayed Him as a wrathful, angry deity—but only to accommodate the primitive understanding of our ancient forefathers. Supposedly the New Testament—and particularly Jesus—corrected this "faulty" concept, emphasizing the love of God. Those who hold this view suggest that the loving God of the New Testament reflects a more sophisticated understanding of God than the patriarchs had.

There is one serious problem with that theory: all the biblical data quite clearly refute it. For one thing, the Old Testament has as much to say about the love of God as the New. Again and again the Old Testament exalts the lovingkindness and goodness of God. In fact, the word for "lovingkindness" is applied to God more than 150 times in the Old Testament alone: "The Lord's lovingkindnesses indeed never cease, for His compassions never fail. They are new every morning; great is Thy faithfulness" (Lam. 3:22–23). That truth is emphasized from the beginning to the end of the Old Testament.

God's love for Israel is revealed over and over, in spite of Israel's rejection. The depiction of that love in the prophecy of Hosea is unmistakable, and even shocking. Hosea became a living illustration of divine love in his relationship with his wife, Gomer. She became a prostitute and bore several illegitimate children. She shattered her husband's heart. She pursued her life of adulterous harlotries until she was totally dissolute. Finally, she was placed for sale in a slave market. Hosea had followed her wretched career, and behind the scenes he made sure her needs were met. When she was placed on the block to be sold, he bought her for his own, took her home, and treated her as if she were a virgin. Hosea's laudable, generous, forgiving love for his evil wife, and his willingness to take her back no matter what she had done, are object lessons to illustrate God's love for sinning Israel. Hosea cites God's own plea to that wayward nation: "My heart is turned over within Me, all My compassions are kindled" (Hos. 11.8). How faithfully He loves!

Throughout the Old Testament God is portrayed in this manner, as a God of tender mercies, infinite lovingkindness, great compassion, and patient longsuffering.

Just to keep the record straight, the New Testament has as much to say about the *wrath* of God as the Old. It was Jesus Himself, in the New Testament, who gave the fullest and most explicit descriptions of the horrors of hell (Matt. 5:29–30; Mk. 9:43–48; Lk. 16:19–31). And the New Testament also records these words of Jesus: "But I will warn you whom to fear: fear the One who after He has killed has authority to cast into hell; yes, I tell you, fear Him!" (Lk. 12:5). The final New Testament description of Christ in His Second-Coming glory says, "From His mouth comes a sharp sword, so that with it He may smite the nations; and He will rule them with a rod of iron; and He treads the wine press of the fierce wrath of God, the Almighty" (Rev. 19:15).

So there is absolutely no basis for the notion that the New Testament changes the concept of God from wrathful to loving. The same God reveals Himself to us in both Testaments. The glorious truth is that "God is love" (1 Jn. 4:8, 16)—yet it is nevertheless "a terrifying thing to fall into the hands of the living God" (Heb. 10:31). Both truths are stressed in both Testaments.

One further clarification needs to be made on this point. When we speak of God's love and God's wrath, we are not talking about anything like human passions. According to the best-known Protestant confession of faith, God is "a most pure spirit, invisible, without body, parts, or passions, immutable. . . ."[2] God's wrath and His love are fixed and steady dispositions. They are not moods or passionate emotions. He does not swing wildly from one temperament to the other. To think of God that way is to deny that He is eternally unchanging. He Himself says: "I, the Lord, do not change" (Mal. 3:6). With God "there is no variation, or shifting shadow" (Jas. 1:17). He is "the same the same yesterday and today, yes and forever" (Heb. 13:8).

Nor do God's wrath and love imply any contradiction in His nature. "He cannot deny Himself" (2 Tim. 2:13). His wrath is not inconsistent with His love. Because He so completely loves what is true and right, He must hate all that is false and wrong. Because He so perfectly loves His children, He seeks what blesses and edifies them, and hates all that curses and debases them. Therefore, His wrath against sin is actually an expression of His love for His people. His chastening for their sin is proof that He is a loving Father (Heb. 12:6–11). And when He exercises vengeance against the enemies of truth, that also reveals His love for His chosen ones. Israel's history is filled with examples of these truths.

One classic example of this was Nineveh, a city that was Israel's nemesis for several centuries. There both the goodness and the severity of God were dramatically put on display. In fact, nowhere are God's lovingkindness and His holy wrath seen side by side more vividly than in the history of Nineveh. In this chapter we will examine God's goodness to the city, and in the chapter that follows we will see how that goodness finally gave way to an awful outpouring of divine wrath.

Sin City

NINEVEH WAS AN ancient city founded by Nimrod. Genesis 10:8–12 records that Nimrod founded the entire Babylonian kingdom, of which Nineveh was a part (cf. Mic. 5:6). Nimrod's Babylon became the source of virtually every false religious system.[3] That is why Scripture makes reference to "Babylon the great, the mother of harlots and of the abominations of the Earth" (Rev. 17:5). From its very beginning, Nineveh was one of the most important cities of the Babylonian empire, steeped in wickedness and debauchery. Nineveh opposed everything the true God stood for and vice versa.

In the eighth century B.C., Nineveh became the capital of Assyria. The Assyrians were known for their wicked ruthlessness. One author says,

> These people ruled with hideous tyranny and violence from the Caucasus and the Caspian to the Persian Gulf, and from beyond the Tigris to Asia Minor and Egypt. The Assyrian kings literally tormented the world. They flung away the bodies of soldiers like so much clay; they made pyramids of human heads; they sacrificed holocausts of the sons and daughters of their enemies; they burned cities; they filled populous lands with death and devastation;

they reddened broad deserts with carnage of warriors; they scattered whole countries with the corpses of their defenders as with chaff; they impaled 'heaps of men' on stakes, and strewed the mountains and choked the rivers with dead bones; they cut off the hands of kings, and nailed them on the walls, and left their bodies to rot with bears and dogs on the entrance gates of cities; they cut down warriors like weeds, or smote them like wild beasts in the forests, and covered pillars with the flayed skins of rival monarchs . . . and these things they did without sentiment or compunction.[4]

Nineveh represented the seat of this evil culture. Understandably, the Israelites hated Nineveh and all that the Assyrians represented.

A Reluctant Prophet and a Great Revival

AT THE VERY HEIGHT of Assyrian power, God commanded a prophet of Israel to go to Nineveh and warn the people there of God's impending judgment. Not surprisingly, the prophet rebelled.

That prophet was Jonah, whose history is familiar to every Sunday school student. Commanded by God to go to Nineveh, Jonah boarded a ship in the Mediterranean—and headed the opposite direction! (Jonah 1:3). "The Lord hurled a great wind on the sea . . . so that the ship was about to break up" (v. 4). The sailors on the ship discovered that Jonah had angered God, and on Jonah's own instructions they threw him overboard (vv. 12–15).

God had prepared a great fish to be at precisely the right spot, and the fish swallowed Jonah (v. 17). After three days and nights in the fish's belly—time spent by the disobedient prophet praying one of the finest prayers of repentance recorded in Scripture— Jonah was miraculously spared (2:1–9). "The Lord commanded the fish, and it vomited Jonah up onto the dry land" (2:10).

Behold the Goodness . . .

Scripture says, "Now the word of the Lord came to Jonah the second time, saying, 'Arise, go to Nineveh the great city and proclaim to it the proclamation which I am going to tell you'" (3:1–2). This time, albeit still reluctantly, "Jonah arose and went to Nineveh according to the word of the Lord" (v. 3).

Have you ever noticed *why* Jonah attempted to flee Nineveh? It was not because he feared the city's inhabitants. It was not that he was intimidated by the thought of preaching God's Word to pagans. Nothing indicated that Jonah was the least bit timid in the face of the Lord's enemies. In fact, what little we know about him proves he was not a particularly shy man.

Jonah was very candid about why he fled his duty. This was the explanation he gave God: "I knew that Thou art a gracious and compassionate God, slow to anger and abundant in lovingkindness, and one who relents concerning calamity" (4:2). In short, because he knew God loves sinners and seeks to save them, Jonah did not want to warn the Gentile Ninevites. He preferred to keep silent and allow God's judgment to take them by surprise. He would have been happiest if God had wiped the Ninevites from the face of the earth without any warning. His worst fear was that the city would repent, and then God would forestall His judgment.

That is, in fact, precisely what happened. Jonah had barely been in Nineveh one day when a remarkable spiritual awakening rocked the place. Jonah's message was short: "Yet forty days and Nineveh will be overthrown" (3:4). At that simple warning, Scripture tells us, "The people of Nineveh believed in God; and they called a fast and put on sackcloth from the greatest to the least of them" (v. 5). This pagan city repented of the evil they had done. The revival went through the entire population (estimated at about 600,000). Even the king "arose from his throne, laid aside his robe from him, covered himself with sackcloth, and sat on the ashes" (v. 6). It was the most extraordinary spiritual revival the world had ever seen. To this day history has never seen another awakening like what happened in Nineveh.

But Jonah was *not* pleased. His worst fear was coming to pass before his eyes. Still, he hoped to see God's judgment carried out. He camped on the east side of the city to see what would happen (4:5). What *did* happen is not as familiar to most people as Jonah's experience with the fish. But it reveals the main point of the Book of Jonah. God was giving Jonah a lesson about the glory of divine compassion.

These are the closing verses of Jonah. Jonah is bivouacked in the desert outside Nineveh, keeping his bitter vigil:

> So the Lord God appointed a plant and it grew up over Jonah to be a shade over his head to deliver him from his discomfort. And Jonah was extremely happy about the plant. But God appointed a worm when dawn came the next day, and it attacked the plant and it withered. And it came about when the sun came up that God appointed a scorching east wind, and the sun beat down on Jonah's head so that he became faint and begged with all his soul to die, saying, "Death is better to me than life."
>
> Then God said to Jonah, "Do you have good reason to be angry about the plant?" And he said, "I have good reason to be angry, even to death." Then the Lord said, "You had compassion on the plant for which you did not work, and which you did not cause to grow, which came up overnight and perished overnight. And should I not have compassion on Nineveh, the great city in which there are more than 120,000 persons who do not know the difference between their right and left hand, as well as many animals?" (Jonah 4:6–11).

That is surely one of the strangest finales in all Scripture. We are not told what became of Jonah. We have no idea whether his attitude changed after this, or if he remained the entire forty days, still hoping for the destruction of Nineveh. We get no glimpse of how Jonah responded in his heart to the Lord's tender admonition. We know nothing of his further ministry. History is even silent about the long-term effects of the revival in Nineveh. But the lesson God was teaching Jonah—and all Israel—was very clear. God is loving, merciful, patient, and compassionate toward sinners.

What happened to the prophecy of Nineveh's destruction? "When God saw their deeds, that they turned from their wicked way, then God relented concerning the calamity which He had declared He would bring upon them. And He did not do it" (3:10). Does this imply some changeableness in God? The *King James Version* is even more forceful: "God *repented* of the evil, that he had said that he would do unto them; and he did it not" (emphasis added). Is that not a contradiction of Numbers 23:19: "God is not a man, that He should lie, nor a son of man, that He should repent; has He said, and will He not do it? Or has He spoken, and will He not make it good?"

But this is no contradiction; it is an *anthropopathism*—a figure of speech that assigns human thoughts and emotions to God. Scripture uses anthropopathisms to explain to us truths about God that cannot be expressed in literal human terms.

Jonah 3:10 does not mean that God actually changed His mind. Quite the contrary; it was the Ninevites who changed. The turning away of God's wrath was perfectly consistent with His eternal loving character. Indeed, if He had *not* stayed His hand against Nineveh, *that* would have signaled a change in God, for this gracious promise overrides all His threatened judgments: "If that nation against which I have spoken turns from its evil, I will relent concerning the calamity I planned to bring on it" (Jer. 18:8).

The prophecy of doom against Nineveh was issued against a people who were haughty, violent, God-hating pagans. No such threat is ever uttered against humble penitents clothed in sackcloth and ashes. The revival utterly changed the people of Nineveh, so God stayed His hand of judgment and forgave them out of His love.

The God Who Loves

What happened was, of course, God's design from the beginning. Jonah seemed to understand this. He sensed that the prophetic warning was intended by God to turn the hearts of the Ninevites. That was why he fled toward Tarshish at the outset. Certainly God, far from being surprised by the turn of events, was sovereign over every detail of the unfolding drama. The One who oversees every sparrow—who even numbers the hairs on our heads—is supremely able to make all things work together for His own perfect ends. In every detail of everything, all His purposes are fulfilled and all His good pleasure is accomplished (Isa. 46:10). Nothing can thwart, frustrate, or improve the perfect plan of God. "Known unto God are all his works from the beginning of the world" (Acts 15:18, KJV). He providentially controls everything that comes to pass, according to a plan He decreed before the foundation of the world.

Throughout the Book of Jonah we see God at work in divine providence, sovereignly orchestrating all events in accordance with His eternal purposes. We are told, for example, that God appointed the fish that swallowed Jonah (1:17). Now in the closing chapter of the book, we read three times that God "appointed" certain things to be graphic illustrations to Jonah as God taught the prophet a lesson about divine compassion. These illustrations demonstrate how God determines even the smallest details of all that happens so that everything works together for His own glory and for the good of those who love Him. Here God was sovereignly directing everything, not only for the Ninevites' good, but for Jonah's good as well—even though what ensued was not entirely to Jonah's liking.

God gave the pouting prophet a series of object lessons to rebuke his lack of love for the people of Nineveh.

First, God *appointed a plant* to grow up over Jonah to shade Him from the desert sun during his vigil. Scripture says "Jonah was extremely happy about the plant" (4:6). Jonah probably saw the plant as a token of God's favor to Him. Perhaps he thought he could read the hand of divine providence in this event. After all, a single plant miraculously shooting up in the middle of the desert in just the right place to provide shade for Jonah *must* signify that God was on his side, not on the side of the Ninevites! Jonah might have even thought it meant God was preparing to destroy Nineveh after all. The prophet's mood immediately changed from anger to delight.

But at dawn of the very next day God *appointed a worm,* which attacked the plant so that it withered and died. Worse, God *appointed a hot wind* that sapped all the prophet's strength and suddenly made his circumstances thoroughly uncomfortable.

God was still working all things for Jonah's good, but the prophet did not see it that way. His mood changed again. Now he was angrier than ever. He even begged God to let Him die.

God rebuked the wayward prophet for his failure to understand divine compassion. He reminded Jonah that Nineveh was filled with young children ("more than 120,000 persons who do not know the difference between their right and left hand"). They would all be destroyed if God poured out His wrath on the city. The Lord pointed out that Jonah was so selfish about his own personal comfort that he had more feeling for the plant than for the people of Nineveh.

Notice how Jonah's irrational feelings for the plant ("for which you did not work, and which you did not cause to grow") contrast with God's compassion for His own creation: "Should I not have compassion on Nineveh, the great city . . . ?" Romans 9 echoes the same idea: "I will have mercy on whom I have mercy, and I will have compassion on whom I have compassion. . . . Does not the potter have a right over the clay?" (vv. 15, 21). If God chose to be merciful to the inhabitants of Nineveh, He had every right to display His saving love that way. On the other hand, Jonah—himself a recipient of God's wondrous grace—had *no* right to resent God's compassion for others. He also had no right to be so devoid of compassion toward these people.

The God Who Loves

From a human perspective, it is certainly understandable that Jonah, together with virtually all of Israel, would have preferred that God simply destroy Nineveh. But the human perspective is flawed. God is a God of patience, compassion, and grace. Because God was willing to show mercy to a wicked society, Jonah's preaching ushered in one of the most remarkable revivals in the history of mankind—in spite of Jonah himself. And God was glorified in such a display of His great love for sinners.

God's Gift of Repentance

GOD'S LOVINGKINDNESS and tender mercies lavished on such an evil culture give us insight into the very heart of God. It is His nature to love, to show mercy, and to have compassion. But mark this carefully: when He stayed His hand of judgment in Nineveh, He did not merely overlook the sins of that society and allow them to continue blithely in their pursuit of evil. He changed the hearts of the Ninevites. The revival was a miracle wrought by God. As Jonah himself testified, "Salvation is of the Lord" (2:9). God is the One who brought the Ninevites to repentance. He awakened them spiritually so that they mourned for their sins (3:8). They turned from their wicked way (3:10)—but it was God who turned them (Lam. 5:21, KJV: "Turn thou us unto thee, O Lord, and we shall be turned").

True repentance from sin is always a gift of God. Paul wrote Timothy a bit of advice that would have been apropos to Jonah: "The Lord's bond-servant must not be quarrelsome, but be kind to all, able to teach, patient when wronged, with gentleness correcting those who are in opposition, *if perhaps God may grant them repentance* leading to the knowledge of the truth" (2 Tim. 2:24–25).

The very act of the Ninevites' repentance was confirmation of the sovereign grace and loving mercy of God. Had He not turned their hearts, they would never have turned.

Yet they *did* turn, and almost immediately. "The people of Nineveh believed in God; and they called a fast and put on sackcloth from the greatest to the least of them" (3:5). The king shed his kingly garments, put on sackcloth, and proclaimed a fast. It was astonishing that a culture of wicked arrogance could be instantly reduced en masse to the lowest humility in sackcloth and ashes.

About this, Hugh Martin, a nineteenth-century preacher from Scotland, wrote,

> Doubtless, the hand of God is to be traced in this, and His power and gracious influence on their hearts. And a very wondrous work it is of the grace of God, that a city such as Nineveh—great, and violent, and proud, and of a haughty spirit—should have been so greatly, so suddenly humbled to believe the message of God. Surely God's Holy Spirit was with God's holy Word among them: and very powerful, though secret, were His operations. It is impossible to account for their faith without attributing it to the operation of God upon their hearts, and the sovereign mercy of God towards them. . . . When the Ninevites believed God, was this not a faith which was "not of themselves"? Was it not "the gift of God"?[5]

Some have suggested that the "faith" of the Ninevites stopped short of true, saving faith. But I do not share that view. It seems obvious from our Lord's own testimony that for multitudes in Nineveh this represented an authentic saving conversion. In fact, Jesus cited Nineveh's repentance as a witness against His own generation: "The men of Nineveh shall stand up with this generation at the judgment, and shall condemn it because they repented at the preaching of Jonah; and behold, something greater than Jonah is here" (Matt. 12:41; Lk. 11:32). An entire generation of Ninevites was thus brought into the kingdom of God solely by His loving grace.

The God Who Loves

What were the long-term effects of this revival? Neither Scripture nor history give us much information. What we know is not encouraging. Sadly, within a generation or so after this revival, Nineveh reverted to her old ways. As we shall see in the following chapter, God finally had to pour out His wrath on the city.

That brings to mind a crucial truth about God's love and goodness. "From everyone who has been given much shall much be required" (Lk. 12:48). God's grace and privileges are not to be taken lightly. With greater privilege comes greater responsibility. And those who sin against God's goodness only deepen their inevitable condemnation.

The history of Nineveh illustrates that truth in a graphic way. That one blessed generation saw the goodness of God when what they deserved was His wrath. Only eternity will reveal how many souls were swept into the kingdom in that glorious revival.

But the glory soon departed. The memory of the revival was short-lived. Tragically, the offspring of that revived generation of Ninevites returned to their forefathers' extreme wickedness. The mercy of God to that generation was soon forgotten. A younger generation returned to the sins of their fathers. God's goodness to the city of Ninevah became a distant memory. The revival was not even mentioned in any of the known records of Assyrian history. There is no evidence that the revival ever penetrated beyond Nineveh into the rest of the Assyrian nation. In fact, what we know of Assyrian history suggests that the revival's impact was limited to one generation and one city. Assyria as a whole remained hostile to the God of Israel. We would know nothing of how God's loving grace was poured out on the wicked city without the Old Testament Book of Jonah.

Those years after Jonah's revival were the very years when Assyria became the dominant world power, increasing in military might and political influence. Riding the crest of God's mercy, Nineveh became the most powerful city in the entire world—the nucleus of Assyrian domination. Meanwhile, Assyria continued to wage war against the people of God. Soon Jehovah God was once again more hated than feared by the Ninevites.

But God was not through with Nineveh. The final page of her history was not yet written. That wretched city, which had tasted so much of divine goodness only to spurn God Himself, was about to learn what a fearful thing it is to fall into the hands of the living God.

. . . And the Severity of God

He Is a God of Inflexible Justice

He Is a God of Irresistible Power

He Is a God of Infinite Mercy

He Is a God of Inconceivable Righteousness

Chapter 4

. . . *And the Severity of God*

MORE THAN A HUNDRED YEARS passed from the time of Jonah until Nahum prophesied the final doom of Nineveh.

Nahum, like Jonah before him, was called specifically to prophesy against that city. The brief book that bears his name is his only known prophecy.

This time God's purpose was vengeance, not mercy. Jonah's message had brought a loving warning to the city. Nahum's message would be a pronouncement of doom. God was about to glorify Himself again, but now He would do it by displaying His *wrath* against Nineveh.

Shortly after Jonah's experience in Nineveh, the Assyrians—led by Sennacherib, whose palace was in Nineveh—stepped up their barbarous treatment of the Israelites. Assyrian rulers of this era were ruthless men who boasted of their own brutalities. They liked to torture their victims with slow, cruel means of death, and they were known for building monuments to their conquests out of mutilated human remains. Sennacherib was the worst of the lot.

Assyria was responsible for dragging the ten northern tribes of Israel off into captivity from which they never returned. The Assyrians under Sennacherib also came in military force against the southern kingdom during Hezekiah's reign. Through Nahum, God was in effect saying He would no longer tolerate the sins of such a nation or the persecution of His people. And since Nineveh was the capital city of Assyria, it was against the Ninevites that God pronounced His judgment.

Under Jonah's ministry—and despite Jonah's unsympathetic attitude—God displayed His love and compassion for the citizens of Nineveh. Now He would pour out His wrath. Either way, He received glory.

Nahum's prophecy gives us lucid insight into the character of God. Lest we behold His mercy and forget His severity, here is a reminder that ultimately a holy God must wreak vengeance against sin. God is a righteous Judge. For Him to fail to carry out judgment would be inconsistent with His glory, untrue to His Word, and a contradiction of who He is. In other words, the basis for His judgment is His own righteous character. His judgment is as essential to His glory as His love.

So in the most candid, vivid terms, Nahum sets forth the majestic character of God as Judge. Nahum's prophecy is noteworthy for its careful balance. The prophet outlines four aspects of God's judgment that show the perfect equilibrium of the divine attributes.

He Is a God of Inflexible Justice

JUSTICE IS A LEGAL term that describes the righteousness of divine government. God is a just God. His justice is as unchanging as any other aspect of His character. God cannot change His mind or lower His moral standards. Since He is utterly perfect, any change at all would diminish His perfection—and that would be unthinkable. So His justice is inflexible; His holy nature demands that it be so.

As Creator, He is entitled to rule over all His creatures any way He pleases. The Potter quite simply has power over the clay to fashion it any way He desires. He makes the laws; He determines the standards; and He judges accordingly. He created everything for His own pleasure; and He has every right to do so. He also has total power to determine the principles by which His creation must function. In short, He has the absolute right to do whatever He determines to do. And because He is righteous, He rules in perfect righteousness, always holding to the highest standard of truth and perfect virtue.

If any creature chafes under God's rule or rebels against divine government, that creature then falls immediately under the judgment of God. Anyone who does not conform to the will of God incurs the inflexible justice of God.

In other words, God's justice is *perfect* because He Himself is absolutely pure, utterly righteous, consummately just—He Himself is perfect. He cannot be unjust. That is precisely why His justice is inflexible.

Here is the description of God with which Nahum introduces his prophecy: "A jealous and avenging God is the Lord; the Lord is avenging and wrathful. The Lord takes vengeance on His adversaries, and He reserves wrath for His enemies. The Lord is slow to anger and great in power, and the Lord will by no means leave the guilty unpunished" (Nah. 1:2–3). Those are powerful statements, giving us an unmistakable look into God's character.

Notice it says God is "jealous." As a child, I was troubled the first time I heard that, because I pictured jealousy as an unwholesome trait. But this speaks of a righteous jealousy unique to God. He is intolerant of unbelief, rebellion, disloyalty, or infidelity. He resents the insults and the indignities of people who worship anything or anyone besides Him. He demands to be given His rightful place above all else that we love or worship.

Thus, someone might say, "God is self-centered."

But, of course; God alone has the *right* to be self-centered. In contrast to all His creatures, He is entitled to demand worship and be jealous of His own glory. He is God, and there is no one else like Him (Isa. 46:9). He, and He alone, has absolute authority to judge those who rebel against His laws, refuse to give Him glory, ridicule His authority, or doubt His Word. And He jealously guards His name against all who would diminish His glory. "I am the Lord, that is My name; I will not give My glory to another, nor My praise to graven images" (Isa. 42:8). *"For My own sake, for My own sake, I will act; for how can My name be profaned? And My glory I will not give to another"* (48:11, emphasis added). What would seem like unacceptable pride in any lesser being is the necessary expression of a holy God who refuses to have His holiness besmirched. God's jealousy is therefore a righteous jealousy.

This truth is taught in the first of the Ten Commandments: "I am the Lord your God, who brought you out of the land of Egypt, out of the house of slavery. You shall have no other gods before Me" (Exod. 20:2–3).

The second commandment forbids idolatry and explicitly describes God as jealous:

> You shall not make for yourself an idol, or any likeness of what is in heaven above or on the earth beneath or in the water under the earth. You shall not worship them or serve them; for I, the Lord your God, am a jealous God, visiting the iniquity of the fathers on the children, on the third and the fourth generations of those who hate Me (vv. 4–5).

The third commandment continues the same theme, warning those who would trifle even with the name of God: "You shall not take the name of the Lord your God in vain, for the Lord will not leave him unpunished who takes His name in vain" (v. 7). In Ezekiel 39:25 He echoes: "I shall be jealous for My holy name."

God's holy jealousy is so descriptive of who He is that He even takes the name "Jealous" as His own. "You shall not worship any other god, for the Lord, *whose name is Jealous,* is a jealous God" (Exod. 34:14, emphasis added).

And in Deuteronomy 4:24 we read, "The Lord your God is a consuming fire, a jealous God."

The message is clear: God is jealous for His glory, and to disgrace His honor in any way—by worshiping a false God, or disobeying the true God, or simply failing to love Him with all the heart, soul, mind, and strength—is to incite the jealousy of God and incur His holy wrath. Simply because of who He is, God is perfectly righteous to be jealous of His glory and to be angry at those who denigrate or defame Him in any way.

Ezekiel 38:18 is a graphic portrayal of God's righteous jealousy: "It shall come to pass at the same time when Gog shall come against the land of Israel, saith the Lord God, that my fury shall come up in my face" (KJV). There, in a classic anthropopathism, Scripture pictures God as so angry that His wrath wells up in His face—like someone who becomes red-faced with fury. Ezekiel's prophecy continues,

> "And in My zeal and in My blazing wrath I declare that on that day there will surely be a great earthquake in the land of Israel. And the fish of the sea, the birds of the heavens, the beasts of the field, all the creeping things that creep on the earth, and all the men who are on the face of the earth will shake at My presence; the mountains also will be thrown down, the steep pathways will collapse, and every wall will fall to the ground. And I shall call for a sword against him on all My mountains," declares the Lord God. "Every man's sword will be against his brother. And with pestilence and with blood I shall enter into judgment with him; and I shall rain on him, and on his troops, and on the many peoples who are with him, a torrential rain, with hailstones, fire, and brimstone. And I shall magnify Myself, sanctify Myself, and make Myself known in the sight of many nations; and they will know that I am the Lord" (vv. 19–23).

The God Who Loves

God tolerates no rivals; He permits no rebels. He is a jealous God.

And when the Lord Jesus Christ returns in glory, the wrath of God will be on display. Jude 14–15 tells us, "Behold, the Lord cometh with ten thousands of his saints, to execute judgment upon all, and to convince all that are ungodly among them of all their ungodly deeds which they have ungodly committed, and of all their hard speeches which ungodly sinners have spoken against him" (KJV).

So why all this attention to God's jealousy in a book that features His love? Quite simply because God's jealousy is an expression of His love. Jealousy is possible only in a love relationship.

God is jealous because He loves. He is jealous when those who are the object of His lovingkindness are drawn away by sin and evil to worship other gods. He is jealous when those who ought to love Him defy Him and set their love on lesser objects.

But the supreme jealousy of God is against those who spurn His beloved Son. Scripture says, "If anyone does not love the Lord, let him be accursed" (1 Cor. 16:22). Those who refuse love to the Lord Jesus Christ abide under God's curse—because He is jealous for His own Son. Thus God's love—particularly the Father's love for the Son—is inextricably linked to His holy jealousy. His love would actually be diminished if He relinquished His jealous anger.

Look again at Nahum's prophecy against Nineveh. Here we see that God's wrath—tempered by His great patience and lovingkindness for so many years—must inevitably give way to His avenging anger against sin. Notice the emphasis placed on divine vengeance in just the second verse of Nahum's prophecy: "A jealous and *avenging* God is the Lord; the Lord is avenging and wrathful. The Lord takes *vengeance* on His adversaries, and *He reserves wrath for His enemies*" (Nah. 1:2, emphasis added).

The repetition of this solemn concept gives the prophecy a tone that is both fearful and serious—and fittingly so. These are no idle threats. God is about to avenge His name against a wicked city that was once the recipient of His patience and compassion. Now Nineveh will find no mercy.

The concept of vengeance, like that of jealousy, often carries less than noble connotations. Jesus forbade us to have a vengeful spirit (Matt. 5:38–44). But again, God—precisely because He is God—has every right to unleash His vengeance against the wicked. In fact, He is righteous to do so. In Deuteronomy 32:35 He says, "Vengeance is Mine, and retribution." He has the exclusive right to judge evildoers, execute vengeance, and pour out His wrath against sin. Those are prerogatives of God and God alone.

In fact, the very reason *we* are not to seek our own vengeance is that judgment and condemnation are divine rights. Paul wrote the Romans, "Never take your own revenge, beloved, but leave room for the wrath of God, for it is written, 'Vengeance is Mine, I will repay,' says the Lord" (Rom. 12:19).

No one violates the glory and the honor of God, no one slights His Son, and no one attacks those He loves—then escapes His wrath. Nahum 1:3 simply says, "The Lord will by no means leave the guilty unpunished."

"The Lord . . . is furious" (v. 2, KJV). "Furious" is translated from two Hebrew words (*ba'al chemah*) that literally mean the Lord is "master of His anger." It speaks of a controlled fury—again, not a transient emotion, not a passion, but a fixed disposition. "God is angry with the wicked every day" (Ps. 7:11, KJV). His wrath is constant, unwavering—but it is a burning fury against all those who rebel against Him.

God's wrath is revealed from heaven against all unrighteousness and ungodliness of men (Rom. 1:18). His justice is inflexible, unbending, always consistent. He will reckon with all who rebel. He will take vengeance on all His adversaries, "He reserves wrath for His enemies" (Nah. 1:2) because it is just for Him to do so. "The Lord will by no means leave the guilty unpunished" (v. 3).

The God Who Loves

Sinners often presume on the mercy and goodness of God. He is slow to anger (v. 3)—patient, longsuffering, kind, and gracious. But no sinner should ever take the goodness of God for granted. No one should mistake His patience for weakness. No one should assume His kindness signifies permission to continue in sin and unbelief. No one should think of His love as an antidote to His wrath. His goodness is not given as a comfort for sinners, but for precisely the opposite reason: "Do you think lightly of the riches of His kindness and forbearance and patience, not knowing that *the kindness of God leads you to repentance?*" (Rom. 2:4, emphasis added).

Yet many *do* misinterpret God's goodness as apathy toward sin and a barrier to judgment. Second Peter 3:4 depicts this error taken to its extreme by mockers who in the last days will scoff at the threat of retribution: "Where is the promise of His coming? For ever since the fathers fell asleep, all continues just as it was from the beginning of creation."

No one should miss the real point of God's longsuffering. Though loving, He has no plan to overlook the transgressions of the wicked. "The Lord knows how . . . to keep the unrighteous under punishment for the day of judgment" (2 Pet. 2:9). He is not slack concerning His promises; just longsuffering (3:9).

Likewise, when Nahum writes, "The Lord is slow to anger" (1:3), he is warning his readers that they must not confuse God's patience with impotence. Look again at Nahum's words: "The Lord is slow to anger *and great in power*" (emphasis added). Those who believe they are safe from judgment because God has not yet poured out His wrath had better think again. His goodness is not weakness; and His forbearance is not indifference. "Vengeance is Mine, and retribution," says the Lord. "In due time their foot will slip; for the day of their calamity is near, and the impending things are hastening upon them" (Deut. 32:35). "The Lord will by no means leave the guilty unpunished" (Nah. 1:3).

. . . And the Severity of God

Nahum's statement that God is "great in power" introduces the second of three aspects of divine judgment that he highlights.

He Is a God of Irresistible Power

NAHUM'S ENTIRE PROPHECY is a verbal display of the divine majesty and a paean to God's power. "In whirlwind and storm is His way, and clouds are the dust beneath His feet" (v. 3). Anyone familiar with the power of a cyclone understands the gist of this. Nahum is describing the majestic power of God's fury, and he uses three aspects of nature to make the point: God's power in the heavens, God's power over the waters, and God's power on the land.

In Psalm 19:1 David wrote, "The heavens are telling of the glory of God; and their expanse is declaring the work of His hands." The glory Nahum sees in the heavens is God's avenging power. God controls the whirlwinds, the storms, and the clouds (v. 3). Those natural wonders are not only displays of divine power, but also are frequently employed as instruments of His judgment. Clouds, for example, are often noted in Scripture as symbols of divine judgment. When Christ returns in judgment, He comes with the clouds and in the midst of great judgment, according to Mark 13:26 and Revelation 1:7.

In Nahum's prophecy not only the heavens, but also the waters represent God's vengeance. "He rebukes the sea" (Nah. 1:4). That, of course, reminds us of the dramatic account of Mark 4:39, when Jesus "rebuked the wind and said to the sea, 'Hush, be still.' And the wind died down and it became perfectly calm." Do you recall the disciples' reactions? "They became very much afraid and said to one another, "Who then is this, that even the wind and the sea obey Him?" (v. 41). They saw the awesome power of God in Christ, and they trembled before that power. They knew it was the power of a holy, omnipotent, avenging Judge. Perhaps their minds even went back to this verse in Nahum, and they remembered the prophecy of divine vengeance.

When Nahum wrote, "He rebukes the sea and makes it dry; He dries up all the rivers. Bashan and Carmel wither; the blossoms of Lebanon wither," he was foretelling the doom of Israel's enemies. Bashan, Carmel, and Lebanon were the boundaries of Israel. Of course, this prophecy had particular reference to Nineveh—a city well beyond Israel's borders, but home to an army that was threatening those very borders.

Nahum next spoke of God's power over the land: "Mountains quake because of Him, And the hills dissolve; Indeed the earth is upheaved by His presence, the world and all the inhabitants in it" (Nah. 1:5). Someday God—according to Revelation 6:12; 11:13; and 16:18–20—will shake the earth with an earthquake from which the world as we know it will never recover. Haggai 2:6–7 contains this prophecy: "For thus says the Lord of hosts, 'Once more in a little while, I am going to shake the heavens and the earth, the sea also and the dry land. And I will shake all the nations.'"

God controls the earth. He can shake it whenever He likes. The mountains quake at His presence (Isa. 64:3). The hills melt like hot wax before Him (Ps. 97:5). When He determines to shake the earth, He shakes it (Jdg. 5:5; Ezek. 38:20). His power is irresistible.

In Nahum 1:6, the prophet asks, "Who can stand before His indignation? Who can endure the burning of His anger?" The answer is that *no one* can stand before Him. This is a description of divine judgment: "His wrath is poured out like fire, And the rocks are broken up by Him."

Divine wrath did finally bring about the doom of Nineveh, and all Nahum's prophecies were dramatically fulfilled.

God's justice is absolutely inflexible. His power is absolutely irresistible. Our God is a consuming fire. No wonder the writer of Hebrews warns,

See to it that you do not refuse Him who is speaking. For
if those did not escape when they refused him who warned
them on earth, much less shall we escape who turn away
from Him who warns from heaven. And His voice shook the
earth then, but now He has promised, saying, "Yet once
more I will shake not only the earth, but also the heaven."
And this expression, "Yet once more," denotes the removing
of those things which can be shaken, as of created things, in
order that those things which cannot be shaken may remain.
. . . For our God is a consuming fire (Heb. 12:25–29).

He Is a God of Infinite Mercy

BUT IN VERSE 7 Nahum introduces a brief interlude into his
prophecy of doom against the enemies of Jehovah. He reminds
the people of Israel, "The Lord is good, a stronghold in the day of
trouble, and He knows those who take refuge in Him." The
Hebrew word translated "take refuge in" conveys the idea of trusting, confiding in, and fleeing to for protection. It speaks of faith.
Those who "take refuge in" the Lord are those who *believe in and
trust* Him. In fact, the *King James Version* translates the verse like
this: "The Lord is good, a strong hold in the day of trouble; and
he knoweth them that trust in him" (emphasis added).

The Lord—the Judge Himself—is a stronghold for those who
seek refuge in Him by faith. Those words in a nutshell contain the
entire gospel of justification by faith. The same God who threatens
judgment against the wicked lovingly, compassionately invites sinful souls in despair to find their refuge in Him. He alone will be their
haven, their stronghold, their protection from divine judgment.

How does He shelter those who trust Him? He covers them
with His own righteousness, which is theirs by faith (Phil. 3:9).
That's why in the Old Testament He is called "the Lord our
righteousness" (Jer. 23:6).

The God Who Loves

The Old Testament repeatedly reveals God as a shelter for believing Israel. Psalm 61 calls Him a refuge and a tower of strength, covering His people as a bird covers its chicks with its wings (vv. 3–4). In Psalm 140:7 the psalmist refers to the Lord as "the strength of my salvation, [who] hast covered my head in the day of battle." He is the rock, the fortress, the deliverer (2 Sam. 22:2). All that imagery has important implications for the doctrine of justification by faith. This theme in the Old Testament reaches its apex in Isaiah 53:11, where the prophet reveals that the Messiah, "the Righteous One, [God's] Servant, will justify the many, as He will bear their iniquities."

The fullness of the doctrine of justification is finally expounded in the New Testament, where the apostle Paul elucidates it most thoroughly in his epistles. There we learn that the very righteousness of God in Christ is imputed to believers—solely by faith and not owing to any works performed by the believing one (Rom. 4:4–6). Christ Himself has already fulfilled the righteous requirements of the law on behalf of believers, and died in their place to pay sin's dreadful price. All believers in Christ are therefore both freed from their guilt and vested with Christ's perfect righteousness. That is the only way guilty sinners can ever find peace with God (Rom. 5:1). This doctrine of justification by faith is the very heart and soul of genuine Christianity. No brand of faith that denies it deserves to be labeled Christianity.

The textbook definition of justification by faith is this: "Justification is a judicial act of God, in which He declares, on the basis of the righteousness of Jesus Christ, that all the claims of the law are satisfied with respect to the sinner."[1] In other words, God *declares* the believing sinner righteous because of Christ—not because of any actual righteousness on the part of the sinner himself. Some might suggest that Nahum 1:3 altogether rules out that sort of justification: "The Lord will by no means leave the guilty unpunished." The *King James Version* is even stronger: "[The Lord] will not at all acquit the wicked." A parallel passage makes the same point, with God Himself stating, "I will not acquit the guilty" (Exod. 23:7). "I will not justify the wicked" (KJV). If God will not justify sinners, we all seem to be in a hopeless state.

But this is precisely where the glorious light of New Testament revelation shines most brightly, revealing the true depth of God's love. He does not merely acquit sinners. He does not overlook their sin. In the Person of Jesus Christ, He made a once-for-all, infinite atonement for their sins. Now He covers them with His own perfect righteousness by imputing it to them through faith (Rom. 4:11). All genuine believers therefore stand completely justified before a righteous God. It is not a future hope but a present reality. It is not a drawn-out process, but an immediate divine act that occurs at the first moment of faith. God's holy wrath is appeased and His love is perfectly fulfilled in the salvation wrought by Christ. Thus, He Himself is truly the stronghold to which sinners may flee from His awful judgments.

Again we see that the love of God and His wrath are inextricably linked. It is impossible to study one without encountering the other. That is why Nahum places his accolade to the goodness and mercy of God in the midst of a passage about God's wrath. This verse is not a digression from his theme; it is at the heart of his message.

This juxtaposition of the wrath and goodness of God is frankly hard for many people to swallow. As we noted in chapter 1, liberal theology flatly denies that a God of wrath can also be loving. Those who hold the liberal view inevitably define God according to their own specifications. They imagine God as benign but impotent—unable to enforce His righteous standards or to stop evil things from happening. In other words, they deny that God is truly sovereign.

Others deny God's essential goodness. They see the effect of evil in the world—poverty, disease, human wretchedness, natural disasters, and other disorders—and they conclude that God is cruel or unloving—or even deny that He exists. They cannot envision that a sovereign being who is truly good would tolerate so much evil.

But Nahum knew God as both sovereign and good. There was no contradiction. The Lord *is* good; forty-one times in the Old Testament we are told that His mercy endures forever. Seven times we find the phrase, "The Lord is good." He alone is good (Matt. 19:17). His goodness is personified in Christ, the Good Shepherd (Jn. 10:11, 14). His universal goodness is revealed in all His works: "The Lord is good to all, and His mercies are over all His works" (Ps. 145:9). Psalm 33:5 says, "The earth is full of the lovingkindness of the Lord." All creation speaks of God's essential goodness.

Consider this simple thought: The Lord could have made everything brown! Brown grass, brown flowers, brown sky, brown sea. But He didn't. There is much for us to enjoy in the variety and the beauty of His creation. These things illustrate His essential goodness. God is good. His goodness is seen in all His works. Don't let the profundity of that truth escape you.

No one appreciates the goodness of God like those who seek their refuge in Him. They are the ones who know Him and love Him. They are the ones on whom He has set His eternal love. They have fled to Him as their stronghold, and found mercy. They experience His goodness like no others. They appreciate His love like no one else.

"And He knows those who take refuge in Him" (v. 7). Does that mean the only people He knows about are the ones who trust Him? Certainly not. Remember that the word "know" and its cognates are often used in Scripture as synonyms for love. "Cain knew his wife" (Gen. 4:17, KJV). The expression speaks of the most intimate kind of love—in this case, the sexual union between a man and his wife. When Scripture says God "knows" those who take refuge in Him, it means He loves them with the deepest, most tender, and most personal affection. It describes the intimacy of divine love, which is unparalleled by any earthly kind of love.

When Jesus said, "My sheep hear My voice, and I know them" (Jn. 10:27), He didn't mean He knows who they are. He meant that He has an intimate relationship with them. Similarly, when Jesus said, "I never knew you; depart from me, you who practice lawlessness" (Matt. 7:23)—He did not mean that He didn't know who those people were. He meant that He had never had the intimacy of a love relationship with them.

God intimately loves those who trust in Him. The knowledge of that love is the greatest of all delights that can be experienced by the human heart.

One of my favorite passages in all of Scripture is found in Micah 7:18–19:

> Who is a God like Thee, who pardons iniquity and passes over the rebellious act of the remnant of His possession? He does not retain His anger forever, because He delights in unchanging love. He will again have compassion on us; He will tread our iniquities under foot. Yes, Thou wilt cast all their sins into the depths of the sea.

That describes the infinite mercy of God displayed in the salvation of His people. If you have never personally known that love but your heart is stirred by the wonder of it, I urge you to turn to Christ in faith and seek refuge in Him.

He Is a God of Inconceivable Righteousness

IT IS TEMPTING TO CAMP on Nahum 1:7 and focus on the goodness of God. But we must note that it is only a one-verse interlude in a chapter that extols the utter righteousness of God in judging the wicked. The Book of Nahum, as we have noted, is a prophecy of doom on a wicked city. Though the Ninevites of Jonah's day found in God a refuge from judgment, their descendants would bear the full brunt of God's wrath. Nahum 1:7 is a clear testimony that God is still good to those who seek refuge in Him, but the Ninevites of Nahum's day would ultimately provide an object lesson of a different sort: "Whatever you devise against the Lord, He will make a complete end of it. Distress will not rise up twice" (1:9).

God's judgment does not negate His essential goodness. Nor does His goodness alter the severity of judgment. God is longsuffering. But when He finally must act in judgment, He makes a complete end of it. Hardened sinners should take note and tremble.

Nahum's message in verses 10–14 foretells the defeat of the Assyrians. God's righteous contempt for their evil works is evident in His pronouncement against them:

> Like tangled thorns, and like those who are drunken with their drink, they are consumed as stubble completely withered. From you has gone forth one who plotted evil against the Lord, a wicked counselor. Thus says the Lord, "Though they are at full strength and likewise many, even so, they will be cut off and pass away. Though I have afflicted you, I will afflict you no longer. So now, I will break his yoke bar from upon you, and I will tear off your shackles." The Lord has issued a command concerning you: "Your name will no longer be perpetuated. I will cut off idol and image from the house of your gods. I will prepare your grave, for you are contemptible."

Like a field of tangled thorns, they were fit only for burning. Like drunkards, they were defenseless. And like dry stubble, they were powerless to withstand the consuming flames of divine wrath. The phrase, "one who plotted evil against the Lord, a wicked counselor," seems to refer to Sennacherib. Against the entire nation and all their idolatrous gods, the Lord prophesied total destruction.

The prophecy was fulfilled to the letter. We read in 2 Kings 19:35–37 that one night "the angel of the Lord went out, and struck 185,000 in the camp of the Assyrians; and when men rose early in the morning, behold, all of them were dead. So Sennacherib king of Assyria departed and returned home, and lived at Nineveh. And it came about as he was worshiping in the house of Nisroch his god, that Adrammelech and Sharezer killed him with the sword; and they escaped into the land of Ararat. And Esarhaddon his son became king in his place."

But that was only the beginning of the judgment of the Assyrians—and of Nineveh in particular.

Beginning in chapter 2, Nahum prophesies the destruction of Nineveh. Space and the limitations of our topic do not permit examination of his prophecy in detail, but note that it was fulfilled exactly as it is recorded. After a series of enemy attacks and natural disasters, Nineveh was overwhelmed by the armies of the Medes, and the city was utterly leveled. When Nineveh fell, the Assyrian Empire toppled along with it.

Twice in Nahum's prophecy the Lord tells Nineveh, "I am against you" (2:13; 3:5). About this, my late mentor, Dr. Charles L. Feinberg, wrote,

> Paul indicates (Ro. 8:31) that if God be for us, no one can successfully be against us. The reverse is true also: if God be against an individual or nation by virtue of sin, then no one can successfully be for that person or nation.
>
> When Assyria touched Israel, God said, "Behold, I am against thee!" This is inevitable if God is to be true to His promise to Abraham. He had solemnly promised that in just such instances He would curse those who had cursed the seed of Abraham. The truth of God's dictum is written in the fate of Nineveh.[2]

The God Who Loves

And so we see again that God's wrath is proof of His love. His judgment is linked to His faithfulness. And He is righteous when He judges.

Nineveh was finished as a city. To this day the site lies in ruins, giving mute testimony to the severity of God's wrath against sin.

But it is also a reminder of God's immeasurable love for His own people. The destruction of Nineveh freed Israel from centuries of grief at the hands of marauding Assyrians. It was God's message to a wayward nation that He still loved them.

God had chastened Israel severely for her sins. But His purpose in afflicting Israel was only corrective. Through Nahum, He assured them, "[The Assyrians] will be cut off and pass away. Though I have afflicted you, I will afflict you no longer" (1:12).

There is a vast and important difference between God's judgment and His discipline. Judgment is severe, final, destructive. Discipline is loving, tender, and corrective. "For those whom the Lord loves He disciplines, and He scourges every son whom He receives" (Heb. 12:6). His discipline has a loving purpose: "He disciplines us for our good, that we may share His holiness. All discipline for the moment seems not to be joyful, but sorrowful; yet to those who have been trained by it, afterwards it yields the peaceful fruit of righteousness" (Heb. 12:10–11).

His judgment against the wicked, however, is of a different character altogether. To the wanton unbeliever, "Our God is a consuming fire" (v. 29). "His calamity will come suddenly; Instantly he will be broken, and there will be no healing" (Prov. 6:15).

No one should be lulled into carelessness by the knowledge that God is loving and gracious. God's love is immeasurable, unfathomable, and inexhaustible. It is perfectly correct to say that God's love is infinite. But that does not mean His love negates His righteousness or overrules His holy wrath.

The Lord is good, and His mercy endures forever (Jer. 33:11). The countless redeemed throughout eternity will give testimony to that. "For the Lord will not abandon His people, nor will He forsake His inheritance" (Ps. 94:14). "But judgment shall return unto righteousness: and all the upright in heart shall follow it" (v. 15, KJV). Those who are not upright in heart—those who spurn God's love and follow their own ways—will ultimately suffer the same fate as Nineveh. That city, where the love of God was once poured out in so great abundance, finally perished in the fury of His wrath.

> Behold therefore the goodness and severity of God: on them which fell, severity; but toward thee, goodness, if thou continue in his goodness: otherwise thou also shalt be cut off (Rom. 11:22, KJV).

Everything I Need to Know
About the Love of God
I Learned in the Nursery?

Wrong Answers to the Hard Questions About God's Love

Wrong Questions Based on the Wrong Perspective of God

Wrong Inferences from a Faulty View of Divine Providence

Two Aspects of the Love of God

Chapter 5

Everything I Need to Know About the Love of God I Learned in the Nursery?

Jesus loves me, this I know,
For the Bible tells me so.

From childhood most of us have heard that God loves us. The Bible tells us that love is at the very heart of who God is: *"God is love"* (1 Jn. 4:8, 16, emphasis added) and He is "the God of love and peace" (2 Cor. 13:11). Those truths are so wonderful that they are always among the first things we teach our children about God. And that is as it should be.

But don't get the idea that God's love is only a child's subject. And don't think that you have mastered the subject by absorbing what you were taught as a child. This subject is certainly *not* child's play. As we have seen already, God's love raises some very complex and sometimes disturbing questions. These questions need to be thought through carefully and answered biblically.

I promised at the very beginning of this book that we would return to deal with some of the hard questions the truth of God's love brings to mind. Even after all we've learned about the issue in the preceding chapters, we must still admit that these questions are among the hardest dilemmas any pastor or theologian will ever be faced with: If God is love, why is the world such a theater of tragedy? If God is so loving, why does He allow His own people to suffer? If "God so loved the world"—then why does He allow all the suffering and torture and pain and sorrow and grief and death? If God is both loving and omnipotent, then why is the world such a mess? Why would a loving God ever allow wars and famines and disasters to cause so much human anguish?

If God is the loving Father of humanity, why doesn't He act like a human father who loves his children? Why does He allow His creatures to make choices that result in their destruction, when He could prevent it or overrule it? If God is a loving God, why did He allow sin in the first place, and why death?

There are more questions, and they get even harder: If God is love, why isn't everyone saved? Why are only *some* said to be "elect," chosen by God to eternal life (cf. Matt. 22:14; 2 Tim. 2:10)? Why would a loving God send people to hell to suffer forever? Why would a loving God devise a plan that has so many people going to hell for all eternity?

What kind of love is it that can control the world but allows the world to suffer the way it suffers? What kind of love is it that is sovereign and yet sends poor, suffering people to an eternal flame? How are we to understand that kind of love?

Wrong Answers to the Hard Questions About God's Love

THOSE QUESTIONS ARE REASONABLE, and they need to be faced honestly. It won't do to pretend such difficulties are easy to answer, or simply ignore them and hope they go away. Anyone who thinks deeply about God will eventually come face-to-face with those very questions and others like them. They are unsettling, vexing, even bewildering questions. Genuinely satisfying answers to them are elusive. There's no point in pretending such questions should pose no problems for the Christian.

In fact, history reveals that those who settle for easy answers to these questions often make shipwreck of the faith. Usually they will cite Scripture selectively and ignore half of some important biblical truth while grossly overemphasizing the other half. And so they tend to go to extremes. The casualty list of those who have run on the rocks over these questions is enough to make the discerning Christian realize that these are hazardous waters to navigate.

Universalism, for example, teaches that in the end everyone will be saved. Universalists believe that because God is love, He cannot eternally condemn anyone. In the end, they believe, hell will not even exist. Some teach that the devil and his fallen angels will be redeemed. As we shall shortly see, Scripture contradicts such a view (Rev. 20:10).

Another attempt to solve the dilemma posed by God's love is a theory known as *annihilationism.* Under this scheme, God takes believers to heaven and puts the rest out of existence. They experience no conscious punishment or suffering; they are judged by having their existence terminated. According to this view, therefore, there is no such place as eternal hell. Many cults and apostate denominations have embraced this doctrine.

A doctrine closely related to annihilationism is a theory known as *conditional immortality.* This view suggests that the human soul is transient until immortality is bestowed upon it. Since eternal life is given only to believers, all others simply pass into oblivion after the final judgment. This view is gaining popularity these days, but it too contradicts Scripture (Matt. 25:46; Rev. 14:11).

Those views may serve to salve human emotion to some degree, but they don't do justice to what Scripture teaches. Therefore, they are errors—and extremely dangerous ones at that, because they give people a false sense of safety. Jesus Himself described hell in graphic terms. In fact, He had more to say about hell than anyone else in Scripture. He described it as a place "where their worm does not die, and the fire is not quenched" (Mk. 9:48). He called hell "outer darkness; [where] there shall be weeping and gnashing of teeth" (Matt. 8:12; 25:30). He warned unbelievers about the judgment to come: "There will be weeping and gnashing of teeth there when you see Abraham and Isaac and Jacob and all the prophets in the kingdom of God, but yourselves being cast out" (Lk. 13:28). He described hell as "unquenchable fire" (Matt. 3:12) and a "furnace of fire" (Matt. 13:42). And He warned those who heard Him preach, "If your hand causes you to stumble, cut it off; it is better for you to enter life crippled, than having your two hands, to go into hell, into the unquenchable fire" (Mk. 9:43).

Furthermore, Revelation 14:11 describes hell's torments as unremitting and eternal: "The smoke of their torment goes up forever and ever; and they have no rest day and night." Revelation 20:10 states, "They will be tormented day and night forever and ever." Matthew 25:46 says, "These [unbelievers] will go away into eternal punishment, but the righteous into eternal life." That verse employs the same Greek word for "eternal" (aionios—meaning "perpetual, everlasting, forever") to describe both the bliss of heaven and the punishments of hell.

Embracing any of these theories also usually has the effect of making people indifferent to evangelism. They begin to feel comfortable that everyone will either be saved or put out of misery, so evangelism loses its urgency. The gospel seems less compelling. It becomes easy to kick back and think less about eternal matters. And that is precisely the effect these theories have had in churches and denominational groups where they have been espoused. As the churches become liberal, the "Christians" influenced by them become cold to spiritual things. Many times they deny the faith altogether. The history of universalism provides abundant evidence of this. Because the doctrine is at its heart a denial of Scripture, it is a sure road to serious apostasy.

But one can easily err in the other direction as well. As I noted earlier, there are some Christians who ponder the hard questions about divine love and conclude that God simply does not love people who aren't His own; He hates them. Under this scheme, there's no tension between the love of God and His wrath. There's no reason to wonder how God can love people whom He ultimately condemns, because you simply conclude that whoever He condemns He hates. The non-elect are people whom God never loved in any sense. People who hold this view are quick to remind that God is angry with the wicked (Ps. 7:11); that He loved Jacob but hated Esau (Rom 9:13); and that He hates those who practice wickedness (Prov. 6:16–19). They conclude that such hatred and genuine love are mutually exclusive. Therefore according to this view, the love of God is limited to the elect alone.

That view doesn't do justice to Scripture, either. It restricts God's love to a remnant, and pictures Him hating the vast majority of humanity. In terms of sheer numbers, it suggests that God's hatred for humanity overwhelms His love. That is not consistent with the God of Scripture, who is "compassionate and gracious, slow to anger, and abounding in lovingkindness and truth" (Exod. 34:6). It doesn't seem befitting for the One whom Scripture describes as "a God of forgiveness, gracious and compassionate, slow to anger, and abounding in lovingkindness" (Neh. 9:17). And it doesn't seem consistent with the truth of Psalm 145:8–9: "The Lord is gracious and merciful; slow to anger and great in lovingkindness. *The Lord is good to all, and His mercies are over all His works*" (emphasis added).

And what about "God so loved the world" (Jn. 3:16)? I realize that there are some good commentators who have tried to limit the meaning of the word "world" in this verse to the elect alone. As noted in chapter 1, however, that view seems to run contrary to the whole thrust of the passage. John Calvin correctly saw this verse as a statement that "the Father loves the human race."[1] In fact, the whole point of verse 17 is to assert that Christ's advent was a search-and-rescue mission, not a crusade for judgment: "For God did not send the Son into the world to judge the world, but that the world should be saved through Him" (v. 17). The point is that God's primary purpose in sending Christ was born out of love, not a design to condemn. Christ's purpose in coming was to save, not to destroy.

Inevitably, those who want to limit the meaning of "world" in verse 16 will suggest that "world" in verse 17 cannot include every individual in the world, unless this passage is teaching a form of universalism. The verse says Christ came so that the *world* might be saved through Him. Obviously not every individual in the world is saved. Therefore, they suggest, "world" in both verses must be limited to the elect alone, and the verse can only mean, "God so loved *the elect.*"

But "world" in this context seems clearly to speak of humanity in general. If we try to make the term mean either "every individual" or "the elect alone," the passage simply makes no sense. The word "world" here is a synonym for the human race. Humanity in general is the object of divine love. And verse 17 simply means that Christ came to redeem this fallen race—not every individual, but humanity as a race. Titus 3:4 also speaks of God's love in these very terms: "The kindness of God our Savior and His *love for mankind* appeared" (emphasis added). The whole sweep of these texts seems to be saying that in a broad sense God's love is set on the whole human race, not just the remnant of elect individuals.

Indeed, to make good sense of this passage, we must interpret the expression "world" in verses 16 and 17 as broadly as we understand the same word in verse 19: "And this is the judgment, that the light is come into the world, and men loved the darkness rather than the light; for their deeds were evil." Clearly the word "world" has a universal and corporate aspect that envelops more than just the elect alone. God's love is for the world in general, the human race, all humanity.

So how are we to understand Romans 9:13: "Jacob I loved, but Esau I hated"? Did God really hate Esau? Yes. He hated the evil Esau represented. He hated Esau's unbelief and sin and worldliness. And in a very real sense, God hated Esau himself. It was not a petty, spiteful, childish kind of hatred, but something far more dreadful. It was divine antipathy—a holy loathing directed at Esau personally. God abominated him as well as what he stood for.

Esau, for his part, hated the things of God. He despised His birthright and sold it for one bowl of lentil stew (Gen. 25:34). He brought nothing but grief to his parents (26:35). He plotted to kill his own brother (27:41). He married pagan women because he knew it displeased his father (28:8–9). He lived a careless, worldly life of utter disregard and disrespect for the God of his ancestors. Certainly God hated all that, as well as Esau himself.

It is worth pointing out that the passage Paul quotes in Romans 9 is Malachi 1:2–3. God was speaking of two nations, Israel and Edom, merely calling them by the names of their respective ancestors. The words "I have hated Esau" (Mal. 1:3) have a meaning that goes beyond Esau himself and encompasses the whole evil nation of Edom. The hatred this describes is not a petty, spiteful loathing, but a holy abhorrence of people who were thoroughly and absolutely debauched.

But God's hatred for Esau and the nation of Edom does not prove that He had no love, no compassion, and no charity whatsoever to Esau or his descendants. In fact, we know from Scripture that God was kind to this despicable nation. When the Israelites left Egypt on their way to Canaan, they passed through the land of Edom. God firmly instructed Moses, "Do not provoke them, for I will not give you any of their land, even as little as a footstep because I have given Mount Seir to Esau as a possession" (Deut. 2:5).

This holy hatred combined with lovingkindness implies no inconsistency or equivocation on God's part. Both love and wrath are reflections of His nature; He is loving, yet holy. He is compassionate, yet indignant over evil. As I have already noted, hatred and love are not necessarily mutually exclusive. Even in the range of human emotions, such feelings are quite common. Most people know very well what it is to hate and love the same object at the same time. One might, for example, have both sincere compassion yet deep revulsion toward a filthy tramp who has lived a life of dissipation.

Furthermore, as any parent knows, wrath and love do not rule out one another. We know that God is often angry with those who are the objects of His everlasting love. After all, before salvation, even the elect are enemies of God (Rom. 5:10); "children of wrath, even as others" (Eph. 2:3). Conversely, God genuinely and sincerely loves those who are the objects of His eternal wrath.

We simply cannot resolve the difficult questions about divine love by concluding that God actually withholds His lovingkindness, compassion, mercy, and goodwill from all but the elect.

So we must reject universalism, annihilationism, and conditional immortality. But we must also refuse the notion that God's hatred for the wicked rules out any love for them. How then shall we answer the hard questions about divine love?

One other solution is often suggested. It is to tell those inclined to ask hard questions, "Shut your mouth. You have no right to ask the question." People who take this approach will point to Romans 9:20–21, where the apostle Paul replied to a skeptic of God's sovereignty by saying, "On the contrary, who are you, O man, who answers back to God? The thing molded will not say to the molder, 'Why did you make me like this,' will it? Or does not the potter have a right over the clay, to make from the same lump one vessel for honorable use, and another for common use?"

Who are we to question God? That is what Paul asks. God is God. He will do whatever He wants to do because He is completely sovereign. He is the Potter. He decides what the pot will be like. And the pot has no right to object.

Obviously, that is all very true. God is God. We cannot comprehend His ways. Many of the questions we ask have answers we could never comprehend. Certainly we have no right to challenge God's motives. We are not entitled to subject Him to our interrogation, as if He were accountable to us. And sometimes the questions we raise do not even deserve to be answered. In the end, we will be left with many unanswered questions. That will bring us to Romans 9:20 and the inevitable place where we must simply close our mouths and stand in awe.

Before we get to that point, there are many things that we *do* need to understand. Romans 9:20 is a fitting response to a skeptic. It is appropriate for the person who will not be satisfied with knowing what God Himself has revealed. But for the truth-seeker sincerely wanting to understand God and His love, there is much in the Bible to help him come to grips with the hard questions before coming to a stop at Romans 9:20.

That is not to say that we can find all the answers to our hardest questions. We can't. Take, for example, the very difficult question of why a loving God does not redeem everyone. *If God is love, why does He send some people to an endless hell?* Why doesn't He redeem everyone?

We simply do not know. Scripture doesn't say. God Himself does not reveal to us the answers to those questions. Anyone who pretends to know more than God has told us is foolish.

Ultimately we reach the place where we must leave our questions to God and trust His essential righteousness, His lovingkindness, His tender mercy, and His justice. We learn to live with the *unanswered* questions in light of what we *know* to be true about God. At that point, Romans 9:20 becomes a satisfying answer, because we know we can trust the Potter. Meanwhile, as we search God's Word with an open heart, God's own self-revelation gives us a wonderful, marvelous, rich, comprehensible understanding of His love.

Wrong Questions Based on a Wrong Perspective of God

IN GRAPPLING WITH THE HARD QUESTIONS about God's love it is crucial to bear in mind that human tendency to see things from the wrong perspective. We cannot comprehend an infinite God with our finite minds. If we attempt to measure God from a human perspective, all our thinking about Him will be out of whack. And we sin against God when we think things of Him that are unbefitting of His glory.

God Himself rebukes those who underestimate Him by thinking of Him in human terms: "You thought that I was just like you; I will reprove you, and state the case in order before your eyes" (Ps. 50:21).

Remember how the book of Job ends? After all Job's suffering, and his friends' counsel that actually added to his sufferings, God rebuked not only Job's counselors, but also Job himself, for entertaining thoughts about God that were not sufficiently high. Both Job and his counselors were attempting to explain God in human terms. They were trying to make sense of what Job was going through, but their failure to see God as far above His creatures had skewed their view of what was happening. The counselors were giving the wrong answers, and Job was asking the wrong questions. God put some questions of His own to Job:

> Who is this that darkens counsel by words without knowledge? Now gird up your loins like a man, and I will ask you, and you instruct Me! Where were you when I laid the foundation of the earth? Tell Me, if you have understanding, who set its measurements, since you know? Or who stretched the line on it? On what were its bases sunk? Or who laid its cornerstone, when the morning stars sang together, and all the sons of God shouted for joy? Or who enclosed the sea with doors, when, bursting forth, it went out from the womb; when I made a cloud its garment, and thick darkness its swaddling band, and I placed boundaries on it, and I set a bolt and doors, and I said, "Thus far you shall come, but no farther; and here shall your proud waves stop"? Have you ever in your life commanded the morning,

and caused the dawn to know its place; that it might take
hold of the ends of the earth, and the wicked be shaken out
of it? (Job 38:2–13).

I love that portion of Scripture! God is recounting His own creative
works, and asking if Job is wise enough to tell God how these
things are to be done. From this point on, for three or four chapters, God lists the marvels of His creation and challenges Job to tell
Him if he knows better than God how the universe ought to be run.
Rather than seeking to vindicate Himself in Job's eyes, God simply
appealed to His own sovereignty. "Will the faultfinder contend with
the Almighty? Let him who reproves God answer it" (40:1).

Job, wise enough to know when he had said too much already,
simply replied, "Behold, I am insignificant; what can I reply to
Thee? I lay my hand on my mouth. Once I have spoken, and I
will not answer; Even twice, and I will add no more" (vv. 4–5).

Then God asked Job, "Will you really annul My judgment?
Will you condemn Me that you may be justified? Or do you have an
arm like God, and can you thunder with a voice like His?" (Job
40:8–9). Job's questions, valid as they may have seemed for someone who had suffered all Job had suffered, actually cast aspersions
on God's character. Job was stepping over the line if he thought
he could justify himself at God's expense.

Job, by God's own testimony, was a blameless and upright
man. There was no one like Job on the face of the earth (Job 1:8).
Yet he suffered—probably more than anyone else had ever suffered. Job was not as deserving of such suffering as anyone else
would have been. Why was he taking the brunt of so much catastrophe? Where was God's love and His sense of justice and fair
play? It was inevitable that Job would struggle with some very difficult questions like those, as people do today.

But the moment his questions reflected misgivings about
God—His wisdom, His love, His goodness, and the equity of His
justice—Job and his friends had crossed the line. They were

appraising God by human standards. They forgot that He is the Potter and we are merely the clay. So God rebuked them.

Job immediately saw his sin: "Therefore I have declared that which I did not understand, things too wonderful for me, which I did not know" (42:3).

We need to bear in mind as we ponder the love and the wrath of God that in many ways these things touch on knowledge "too wonderful" for us. "It is too high, [we] cannot attain to it" (Ps. 139:6). "Who has known the mind of the Lord, or who became His counselor?" (Rom. 11:34). "Who has directed the Spirit of the Lord, or as His counselor has informed Him? With whom did He consult and who gave Him understanding? And who taught Him in the path of justice and taught Him knowledge, and informed Him of the way of understanding?" (Isa. 40:13–14). And "Who has known the mind of the Lord, that he should instruct Him?" (1 Cor. 2:16). Those are the same kinds of questions with which God confronted Job.

Therefore as we ponder our own hard questions about God's love, we must take great care lest the very questions themselves provoke us to think inadequate or inappropriate thoughts about God or develop sinful attitudes toward His love and wisdom.

Wrong Inferences from a Faulty View of Divine Providence

WE DARE NOT make the error Job's counselors made, thinking we can observe the workings of providence and thereby discern the mind of God. Job's friends thought his sufferings were proof that Job was guilty of some secret sin. In reality, the opposite was true. Since it is clear from many scriptures that we cannot know God's mind, we must not try to read too much into His works of providence.

By that, I mean we cannot assume we know the meaning or purpose of every fortune or disaster that befalls. Often the unrighteous seem to prosper and experience God's goodness: "The tents of the destroyers prosper, and those who provoke God are secure, whom God brings into their power" (Job 12:6). "I have seen a violent, wicked man spreading himself like a luxuriant tree in its native soil" (Ps. 37:35). "Behold, these are the wicked; and always at ease, they have increased in wealth" (Ps. 73:12). So what often seems like divine blessing is no proof of God's favor. Don't think for a moment that prosperity is proof of divine approval. Those who think in those terms are prone to go astray.

On the other hand, the righteous frequently suffer: "Indeed, all who desire to live godly in Christ Jesus will be persecuted" (2 Tim. 3:12). "Unto you it is given in the behalf of Christ, not only to believe on him, but also to suffer for his sake" (Phil. 1:29). But God uses such suffering to accomplish much good: "God causes all things to work together for good to those who love God" (Rom. 8:28).

In other words, the very thing that seems good will end in evil for the impenitent and unbelieving. But for God's own children, even trouble and discipline are intended for good (Gen. 50:20). Therefore the greatest disaster from our perspective may actually be a token of God's lovingkindness.

The area where I live is active with earthquakes. Over the years we have experienced regular tremors. I never feel the earth shake that I don't also think of the infinite might of our God. At 4:31 A.M. on January 17, 1994, I was suddenly awakened by the most severe tremor I have ever felt. That earthquake, which lasted less than ninety seconds, leveled several freeway overpasses very close to my home. A high-rise medical office building in the vicinity dropped ten feet when the second floor collapsed. A large shopping mall was virtually destroyed. Hundreds of apartment buildings and homes were demolished. Sadly, several people asleep in one building were crushed to death when the ground floor crumbled underneath the weight of two upper stories. From a financial perspective it was the most costly natural disaster in the history of our nation.

Everyone seems to see the hand of God in such an event. In the midst of our city's crisis, we suddenly heard newscasters and civic officials openly discussing the awesome power of God and speculating on whether the earthquake (and a wave of other civic and natural disasters that had befallen southern California in recent years) might contain some message from the Almighty.

Someone noted that the epicenter of the earthquake was in an area well-known as a major production center for pornography. Sadly, many Christians were confidently declaring that the earthquake was God's judgment on the community. It was proof, they said, that God was finally fed up with the sins of southern California. This was such a topic of conversation that one of the major networks sent their top news anchor to interview me for a story on the earthquake as a judgment of God. One of the first questions the anchorman asked was whether I thought the earthquake was a divine judgment.

My response surprised him. I said I thought God had shown more mercy than judgment in the earthquake. After all, it occurred at an hour when most people were at home in bed, on a Monday that was a government holiday. Fewer people were on the roads than at any other time during the week. The national media had shown scenes of vehicles trapped on islands of roadway where portions of a bridge had collapsed in front of and behind them. Incredibly, not one vehicle had fallen to the ground below. Freeways collapsed, parking structures crumbled, and high-rise office buildings fell. Many people I know narrowly escaped death or serious injury. But of the millions of people living in the quake area, fewer than sixty were killed! In fact, the most remarkable thing of all about the earthquake was the low death toll.

On reflection, then, what most of the world saw as a catastrophe, what most Christians assumed was a severe judgment, was undoubtedly a token of divine mercy. It surely was a warning of greater judgment to come. But like most incidents that we deem tragedies, the quake undoubtedly held a mixture of both the goodness *and* the severity of God. In my estimation, the blessings far outweighed the calamity.

Clearly, however, we cannot know the mind of God. There are, therefore, many pitfalls to avoid in both asking and answering the hard questions about God's love. The subject is *not* child's play. With those things in mind, we can delve into what God Himself reveals in His Word—and surely we will find that it is a very fruitful study.

Two Aspects of the Love of God

IN THE CHAPTERS THAT FOLLOW, we're going to examine the love of God in even greater depth. We'll attempt to keep a balanced perspective of God's universal love for all men and women, and His particular love—a saving love—for His chosen ones, the elect. As we weave together many threads of thought, please try to avoid jumping to preliminary conclusions. Once we have a full picture of all that Scripture has to say about the love of God, all the different strands of truth will make a rich tapestry. Some things may not seem to make sense until we step back and look at the finished work. But when we see the big picture, it is breathtaking.

These two aspects of God's love—His universal love for all humanity, and His particular love for the elect—must not be confounded. To affirm that God loves the elect with a saving love is not to suggest that He has no love whatsoever for the rest of humanity. And to acknowledge that God genuinely loves even those whom He does not save is not to impute any kind of feebleness to God. In the end, none of His purposes are thwarted, and every aspect of His love perfectly declares His glory.

The Love of God for Humanity

Does God Love the Whole World?

Is God Sincere in the Gospel Offer?

Can God Really Love Those Whom He Does Not Save?

In What Sense Is God's Love Universal?

Chapter 6

■

The Love of God for Humanity

Perhaps you have noticed that someone shows up at almost every major American sporting event, in the center of the television camera's view, holding a sign that usually reads "John 3:16." At the World Series, the sign can normally be spotted right behind home plate. At the Super Bowl, someone holding the sign inevitably has seats between the goalposts. And in the NBA playoffs, the ubiquitous "John 3:16" banner can be seen somewhere in the front-row seats. How these people always manage to get prime seats is a mystery. But someone is always there, often wearing a multicolored wig to call attention to himself.

A couple of years ago, one of the men who had gained some degree of fame from holding up these "John 3:16" signs barricaded himself in a Los Angeles hotel and held police at bay until he was permitted to make a statement on television. It was a surrealistic image—here was someone who felt his mission in life was declaring John 3:16, and he was waving a gun and threatening police, while spouting biblical slogans. His career of attending major sporting events abruptly ended when police took him into custody without further incident.

As I watched the sordid episode unfold on television, I was

embarrassed that someone whom the public identified as a Christian would so degrade the gospel message. It occurred to me that I was watching someone whose approach to "evangelism" had never really been anything more than a quest for publicity. This stunt, it seemed, was nothing more than a large-scale attempt to get himself into the camera's eye once more. Sadly, he brought a horrible reproach on the very message he was seeking to publicize.

I also realized while watching that episode that John 3:16 may be the most familiar verse in all of Scripture, but it is surely one of the most abused and least understood. "God so loved the world"—waved like a banner at a football game—has become a favorite cheer for many people who presume on God's love and who do not love Him in return. The verse is often quoted as evidence that God loves everyone exactly the same and that He is infinitely merciful—as if the verse negated all the biblical warnings of condemnation for the wicked.

That is not the point of John 3:16. One has only to read verse 18 to see the balance of the truth: "He that believeth not is condemned already, because he hath not believed in the name of the only begotten Son of God" (KJV). Surely this is a truth that needs to be proclaimed to the world at least as urgently as the truth of John 3:16.

Does God Love the *Whole* World?

NEVERTHELESS, while acknowledging that some people are prone to abuse the notion of God's love, we cannot respond by minimizing what Scripture says about the extent of God's love. John 3:16 is a rich and crucial verse. In chapter 1, I noted that some Christians actually deny that God truly loves the whole world. I referred to Arthur Pink's famous attempt to argue that "world" in John 3:16 refers to *"the world of believers"* rather than *"the world of the ungodly.*"[1] I pointed out that this notion seems to have gained popularity in recent years.

Perhaps it's worth revisiting this subject for a closer look. As I said, I am encountering more and more Christians who want to argue that the only correct interpretation of John 3:16 is one that actually limits God's love to the elect and eliminates any notion of divine love for mankind in general.

A friend of mine recently gave me seven or eight articles that have circulated in recent months on the Internet. All of them were written and posted in various computer forums by Christians. And all of them deny that God loves everyone. It is frankly surprising how pervasive this idea has become among evangelicals. Here are some excerpts taken from these articles:

- ❐ The popular idea that God loves everyone is simply not to be found in the Scripture.

- ❐ God does love many, and those whom He loves, He will save. What about the rest? They are loved not at all.

- ❐ *Sheer logic alone* dictates that God would save those whom He loves.

- ❐ If God loved everyone, everyone would be saved. It is as simple as that. Clearly, not everyone is saved. Therefore, God does not love everyone.

- ❐ Scripture tells us that the wicked are an abomination to God. God Himself speaks of hating Esau. *How can anyone who believes all of Scripture claim that God loves everyone?*

- ❐ God loves His chosen ones, but His attitude toward the non-elect is pure hatred.

- ❐ The concept that God loves all humanity is contrary to Scripture. God clearly does *not* love everyone.

❏   All who are not keeping the Ten Commandments of God can be certain that God does not love them.

❏   Not only does God not love everyone, there are multitudes of people whom He utterly loathes with an infinite hatred. Both Scripture and consistent logic force us to this conclusion.

But neither Scripture *nor* sound logic will support such bold assertions.

I want to state as clearly as possible that I am in no way opposed to logic. I realize there are those who demean logic as if it were somehow contrary to spiritual truth. I do not agree; in fact, to abandon logic is to become irrational, and true Christianity is not irrational. The only way we can understand any spiritual matter is by applying careful logic to the truth that is revealed in God's Word. Sometimes logical deductions are necessary to yield the full truth on matters Scripture does not spell out explicitly. (The doctrine of the Trinity, for example, is implicit in Scripture but is never stated explicitly. It is a truth that is deduced from Scripture by good and necessary consequence—and therefore it is as surely true as if it were stated explicitly and unambiguously.)[2] There is certainly nothing whatsoever wrong with sound logic grounded in the truth of Scripture; in fact, logic is essential to understanding.

But surely we ought to be wary lest "sheer logic alone" lead us to a conclusion that runs counter to the whole thrust and tenor of Scripture. Applying logic to an incomplete set of propositions about God has often yielded the bitter fruit of false doctrine. We must constantly check our logical conclusions against the more sure word of Scripture. In this case, the notion that God's love is reserved for the elect alone does not survive the light of Scripture.

As we have seen throughout this study, Scripture clearly says that God is love. "The Lord is good to all, and His mercies are over all His works" (Ps. 145:9). Christ even commands us to love our enemies, and the reason He gives is this: "In order that you may be sons of your Father who is in heaven; for He causes His sun to rise on the evil and the good, and sends rain on the righteous and the unrighteous" (Matt. 5:45). The clear implication is that in some sense God loves His enemies. He loves both "the evil and the good," both "the righteous and the unrighteous" in precisely the same sense we are commanded to love our enemies.

In fact, the second greatest commandment, "You shall love your neighbor as yourself" (Mk. 12:31; cf. Lev. 19:18) is a commandment for us to love *everyone*. We can be certain the scope of this commandment is universal, because Luke 10 records that a lawyer, "wishing to justify himself . . . said to Jesus, 'And who is my neighbor?'" (Lk. 10:29)—and Jesus answered with the Parable of the Good Samaritan. The point? Even Samaritans, a semi-pagan race who had utterly corrupted Jewish worship and whom the Jews generally detested as enemies of God, were neighbors whom they were commanded to love. In other words, the command to love one's "neighbor" applies to *everyone*. This love commanded here is clearly a universal, indiscriminate love.

Consider this: Jesus perfectly fulfilled the law in every respect (Matt. 5:17–18), including this command for universal love. His love for others was surely as far-reaching as His own application of the commandment in Luke 10. Therefore, we can be certain that He loved everyone. He *must* have loved *everyone* in order to fulfill the Law. After all, the apostle Paul wrote, "The whole Law is fulfilled in one word, in the statement, 'You shall love your neighbor as yourself'" (Gal. 5:14). He reiterates this theme in Romans 13:8: "He who loves his neighbor has fulfilled the law." Therefore, Jesus must have loved His "neighbor." And since He Himself defined "neighbor" in universal terms, we know that His love while on earth was universal.

Do we imagine that Jesus as perfect man loves those whom Jesus as God does not love? Would God command us to love in a way that He does not? Would God demand that our love be more far-reaching than His own? And did Christ, having loved all humanity during His earthly sojourn, then revert after His ascension to pure hatred for the non-elect? Such would be unthinkable; "Jesus Christ is the same yesterday and today, yes and forever" (Heb 13:8).

Look once again at the context of John 3:16. Those who approach this passage determined to suggest that it *limits* God's love miss the entire point. There is no delimiting language anywhere in the context. It has nothing to do with how God's love is distributed between the elect and the rest of the world. It is a statement about God's demeanor toward mankind in general. It is a declaration of *good* news, and its point is to say that Christ came into the world on a mission of salvation, not a mission of condemnation: "For God did not send the Son into the world to judge the world, but that the world should be saved through Him" (v. 17). To turn it around and make it an expression of divine hatred against those whom God does not intervene to save is to turn the passage on its head.

John Brown, the Scottish Reformed theologian known for his marvelous studies on the sayings of Christ, wrote,

> The love in which the economy of salvation originates, is love *to the world*. "God so loved the world, as to give His only begotten Son." The term "world," is here just equivalent to mankind. It seems to be used by our Lord with a reference to the very limited and exclusive views of the Jews. . . .

Some have supposed that the word "world" here, is descriptive, not of mankind generally, but of the whole of a particular class, that portion of mankind who, according to the Divine purpose of mercy, shall ultimately become partakers of the salvation of Christ. But this is to give the term a meaning altogether unwarranted by the usage of Scripture.[3]

B. B. Warfield takes a similar position:

Certainly here "the world" and "believers" do not seem to be quite equipollent terms: there seems, surely, something conveyed by the one which is not wholly taken up by the other. How, then, shall we say that "the world" means just "the world of believers," just those scattered through the world, who, being the elect of God, shall believe in His Son and so have eternal life? There is obviously much truth in this idea: and the main difficulty which it faces may, no doubt, be avoided by saying that what is taught is that God's love of the world is shown by His saving so great a multitude as He does save out of the world. The wicked world deserved at His hands only total destruction. But He saves out of it a multitude which no man can number, out of every nation, and of all tribes, and peoples and tongues. How much must, then, God love the world! This interpretation, beyond question, reproduces the fundamental meaning of the text.[4]

Warfield goes on to make the crucial point that our primary concern as we interpret the word "world" in John 3:16 should not be to limit the *extent* of God's love, as much as to magnify the rich *wonder* of it:

The key to the passage lies . . . you see, in the significance of the term "world." It is not here a term of extension so much as a term of intensity. Its primary connotation is ethical, and the point of its employment is not to suggest that it takes a great deal of love to embrace it all, but that the world is so bad that it takes a great kind of love to love it at all, and much more to love it as God has loved it when He gave His Son for it.[5]

In fact, as we noted in an earlier chapter, if the word "world" holds the same meaning throughout the immediate context, we see in verse 19 that it cannot refer to the "world of the elect" alone: "this is the condemnation, that light is come into the world, and men loved darkness rather than light, because their deeds were evil." About this, Robert L. Dabney wrote,

> A fair logical connection between verse 17 and verse 18 shows that "the world" of verse 17 is inclusive of "him that believeth" and "him that believeth not" of verse 18. . . . It is hard to see how, if [Christ's coming into the world] is in no sense a true manifestation of divine benevolence to that part of "the world" which "believeth not," their choosing to slight it is the just ground of a deeper condemnation, as is expressly stated in verse 19.[6]

So John 3:16 demands to be interpreted as speaking of God's love to sinful mankind in general. Calvin's interpretation is worth summarizing again here. You'll recall that he saw two main points in John 3:16: "Namely, that faith in Christ brings life to all, and that Christ brought life, because the Father loves the human race, and wishes that they should not perish."[7]

Now take a fresh look at John 3:16 and try to absorb the real sense of it: "God so loved *the world*," wicked though it was, and despite the fact that nothing in the world was worthy of His love. He nevertheless loved the world of humanity so much "that He gave His only begotten Son," the dearest sacrifice He could make, so "that *whoever believes in Him* should not perish, but have eternal life." The end result of God's love is therefore the gospel message—the free offer of life and mercy to anyone who believes. In other words, the gospel—an indiscriminate offer of divine mercy to everyone without exception—manifests God's compassionate love and unfeigned lovingkindness to all humanity.

And unless we mean to ascribe unrighteousness to God, we must affirm that the offer of mercy in the gospel is sincere and well-meant. Surely His pleas for the wicked to turn from their evil ways and live must in some sense reflect a sincere desire on God's part. As we shall see, however, there are some who deny that this is the case.

Is God Sincere in the Gospel Offer?

OF COURSE, PEOPLE who assert that God's love is exclusively for the elect will usually acknowledge that God nevertheless shows mercy, longsuffering, and benevolence to the unrighteous and unbelievers. But they will insist that this apparent benevolence has nothing whatsoever to do with love or any sort of sincere affection. According to them, God's acts of benevolence toward the non-elect have no other purpose than to increase their condemnation.

Such a view, it seems to me, imputes insincerity to God. It suggests that God's pleadings with the reprobate are artificial, and that His offers of mercy are mere pretense.

Often in Scripture, God makes statements that reflect a yearning for the wicked to repent. In Psalm 81:13 He says, "Oh that My people would listen to Me, that Israel would walk in My ways!" And, again, in Ezekiel 18:32 He says, "'I have no pleasure in the death of anyone who dies,' declares the Lord God. 'Therefore, repent and live.'"

Elsewhere, God freely and indiscriminately offers mercy to all who will come to Christ: "Come to Me, all who are weary and heavy-laden, and I will give you rest. Take My yoke upon you, and learn from Me, for I am gentle and humble in heart; and you shall find rest for your souls. For My yoke is easy, and My load is light" (Matt. 11:28–30). "And the Spirit and the bride say, 'Come.' And let the one who hears say, 'Come.' And let the one who is thirsty come; let the one who wishes [whosoever will—KJV] take the water of life without cost" (Rev. 22:17).

God Himself says, "Turn to Me, and be saved, all the ends of the earth; for I am God, and there is no other" (Isa. 45:22). And,

"Ho! Every one who thirsts, come to the waters; and you who have no money come, buy and eat. Come, buy wine and milk without money and without cost" (Isa. 55:1). "Let the wicked forsake his way, and the unrighteous man his thoughts; and let him return to the Lord, and He will have compassion on him; and to our God, for He will abundantly pardon" (v. 7).

There are some who flatly deny that such invitations constitute any sincere offer of mercy to the non-elect. As far as they are concerned, the very word *offer* smacks of Arminianism (a name for the doctrine that makes salvation hinge solely on a human decision). They deny that God would "offer" salvation to those whom He has not chosen. They deny that God's pleadings with the reprobate reflect any real desire on God's part to see the wicked turn from their sins. To them, suggesting that God could have such an unfulfilled "desire" is a direct attack on divine sovereignty. God is sovereign, they suggest, and He does whatever pleases Him. Whatever He desires, He does.

Let us be completely honest: this poses a difficulty. How can unfulfilled desire be compatible with a wholly sovereign God? For example, in Isaiah 46:10, God states, "My purpose will be established, and I will accomplish all My good pleasure." He is, after all, utterly sovereign. Is it not improper to suggest that any of His actual "desires" remain unfulfilled?

This issue was the source of an intense controversy among some Reformed and Presbyterian denominations about fifty years ago—sometimes referred to as the "free offer" controversy. One group denied that God loves the non-elect. They also denied the concept of common grace (God's non-saving goodness to mankind in general). And they denied that divine mercy and eternal life are offered indiscriminately to everyone who hears the gospel. The gospel offer is not free, they claimed, but is extended to the elect alone. That position is a form of hyper-Calvinism.

Scripture clearly proclaims God's absolute and utter sovereignty over all that happens. He declared the end of all things before time even began, so whatever comes to pass is in perfect accord with the divine plan.

What God has purposed, He will also do (Isa. 46:10–11; Num. 23:19). God is not at the mercy of contingencies. He is not subject to His creatures' choices. He "works all things after the counsel of His will" (Eph. 1:11). Nothing occurs but that which is in accord with His purposes (cf. Acts 4:28). Nothing can thwart God's design, and nothing can occur apart from His sovereign decree (Isa. 43:13; Ps. 33:11). He does all His good pleasure: "Whatever the Lord pleases, He does, in heaven and in earth, in the seas and in all deeps" (Ps. 135:6).

But that does not mean God derives pleasure from every aspect of what He has decreed. God explicitly says that He takes no pleasure in the death of the wicked (Ezek. 18:32; 33:11). He does not delight in evil (Isa. 65:12). He hates all expressions of wickedness and pride (Prov. 6:16–19). Since none of those things can occur apart from the decree of a sovereign God, we must conclude that there is a sense in which His *decrees* do not always reflect His *desires;* His *purposes* are not necessarily accomplished in accord with His *preferences.*

The language here is necessarily anthropopathic (ascribing human emotions to God). To speak of unfulfilled desires in the Godhead is to employ terms fit only for the human mind. Yet such expressions communicate some truth about God that cannot otherwise be expressed in human language. As noted in chapter 3, God's own Word uses anthropopathisms to convey truth about Him that cannot adequately be represented to us through any other means. To give but one example, consider Genesis 6:6: "The Lord was sorry that He had made man on the earth, and He was grieved in His heart." Yet we know that God does not change His mind (1 Sam. 15:29). He is immutable; "with [Him] there is no variation, or shifting shadow" (Jas. 1:17). So whatever Genesis 6:6 means, it cannot suggest any changeableness in God. The best we can do with such an anthropopathism is try to grasp the

The God Who Loves

essence of the idea, then reject any implications we know would take us to ideas about God that are unbiblical.

That same principle applies when we are grappling with the question of God's expressed desire for the wicked to repent. If God's "desire" remains unfulfilled (and we know that in some cases, it does—Lk. 13:34), we cannot conclude that God is somehow less than sovereign. We know He is fully sovereign; we do not know why He does not turn the heart of every sinner to Himself. Nor should we speculate in this area. It remains a mystery the answer to which God has not seen fit to reveal. "The secret things belong to the Lord our God"; only "the things revealed belong to us" (Deut. 29:29). At some point, we must say with the psalmist, "Such knowledge is too wonderful for me; It is too high, I cannot attain to it" (Ps. 139:6).

Can God Really Love Whom He Does Not Save?

I REALIZE, OF COURSE, that most readers have no objection whatsoever to the idea that God's love is universal. Most of us were weaned on this notion, being taught as children to sing songs like, "Jesus loves the little children; all the children of the world." Many may never even have encountered anyone who denies that God's love is universal.

Yet if I seem to dwell on this issue, it is because I want to acknowledge that it poses a perplexing difficulty for other aspects of God's revealed truth. Let us honestly admit that on the face of it, the universal love of God is hard to reconcile with the doctrine of election.

Election is a biblical doctrine, affirmed with the utmost clarity from beginning to end in Scripture. The highest expression of divine love to sinful humanity is seen in the fact that God set His love on certain undeserving sinners and chose them for salvation before the foundation of the world. There is a proper sense in which God's love for His own is a unique, special, particular love determined to save them at all costs. (We will delve more deeply into this truth in forthcoming chapters.)

It is also true that when Scripture speaks of divine love, the focus is *usually* on God's eternal love toward the elect. God's love for mankind reaches fruition in the election of those whom He saves. And not every aspect of divine love is extended to all sinners without exception. Otherwise, all would be elect, and all would ultimately be saved. But Scripture clearly teaches that *many* will *not* be saved (Matt. 7:22–23). Can God sincerely love those whom He does not intervene to save?

British Baptist leader Erroll Hulse, dealing with this very question, has written,

> How can we say God loves all men when the psalms tell us He hates the worker of iniquity (Ps. 5:5)? How can we maintain that God loves all when Paul says that He bears the objects of His wrath, being fitted for destruction, with great patience (Rom. 9:22)? Even more how can we possibly accept that God loves all men without exception when we survey the acts of God's wrath in history? Think of the deluge which destroyed all but one family. Think of Sodom and Gomorrah. With so specific a chapter as Romans [1,] which declares that sodomy is a sign of reprobation, could we possibly maintain that God loved the population of the two cities destroyed by fire? How can we possibly reconcile God's love and His wrath? Would we deny the profundity of this problem?[8]

Yet Hulse realizes that if we take Scripture at face value, there is no escaping the conclusion that God's love extends even to sinners whom He ultimately will condemn. "The will of God is expressed in unmistakable terms," Hulse writes. "He has no pleasure in the destruction and punishment of the wicked (Ez. 18:32; 33:11)." Hulse also cites Matthew 23:37, where Jesus weeps over the city of Jerusalem, then says, "We are left in no doubt that the desire and will of God is for man's highest good, that is his eternal salvation through heeding the gospel of Christ."[9]

It is crucial that we accept the testimony of Scripture on this question, for as Hulse points out,

> We will not be disposed to invite wayward transgressors to Christ, or reason with them, or bring to them the overtures of the gospel, unless we are convinced that God is favorably disposed to them. Only if we are genuinely persuaded that He will have them to be saved are we likely to make the effort. If God does not love them it is hardly likely that we will make it our business to love them. Especially is this the case when there is so much that is repulsive in the ungodliness and sinfulness of Christ-rejecters.[10]

Biblically, we cannot escape the conclusion that God's benevolent, merciful love is unlimited in extent. He loves the *whole* world of humanity. This love extends to all people in all times. It is what Titus 3:4 refers to as "the kindness of God our Savior and His love for mankind." God's singular love for the elect quite simply does not rule out a universal love of sincere compassion—and a sincere desire on God's part to see every sinner turn to Christ.

Mark 10 relates a familiar story that illustrates God's love for the lost. It is the account of the rich young ruler who came to Jesus and began asking Him a great question: "Good Teacher, what shall I do to inherit eternal life?" Scripture tells us:

> And Jesus said to him, "Why do you call Me good? No one is good except God alone. You know the commandments, 'Do not murder, Do not commit adultery, Do not steal, Do not bear false witness, Do not defraud, Honor your father and mother'" (vv. 18–19).

Every aspect of Jesus' reply was designed to confront the young man's sin. Many people misunderstand the point of Jesus' initial question: "Why do you call Me good?" Our Lord was not denying His own sinlessness or deity. Plenty of verses of Scripture affirm that Jesus was indeed sinless—"holy, innocent, undefiled, separated from sinners and exalted above the heavens" (Heb. 7:26). He is therefore also God incarnate (Jn. 1:1). But Jesus' reply to this young man had a twofold purpose: first, to underscore His own deity, confronting the young man with the reality of who He was; and second, to gently chide a brash young man who clearly thought of *himself* as good.

To stress this second point, Jesus quoted a section of the Decalogue. Had the young man been genuinely honest with himself, he would have had to admit that he had not kept the law perfectly. But instead, he responded confidently, "Teacher, I have kept all these things from my youth up" (v. 20). This was unbelievable impertinence on the young man's part. It shows how little he understood of the demands of the law. Contrast his flippant response with how Peter reacted when he saw Christ for who He was. Peter fell on his face and said, "Depart from me, for I am a sinful man, O Lord!" (Lk. 5:8). This rich young ruler's response fell at the other end of the spectrum. He was not even willing to admit he had sinned.

So Jesus gave him a second test: "One thing you lack: go and sell all you possess, and give to the poor, and you shall have treasure in heaven; and come, follow Me" (Mk. 10:21).

Sadly, the young man declined. Here were two things he refused to do: he would not acknowledge his sin, and he would not bow to Christ's lordship. In other words, he shut himself off from the eternal life he seemed so earnestly to be seeking. As it turned out, there were things more important to him than eternal life, after all. His pride and his personal property took priority in his heart over the claims of Christ on his life. And so he turned away from the only true Source of the life he thought he was seeking.

The God Who Loves

That is the last we ever see of this man in the New Testament. As far as the biblical record is concerned, he remained in unbelief. But notice this significant phrase, tucked away in Mark 10:21: "Looking at him, Jesus felt a love for him." Here we are explicitly told that Jesus loved an overt, open, non-repentant, non-submissive Christ-rejector. He loved him.

That's not the only Scripture that speaks of God's love for those who turn away from Him. In Isaiah 63:7–9 the prophet describes God's demeanor toward the nation of Israel:

> I shall make mention of the lovingkindnesses of the Lord, the praises of the Lord, according to all that the Lord has granted us, and the great goodness toward the house of Israel, which He has granted them according to His compassion, and according to the multitude of His lovingkindnesses. For He said, "Surely, they are My people, Sons who will not deal falsely." So He became their Savior. In all their affliction He was afflicted, and the angel of His presence saved them; in His love and in His mercy He redeemed them; and He lifted them and carried them all the days of old.

Someone might say, Yes, but that talks about God's redemptive love for His elect alone. No, this speaks of a love that spread over the entire nation of Israel. God "became their Savior" in the sense that He redeemed the entire nation from Egypt. He suffered when they suffered. He sustained them "all the days of old." This speaks not of an eternal salvation, but of a temporal relationship with an earthly nation. How do we know? Look at verse 10: "But they rebelled and grieved His Holy Spirit; therefore, He turned Himself to become their enemy, He fought against them."

That is an amazing statement! Here we see God defined as the Savior, the lover, the redeemer of a people who make themselves His enemies. They rebel against Him. They grieve His Holy Spirit. They choose a life of sin.

The Love of God for Humanity

Now notice verse 17: "Why, O Lord, dost Thou cause us to stray from Thy ways, and harden our heart from fearing Thee?" That speaks of God's judicial hardening of the disobedient nation. He actually hardened the hearts of those whom He loved and redeemed out of Egypt.

Isaiah 64:5 includes these shocking words: "Thou wast angry, for we sinned, we continued in them a long time; and shall we be saved?"

How can God be Savior to those who will not be saved? Yet these are clearly unconverted people. Look at verses 6–7, which begins with a familiar passage:

> For all of us have become like one who is unclean, and all our righteous deeds are like a filthy garment; and all of us wither like a leaf, and our iniquities, like the wind, take us away. And there is no one who calls on Thy name, who arouses himself to take hold of Thee; for Thou hast hidden Thy face from us, and hast delivered us into the power of our iniquities.

These are clearly unconverted, unbelieving people. In what sense can God call Himself their Savior?

Here is the sense of it: God revealed Himself as Savior. He manifested His love to the nation. "In all their affliction He was afflicted" (63:9). He poured out His goodness, and lovingkindness and mercy on the nation. And that divine forbearance and longsuffering should have moved them to repentance (Rom. 2:4). But instead they responded with unbelief, and their hearts were hardened.

Isaiah 65 takes it still further:

> I permitted Myself to be sought by those who did not ask for Me; I permitted Myself to be found by those who did not seek Me. I said, "Here am I, here am I," To a nation which did not call on My name. I have spread out My hands all day

long to a rebellious people, who walk in the way which is not good, following their own thoughts. (vv.1–2)

In other words, God turned away from these rebellious people, consigned them to their own idolatry, and chose a people for Himself from among other nations.

Isaiah reveals the shocking blasphemy of those from whom God has turned away. They considered themselves holier than God (v. 5); they continually provoked Him to His face (v. 3), defiling themselves (v. 4) and scorning God for idols (v. 7). God judged them with the utmost severity, because their hostility to Him was great, and their rejection of Him was final.

Yet these were people on whom God had showered love and goodness! He even called Himself their Savior.

In a similar sense Jesus is called "Savior of the world" (Jn. 4:42; 1 Jn. 4:14). Paul wrote, "We have fixed our hope on the living God, who is the Savior of all men, especially of believers" (1 Tim. 4:10). The point is not that He actually saves the whole world (for that would be universalism, and Scripture clearly teaches that not all will be saved). The point is that He is the only Savior to whom anyone in the world can turn for forgiveness and eternal life— and therefore, all are urged to embrace Him as Savior. Jesus Christ is proffered to the world as Savior. In setting forth His own Son as Savior of the world, God displays the same kind of love to the whole world that was manifest in the Old Testament to the rebellious Israelites. It is a sincere, tender-hearted, compassionate love that offers mercy and forgiveness.

In What Sense Is God's Love Universal?

WHAT ASPECTS OF GOD'S LOVE and goodwill are seen even in His dealings with the reprobate? There are at least four ways God's love is manifest universally to all people.

The Love of God for Humanity

Common Grace

COMMON GRACE is a term theologians use to describe the goodness of God to all mankind universally. Common grace restrains sin and the effects of sin on the human race. Common grace is what keeps humanity from descending into the morass of evil that we would see if the full expression of our fallen nature were allowed to have free reign.

Scripture teaches that we are totally depraved—tainted with sin in every aspect of our being (Rom. 3:10–18). People who doubt this doctrine often ask, "How can people who are supposedly totally depraved enjoy beauty, have a sense of right and wrong, know the pangs of a wounded conscience, or produce great works of art and literature? Aren't these accomplishments of humanity proof that the human race is essentially good? Don't these things testify to the basic goodness of human nature?"

And the answer is no. Human nature is utterly corrupt. "There is none righteous, not even one" (Rom. 3:10). "The heart is more deceitful than all else and is desperately sick" (Jer. 17:9). Unregenerate men and women are "dead in . . . trespasses and sins" (Eph. 2:1). All people are by nature "foolish . . . disobedient, deceived, enslaved to various lusts and pleasures, spending [their lives] in malice" (Titus 3:3). This is true of all alike, "For all have sinned and fall short of the glory of God" (Rom. 3:23).

Common grace is all that restrains the full expression of human sinfulness. God has graciously given us a conscience, which enables us to know the difference between right and wrong, and to some degree places moral constraints on evil behavior (Rom. 2:15). He sovereignly maintains order in human society through government (Rom. 13:1–5). He enables us to admire beauty and goodness (Ps. 50:2). He imparts numerous advantages, blessings, and tokens of His kindness indiscriminately on both the evil and the good, the righteous and the unrighteous (Matt. 5:45). All of those things are the result of common grace, God's goodness to mankind in general.

Common grace *ought* to be enough to move sinners to repentance. The apostle Paul rebukes the unbeliever: "Do you think lightly of the riches of His kindness and forbearance and patience, not knowing that the kindness of God leads you to repentance?" (Rom. 2:4). Yet because of the depth of depravity in the human heart, all sinners spurn the goodness of God.

Common grace does not pardon sin or redeem sinners, but it is nevertheless a sincere token of God's goodwill to mankind in general. As the apostle Paul said, "In Him we live and move and exist . . . for we also are His offspring" (Acts 17:28). That takes in everyone on earth, not just those whom God adopts as sons. God deals with us all as His offspring, people made in His image. "The Lord is good to all, and His mercies are over all His works" (Ps. 145:9).

If you question the love and goodness of God to all, look again at the world in which we live. Someone might say, "There's a lot of sorrow in this world." The only reason the sorrow and tragedy stand out is because there is also much joy and gladness. The only reason we recognize the ugliness is that God has given us so much beauty. The only reason we feel the disappointment is that there is so much that satisfies.

When we understand that all of humanity is fallen and rebellious and unworthy of any blessing from God's hand, it helps give a better perspective. "Because of the Lord's great love we are not consumed, for His compassions never fail" (Lam. 3:22, NIV). And the only reason God ever gives us anything to laugh at, smile at, or enjoy is because He is a good and loving God. If He were not, we would be immediately consumed by His wrath.

Acts 14 contains a helpful description of common grace. Here Paul and Barnabas were ministering at Lystra, when Paul healed a lame man. The crowds saw it and someone began saying that Paul was Zeus and Barnabas was Hermes. The priest at the local temple of Zeus wanted to organize a sacrifice to Zeus. But when Paul and Barnabas heard about it, they said,

> Men, why are you doing these things? We are also men of the same nature as you, and preach the gospel to you in order that you should turn from these vain things to a living God, who made the heaven and the earth and the sea, and all that is in them. *And in the generations gone by He permitted all the nations to go their own ways; and yet He did not leave Himself without witness, in that He did good and gave you rains from heaven and fruitful seasons, satisfying your hearts with food and gladness* (vv. 15–17, emphasis added).

That is a fine description of common grace. While allowing sinners to "go their own ways," God nevertheless bestows on them temporal tokens of His goodness and lovingkindness. It is not saving grace. It has no redemptive effect. Nevertheless, it is a genuine and unfeigned manifestation of divine lovingkindness to all people.

Compassion

GOD'S LOVE to all humanity is a love of *compassion*. To say it another way, it is a love of pity. It is a broken-hearted love. He is "good, and ready to forgive, and abundant in lovingkindness to all who call upon [Him]" (Ps. 86:5). "To the Lord our God belong compassion and forgiveness, for we have rebelled against Him" (Dan. 9:9). He is "compassionate and gracious, slow to anger, and abounding in lovingkindness and truth" (Exod. 34:6). As we saw in an earlier chapter, "God is love" (1 Jn. 4:8, 16).

Again, we must understand that there is nothing in any sinner that compels God's love. He does not love us because we are lovable. He is not merciful to us because we in any way deserve

His mercy. We are despicable, vile sinners who if we are not saved by the grace of God will be thrown on the trash heap of eternity, which is hell. We have no intrinsic value, no intrinsic worth—there's nothing in us to love.

I recently overheard a radio talk-show psychologist attempting to give a caller an ego-boost: "God loves you for what you are. You *must* see yourself as someone special. After all, you are special to God."

But that misses the point entirely. God *does not* love us "for what we are." He loves us *in spite of what we are.* He does not love us because we are special. Rather, it is only His love and grace that give our lives any significance at all. That may seem like a doleful perspective to those raised in a culture where self-esteem is elevated to the supreme virtue. But it is, after all, precisely what Scripture teaches: "We have sinned like our fathers, we have committed iniquity, we have behaved wickedly" (Ps. 106:6). "All of us have become like one who is unclean, and all our righteous deeds are like a filthy garment; and all of us wither like a leaf, and our iniquities, like the wind, take us away" (Isa. 64:6).

God loves because He *is* love; love is essential to who He is. Rather than viewing His love as proof of something worthy in us, we ought to be humbled by it.

God's love for the reprobate is not the love of value; it is the love of pity for that which *could* have had value and has none. It is a love of compassion. It is a love of sorrow. It is a love of pathos. It is the same deep sense of compassion and pity we have when we see a scab-ridden derelict lying in the gutter. It is not a love that is incompatible with revulsion, but it is a genuine, well-meant, compassionate, sympathetic love nonetheless.

Frequently the Old Testament prophets describe the tears of God for the lost:

> Therefore my heart intones like a harp for Moab, and my
> inward feelings for Kir-hareseth. So it will come about when
> Moab presents himself, when he wearies himself upon his

high place, and comes to his sanctuary to pray, that he will not prevail. This is the word which the Lord spoke earlier concerning Moab (Isa. 16:11–13).

"And I shall make an end of Moab," declares the Lord, "the one who offers sacrifice on the high place and the one who burns incense to his gods. Therefore My heart wails for Moab like flutes; My heart also wails like flutes for the men of Kir-heres. Therefore they have lost the abundance it produced. For every head is bald and every beard cut short; there are gashes on all the hands and sackcloth on the loins" (Jer. 48:35–37).

Similarly, the New Testament gives us the picture of Christ, weeping over the city of Jerusalem: "O Jerusalem, Jerusalem, who kills the prophets and stones those who are sent to her! How often I wanted to gather your children together, the way a hen gathers her chicks under her wings, and you were unwilling" (Matt. 23:37). Luke 19:41–44 gives an even more detailed picture of Christ's sorrow over the city:

> And when He approached, He saw the city and wept over it, saying, "If you had known in this day, even you, the things which make for peace! But now they have been hidden from your eyes. For the days shall come upon you when your enemies will throw up a bank before you, and surround you, and hem you in on every side, and will level you to the ground and your children within you, and they will not leave in you one stone upon another, because you did not recognize the time of your visitation."

Those are words of doom, yet they're spoken in great sorrow. It is genuine sorrow, borne out of the heart of a divine Savior who "wanted to gather [them] together, the way a hen gathers her chicks under her wings," but they were "unwilling."

The God Who Loves

Those who deny God's love for the reprobate usually suggest that what we see here is the human side of Jesus, not His divinity. They say that if this were an expression of sincere desire from an omnipotent God, He would surely intervene in their behalf and save them. Unfulfilled desire such as Jesus expresses here is simply incompatible with a sovereign God, they say.

But consider the problems with that view. Is Christ in His humanity more loving or more compassionate than God? Is tenderness perfected in the humanity of Christ, yet somehow lacking in His deity? When Christ speaks of gathering the people of Jerusalem as a hen gathers her chicks, is this not deity speaking, rather than humanity? Do not these pronouncements of doom necessarily proceed from His deity as well? And if the words are the words of deity, how can anyone assert that the accompanying sorrow is the product of Christ's human nature only, and not the divine? Do not our hearts tell us that if God is love—if His tender mercies are over all His works—then what we hear in Jesus' words must be an echo of the divine?

Admonition

GOD'S UNIVERSAL LOVE is revealed not only in common grace and His great compassion, but also in His admonition to repent. God is constantly warning the reprobate of their impending fate, and pleading with them to turn away from sin. Nothing demonstrates God's love more than the various warnings throughout the pages of Scripture, urging sinners to flee from the wrath to come.

Anyone who knows anything about Scripture knows it is filled with warnings about the judgment to come, warnings about hell, and warnings about the severity of divine punishment. If God really did *not* love the reprobate, nothing would compel Him to warn them. He would be perfectly just to punish them for their sin and unbelief with no admonition whatsoever. But He *does* love and He *does* care and He *does* warn.

God evidently loves sinners enough to warn them. Sometimes the warnings of Scripture bear the marks of divine wrath. They sound severe. They reflect God's hatred of sin. They warn of the irreversible condemnation that will befall sinners. They are unsettling, unpleasant, even terrifying.

But they are admonitions from a loving God who as we have seen weeps over the destruction of the wicked. They are necessary expressions from the heart of a compassionate Creator who takes no pleasure in the death of the wicked. They are further proof that God is love.

The Gospel Offer

FINALLY, WE SEE PROOF that God's love extends to all in *the gospel offer*. We saw earlier that the gospel invitation is an offer of divine mercy. Now consider the unlimited breadth of the offer. No one is excluded from the gospel invitation. Salvation in Christ is freely and indiscriminately offered to all.

Jesus told a parable in Matthew 22:2–14 about a king who was having a marriage celebration for his son. He sent his servants to invite the wedding guests. Scripture says simply, "they were unwilling to come" (v. 3). The king sent his servants again, saying, "Behold, I have prepared my dinner; my oxen and my fattened livestock are all butchered and everything is ready; come to the wedding feast" (v. 4). But even after that second invitation, the invited guests remained unwilling to come. In fact, Scripture says, "They paid no attention and went their way, one to his own farm, another to his business, and the rest seized his slaves and mistreated them and killed them" (vv. 5–6). This was outrageous, inexcusable behavior! And the king judged them severely for it.

Then Scripture says he told his servants, "The wedding is ready, but those who were invited were not worthy. Go therefore to the main highways, and as many as you find there, invite to the wedding feast" (v. 9). He opened the invitation to all comers. Jesus closes with this: "Many are called, but few are chosen" (v. 14).

The parable represents God's dealing with the nation of Israel. They were the invited guests. But they rejected the Messiah. They spurned Him and mistreated Him and crucified Him. They wouldn't come—as Jesus said to them, "You search the Scriptures, because you think that in them you have eternal life; and it is these that bear witness of Me; and *you are unwilling to come to Me,* that you may have life" (Jn. 5:39–40).

The gospel invites many to come who are unwilling to come. Many are called who are not chosen. The invitation to come is given indiscriminately to all. Whosoever will may come—the invitation is not issued to the elect alone.

God's love for mankind does not stop with a warning of the judgment to come. It also invites sinners to partake of divine mercy. It offers forgiveness and mercy. Jesus said, "Come to Me, all who are weary and heavy-laden, and I will give you rest. Take My yoke upon you, and learn from Me, for I am gentle and humble in heart; and you shall find rest for your souls" (Matt. 11:28–29). And Jesus said, "The one who comes to Me I will certainly not cast out" (Jn. 6:37).

It should be evident from these verses that the gospel is a *free offer* of Christ and His salvation to all who hear. Those who deny the free offer therefore alter the nature of the gospel itself. And those who deny that God's love extends to all humanity obscure some of the most blessed truth in all Scripture about God and His lovingkindness.

God's love extends to the whole world. It covers all humanity. We see it in common grace. We see it in His compassion. We see it in His admonitions to the lost. And we see it in the free offer of the gospel to all.

God *is* love, and His mercy is over all His works.

But that's not all there is to know about God's love. There is an even greater aspect of the love of God that is made manifest in His sovereign election and salvation of certain sinners. And it is to this higher kind of love that we now turn our attention.

The Love of God for His Elect

The Limits of Universal Love

■

The Magnitude of God's Saving Love

■

A Love That Is Sovereignly Bestowed

■

A Graphic Picture of Unfailing Love

■

God's Enduring Faithfulness

Chapter 7

The Love of God for His Elect

No ONE OUGHT TO CONCLUDE that because God's love is universally extended to all that God therefore loves everyone equally. The fact that God loves every man and woman does not mean that He loves all *alike*. Clearly, He does not. In Romans 9:13, the apostle Paul, quoting a prophecy from the Old Testament Book of Malachi, describes God's demeanor toward the twin sons of Isaac: "Jacob I loved, but Esau I hated."

Moreover, Paul says God made His choice when "the twins were not yet born, and had not done anything good or bad" (v. 11). Why? Why would God choose to love one and hate the other, before either of them could do anything to merit God's love or hatred?

Paul tells us why: "In order that God's purpose according to His choice might stand, not because of works, but because of Him who calls" (v. 11). Paul is teaching that God is sovereign in the exercise of His love. God has set His love on certain individuals in eternity past and *predestined* them to eternal life. Here, of course, we touch on the biblical doctrine of election.

Most people struggle with this doctrine when they first encounter it. Yet as we shall see, the doctrine is clearly taught in

Scripture. And it is so crucial to understanding the love of God that we must address it here.

The Limits of Universal Love

THE COMPASSIONATE LOVE and goodness God bestows on all humanity has its limits. It may be resisted. It may be rejected. It may be spurned. As we noted in the previous chapter, God's love and goodness *ought* to lead the sinner to repentance (Rom. 2:4), but because of the utter wickedness of the sinful heart, the sinner stubbornly persists in his sin and unbelief. Therefore, God's compassionate love and His goodness ultimately give way to hatred and judgment. The apostle Paul wrote in 1 Corinthians 16:22, "If any man love not the Lord Jesus Christ, let him be accursed." That is literally a pronouncement of damnation against those who spurn the love of God.

As we noted in an earlier chapter, some people would like to believe that God loves everyone so much that ultimately everyone will be saved. They suggest that even those who reject Him here on earth will be given a second chance on the other side of the grave— or that God will just summarily forgive everyone and take everyone to heaven. But Scripture holds forth no such hope. According to Jesus, the wicked are ushered into "eternal punishment" (Matt. 25:46). God's love spurned gives way to divine hatred, manifested in the animosity and vengeance of eternal judgment.

Others deny that God truly hates anyone. They will say that God hates the sin, but not the sinner. That is a false dichotomy, however. Remember that it is the sinner himself who is judged and condemned and punished. If God hated only the sin and not the sinner, He would strip the sin away and redeem the sinner, rather than casting the whole person into hell (Matt. 5:29; 10:28). Hell is, after all, the final expression of God's hatred. God does hate the reprobate sinner in a very real and terrifying sense.

I would never say such a thing were it not clearly taught in Scripture. Psalm 5:5-6 says, "The boastful shall not stand before Thine eyes; Thou dost hate all who do iniquity. Thou dost destroy those who speak falsehood; The Lord abhors the man of bloodshed and deceit." Psalm 11:5 says, "The Lord tests the righteous and the wicked, and the one who loves violence His soul hates."

The psalmist himself reflects the divine attitude when he writes, "Do I not hate those who hate Thee, O Lord? And do I not loathe those who rise up against Thee? I hate them with the utmost hatred; they have become my enemies" (Ps. 139:21–22).

As we have noted previously, this is not a malevolent hatred; it is a holy abhorrence for that which is vile, loathsome, and evil. But it is true hatred nonetheless.

So while there is a genuine sense in which God's love is universal in its extent, there is another sense in which it is limited in degree. The love of God for all humanity is not the sort of love that guarantees everyone's salvation. It is not a love that nullifies His holy abhorrence of sin. It is not a saving love.

The Magnitude of God's Saving Love

THERE IS AN EVEN GREATER LOVE of God, however, that does accomplish the salvation of sinners. It is a special love, bestowed from all eternity on those whom He has chosen as His own. God's love for those who believe—His love for the elect—is infinitely greater in degree than His love for humanity in general. Here we are talking about a very, very important doctrine of Scripture.

An entire chapter has already been devoted to demonstrating that God loves all humanity. For obvious reasons, that universal aspect of God's love is important to affirm. But it is even more crucial that we see that God has a special love for *His own,* His chosen people, and that He loves them with an eternal, unchanging love.

The God Who Loves

John 13:1 describes the love of Christ for His disciples: "Having loved His own who were in the world, He loved them to the end." Another version translates that same verse this way: "Having loved his own who were in the world, he now showed them the full extent of his love" (NIV).

That little phrase "to the end" (Jn. 13:1) is an important phrase. The Greek expression is *eis telos*. "To the end" is an acceptable translation, but idiomatically this is an expression that carries the meaning "completely, perfectly, fully, or comprehensively—to the uttermost."

God loves the world, but He loves "His own" perfectly, unchangingly, completely, fully, comprehensively—*eis telos*. Let me say it simply: He loves His own to the complete extent of His capacity to love His creatures. He loves them enough to make them joint-heirs with Christ. He loves them enough to make them into His very image. He lavishes them with all the riches of His grace for all of eternity. He loves them as fully and completely as any human could ever be loved by God—and His love knows no limits. That's what *eis telos* conveys.

This is also an unconditional love. Look at the context: Jesus was in the Upper Room with the disciples on the night He was betrayed. At this moment He was very much aware of their failures and weaknesses and their disappointing actions. They seemed to struggle to comprehend the simplest truths. They were a cowardly, disloyal, frightened group who would very soon scatter when He was taken prisoner. Christ knew this. He predicted that Peter would shamefully deny Him three times. He knew that when He hung on the cross the next day, most of the disciples would not even be present.

His love for them had never failed. He had proved it time and again. He even began their final evening together in the Upper Room by washing their feet, as if He were a lowly servant to them. Even after that, however, they interrupted the meal with an argument about which one of them was the greatest (Lk. 22:24)! He had loved them as magnanimously as was reasonable, and this is what He got in return.

To put it simply, His love for them was not repaid as it should have been. The disciples had ignored His love, taken it for granted, and abused it. But He loved them to the end. In other words, this was a love that would never die. It would never wane. It was *unconditional*.

But the expression *eis telos* also carries the idea of eternality. Here it speaks of a love that lasts forever. Not only did Christ love His own to the end of their lives; not only did He love them to the end of *His* earthly life; but He would love them eternally. In this same context, He tells them, "I go to prepare a place for you . . . that where I am, there you may be also" (Jn. 14:2–3). His love for His own will be manifest throughout eternity.

So the phrase *eis telos* is rich with meaning. "Having loved His own who were in the world, He loved them *[eis telos]*"—to the uttermost in every respect.

This, of course, speaks of the particular love of God for the elect. It is not the general love that extends to all humanity. It is not a conditional love that can give way to hatred. This is the love He has for "His own." It is a love that extends from eternity past to eternity future. And it is a love that will stop at nothing to redeem its object.

"Greater love has no one than this," Jesus said, "that one lay down his life for his friends" (Jn. 15:13). That is precisely what He would do for them the day after He spoke these words.

This love of God for His own is not bestowed on people because they show themselves worthy of it. In fact, there is *nothing* worthy in the recipients of this love:

> Christ died for the ungodly. For one will hardly die for a righteous man; though perhaps for the good man someone would dare even to die. But God demonstrates His own love toward us, in that while we were yet sinners, Christ died for us (Rom. 5:6–8).

The God Who Loves

These are not people who have somehow earned God's love. It is a wholly gracious love, not something anyone could ever earn through any kind of merit system.

Here is where the true greatness of divine love is seen. Christ faces the cross. He will bear their sin. And He will undergo the agonizing wrath of God on their behalf. He will suffer the painful, lonely sense of being forsaken by the Father, not to mention the human pain of execution and murder and public shame. And yet He is totally immersed in His love for His own, and as He faces death, He wants to affirm how much He loves these utterly unworthy men.

This is a love that only those who belong to Christ can possibly know. It is a unique and marvelous love. It is a life-giving love. It is a love that pursues its object, no matter what. It is a love that saves forever.

A Love That Is Sovereignly Bestowed

IN DEUTERONOMY 7:6, God told Israel, "You are a holy people to the Lord your God; the Lord your God has chosen you to be a people for His own possession out of all the peoples who are on the face of the earth." Here God is speaking about Israel, His chosen people. He says,

> The Lord did not set His love on you nor choose you because you were more in number than any of the peoples, for you were the fewest of all peoples, but because the Lord loved you and kept the oath which He swore to your forefathers, the Lord brought you out by a mighty hand, and redeemed you from the house of slavery, from the hand of Pharaoh king of Egypt (vv. 7–8).

God chose Israel not because they were better than the other nations, not because they were more worthy of His love, not because they were a greater or more impressive nation than any other, but simply because of His grace.

Someone might suggest that the words of Deuteronomy 7 are directed to an entire nation, including many who evidently were not numbered among the elect. After all, only a remnant from Israel was saved (Rom. 9:27–29). The apostle Paul, replying to a similar objection, wrote, "But it is not as though the word of God has failed. For they are not all Israel who are descended from Israel; neither are they all children because they are Abraham's descendants" (Rom. 9:6–7). In other words, election is not determined by blood descent. So taken in light of everything Scripture has to say about Israel, we know that the words of Deuteronomy 7 are actually addressed to the elect remnant.

Moreover, national Israel was only *representative* of all the elect of all time. God in His grace actually chose for Himself a people "from every nation and all tribes and peoples and tongues" (Rev. 7:9). When God speaks in Deuteronomy 7 of His eternal love for Israel, He is speaking of the spiritual children of Abraham. "Therefore, be sure that it is *those who are of faith* who are [true] sons of Abraham" (Gal. 3:7).

So the love God describes in Deuteronomy 7:6–7 is a particular love for the elect, and these verses therefore describe His love for *all* the elect. It is an eternal love, bestowed on the Israelites not because of anything worthwhile in them, but simply because it was the sovereign will of God to love them.

Why, of all nations, was Israel chosen as God's people? Because they chose God? No, because *God* chose *them*. That's exactly what Deuteronomy 7:7 means. It was God's sovereign choice to set His eternal love on Israel. In no way were they to think they were any more deserving than any other nation. It was a sovereign act of God's own will that He loved Israel. And out of His love, He chose.

The God Who Loves

A Graphic Picture of Unfailing Love

GOD HIMSELF, speaking through Ezekiel, explained His unique love for the elect in graphic terms. In Ezekiel 16, He pictures Israel in such loathsome and sordid terms that within Judaism itself this chapter is not permitted to be read in any public meeting. But this passage is not really about Israel's iniquity. It is about the eternality of God's love:

> Then the word of the Lord came to me saying, "Son of man, make known to Jerusalem her abominations, and say, 'Thus says the Lord God to Jerusalem, "Your origin and your birth are from the land of the Canaanite, your father was an Amorite and your mother a Hittite" (vv. 1–3).

Here God speaks to the city of Jerusalem, representing the Israelite nation. Jerusalem was God's own city, His dwelling place (Ps. 135:21). It was the center of Israel's life and worship. The temple was located there.

But something tragic had happened. Jerusalem was full of abominations. Idolatry was rampant. So the Lord instructed Ezekiel to make known to Jerusalem her own abominations. Ezekiel was to tell Israel that her father was an Amorite, and her mother was a Hittite (Amorite and Hittite being general names for the pagan dwellers of Canaan). The point was not literally that Israel descended from these tribes; they didn't. God was simply lamenting the fact that Jerusalem under Israel was no better off than when pagan tribes ruled Canaan. Israel had allowed things to regress to a state of paganism. They were acting like children of pagans rather than children of God.

In verses 44-45, Ezekiel repeats the same accusation, "Behold, everyone who quotes proverbs will quote this proverb concerning you, saying, 'Like mother, like daughter.' You are the daughter of your mother, who loathed her husband and children. You are also the sister of your sisters, who loathed their husbands and children. Your mother was a Hittite and your father an Amorite." This was a scathing rebuke, suggesting that as the daughter of Hittites, the Israelites were repeating the Hittites' gross spiritual harlotries. They were acting like the offspring of idolaters.

Notice, now, the Lord's description of the nation as a helpless, outcast infant in verses 4–6. This is graphic, disturbing imagery:

> As for your birth, on the day you were born your navel cord was not cut, nor were you washed with water for cleansing; you were not rubbed with salt or even wrapped in cloths. No eye looked with pity on you to do any of these things for you, to have compassion on you. Rather you were thrown out into the open field, for you were abhorred on the day you were born. When I passed by you and saw you squirming in your blood, I said to you while you were in your blood, 'Live!'"

God pictured Israel as the unwanted child of a prostitute, thrown out immediately after its birth into an open field, the umbilical cord still attached to the afterbirth. The child was not even washed. Left for the dogs to devour. No chance of survival.

That, God said, was how Israel was "when I found her." He was speaking of Israel during captivity in Egypt. They were a despised and helpless people. No one cared about them. They were defenseless, pathetic, loathed, and abhorred by everyone— and doomed to perish. They were unwanted outcasts with no hope in the world, not even a land of their own.

But God decided to set His love on that helpless child. "When I passed by you and saw you squirming in your blood, I said to you while you were in your blood, 'Live!' I said to you while you were in your blood, 'Live!'" (v. 6). God picked them up and rescued them. He delivered them out of Egypt and gave them life. Why? Because there was something lovable about them? No, as

The God Who Loves

He described the Israelites, they were ugly and bloody and dirty. Nobody wanted them. There was nothing about them to compel God to show compassion on them. But He passed by and saw them squirming in the dirt, and He gave them life.

He continues,

> "I made you numerous like plants of the field. Then you grew up, became tall, and reached the age for fine ornaments; your breasts were formed and your hair had grown. Yet you were naked and bare. Then I passed by you and saw you, and behold, you were at the time for love; so I spread My skirt over you and covered your nakedness. I also swore to you and entered into a covenant with you so that you became Mine," declares the Lord God (vv. 7–8).

Here the Lord depicted Israel as a girl who had reached puberty and was ready for marriage ("you were at the time for love"). Israel had reached maturity. She was like a pubescent child who has reached the age where it was now inappropriate to be unclothed, so the Lord Himself covered her: "I spread My skirt over you." This was an emblem of protection, like a bird that spreads its wings to cover its young. Jesus used similar imagery when He wept over Jerusalem (Lk. 13:34).

The spreading of one's "skirts"—the *tallith,* or prayer shawl—was a custom that signified espousal for marriage (Ruth 3:9). It showed that the husband was taking the bride under his protection. God was saying to Israel, "I not only picked you up out of the field when you were a bloody, dirty infant—but I carried you until you grew. And then when you became mature enough, I deemed it proper to marry you."

That is also the sense of the final phrase of verse 8: "I also swore to you and entered into a covenant with you so that you became Mine."

So this described the marriage of God to Israel. He chose her according to His sovereign will to love with an everlasting covenant. He treated her with the utmost tenderness, caring for her in her helplessness: "Then I bathed you with water, washed off your blood from you, and anointed you with oil" (v. 9). He bestowed on her all the favors that the wealthiest king might give his bride, lavishing her with the riches of His grace:

> "I also clothed you with embroidered cloth, and put san-
> dals of porpoise skin on your feet; and I wrapped you with
> fine linen and covered you with silk. And I adorned you
> with ornaments, put bracelets on your hands, and a necklace
> around your neck. I also put a ring in your nostril, earrings
> in your ears, and a beautiful crown on your head. Thus you
> were adorned with gold and silver, and your dress was of
> fine linen, silk, and embroidered cloth. You ate fine flour,
> honey, and oil; so you were exceedingly beautiful and
> advanced to royalty" (vv. 10–13).

The love He showed Israel was extraordinary. This is what we would call today a "makeover" of major proportions. He turned this foundling riffraff into the most beautiful queen! In fact, this is precisely what God did when He brought Israel out of the slavery of Egypt to the brilliance and splendor of the Solomonic kingdom. Remember that the Queen of Sheba came just to see the glories of Solomon's kingdom (1 Ki. 10:1–13). All the beauty and magnificence of Israel at her height of glory were only because of the goodness of God.

But notice Ezekiel 16:15, "But you trusted in your beauty and played the harlot because of your fame, and you poured out your harlotries on every passer-by who might be willing." Israel became enamored with her beauty and greatness—and began having relationships with "every passerby who might be willing." That, of course, describes the spiritual harlotries of Israel, who after the reign of David repeatedly fell into sins such as worshiping idols and mixing pagan religious ideas with the worship God had commanded. Even Solomon himself "went after Ashtoreth the goddess of the Sidonians and after Milcom [Moloch] the detestable idol of the Ammonites" (1 Ki. 11:5).

God had chosen the nation in her helplessness, nurtured and cared for her until she was marriageable—and then wed her and adorned her with royalty. Now all of a sudden she was like a harlot on the street offering to commit adultery with any person who passed by. This is a disgusting, loathsome picture. But these are God's own words to Israel:

> "And you took some of your clothes, made for yourself high places of various colors, and played the harlot on them, which should never come about nor happen. You also took your beautiful jewels made of My gold and of My silver, which I had given you, and made for yourself male images that you might play the harlot with them. Then you took your embroidered cloth and covered them, and offered My oil and My incense before them. Also My bread which I gave you, fine flour, oil, and honey with which I fed you, you would offer before them for a soothing aroma; so it happened," declares the Lord God (Ezek. 16:16–19).

Israel took the very advantages God had graciously granted her, and turned those blessings into the instruments of her spiritual adulteries. She used God's gifts and His blessings in her own acts of unfaithfulness. She used the riches He gave to buy idols. She used her national stature to make alliances with pagan nations. The Israelites took the abundant goodness they derived from that land that flowed with milk and honey—and they offered it to foreign gods.

Worst of all, they engaged in the grossest kind of godlessness:

> "Moreover, you took your sons and daughters whom you had borne to Me, and you sacrificed them to idols to be devoured. Were your harlotries so small a matter? You

slaughtered My children, and offered them up to idols by causing them to pass through the fire" (vv. 20–21).

In other words, they took their own babies—helpless infants just as Israel was when God found her—and they put them on a fire to appease Moloch, the horrible god of the Ammonites. It was the Ammonites' practice to sacrifice their own children to Moloch by placing the infants on an open fire and roasting them alive (Lev. 20:2–5). This was one of the very reasons the Lord had ordered the Israelites to utterly destroy the inhabitants of the land before them (Lev. 18:21, 24–26).

On top of all this, Israel forgot the grace of God: "And besides all your abominations and harlotries you did not remember the days of your youth, when you were naked and bare and squirming in your blood" (Ezek. 16:22). She had returned the land to the sins of its pagan inhabitants. And as the Lord Himself said, "Yet you have not merely walked in their ways or done according to their abominations; but, as if that were too little, you acted more corruptly in all your conduct than they" (v. 47). Verse 27 says the sins of Israel were enough to shame even the Philistines!

Israel had made her own God a laughingstock among the nations. Try to dream up the grossest, most heinous imaginable kind of idolatry, and it would not outdo what Israel had done. It was as if they had gone out of the way to make their sins as public and as shameful as they could. They then sought more ways to indulge in idolatry:

> "Then it came about after all your wickedness, 'Woe, woe to you!' declares the Lord God), that you built yourself a shrine and made yourself a high place in every square. You built yourself a high place at the top of every street, and made your beauty abominable; and you spread your legs to every passer-by to multiply your harlotry" (vv. 23-25).

God continues to recount how Israel sought to commit her spiritual adulteries with the Egyptians (v. 26), the Assyrians (v. 28), and the Chaldeans (v. 29). "How languishing is your heart," declares the Lord God, "while you do all these things, the actions of a bold-faced harlot" (v. 30).

But this was even *worse* than harlotry! A harlot was paid for her favors God said to Israel, "In disdaining money, you were not like a harlot" (v. 31). Israel was willing to commit wanton adultery shamelessly, and for nothing in return. They weren't "selling out"; they were being unfaithful to God out of sheer lust for idolatry! Worse still—

> "You adulteress wife, who takes strangers instead of her husband! Men give gifts to all harlots, but *you give your gifts to all your lovers to bribe them to come to you* from every direction for your harlotries. Thus you are different from those women in your harlotries, in that *no one plays the harlot as you do, because you give money and no money is given you;* thus you are different" (vv. 32–33, emphasis added).

Israel was like a woman so lustful, she was paying for illicit lovers.

Do you see the degree to which Israel had gone in sinning against the Lord? Her lust for idolatry was insatiable. She had sinned against God in every conceivable fashion—and was still thirsting for more ways of committing her spiritual adulteries.

And so in verses 35–59, God pronounced a stern judgment on Israel. Her own lovers would abuse her:

> "I shall also give you into the hands of your lovers, and they will tear down your shrines, demolish your high places, strip you of your clothing, take away your jewels, and will leave you naked and bare. They will incite a crowd against you, and they will stone you and cut you to pieces with their swords" (vv. 39–40).

Israel had been haughty in her sinning. She had dishonored God and profaned His name before all the nations. Now God would dishonor her openly as well:

> "So I shall calm My fury against you, and My jealousy will depart from you, and I shall be pacified and angry no more. Because you have not remembered the days of your youth but have enraged Me by all these things, behold, I in turn will bring your conduct down on your own head," declares the Lord God, "so that you will not commit this lewdness on top of all your other abominations" (vv. 42–43).

This was a prophecy foretelling the Babylonian captivity. Israel was defeated by the Babylonians. Her cities and towns were plundered and burned. Her sons and daughters were taken captive into a foreign land. Her sin bore the inevitable fruit of shame and degradation and ultimate earthly disgrace. Having "despised the oath by breaking the covenant" (v. 59), Israel returned herself to a worse state than when the Lord originally found her.

But here is the astonishing part—though it may appear to the observer as if God had cast off His own people at this point, His love for Israel still moved Him:

> "Nevertheless, I will remember My covenant with you in the days of your youth, and I will establish an everlasting covenant with you. Then you will remember your ways and be ashamed when you receive your sisters, both your older and your younger; and I will give them to you as daughters, but not because of your covenant "(vv. 60–61).

Note that God did *not* say, "I will hate you with a holy hatred." Why? Why did He not treat Israel as He had treated the Sodomites, if as He said in verse 48, Israel's sins were worse than Sodom's? And why did He not forgive Samaria for their sins, if as the Lord Himself said in verse 51, "Samaria did not commit half of [Israel's] sins"?

It was simply and only because God had set His eternal love on Israel. These were the people whom He had chosen to love and with whom He had made an everlasting covenant. He loved them as fully as He had a capacity to love. Since in the first place His love was not because of anything *worthy* He found in the Israelites, nothing *unworthy* in them could destroy His love. His love for them was eternal and unconditional. Therefore it was a love rooted in God Himself. This is the particular love of God for His elect.

Notice, now, the conclusion of this chapter in verses 62–63:

> "Thus I will establish My covenant with you, and you shall know that I am the Lord, in order that you may remember and be ashamed, and never open your mouth anymore because of your humiliation, when I have forgiven you for all that you have done," the Lord God declares.

God silenced Israel. He reduced her to humiliation. How? By forgiving her. He accomplished it with His love.

Why didn't God forgive Sodom? They weren't His elect. Why didn't He forgive Samaria? He never made a covenant with them.

God loves whom He chooses to love. He makes a covenant with those people, and that covenant is an everlasting covenant made in eternity past. It guarantees redemption for the objects of God's particular love. Sodom was destroyed and unredeemed. Samaria was likewise condemned. But Israel, whose sins were worse than both, God forgave.

God's Enduring Faithfulness

WHY IS IT that God would so forgive Israel? Because He set His love on her *and made Israel His own possession.* They were *His own* in a unique sense—the same sense in which Jesus says of all the elect, "I am the good shepherd; and I know My own, and My own know Me" (Jn. 10:14). His love for His own is a far greater degree of love than the compassionate love He has for the whole world. This love is perfect. This love is comprehensive. This love is complete. This love is redemptive. This love is eternal. It is this love that caused Him to lay down His life for His own (Jn. 10:15).

The example we've looked at in Ezekiel 16 applies this special love of God in a national sense. Remember, however, that "For they are not all Israel who are descended from Israel" (Rom. 9:6). God's election of Israel was not a blanket choosing of every individual in the nation. But as the apostle Paul says, the promise is confirmed only to "those who are of the faith of Abraham."

Yet there *is* nevertheless a sense in which the *nation* of Israel was chosen by God above every other earthly race or tribe or tongue. "They were entrusted with the oracles of God" (Rom. 3:2). So, we might legitimately ask, "If some did not believe, [does] their unbelief . . . nullify the faithfulness of God?" (v. 3). If Israel is elect, how is it that the vast majority of Jews now reject their own Messiah? "God has not rejected His people, has He?" (Rom. 11:1). Paul spends three chapters addressing this very issue (Rom. 9–11), just after he expounds the great truth that God's love for His elect is inviolable (Rom. 8:35–39). Paul's answer: Israel's current unbelief does not nullify the faithfulness of God. God for His own purposes is currently "taking from among the Gentiles a people for His name" (Acts 15:14). But His love for Israel is undiminished.

In the first place, Paul says, there is "at the present time a remnant according to God's gracious choice" (Rom. 11:5). God still graciously calls a faithful remnant from among Israel. There are many, many Jews who do recognize Jesus as the true Messiah.

But in the second place, Paul tells us, there is coming a day when "all Israel will be saved; just as it is written, 'The Deliverer will come from Zion, He will remove ungodliness from Jacob'" (v. 26). In the greatest revival the world has ever seen, God will one day turn the entire Jewish nation to faith in their true Messiah. As Isaiah wrote, "Israel shall be saved in the Lord with an everlasting salvation: ye shall not be ashamed nor confounded world without end" (Isa. 45:17, KJV). Speaking of that glorious day, Jeremiah adds, "At that time they shall call Jerusalem 'The Throne of the Lord,' and all the nations will be gathered to it, to Jerusalem, for the name of the Lord; nor shall they walk anymore after the stubbornness of their evil heart. In those days the house of Judah will walk with the house of Israel, and they will come together from the land of the north to the land that I gave your fathers as an inheritance" (Jer. 3:17–18).

How can we be certain that God will do this? "This is My covenant with them, when I take away their sins" (Rom. 11:27). He has eternally covenanted to do it, and "the gifts and the calling of God are irrevocable" (v. 29). Therefore, "God has not rejected His people whom He foreknew" (v. 2). The current apostasy of Israel does not invalidate the eternality of God's love.

Bear in mind also that God's electing love is individual as well as corporate. Those whom God has elected are *individuals*. Even the election of Israel involves the choosing of a remnant of individuals. Within the nation, God deals with people individually: "That which Israel is seeking for, it has not obtained, but *those who were chosen obtained it,* and the rest were hardened" (Rom. 11:7, emphasis added).

A powerful example of this is found in the Old Testament account of the sordid tale of David's adultery with Bathsheba. Remember that David lusted after Bathsheba, committed adultery with her, impregnated her, then had her husband killed to try to cover the sin. Bathsheba became David's wife, but David did not repent of his sin until after the birth of the child. Moreover, the child conceived in that act of adultery died soon after birth. Scripture describes David's horrible agony over the death of his son, made all the more bitter by his shame for his own sin. Bathsheba, we assume, was equally distraught.

But 2 Samuel 12 records in a poignant verse what happened after the death of that child: "David comforted his wife Bathsheba, and went in to her and lay with her; and she gave birth to a son, and he named him Solomon. *Now the Lord loved him*" (v. 24, emphasis added).

Here is an explicit statement of the special love of God for an individual. The Lord *loved* Solomon. The prophet Nathan even nicknamed Solomon "Jedidiah," meaning "beloved of the Lord," to signify the Lord's love for him (v. 25).

Solomon was a newborn infant. He was not yet a believer. He had not yet done good or evil. Yet the Lord set His love on Solomon, even though he was the child of a sinful union that should never have been.

Nor was Solomon's life free from sin. Solomon was drawn to the same kind of sin that caused his father to fall. Scripture tells us Solomon took hundreds of wives. He dabbled in idolatry. Despite his great wisdom, he often behaved foolishly. One thing is certain: God did not set His love on Solomon because Solomon deserved it.

But the Lord delights in pouring out the riches of His love on undeserving sinners. He is a God of grace. He sets His love on whom He chooses, and draws them to Himself in love. Solomon, despite the abundance of sin in his life, *did* love the Lord (1 Ki. 3:3). God's love for Solomon guaranteed Solomon's love for God. "We love him, because he first loved us" (1 Jn. 4:19).

Years after Solomon, Nehemiah would return from Persia to rebuild the walls of Jerusalem. When Nehemiah discovered Israelites were marrying foreign women, he outlawed such marriages, saying, "Did not Solomon king of Israel sin regarding these things? Yet among the many nations there was no king like him, and *he was loved by his God,* and God made him king over all Israel; nevertheless the foreign women caused even him to sin" (Neh. 13:26, emphasis added).

Odd, isn't it, that in the midst of holding Solomon's sin up as a negative example not to be emulated, Nehemiah would say, "He was loved by his God"? But here's the point: God chooses to love those whom He chooses to love. He chooses *in spite of* our sin. The fact that He loves us does not mean that we are worthy. But when He chooses to love redemptively and eternally, He forgives and redeems and keeps us in the faith. His love simply will not let us go. It will bless us and chasten us and perfect us through pain—but it will never release us.

Furthermore, it is *only* by His grace that we are not left to reap the bitter consequences of our own sin. It is only by His grace that we are not *all* consumed by divine wrath (Lam. 3:22–23). People seem to get hung up asking why God did not elect everyone. But the more reasonable question is why He chose anyone at all, much less a great multitude which no man can number (cf. Rev. 7:9).

Someone will say, "But how can I know if I'm chosen?"

Do you believe? Do you love the Lord Jesus Christ and trust Him alone (not your own good deeds) to save you? Do you believe that He came into the world as God in human flesh? That He died on a cross as an atonement for sins and rose again the third day? Do you believe that He is the only one who can erase your guilt and enable you to be forgiven and clothed in right-eousness? Then you were chosen to be loved everlastingly.

The particular love of God for His own is overwhelming. It is powerful. If you don't stand in awe of it, then you don't really grasp its significance.

We ought to be in awe, and like Israel, humiliated before such love. We have no right to God's love. He does not owe it to us. Yet He condescends to love us nonetheless. If our hearts aren't stirred with love for God in return, then there's something terribly wrong with us.

No wonder Paul told the Ephesians,

> For this reason, I bow my knees before the Father, from
> whom every family in heaven and on earth derives its name,
> that He would grant you, according to the riches of His

glory, to be strengthened with power through His Spirit in the inner man; so that Christ may dwell in your hearts through faith; and that you, being rooted and grounded in love, may be able to comprehend with all the saints what is the breadth and length and height and depth, and to know the love of Christ which surpasses knowledge, that you may be filled up to all the fulness of God (Eph. 3:14–19).

Finding Security in the Love of God

The Illustration: The Prodigal Son

■

The Doctrine: Romans 8

■

*The Conclusion: Nothing Can Separate Us
from the Love of God in Christ Jesus*

■

The Sum of It All: God Is Love

Chapter 8

Finding Security in the Love of God

GEORGE MATHESON, a brilliant nineteenth-century Scottish pastor and hymn writer, was born with an eye defect that developed into total blindness by the time he was eighteen. Shortly thereafter, his fiancée left him, deciding she would not be content to be married to a blind man. And so it was in response to one of the gloomiest episodes of his life that Matheson penned his great hymn about the security of God's love, "O Love that Wilt Not Let Me Go." Spurned by what he thought was true love, he sought—and found—solace in the unchanging love of God:

> *O love that wilt not let me go,*
> *I rest my weary soul in thee.*
> *I give thee back the life I owe*
> *That in thine ocean-depths its flow*
> *May richer, fuller be.*

God's love for His own simply has no parallel in human experience. As we have seen, it is a powerful, immutable love that extends from eternity past to eternity future. It is a love that is not deterred by our race's sinful rebellion against God. Because of this love God pursues and redeems us even when we are morally and spiritually reprehensible and unworthy of His love in every way: "God demonstrates His own love toward us, in that while we were yet sinners, Christ died for us" (Rom. 5:8).

In other words, God's love is so great that He would stop at nothing to redeem those whom He loved—even though it meant giving His own beloved Son. In fact, the love of God is the supreme guarantee of the believer's security. Many passages of Scripture explicitly teach this. In this chapter, I want to examine two key passages that highlight the security that is to be found in God's love. One of these is an illustration of God's love by way of a parable; the other is a doctrinal treatment extolling the security of divine love.

The Illustration: The Prodigal Son

WE BEGIN BY LOOKING at the most familiar parable of all—the parable of The Prodigal Son, found in Luke 15. The parable's centerpiece is actually not the son's prodigality, but the father's longing love and ready forgiveness for a wayward son:

> A certain man had two sons; and the younger of them said to his father, "Father, give me the share of the estate that falls to me." And he divided his wealth between them. And not many days later, the younger son gathered everything together and went on a journey into a distant country, and there he squandered his estate with loose living.
>
> Now when he had spent everything, a severe famine occurred in that country, and he began to be in need. And he went and attached himself to one of the citizens of that country, and he sent him into his fields to feed swine. And he was longing to fill his stomach with the pods that the swine were eating, and no one was giving anything to him.
>
> But when he came to his senses, he said, "How many of my father's hired men have more than enough bread, but I

am dying here with hunger! I will get up and go to my father, and will say to him, "'Father, I have sinned against heaven, and in your sight; I am no longer worthy to be called your son; make me as one of your hired men.'" And he got up and came to his father. But while he was still a long way off, his father saw him, and felt compassion for him, and ran and embraced him, and kissed him (Lk. 15:11–20).

The father represents God. The younger son is the irreligious, worldly sinner. He represents the sinner who squanders everything he has in a dissolute, irreligious life. He takes everything good his father has ever given him, spurns the father himself, and fritters away his entire legacy in loose living, immorality, and drunkenness.

He finally comes to a point in the midst of his debauchery where he realizes he has hit bottom. He's serving pig slop—hardly an acceptable job for a Jewish son—and worse, he is reduced to taking his own meals from the slop he feeds to the hogs.

Suddenly, he realizes that this is no way to live. He decides to come home. He represents the penitent sinner. He is sorrowful over his wasted life, grieving that he has squandered all his father's goodness, and very aware that he has spent his youth fruitlessly on wickedness and dissipation. He is humiliated. He knows precisely where he stands. He has had his fill of iniquity. Perhaps he once felt that facing up to his sin before his father would cost him everything; but now he knows he has nothing left to lose. He decides to go back and make things right with his father—or at least throw himself on his father's mercy.

The father's response illustrates God's love toward a penitent sinner. Even while the profligate boy is still a long way off, the father sees him (which means the father must have been looking for his wayward son). He "ran and embraced him, and kissed him" (v. 20). The verb tense indicates that he kissed him over and over. Here is tender mercy. Here is forgiveness. Here is compassion. Here is a father treating the son as if there were no past, as if his sins had been buried in the depths of the deepest sea, removed as far as the east is from the west, and forgotten. Here is unrestrained affection, unconditional love.

The father's response is remarkable. There is no diffidence. There is no hesitation. There is no withholding of emotion, no subtle coolness. There is only sympathetic, eager, pure, unbridled love. The father loves his wayward child lavishly. He loves him profusely. He loves him grandly.

The son seems shocked by this. He begins the speech he had rehearsed: "Father, I have sinned against heaven and in your sight; I am no longer worthy to be called your son" (v. 21). It's almost as if he can't deal with his father's tender affection. He is consumed by his own sense of unworthiness. He is in the throes of profound humiliation. He is fully aware of the seriousness of his sin. After all, he had been reduced to eating with pigs. Now, being showered with a loving father's kisses must have only increased his sense of utter shame.

The father's grace was, if anything, even more humbling than the prodigal son's awareness of his own sin. The young man knew in his heart that he was completely undeserving. And so he confessed, "I am no longer worthy to be called your son."

But here we are concerned primarily with the father's response. Notice that he doesn't even respond to the son's hesitancy:

> But the father said to his slaves, "Quickly bring out the best robe and put it on him, and put a ring on his hand and sandals on his feet; and bring the fattened calf, kill it, and let us eat and be merry; for this son of mine was dead, and has come to life again; he was lost, and has been found." And they began to be merry (vv. 22–24).

He pays no attention whatsoever to the penitent young man's confession of unworthiness. He just orders his servants to start the celebration. He showers the prodigal son with favors. He gives him the best robe. He puts a ring on his hand. He gets sandals for his feet. And he kills the fatted calf.

There's much more that could be said about this parable, of course. There are rich spiritual lessons to be drawn from the nature of the prodigal's repentance, the response of the elder brother, and many other aspects of the parable. But the point that interests us here is how Jesus pictured the love of God toward a penitent sinner.

God's love is like the love of this father. It is not minimal; it is unreserved. It is unrestrained. It is extravagant. It is not bestowed in moderation. There is no holding back—just pure love undiluted, without any resentment or disaffection. The father receives the wayward boy as a privileged son, not as a lowly servant.

Above all, the love of the father was an unconditional love. It was undiminished by the rebellion of the son. Despite all that this boy had done to deserve his father's wrath, the father responded with unrestrained love. Though the young man may not have realized it while he was languishing in the far country, he could not be estranged from so loving a father. Even his great sins could not ultimately separate him from his father's love.

The apostle Paul taught a similar lesson in one of the great doctrinal sections of Scripture—Romans 8:31–39. That passage makes a fitting climax for our study.

The Doctrine: Romans 8

ALL THE WRITINGS of the apostle Paul are didactic and doctrinal. Most of his epistles begin with a section of pure doctrine and culminate with a section of practical application. The book of Romans is Paul's great treatise on justification by faith. The doctrinal section of this book is a full, systematic, logical exposition of the doctrine of justification. It reaches its pinnacle at the end of Romans 8, where Paul discusses the security of the believer:

The God Who Loves

> What then shall we say to these things? If God is for us, who is against us? He who did not spare His own Son, but delivered Him up for us all, how will He not also with Him freely give us all things? Who will bring a charge against God's elect? God is the one who justifies; who is the one who condemns? Christ Jesus is He who died, yes, rather who was raised, who is at the right hand of God, who also intercedes for us (Rom. 8:31–34).

Let's set this passage in its immediate context: One of the main themes of Romans 8 is that salvation is entirely God's work. Verses 7–8 declare the hopeless state of every unredeemed person: "The mind set on the flesh is hostile toward God; for it does not subject itself to the law of God, for it is not even able to do so; and those who are in the flesh cannot please God." The sinner is therefore trapped in his own insuperable lostness, unless God intervenes to save him.

And as Paul states, that is precisely what happens. God Himself orchestrates salvation from eternity past to eternity future: "Whom He foreknew, He also predestined to become conformed to the image of His Son, that He might be the first-born among many brethren; and whom He predestined, these He also called; and whom He called, these He also justified; and whom He justified, these He also glorified" (vv. 29–30).

Every stage of the process is God's work. There's a tremendous amount of security in that. If our salvation is God's work, not our own, we can be sure that He will see it to full fruition. "He who began a good work in you will perfect it until the day of Christ Jesus" (Phil. 1:6). Believers are "protected by the power of God through faith for a salvation ready to be revealed in the last time" (1 Pet. 1:5). God is both the Author and the Finisher of our salvation, and He personally guarantees that we will persevere in faith to the end.

That does not mean, incidentally, that believers will never fall into sin. We know from the lives of saints such as David and

Solomon that it is possible for believers to sin in shameful ways. But what is guaranteed is that no true believer can ever fall away totally and finally from the faith. Genuine believers cannot lapse into unbelief. They cannot turn from Christ completely. God will discipline His children who sin (Heb. 12:7–8), but even that discipline is a token of God's love, not His wrath: "For those whom the Lord loves He disciplines, and He scourges every son whom He receives" (Heb. 12:6). True believers can never be separated from the love of God. God Himself guarantees it. As Jesus said, "I give eternal life to them, and they shall never perish; and no one shall snatch them out of My hand. My Father, who has given them to Me, is greater than all; and no one is able to snatch them out of the Father's hand" (Jn. 10:28–29).

Professing believers who do fall away only prove that their faith was never genuine to begin with: "They went out from us, but they were not really of us; for if they had been of us, they would have remained with us; but they went out, in order that it might be shown that they all are not of us" (1 Jn. 2:19). That verse speaks not of people who fall into temptation and sin, but of those who fall away totally and finally from the faith. These are people who utterly abandon the faith. True believers are not capable of such spiritual treachery. God graciously and lovingly insures their perseverance. Like Peter, we can be sifted like wheat, but if our faith is genuine, it will not fail (cf. Lk. 22:31–32).

Here in Romans 8, Paul declares that God's love is the greatest guarantee that every true believer will persevere in the faith. He uses a succession of arguments, all based on the truth that salvation is solely God's work.

God Is for Us

"WHAT THEN SHALL WE SAY to these things? If God is for us, who is against us?" (v. 31). The argument is simple: If God is working to save us, nothing will thwart the work. Whatever God undertakes will most certainly be accomplished. And if God is on our side, it doesn't matter who is on the other side. God's side will be victorious. If God is for us, no one can stand against us.

Someone has said that God plus one equals a majority. The truth is that God alone makes a majority. If every creature in the material and immaterial universe combined to oppose God together, still He would not be defeated. He is infinitely greater, and holier, and wiser, and more powerful than the aggregate of all His creation.

So the fact that He is working to save me makes the outcome certain. If my salvation were ultimately up to me, I would have much to fear. If my redemption hinged in any way on my abilities, I would be lost. Like any sinner, I'm prone to disobedience, unbelief, and weakness. If it were up to me alone to keep myself in the love of God, I would surely fail.

At this point someone might point out that Jude 21 does say, "Keep yourselves in the love of God." Does that mean we're dependent on our own staying power to remain within the purview of God's love? Of course not. Jude acknowledges just three verses later that only God "is able to keep you from stumbling, and to make you stand in the presence of His glory blameless with great joy" (v. 24).

And with God on our side, Paul says, no one can stand against us. This echoes a recurring theme of the Psalms. David wrote, "The Lord is my light and my salvation; whom shall I fear? The Lord is the defense of my life; whom shall I dread?" (Ps. 27:1). Psalm 46 says, "God is our refuge and strength, a very present help in trouble. Therefore we will not fear. . . . The Lord of hosts is with us; the God of Jacob is our stronghold" (vv. 1–2, 11). And the repeated refrain of Psalm 80 suggests that when the Lord causes His face to shine upon us, *we will be saved* (vv. 3, 7, 19, emphasis added). No doubt about it. When the Lord sets out to accomplish something, who can oppose Him?

If anyone could rob us of our salvation, that person would have to be greater than God Himself. God is for us. He has set His love on us. No human, no angel, not even Satan himself can alter that. So if God is for us, it matters not who is against us.

Yes, someone says, but can't Christians put themselves outside God's grace? What about those who commit abominable sins? Don't they nullify the work of redemption in themselves? Don't they forfeit the love of God?

Certainly not. That kind of thinking posits an impossible situation. Remember that we did not gain salvation by our own efforts, so it's preposterous to think that we can forfeit it by anything we do. We did not choose God in the first place; He chose us (Jn. 15:16). We are drawn to Christ only by God's redeeming love (Jer. 31:3). His love continues to draw us and hold us. This is Paul's very point in Romans 8. God's love guarantees our security. That same love also guarantees our perseverance. "We love him, because he first loved us" (1 Jn. 4:19, KJV). Now "The love of Christ controls us" (2 Cor. 5:14). And we continue in the faith because we are protected by His power (1 Pet. 1:5). Thus, His own love insures that we cannot do anything to remove ourselves from His grace.

We can no more forfeit the love of God than the prodigal son could destroy his father's love for him. Like the father of the prodigal son, God loves us constantly. He forgives eagerly, loves lavishly, and does not deal with us according to our sins, or reward us according to our iniquities (Ps. 103:10). Moreover, He does something the prodigal son's father could not do: He sovereignly draws us to Himself. His love is like a cord that draws us inexorably to Him (Hos. 11:4). "He chose us in [Christ] before the foundation of the world, that we should be holy and blameless before Him. In love He predestined us to adoption as sons through Jesus Christ to Himself, according to the kind intention of His will" (Eph. 1:4–5). And "whom He predestined . . . these He also glorified" (Rom. 8:30). He sees the process through to the end.

Our salvation is the work of God. God is "for us," and no one can deter Him from accomplishing what He has determined to do.

The God Who Loves

Christ Died for Us

HERE'S MORE PROOF that we are eternally secure: "He who did not spare His own Son, but delivered Him up for us all, how will He not also with Him freely give us all things?" (Rom. 8:32). God loves us regardless of the cost. Consider what God's love for us has already cost Him: He gave His own beloved Son to die in order to accomplish our salvation. Having already paid so great a price to redeem us, He won't allow the process to stop short of the goal. And if He has already given His best and dearest on our behalf, why would He withhold anything from us now?

Would God redeem sinners at the cost of His own Son's blood, then cast those same blood-bought believers aside? Having brought us to salvation at so great a price, would He then withhold any grace from us? Won't He finish what He started?

And consider this: God gave Christ to die for us "while we were yet sinners" (Rom. 5:8). Would He turn His back on us now that we are justified? If He didn't spurn us when we were rebellious sinners, would He then cast us aside now that we are His children? "If while we were enemies, we were reconciled to God through the death of His Son" (Rom. 5:10), doesn't it seem reasonable that He will do everything necessary to keep us in the fold now that we are reconciled? If He gave us grace to trust Christ in the first place, He will assuredly give grace to keep us from falling away.

Psalm 84:11 says, "For the Lord God is a sun and shield: the Lord will give grace and glory: no good thing will he withhold from them that walk uprightly." God is not stingy with His grace, and the proof of that is seen in the sacrifice of Christ on our behalf. "But he giveth more grace" (Jas. 4:6, KJV).

The sacrifice of Christ is eternally bound up in God's love for the elect. Did you know that in eternity past, before God had even begun the work of creation, He promised to redeem the elect? Titus 1:2 says the promise of eternal life was made "before the world began" (KJV)—literally, before the beginning of time. So this speaks of a divine promise made before anything was created.

Who made this promise and with whom was it made? Since it was made before creation commenced, there is only one possible answer: it was a promise made between the triune Members of the Godhead. God the Father, God the Son, and God the Spirit promised among themselves to redeem fallen humanity.

The plan of redemption was made not after Adam fell but before the beginning of creation. This is consistent with everything Scripture says about election. The saved are chosen in Christ "before the foundation of the world" (Eph. 1:4). God called us . . . in Christ Jesus from all eternity" (2 Tim. 1:9). The eternal kingdom is prepared for them "from the foundation of the world" (Matt. 25:34). Christ was foreordained to shed His blood on their behalf "before the foundation of the world" (1 Pet. 1:20). The names of the elect are written in the Book of Life "from the foundation of the world" (Rev. 13:8; 17:8).

This means the plan of redemption is no contingency. It is not Plan B. It is no alternative strategy. It *is* God's plan, the very purpose for which He created us.

Furthermore, it means that the elect are God's gift of love to His Son. That's why Christ refers to them as "those whom Thou hast given Me" (Jn. 17:9, 24; 18:9). The Father has given the elect to Christ as a gift of love, and therefore not one of them will be lost. Both the Father and the Son work together to insure the fulfillment of their eternal plan of redemption. This further assures the salvation of all the elect, for as Jesus said, "All that the Father gives Me shall come to Me, and the one who comes to Me I will certainly not cast out. . . . For this is the will of My Father, that everyone who beholds the Son and believes in Him, may have eternal life; and I Myself will raise him up on the last day" (John 6:37, 40).

So Christ Himself promises to see God's plan of redemption through to the end. Having died as a substitute for those whom the Father gave Him, He promises to see the process through to the final consummation in glory. Likewise, the Father, having already given His Son to die on our behalf, will not now withhold anything necessary to complete our redemption.

God Himself Justifies Us

REMEMBER THAT THE THEME of Paul's epistle to the Romans is justification by faith. Paul began chapter 8 with a crucial statement about justification: "There is therefore now no condemnation for those who are in Christ Jesus." There is a wealth of theology in that verse. It draws together all the threads of truth about justification that the apostle had been weaving in the preceding chapters.

Paul had been teaching the Romans that justification is a forensic event whereby God forgives the sins of those who believe and imputes to them a perfect righteousness. In chapter 4, for example, he spoke of believers as "Those whose lawless deeds have been forgiven, and whose sins have been covered" (Rom. 4:7). The Lord does not take their sins into account (v. 8). And what's more, righteousness is reckoned to their account (v. 11). Therefore, they stand before God without fear of His righteous judgment (Rom. 8:1).

All this hinges on the fact that they are "in Christ;" that is, they have been united with Him by faith. Paul has already outlined this doctrine in Romans 6:3–5.

So consider the implications of this doctrine: Those who are "in Christ" have their sins completely forgiven; they have all the merit of Christ Himself imputed to their account. God Himself has undertaken to justify them. Christ has accomplished redemption on their behalf. They stand in God's favor solely because He decided to show grace to them, not because of anything they did to earn it. Therefore, Paul asks, if God declares them not guilty, who is going to condemn them? "Who will bring a charge against

God's elect? God is the one who justifies; who is the one who condemns? (8:33–34).

There's a tremendous amount of security in the doctrine of justification by faith. It is because of this doctrine that we can rest in our salvation as an accomplished fact. Jesus said, "Truly, truly, I say to you, he who hears My word, and believes Him who sent Me, has eternal life, and does not come into judgment, but has passed out of death into life" (Jn. 5:24, emphasis added). As Paul says, *"There is therefore now no condemnation for those who are in Christ Jesus"* (Rom. 8:1, emphasis added). It is a done deal, not a goal we work toward. Eternal life is a present possession, not a future hope. And our justification is a declaration that takes place in the court of heaven, so no earthly judge can alter the verdict. When God Himself says "not guilty," who can say otherwise?

Our Heavenly High Priest Intercedes for Us

THE ONGOING WORK OF CHRIST is yet another reason we cannot fall out of favor with God. Paul writes, "Christ Jesus is He who died, yes, rather who was raised, who is at the right hand of God, who also intercedes for us" (v. 34).

Did you realize that Jesus makes continuous intercession for all believers? Hebrews 7:25, echoing Paul's thought in Romans 8:34, says, "He is able to save forever those who draw near to God through Him, since He always lives to make intercession for them." Jesus' ongoing intercession on our behalf guarantees our salvation "forever"—literally, to the uttermost.

How does Christ pray on our behalf? Surely what He prays is similar to the great high priestly prayer recorded in John 17. He prays for our security (Jn. 17:11–12). He prays that we might be in the world but not of the world (vv. 14–15). He prays that we might be kept from evil (v. 15). He prays for our sanctification (v. 17). He prays that we will be one with Him, one with the Father, and one with one another (vv. 21–23). In short, He is praying that we will be kept in the faith, that we might "never perish," and that no one would snatch us out of His hand (John 10:28).

Will that prayer be answered? Certainly. In fact, to deny that the believer is secure in Christ and secure in the love of God, is to deny that Christ's priestly work is sufficient. And to doubt whether the believer might fall out of favor with God is to misunderstand God's love for His elect.

The Conclusion: Nothing Can Separate Us from the Love of God in Christ Jesus

THE ENERGY that has driven God's plan of redemption from eternity past flows from the power of His love. He chose us and predestined us "in love" (Eph. 1:4–5). It is solely "because of His great love with which He loved us" that He raised us from our hopeless state of spiritual death (Eph. 2:4). It is because He loved us with an everlasting love that He drew us to Himself (Jer. 31:3). Christ died because of God's love for us (Rom. 5:8).

In other words, election is the highest expression of God's love to sinful humanity. Some people hate this doctrine. They fight against it, try to explain it away, or claim it's not fair. Some even claim it is a form of tyranny, or that it is fatalistic, or that it violates the human will. But in reality the doctrine of election is all about the eternal, inviolable love of God.

Is it tyranny? Certainly not. God's sovereignty is not the sovereignty of a tyrant, but the loving providence of a gracious God. As we have seen, He finds no pleasure in the destruction of the wicked, but pleads with them to repent and turn to Him for mercy (Ezek. 33:11). He showers blessings on the wicked *and* the righteous alike (Matt. 5:45). His very goodness is an appeal to the wicked that they should repent (Rom. 2:4). He weeps over those who refuse His mercies (Lk. 13:34). Why does He not elect everyone for salvation? We are not told, but the answer is certainly not because of any deficiency or lack in God's love.

What about the charge that the doctrine of election is fatalism? B. B. Warfield said this charge is usually leveled by people who "wish to be the architects of their own fortunes, the determiners of their own destinies; though why they should fancy they could do that better for themselves than God can be trusted to do it for them, it puzzles one to understand."[1] Fatalism is the notion that all things are controlled by an impersonal or irrational force—Fate. God is sovereign, but He is by no means impersonal or irrational. The difference between fatalism and the biblical doctrine of divine sovereignty is really quite profound. It is true, as Scripture teaches, that God "works all things after the counsel of His will" (Eph. 1:11), and that He will accomplish all His good pleasure (Isa. 46:10). But He does not govern arbitrarily or whimsically.

Nor does God impose His sovereign will in a way that does violence to the will of the creature.[2] The outworking of His eternal plan in no way restricts the liberty of our choices or diminishes our responsibility when we make wrong choices. Unbelief is forced on no one. Those who go to a Christless eternity make their own choice in accord with their own desires. They are not under any compulsion from God to sin. "Let no one say when he is tempted, 'I am being tempted by God'; for God cannot be tempted by evil, and He Himself does not tempt anyone" (Jas. 1:13). People who choose unbelief make that choice in full accord with their own desires.

What about the charge that the doctrine of election is not fair? In one sense, there's some truth in this. "Fair" would mean that everyone gets precisely what he deserves. But no one really wants that. Even the non-elect would face a more severe punishment if it were not for the restraining grace of God that keeps them from expressing their depravity to its full extent.

Fairness is not the issue; *grace* is the issue. Election is the highest expression of God's loving grace. He didn't have to choose anyone. And He is, after all, God. If He chooses to set His love in a particular way on whomever He chooses, He has every right to do so.

The God Who Loves

But for Christians, the knowledge that we are saved because of God's choice is the supreme source of security. If God loved us from eternity past, and He is unchanging, then we can know that His love for us in eternity future will be undiminished.

This is precisely Paul's point in Romans 8 as he wraps up his discourse on the believer's security. The closing verses of this passage read like a hymn on the love of God:

> Who shall separate us from the love of Christ? Shall tribulation, or distress, or persecution, or famine, or nakedness, or peril, or sword? Just as it is written, "For Thy sake we are being put to death all day long; we were considered as sheep to be slaughtered." But in all these things we overwhelmingly conquer through Him who loved us. For I am convinced that neither death, nor life, nor angels, nor principalities, nor things present, nor things to come, nor powers, nor height, nor depth, nor any other created thing, shall be able to separate us from the love of God, which is in Christ Jesus our Lord (Rom. 8:35–39).

Writing to the Ephesians, Paul described the Christian life as spiritual warfare. "Our struggle is not against flesh and blood, but against the rulers, against the powers, against the world forces of this darkness, against the spiritual forces of wickedness in the heavenly places" (Eph. 6:12). Wicked forces, diabolical persons, and evil circumstances all conspire to attack each believer. At times it seems as if all the forces of hell are arrayed against us. That would be daunting, except as Paul points out in Romans 8, the outcome is guaranteed.

Nothing can separate us from the love of God in Christ—not earthly trials, such as "tribulation, or distress, or persecution, or famine, or nakedness, or peril, or sword" (v. 35), and not even heavenly foes—"neither death, nor life, nor angels, nor principalities, nor things present, nor things to come, nor powers, nor height, nor depth, nor any other created thing" (vv. 38–39). "In all these things we overwhelmingly conquer through Him who loved us" (v. 37). It's a no-lose situation—because of the love of God.

The various threats Paul outlined were not hypothetical dilemmas as far as he was concerned. Tribulation, distress, persecution, famine, sword—Paul had faced those very hardships—and others as well.

> . . . beaten times without number, often in danger of death. Five times I received from the Jews thirty-nine lashes. Three times I was beaten with rods, once I was stoned, three times I was shipwrecked, a night and a day I have spent in the deep. I have been on frequent journeys, in dangers from rivers, dangers from robbers, dangers from my countrymen, dangers from the Gentiles, dangers in the city, dangers in the wilderness, dangers on the sea, dangers among false brethren; I have been in labor and hardship, through many sleepless nights, in hunger and thirst, often without food, in cold and exposure (2 Cor. 11:23–27).

And Paul had emerged from those trials with an unshaken confidence in the love of God.

The people of God have always suffered. In Romans 8:36 Paul quotes Psalm 44:22 by way of reminder: "For Thy sake we are killed all day long; we are considered as sheep to be slaughtered." God's love does not necessarily guarantee earthly comfort. But the sufferings of this world are more than compensated by the rewards of divine love in eternal bliss. As Paul wrote earlier in Romans 8, "I consider that the sufferings of this present time are not worthy to be compared with the glory that is to be revealed to us" (v. 18; cf. 2 Cor. 4:17).

"The glory that is to be revealed to us" is God's glory. As we said at the close of chapter 5, every aspect of God's love declares His glory. The general love God has toward all humanity reveals

His basic goodness. The fact that it is spurned by those who do not believe in no way diminishes God's glory. Even the wrath of sinful men shall praise Him (Ps. 76:10).

But the riches of His goodness and glory are revealed most clearly in the salvation of the elect, a great multitude that no man could ever number (Rev. 7:9).

"This hope we have as an anchor of the soul, a hope both sure and steadfast" (Heb. 6:19).

The Sum of It All: God Is Love

GOD IS LOVE. His mercy is over all His works. He manifests His love to all. But the highest expression of His love is manifest to those who by sheer grace He lovingly draws to Himself.

Therefore to those of us who believe, God's love is a uniquely precious reality, albeit an unfathomable one. There is no way we can scale the height of it. There is no way we can imagine the breadth of it or span the width of it. Nevertheless, by God's grace we can know the love of Christ, which passes knowledge (Eph. 3:18–19).

We daily benefit from the goodness of His love. He gives us richly all things to enjoy (1 Tim. 6:17). More than that, His love is shed abroad in our own hearts (Rom. 5:5). I know of no greater source of comfort, no more sure foundation for our security, no richer source of contentment.

Why is all this so important? Ultimately the love of God is the basis for all our hopes. It is the object of our deepest longings. It is the source and fulfillment of our faith. It is the very basis for His grace to us. After all, we love Him only because He first loved us (1 Jn. 4:19). And His love is also our guarantee of eternal bliss. Since He loved us enough to send His own Son to die for us while we were yet His enemies—we have no reason to fear losing that love, now that His Spirit has been sent forth into our hearts, enabling us to cry, "Abba, Father!" (Gal. 4:5). His love absolutely permeates and envelops every aspect of our lives in Christ.

As Christians, then, we ought to see that everything we enjoy in life—from our tiniest pleasures to the eternal redemption we have found in Christ—is an expression of the great love wherewith God loved us (Eph. 2:4). The blessing of His love comes to us not because we deserve it, but simply and only because of His sovereign grace. For certainly we do not deserve His blessing, but the very opposite. Yet He pours out His love without measure, and we are invited to partake of its benefits freely.

As recipients of love like that, we can only fall on our faces in wonder. When we contemplate such love, it ought to make us feel unworthy. Yet at the same time it lifts us to unimaginable heights of joy and confidence, because we know that our God, the righteous judge of all the universe, the One to whom we have by faith committed our very souls' well-being—has revealed Himself as a God of immeasurable love. And *we* are the objects of that love—despite our unworthiness and despite our sin! In light of the glories of divine love, how can we not be utterly lost in wonder, love, and praise?

Appendices

Appendix 1: Fury Not in God

▧

Appendix 2: On the Love of God, and Whether it Extends to the Non-Elect

▧

Appendix 3: Christ the Savior of the World

▧

Appendix 4: The Love of God to the World

Appendix 1

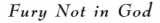

Fury Not in God

EDITOR'S NOTE: This classic tract by Thomas Chalmers, a Glasgow pastor and professor of theology at the University of Edinburgh in the first half of the 1800s, was adapted from one of his best-known sermons.

All Scripture references in this Appendix are from the King James Version of the Bible.

"Fury is not in me: who would set the briers and thorns against me in battle? I would go through them, I would burn them together. Or let him take hold of my strength, that he may make peace with me; and he shall make peace with me" (Isaiah 27:4–5).

THERE ARE THREE DISTINCT LESSONS in this text. The first, that fury is not in God; the second, that He does not want to glorify Himself by the death of sinners ("Who would set the briers and thorns against me in battle?"); the third, the invitation ("Take hold of my strength, that you may make peace with me; and you shall make peace with me").

The God Who Loves

Fury Is Not in God

"FURY IS NOT IN ME," the Lord states. But how can this be? Isn't fury one manifestation of His essential attributes? Do we not repeatedly read of His fury—of His fury being poured forth in the streets of Jerusalem (Jer. 44:6); of God casting the fury of His wrath upon the world (Job 20:23); of Him rendering His anger upon His enemies with fury (Isa. 59:18); of Him kindling the fire of His fury in Zion (Lam. 4:11); of Him pouring out His fury like a fire (Lam. 2:4)? We are not therefore to think that fury is banished altogether from God's administration. There are occasions when this fury is discharged against the objects of God's wrath; and there must be other times when there is no fury in Him.

Now what is the occasion our text refers to when He disclaims all fury? He is inviting men to reconciliation. He is calling them to make peace with Him. He is assuring them that if they will only take hold of His strength, they can make peace with Him.

In the preceding verses, the Lord speaks of a vineyard. When He invites people to lay hold of His strength, He is in fact inviting those who are outside the boundaries of the vineyard to enter in. Fury will be discharged on those who reject the invitation. But we cannot say that there is any exercise of fury in God at the time of giving the invitation. In fact, our text explicitly and directly states God's assurance to the contrary.

Instead of fury, there is a longing desire after you. There is a wish to save you from that awful day in which the fury of a rejected Savior will be spread abroad over all who have despised Him. The tone of God's invitation is not a tone of anger—it is a tone of tenderness. The look that accompanies the invitation is not a look of wrath—it is a look of affection. There will certainly be an occasion when the fury of God will be poured forth on those who have held out against Him and turned away in unbelief and contempt from His beseeching voice. But while He is lifting this voice—while He is sending messengers over the face of the earth to

Appendix 1

circulate His gracious invitation among the habitations of men—especially at this time, when Bibles are within the reach of every family and ministers in every pulpit are sounding forth the overtures of the gospel—surely at such a time and upon such an occasion, it may well be said of God to all who are now seeking His face and favor, that there is no fury in Him.

It is just as in the parable of the marriage feast many rejected the king's invitation (Matt. 22:2–7). The king was rightfully angry with many of them, and sent forth his armies and destroyed them, and burned up their city (v. 7). On that occasion there was fury in the king, and on the like occasion will there be fury in God. But He can truthfully say at the time when He is now giving the invitation, "Fury is not in Me."

In His invitation is kindness, a desire for peace and friendship, and a longing earnestness to erase the enmity which now exists between the Lawgiver in heaven and His yet impenitent and unreconciled creatures.

This very process was all gone through before the destruction of Jerusalem. Israel rejected the warnings and invitations of the Savior, and at length experienced His fury. But there was no fury at the time of His giving the invitations. The tone of our Savior's voice when He uttered "O Jerusalem, Jerusalem" (Lk. 13:34) was not the tone of a vindictive and irritated fury. There was compassion in it—a warning and pleading earnestness that they would repent and make peace with God. He testified that He would willingly have gathered them as a hen gathers her chickens under her wings, so it may well be said that there was no fury in the Son of God, no fury in God.

Let's make the application to ourselves in the present day. On the last day there will be a tremendous discharge of fury. All the wrath that sinners are now treasuring up will be poured forth on them. The season of God's mercy will then have come to an end. After the sound of the last trumpet, there will nevermore be heard the sounding call of reconciliation. Oh, my brethren, God will in the last day pour forth His wrath in one mighty torrent on the heads of the impenitent. That wrath is now gathering and accumulating in a storehouse of vengeance; and at some awful point in the future, when time shall be no more, the door of that storehouse will be opened and the fury of the Lord will break loose against the guilty. Then His righteous fury will execute the full weight and the terror of all His threatenings.

Therefore, my brethren, you misunderstand the text if you infer from it that fury has no place in the history or methods of God's administration. God's wrath does have its time and its occasion. And the very greatest display of it is yet to come, when "the heavens shall pass away with a great noise, and the elements shall melt with fervent heat, the earth also and the works that are therein shall be burned up" (2 Pet. 3:10). In that day, "the Lord Jesus shall be revealed from heaven with his mighty angels, in flaming fire taking vengeance on them that know not God, and that obey not the gospel of our Lord Jesus Christ: Who shall be punished with everlasting destruction from the presence of the Lord, and from the glory of his power" (2 Thess. 1:7–9).

It makes one shudder seriously to think that there may be some reading these words whom the devouring torrent of divine wrath shall sweep away. Some who read these words will be drawn into the whirl of destruction, and forced to take their descending way through the mouth of that pit where the worm dies not, and the fire is not quenched. In fact, some foolishly presume there is no fury in God whatsoever, or at any time. Tragically, they will discover throughout the dreary extent of one hopeless and endless and unmitigated eternity, that God's fury is the only attribute of His they will ever really know.

So hear me. Hear me before you take your bed in hell. Hear me before that prison door be shut against you never, never again to be opened. Hear me before the great day of the revelation of God's wrath comes around, and there shall be a total breaking up of the system that now looks so stable and so unalterable. On that awful day we will not be able to take up the text and say there is no fury in God.

But hear me now—for your lives, hear me. On this day I can say it. At this moment I can throw abroad among you the wide announcement that there is no fury in God. There is not one of you into whose heart this announcement may not enter. You will be welcome to make eternal peace with your beseeching God. Surely as long as I am called by God to hold out the language of entreaty, and to sound in your ears the tidings of gladness, and to invite you to enter into the vineyard of God—surely when the messenger of the gospel is thus executing the commission with which he is charged and warranted, he may well say that there is no fury in God. Surely when the Son of God is inviting you to kiss Him and to enter into reconciliation, there is neither the feeling nor the exercise of fury.

It is only if you refuse, and if you persist in refusing, and if you suffer all these calls and entreaties to be lost upon you—it is only then that God will execute His fury and put forth the power of His anger. And therefore He says to us, "Kiss the Son, lest he be angry, and ye perish from the way, when his wrath is kindled but a little. Blessed are all they that put their trust in him" (Ps. 2:12).

This, then, is the point of time at which you stand: there is no fury in God; in fact, He is inviting you to flee from it. He is uttering no blasting curse upon the fig tree (cf. Matt. 21:19–20), even though it has so far borne no fruit. Instead, He says, "Let it alone this year also, till I shall dig about it, and dung it: and if it bear fruit, well: and if not, then after that thou shalt cut it down" (Lk. 13:8–9).

Now, my brethren, you are all in the situation of this fig tree. You are for the present let alone. God has purposes of kindness toward every one of you; and as one of His ministers, I can now say to all who read this that there is no fury in God. When the proclaimer of the good news is trying to soften your hearts, he is warranted to make full use of the argument of my text—that there is no fury in God.

The God Who Loves

When the ambassador of Christ is imploring you with the offers of grace, he is surely charged with matter of far different import from wrath and threatening and vengeance. Oh, let not all this pleading turn out to be unavailing! Let not the offer be made now, and no fruit appear afterwards; let not yours be the fate of the barren and unfruitful fig tree.

The day of the fury of the Lord is approaching. The burning up of this earth and the passing away of these heavens is an event to which we are continually drawing nearer. On that day when the whole of the universe shall be turned into a heap of ruins, we shall see the gleam of a mighty conflagration. We shall hear the noise of the framework of creation rending into fragments. On that day a cry shall be raised from a despairing multitude from all generations who have just awoke from their resting places. The terror at His wrath on that day will be more horrible than all the rest of the destruction of the universe.

Oh, my brethren, on that day the Judge will appear charged with the mighty object of vindicating before men and angels the truth and the majesty of God. And on that day the fury of God will appear in a bright and burning manifestation.

But what I have to tell you on this day is this: such fury is not now in God. Now is an opportunity to make peace with God for all eternity. And if you will only hear on this the day of your merciful visitation, you will be borne off in safety from all those horrors. Amid the wild war and frenzy of the reeling elements of divine judgment, you will be carried by the arms of love to a place of security and everlasting triumph.

God Is Not Wanting to Glorify Himself by the Death of Sinners

THAT BRINGS US TO THE second point of this text: "who would set the briers and thorns against me in battle?" Both the wicked and the righteous are often represented in Scripture by figures from the plant kingdom. For example, the saved and sanctified are called trees of righteousness, planted by the Lord that He might be glorified (Isa. 61:3). The godly man is said to be like a tree planted by the rivers of water, bringing forth its fruit in its season (Ps. 1:3). The judgment that comes upon a man is compared to an ax laid to the root of a tree (Matt. 3:10). A tree is said to be known by its fruit, and as a proof that the character of men is symbolized by the tree, we read, "of thorns men do not gather figs, nor of a bramble bush gather they grapes" (Lk. 6:44).

Observe that the thorn is specifically referred to in our text from Isaiah 27:4–5. When God says, "I would go through them, I would burn them together," He speaks of the destruction that comes on all who remain in the state of thorns and briers. This agrees with what we read in Hebrews 6:8: "that which beareth thorns and briers is rejected, and is nigh unto cursing; whose end is to be burned."

Thorns and briers are in other places even more directly employed to signify the enemies of God. "And the light of Israel shall be for a fire," says Isaiah 17:10, "and his Holy One for a flame: and it shall burn and devour his thorns and his briers in one day."

Therefore, when God says, "Who would set the briers and thorns against me in battle? I would go through them, I would burn them together," He speaks of the ease with which He could accomplish His wrath upon His enemies. They would perish before Him like the moth. They could not stand the lifting up of the red right arm of the displeasure of Almighty God.

Why set up, then, a contest so unequal as this? Why put the wicked in battle array against Him who could go through them and devour them in an instant by the breath of His fury? *God is saying in the text that this is not what He is wanting.* He does not want to set Himself forth as an enemy, or as a strong man armed against them for the battle—it is a battle He is not at all disposed to enter into. The glory He would achieve by a victory over a host so feeble is not a glory that His heart is at all set upon.

Oh, no, children of men! He has no pleasure in your death. He is not seeking to magnify Himself by the destruction of so paltry a foe. He could devour you in a moment. He could burn you up like stubble. And you are mistaken if you think renown on so poor a field of contest is a renown that He aspires after.

Who would set the grasshoppers in battle array against the giants? Who would set thorns and briers in battle array against God? This is not what He wants. He would rather something else. Be assured, He would rather you turn, and live, and come into His vineyard, and submit to Him in faith, and receive His offer of mercy. In the language of verse 5, He would rather that sinners take hold of His strength and make peace with Him.

Now tell me if this does not open up a most wonderful and a most inviting view of God? It is the real attitude in which He puts Himself forth in the gospel of His Son. It is why He says, in the hearing of all to whom the Word of this salvation is sent, *"Why will ye die?"* (Ezek. 18:31).

It is true that by the death of a sinner God *could* manifest the dignity of His Godhead. He *could* make known the power of His wrath. He *could* spread the awe of His truth and His majesty over the whole territory of His government, and send forth to its uttermost limits the glories of His strength and His immutable sovereignty. But He does not want to magnify Himself over men in this way. He has no ambition whatever after the renown of such a victory over such weak and insignificant enemies. Their resistance is no trial whatever to His strength or to His greatness. There is nothing in the destruction of creatures so weak that can at all bring Him any distinction, or throw any aggrandizement around Him. And thus we see Him pleading and protesting with sinners everywhere in Scripture. He does not want to signalize Himself upon the ruin of any, but would rather that they should turn and be saved.

Appendix 1

And now, my dear readers, what remains for you to do? God is willing to save you. Are you willing to be saved? The way is set before you most patiently and clearly in the Bible. In fact, our very text, brief as it is, points out the way, as I shall endeavor to explain and set before you under my third point. But meanwhile, and all the better to secure a hearing from you, let me ask you to lay it upon your consciences: Are you in a state of readiness to stand before God?

If not, then I beseech you to think how certainly death will (and how speedily it may) come upon you. Even the youngest among us should be aware that death can come quickly. The agony of the parting breath will come. The time when you are stretched a lifeless corpse before the eyes of weeping relatives will come. The coffin that will enclose you will come. The hour when the company assemble to carry you to the burial ground will come. The minute when you are put into the grave will come. The throwing in of the loose earth into the narrow house where you are laid, and the spreading of the green sod over it—all, all will come on every living creature who now reads these words. In a few short years both I who now write, and you who read my words, will both be in our graves, and another generation will populate the earth.

Now you know that all this must and will happen—your common sense and common experience serve to convince you of it. Perhaps it may have been little thought of in the days of careless and thoughtless and thankless unconcern which you have spent until now. But I call on you to think of it, to lay it seriously to heart, and no longer to trifle and delay, when the high matters of death and judgment and eternity are thus set so evidently before you. This message I am commissioned to proclaim—and the blood lies on your own head and not upon mine if you will not heed the warning. The object of my message is to let you know what things are to come. It is to carry you beyond the regions of sight and of sense to the regions of faith—and to assure you, in the name of Him who cannot lie, that as surely as the hour of placing the body in the grave comes, so surely will also come the hour of the spirit returning to the God who gave it.

Yes, the day of final reckoning will also come. The appearance of the Son of God in heaven, and His mighty angels around Him, will come. The opening of the books will come. The standing of the men of all generations before the judgment seat will come. And the solemn passing of sentence that will seal your eternity will come.

Yes, and if you refuse to be reconciled in the name of Christ, now that He is beseeching you to be so, and if you refuse to turn from the evil of your ways, and to turn to your Savior in faith, I must tell you what sentence you will hear pronounced against you: "Depart from me, ye cursed, into everlasting fire, prepared for the devil and his angels" (Matt. 25:41).

There is a way of escape from the fury of this tremendous storm. There is a pathway of deliverance from the state of condemnation to the state of justification. There is a means pointed out in Scripture by which we, who by nature are the children of wrath, may come to be at peace with God. Let all ears be open then to our explanation of this way, as we bid you in the language of our text, "let him take hold of [God's] strength, that he may make peace with [Him]" (Isa. 27:5).

The Way of Salvation Is Open Before You

THE WORD *rather* signals the change between verses 4 and 5. Rather than engaging in battle with His enemies—rather than going through them and burning them with eternal destruction—God would greatly prefer that they took hold of His strength in order to make peace with Him. And He promises, as the sure effect of their turning to Him in faith, that they "shall make peace with me."

Appendix 1

We don't have to look far to discover what this "strength" is that sinners are called to take hold of. Isaiah himself speaks of the strength of *salvation* (33:6). It is not your destruction but your salvation that God wants to put forth His strength into. Strength has already been put forth in the deliverance of a guilty world, and this is the very strength which He bids you lay hold of.

God will certainly be glorified in the destruction of the sinner, but He prefers the glory that is His through the salvation of sinners. To destroy you is to do no more than to set fire to briers and thorns and consume them. But to save you—this is indeed the power of God and the wisdom of God. This is the mighty achievement which angels desire to look into (1 Pet. 1:12). This is the enterprise upon which Christ embarked from His heavenly glory. This is the mission on which He spent all His strength and labored with distress in His soul until He accomplished it (Lk. 12:50). Now that it is accomplished, God will be glorified both in the destruction of sinners (2 Thess 1:7) and in the salvation of His saints (v. 10). But God prefers the latter to the former. He shows His wrath and makes His power known in the destruction of the sinner (Rom. 9:22). But the glory of God will redound in an even greater way forever in the eternal praise shown forth by His redeemed people (1 Pet. 2:9).

And so He pleads with you to take hold of His strength. He would greatly prefer this way of making His power known. He does not want to enter into the battle with you, or to consume you like stubble by the breath of His indignation. No; He delights to transform sinners into saints. He delights to transform vessels of wrath into vessels of mercy, and to make known the riches of His glory on those whom He had before prepared unto glory (Rom. 9:23).

There is a glorious strength put forth in the destruction of the sinner, but there is *a more glorious* strength put forth in the salvation of a sinner. This saving strength is the strength He bids you lay hold of. He would rather decline entering into a contest with sinners; for to gain a victory over them would be no more to Him than to fight with the briers and the thorns, and to consume them. But to make friends from enemies; to transform the children of wrath into children of adoption; to accomplish such a mighty and a wonderful change from the state of guilt to the state of justification; to make servants of sin into willing servants of God; to chase away the darkness of sinful nature and make everything light and comfort around the redeemed; to take people who are slaves of their feelings and invest them with a preference for the things of eternity; to pull down the strongholds of corruption within and raise one who was spiritually dead to a life of new obedience—this is the victory that God delights in! The destruction of the wicked brings Him no pleasure.

Let me now, in what remains, first say a few things more upon this strength—the strength of salvation spoken of in our text—and then allow me to state very briefly what it is to lay hold of it.

First we read of a mighty strength that had to be put forth in the work of a sinner's justification. You know that all men are sinners, and so all are under the righteous condemnation of God. How, in the name of all that is difficult and wonderful, can these sinners ever get this condemnation removed from them?

By what new and unheard of process can the guilty before God ever again become justified in His sight? How can the sentence of acquittal ever be heard on the children of iniquity from God's own throne of judgment and justice? How can God's honor be kept entire in the sight of angels, if we who have repeatedly mocked Him and insulted Him, are pardoned? How can we justly be forgiven, with all our contempt of the Law and of the Lawgiver, and with all this character of rebellion against Him written upon our foreheads? How can sinners such as we are be admitted to a place of distinction in heaven?

After all, God has committed Himself to full justice in the hearing of angels. He declared that He "will by no means clear the guilty" (Exod. 34:7). After He had given us a law by the disposition of angels, and we had not kept it, He said, "I will not justify the wicked" (Exod. 23:7). Over and over He has said things like, "The wicked shall not be unpunished" (Prov. 11:21), and, "Cursed is every one that continueth not in all things which are written in the book of the law to do them" (Gal. 3:10).

But what is more, it was not merely the good and the obedient angels who knew our rebellion. The malignant and fallen angels not only knew it, but they devised and prompted it. And how, I would ask, can God keep the awful majesty of His truth and justice entire in the sight of His adversaries, if Satan and the angels of wickedness along with him shall have it in their power to say, "We prevailed on man to insult God by sin, and now we have compelled God to put up with the affront?"

But as great as the weight and magnitude of that obstacle, so is the greatness of the strength put forth by the Savior in the mighty work of removing the obstacle. We have no adequate conception upon this matter; all we can know about it is what Scripture says. And whether we take the prophecies that foretold the work of our Redeemer, the history that recounts it, or the doctrine that expounds on its worth and its efficacy—all go to establish that there was the operation of a tremendous power in obtaining our salvation. There was the severity of a conflict; there was an arduous and mighty warfare; there were all the throes and all the exertions of a struggling (and at length a prevailing) energy in the execution of that work which our Saviour had to do. He had a barrier to surmount, and that, too, with the cries and the pains and the sorrows of heavy suffering and labor. A mighty obstacle lay before Him, and He, in the business of removing it, had to exert all the power of the faculties that belonged to Him. There was a burden laid upon His shoulders which no one else but the Prince of Peace could have borne. And there was a task placed in His hand which none but He could ever fulfil.

If all the angels in paradise had contemplated how our salvation might be accomplished, they would no doubt have concluded such a work was impossible. Who can bend the unchangeable attributes of God? Who can give them a shift so wonderful that the sinners who have insulted Him may be taken into forgiveness while His honor is kept untainted and entire? There is not one of the mighty hosts of heaven who would not have shrunk from an enterprise so lofty. Not one of them could have at once magnified the Law and released man from its violated sanctions. Not one of them could turn its threatening away from us and at the same time give truth and justice of God their brightest manifestation. Not one of them could unravel the mystery of our redemption through all the difficulties that surround it. Not one of them, by the strength of his arm, could have obtained the conquest over these difficulties.

And though you may never have contemplated such questions, let us forget not that these matters were not merely between God and man—they were between God and all the creatures He had formed. They saw the dilemma. They felt how deeply it involved the character of the Deity. They perceived its bearing on the majesty of His attributes and on the stability of the government that was upheld by Him. With them it was a matter of deep and substantial interest. And when the Eternal Son stepped forward to carry the undertaking to its end, the feeling among them all was that a battle behooved to be fought, and that the strength of this mighty Captain of our salvation alone was equal to the achievement of the victory.

> Who is this that cometh from Edom, with dyed garments from Bozrah? this that is glorious in his apparel, travelling in the greatness of his strength? I that speak in righteousness, mighty to save. Wherefore art thou red in thine apparel, and thy garments like him that treadeth in the winefat? I have trodden the winepress alone; and of the people there was none with me: for I will tread them in mine anger, and trample them in my fury; and their blood shall be

sprinkled upon my garments, and I will stain all my rai-
ment. For the day of vengeance is in mine heart, and the
year of my redeemed is come. And I looked, and there was
none to help; and I wondered that there was none to
uphold: therefore mine own arm brought salvation unto
me; and my fury, it upheld me (Isa. 63:1–5).

A way of redemption has been found out in the unsearchable
riches of divine wisdom. Christ Himself is called the wisdom of
God. The same Christ is also called the power of God:

> We preach Christ crucified, unto the Jews a stumbling-
> block, and unto the Greeks foolishness; But unto them
> which are called, both Jews and Greeks, *Christ the power of
> God,* and the wisdom of God (1 Cor. 1:23–24, emphasis
> added).

In the mighty work of redemption He put forth a strength, and it
is that strength that we are called to take hold upon. There was a
wonderful strength in bearing the wrath that would have fallen
on the millions and millions more of a guilty world. There was a
strength that carried Him in triumph through the contest over
Satan, when he buffeted Him with his temptations. There was a
strength that bore Him up under the agonies of the garden. There
was a strength that supported Him when His Father's countenance was hidden from Him. There was a strength that upheld
Him in the dark hour of the travail of His soul. There was a
strength observers might think had well-nigh given way when He
called out, "My God, my God, why hast thou forsaken me?"
(Matt. 27:46).

There was a strength far greater than we know in that mysterious struggle which He held with the powers of darkness, when
Satan fell like lightning from heaven, and the Captain of our salvation spoiled principalities and powers, and made a show of

them openly, and triumphed over them. There was strength in overcoming all the mighty difficulties which lay in the way between the sinner and God, in unbarring the gates of acceptance to a guilty world, in bringing truth and mercy to meet, and right-eousness and peace to enter into fellowship—so that God might be just, while He is the justifier of him who believeth in Jesus (Rom. 3:26).

So much for the strength which is put forth in the work of man's redemption. There is also strength put forth in the work of man's sanctification. Christ has not only done a great work for us in making good our reconciliation with God—He further does a great work in us when He makes us like unto God. But I have not the time to dwell upon this last topic, and must content myself with referring you to the following Scriptures: Ephesians 1:19; 2:10; Philippians 4:13; 2 Corinthians 12:9–10; and John 15:5. The same power that raised Jesus from the dead is the power that raises us from our death in trespasses and sins. The power that was put forth on creation is the power that makes us new creatures in Jesus Christ our Lord.

Neither have I time to make out a full demonstration of what is meant by laying hold of that strength. When you apply to a friend for some service, some relief from distress or difficulty, you may be said to lay hold of him. And when you place firm reliance both on his ability and willingness to do you the service, you may well say that you have taken hold of your friend. The expression becomes all the more appropriate should *he promise* to do what you are trusting him to do. In such a case your hold is not upon his power only, but also upon his faithfulness.

And it is even so with the promises of God in Christ Jesus— you have both a power and a promise to take hold of. If you believe that Christ is able to save to the uttermost all who come unto God through Him (Heb. 7:25), and if you believe the hon-esty of His invitation to all who are weary and heavy-laden that they might come unto Him and find rest for their souls (Matt.

11:28–30), then you have judged Him to be faithful who has promised, and then indeed you will lay hold of Christ as the power of God unto salvation. According to the faith that has led you to fix your hope on the Saviour, so will it be done unto you. In the language of Scripture, "hold fast the confidence and the rejoicing of the hope firm unto the end" (Heb. 6:3). "Cast not away therefore your confidence, which hath great recompense of reward" (Heb. 10:35).

And if you have not yet begun to place this confidence in the assurances of the gospel, lay hold of them now. They are addressed to you. "The Spirit and the bride say, Come. And let him that heareth say, Come. And let him that is athirst come. And *whosoever will,* let him take the water of life freely" (Rev. 22:17, emphasis added). It is not a vague generality of which I am speaking. You are invited to take up with Christ, and trust in Him for yourself. God Himself urges you to repent and live (Ezek. 18:31).

I am well aware that unless the Spirit reveal to you, all I have said about Him will fall fruitless upon your ears, and your hearts will remain as cold and as heavy and as alienated as ever. Faith is His gift, and it is not of ourselves. But the minister is at his post when he puts the truth before you; and you are at your posts when you hearken diligently, and have a prayerful spirit of dependence on the Giver of all wisdom, that He will bless the Word spoken, and make it reach your souls in the form of a salutary and convincing application.

And it is indeed incredible—it is more than incredible—that we should entertain any thought that our Father who is in heaven is less than benevolent. With all the ways He sets Himself forth to us, isn't it disgraceful that we do not have more confidence in His goodness and His willingness to save? How can we account for the barrier of unbelief that stands so obstinately firm in spite of His every remonstrance? Why does the hardness continue? Not the hardness of God toward us, for He has said everything to woo us to put our trust in Him, but our hardness toward God. In the face of His kind and compassionate entreaties, how can we persist in being cold and distant and afraid of Him?

I know not, my brethren, in how far I may have succeeded, as an humble and unworthy instrument, in drawing aside the veil which darkens the face of Him who sits on the throne. But oh, how imposing is the attitude, and how altogether affecting is the argument with which He comes forward to us in the text we are considering! "Fury is not in me."

It is not so much His saying that there is no fury in Him whatsoever. He often tells us of His wrath in other passages of Scripture. But the striking peculiarity of the words now before us is the way He would convince us how little interest He can have in our destruction. He is reassuring us how far it is from His thoughts to aspire after the glory of such an achievement.

It is as if He had said, "It would be nothing to Me to consume you all by the breath of My indignation. It would throw no honor over Me to sweep away the whole strength of that rebellion which you have mustered up against Me. It would make no more to My glory than if I went through the thorns and briers and burned them before Me. This is not the battle I want to engage in—this is not the victory by which I seek to signalize Myself. And you mistake Me, you mistake Me, feeble children of men, if you think that I aspire after anything else with any one of you than that you should be prevailed on to come into My vineyard, and lay hold of My strength, and seek to make peace with Me.

"The victory that My heart is set upon is not a victory over your persons. That is a victory that will easily be gotten in the great day of final reckoning over all who have refused My overtures, and would none of My reproof, and have turned them away from my beseeching offers of reconciliation. In that great day of the power of My anger, it will be seen how easy it is to accomplish such a victory. How rapidly the fire of My conflagration will involve the rebels who have opposed Me in that devouring flame from which they never, never can be extricated! How speedily the execution of the condemning sentence will run through the multitude who stand at the left hand of the Avenging Judge! And rest assured, you who are now hearing Me, and whom I freely invite all to enter into the vineyard of God, that this is not the triumph that God is longing after."

It is not the victory over your persons in judgment that brings Him pleasure. It is the victory over your wills now. It is that you do honor to His testimony by placing your reliance on Him. It is that you accept of His kind and free assurances that He has no ill-will to you. It is that you cast the whole burden of sullen fear and suspicion away from your hearts, and that now, even now, you enter into a fellowship of peace with the God whom you have offended.

Oh, be prevailed upon! I know that terror will not subdue you. I know that all the threatenings of the Law will not reclaim you. I know that no direct process of pressing home the claims of God upon your obedience will ever compel you to the only obedience that is of any value in His estimation—even the willing obedience of the affections to a Father whom you love.

But surely when He looks on you with the countenance of a Father; when He speaks to you with the tenderness of a loving Parent; when He tries to woo you back to that house of His from which you have wandered; and when, to persuade you of His goodwill, He descends so far as to reason the matter, and to tell you that He is no more seeking any glory from your destruction than He would seek glory from lighting into a blaze the thorns and the briers, and burning them together—ah! My brethren, should it not look plain to the eye of faith how honest and sincere the God of your redemption is, who is thus bowing Himself down to the mention of such an argument?

Do lay hold of it, and be impressed by it, and cherish no longer any doubt of the goodwill of the Lord God, merciful and gracious. Let your faith work by love to Him who has done so much and said so much to call you to loving faith. And let this love manifest all the power of a commanding principle within you, by urging your every footstep to the new obedience of new creatures in Jesus Christ your Lord.

Thus, the twofold benefit of the gospel will be realized by all who believe and obey that gospel. Reconciled to God by the death of His Son, regenerated by the power of that mighty and all-subduing Spirit who is at the giving of the Son, your salvation will be complete. You will be washed, and sanctified, and justified in the name of the Lord Jesus, and by the Spirit of our God.[1]

Appendix 2

On the Love of God, and Whether It Extends to the Non-Elect

EDITOR'S NOTE: This text by Andrew Fuller, influential Baptist pastor and writer from England in the late seventeen hundreds, was excerpted from a letter to a friend.

QUESTION: Since God never intended those whom He did not elect to know the power of His grace in Christ Jesus, how can we extol the love of God in seeking the salvation of men, except in relation to those whom He designed to save?

And how can we speak of the love of God to men at large, except on the general ground that it is among the mass of mankind that His chosen can be found?

In fewer words, What is it the love God has for those whom He has not chosen to eternal life?

ANSWER: I cannot undertake to free this subject or any other from difficulty; nor do I pretend to answer it on the principles of reason. If I can ascertain certain principles to be taught in the Word of God, I feel it safe to reason from them; but if I proceed beyond this, I am at sea.

The God Who Loves

Respecting the first member of this question, I am not aware of having represented God as "seeking the salvation of those who are not saved." If by the term seeking were meant no more than His furnishing them with the means of salvation, and, as the moral Governor of His creatures, sincerely directing and inviting them to use them, I should not object to it. In this sense He said of Israel, "O that thou hadst hearkened to my commandments!" (Isa. 48:18). In this sense the Lord of the vineyard is described as seeking fruit where He finds none (Lk. 13:7). But if it be understood to include such a desire for the salvation of men as to do all that can be done to accomplish it, I do not approve of it. I see no inconsistency between God's using all proper means for the good of mankind as their Creator and Governor, and His withholding effectual grace, which is something super-added to moral government, and to which no creature has any claim,

As to the second part of the question above, God may certainly be said to exercise love to mankind, being the mass containing His chosen people. But I cannot think this idea gives a complete answer.

It appears to me an incontrovertible fact that God is represented in His Word as exercising goodness, mercy, kindness, long-suffering, and even love towards men as men. The bounties of Providence are described as flowing from *kindness* and *mercy*. Moreover, God's own kindness and mercy is held up to us as an example of how we should love our enemies (Matt. 5:44–45; Lk 6:35–36). And this the apostle extols, calling it, "the riches of his goodness," keenly censuring the wicked for despising it, instead of being led to repentance by it (Rom. 2:4).

And what if God never intended to render His goodness, forbearance, and long-suffering effectual to the leading of them to repentance? Does it follow that it is not goodness?

I read such language as this: "God so loved the world that He gave His only begotten Son, that whosoever believeth in Him should not perish, but have everlasting life." Also, the ministry of reconciliation was in this strain: "We are ambassadors for Christ, as though God did beseech [men] by us: we pray [them] in Christ's stead, be ye reconciled to God" (2 Cor. 5:20). I can draw no conclusion short of this: Eternal life through Jesus Christ is freely offered to sinners as sinners. Or as Calvin, on John 3:16, expressed it:

> He useth the universal note both that He may invite all men in general unto the participation of life, and that He may cut off all excuse from unbelievers. To the same end tendeth the term world; for although there shall nothing be found in the world that is worthy of God's favour, yet He showeth that He is favorable unto the whole world, when He calleth all men without exception to the faith of Christ. But remember that life is promised to all who shall believe in Christ, so commonly, that yet faith is not common to all men; yet God doth only open the eyes of His elect, that they may seek Him by faith.

> Although God sent His Son to die for the whole world and offers pardon and eternal life to all who should believe in Him, if He had done so without making effectual provision for the reception of Him by electing certain people to salvation, what would have been the consequence? Not one of the human race, you may say, would have been saved, and so Christ would have died in vain. Be it so.

> Though this would not have comported with the wise and gracious designs of God, yet it does not appear to me inconsistent with His justice, goodness, or sincerity. If He had called sinners to repent, believe, and be saved, while He withheld the means of salvation, it would have been so; but not in His merely withholding the grace necessary to turn the sinner's heart.

If I am not mistaken, this second member of the question proceeds on the principle that there can be no true goodwill exercised towards a sinner in inviting him to repent, believe, and be saved, unless effectual grace be given him for the purpose. But that principle appears to me unscriptural and unfounded. Supernatural, effectual, saving grace is indeed necessary to the *actual production of good* in men; but it is never represented as necessary to justify the goodness of God in *expecting or requiring it*. All that is necessary to this end is that He furnish them with rational powers, objective light, and outward means. In proof of this, let all those scriptures be considered in which God complains of men for not repenting, believing, or obeying. For example, in the complaint against Chorazin and Bethsaida, no mention is made of supernatural grace given to them: but merely of the "mighty works" wrought before them (Matt. 11:20–24).

Similarly, in the parable of the landowner, the complaint that the vinegrowers lacked reverence for the landowner's Son was not founded on his having furnished them with supernatural grace (Matt. 21:33–38). Instead, it was justified because he had provided them with objective light, means, and advantages. Likewise God gave no effectual grace to those who are accused of bringing forth wild grapes instead of grapes; yet *He looked for* and asked what He could have done more for His vineyard that He had not done (Isa. 5:4).

The strivings of the Spirit, which sinners are described as "resisting," (Acts 7:51; cf. Gen. 6:3) could not for this reason mean the effectual grace of the Holy Spirit, nor indeed any thing wrought in them, but the impressive motives presented to them by the inspired messages of the prophets (see Neh. 9:30).

That is the same way I conceive we are to understand the complaint in Deuteronomy 29:4: "The Lord hath not given you an heart to perceive, and eyes to see, and ears to hear, unto this day." It is inconceivable that Moses should complain of them for the Lord's not having given them *supernatural grace*. The complaint appears to be founded on the non-success of the most impressive *outward means,* which ought to have produced in them a heart to perceive, eyes to see, and ears to hear. Such is the scope of the passage— "Moses called unto all Israel, and said unto them, Ye have seen all that the Lord did before your eyes in the land of Egypt unto Pharaoh, and unto all his servants, and unto all his land; the great temptations which thine eyes have seen, the signs, and those great miracles: yet the Lord hath not given you an heart to perceive, and eyes to see, and ears to hear, unto this day" (Deut. 29:2–4).

From the whole, I conclude that there are two kinds of influence by which God works on the minds of men: First, *that which is common,* and which is effected by the ordinary use of motives presented to the mind for consideration. Secondly, *that which is special and supernatural.* The one is exercised by Him as the moral Governor of the world; the other as the God of grace, through Jesus Christ. The one contains nothing mysterious, any more than the influence of our words and actions on each other; the other is such a mystery that we know nothing of it but by its effects. The former *ought* to be effectual; the latter *is* so.

Finally, you sum up the question in fewer words by asking, "What is the love which God hath for those whom He hath not chosen to eternal life?" I reply, It is the goodwill of the Creator, whose tender mercies are over all His works (Ps. 145:9). It is that tender regard for the work of His hands which nothing but sin could extinguish. That is why the infliction of the most tremendous punishments is proof of sin's malignity.

Scripture implies that God's wrath is against the grain of His native goodness. Since God's tender mercies are over all His works, we know that He would not punish offenders with eternal destruction if the inalienable interests of His character and government did not require it. Such are the ideas conveyed by implication in Genesis 6:7: "I will destroy man *whom I have created* from the face of the earth" and Isaiah 27:11: *"He that made them* will not have mercy on them, and *He that formed them* will show them no favour" (emphasis added).[1]

Appendix 3

▪

Christic the Savior of the World

EDITOR'S NOTE: This sermon by Thomas Boston, Scottish pastor and author, was preached at Ettrick, Scotland on June 7, 1724.

And we have seen and do testify that the Father sent the Son to be the Saviour of the world (1 John 4:14).

John, the beloved disciple, in his epistles, is still breathing love. Love is the string he delights peculiarly to harp upon. He is always either magnifying God's love to us, or pressing our love to God and to one another.

But his favorite subject, love, is no narrow one, but most comprehensive. It comprehends both the gospel and the law, both faith and works. The love of God to man is the great doctrine of the gospel and the object of faith. Men's love to God and to one another is the great doctrine of the law of the Ten Commandments and the object of holy practice.

There is a near relation between the two: God's love is the fountain—our love the stream. The former is the original holy fire; the latter the flame kindled by it. Accordingly, the context of

1 John 4:14 asserts how the love of God moves us to love one another. But the verse itself displays how divine love is the substance of the gospel.

Here, then, we have the gospel, which all the apostles were in one voice to preach unto the world: "We have seen and do testify that the Father sent the Son to be the Saviour of the world." And therein we may consider two things:

First, *the gospel or glad tidings itself:* that the Father sent the Son to be the Savior of the world. Here is indeed glad news to the world—Christ's mission. The promise of this mission was made to fallen Adam in paradise. Believers under the Old Testament lived and died in the faith of it. But the apostles testified it as a thing performed. Past tense: the Father sent, or has sent, the Son.

The party sent is the Son of God, our Lord Jesus Christ. No other was fit for this mission. The party sending, from whom He had His commission, was the Father—the First Person of the glorious Trinity. None of a lower dignity could send one of His dignity. The character in which He was sent, is as "Saviour of the world." The words are without any supplement; of which there is no need here. Christ was constituted, nominated, and appointed by his Father as "Saviour of the world." And thus was He sent away into the world in that character.

"The world" is the world of mankind indefinitely, ruined by Adam's sin (Jn. 3:16 ff.). Therein God's love toward mankind appeared (Tit. 3:4).

Second, we note *the certainty of this gospel or glad tidings.* All the apostles witnessed with one mouth this great truth—and they testified to it as eyewitnesses. They had seen the Savior, conversed with Him, read His commission as He unfolded it to them from the Old Testament, and beheld heaven's seal of authentication again and again in His miracles. This matter of their witnessing from their own eyesight was so crucial to the apostolic testimony that the apostle Paul, who was not called to be an apostle until after Christ's ascension, was allowed first to see with his eyes, before he should bear witness. Jesus told him, "I have appeared unto thee for this purpose, to make thee a minister and a witness both of these things which thou hast seen, and of those things in the which I will appear unto thee" (Acts 26:16).

The Doctrine

IT IS THE GREAT TRUTH AND TESTIMONY *of the gospel that the Father hath sent his Son Jesus Christ in the character of Savior of the world.*

In examining this doctrine, I shall first take notice of some things signified in the apostle John's testimony; second, unwrap the sense of the title "Savior of the world"; and third, probe the applications of this truth.

Some things signified in this testimony. First, the world needed a Savior. Otherwise one would not have been provided for them by Him who does nothing in vain. It was a sick world, cast into a desperate illness by eating of the forbidden fruit. Humanity needed a physician to cure the distemper. Jesus said, "They that be whole need not a physician, but they that are sick" (Matt. 9:12). It was a cursed world, staked down under wrath by the sentence of the broken law. Such a world needed a Savior to remove the curse and bring in the blessing. So "God, having raised up his Son Jesus, sent him to bless you" (Acts 3:26). It was a lost world—lost to God, lost to themselves, lost to all good, lost and perishing under the wrath of God. It needed Someone to seek and save: "For the Son of man is come to seek and to save that which was lost" (Luke 19:10).

Second, no one of inferior dignity to the Son of God could be the Savior of the world. No man or angel would be able to sustain the character of Savior of a lost world. The work of that office was above the reach of the whole creation (cf. Rev. 5:3). Here was a trial of the divine love to man. Humanity's case was hopeless and helpless from all the creatures. But "God so loved the world, that he gave his only begotten Son, that whosoever believeth in him should not perish, but have everlasting life" (Jn. 3:16).

Third, Christ was sent to be Savior of the world from God's own initiative. The plot to save humanity was conceived entirely without humanity's input. The world did not meet, and send someone to the court of heaven with a petition for a Savior. The Savior was not granted in response to sinners' earnest entreaties and supplications. Instead, the Father, purely out of free love, sent his Son to be the Savior of the world. The world's needs spoke loud, but they themselves were quite silent; and yet their needs spoke no louder than those of the fallen angels. Sovereign, free grace heard the voice of man's need, while it stopped its ears to the needs of fallen angels. "For verily he took not on him the nature of angels; but he took on him the seed of Abraham" (Heb. 2:16). "But after that the kindness and love of God our Savior toward *man* appeared" (Tit. 3:4, emphasis added).

Fourth, Christ is fully furnished for the saving of a lost world. His being sent in that character proves His ability to answer it. "Wherefore he is able also to save them to the uttermost that come unto God by him, seeing he ever liveth to make intercession for them" (Heb. 7:25). There is nothing wrong in the world but what there is a remedy to be found in Christ for. Whosoever in the world shall die, they shall not die because there was no help for their case in the Savior, but because they did not put their case in His hand. The Savior of the world is certainly able to save the world; since He was sent of God in that character.

Finally, the salvation of lost sinners of the world of mankind is very acceptable to the God and Father of our Lord Jesus, as well as to Jesus Himself. Otherwise God would not have sent His Son to be Savior of the world. "For this is good and acceptable in the sight of God our Saviour; who will have all men to be saved, and to come unto the knowledge of the truth" (1 Tim. 2:3–4). Hence, the salvation of sinners is called "the pleasure of the Lord," (Isa. 53:10). So He is said to make the marriage for His Son, and to send forth His servants to bid all to come to that marriage (Matt. 22:9). From this it is evident that there is no impediment on Heaven's part to the salvation of sinners by Jesus Christ. Saving sinners is pleasing to the Father, to His Son, and to His Spirit.

The sense of the title *Savior of the world*. In what sense is Christ Savior of the world? *Savior* is a name of honor, and a name of business. It is an honorable thing to save and help the miserable—to be destined, appointed, and called to that employment. Every such honorable post has some work annexed to it, which success is expected to attend—as in the case of a teacher, physician, and the like. In fact, teachers or physicians *are* types of "saviors" in society. They are saviors in two ways: in respect of office, and in respect of actuality. In the first sense, "savior" speaks of one called to and invested with the office of saving, teaching, or curing society. Those appointed to such an office are called teachers or physicians—saviors—even before they ever teach or cure or save anyone. In this respect one may be called an *official* savior. There is another sense in which we speak of an *actual* savior. In such cases the term is applied with respect to the actuality of saving, teaching, or healing. As the former arises from an appointment put upon such a one, this arises from the work He manages in virtue of that appointment. Thus, Nehemiah 9:27 says, "When they cried unto thee, thou heardest them from heaven; and according to thy manifold mercies thou gavest them saviours, who saved them out of the hand of their enemies."

Our Lord Jesus is the *actual* Savior of the elect only, in whose room and stead only He died upon the cross, according to the eternal covenant between Him and the Father—the covenant of grace, otherwise called the covenant of redemption (these are not two, but one and the same covenant). Thus, the apostle calls Him "the Saviour of the body," (Eph. 5:23). That is, in a particular sense He is Savior of the elect, who make up the body whereof He was appointed Head from eternity. They are the ones on whose behalf He covenanted with the Father in the eternal covenant. And He is their Savior in the sense that He actually saves them: "She shall bring forth a son, and thou shalt call his name Jesus: for he shall save his people from their sins" (Matt. 1:21). None but these will ever truly put their case in His hand or know Him as Savior. And every one of them will certainly trust Him as Savior sooner or later. "As many as were ordained to eternal life believed" (Acts 13:48). "All that the Father giveth me shall come to me" (Jn. 6:37).

Our Lord Jesus Christ is the *official* Savior, not of the elect only, but of the world of mankind indefinitely. Thus, our text calls Him "saviour of the world." In a cross reference, God in Christ is called "the saviour of all men," but in a special sense, the Savior of "those that believe," (1 Tim. 4:10).

When a governmental ruler, out of regard for his people's welfare, commissions a qualified physician to be surgeon general to all of society, the commission itself constitutes him surgeon general of that whole society. Even though many individuals should never employ him, but call other physicians, yet still there is a relation between him and them; he is their surgeon general by office.

In the same way, God, looking on the ruined world of mankind, has constituted and appointed Jesus Christ His Son Savior of the world. Christ has Heaven's patent for this office, and wherever the gospel comes, He is held up as Savior by office. By this office a relation is constituted between Him and the world of mankind. He is their Savior, and they the objects of His administration. Any of them all may come to Him as Savior, without money or price, and be saved by Him as their own Savior appointed to that office by the Father.

So the matter lies here: in this official sense, Christ is Savior of the whole world.

This appears even more clearly when we consider Scripture testimony, which is plain. Our text expressly calls Him Savior of the world. The believing Samaritans likewise profess their faith in Him: "Now we believe, not because of thy saying: for we have heard him ourselves, and know that this is indeed the Christ, the Saviour of the world" (Jn. 4:42). You have the appointment of Heaven very plainly in John 3:16: "God so loved the world, that he gave his only begotten Son, that whosoever believeth in him should not perish, but have everlasting life"—even as the brazen serpent lifted up on the pole in the wilderness was ordained by God for healing to the snake-bitten persons of the whole camp of Israel. Hence, Christ's salvation is called "the common salvation" in Jude 3; any of mankind's sinners may lay hold on this salvation. Even so the Savior's birth is said to be "good tidings of great joy, which shall be to all people" (Lk. 2:10)—which it could not have been, if He had not been a Savior to all people. And for this reason He Himself testifies that He came to save the world: "God sent not his Son into the world to condemn the world; but that the world through him might be saved" (Jn. 3:17).

In John 12:47 He states, "I came not to judge the world, but to save the world." This is His office. He is held up as Savior to all sinners generally; not to this or that sort of sinner, but to all sinners of mankind indefinitely, without exception. "This is a faithful saying, and worthy of all acceptation, that Christ Jesus came into the world to save sinners" (1 Tim. 1:15). "This is a faithful saying, and worthy of all acceptation, that Christ Jesus came into the world to save sinners." He came "to seek and to save that which was lost" (Lk. 19:10). To the same purpose He declares Himself "the light of the world" namely, by office (Jn. 8:12). And whosoever will follow Him "shall not walk in darkness, but shall have the light of life" (Jn. 8:12). That is why the gospel message He has committed to us is a message of reconciliation. We are to beseech men in Christ's stead to be reconciled to God (2 Cor. 5:19–20).

If it were not so that Christ is Savior of the world, He could not warrantably be offered with His salvation to the world indefinitely, but to the elect only. If He were not commissioned to the office of Savior of all men, it would be no more appropriate to call all men to trust Him as Savior any more than He could be offered lawfully to fallen angels (who are *not* within His commission as Savior). The gospel offer could never lawfully carry the matter beyond the bounds of Christ's commission from His Father.

But we know from Scripture that Christ and His salvation may be warrantably offered to the whole world of sinners, with assurance that whoever of them will turn in faith to Him as Savior, he shall be saved (Mark 16:15–16). Moreover, if it were not so, the unbelief of hearers of the gospel, their not coming to Christ for salvation, could not be their sin. It can never be one's sin not to do a thing he has no legitimate warrant for. No one could be held guilty for not turning to Christ for salvation, unless there is a sense in which God has appointed Him to be Savior of that guilty one. It is no sin for fallen angels not to believe in Christ for salvation, because they are not within the Savior's commission. They are not commanded to turn to Him as Savior, and even if they did so, they would find Him their judge only, and no Savior to them.

But Scripture tells us that not believing in Christ the Savior is the very sin that ruins the hearers of the gospel who ultimately perish: "And this is the condemnation, that light is come into the world, and men loved darkness rather than light, because their deeds were evil" (Jn. 3:19).

Finally, if it were not so that Christ is Savior of the world, the elect themselves could never believe in Christ until their election were revealed to them. That is contrary to the stated method of grace, for no one can believe on Christ for salvation, until that person sees Him to be a Savior for them.

There are two things further to be remarked on before we move on:

❒ First, the ground on which Christ is constituted Savior of the world is nothing but the infinite sufficiency of the merit of His death and sufferings. Christ died as a substitute for His elect in particular. The Good Shepherd lay down His life "for the sheep" (Jn. 10:15). Yet the price He paid for them was of infinite worth. It was therefore sufficient in itself to save the whole world. The bread provided for them—a crucified Christ—was sufficient to give life to and feed, not them only, but the whole world of mankind. Therefore He is appointed Savior of the world: "For the bread of God is he which cometh down from heaven, and giveth life unto the world. . . . I am the living bread which came down from heaven: if any man eat of this bread, he shall live for ever: and the bread that I will give is my flesh, which I will give for the life of the world" (Jn. 6:33, 51).

❐ Second, the title "Savior of the world" is a title of honor Christ merited by laying down His life on behalf of sinners. The Father speaks thus: "I will also give thee for a light to the Gentiles, that thou mayest be my salvation unto the end of the earth" (Isa. 49:6). The Father invested Him with "all power . . . in heaven and in earth" (Matt. 28:18). "For the Father judgeth no man, but hath committed all judgment unto the Son: That all men should honour the Son, even as they honour the Father (Jn. 5:22–23). It was a reward suitable to His work.

The business committed to Him as Savior of the world. Christ's work is to save sinners from their sin: "Thou shalt call his name Jesus: for he shall save his people from their sins" (Matt. 1:21). Satan ruined the world of men by bringing sin upon them. They were bound with the cords of guilt. The image of God in them was defaced. They were polluted and made loathsome and shut up in bondage to a strange lord.

But God has appointed Christ Savior of the world so that sinners may come to Him and be delivered from their sins. "He that committeth sin is of the devil; for the devil sinneth from the beginning. For this purpose the Son of God was manifested, that he might destroy the works of the devil" (1 John 3:8). Sin is an inveterate disease, the care of which was as far beyond the reach of any mere creature as the raising of the dead is. So He was appointed Savior in the case: "I have laid help upon one that is mighty; I have exalted one chosen out of the people" (Ps. 89:19).

Christ's work is also to save sinners from misery and to free them from destruction. "O Israel, thou hast destroyed thyself; but in me is thine help" (Hos. 13:9). People are by sin made objects of wrath, laid under the curse of the broken law, liable to revenging wrath for time and for eternity. But Christ is appointed to save them from all this, upon their coming to Him and trusting Him for that purpose. "And a man shall be as an hiding place from the wind, and a covert from the tempest; as rivers of water in a dry place, as the shadow of a great rock in a weary land" (Isa. 32:2).

Sin let in a deluge of miseries on the world. These miseries flow about the sinner continually in greater or lesser measure. But He is a Savior to deliver them from those miseries. "Of him are ye in Christ Jesus, who of God is made unto us wisdom, and righteousness, and sanctification, and redemption" (1 Cor. 1:30).

The Application

Believe. Behold here, admire, and believe the great love of God to a lost world, in providing a Savior, and such a Savior, for them— even His own Son. Scripture speaks of this in a very high strain: "God so loved the world, that he gave his only begotten Son, that whosoever believeth in him should not perish, but have everlasting life" (Jn. 3:16). There was a man-love in God: "The kindness and love of God our Saviour toward man appeared" (Tit. 3:4). That speaks of a love of the species mankind. God's love for humanity has appeared in two eminent instances: First, in securing, by an irreversible decree, the salvation of some of them; and second, in providing a Savior for the whole of the kind, constituting His own Son Savior to the lost family of Adam indefinitely.

Believe this truth with application to yourselves. If upon this a secret murmur begins to go through your heart, *But it was not for me*—crush it in the bud, for it is a bud of hell. If you are not one of the demon-kind, but one of sinful mankind, it was indeed for you. The Father gave Christ as a Savior for you, that if you would believe on Him, you should not perish. He sent His Son from heaven with full instructions and ample powers to save you, if you will believe. And is not this love? Believe it, and it will be the way to let you in to a sight of more love.

Behold here a broad and firm foundation of faith for all and every one of you. You may come to Christ whatever your case is, and you may claim His righteousness and His whole salvation for yourselves. You may hide yourselves in Him as the refuge appointed for you by the Father—a holy refuge from sin and wrath. You are as free to lay hold of Him as Savior as the bitten Israelites were to look to the brazen serpent. You may wholly trust Him to save you from sin and wrath. For He was sent by the Father as Savior of the world. And if by the Father's appointment He is Savior of the world, He is by office *your* Savior, and *my* Savior, since we are members of that world of mankind. Therefore we may by faith claim His saving us from sin and wrath.

As a child who lives in a school district may claim teaching from one who is appointed teacher of a public school; as those of a congregation may claim the preaching of their own minister; and as the wounded in battle may claim the services of a physician who has been appointed to their regiment. We "testify that the Father sent the Son to be the Saviour of the world" (1 John 4:14).

Sinners living in their sins, pining away, and about to perish eternally in sin, are without excuse. For "the Father sent the Son to be the Saviour of the world." Jesus said, "If I had not come and spoken unto them, they had not had sin: but now they have no cloak for their sin" (Jn. 15:22). Sinners are destroyed with their living and raging lusts. They are run down with them as with running sores; their souls are bleeding to death with them as with mortal wounds. In this state they hold on over the belly of their guilt and they say they cannot help it. One cannot help his swearing; another his sensuality; another his pride, passion, covetousness, gross ignorance, his old corrupt unrenewed heart. But the truth is, they do not want it helped. Jesus said, "Ye will not come to me, that ye might have life" (Jn. 5:40). If you cannot help it, you have a Savior who can help it, and would certainly help it if you would come to Him. But if you will not come, you will perish in your sin. Jesus warned, "I said therefore unto you, that ye shall die in your sins: for if ye believe not that I am he, ye shall die in your sins" (Jn. 8:24).

Know with certainty that if any of you *shall* perish—and if you go on in your sins ye shall perish—you shall not perish for want of a Savior. At the tribunal of God, the devils may say, "We could not be saved from our sins—for there was no Savior appointed for us." The pagans may say, "We could not be saved, for though we were within the compass of the Savior's commission, yet we never heard of it. It was never intimated to us." But what will *you* have to say when your Savior shall sit judge upon you and condemn you to suffer the vengeance of eternal fire? Your only reply will be that you would have none of Him or His salvation. You did not want to be saved from your sins. You would not trust Him as Savior, though He had His Father's commission to be Savior of the world—and your Savior. Though this was explained to you, you would not receive Him as your Savior. You would rather die in your sins than trust Him.

Examine yourself. Is the Savior of the world by office your actual Savior? Has He saved you? Do not think that Christ puts off His saving of sinners until they come to heaven. True, they are not *completely* saved until they see Him (1 Jn. 3:2). But if your salvation by Christ is not begun here, you shall never get there. "For it is not by works of righteousness which we have done, but according to his mercy he saved us, by the washing of regeneration, and renewing of the Holy Ghost; which he shed on us abundantly through Jesus Christ our Saviour; that being justified by his grace, we should be made heirs according to the hope of eternal life" (Tit. 3:5–7).

You have no right before the Lord to His table, if He has not been an actual Savior to you. If He has not saved you from sin and wrath initially (though not completely) you have no part with Him.

But as soon as a sinner turns to Him, He fully justifies that sinner. What are the marks of faith that follow?

First, if Christ has really begun to save you, you will have the saved man's thoughts of sin, and of the wrath of God. If a drowning man were pulled alive out of a water—or a filthy stinking puddle—and standing at the side of it, looking to it after his narrow escape, what would be his thoughts of that water, that puddle, where be was once over head and ears, and almost gone? Such will be your thoughts of sin, and of the wrath of God. You will have solemn and devout thoughts of the wrath of God above all the things you fear. "Wherefore we receiving a kingdom which cannot be moved, let us have grace, whereby we may serve God acceptably with reverence and godly fear for our God is a consuming fire" (Heb. 12:28–29). Jesus said, "Fear not them which kill the body, but are not able to kill the soul: but rather fear him which is able to destroy both soul and body in hell" (Matt 10:28). Of all terrors, divine wrath will be to you the most terrible.

Those in the state of wrath either have lost their sense of God's wrath; or they know not where they are; or they are dreaming of some pleasant place. And so they go on peacefully in their sins, undisturbed with thoughts of wrath. Or else they have some terrible apprehensions of it, but they may think there is something more terrible. Therefore they will rather sin than suffer the hardships attending the mortification of sin. Or else their heart is fire-hot with the terror of the wrath of God, and in the meantime, at least, stone-cold of love and childlike affection to the God whose wrath it is. But the saved soul looks on God's wrath as of all things the most awful, yet with a childlike reverence and affection toward that God whose wrath it is.

Second, if Christ is your Savior actually, you will have a transcendent esteem of and love to your Savior. "Unto you therefore which believe he is precious " (1 Pet. 2:7). His conscience-purifying blood, His soul-sanctifying Spirit will be more valuable to you than a thousand worlds. You will desire them above all things, pant and long after them, and seek more and more of them. In comparison of them, all the world will be but trifles in your eyes, which you would be content to part with in order to gain the riches of Christ: "[The merchant man] when he had found one pearl of great price, went and sold all that he had, and bought it" (Matt. 13:46). Jesus Himself said, "If any man come to me, and hate not his father, and mother, and wife, and children, and brethren, and sisters, yea, and his own life also, he cannot be my disciple" (Luke 14:26). But those who know Him know He is worth any price:

> "Yea doubtless, and I count all things but loss for the excellency of the knowledge of Christ Jesus my Lord: for whom I have suffered the loss of all things, and do count them but dung, that I may win Christ, and be found in him, not having mine own righteousness, which is of the law, but that which is through the faith of Christ, the righteousness which is of God by faith" (Phil. 3:8).

Third, if you have trusted Christ as your actual Savior, you will be groaning under the remains of the disease of sin you are saved from. Your conscience will bear witness that you would eagerly be wholly rid of it. "O wretched man that I am! who shall deliver me from the body of this death?" (Rom. 7:24). Your souls will be longing for the complete salvation, so that the enemies you see today you may see no more for ever. You will long for that complete victory over all your corruptions: "We ourselves groan within ourselves, waiting for the adoption, to wit, the redemption of our body" (Rom. 8:23).

Receive the Lord Jesus. Lay hold of Christ as *your* Savior, O sinners. Receive Him in that character wherein His Father sent Him—as the Savior of the world, and as your Savior. You are lost in your sins. Lost under the wrath of God. Lost under the curse of the law. So come to Him for His whole salvation. Put your case in His hand as your Savior by the Father's appointment; and slight Him no more.

Consider, first of all, that you need a Savior. Your disease of sin will ruin you, if you be not saved from it. The guilt of it will stake you down under wrath, and the wrath of God will sink you into hell. And as long as sin keeps its unbroken dominion over you, you can be sure the guilt is not removed. "They that be whole need not a physician, but they that are sick" (Matt. 9:12). "But of the tree of the knowledge of good and evil, thou shalt not eat of it: for in the day that thou eatest thereof thou shalt surely die" (Gen. 2:17).

There is no Savior besides Christ. "Neither is there salvation in any other: for there is none other name under heaven given among men, whereby we must be saved" (Acts 4:12). All others are physicians of no value. All your own endeavors will not save you—nor any thing any creature can do for you.

Moreover, He is able to save you. "He is able also to save them to the uttermost that come unto God by him, seeing he ever liveth to make intercession for them" (Heb. 7:25). Whatever be your case, there is infinite merit in His blood to take away the deepest guilt. "The blood of Jesus Christ his Son cleanseth us from all sin" (1 Jn. 1:7). There is an infinite efficacy of His Spirit to sanctify the most unholy: "And such were some of you: but ye are washed, but ye are sanctified, but ye are justified in the name of the Lord Jesus, and by the Spirit of our God" (1 Cor. 6:11). If you doubt that, you dishonor Christ and His Father who sent Him. "Then thou spakest in vision to thy holy one, and saidst, I have laid help upon one that is mighty; I have exalted one chosen out of the people" (Ps. 90:19).

He is willing to save you: "And the Spirit and the bride say, Come. And let him that heareth say, Come. And let him that is athirst come. And whosoever will, let him take the water of life freely" (Rev. 22:17). The only thing wanting is your willingness to be saved. "Woe unto thee, O Jerusalem! wilt thou not be made clean?" (Jer. 13:27). You need not fear being rejected if you come. He says, "Him that cometh to me I will in no wise cast out" (Jn. 6:37). He has taken on Him the office of Savior of the world, and He cannot refuse the business of it.

Finally, you must either receive Him as your Savior from sin and wrath, according to His commission from heaven, or you will be held guilty for refusing Him as your Savior, after His own Father—our God—has appointed and commissioned Him for that effect.

Consider how you will answer that before the judgment.

How can you receive Him and lay hold of Him? Only by faith. Only by believing on Him, by being convinced of your sin and hopeless state, and by desiring to be saved from both. Believe Christ is *your* Savior by His Father's appointment; and so wholly trust on Him as a crucified Savior, for His whole salvation, on the ground of God's faithfulness in His Word.[1]

Appendix 4

The Love of God to the World

EDITOR'S NOTE: The following text was excerpted from an essay by John Brown, one of several Scottish preachers who bore that name. He is remembered best for the work from which this text is taken.

> For God so loved the world, that he gave his only begotten Son, that whosoever believeth in him should not perish, but have everlasting life (Jn. 3:16).

Let us now proceed to consider the primary source of this economy of salvation, as stated by our Lord. The love of God—the love of God to the world. "God so loved the world" (Jn. 3:16).

The advocates for the doctrine of the atonement—the doctrine that the death of the incarnate Only-begotten of God, as the victim for the sins of men, was necessary in order to the Divine mercy manifesting itself to sinners in the communication of pardon and salvation, consistently with the righteousness of his character and law; the advocates of this doctrine, have often been accused of holding that the interposition of the divine Son was necessary to produce in the bosom of His divine Father, a disposition to pity, and to save, man; and, as it has been forcibly put, "that the compassion of God rather than the souls of men, was the purchase made by the incarnate Son, when He laid down His life as a ransom." It has been said that they represent the Divinity, as a being of resentments so fierce that nothing could mitigate them but the tears and prayers, the blood and death, of His own Son.

It must be acknowledged that the doctrine of the atonement has not always been taught in "the words which become sound doctrine," and that language has sometimes been employed on the subject, by good men, which seemed to intimate rather that Christ died, in order that God might be induced to pity and save man, than that He died, because God pitied man, and was determined to save him.

The doctrine of the atonement, as taught in Scripture, however, lays no foundation for such conclusions. "God," according to its declarations, "is love," perfect in benignity, "rich in mercy." In forming conceptions on this subject, when we err, it is by defect, not by excess. Our ideas fall beneath, instead of rising above, the truth.

There was, there could be, no discordance among the persons of the Godhead, in reference to the salvation of man. The will of the Godhead is, and necessarily must be, one. We are not for a moment to suppose that the Father and the Spirit were disinclined to the salvation of man; and that the Son became incarnate, and suffered, and died, to induce Them to comply with His disposition to show favour to the guilty and ruined race. The wondrous economy of redemption is the fruit of that sovereign benignity which equally belongs to the Father, and to the Son, and to the Holy Ghost. In that economy, the Father sustains the majesty of Divinity. All is represented as originating in Him. But His holiness is the holiness of the Divinity; His justice, the justice of the Divinity; His love, the love of the Divinity.

Christ did not die that God might love man; He died because God loved man. "God commendeth His love to us in that, while we were yet sinners, Christ died for us" (Rom. 5:8).

> In this was manifested the love of God toward us,
> because that God sent his only begotten Son into the world,
> that we might live through him. Herein is love; not that we
> loved God, but that he loved us, and sent his Son to be the
> propitiation for our sins (1 Jn. 4:9-10).

The atonement is thus not the cause, but the effect, of the love of God. It is the wonderful expedient devised by infinite wisdom, to render the manifestation of sovereign kindness to a guilty race, not merely consistent with, but gloriously illustrative of, the righteousness of the Divine character, as displayed both in the requisitions and sanctions of that holy law which man had violated.

That law is not an arbitrary institution. It is simply the embodiment of those principles which are necessary to the happiness of intelligent, responsible beings, while they continue what they are, and God continues what He is. That law originates not in sovereignty, but in that union of perfect wisdom, holiness, and benignity, which forms the moral character of God; and to uphold that law is a necessity of His nature; He cannot but require truth, righteousness, and benignity of man. This law had been violated by man. The consequence was, man became liable to the dreadful consequences of transgression. He had sinned, and he deserved to die. The hopeless, the everlasting, destruction of the sinner, must have seemed to every created mind the necessary result of this state of things. But "God who is rich in mercy," and infinite in wisdom, devised and executed a plan by which the honor of the law might be vindicated, and yet the violators of that law pardoned and saved; by which the evil of sin might be exhibited to the intelligent universe in a light far stronger than if the whole race of man bad perished for ever, and yet an innumerable multitude of that self-ruined race be rescued from destruction, and "saved . . . with an everlasting salvation" (Isa. 45:17).

The only begotten Son, in glad compliance with the merciful appointment of His Father, having taken the place of the guilty;

and in their nature, and in their room, yielded a perfect obedience, in circumstances of the greatest temptation and difficulty, to that law which they had violated, thus showing the reasonableness and excellence of all its requisitions; and submitted in their room to such sufferings as, in the estimation of infinite wisdom and righteousness, more signally honored the sanctionary part of the Divine law, than the everlasting punishment of sinful men could have done:—"God hath set forth his Son to be a propitiation through faith in his blood, to declare his righteousness for the remission of sins, that he might be just, and the justifier of him that believes in Jesus" (Rom. 3:25-26); "a just God, and a Saviour" (Isa. 14:21).

Having thus endeavored to show that the atonement of Christ is not the procuring cause of God's love to sinners, but the means which God in his wisdom devised for rendering the display of his love consistent with his righteousness, I go on to illustrate, somewhat more particularly, the great truth upon which, in this part of the subject, I wish to fix your attention: that the whole of that wondrous economy of salvation unfolded by our Lord, proceeds from the love of God, from the love of God to the world.

The Love of God, the Origin of the Plan of Salvation

WE MAY BEGIN WITH asking in what could the plan of salvation originate but in love—pure, sovereign benignity? Contemplate the attributes and relations of God, and then contemplate the character and circumstances of man. Look first at the bestower, and then look at the recipients of salvation, and say, from what source it could flow but from spontaneous kindness?

Look upwards to Divinity and say if anything but sovereign kindness could have actuated Him in devising and executing the plan of human salvation? It could not be strict justice that influenced him: that would have led to the infliction of punishment, not the conferring of benefits; that would have led to man's destruction, not his salvation. Selfish considerations are, from the absolute independence of the Divine Being, entirely out of the question. The sources of the Divine happiness, like the sources of the Divine excellence, are in the Divine nature. No creature can either advance or diminish the happiness of God. Our gratitude, obedience, and praise for the benefits of salvation, cannot increase His felicity. Our goodness extendeth not to him (Ps. 16:2). "Can a man be profitable to God, as he that is wise is profitable to himself? Is it any pleasure to the Almighty, that thou art righteous? or is it gain to him, that thou makest thy ways perfect?" (Job 22:2-3). And if this wondrous plan of salvation could not originate in a selfish desire for our services and praises, it could as little originate in a selfish fear of our enmity, reproaches, or rebellious attempts against His government. The very idea is as absurd as it is blasphemous. "Will he reprove thee for fear of thee?" (Job 22:4). "If thou sinnest, what doest thou against him? or if thy transgressions be multiplied, what doest thou unto him?" (Job 35:6). "Thy wickedness may hurt a man as thou art" (v. 8)—but not God. He can easily render all the attempts which men and devils can make against His government, but so many occasions for the display of his wisdom, his power, and his righteousness. Had the whole sinning race of man been consigned to endless perdition, would He not have gathered through eternity a revenue of praise from their sufferings, as illustrations of His immaculate holiness, His inflexible justice, His inviolable faithfulness, without any disparagement of His benignity, which would indeed have been manifested in their interminable sufferings, as in those of the "angels who kept not their first estate" (Jude 6) such inflections being direct means of upholding that law, which is as necessary to the happiness of His intelligent creatures, as it is to the honor of His character, or the stability of His throne?

The God Who Loves

When we thus look upward to God, the giver of the blessings of the Christian salvation, we are constrained to say, "Nothing but love could influence Him in bestowing them." And when we direct our thoughts to the recipients of these benefits, we are conducted by a very short process of reasoning to the same conclusion. There is nothing in the situation or character of man which can lead us to trace blessings conferred on him to anything but pure benignity.

Man is a creature, and therefore, strictly speaking, he can have no claim on God. It was of God's free sovereign pleasure to create him, or not to create him; and when He created him, it was of His sovereign pleasure that He made him a living, thinking, immortal being, rather than an irrational brute, or an inanimate clod. As a creature, man, in common with all creatures, must be a pensioner on Divine bounty for every blessing. But though in no case could man have had a claim on God, had he continued what God made him, an innocent, a holy being, we may safely affirm that the equity as well as the benignity of God, would have secured for him everything necessary to true and permanent happiness.

But man is a sinner. He is guilty of innumerable violations of that holy law, one transgression of which deserves everlasting destruction; and he is not, as the economy of grace finds him, a penitent sinner. No, he is a hardened rebel, "going on in his trespasses," receding farther and farther from God. When God looks down from heaven on the children of men, what does He see? They have all gone aside; they have altogether become filthy; there is none that doeth good, no, not one (Ps. 14:2-3)

What could induce God to spare, what could induce Him to save, such beings? Holiness, justice, wisdom, had they not in the Divine nature been conjoined with infinite benignity, would have suggested anything rather than "thoughts of good" towards such a polluted, rebellious, worse than useless, mischievous, class of creatures; a set of beings whom a mere act of will could have annihilated, or punished with "everlasting destruction." What but love, pure sovereign compassion, could have said, "Deliver these from going down to the pit; I have found a ransom" (Job 33:24).

As it is thus plain that nothing but love could have been the source of the economy of human salvation, so it is equally evident, that that love must have had "a height and a depth, a length and a breadth" that exceeds the computing powers of created intelligences (Eph. 3:17-19). Well may we with the apostle stand in adoring wonder and exclaim, "Behold what manner of love!" (1 Jn. 3:1). "Herein"—herein indeed—"is love" (1 Jn. 4:10), as if all the other displays of Divine benignity were unworthy of regard when compared with this.

There are two ways by which we naturally measure the strength of a benevolent affection: the intrinsic value of the benefits bestowed on the objects of it; and the expense, labour, and suffering at which these benefits are obtained for them. Let us apply, or rather attempt to apply, these measures to the case before us, and we shall be obliged to confess, that this love it passes knowledge (Eph. 3:19).

The salvation which is by Christ includes deliverance from numerous, varied, immense, unending evils. It is deliverance from "perishing." It includes also restoration to numerous, varied, immense, unending blessings. It is the enjoyment of "eternal life." It is deliverance from evil, moral and physical, in all its forms, and in all its degrees, for ever and ever; and the possession of a happiness suited to, and filling to an overflow, all our capacities of enjoyment during the whole eternity of our being. When we think of the number, and variety, and value of the heavenly and spiritual blessings bestowed on us, we must acknowledge that it is "great love" wherewith God loves us; when we reflect on the inheritance, incorruptible, undefiled, and that fadeth not away, we are constrained to say, the mercy which bequeaths it, "is abundant mercy." This measure we can but very inadequately apply. Only the hopelessly lost know what the salvation of Christ delivers from. Only the blessed in heaven know what the salvation of Christ exalts to.

Even they know these things imperfectly. Eternity will be ever disclosing new horrors in the one, new glories in the other.

If we attempt to apply the second principle, we soon arrive at the same result. To obtain these blessings, the Son of God must become incarnate, and obey, and suffer, and die. God spared not his own Son, but delivered him up in our room as the victim for our transgressions (Rom. 8:32). He made Him who knew no sin, a sin offering in our room (2 Cor. 5:21). He made to meet on Him the iniquities of us all. It pleased the Lord to bruise Him; and He was wounded for our iniquities, bruised for our transgressions, and the chastisement of our peace was on Him (Isa. 53:5-6). He who was in the form of God, and who thought it not robbery to be equal with God, made himself of no reputation, took on him the form of a servant, humbled himself, and became obedient to death, even the death of the cross (Phil. 2:6-8). If it was a strong proof of the regard of Abraham to God, that he did not withhold his son, his only son, from Him, how shall we estimate the love of God to a lost world, which led Him to give His own, His only begotten, His beloved Son, that He might give Himself, a sacrifice and an offering for man's salvation!

Love of God to the World: The Origin of the Plan of Salvation

THERE IS ANOTHER IDEA to which I wish for a little to turn your attention on this part of the subject. The love in which the economy of salvation originates, is love to the world. God so loved the world as to give His only begotten Son. The term "world" is here just equivalent to mankind. It seems to be used by our Lord with a reference to the very limited and exclusive views of the Jews. They thought God loved them, and hated all the other nations of mankind. These were their own feelings, and they foolishly thought that God was altogether such an one as themselves. They accordingly expected that the Messiah was to come to deliver Israel, and to punish and destroy the other nations of the earth. But God's ways were not their ways, nor His thoughts their thoughts. As the heavens are high above the earth, so were His ways above their ways, and His thoughts above their thoughts (Isa. 55:8-9).

Some have supposed that the word "world" here is descriptive not of mankind generally, but of the whole of a particular class, that portion of mankind who, according to the Divine purpose of mercy, shall ultimately become partakers of the salvation of Christ. But this is to give to the term a meaning altogether unwarranted by the usage of Scripture. There can be no doubt in the mind of a person who understands the doctrine of personal election, that those who are actually saved are the objects of a special love on the part of God; and that the oblation of the Savior had a special design in reference to them. But there can be as little doubt, that the atonement of Christ has a general reference to mankind at large; and that it was intended as a display of love on the part of God to our guilty race. Not merely was the atonement offered by Christ Jesus sufficient for the salvation of the whole world, but it was intended and fitted to remove out of the way of the salvation of sinners generally every bar which the perfections of the Divine moral character and the principles of the Divine moral government presented. Without that atonement, no sinner could have been pardoned in consistency with justice. In consequence of that atonement, every sinner may be, and if he believe in Jesus certainly shall be, pardoned and saved. Through the medium of this atonement, the Divine Being is revealed to sinners, indiscriminately, as gracious and ready to forgive; and the invitations and promises warranting men to confide in Christ for salvation, are addressed to all, and are true and applicable to all without exception or restriction.

The revelation of mercy made in the gospel refers to men as sinners, not as elect sinners. Their election or their non-election is something of which, when called on to believe the gospel, they are necessarily entirely ignorant, and with which they have nothing to do. "The kindness and love of God . . . toward man," the Divine philanthropy, is revealed (Tit. 3:4). "God was in Christ, reconciling the world unto himself" (2 Cor. 5:19). He appears in the revelation of mercy as the God who has no pleasure in the death of the wicked; who willeth all men to be saved and to come to the knowledge of the truth (Ezek. 33:11; 1 Tim. 2:3-4). "The grace of God" revealed in the gospel "brings salvation to all," without exception, who in the faith of the truth will receive it (Tit. 2:11).

I am persuaded that the doctrine of personal election is very plainly taught in Scripture; but I am equally persuaded that the minister misunderstands that doctrine who finds it, in the least degree, hampering him in presenting a full and a free salvation as the gift of God to every one who hears the gospel; and that the man abuses the doctrine who finds in it anything which operates as a barrier in the way of his receiving, as a sinner, all the blessings of the Christian salvation, in the belief of the truth. Indeed, when rightly understood, it can have no such effect. For what is that doctrine, but just this, in other words—It is absolutely certain that a vast multitude of the race of man shall be saved through Christ? And it is as certain, that if any one of those to whom that salvation is offered, remains destitute of it, and perishes eternally, it is entirely owing to his own obstinate refusal of what is freely, honestly, presented to him. The kindness of God, as manifested in the gift of His Son, is kindness to the race of man; and when, as an individual, I credit the kindness of God to man, so strangely displayed, so abundantly proved, I cannot find any reason why I should not depend on this kindness, and expect to be saved even as others.

Whenever a man hesitates about placing his dependence on the mercy of God, because he is not sure whether he be elected or not, he gives clear evidence that he does not yet understand the gospel. He does not apprehend the manifestation of the love of God to man. When he sees God in Christ reconciling the world to Himself, he does not need to ask, *Is the plan of mercy such as I am warranted to embrace? may I not somehow be excluded from availing myself of it?* These, and similar suggestions, which draw away his mind from the voice of God to the speculations of his own mind, are no more regarded." He sees God rich in mercy, ready to forgive; just, and the justifier of the ungodly. He cannot but place his confidence in Him. "Jehovah," as it has been happily said, "by the manifestation of what he has done, especially in sending Christ, and delivering Him up, the just in the room of the unjust, pleads His own cause with such subduing pathos that there is no more power of resistance: but the person who is the object of the demonstration yields himself up to the authority and glory of the truth. The sinner, thus cordially believing the Gospel, gladly and gratefully receives "the Savior of the world" as his Savior, and trusts that by the grace of God he shall partake of "the common salvation."

Notes

Chapter 1 ■ God So Loved the World

1. Cited in Iain H. Murray, Jonathan Edwards: *A New Biography* (Edinburgh: Banner of Truth, 1987), 169.

2. Charles G. Finney, *Revivals of Religion* (Old Tappan, New Jersey: Revell, n. d.), 4-5.

3. Ibid., 220-21 (emphasis added).

4. J. C. Pollock, Moody: *A Biographical Portrait of the Pacesetter in Modern Evangelism* (New York: Macmillan, 1963), 72-73.

5. D. L. Moody himself was undoubtedly guilty of an overemphasis on divine love. "His [one] message, aside from the constant stress on the need for conversion, was of the love of God. His theology, although basically orthodox, was ambiguous to the point of seeming not to be theology at all." George M. Marsden, *Fundamentalism and American Culture* (Oxford: Oxford, 1980), 32, cf. 35.

As a result, Moody failed to reckon with the dangers of liberalism. "While he disapproved of liberalism in the abstract, he cultivated friendships with influential liberals in the hope that peace would prevail." Ibid., 33.

The schools Moody founded in Northfield, Massachusetts, and

with which he was associated until his death, were totally dominated by liberal leadership within a generation of Moody's passing. The Moody Bible Institute in Chicago, which Moody entrusted to sound leadership several years before his death, remains strongly evangelical to this day.

6. This method of biblical criticism is still followed today by such groups as the highly publicized "Jesus Seminar," whose scholars have concluded that only thirty-one of the more than seven hundred sayings attributed to Jesus were really spoken by Him.

7. Harry Emerson Fosdick, *Christianity and Progress* (New York: Revell, 1922), 173-74 (emphasis added).

8. Ibid., 174.

9. Ibid (emphasis added).

10. That is precisely the language used by Harold Kushner, *When Bad Things Happen to Good People* (New York: Shocken, 1981).

11. Arthur W. Pink, *The Sovereignty of God* (Grand Rapids: Baker, 1930), 29-31, 245-52, 311-14.

12. Ibid., 29-30.

13. Ibid., 246.

14. Ibid., 314. The sections I quote here were removed in the edition of Pink's work published by *The Banner of Truth Trust* (1961). In his biography of Arthur Pink, editor Iain Murray called Pink's denial of God's love for the non-elect an "area of serious weakness." Iain Murray, *The Life of Arthur W. Pink* (Edinburgh: Banner of Truth, 1981), 196.

15. This is not to suggest that God is ambivalent. God is perfectly consistent with Himself (2 Tim. 2:13). Contradictory volitions cannot exist in His mind. What I am saying is this: God in a real and sincere sense hates the wicked because of their sin; yet in a real and sincere sense He also has compassion, pity, patience, and true affection for them because of His own loving nature.

16. John Calvin, *Commentary on a Harmony of the Evangelists, Matthew, Mark, and Luke,* William Pringle, trans. (Grand Rapids: Baker, 1979 reprint), 123.

17. Ibid., 125 (italics in original).

18. See appendix 3 for specific quotations from these authors.

Chapter 2 ■ God Is Love

1. Mary Baker Eddy, *Science and Health with Key to the Scriptures* (Boston: Trustees of MBE, 1875), 473.

2. The Children of God sect, otherwise known as the Family of Love, have been known to practice an evangelistic technique they call "love bombing," where cult members offer potential recruits sex "to show them the love of God." [Maurice C. Burrell, *The Challenge of the Cults* (Grand Rapids: Baker, 1981), 44–45.]

3. Gordon H. Clark, *First John: A Commentary* (Jefferson, Maryland: Trinity Foundation, 1980), 131.

4. John R. W. Stott, *The Epistles of John* (Grand Rapids: Eerdmans, 1964), 160.

5. Ibid.

6. Donald W. Burdick, *The Letters of John the Apostle* (Chicago: Moody, 1985), 351.

7. D. Martyn Lloyd-Jones, *The Love of God* (Wheaton: Crossway, 1994), 45.

8. Ibid., 150-53.

9. Ibid., 153-54.

10. Ibid., 51.

11. Ibid., 52 (emphasis added).

Chapter 3 ■ Behold the Goodness . . .

1. A. W. Tozer, *The Knowledge of the Holy* (New York: Harper & Row, 1961), 9.

2. *Westminster Confession of Faith,* chap. 2 sec. 1.

3. See Alexander Hislop, *The Two Babylons* (Neptune, New Jersey: Loizeaux, reprint of 1916 edition) for abundant historical evidence that the Babylonian religion founded by Nimrod is the basis for virtually all subsequent false religious systems.

4. W. Graham Scroggie, *The Unfolding Drama of Redemption,* 3 vols. (Grand Rapids: Zondervan, 1970) 1:383.

5. Hugh Martin, *The Prophet Jonah: His Character and Mission to Nineveh* (Grand Rapids: Baker, 1979 reprint).

Chapter 4 ■ . . .And the Severity of God

1. Louis Berkhof, *Systematic Theology* (Grand Rapids: Eerdmans, 1941), 513.

2. Charles Lee Feinberg, *The Minor Prophets* (Chicago: Moody, 1977), 197.

Chapter 5 ■ Everything I Need to Know About the Love of God I Learned in the Nursery?

1. John Calvin, *Commentary on a Harmony of the Evangelists,* Matthew, Mark, and Luke, William Pringle, trans. (Grand Rapids: Baker, 1979 reprint), 123.

Chapter 6 ■ The Love of God for Humanity

1. Arthur W. Pink, *The Sovereignty of God* (Grand Rapids: Baker, 1930), 314.

2. This is the formulation of the Westminster Confession of Faith with regard to the sufficiency of Scripture: "The whole counsel of God, concerning all things necessary for his own glory,

man's salvation, faith, and life, is either expressly set down in scripture, or by good and necessary consequence may be deduced from scripture: unto which nothing at any time is to be added, whether by new revelations of the Spirit, or traditions of men" (1:6, emphasis added).

3. John Brown, *Discourses and Sayings of Our Lord*, 3 vols. (Edinburgh: Banner of Truth, 1990 reprint), 1:34.

4. B. B. Warfield, *The Saviour of the World* (Edinburgh: Banner of Truth, 1991 reprint), 114.

5. Ibid., 120-21.

6. R. L. Dabney, *Discussions: Evangelical and Theological*, 3 vols. (Edinburgh: Banner of Truth, 1982 reprint), 1:312.

7. John Calvin, *Commentary on a Harmony of the Evangelists*, Matthew, Mark, and Luke, William Pringle, trans. (Grand Rapids: Baker, 1979 reprint), 123.

8. Erroll Hulse, "The Love of God for All Mankind," *Reformation Today* (Nov-Dec 1983), 18-19.

9. Ibid., 21-22.

10. Ibid., 18.

Chapter 7 ■ The Love of God for His Elect

No *Notes*.

Chapter 8 ■ Finding Security In the Love of God

1. B. B. Warfield, *Selected Shorter Writings* (Phillipsburg, New Jersey: Presbyterian & Reformed,), 393.

2. *The Westminster Confession of Faith*, a strongly Calvinistic document, underscores this very point: "God from all eternity did, by the most wise and holy counsel of his own will, freely and

unchangeably ordain whatsoever comes to pass: yet so, as thereby neither is God the author of sin, nor is violence offered to the will of the creatures, nor is the liberty or contingency of second causes taken away, but rather established" (3.1).

Appendix 1: Fury Not in God

1. Thomas Chalmers was a Glasgow pastor and professor of theology at the University of Edinburgh in the first half of the 1800s. He led the formation of the Free Church of Scotland in 1843, after seceding from the Church of Scotland because of encroaching unbelief in the state church. He is remembered as one of the finest preachers Scotland has ever produced. His evangelistic fervor, for which he is well remembered, is evident in this tract adapted from one of his best-known sermons. It has been edited slightly, chiefly to update some of the archaic expressions.

Appendix 2: On the Love of God, and Whether It Extends to the Non-Elect

1. This is excerpted from a letter to a friend, by Andrew Fuller (1754-1815). Fuller was an influential English Baptist pastor and writer. A Calvinist who strongly opposed hyper-Calvinism, Fuller helped found the Baptist Foreign Missionary Society, which sent William Carey to India.

Appendix 3: Christ the Savior of the World

1. A sermon by Thomas Boston, preached immediately before the celebration of the Lord's Supper, at Ettrick, Scotland, on June 7, 1724. Boston was a Scottish pastor and author, best

known today for his book *Human Nature in Its Fourfold State* (Edinburgh: Banner of Truth).

Appendix 4: The Love of God to the World

1. John Brown (1784-1858) was one of several Scottish preachers who bore that name. He was known for his biblical exposition and is remembered best for the work from which this essay is excerpted—Discourses and Sayings of Our Lord Jesus Christ, 3 Vols. (Edinburgh: Banner of Truth, 1990 reprint), 1:28-36.

Scripture Index

Scripture Index

Scripture Index

Scripture Index

Subject Index

Subject Index

Subject Index

Subject Index

ABOUT THE AUTHOR . . .

DR. JOHN MACARTHUR, JR. is the dynamic pastor/teacher of Grace Community Church in Sun Valley, California. His unwavering advocacy for a restoration of biblical theology in our time has won him the respect of both serious students of the Word and "people in the pew." His numerous books include *The Vanishing Conscience, Rediscovering Expository Preaching, Ashamed of the Gospel,* and *Our Sufficiency in Christ.* Dr. MacArthur is heard daily on the nationally syndicated radio broadcast, "Grace to You," which has sold more than ten million tapes.